D0954385

The Hour I First Believed

→►ALSO BY WALLY LAMB◄←

I Know This Much Is True

She's Come Undone

→►BY WALLY LAMB AND THE WOMEN OF
YORK CORRECTIONAL INSTITUTION◄←

Couldn't Keep It to Myself:
Testimonies from our Imprisoned Sisters

I'll Fly Away: Further Testimonies from
the Women of York Prison

The Hour I First Believed

A NOVEL

Wally Lamb

HARPER

An Imprint of HarperCollins*Publishers*

*This novel is a work of fiction. References to real people, events, establish-
ments, organizations, or locales are included for the reasons fully described in the
Author's Note. All other names, characters, places, and dialogue and all dialogue
and incidents portrayed in this book are the product of the author's imagination.*

THE HOUR I FIRST BELIEVED. Copyright © 2008 by Wally Lamb. All rights
reserved. Printed in the United States of America. No part of this book may
be used or reproduced in any manner whatsoever without written permission except in the case of brief quotations embodied in critical articles and
reviews. For information, address HarperCollins Publishers, 10 East 53rd
Street, New York, NY 10022.

Pablo Picasso, *Minotauromachia*, © 2008 Estate of Pablo Picasso / Artists
Rights Society (ARS), New York, courtesy of The Brooklyn Museum.

"Boston's Worst" © 2008 Time Inc. All rights reserved. Reprinted from
Time magazine with permission.

Dante's *Inferno*, Canto 3, 118–120, translated by Chad Davidson, Associate
Professor of English at the University of West Georgia.

Designed by Leah Carlson-Stanisic

ISBN-13: 978-1-61523-083-9

FOR ANNA

A SERIES OF DEBILITATING STROKES and the onset of dementia necessitated the agonizing conversation I had with my mother in the winter of 1997. When I told her she'd be moving to a nearby nursing home, she shook her head and, atypically, began to cry. Tears were a rarity for my stoic Sicilian-American mother. The next day, she offered me a deal. "Okay, I'll go," she said. "But my refrigerator comes with me." I couldn't meet her demand, but I understood it.

Ma's refrigerator defined her. The freezer was stockpiled with half-gallons of ice cream for the grandkids, and I do mean stockpiled; you opened that freezer compartment at your peril, hoping those dozen or so rock-hard bricks, precariously stacked, wouldn't tumble forth and give you a concussion. The bottom half of Ma's "icebox" was a gleaming tribute to aluminum—enough foil-wrapped Italian food to feed, should we all show up unexpectedly at once, her own family and the extended families of her ten siblings. But it was the outside of Ma's fridge that best spoke of who she was. The front and sides were papered with greeting cards, holy pictures, and photos, old and new, curling and faded, of all the people she knew and loved. Children were disproportionately represented in her refrigerator photo gallery. She adored kids—her own and everyone else's. My mother was a woman of strong faith, quiet resolve, and easy and frequent laughter.

This story's been a hard one to write, Ma, and it got harder after you left us. But I had the title from the very beginning, and when I reached the end, I realized I'd written it for you.

(P.S. Sorry about all those four-letter words, Ma. That's the characters speaking. Not me.)

AND SO, THEY MOVED OVER THE DARK WAVES,
AND EVEN BEFORE THEY DISEMBARKED,
NEW HORDES GATHERED THERE.

Dante's *Inferno*, canto 3, lines 118–120

PART ONE

Butterfly

THEY WERE BOTH WORKING THEIR final shift at Blackjack Pizza that night, although nobody but the two of them realized it was that. Give them this much: they were talented secret-keepers. Patient planners. They'd been planning it for a year, hiding their intentions in plain sight on paper, on videotape, over the Internet. In their junior year, one had written in the other's yearbook, "God, I can't wait till they die. I can taste the blood now." And the other had answered, "Killing enemies, blowing up stuff, killing cops! My wrath will be godlike!"

My wrath will be godlike: maybe that's a clue. Maybe their ability to dupe everyone was their justification. If we could be fooled, then we were all fools; they were, therefore, superior, chaos theirs to inflict. But I don't know. I'm just one more chaos theorist, as lost in the maze as everyone else.

It was Friday, April 16, 1999, four days before they opened fire. I'd stayed after school for a parent conference and a union meeting and, in between, had called Maureen to tell her I'd pick up takeout. Blackjack Pizza was between school and home.

It was early still. The Friday-night pizza rush hadn't begun. He was at the register, elbows against the counter, talking to a girl in a hairdresser's smock. Or not talking, pretty much. There was a cell phone on the counter, and he kept tapping it with his index finger to make it spin—kept looking at the revolving cell phone instead of at the girl. I remember wondering if I'd just walked in on a lover's spat. "I better get back," the girl said. "See you tomorrow." Her smock said "Great Clips," which meant she worked at the salon next door—the place where Maureen went.

"Prom date?" I asked him. The big event was the next night at the Design Center in Denver. From there, the kids would head back to school for the all-night post-prom party, which I'd been tagged to help chaperone.

"I wouldn't go to that bogus prom," he said. He called over his shoulder. "How's his half-mushroom-half-meatball coming?" His cohort opened the oven door and peered in. Gave a thumbs-up.

"So tell me," I said. "You guys been having any more of your famous Blackjack flour wars?"

He gave me a half-smile. "You remember that?"

"Sure. Best piece you wrote all term."

He'd been in my junior English class the year before. A grade-conscious concrete sequential, he was the kind of kid who was more comfortable memorizing vocab definitions and lines from Shakespeare than doing the creative stuff. Still, his paper about the Blackjack Pizza staff's flour fights, which he'd shaped as a spoof on war, was the liveliest thing he'd written all term. I remember scrawling across his paper, *"You should think about taking creative writing next year."* And he had. He was in Rhonda Baxter's class. Rhonda didn't like him, though—said she found him condescending. She hated the way he rolled his eyes at other kids' comments. Rhonda and I shared a free hour, and we often compared notes about the kids. I neither liked nor disliked him, particularly. He'd asked me to write him a letter of recommendation once. Can't remember what for. What I *do* recall is sitting there, trying to think up something to say.

He rang up my sale. I handed him a twenty. "So what's next year looking like?" I asked. "You heard back from any of the schools you applied to?"

"I'm joining the Marines," he said.

"Yeah? Well, I heard they're looking for a few good men." He nodded, not smiling, and handed me my change.

His buddy ambled over to the counter, pizza box in hand. He'd lost the boyish look I remembered from his freshman year. Now he was a lanky, beak-nosed adult, his hair tied back in a sorry-looking ponytail, his chin as prominent as Jay Leno's. "So what's *your* game plan for next year?" I asked him.

"University of Arizona."

"Sounds good," I said. I gave a nod to the Red Sox cap he was wearing. "You follow the Sox?"

"Somewhat. I just traded for Garciaparra in my fantasy league."

"Good move," I said. "I used to go to Sox games all the time when I was in college. Boston University. Fenway was five minutes away."

"Cool," he said.

"Maybe this is their year, huh?"

"Maybe." He didn't sound like he gave a shit either way.

He was in Rhonda's creative writing class, too. She'd come into the staff room sputtering about him one day. "Read this," she said. "Is this sick or what?" He'd written a two-page story about a mysterious avenger in a metal-studded black trench coat. As jocks and "college preps" leave a busy bar, he pulls pistols and explosives out of his duffel bag, wastes them, and walks away, smiling. "Do you think I should call his parents?" Rhonda had asked.

I'd shrugged. "A lot of the guys write this kind of crap. Too many video games, too much testosterone. I wouldn't worry about it. He probably just needs a girlfriend." She *had* worried, though, enough to make that call. She'd referred to the meeting, a week or so later, as "a waste of time."

The door banged open; five or six rowdy kids entered Blackjack. "Hey, I'll see you later," I said.

"Later," he said. And I remember thinking he'd make a good Marine. Clean-cut, conscientious, his ironed T-shirt tucked neatly into his wrinkle-free shorts. Give him a few years, I figured, and he'd probably be officer material.

———

AT DINNER THAT NIGHT, MAUREEN suggested we go out to a movie, but I begged off, citing end-of-the-week exhaustion. She cleaned up, I fed the dogs, and we adjourned to our separate TVs. By ten o'clock, I was parked on my recliner, watching *Homicide* with the closed-caption activated, my belly full of pizza. There was a *Newsweek* opened on my lap for commercial breaks, a Pete's Wicked ale resting against my crotch, and a Van Morrison CD reverberating inside my skull: *Astral Weeks*, a record that had been released in 1968, the year I turned seventeen.

I was forty-seven that Friday night. A month earlier, a guy in a music chat room I'd begun visiting had posed the question, "What are the ten masterworks of the rock era?" Dozens of us had begun devising our lists, posting them as works in progress and busting each other's chops about our selections. (I came to picture my cyber-rockin' brethren as a single balding fat guy in a tie-dye T-shirt— size XL when XXL would have been a better fit.) My masterwork choices were as controversial as the next guy's. I incurred the good-natured wrath of several of my cyberbuddies, for instance, when I named to my list Springsteen's *Nebraska* while excluding *Born to Run* and *Born in the U.S.A.* "Dude, as spokesman for the Boss's TRUE fans," a trash-to-energy engineer from Michigan messaged me, "I regret to inform you that you're more f***ed up than a soup sandwich!" I dished it out, too, of course, not always successfully. I learned that I'd deeply offended a professor of medieval litera-ture by stating that the bloodline of the Backstreet Boys could be traced to that *other* vapid and overrated boy band of an earlier era, the Beach Boys. The scholar asked if he could communicate with me privately, and I obliged him with my address. A week later, I received a FedEx envelope, postage paid by Princeton University, which contained an erudite (if unconvincing) eleven-page defense of the album *Pet Sounds*.

For weeks, listening and list-making had consumed me: *Sgt. Pepper* or *Songs in the Key of Life*? Aretha or Etta James? I'd saved my tenth and final berth for the unorthodox but always interesting Van Morrison but was having trouble deciding between Van the Man's elegant *Moondance* and his more emotionally raw *Astral Weeks*. Thus, that Friday night, the earphones.

But it was armor, all of it, I see that now: the TV, the open magazine, the aural review of my life, the keyboard chatter. I'd safeguarded myself in multimedia chain mail to prevent emotional penetration from Maureen.

A shadow moved across the carpet, and I looked up from *Homicide* to her. "Caelum?" her lips said. She was holding our wicker tray, two glasses of red wine counterbalanced by a lit candle. I watched the wine rock in the glasses while she waited. The candle was scented—spice of some kind. She was into Enya and aromatherapy back then.

I lifted my left earphone. "Yeah, give me a few minutes," I said. "I want to let the dogs out, catch a little of the news. I'll be up."

Maureen, her wines, and her defeated shoulders turned and started up the stairs. I could read Mo from the back, same as I could the other two. But reading and responding are two different things. "Look, don't just stare at the pages," I used to tell my students. "*Become* the characters. Live *inside* the book." And they'd sit there, staring back politely at the alien from Planet Irrelevance.

Maureen's my three-strikes-and-you're-out spouse and, as far as I know, the only one of the trinity who ever cheated on me. That lit candle on the tray? It's one of the signals she and I came up with back in Connecticut, back in 1994, during the sensitizing humiliation of couples counseling—those seven sessions we attended in the aftermath of her Courtyard Marriott fuck-fests with Paul Hay.

Whom I'd met a few times at her staff parties. Who was in our

Rolodex. Come to think of it, we must have been in the Hays' Rolodex, too.

HELLO?" I SAID. ORDINARILY, WHEN the phone rang while I was grading papers, I'd let the machine get it. But the rain that March night had started making clicking sounds against the floorboards of the deck and the dogs had come back inside wearing ice crystals on their backs. Nervous about Mo's driving home from tai chi on treacherous roads, I was half waiting for a call.

"May I speak to Maureen Quirk?" the woman asked.

"She's out," I said.

"Are you Mr. Quirk?"

"Yeah, but look. No telemarketing at this number. Take us off your—"

"Do you know who Maureen's out *with*?"

I uncapped my pen. Tore off a piece of some kid's blue book to jot down her number. "Excuse me," I said. "Who'd you say this is?"

She identified herself not by name but by association: she was Trina Hay's best friend. Trina was sitting right there next to her, she said, but too upset to talk on the phone. "We just wanted you to know, in case you *don't* know, that your wife's having an affair with Paul."

I said nothing for several seconds, but when I finally did speak, all I could come up with was, "Paul who?"

"Paul *Hay*," she said. "Trina's *husband*. Did you know they have a little boy named Casey? Or that Trina has lupus? Or that they're building a *house*?" Jesus, she was giving me the whole *A&E Biography*, and I was still on *Paul Hay? Paul Hay? Where do I know that name from?* Maureen's betrayal hadn't broken the surface yet. Or maybe it had, because my instinct was to kill the messenger.

"So what are you—some no-life chick's gotta borrow her friend's business?" I asked.

"This *is* my business, okay?" she said. "I'm Casey's *god*mother."

"You're fat, aren't you? You have a fat voice."

"Do you know who bought Trina and Paul the lot they're building their house on? Trina's *father*, that's who. The month before he *died*."

"Your options are limited, right? It's either Tina's problems or a spoon, a pint of Ben & Jerry's between your knees, and *Touched by an Angel*."

"Her name's Trina, *okay*? And my personal life is none of your business. Just tell your little slut of a wife that if she thinks she's moving into Trina's new house when it's finished, she's . . . she's . . ."

There was dead air for a few seconds, some muffled whispering. Then the avenger was back on the line, blubbering. "I am *trying* to stop your wife from destroying my friend's marriage. *Okay?*"

"Yeah, sure, Fat Chunks. Your Nobel Peace Prize is in the mail." I can't remember which of us hung up on the other.

I paced, muttered. Sent my students' blue books flying and the dogs running for cover. When I realized the cordless phone was still clenched in my hand, I whacked it five or six times against the refrigerator door. My car keys were on the counter. I stared at them for several seconds, then grabbed them.

The trucks hadn't sanded Bride Lake Road yet, but I kept mislaying the fact that the road was icy. Passing the entrance to the women's prison, I spotted oncoming headlights and hit the brakes. The fishtail I went into nearly sent me crashing into the security gate. My heart thumped. My breath came out in short blasts. I remembered who Paul Hay was.

I'd met him a couple of times at her staff parties. Reddish hair, bearish build. We'd small-talked. He'd tried home brewing once, but it had come out watery. He liked the Mets. Maureen was nurse-supervisor at Rivercrest Nursing Home back then, and Lover Boy was in her pool of per diem LPNs.

The karate school where she took tai chi was in a strip mall near the Three Rivers depot. There's a convenience store, a bike shop, Happy

Joy Chinese, and Caputo's Martial Arts. The plate-glass window was foggy. I got out, walked to the door, opened it a crack. Twenty or so little kids in karate suits stood with their hands clasped as if in prayer. "Bow to the master, bow to the flag," the instructor said. Well, okay, I thought. She's guilty.

I slipped and slid my way back home. No car in the garage. I fed the dogs, picked the exam booklets off the floor, picked up the phone. No dial tone; I'd killed it. Two Johnny Walkers later, she came through the door with Chinese food. "Hey," I said. "How was it driving?"

"Not great, but I lucked out. I followed the sand truck all the way up Bride Lake Road. You eat yet?"

"Nope."

She hit the message machine. Her J. C. Penney order was in, one of her first-shift nurses was taking a "mental health day" and needed a sub. She put on a pot of tea, set two places, and opened the cardboard containers. "Look at this," she said. Her open palm was piled with soy sauce and mustard packets. "If someone consumed all this sodium, they'd have a stroke."

"So why'd you drive across town to the other place when you were right next door to Happy Joy?" I said.

"Because last time you said Happy Joy's too greasy."

Which was true—I had. It was.

We spooned out the food. The kettle whistled. Maureen got up to get our tea. "What happened here?" she asked. Her fingers were skidding along the refrigerator door.

"What?"

"These dents?"

"Tell me," I said. "Who gets on top, you or him? Or do you alternate?"

Okay, this next part's hard. I'm not proud of the moo shu and orange chicken dripping down the wall. Or the fact that when she tried to leave the room, I grabbed her so hard by the wrist that I sprained it. Or the fact that she totaled her car on her way to her friend Jackie's apartment.

She wouldn't come back. She wouldn't take my calls. Each day, I went to school, taught classes, endured staff meetings, drove home, and walked the dogs. I spent my evenings calling Jackie's number on our brand-new phone. Redial, redial, redial, redial. When Jackie's boyfriend warned me to stop calling or else he'd *have* the calling stopped, I said okay, fine, I didn't want any trouble. I just needed to talk to my wife.

Next day after school, I drove over to the town hall and found out where Hay was building their dinky little shoebox of a house. It was out in the sticks, out past the old gristmill. I drove out there around dusk. The place was framed; the chimney was up. Overhead was a pockmarked moon.

I drove back there the next morning, a Saturday. His truck was there. He was up on the second floor. He squinted down at me, puzzled. I cut the engine. That's when I saw it, in the seat well on the passenger's side: the pipe wrench I'd borrowed from Chuck Wagner to tighten our leaky hallway radiator valve. It wasn't premeditated. I'd meant to return that wrench for a week or more. But suddenly its being there seemed just and right. There was a fire in my head.

Six weeks after that moment, in a darkened classroom at Oceanside Community College, I would learn via an anger management class video about the cardiology, neurology, and endocrinology of rage—about how, as I reached for that wrench, my hypothalamus was instant-messaging my adrenal glands to secrete cortisol and adrenaline. How stored fat was dumping into my bloodstream for an energy turbocharge. How my heart was pumping overtime, sending a surge of blood to my muscles and lungs in preparation for what that instructional video called "the evolutionary miracle of fight-or-flight." That morning, I saw Hay and took the former option.

Took out his windshield. Took the wrench to his stacks of not-yet-installed Andersen windows. When he came flying at me, I took a swing at his head that, thank God, didn't connect. He head-butted me, knocked me backward, gave me a cracked rib and a busted lip, a bruised tailbone.

They arrested me that afternoon. Hay got a restraining order. Maureen got me out of the house and would not let me take the dogs. We all got lawyers. Mine, Lena LoVecchio, was a friend of my Aunt Lolly's. Her manner was brusque, her hairstyle a shellacked mullet. There were two framed posters on the wall behind her desk: the UConn women's basketball team with their championship trophy and Kramer from *Seinfeld*.

"How come he gets to screw my wife *and* be the victim?" I asked Lena.

"It's all about the wrench," she said.

I tried to explain to Lena how I'd reached the point where there was nothing between me and the pain of my wife's betrayal. She kept nodding, sad-eyed, her fingers stretching a rubber band. When I stopped talking, she said, "I'm your attorney, Caelum. Not your therapist."

Pending disposition of the case, I took a mandatory unpaid leave of absence from teaching. Took Aunt Lolly up on her offer to have me come stay at the family farm with her and her don't-ask-don't-tell companion, Hennie. (It was April, and my aunt was as practical as she was sympathetic; I got room, board, and laundry service in exchange for plowing and manure spreading.) I took the deal the lawyers hammered out. In exchange for two hundred hours of community service, completion of the anger management class, and restitution on all that broken glass out at the Hays' hacienda, I got the assault and damage charges reduced to misdemeanors. That meant probation instead of prison and a shot at qualifying for "accelerated rehabilitation." It would be the judge's call. If I got it and behaved myself for a year, my criminal record would be wiped clean and I could teach again. My case was on the docket for August the first.

I missed school—the kids, the daily grind. Had Melanie DeCarlo gotten into one of her dream schools? Had Mike Jacaruso gotten that soccer scholarship? When the Wildcats made it to the semifinals in basketball, I drove up to their big game against Wethersfield. Made the mistake of sitting in the Three Rivers section. I left at the half, though. I couldn't take the fact that, although everyone was packed in tight on those bleachers, I had room on either side of me. Couldn't take the whispering, the swiveling heads: *that's that teacher who . . .*

The community service piece was punishment by acute tedium. I'd have been okay with a soup kitchen or group home assignment, but they gave me data entry at the DMV—six mind-numbing hours every Saturday for thirty-three weeks.

Hey, you think those Motor Vehicle employees are charmers when you're in line? You should feel the love when you're one of their community service penitents. This one woman? Had Disney crap pinned up all over her cubicle walls? She goes to her supervisor and accuses me of helping myself to the M&Ms in the glass canister on her desk. Which was bullshit. She's blowing her nose every two minutes and leaving used Kleenex all over her desk, and she thinks I want to get within ten feet of that germ pool?

And then there was anger management: twelve three-hour sessions run by Beth the Ballbuster and Dredlock Darnell, who, I'm guessing, must have been at least a *semi*finalist for Dunkin' Donuts' Customer of the Decade. They had this good cop/bad cop thing going, those two. He'd expound on "our feelings as messengers" and play the pathetically dated videos—*The Blame Game, Slaying the Dragon Within.* She'd try her best to incite us, drill-sergeant style, cutting off at the knees any guy clueless enough to claim that he didn't really have to be there or that, on some level at least, his wife or girlfriend had asked for it. "Bull*shit!*" Beth declared, in the middle of one sap's poor-me ramble about the connection between his mother's ridicule and the fact that he'd sunk a barbecue fork into his nagging wife's leg. "Stop using your lousy childhood as an excuse, and stop calling her 'the wife.' She has a name, doesn't she? Use it. And face the fact that you're a domestic terrorist." During break midway through our second session, I'd rolled my eyes and quipped sotto voce to Beth that some of the bulletheads in our class probably needed stupidity management more than anger management. "Mr. Quirk, are you under the mistaken impression that we facilitators are your peer group?" she asked. "Because we're not. You're in the abusers' group." After that icing, I joined the smokers and gripers outside, neither nodding at nor challenging their mumblings about wasted time, whale blubber, and femiNazis.

I learned things, though. The curriculum may have been redundant, Darnell may have had food issues, and Beth may have bulldozed her way through resistance rather than dismantling it the way a more skillful teacher might have done. ("Hey, you don't *want* to fix yourself? Fine. Drop out. *I'm* not the one who needs the signed certificate.") Still, I went away with a better understanding of the biology of anger, what triggers it, and what I could do to short-circuit it. More than that, I had a twelve-week dose of humility. Man, I hated the sick-to-my-stomach feeling I got driving to that class every week. Hated the beat-up/riled-up feeling I always had afterward. Hated facing up to the fact that, whether she'd been unfaithful to me or not, if Maureen had gotten killed that icy night when she totaled her Toyota, it would have been my fault because she'd left out of fear. If I'd bashed in Hay's skull with that pipe wrench, his death would have been on me. I *was* in the abusers' group, not the group for the abused; that's what I learned. My childhood grudges, my righteous indignation, and my master's degree didn't count for squat. My Phi Beta Kappa key unlocked nothing. I was my failings and my actions, period. Like I said, it was a humbling experience.

In court, Hay's lawyer stood and asked the judge if his client could speak. Attorney LoVecchio and I exchanged uh-oh looks; this wasn't in the script. This couldn't be good.

In the months since the incident, Hay said, he had rediscovered His Lord and Savior Jesus Christ. He had broken the ninth commandment and had come to understand that he bore responsibility for the outcome of those trespasses. He was not a vindictive man, he said. He was sorry for the hurt he'd caused. He hoped *I* could forgive him as *he* had forgiven me. He looked right at me when he said that last part. I looked away from him. Looked back and nodded. The judge granted me my "accelerated rehab."

Maureen had filed for divorce by then. That fall, I helped Lolly and Hennie with the milking and the apple and pumpkin sales. I also resurrected the Bride Lake Farms corn maze. During the fifties and early sixties, the maze had been a Three Rivers tradition; we'd get a couple thousand paying customers going through that thing in season. "People *like* to get lost for a little while," my grandfather used to say. But the maze's popularity had petered out during the late sixties, maybe because, by then, most of us were already more lost than we wanted to be. Out in the old desk in the barn, I found my father's pencil sketch for the original three-acre labyrinth, dated 5/12/56, and duplicated that. Did a decent enough job of it, so I went down to the newspaper and tried to get the features editor interested in doing a nostalgic story. "The Return of the Bride Lake Farm Corn Maze," something like that. She wasn't interested, though, and we couldn't afford *paid* advertising, so the whole thing kind of fizzled. I mean, we got some families on the few weekends that weren't rained out, and a few school groups during the week, but it was nothing like when I was a kid, when the cars would be parked a quarter of a mile down Bride Lake Road.

I took a stop-gap second job as night baker at Mama Mia Pastry, which was how I'd put myself through school back in the seventies. Mr. and Mrs. Buzzi had both retired by then, and their surviving son, Alphonse, was running the biz. The Buzzis' older son, Rocco, and I had been high school buddies, then roommates at BU, seatmates at Sox games. Being back at the bakery felt like a demotion, especially since, technically, Alphonse Buzzi was now my boss. When he was a kid, his brother and I used to tease Alphonse mercilessly. He'd ask for it, you know? Squeal on us, ambush us with water balloons.

"Baby Huey," we used to call him, and he'd go crying to his mother. After Rocco died, Alphonse became a friend by default, I guess you could say. He was still annoying, though. Still a baby. My first wife? Patti? She was always trying to fix him up with women from her bank, but nothing ever took. I mean, even now, the guy's in his mid-forties—runs a *business*, for Christ's sake—and you know what he's into? Paintball. You know what's sitting on top of the file cabinet in his office? His friggin' Super-Soaker.

But anyway, nighttime baking suited me okay; I wasn't sleeping for shit anyway. I kept telling myself that my year away from teaching gave me the perfect opportunity to write again—kept feeding myself that "Life gives you lemons, make lemonade" crap. I bought a three-ring binder and a three-hundred-sheet package of loose-leaf paper. Put the paper in the binder, snapped the rings shut, put a pen in the pocket, and put it on the nightstand next to my bed. But I *didn't* write again. Didn't open that fucking loose-leaf binder once.

And then Maureen called me. Out of the blue, on Halloween night. Well, it was one in the morning, so, technically, it was already November the first. All Saints Day, I remembered, from my Catholic childhood. Mo was crying. She was scared, she said. Sophie, the older and needier of our two mutts, was sick. Dying, maybe. Dogs could die from too much chocolate, right? Maureen had overplanned for trick-or-treaters, then gone to bed, leaving most of the unclaimed candy in a bowl by the door. Sophie had chowed down on thirty or forty of those miniature Hershey bars, wrappers and all. She'd been vomiting chocolate, paper, and foil nonstop for two hours. The vet's answering service wouldn't pick up. Could I come over?

I stopped at the all-night convenience store on my way and bought Pepto-Bismol. Sent Maureen to bed and stayed up with Soph for the rest of the night. She stopped retching around three in the morning. I sat there, watching her sleep, her chest heaving. By dawn, her breathing had normalized. By seven, she was up again, looking better and wanting breakfast.

One thing led to another with Mo and me. She'd tell me okay, I could come over for a cup of coffee. "One hour," she'd insist. The first time, she even set the stove timer. Then she let me take her out to dinner. Then we started walking the dogs out by the reservoir. Started watching UConn basketball on TV. One night when I went over there, I brought a bottle of wine, and we drank it and made out on the couch. Made our way to the bedroom. We were awkward with each other, out of synch. I came before she was anywhere near ready. "It's okay," she kept saying. "It's fine."

Later, after I'd started dozing, she said, "Caelum?"

"Hmm?"

"Tell me a secret."

At first I didn't say anything. Then I said, "What kind of secret?"

"Something you've never told anyone before."

Mr. Zadzilko, I thought. I saw his broad face before me, the bare lightbulb hanging from the ceiling of the utility closet. "I don't . . . I can't think of anything."

"Tell me something about your ex-wife."

"Patti?"

"Francesca. You never talk about her."

I rolled toward her, onto my side. And because I wanted to come home again, I complied. "Well," I said. "When I started writing my book? She bought me a computer. My first computer."

Mo said that wasn't a secret. It didn't count.

"Yeah, but wait. The day she left me? She took her house key—the one she left behind—and scratched something onto the face of the monitor."

"What?"

"Two words: emotional castrato. . . . Like our whole marriage was my fault. Like her living in New York all week and coming home on weekends—*some* weekends, I should say, fewer and fewer, actually—like that had nothing to do with it. And here's what a freaking masochist *I* was: I lived with that goddamned monitor. Kept typing away, squinting around and past those words. It was four or five months before I unplugged the fucker and hefted it out to the curb. Lifted it over my head and dropped it face-first onto the sidewalk, just so I could hear the pleasure of it crash. Spring cleanup, it was, and the town trucks were driving around, picking up people's bulky waste. And the next morning, I heard the truck and stood at the window. Had the pleasure of watching them haul it away. . . . So there's your secret."

"Who else knows about it?" she asked.

"No one else. Just you."

She reached over. Stroked my hair, my cheek. "After my parents split up?" she said. "When I used to spend weekends with my father? He'd come into my room some nights, sit in the chair across from my bed and . . . "

"What?"

"Masturbate." My mind ricocheted. She anticipated the question I wanted and didn't want to ask. "That was as far as it ever went. He never . . . you know."

"Did he think you were asleep?"

"No. He used to watch me watching him. Neither of us ever said anything. He'd just do it, finish up, and leave. And in the morning, he'd be Daddy again. Take me out and buy me chocolate chip pancakes for breakfast."

"That's sick," I said. "How many times did it happen?"

"Two or three, maybe. Then he started seeing the Barracuda, and it stopped." The Barracuda was Evelyn, her stepmother, a high-stakes real estate broker. From the start, Evelyn and Mo had kept their distance.

"You tell your mother?"

"No. You're the first person I've ever told. . . . It was pretty confusing. I was only eleven. I mean, most of the time he was so distant. So unavailable. Then he'd . . . I knew it was wrong to watch him. Dirty or whatever, but . . . "

"But what?"

"It was this thing we shared. This secret. It messed me up, though. I slept around a lot in high school."

I put my arm around her. Squeezed her tight, then tighter.

"Caelum? Do you think you could trust me again? I know I've given you good reason not to, but . . . I mean, if you're going to be all Sherlock Holmes every time I go out . . ."

I told her I *wanted* to be able to trust her—that working on it was the best I could promise.

"Okay," she said. "That's fair."

On our next date, she told me I could come back home if I wanted to. There was one condition, though: couples counseling.

Our therapist, the sari-wearing, no-nonsense Dr. Beena Patel, was a dead ringer for Supreme Court justice Ruth Bader Ginsburg. I'd assumed Mo was going to be the one to take the heat, since she was the one who'd cheated, but within the first fifteen minutes of session one, I realized that Dr. Patel was going to be an equal-opportunity nutcracker. Besides, Dr. Patel said, she thought it would be more profitable for us to focus on the future than the past. And speaking of profitable, her fee was a hundred and fifteen a pop.

Dr. Patel assigned homework. She made Mo and me design a series of nonverbal requests we could use when asking directly for something made either one of us feel too vulnerable. Universally recognizable signals weren't permitted. No raised middle finger in response to a cutting remark, for instance; no ass-grabbing if, walking into the kitchen and seeing her in those cutoffs of hers, I suddenly got in the mood. "The creation of signs exclusive to you as a couple is as much a part of the therapy as the employment of them," Dr. P explained. "And, of course, with that, the careful honoring of each other's reasonable requests." So, a tug of the earlobe came to mean: *Please listen to me.* A hand over the heart: *What you just said hurts.* A lit candle: *Come upstairs. Be with me. Love me.* And I did love Maureen. I do. Ask any of us cynical bastards to lift up our shirt, and we'll show you where we got shot in the heart.

"You can't just *say* you forgive her, Mr. Quirk," Dr. Patel used to insist during the solo sessions she requested because, at our regular appointments, Maureen was averaging 75 percent of the talking. "If you truly want to live inside this marriage, then you must shed your carapace of bitterness and *embrace* forgiveness."

"My carapace?" I said. "What am I? An insect?"

Dr. Patel didn't smile. "Or else, my friend, move on."

But rather than move on, we'd moved. Maureen's mom was dead; her father and the Barracuda had a grown daughter and a grandchild. They had nothing more than a birthday- and Christmas-card relationship with Mo, and even then, the good wishes were always in Evelyn's handwriting. But Mo had this fantasy that she and her dad might become closer if she was back in Colorado. I couldn't see why she wanted that, frankly. I mean, by rights, the guy should have been registered as a sex offender. But I never said that, and Maureen had never wanted to talk about Daddy with Dr. Patel. And as for me, the thought of standing in front of classes of high school kids who *hadn't* heard about my arrest—as opposed to kids who *had*—well, that had a certain appeal. So we made umpteen phone calls. My Connecticut teaching license was transferable, and Maureen had never let her Colorado nursing credentials lapse. We flew out there in late June, interviewed, found a house we liked in Cherry Knolls. By mid-July, we had jobs at the same high school—me as an English teacher and Maureen as a backup school nurse. And so we hired movers, closed our bank accounts, sedated the dogs for the trip west, and went.

If, for Maureen, Colorado was coming home, I was a stranger in a strange land. "Welcome to God's country," people kept saying, usually with a nod to those ubiquitous goddamn mountains. "Drink water, or the altitude'll do a number on you." And it did, too. I'd get nosebleeds out of nowhere for the first month or so.

It was the small things I missed: the family farm in October, Aunt Lolly's chuckle, my old jogging route, Fenway Park. I'd held on to those same Red Sox seats (section 18, row double-N, seats 5 and 6) since my BU days. I'd sat with Rocco Buzzi in the early years, and later with his brother, Alphonse. I mean, I'd *go* to a Rockies game, but it wasn't the same. They're home-run-happy out there, for one thing; someone dings one, and the altitude takes care of the rest. Maureen would go with me to Coors Field sometimes in the beginning, but she'd usually bring a book, or drag me to some LoDo art gallery afterwards. "How many points do we have now?" she'd ask, and I'd have to remind her it was runs, not points. I don't know. It's just different out there. You know what you can get on a pizza in metro Denver? Mesquite-flavored tilapia, with or without goat cheese. Jesus God.

Hey, in my own defense? I was respectful of those signals of ours for a while. I'd see her hand on her heart and comfort her. I'd *act* on a lit candle. Light one myself from time to time. And it worked; it *was* better. I'll give counseling that much. But over time, I got careless. Got bitter again, gummed up in the flypaper of what I was supposed to be beyond: the fact that those Monday and Thursday nights when she was supposed to be taking tai chi, she'd been opening her legs and taking Paul Hay inside her instead. I don't know. Maybe that stuff with her father *had* messed her up. I mean, it had to have, right? But after that tell-me-a-secret night, we never went near the subject again—not even with Dr. Patel.

I tell you one thing, though: Mo's moving back to Colorado didn't get her what she wanted, father-wise. She went over to their house three or four times at the beginning. She'd get all dressed up, buy them gifts. I chose not to go with her. The thing was, I didn't trust myself. Figured seeing Daddy Dearest might trigger something, and I'd go off on the guy. Coldcock him or something. It's not like I didn't have a history. Maureen would always come back from those visits saying she'd had a good time, or that their house was beautiful, or that their granddaughter, Amber, was so adorable. She'd be down, though—in a slump for the next few days. Sometimes, I'd eavesdrop when she called them. Maureen would small-talk with Evelyn for a while and then ask to speak to her father. He'd oblige her—come to the phone maybe half the time. And when he did, it made me sad to hear Mo doing most of the talking. He never called her. Neither did Evelyn. Or Cheryl, the half-sister. Somewhere during our second year out there, Maureen stopped calling, too. It was hard for her, as it had been hard for me. I knew a thing or two about abdicating fathers.

<hr>

BUT ANYWAY, THAT FRIDAY NIGHT? In our Colorado living room? *Homicide* ended on its usual note of moral ambiguity, Van Morrison's "Slim Slow Slider" faded to silence, and the news came on. There was relative calm in the world that night. Nothing you'd stay glued to your recliner over. No sign of the trouble those two rage-filled little motherfuckers were planning. Channel Nine had a convenience-store stickup in Lakewood, an environmental protest in Fort Collins. There was the usual numbing news from Kosovo. Get up, I kept telling myself. Go to her. Instead, I'd stuck around for the Sox and Celtics scores, checked in with the Weather Channel for the national temperatures. We'd been out there for four years by then, and I was still keeping tabs on Connecticut weather.

Still, I meant to go up to her. I was going to. But the news led into *Letterman*, and since James Brown was the musical guest, I decided to open a beer and catch that soulful old reprobate, too. Should I add the Godfather of Soul to my masterworks list, I wondered. And if so, who should I bump? . . .

My eyes cracked open some time after three. I looked around until I recognized the room. Got up, got the dogs taken care of and the downstairs locked up. Went up there.

Our bedroom was lit by dying candlelight and aromatic with ginger. Wax had dribbled down the front of the bureau and cooled. Carapaced the carpet. Maureen was scowling in her sleep. She'd drunk both of the wines.

I dropped my clothes beside our bed and got in next to her. She rolled onto her side, away. *Moondance*, I thought. No, *Astral Weeks*. And in the midst of my indecision, I suddenly saw the long view of my inconsequential life: Mouseketeer, farm kid, failed husband, mediocre teacher. Forty-fucking-eight years old, and what had *I* accomplished? What had *I* come to know?

IN THE AFTERMATH, I'D LEARN that he lied to me on two counts that afternoon at Blackjack Pizza. First, he hadn't been as anti-prom as he let on; he'd asked a couple of girls and been refused. As was his habit when one of his peers displeased or slighted him, he'd gone home, grabbed a marking pen, and X-ed out their faces in his yearbook. Second, he was not headed for the Marines. The *Rocky Mountain News* would report that the antidepressant he was taking for obsessive-compulsive disorder had disqualified him. The recruiter had dropped by his home and delivered the news on Thursday, the night before I'd bought that pizza. His buddy *had* made plans to go to the University of Arizona, though; he and his dad had driven there a few weeks earlier and chosen his dorm room. Had that been part of the deceit? Had he been playing both fantasy baseball and fantasy future? Playing his parents along with everyone else? His computer offered no clues; they confiscated it within the first few hours, but he'd erased the hard drive the night before.

Over and over, for years now, I have returned to that Friday night: when I can't sleep, when I can, when the steel door slides open and I walk toward her, Maureen looking sad-eyed and straggly-haired, in her maroon T-shirt and pocketless jeans. Mo's one of the victims you've never read about in the Columbine coverage, or seen interviewed on the *Today* show or *Good Morning America*. One of the collaterally damaged.

I just wish to Christ I'd gotten up the stairs that night. Made love to her. Held her in my arms and made her feel safe. Because time was almost up. They'd bought their guns, taped their farewell videos, finalized their plans. They'd worked their last shift together at Blackjack—had made and sold me that pizza that, piece by piece, Mo and I had lifted out of the box and eaten. Chaos was coming, and it would drive us both so deeply into the maze that we'd wander among the corpses, lost to each other for years. Yet there Maureen was on that long-ago night, up in our bed, waiting for me.

Get up those stairs! I want to scream to my clueless April-seventeenth-of-nineteen-ninety-nine self. *Hold her! Make her feel safe!* Because time was running out. Their first shots were eighty hours away.

→→ *chapter two* ←←

ON SATURDAY MORNING, I AWOKE to the sound of whimpering. Eyes closed, I groped. Felt, on my left, Maureen's hipbone. On my right, fur. I'd swum up from sleep on my back, the sheet knotted around my ankles, a hard-on tent-poling the front of my boxers. I cracked open my eyes and looked into the eyes of the perp. The whimperer: Sophie. Her muzzle rested against the mattress. Her face was a foot from mine. I blinked; she blinked. I sighed; she sighed. The plea in her eyes was readable: *Get up. Feed me. Love me the most.*

Sophie was the needier of our two mutts—mother and son golden retrievers we'd brought with us from Connecticut. Soph had gotten neurotic as she aged—whiny, fixated on food, and, out of nowhere, possessive of me. I'd grab Maureen by the kitchen sink or in the bathroom, give her a smooch, and Sophie would appear at our feet, head-butting her away. It was funny but creepy, too, like living with a canine version of what's-her-name in *Fatal Attraction*. Not Meryl Streep. The other one. Cruella De Vil.

Maureen's arm swung back. "Mmph," she said. Her hand found me, her fingertips skidding across my throat. I rolled toward her and hitched my chin over her shoulder. Placed my stiffness against her. "Hey, toots," I whispered.

"Bad breath," she mumbled back, stuffing her pillow between us. Sophie's whimper became a guttural grunt. *Yoo hoo. Remember me?*

The clock radio said 7:06. The wineglasses on the wicker tray by the window said I'd failed Maureen the night before. Sophie's wet nose poked my wrist. "Yeah, yeah, wait a minute," I muttered. Swung my feet to the floor and padded toward the bathroom, Sophie following. Chet groaned and stretched, wagged his tail, and joined the pissing party. You almost never saw that dog without a grin on his face.

Mid-leak, Maureen came in, a wineglass stem in each fist. She dumped the dregs with so much determination that wine spattered on the wall.

"Hey," I said. "What do you say I give the dogs a quick run, then we go someplace for breakfast?"

She rinsed the glasses, kept me waiting. "Can't," she finally said.

"You can't, or you'd rather not eat eggs with a shithead like me?"

No forgiving smile. No look in my direction. She grabbed a washcloth, wiped the glasses so hard they squeaked. "I'm taking Velvet to breakfast."

I stood there, nodding. Touché.

In that system of signals Mo and I had worked out with Dr. Patel, there was no shorthand for "I'm sorry." You were obliged to *speak* those two words. But the mention of Maureen's breakfast buddy short-circuited any contrition I'd been generating.

Mo's field was gerontology, but after we moved out West and she took the school nurse's job, she found she enjoyed working with the high school kids. She liked the needy ones, particularly. "Just give them an aspirin and send them back to class," I kept advising her. Instead, she'd help them with their math, counsel them on their love lives, give them rides and lunch money. I'd warned Mo to observe boundaries with Velvet, especially. Velvet Hoon was like a Cape Cod undertow: if you weren't careful, she'd pull you in deeper than you meant to go. I spoke from experience.

I pulled on my sweats, laced up my running shoes. If she wanted to spend her weekend morning with a dysfunctional sixteen-year-old instead of with her husband, then fine. Fuck it. Maybe I'd leave the dogs home, do a long run—the eight-miler out to Bear Creek Lake and back. I was halfway out the door when she said something about a rain check.

I stopped. Our eyes met for a nanosecond. "Yeah, whatever," I said. Bounding past me down the stairs, the dogs almost sent me tumbling.

Outside, it was see-your-breath cold. Flurries possible tomorrow, they said. Goddamn thin Colorado air. It was different back in Connecticut. By mid-April, the sea breezes began to cut you some slack. Aunt Lolly had probably gotten her garden rototilled by now, I figured. She may have even put her peas in the ground. When she called on Sunday, I'd be sure to get the weekly farm and weather reports, along with a complaint or two about her hired man, Ulysses—"Useless," she called him—and an update on the latest shenanigans being pulled by "those goddamned toy soldiers down the road." Lolly had it in for the paramilitary regime that now ran the maximum-security version of what she still stubbornly referred to as "Grandma's prison." Like her paternal grandmother, who had served as superintendent of the Bride Lake State Farm for Women from 1913 to 1943, Aunt Lolly, too, had been a Bride Lake long-timer, albeit a rank-and-filer. For forty of her sixty-eight years, she'd been a second-shift custody officer—a CO. "Of course, that was back when they let us treat the gals like human beings instead of cockroaches," she'd say. "Nowadays they've got all those captains and majors and lieutenants strutting around like it's May Day in Moscow, and they don't know shit from Shinola about how to run a ladies' jail."

Out in the backyard, I was doing my stretches and deliberating about whether or not to go back in for a cap and gloves when I heard leaves crackling in the woods behind our place. The dogs heard it, too. They stood rigid, staring at the clearing, Chet emitting a low, throaty growl. Deer, I figured. Too heavy-footed for squirrels. "Easy, boy," I told Chet, and the three of us stood there, listening to the silence. A few seconds later, the crackling recommenced and she emerged from the woods in all her chaotic glory: Velvet Hoon.

Remembering that our dogs freaked her out, I grabbed them by their collars. "Got 'em!" I called. The phrase "all bark, no bite" could have been coined for our mutts; couple of wimps, those two. But to tell you the truth, it was a relief to see Velvet afraid of *some*thing. Eyeing my hold, she entered the yard in full freak regalia: halter top, exposed flab, hacked-off tuxedo pants, and those Bozo-sized men's workboots of hers, spray-painted silver. Her shaved head had grown out in the months I hadn't seen her. Now she was sporting a butch cut, dyed bread-mold blue. Watching her make a beeline for the picnic table, I couldn't help but crack a smile. Short and squat, she moved like R2-D2. She climbed from the bench to the tabletop and fumbled for a cigarette. Having secured higher ground and sucked in a little nicotine, her cocky stance returned.

"Maureen home?" she called.

"Mrs. Quirk, you mean?" I nodded. Watched a shiver pass through her. What did she expect, exposing that much belly in weather where you could see your breath? "I'll tell her you're out here." I'd be damned if I was going to let her back in the house. "You need a jacket?"

Instead of answering me, she screamed at the barking dogs. "Peace *out*! Shut the fuck *up*!" Her shouting made them nuts.

Back inside, I called up the stairs. "Cinderella's here!"

"Already? I told her nine o'clock."

"Must have been a hell of a shortcut. She arrived through the woods."

No response.

"I'm heading out now. Gonna run out to Bear Creek and back."

Nothing.

"Don't let her in here unsupervised, okay?" One thousand one, one thousand two, one thousand . . . "Mau*reen*!"

"Okay! Okay!"

In the mud room, I grabbed my wool-lined jacket and headed back out. Velvet was still on the picnic table, but sitting now, smoking.

"Here's a loaner," I called. I balled up the jacket and tossed it under-hand. It fell short by a foot or two, landing on the frosty grass. She looked down at it but didn't move. "Make sure you stub out that ciga-rette when you're done," I said. She took a drag, blew smoke toward the sky.

"You find my book yet?" I said.

"I didn't *take* your freakin' book."

She looked away before I did. I turned and jogged down the drive-way. If she wanted to freeze out there rather than pick up the jacket, then let her. It wasn't like she was doing *me* any favors.

It was a tough run. My lungs burned, my throat felt fiery from what was probably a cold coming on. Even at the top of my game, I'd never fully acclimated to running at those altitudes. "Your red blood cells adjust in a few days, Caelum," Andy Kirby had told me once. "It's your head that's the problem." Andy's a marathoner and a math teacher. Andy, Dave Sanders, and I used to eat lunch together during my first year on the faculty. Dave was the girls' basketball coach, and he followed the UConn women pretty closely—closer than I did. Good guys, Dave and Andy were, but during my second year at Columbine, I started bringing my lunch and eating in my room. I don't know why, really; I just did. For a while, the kids—the needy ones—would squint through the window in my classroom door and want to visit me during my duty-free lunch. After a while, though, I got smart. Cut a piece of black construction paper and taped it over the glass. With the lights off, the door locked, and the view blocked, I was able to eat in peace.

See, that's what Maureen didn't get: that sometimes you had to play defense against that wall of adolescent neediness. Her job in the nurse's office was half-time, which meant she could leave at noon. But more often than not, she was still there at the end of the school day. "Accept your limitations," I'd warn her. "A lot of these kids are damaged beyond repair." And you know what her response was? That I was cynical. Which hit a nerve, I have to admit. I *wasn't* a cynic; I was a banged-up realist. You live to middle age, you begin to reckon with life's limits, you know? You lace up your sneakers and run it out.

From West Belleview, I took a left onto South Kipling. My destination, the park entrance at Bear Creek Lake, was a haul, and eight miles there meant eight miles back. I'd forgotten to grab my gloves, and my hands felt cold and raw. I was raw on the subject of Velvet Hoon, too.

Velvet had been *my* project before she was Maureen's. The year before, she'd clomped into my second-hour creative writing class in those silver boots, waving an add-to-class slip like a taunt. Hoo boy, I remember thinking, my eyes bouncing from the nose stud to the neck tattoo to the horizontal scar peeking through her stubbled scalp. The kids were seated in a circle, freewriting in their journals. Twenty-two, twenty-three kids in that class, and I don't think there was a single pen that didn't stop dead on the page.

"We're finishing up a writing exercise," I whispered. "Have a seat." She ignored the empty one in the circle I indicated and, instead, exiled herself to a desk in back. Someone made a crack about *Star Trek: Voyager*, but because the put-down was borderline inaudible and the reaction from the others minimal, I decided to let it lie. Velvet didn't. Her arm shot into the air and gave an unspecified middle-finger salute. Most of the kids didn't notice, but the few who did—Becca, Jason, Nate—looked from Velvet to me. I stared them down, one by one. "Five more minutes," I announced. "Keep those pens moving."

When the bell rang and the others exited, Velvet stayed seated. She took an inhaler out of her pocket and gave herself a couple of puffs. She kept looking from her schedule to her photocopied floor plan of the building. "Big school," I said. "It's like a maze when you're new, isn't it? Can I help?"

She shook her head and prepared to go. As she approached, I looked past the "fuck you" accoutrements to the kid herself: broad nose, freckles, skin the grayish tan of Earl Grey tea with milk. I wondered why someone with a six-inch scar running along the side of her skull would choose to shave her head.

"So where you from?" I asked.

"Vermont."

"Really? I'm a transplanted New Englander, too. Where in Vermont?"

"Barre."

"That's where they have the big granite quarries, right?" I caught the slightest of nods. "Oh, and by the way, your inhaler? You're supposed to leave it at the nurse's office. School rule: they have to monitor everyone's medication. My wife's one of the nurses here, so she can help you. Mrs. Quirk."

Without responding, she trudged past me and entered the crowded corridor. "Holy crap!" someone shouted. "Shoot it before it breeds!"

The non-jocks, the readers, the gay kids, the ones starting to stew about social injustice: for these kids, "letting your freak flag fly" is both self-discovery and self-defense. You cry for this bunch at the mandatory pep assemblies. Huddled together, miserably, in the upper reaches of the bleachers, wearing their oversized raincoats and their secondhand Salvation Army clothes, they stare down at the school-sanctioned celebration of the A-list students. They know bullying, these kids—especially the ones who refuse to exist under the radar. They're tripped in the hallway, shoved against lockers, pelted with Skittles in the lunchroom. For the most part, their tormenters are stealth artists. A busy teacher exiting the office or hustling between classes to the copying machine may shoot a dirty look or issue a terse "Cut it out!" but will probably keep walking. And if some unsubtle bully goes over the line and gets hauled to the office, there's a better-than-average chance the vice principal in charge of discipline is an ex-jock and an ex-intimidator, too—someone who understands the culture, slaps the bully's wrist, and sends him back to class. The freaks know where there's refuge: in the library, the theater program, art class, creative writing. So maybe if Velvet had ratcheted down the hostility a couple of notches, or laid low for a week or so, or worn clothes a little less assaultive, my creative writers might have embraced her. But it didn't happen.

A few weeks after her arrival, Velvet's guidance counselor, Ivy Shapiro, appeared at my door in the middle of class. A pint-sized New Yorker in her early sixties, Ivy had a no-nonsense style that a lot of the faculty found abrasive. There were grumblings that she always took the kid's side against the teacher's, no matter what the issue. I liked Ivy, though, despite the fact that she was an obnoxious New York Yankees fan. "Excuse me a minute," I told the kids.

"Velvet Hoon," Ivy said. "Attendance?"

"She shows up."

"She working?"

"Sometimes. She handed in a story today, which sort of surprised me."

"Why's that?"

I told her about the ten-minute warm-ups we do at the beginning of each class. I collect them and keep them in the kids' folders, so they can look back and see if they want to expand something into a longer piece. "Velvet'll do the exercises, but she won't hand them in. The one time I pressed her on it, she balled up her paper and stuffed it in her pocket."

"She doesn't trust men," Ivy said. "What's her story about?"

I shrugged. "Just got it."

She nodded, asked about Velvet's interaction with the other kids.

"Zilch," I said. "Unless you count the sneering."

"Theirs or hers?"

"Goes back and forth."

Ivy asked if I could make it to an after-school meeting on Velvet the next day. "Depends," I said. "You serving refreshments?"

"Sure. And crying towels for Red Sox fans."

That night, after dinner, I read Velvet's story. She'd titled it "Gorilla Grrrrl," so I was expecting some Jane Goodall living-with-the-apes thing. Instead, I'd gotten a handwritten twelve-pager about a badass female outlaw whose mission in life was to wipe out every Gap store in the country. Bombs detonate. Merchandise goes up in flames. Preppy kids and store managers get expended. At the end, the unnamed heroine kills herself rather than let an Army SWAT team take her. But she goes down victorious. Everyone in America's become too scared to shop at the Gap, and the corporation sinks like the *Titanic*.

It was usually the guys who gravitated toward violent revenge fantasies. The girls skewed more toward poetry of the I'm-a-bird-in-a-cage-because-you're-my-boyfriend variety. So Velvet's out-of-the-box yarn caught my attention. At the end of her story, I wrote.

GOOD	NEEDS WORK
1. The story's well shaped.	*1. Tone unclear. Is this a parody?*
2. Political aspects are interesting.	*2. Characterization. Who is she? Why is she so angry?*
3. Original!	*3. Grammar, spelling*

Let's talk about this. For a first draft, you've accomplished quite a bit. A-P.S. I think you mean <u>Guerrilla</u> Grrrl. Look it up.

Later, in bed, I aimed the remote at *Law & Order* and turned off my light. The dogs were already asleep, and I thought Maureen was, too. But in the dark, she started talking about Velvet. By virtue of the kid's twice-per-school-day asthma treatments, she'd become one of Mo's regulars. "She scares the other kids," Maureen said. "When she walks in, my hypochondriacs suddenly feel better and want to go back to class."

"Could be the shaved head," I said. "The Uncle Fester look's a little over-the-top, don't you think?"

Mo shifted positions. Pulled the blanket around her. "Her medical records came in today," she said. "The poor kid's life *has* been a horror show."

I was just dozing off when Mo did something she rarely did: initiated lovemaking rather than following my lead. She was insistent, too, stroking me, straddling me, rubbing the head of my stiff cock back and forth against her belly, her thigh. At the side of the bed, Sophie started whimpering.

"Hey, slow down," I whispered. "Or I'm going to—" When she put me inside of her, I started coming. She came, too, fast and hard. Hers lasted and lasted. I'd think she was done, and she'd shudder some more.

While she was in the bathroom, I lay there wondering who she'd just fucked. Me? Paul Hay? Some new guy I didn't know about? The toilet flushed. Her shadow moved across the wall. She climbed back into bed and scooched up against me. "So what did all that just mean?" I said.

"Nothing," she finally said. "I got scared."

"Of what?"

"I don't know. Nothing. Can you hold me?"

———

AT THE MEETING THE NEXT afternoon, the six of us waited ten minutes for the school psychologist to show. Dr. Importance, a lot of us called him. "Well, screw it," Ivy finally said. "We've all got lives. Let's get started."

Ivy said she hoped a little context might help us cope with someone who, admittedly, was a very complicated young woman. "Now to begin with, she's an emancipated minor. That's always an iffy situation, but in Velvet's case, it may be for the best. Her experiences with adult caretakers—"

"Okay, hold it," Henry Blakely said. "I apologize for wanting to take twenty-five kids through an American history curriculum, but frankly I don't care to know who spanked her or looked at her cross-eyed when she was little." My space in the teachers' parking lot was next to Henry's. His back bumper had two stickers: "*I'd Rather Be Golfing*" and "*He who dies with the most toys WINS!*"

"Trust me, Henry," Ivy said. "It goes way beyond spanking."

"So that gives her a get-out-of-jail-free card?"

"Of course it doesn't. What I'm saying is—"

"No, here's what *I'm* saying. She's combative, she refuses to do the work, and if she shows up in my class wearing those penis earrings again, she's going to get the boot, same as she got today. Now if you'll excuse me, I have two *decent* kids in my room, waiting to take their makeups."

Ivy sat there for a moment, gathering herself. "Decent and inde-cent," she said. "I guess it makes life easier when you can put kids in two camps and write off half of them." She reached into her big canvas bag. "Almost forgot. Mr. Quirk wanted refreshments." We passed the Mint Milanos around the conference table and told our tales of woe.

Audrey Gardner said she had trouble getting past the swastika tattoo on Velvet's calf. "It's upsetting for some of the students, too," she said. "Poor Dena Gobel came to me in tears."

Ivy said she was "all over" that one—that she and Velvet had just had a heart-to-heart about the Holocaust. "It was a case of stupid judgment, not anti-Semitism. When she was living in Fort Collins, she got mixed up with some skinhead assistant manager at the Taco Bell where she used to hang out. Getting the swastika was apparently some kind of love test. It shouldn't be a problem anymore, Audrey. I bought her more Band-Aids than there are days left in the school year, and she says she'll wear them. What else we got?"

Bill Gustafson said most days Velvet came back from lunch "on cloud nine." Andy Kirby said that, on her second day in his class, Velvet declared algebra irrelevant to her life and strolled out the door. "Haven't seen her since," he said. Gerri Jones said Velvet had *never* shown up for gym.

"How about you, Quirk?" Ivy asked.

I reported that on the bad days, Velvet was openly hostile, and on the good ones, she was merely passive-aggressive.

"But she comes to class, right?"

"Yup."

"You get a chance to read her story yet?"

I nodded. Summarized the plotline of Velvet's revenge fantasy.

"Wow," Audrey said. "Quite an imagination." No one else said a thing.

Dr. Importance showed up at the one-hour mark and signed off on the decision to pull Velvet from the mainstream. She'd receive her education, instead, seated at a study carrel in the in-school suspension room. Teachers would forward Velvet's work to Ivy, who'd see to it that it was completed and returned. It was a house arrest of sorts.

Ivy said what Velvet needed was a faculty "buddy," one of us who'd be willing to check in with her each day—say at lunchtime—so that she'd have adult contact with someone other than herself and Mrs. Jett, the detention room monitor, aka "Hatchet Face." "How about it, Caelum?" Ivy asked. "She seems to have opened the door a crack to you. You want to give it a shot?"

"Can't," I said. "Cafeteria duty."

"Well, what if I talk to Frank? See if we can get you reassigned?"

My crucial mistake was shrugging instead of shaking my head.

After the meeting broke up, Ivy said she wanted to share some of the particulars of Velvet's biography off the record, provided I thought I had stomach enough to hear them.

Mom and Dad, both drug addicts, had had their parental rights revoked when Velvet was seven. For fun, they and their friends had gotten her drunk, taken her to a carnival, and put her by herself on the Tilt-a-Whirl. Velvet had tried to get off the ride mid-spin and ended up with a concussion and a gash on the side of her head.

"I've seen the scar," I said.

"There was a grandmother in Vermont. She took her in for a while. Decent enough person, I guess, but Velvet was too much for her to handle. She kept running away, back to her mom. The family shipped her out here five or six years ago. An uncle up in Fort Collins said he'd take a crack at her. Which he did, literally, many times over. She was twelve when she moved back to the grandmother's. Then Grandma died and she came back to Colorado. She landed in the emergency room, then bounced into the foster care system. When she was fourteen, she had an abortion."

"The skinhead?" I asked.

"No, he came along later. It was one of her foster brothers or their friends—she couldn't say who. She only knew it wasn't the dad, who'd never touched her, or the upstairs uncle, who'd never penetrated. His thing was urinating on her."

"Good God. And we're supposed to save her with academics?"

What was hopeful, Ivy said, given Velvet's history with men, was that she'd singled me out as someone at the school who she might risk trusting.

"She *doesn't* trust me," I said. "She's not even civil."

"But that story of hers," Ivy said. "The character's angry, alienated, self-hating. That's a form of disclosure, isn't it? Maybe she's testing the waters with you, Quirk. And wouldn't that be awesome, if she could establish a trustworthy relationship with an adult male? Begin to build on that?"

"Well, she and I have one thing in common," I said.

"What's that?"

"Drunken fathers."

Ivy smiled. "Yours, too, huh? Listen, I'm in a great ACOA group, if you ever want to go to a meeting."

I shrugged. Told her I had no talent for acronyms.

"Adult Children of Alcoholics," she said.

"Oh, right. Thanks. But no."

"It helps," she said.

"Probably does," I said. "But my dad died when I was a kid. I buried all that stuff a long time ago."

"Oh," she said. "So was *I* the one who just brought him up?"

———————

VELVET AND I BEGAN OUR sessions by examining "Guerrilla Grrrrl." She said it was neither a parody nor a reflection of herself; it was just some stupid story she'd made up because she had to. No, she didn't want to revise it. With deep sighs of disgust, she fixed the spelling and run-on sentences and declared the job done. In the next few weeks, I gave her two more writing assignments. For each, she wrote variations on the first story.

She was a reader, so there was that to build on. During one of our early go-arounds, I asked her what kind of books she liked. "I don't know," she said. "Different kinds. But not that Shakespeare shit."

"So what's your favorite book?" I asked. I was grasping, frankly. A dialogue between "buddies" is tough when you're the only bud who's talking. Velvet answered my question with an indifferent shrug. So I was pleasantly surprised when, the next day, she took a Chiclet-sized piece of paper out of her back pocket, unfolded and unfolded it, and handed it to me. "These are my top four," she said. "I like them all the same." She had scrawled fifteen or sixteen book titles and crossed out all but *Dune*, *Interview with the Vampire*, *The Hitchhiker's Guide to the Galaxy*, and *To Kill a Mockingbird*. I told her that *Mockingbird* was one of my favorites, too. She nodded soberly. "Boo Radley rocks," she said.

That weekend, in Denver, I wandered into the Tattered Cover. I'd meant to browse for myself. Instead, I filled my arms with books for Velvet.

She read them, too: Tolkien, Ursula K. Le Guin, H. G. Wells. She balked at Dickens at first, but after she'd read everything else, she picked up *Great Expectations*. "I thought this was gonna suck, but it doesn't," she told me, halfway through the book. "This dude *gets* it."

"Gets what?" I said.

"All the different ways adults fuck with kids' heads."

It was a pretty perceptive observation, but her jailer, Mrs. Jett, heard the f-bomb and approached, pointing to a hand-lettered sign on the wall titled "The Ten Commandments of In-School Suspension." The woman had actually cut cardboard into the shape of Moses' stone tablets. She stared hard at Velvet, her pencil point tapping against Commandment Number Five, "Thou Shalt Not Use Profanity."

Goddamnit, I thought. Back off. Let the kid breathe. "Hey, let me ask you something," I said. "Did you have to climb into the Rockies and pick that up personally, or did God the Father FedEx it to you?"

"Whoa, dude! He just *iced* her!" a kid in another cubicle announced. Mrs. Jett's chin quivered. She asked to speak to me in the hallway.

"I don't appreciate your sarcasm," she said. I told her I didn't appreciate her eavesdropping. "I don't *have* to eavesdrop, Mr. Quick. When you and Miss Hoon are having your lunchtime tête-à-têtes, we can all hear you plain as day."

"Yeah, first of all, it's Quirk, not Quick," I said. "And they're not tête-à-têtes. They're literary discussions." If she wanted to get on *her* high horse, I figured, then I sure as hell could climb up on mine.

"I don't consider the word I heard her use to be 'literary.' Nor do I appreciate your casual attitude about my standards. I'd like you to consider the fact that you're a guest in my classroom."

"So this is a turf thing?" I said.

"No, sir. This is an education thing. I work with children who are largely in the dark about the rules of acceptable social behavior. Now I may not be as well-versed in lit'rature as you are, but I can certainly guide them in *decency*."

"Lady," I said. "Loosen up."

When I returned from the hallway, Velvet slipped me a note. "That rocked!" it said. "She's a fucken bitch." And that, more than the books, was our big breakthrough.

I began signing Velvet out of jail at lunchtime. We'd swing by the nurse's office first, so that she could take her asthma medicine and pick up the bag lunch Maureen had started bringing in for her. Then we'd head down to the English wing.

I started letting Velvet borrow my books: Vonnegut, Kesey, Pirsig, Plath. One morning, I took my prize possession out of our bookcase, dropped it into a Ziploc bag, and brought it in to school.

"It's a first edition," I said. "And look. She signed it."

Velvet ran her finger over Harper Lee's signature. "Dude," she said. "This is a fake."

"No, it isn't. I bought it from a reputable dealer. It's authenticated."

"Whatever that means, it probably don't mean dick," she said.

"Dude," I said. "Watch your language." She kept touching the signature, staring at it in disbelief.

Ivy popped in one day after school. "Looks like things are going well with Velvet," she said. "I walked by at lunchtime today and you two were deep in conversation. I almost didn't recognize her without the scowl."

"Yeah, the glacier's starting to melt a little," I said. "She's bright."

Ivy smiled. "One suggestion, though, Red Sox. Keep your door open."

"Because?"

"Because kids like Velvet can manipulate situations. And people. It's one of the ways they learn how to survive."

"Look," I said. "I've been teaching for twenty years. I've seen plenty of kids play plenty of teachers, but I've never been one of them, okay? So unless you want to tell me *how* she's manipulating me—"

"I'm not saying she is, Quirk. I think you're doing a great job with her. All I'm suggesting is that you leave your door open."

Our conversation left a bad taste in my mouth. Wasn't *she* the one who'd set up this "faculty buddy" thing? Wasn't *she* the one who'd gotten all revved up about the idea of Velvet trusting a male teacher? Now that the kid was moving in that direction, it was a problem?

I *did* leave the door open for the next few sessions, and it was hall-way racket and one interruption after another. "Hey, Mr. Quirk, you busy?" "Yo, Mr. Quirk, what's happening?" So I started closing it again, and locking it. I suggested we sit at the back of the classroom where no one would bother us.

Writing-wise, I wanted to wean Velvet away from those comic-book plots she kept cooking up, so I bought her a copy of Anne La-mott's *Bird by Bird: Some Instructions on Writing and Life.* Velvet's conclusion was that Lamott was "pretty wacked but pretty cool." She reread the book, underlined her favorite parts, Post-it-noted pages. "No offense," she said, "but too bad *she's* not my teacher." By the third week, her copy was held together with rubber bands, and Velvet had started writing about her life.

She steered clear of the really tough stuff—her parents, the foster home horrors—but what she wrote was still pretty compelling. She had this tough-vulnerable *voice,* you know? And an instinct about detail. She wrote this one piece about running away, and it was *you* getting into those cars that pulled over to the side of the road. It was *you* sitting in those Wal-Mart snack bars, waiting for folks to get up and walk away from their half-eaten food rather than tossing it. I don't mean to overstate it. She wasn't a genius or anything. But for better or worse, she'd lived more—suffered more—than most kids, so she had more to draw on. Reflect on. And she'd take feedback and run with it. Come back with a revision twice as good as her first draft. And damn if *that* wasn't a rush.

One day, I asked Velvet to write about her favorite place. "My fa-vorite place now or ever?" she asked.

"Ever," I said.

The following Monday, she handed me an essay titled "Hope Cem-etery." I asked her where it was. "Near my grandmother's house in Vermont," she said. "I used to go there to think and shit. I couldn't make it come out like I wanted. If you don't like it, just rip it up."

I'd been telling Velvet to grab the reader's attention from the beginning, and "Hope Cemetery" sure accomplished that. It opened with her fitting a condom over some kid's dick. During her second try at living in harmony with Grandma, Velvet had begun giving blow jobs behind a mausoleum at the back of the graveyard, ten bucks a pop. I stopped reading. Put the paper down and walked away from it. Was she starting to trust me *too* much? Was she playing Shock the Teacher?

But I sat back down and kept reading, and after the raunchy opening, "Hope Cemetery" took an unexpected turn. Became a meditation on Velvet's grandfather, a stonecutter whom she knew only from his graveyard sculpture. (Later on, I Googled the guy. Three different hits verified that Angelo Colonni had been more artist than artisan, one of the best of the breed.) Velvet describes the change Hope Cemetery triggers in her. She stops doing business there and starts going, instead, to visit her grandfather's art: floral bouquets, weeping angels, replicas of dead children, all of them released from blocks of granite. The essay ends back at her grandmother's garage, where Velvet handles the chisels, mallets, and rasps that Colonni had used. In the last sentence, she slips one of her hands inside her grandfather's battered leather work glove. And with that simple act, she feels a connection across time that's both tactile and spiritual. It was a poignant piece of writing, better than she knew. I told her so.

She said she thought it kind of sucked.

"Well, it doesn't," I said. "Look, the Colorado Council of the Arts is sponsoring a writing contest for high school kids. The winners get cash awards. You should work on this some more and enter it. I think you'd have a shot."

She snorted. Some snobby rich kid would win, she said; it would be a waste of time and stamps.

"Guess that lets you off the hook then," I said. "Pretty convenient."

"Should I take out the beginning?" she asked. "If I enter that contest, or whatever."

I said I wasn't sure. "It's pretty raw. Might be off-putting to some straitlaced judge. But there's a strange resonance between the beginning and the end. The glove thing, you know?"

"What's resonance?"

"It's like when something echoes something else and . . . *deepens* it. Makes it mean something more than it meant at first. See, there's the initial effect of you putting the condom on the nameless boy, and it's strictly business, right?"

"Those guys were douchebags," she said.

"Yeah, well . . . but at the end, when you slip your hand into your granddad's glove, it's a *loving* act. So from the beginning of the essay to the end, you've changed, see? And it's the sculpture that took you there. You get it?"

She nodded.

"So, to answer your question, it's up to *you* whether or not you want to leave the opening image in or take it out."

"Yeah, but what do *you* think I should do?"

"I think you should figure it out for yourself. You have good writing instincts. Use them."

At the end of that session, she thanked me for my help. First time. "You know a lot about writing," she said. "You should write a book."

I told her I had—a novel.

"Shut up! Did it get published?"

"It was accepted for publication, but then it never happened."

"Why not?"

"Long story."

"What's it about?"

The disappearance of a little boy, I told her.

"Cool. Can I read it sometime?"

"No."

"Has Maureen read it?"

"Mrs. Quirk, you mean? No, she hasn't."

"Why not?"

Because it made me too vulnerable. "Because it's asleep in a file cabinet in Connecticut," I said. "I don't want to wake it up."

She smirked at that. "So now you don't have to work on it no more, right?" I told her I was beginning to feel like I'd created a monster.

"What's the title?"

"Hey," I said. "Let's get back to *your* writing." But she persisted. Pestered me until I told her. "*The Absent Boy*," I said.

She repeated the title, nodding in agreement. "Cool," she said.

On our walk back to the in-school suspension room, I brought up the subject of those graveyard blow jobs. "You're not doing anything like that now, are you?" I asked. She looked away. Shook her head. "Because that's pretty risky behavior, you know? You deserve better."

"I made them use a condom," she said.

"Which was good. But still—"

"Except this one older dude. He wouldn't use one, so I charged him extra. Plus, he worked at Radio Shack, so he used to boost me some cool stuff. Handheld video games and shit."

———————

A FEW DAYS LATER, VELVET handed me a revision of "Hope Cemetery." The sex act was intact, but she'd sanded down the rough edges and sharpened the connection between the opening and closing images. She'd grasped the concept of resonance, all right. At the bottom of her paper, I wrote, "This essay is as polished as one of your grandfather's sculptures." Sitting across from her at lunchtime the next day, I watched her read the comment. When she was done, she looked up, expressionless. She stared at me for a few seconds more than felt comfortable.

That night, I had Maureen read Velvet's essay. "It's unbelievable, isn't it?" I said. "I mean, unless Jerry Falwell's the judge, how could she not win this thing? . . . What? Why are you smirking?"

"Sounds like Mr. Neutral's misplaced his objectivity," she said.

"Yeah, well . . . if some kid comes up with a piece that's better than 'Hope Cemetery,' I'd really like to read it."

VELVET'S SIXTEENTH BIRTHDAY WAS COMING up, so we invited her over to the house for dinner. It was Maureen's idea. I felt a little iffy about it—mixing school and home—but it wasn't as if anyone else was going to do anything for the kid. Mo ordered a cake and one of those balloon bouquets. She made a vegetable lasagna. We shopped together for Velvet's presents: dangly earrings, jazzy socks, a leather-bound journal for her writing.

Velvet wanted to be picked up in front of Wok Express, the takeout place near where the State of Colorado rented her a room. Mo drove over there, waited half an hour, and then called me. "Should I just come home?" she asked. "Oh, wait a minute. Here she comes."

Back at the house, things got off to a bumpy start. Velvet took one look at Sophie and Chet and headed for higher ground—her butt on the back of our sofa, her big silver boots on the seat cushions. She'd been bitten by a rottweiler once, she said; she didn't trust *any* dogs. We kept trying to convince her that ours were friendly, but she wasn't buying it. I had to put them out in the garage and let them bark.

And then there was Velvet's party outfit: cargo shorts, fishnet stockings crisscrossing the uncovered swastika tattoo, and a stained T-shirt with a cartoon picture of Santa Claus raising his middle finger. "Fuck You and the Sleigh You Rode In On," it said. Maureen handled the situation gracefully. She asked Velvet if she wanted a house tour. On their way upstairs, I heard Mo suggest how chilly it was at our house. When they came back down again, the kid was wearing Mo's blue pullover sweater.

We'd planned to have her open her gifts after dinner and birthday cake, but the minute she saw them, she tore into them. She put on her new earrings, pulled off her boots so that she could wear her new socks. She kept picking up the journal and rubbing its soft leather against her cheek.

"This dinner's good, Mom," Velvet told Maureen, even though she performed an autopsy on her square of lasagna, piling all traces of vegetable matter onto the cloth napkin beside her plate. Two or three times, she got out of her chair to whack her balloon bouquet. When we lit the candles and sang "Happy Birthday," she wouldn't look at her cake. She blew out her candles with such ferocity, I thought the frosting might fly across the room.

When Velvet went outside for a smoke, Maureen and I cleared the table. "This is going well, don't you think?" Mo said.

"Uh-huh. She calls you Mom?"

"She just started doing that. I don't think anyone's ever had a party for her. Do you?"

"From the way she's behaving, I'd say no. Do you think we can let the dogs back in? They're going crazy out there."

Mo shook her head. "She's really scared of them."

We ended things a little after nine. Mo stayed home to clean up and I drove Velvet back, the balloons bobbing and blocking my view from the rearview mirror. En route, I asked her if she'd had a good time.

"Yeah," she said. "You and Mom are awesome."

"Why do you call her Mom?" I asked.

"I don't know. Cuz she's my mom."

"Yeah? How so?"

She didn't answer for several seconds. Then, she said, "I'll give you a blow job if you want. I'm good at it." At first, I didn't say anything. Couldn't think of anything *to* say. "You know the Salvation Army store? Just drive around back where the drop-off bins are."

"Velvet," I said. "That's so inappropriate, so disrespectful of . . . How can you spend the evening with us, call her *Mom*, for Christ's sake, and then—"

"Okay, okay," she snapped. "You don't have to get all moral about it. It's not like you're doing *me* any favors."

When I stopped for a red light, she swung the door open and jumped out. "Hey, come back here!" I called.

She did, but only to snatch up her gifts, minus the balloon bouquet. I followed her for about a block, trying to coax her back into the car. It was dark. It was late. We were a mile or more from where she lived. "Get away from me, you perv!" she screamed. Hey, I didn't need *that* bullshit. I hung a U-turn and gunned it in the opposite direction.

I didn't get it. She'd enjoyed the evening. Why did she have to sabotage it? I was sure her come-on was going to piss off Maureen as much as it did me.

Except when I got home, I didn't tell Mo. "That was quick," she said.

"Yeah. No traffic. The dogs need to go out?"

"Just came back in. I see she forgot her balloons."

"That's a red flag, isn't it?" I said. "That 'Mom' business?"

"Well, I'm not going to make an issue of it, Caelum. If she wants to call me Mom, what's the big deal?"

I let go of Velvet's bouquet. It rose and bumped the ceiling.

The next morning, the balloons were floating halfway between the ceiling and the floor. By the time Aunt Lolly called for her Sunday check-in, they were grazing the carpet. You moved, they moved; they were like wraiths. I kept losing track of what Lolly was saying. Kept wondering why I'd let the whole day slip by without telling Mo what Velvet had said. Which of the two was I trying to protect? Or was it myself I needed to shield from Velvet's sleazy offer? . . . "You know what Shirley Pingalore told me the other day?" Lolly was saying. "That they had to cancel the sports program because of overcrowding. They're using the gym as a dormitory. Seventy-five beds and two toilets. It's pathetic." I opened the cutlery drawer and grabbed a steak knife.

"What's that?" Lolly said.

"What?"

"Sounds like gunfire."

AT SCHOOL ON MONDAY, VELVET was a no-show. She was MIA for the rest of that week. I kept meaning to say something to Maureen, but then I kept not doing it. I didn't want to say anything to Ivy Shapiro, either—have *her* start playing twenty questions. Velvet's proposition had come so out of nowhere, and had been so goddamned embarrassing, I decided to just bury it.

She resurfaced the following week, but when I went to pick her up for our noontime discussion, she told me she didn't want to meet with me anymore—that she was sick of it. Mrs. Jett had left the room to get some tea, and the other kids had been dismissed to lunch.

"You're sick of it, or you feel ashamed about what you said during that ride home?" I said. "Because if it's that, then—"

"What'd I say?" she asked. "I don't even remember."

"Yes, you do."

She told me she wanted to read what *she* wanted to read, not the boring crap I gave her. Writing was boring, she said. *I* was boring. She'd just written all that corny shit because she knew that's what I wanted to hear. She felt sorry for Maureen, she said, married to a geek like me.

"Well," I said. "I guess we're both wasting our time, then. Good luck."

"Wait," she said. "Just *listen* to me." I kept going.

Before I left school that afternoon, I wrote a note to Ivy, resigning as Velvet's "faculty buddy." I was vague about why—spoke in general terms about how it had worked for a while, but then she'd shut down. I kept thinking about what Ivy had said: that kids like Velvet manipulate situations. All I needed was for the kid to claim *I* was the one who'd suggested sex to *her*.

At home, I told Mo I'd packed it in as Velvet's tutor. "Why?" she said.

"Because she's an unappreciative little brat," I said. "I'm sick of her rudeness, and I'm sick of doing all the heavy lifting with this 'buddy' thing."

"You know, ever since her birthday, she's been standoffish with me," Mo said. "I don't get it."

I shrugged. Said we never should have had her over.

I had trouble sleeping that night but didn't want to wake Maureen. I went downstairs to read. Passing by the bookcase in the study, I noticed the space where my signed *To Kill a Mockingbird* was supposed to be.

———————

THE COLORADO ARTS COUNCIL NOTIFIED the school that Velvet Hoon had won the writing award in her division. "I thought you might want to be the one to give her the news," Ivy said. I suggested we do it together.

Velvet was asleep at her cubicle, her cheek against the desktop. When she heard she'd won, she looked more jarred than happy. "What do I have to do?" she asked Ivy. She wouldn't look at me.

"There's a ceremony in downtown Denver," Ivy said. "At the State Capitol. You and the other winners each read a five-minute excerpt from your essays. Then you accept your award, get your picture taken, get fussed over."

"I don't *want* my picture taken," she insisted.

"You get a check for two hundred dollars," I said. "That's not too hard to take, is it?" Velvet ignored the question. When I mentioned that we should go over what was appropriate to read at the event, she finally looked at me. "For instance, you'd want to omit the opening paragraph," I said. "There'll be younger kids there."

"And assholes," Velvet said.

Ivy looked from Velvet to me, then back again. "What I thought," she said, "was that you, Mr. Quirk, and I could drive downtown together. The ceremony's at five. And after, maybe we could take you out to dinner to celebrate. There are some nice restaurants at the Sixteenth Street Mall. Or how about the Hard Rock Café at the Denver Pavilions?"

Velvet nodded in my direction. "Can his wife come?"

"Sure. Sure she can."

From across the room, Mrs. Jett asked what all the excitement was about. When Ivy told her, she wanted to know if she could photocopy the letter of congratulations for her bulletin board.

"No!" Velvet said.

Walking back down the corridor, I remarked to Ivy that Velvet was the most miserable award winner I'd ever seen.

"Not uncommon for kids with her kind of history," she said. "So many bad things have happened to them that they can't trust the good things. They have to shove them away before someone can snatch them back."

At the end of the day, I stopped in the health office to see Maureen. Velvet was with her. "Velvet was just telling me the good news," she said. "Congratulations to you both."

"She's the one who wrote the essay," I said.

A kid appeared in the doorway, asking for a form for his sports physical. When Mo went to the outer office to get it, it was just Velvet and me in there.

"Didn't I tell you you'd written a prize-winner?" I said. She shrugged. "Hey, by the way. When you were over at our house that night? Did you borrow my book?"

"What book?"

"*To Kill a Mockingbird*."

She shook her head.

"Because it's missing. And I know you really love—"

"I didn't steal your freakin' book!" she shouted. She practically plowed Maureen down getting out of there.

———————

ON THE DAY OF THE award ceremony, Velvet was absent from school. Ivy caught up with her by phone in the afternoon. Velvet knew where the Capitol building was, she said; she'd meet us there. Some of her friends were going, too, so they could give her a ride. Ivy reminded her to practice what she was planning to read, to wear something appropriate for the occasion, and to make sure her swastika tattoo was covered.

The Capitol was stately and grand: polished brass, stained glass, marble floors, and pillars. The granite carvings depicting Colorado history made me think of Velvet's grandfather. They'd set things up just inside the west entrance: rows of cushioned folding chairs, a podium atop a riser, refreshments. The other winners, spiffed-up Type A's, sat with their Type A parents. "Think she'll show?" Maureen asked. I said I wasn't going to hold my breath. When I spotted Mrs. Jett in the crowd, I walked over to her. "Thanks for coming," I said. "It'll mean a lot to her. *If* she gets here."

Mrs J. said she was rooting for Velvet, too—that she rooted for all of her ISS kids. "Come sit with us," I said.

A woman in a red and purple caftan mounted the riser, tapped the mic, and asked if we'd all be seated so that the program could begin. There was still no sign of Velvet.

She arrived, boisterously, during some seventh-grade girl's cello intercession. Her entourage consisted of an emaciated woman in black leather pants, late twenties maybe, and a stocky young man wearing a prom gown. The prizewinners and their parents craned their necks to watch the commotion. Velvet was wearing zebra-striped tights, a black bustier, an Army camouflage jacket, and her silver boots. A torn bridal veil hung from her rhinestone tiara; she'd attached plastic spiders to it. No doubt about it: the three of them were high on some-thing.

The caftan woman stood and asked them twice to please respect the other readers. When it was Velvet's turn to read, she kept look-ing back at her friends, exchanging private remarks with them, and breaking into fits of laughter. Maureen reached over, took my hand, and squeezed it.

Instead of reading "Hope Cemetery," Velvet rambled nonsensi-cally about freedom of speech, Kurt Cobain, and "asshole" teachers who try to brainwash their students. I sat there, ramrod straight, paralyzed by her betrayal of herself and me. When she left the podium, she lost her balance, stumbling off the riser and crashing into the lap of a frightened fellow prizewinner, one of the middle school boys.

I stood and left. Waited in the car for the others. Told Ivy and Mo, when they came out, that I'd rather go home than out to dinner. Never again, I promised myself. Never, ever again.

————————

VELVET NEITHER WITHDREW FROM SCHOOL nor showed up for the rest of that year. Maureen said she heard she'd left town. But the following year, she reenrolled after midterm exams and resumed her relationship with Maureen. I spotted her name on the ab-sentee list as often as not. I hardly ever saw her, and when I did, neither of us spoke. So when she emerged from the woods behind our house that morning, climbing the picnic table to be safe from dogs who were never going to hurt her, it was the first exchange the two of us had had in over a year.

I ran all the way out to Bear Creek that morning, ate a PowerBar, took a whiz, and ran all the way back. Maureen's Outback was in the driveway. She was at the kitchen table, working on our bills.

"How was your run?" she asked.

"Hard," I said. "How was your breakfast?"

"Hard. She's trying, though. She just got a job with an industrial cleaning company. But it's night shift work, so—"

"Yeah, well, just remember, Maureen, you're not her fairy godmother. You can't wave your magic wand and fix her fucked-up life. And if you *think* you can, you better put a check on your ego before she body-checks it the way she did mine."

"That was terrible, the way she treated you," she said. "But she's reaching out to me, Cae. I can't just write her off. The *last* thing that kid needs is more rejection."

"I'm going to grab a shower," I said. It was either leave the room immediately or risk telling her about Velvet's come-on for no better reason than because I was pissed about her innocence of what I'd protected her from.

I was toweling off when Mo entered the bathroom. She put her arms around me and rested her forehead against my chest. "I need a friend," she said. I lifted her face to mine. Kissed her. Kissed her harder.

We made it over to the bed. I lay there, watching her undress. She got in and pulled the covers over us. Snuggled beside me. Kissed my shoulder, my mouth. Ran her fingers across my chest, my belly. "Suck me," I said.

She looked at me, puzzled, then repositioned herself to oblige.

I was impatient with her gentle preliminaries. "Come on," I said. "*Do* it!" She pulled away. Got off the bed. Grabbed her clothes and started for the door. "Hey," I said. "Where you going?"

Her back to me, she said it over her shoulder. "I'm your wife, Caelum. Not your whore."

"Fuck *this*," I said. Reached down and started jerking myself off. I mean, I had to get release from *some*where. Sophie was on the side of the bed, watching me. "Get out of here!" I screamed. "Get the fuck—" I whacked her with a pillow and she fled.

After I'd ejaculated the anger out of me, I lay there with my puddle of regret. I'd apologize later, I told myself, but for now . . . I grabbed a magazine, got through a paragraph or two of some article that held no interest, and let my fatigue rescue me. . . .

———————

MO WOKE ME OUT OF a sound sleep. She was seated beside me on the bed. "I'm so sorry, Caelum," she said.

"No, *I'm* sorry," I said. "I was being a total asshole. You had every right to—" She was shaking her head.

"Ulysses just called. He stopped in to get his paycheck this morning and found Lolly out in the yard near the clothesline. She was talking incoherently. Trying to put her socks on her hands."

"What . . ."

"He got her back inside and called nine-one-one. I think she's had a stroke."

chapter three

FIGURING IT WAS BETTER IF they talked with someone who could speak "medical," I had Maureen call the hospital. She tried twice but couldn't get past "Louella's resting comfortably" and "Someone from the medical team will be calling" and "Can you verify that her insurance provider is Blue Cross/Blue Shield?" And goddamnit, by the time the medical team *did* call, Mo'd gone out.

"Mr. Quirk? This is Dan, one of the nurses over at Shanley Memorial." Over at? Three Rivers was two time zones away. "I've been caring for your mother today and—"

"She's my aunt," I said.

A pause, a shuffling of paperwork. "But you're her next of kin, right?"

"Yes. Why? Did she . . . "

"Oh, no, no. She's hanging in there, Mr. Quirk. Dr. Salazar will be speaking to you in just a few minutes about her test results. But first, I wonder if you could answer some questions for us about Louella's medical profile."

"Yeah, well, the thing is, my wife's a nurse, so she's more on top of Lolly's medical stuff. I can have her call you back."

Dan said he was going off-shift soon. Whatever I could help him with. "Okay," I said.

No, I wasn't sure what medications she was taking. No, I didn't know which medical practice she'd switched to after Dr. Oliver died. (I hadn't known he'd died.) Surgeries? None that I could recall. Yes, she smoked: one Marlboro a day, after her evening meal; she'd done that for years. No, she wasn't much of a drinker. A beer every now and then. Brandy on special occasions. Diabetes? No, not that I knew of.

Dan wanted to know if there was anything else I could think of.

"Just hearing loss. The TV's always shouting when I call her. She claims I mumble." When *I* call *her*: now there was a face-saving lie.

"That's helpful," Dan said. "We've been assuming Louella's incomprehension is stroke-related, but maybe she's having trouble hearing us."

"She goes by Lolly, actually. Not Louella."

"I'll make a note of that. Now, let's talk about her family history. I'm assuming both her parents are deceased. Can you tell me what they died of?"

"Well, let's see. Her father—my grandfather—died of Alzheimer's."

"At what age?"

"I'm not sure. His late seventies, maybe?"

"What about her mother?"

"She died during childbirth."

"Of?"

"I don't know. Childbirth, I guess. Lolly and my father were raised by their grandmother."

"So she has a brother. Any other siblings?"

"No. My father was Lolly's twin."

"Was? He's deceased?"

"Yeah. . . . Yup."

"And what was the cause of his death?"

The question tightened my grip on the phone. "Officially? Officially, it was internal injuries and . . . loss of blood. His legs were severed."

"Were these war injuries?"

"No. He was a drunk. He was fishing off a trestle bridge, and they think he must have passed out or something. And a train came along."

"Whoa. That's tough. And how old was—"

"Thirty-three. But look, like I said, my wife can fill you guys in a lot better about Lolly's medical stuff. And as far as her medications, what I can do is get hold of her handyman. Have him go by the house and look around. Make a list, or bring you her prescription bottles, or whatever."

Dan said that would be super. One more thing. Did I think I was going to be able to make the trip back to be with my aunt?

"Oh, well, it would be tough. . . . But if it becomes necessary."

Dan said he understood. Were there friends or other family who might be able to check in on her? Stroke was such an upheaval. So frightening. Familiar faces were reassuring at a time like this.

"Uh, well . . . I know she gets together, plays cards with some of the gals she used to work with. And they go down to the casino once or twice a month. Eat at the buffet or whatever."

"Sounds like my mother," he said. "Is one of her friends Kay? She keeps asking for Kay."

"I don't know. There's a Hilda. And a Marie. A Shirley."

Dan thanked me. I thanked him. "Dr. Salazar will be coming to the phone shortly," he said. "Can you hold?"

Maybe the lite-rock station Dan switched me to was penance for my shortcomings as next-of-kin. I bit at some ragged skin on my thumb. Grabbed a beer out of the fridge. The deejay had a theme going: "The Wind Beneath My Wings," "Colors of the Wind," "Windy." When was it that FM radio had started sucking? The eighties, right? The Reagan era?

That morning's newspaper was on the counter. "NATO Air Strikes in Yugoslavia Intensify" . . . "Hockey Great Gretzky to Retire" . . . "Love Bug Computer Virus Delivers 'Fatally Attractive' Message"

... Before we moved west, I'd promised Lolly I'd get back to see her twice a year—summertime and Christmastime—but I'd reneged. Hadn't even gone back for Hennie's funeral. . . . And what did my father's shit-canning his life have to do with Lolly's stroke? Nothing, that's what. I should have kept my fucking mouth shut. . . . I saw Lolly, standing at the doorway of my algebra class, freshman year— not Ma, not Grandpa. As soon as I saw her there, I knew Daddy was dead.

I crooked the cordless against my shoulder. Filled the dogs' water dish. Finished my beer. . . . *Stroke is such an upheaval, so frightening.* . . . This Dr. Salazar was taking *his* sweet time. They must teach that tactic in medical school: keep the loved ones waiting, so that by the time you pick up the phone, it'll seem like the voice of God.

"And the lite favorites just keep on rolling," the radio said. "*If you like pina coladas, getting caught in the rain . . .*" Oh, God, not *that* stupid song. Guy decides to cheat, so he answers his own wife's personal ad? Yeah, like *that's* going to happen. In real life, some psycho chick would be waiting at that bar, and they'd go to a Motel Six, and he'd have erectile dysfunction. Have to call Bob Dole for some Viagra. Shit, he goes from running for president to being the poster boy for the All-American boner? How much did he get for *that* gig? . . .

"*If you like making love at midnight, in the dunes of the Cape . . .*" No, thanks. Too many sand fleas. Now that shitty song was going to be stuck in my head for the rest of the day. And if that Dan guy thought I was indifferent because I couldn't make it back to Connecticut, then fuck him. I *loved* Lolly. She'd been more of a father to me than my father ever had. Taken me fishing, taken me on my first trip to Fenway. I had almost total recall of that trip. Boston versus Milwaukee, an exhibition game. Lolly'd won tickets on the radio, and we'd gone up in her old green Hudson. Nineteen sixty-one, it was. Yastrzemski and Chuck Schilling in their rookie year, Monbouquette on the mound. We'd had a blowout on the way home, and Lolly'd given me a lesson on how to fix a flat. . . . But shit, this was the busiest stretch of the school year. Curriculum meetings, placement meetings for the special needs kids, term papers to grade, exams to write. I could get back there once school was over, but—

"Hey there," a woman's voice said. "You're the nephew?"

Dr. Salazar was a fast talker, devoid of personality. Lolly's vitals had stabilized, she said. Her stroke was ischemic, caused by a clot rather than a rupture. She'd come in exhibiting classic symptoms: weakness on her left side, double vision, aphasia.

"What's aphasia?" I said.

"A disconnect between what the patient's trying to say and what's being communicated. For instance, Louella thinks to herself, I'm thirsty. I want more ice chips. But when she verbalizes it, it comes out as gibberish."

"So you're saying she's incoherent?"

"Less so than when she first came in."

The EMTs had given Lolly magnesium on the ride in, Dr. Salazar said, and that had put the injury in "slo-mo." And with stroke victims, "time was brain," she said; the quicker there was treatment, the better the odds of avoiding permanent damage. "When she got here, we gave her a clot-buster called tPA. Great drug if the patient gets it in time—acts like Drano on clogged arteries—but the operative word here is *if*. Time-wise, there's only a small window of opportunity. When the blood supply's cut off, brain cells begin to die. I think you'd better prepare yourself for the fact that your aunt will most likely have an altered life."

"Altered how?"

"Too soon to tell. We'll know more in the next forty-eight to seventy-two hours. Are you coming to be with her?"

"I don't . . . We're out in Colorado. The timing's not great."

"No, it never is."

After I hung up, I paced. Let the dogs out. Let them back in. I had to chaperone the post-prom party that night. Two of my classes were handing in their term papers on Monday. I had meetings all week. . . .

When Maureen got back, I showed her what I'd scrawled in the margins of the newspaper: "Salazar, ischemic, magnesium, Drano." Mo rattled off Lolly's medications: Lipitor for her cholesterol, Triamterene for her blood pressure, an antidepressant called Trazodone.

"She takes an antidepressant?"

She nodded. "Since Hennie died. You knew that, didn't you?"

Did I?

"They're pressuring me to fly back there and be with her," I said.

"Are you going to?"

"I can't. Not until the school year's over."

For several seconds, she said nothing. Then she volunteered to fly back and be with Lolly herself. I sighed. Drummed my fingers against the counter. "Who's Kay?" I said. "One of her bridge buddies?"

"Kay?"

"They said she keeps asking for Kay."

Mo's eyes met mine. Her smile was sympathetic. "She's saying 'Caelum.' Lolly wants *you*."

I SKETCHED OUT A WEEK'S worth of lesson plans for the sub. Mo went online and found me a beggars-can't-be-choosers flight out of Denver: a 5:45 a.m. takeoff, a three-hour layover at O'Hare. I'd land in Hartford by late afternoon, rent a car, drive to Three Rivers. Maybe I'd go out to the farm first—get her medications, see if anything else needed doing. Barring complications, I'd be with her at the hospital by six or so.

Mo tried to talk me out of chaperoning the post-prom.

"I'll be fine," I said. "Drink a lot of coffee, drive right from school to the airport. I can crash once I get on the plane." She frowned. "Okay, let me rephrase that. I can *sleep* once I get on the plane."

I opened my closet door and stared. Should I pack my good suit and black loafers? Uh-uh. Travel light. Think positive. Go there, get done whatever there was to do, and get back. I loved Lolly, but I couldn't let her stroke hijack my life. How many guys would do *this much* for their aunt? . . . I saw the two of us out there, stranded on that rural road between Boston and home with that flat tire. It was pitch-black except for her flashlight beam. She was aiming it at the lug nut, at my hands on the wrench.

"Come on, kiddo," she'd coaxed. "Just a little more elbow grease. You can do it."

"I can't!" I'd insisted. I was Caelum Quirk, the kid who sucked at sports and walked around by himself during recess. The kid whose father was a drunk.

"Sure you can. I know you can." And so I'd strained. Grunted. And the nut had given way.

POST-PROMS ARE BRIBES, REALLY: PARENTS and teachers induce their kids to party the night away at the school gym so that they won't drink and drive. Kill themselves, their friends, their futures. The enticements that night included raffles, a deejay, a hypnotist, and nonstop food: burgers, pizzas, six-foot subs. I was put to work as a roving patroller in search of alcohol and, later, as an ice cream scooper at the make-your-own-sundae station.

They were together in the sundae line, I remember. I served them both. "One scoop? Two scoops?" Dylan had requested three, but Eric wanted just one, vanilla. I asked him if he thought they'd have a sundae line like this at boot camp. He shook his head. Half-smiled.

"When do you leave?" I said.

"July one." In another sixty hours, he'd be lying dead in the midst of the chaos, half of his head blown away. And he knew it, too. It was in the videotape they left to be discovered. Their suicides were part of the plan.

There was one other thing that night. It happened during one of the raffles. The winner got free passes to Bandimere Speedway or Rock'n'Bowl or some such, and Dylan's number got called. I was standing on the periphery. Saw the whole thing. Instead of saying, "That's me," or just walking up to get his prize, he showed Eric his ticket and the two of them high-fived. *"Sieg Heil!"* they shouted. A few of the other kids laughed; most just looked. "Assholes," someone near me muttered. I considered taking the two of them aside, saying something about the inappropriateness of it. But it was late at night, late in the school year. I was a few hours away from my flight. I let it go.

God, that's *always* the thing you have to decide with high school kids: what to make an issue of, what to let go. In the aftermath, in the middle of all those sleepless nights, I did plenty of soul-searching about that. We all did, I guess. Had it been preventable? Could those kids have been spared? . . .

I left the school a little after four a.m. Got my overnight bag out of the trunk and threw it onto the passenger seat next to me. Drove northeast toward a lightening sky. My eyes burned; my stomach felt like I'd swallowed fishhooks. As usual, Maureen had been right. I should have skipped the chaperoning detail and grabbed some sleep.

So why hadn't I?

Punishment, maybe? Self-flagellation?

For what?

For having defaulted on her. For having sent Maureen to Hennie's funeral the year before instead of going myself. They'd been common-law spouses for forty-something years, those two. She was depressed. She called me every Sunday night. It was my guilt that was flying me home. . . . And once I got there, then what? How bad off was this stroke going to leave her? How much of my summer was going to get gobbled up by Lolly's "altered life"?

At Denver International, I opted for the garage instead of the Pike's Peak shuttle lot, even though I'd pay through the nose for the convenience. The machine spat me a ticket. The arm lifted. At this hour, there were plenty of empty spaces.

I passed from the jaundiced lighting of the parking garage to the halogen glare of the walkway. Passed two porters, slumped on plastic chairs. Both glanced at my carry-on luggage, then blinked me away, as disinterested as sunning lizards. And right inside the terminal, who do I see but Velvet Hoon. Hard to miss a girl in a blue crew cut.

She was wearing a gray uniform, part of a cleaning crew. A hippie-looking guy with a gray beard was buffing the floor. A scrawny black woman was running a vacuum. Velvet had a squirt bottle and a cleaning cloth and was wiping down plastic chairs. I thought about the kids I'd just left at the post-prom party—their fun and games, their Gummy Bear sundaes and college plans. But, hey, Velvet was her own worst enemy. I walked a little faster, relieved that she didn't see me. Better for both of us. I had to talk to Maureen again about not getting sucked into the black hole of Velvet's needs. She'd just get used and abused. You can't undo that kind of damage. You *can't*.

No line at my airline counter. Just two attendants keeping each other company. They were both good-looking women. The buxom redhead was in her forties, the little blonde maybe two or three years out of high school. A phrase bubbled up from my college days, something Rocco Buzzi and I used to say about pretty girls: *I wouldn't throw her out of bed*. Big Red took the lead.

"Good morning, sir."

"Morning. I have an e-ticket. Last name's Quirk." Red nodded. Her fingers whizzed across her keyboard.

"*Caelum* Quirk?"

"Yes."

"And your final destination today is Hartford-Springfield?"

"That's right."

The blonde squinted at the screen. "I never heard the name Caelum before," she said. "Is it from the Bible?"

I shook my head. "Old family name."

"Well, at least you weren't named after some stupid song on the radio."

I squinted to read her name tag: Layla. My eyes bounced over to

Big Red's, too: Vivian. That's the tricky part about women and name tags: to read them is to check out the frontal real estate. Which I was doing when Vivian caught me. "Well," I told Layla. "You could do worse than being named after a Clapton song."

"Picture ID, sir?" Viv said.

I nodded. Fumbled for my wallet. Handed her my driver's license. Layla asked me if I was traveling for business or pleasure.

"Neither," I said. "Sick relative." Freshman year, Rocco and I had had four classifications for the girls we scoped out from afar in the BU cafeteria: wouldn't screw her blindfolded; *would* screw her blindfolded; wouldn't throw her out of bed; and, for girls of the highest order, would screw her grandmother to screw *her*. Rocco and I were both virgins back then, of course—huddled together, eating our turkey à la king and room-temperature Jell-O and rating girls we were too chicken-shit to approach.

"My son's sick, too," Layla said. "Four ear infections in one year. Wanna see his picture?"

Viv's nostrils flared. "I think what Mr. Quirk wants is to get to his gate," she said. She gave me a professional smile. "This is her first day on the job."

"That's fine," I said. "And actually, I'd *like* to see her son's picture."

Viv's smile became a grimace. Layla produced her purse. Her son dangled from her key ring, in a little plastic frame. Nappy hair, coffee skin.

"He's cute," I said. "How old?"

Three, she said. His name was Shabbaz. Vivian asked if I was checking any bags with them today.

"Uh, no. I just have the one carry-on."

"And has anyone asked you to hold anything for them since you entered airport property, sir?"

Only the heroin smuggler, Viv. "Uh, no. Nope."

"And has the bag you're carrying on board been in your possession at all times since you packed it?"

Pretty much, except when I left it with the Unabomber. "Uh-huh."

She looked up, concerned. "What?"

Had I just said *Unabomber?* "Yes. Yes, it has."

She nodded. "Aisle seat? Window seat?"

"Window, I guess. Better for sleeping."

"Try sleeping when you're a single mom," Layla said. "Last night—"

"Well, then," Viv interrupted. "You're all set. Concourse B, gate thirty-six." She handed me my boarding pass. "Have a nice flight."

"Have a nice flight," Layla echoed.

Ten or twelve steps toward the security gate, I looked back. Layla was getting chewed out in spades.

AT GATE 36, I JOINED my fellow sojourners: guys with laptops, guys on cell phones, tanned retirees in jogging suits and gold jewelry. A college-age couple leaned against each other, napping. A Mexican dad passed out churros to his kids. I caught a whiff of the fried dough and started thinking about the Mama Mia Bakery. Maybe I'd stop by, check in with Alphonse while I was home. Or maybe not. Alphonse's e-mails were depressing: all those politically incorrect jokes, all that silent salivating over some latest counter girl he'd just hired. Pushing fifty, Alphonse was still afraid to approach women. Still searching for his holy grail, too: a 1965 yellow Mustang hardtop with 289-cubic-inch engine, four-barrel carburetor, and solid-lifter valve train. He belonged to something called the Yellow Mustang Registry. Checked eBay five or six times a day. *Phoenician* Yellow, his dream car had to be, not the paler Springtime Yellow, also available back in '65. "Eat your breakfast now," the Mexican dad said.

"Whoever don't finish theirs don't get on the plane." One of the kids began to cry.

I got up, grabbed a seat closer to the TV. CNN Sports. Tim Couch had gone number one in the NFL draft. The Eagles had nabbed McNabb. Darryl Strawberry was in trouble again.

I watched the approach of a freaky-looking couple. Early twenties, maybe. She was fat, her hair a bunch of pigtail stubs. He was rat-faced. Nose ring, tattooed hands and fingers, missing teeth. She was eating a churro, too. They plopped down across from the napping college couple, whose eyes cracked open, then opened wider.

"Hi," Pigtails said.

"Hey," College Guy said.

"What are you guys going to Chicago for?"

They answered in unison. "Back to school."

"Guess why me and him are going?" The college kids both shrugged. "We're gonna be on *Jerry Springer.*"

"Really?" College Girl said. College Boy leaned forward.

"They're picking us up in a limo and paying for our hotel. The chauffeur's meetin' us at the baggage pickup. He's gonna have a sign with my name on it."

"That's awesome," College Boy said. "What are you going to be on for?"

Pigtails smiled at Ratso. Her fingers grazed his chest. "Me and him are lovers. And first cousins. Which is fine, because he got fixed."

The airline rep announced that boarding would begin, small children and passengers with special needs first.

"Acourse, what's fixed can get *un*fixed," Ratso assured College Guy. "You know what I'm saying?"

"See that fat cow sitting over there?" Pigtails said. "That's my mom. She's gonna be on the show, too." College Boy, College Girl, and I followed her gaze to a sad, puffy-looking woman with dyed black hair, seated by herself in the otherwise empty sea of chairs at gate thirty-seven. She was glaring back. "He done her, too. When we get on *Springer*, there's gonna be a showdown!"

"This so rocks," College Boy said. He raised his fist and punched the air. "Jer-ry! Jer-ry! Jer-ry!"

"She had sex with her own *nephew*?" College Girl said. "Eww."

"It's gross, ain't it?" Pigtails said. "I don't blame *him*, though. She was always strutting around our apartment half-naked. Throwing it at him like Thanksgiving dinner. His mom? Her sister? She *disowned* her." She shouted across the walkway. "What are *you* looking at, slut?" Now she had everyone's attention, the gate attendants included. Her mother stood, turning her back to her daughter. The boarding of first-class customers began.

"If she flashes titty, they give her a bonus," Ratso said.

"Not money, though," Pigtails added. "Restaurant coupons. I may do it, I may not. Depends on how I feel. They blur it, so no one sees nothing."

"What about the studio audience?" Ratso said. "Ain't nobody blurring nothin' out for them."

"So?" she said. "Shut up."

Rows thirty through forty were called to board. I was both relieved and disappointed when the *Springer* guests stood up. There went Mexican Guy and his brood, too. Pigtails' mom was in the rows-twenty-to-thirty group. I found her strangely sympathetic. Well, *path*etic, I guess. What, other than dim-wittedness, would have ever motivated her to go on that show?

My row was among the last called. I grabbed my breakfast tote from the self-serve cart, got through the tunnel, and made it to my window seat, 10A. This morning's flight was a full one, the intercom voice told us. Would we please be seated, seatbelts secured, as soon as possible?

Through the magazine and blanket distribution, the headset sales and overhead baggage jockeying, the seat next to mine remained empty. With any luck, I'd be able to flip up the armrest and stretch out a little, the better to sleep my way to Chicago.

I heard him before I saw him. "'Scuse me. 'Scuse me, please. Oops, sorry. 'Scuse me." He negotiated the aisle with the grace of a buffalo and stopped dead at row 10. "Howdy doody," he said. "Hold these for a sec?"

I took his coffee in one hand, his pastry in the other—a catcher's-mitt-sized cinnamon bun. His suitcase was cinched with leather belts. As he jammed and whacked it into the overhead space, his shirt untucked, exposing a jiggling, tofu-colored stomach. Mission accomplished, he crash-landed into seat 10B.

"Whoa," he said, adjusting his safety belt. "I think an anorexic must have had this seat before I did." He buckled the belt, flopped down his tray table, reclaimed his coffee and pastry. "Oh, geez," he said. "Forgot to take my jacket off. Do you mind doing the honors again?" He folded his tray, unbuckled his belt. Struggling out of his sleeves, he whacked my arm, sloshing coffee onto my shirt. "Oops, me bad boy," he said. His giggle was girlish.

He was Mickey Schmidt, he said. I told him my name. We shook hands. His was sticky. "And what does Caleb Quirk do for a living?" he asked.

It's Caelum, douchebag. "I teach."

"At Colorado State? Me, too!"

I shook my head. "I teach high school."

"High school!" He groaned. "I almost didn't survive the experience." I nodded, half-smiled. Told him a lot of people remembered it that way.

"No, I *mean* it," he said. "Freshman year, I tried to kill myself. *Twice*."

"Gee," I said. I mean, what *can* you say?

"The first time, I filled the bathtub and climbed in with my father's electric shaver. It kept shutting off. I thought it was God, willing me to live. But come to find out, it had a safety switch." That giggle again. He took another slug of coffee, another mouthful of cinnamon bun. He talked and ate simultaneously. "The second time, I tried to OD on my mother's Kaopectate. She used to buy it by the case. I drank five bottles. I was going for six, but I couldn't do it. You ever have your stomach pumped? I don't recommend it."

I fished out the in-flight magazine. Thumbed through it to shut him up. He reached into his shirt pocket and pulled out a small vial of pills. Popped one. "Flight anxiety," he said. "Takeoffs and landings, mostly. Once I'm in the air, I'm calmer. Want one?" The pill vial hovered in front of my nose. I shook my head. "Well, Mickey, how about you? Would you like another to help you fly a little higher through the friendly skies? Why, yes, please. Don't mind if I do." He took a second tablet, a slurp of coffee. "So what do you know about chaos-complexity theory?" he said.

"Excuse me?"

"Chaos-complexity theory."

"Uh . . . is that the one where a butterfly flaps its wings in Africa and—"

"And it triggers a tornado in Texas. Yup, that's it. Sensitive dependence on initial conditions. Of course, that's an oversimplification. It's all about bifurcation, really. Three types: subtle, catastrophic, and explosive. See, when bifurcation occurs, a dynamical system destabilizes. Becomes *perturbed*, okay? You with me so far?"

A crowded flight probably meant no seat-switching. And who would I end up next to if I *did* switch? The incest aunt?

Mercifully, the video screens blinked on and the emergency landing spiel began. At the front of the plane, a flight attendant mimed the on-screen instructions. You'd think someone with "flying anxieties" would shut up and listen, but Mickey talked over the audio. "Of course, the fascinating thing is that there's a self-organizing principle at the *edge* of chaos. Order breeds habit, okay? But chaos breeds life."

"Yeah, hold on," I said. "I want to hear this."

He resumed as soon as the video was over. "But anyhoo, that's my area of expertise. I'm adjunct at Colorado State. I teach one course in math, another in philosophy, which makes perfect sense, see, because chaos-complexity cuts across the disciplines. Actually, I could teach in the theology department, too, because chaos theory's entirely applicable to the world's religions. That's not a concept Pat Robertson and the pope would embrace, but hey. Don't shoot the messenger!" The giggle. "Of course, three classes is full time, so they'd have to give me the benefits package, which would kill them. Screw the adjuncts, right? We're the monks of higher education. How much do *you* make?"

I flinched a little. "Rather not say."

He nodded. "Thank God I have another income stream. Whoops, there I go again. I'm the only atheist I know who keeps thanking God. Well, what do you expect, growing up with *my* mother? I mean, she made my father put a *shrine* to the Blessed Virgin in our backyard. Immaculate conception? Yeah, *sure*, Mom. So what do you teach?"

"American lit," I said. "And writing."

"Really? So you're a writer?"

"Uh, yeah. Yes." My answer surprised me.

"That's what I'm doing this summer: writing a book."

I nodded. "Publish or perish, right?"

"Oh, no, no, noooo. This isn't part of my scholarly work. It's a manual for the casino gambler. I'm going to show how the principles of chaos theory can be employed to beat the house. Gambling's my *other* income stream, see? Know how much I pull in in a year? Go ahead, guesstimate."

I shrugged. "Five thousand?"

"Try *fifty* thousand."

I'd seen that suitcase of his. Who did he think he was kidding? "Well," I said, "if you can teach people how to hit the jackpot, you'll have a best-seller."

"Oh, I can teach them, all right. Not that I'm going to give away *all* of my trade secrets. In Vegas? I'm banned at Harrah's, the Golden

Nugget, and Circus Circus." I nodded, then closed my eyes and shifted my body toward the window. Mickey didn't take the hint. "I get ten steps in the front door, disguised or not, and security approaches me. Escorts me out of the building. It's all very cordial, very gentlemanly. They don't make trouble and neither do I. I could, though, because it impedes my research. Life, liberty, and the pursuit of publication, right? That's why I'm flying to Connecticut. To do research for my book. The Indians have a casino there called—"

I opened my eyes. "Wequonnoc Moon," I said.

"Right. You've been there?"

I nodded. "It's about ten minutes from where I grew up."

"Biggest single gaming venue in the country," Mickey said. "Or so I've heard. I've never been there before. Been to Atlantic City many times over. I'm no longer welcome at Mr. Trump's venues either. Now I ask you: is it legal to ban me, simply because I've figured out how to beat them at their own game? If I could afford to do it, I'd sue the bastards."

The plane lurched forward. The intercom clicked on. The captain said we'd been cleared for takeoff. Would the flight attendants prepare the cabin?

"Oh, boy, here we go," Mickey said. He pulled the vomit bag from his seat pocket. "Don't worry. I'm not going to puke. I use these for my breathing exercise."

"Right," I said. Closed my eyes.

Mickey grabbed my arm. "I was wondering if, when we lift off, would you hold my hand? It helps."

"Uh, well . . ."

The plane began to taxi. "Oh, boy," Mickey muttered. "Oh, boy, oh, boy." Paper crinkled in my right ear. In my peripheral vision, I saw his vomit bag expand and contract like a lung. The plane turned right and started down the runway, picking up speed. "Please," he said, his shaky hand groping for mine. Instead of taking it, I pushed it down against the armrest between us.

The cabin rattled. Mickey's hand gripped the armrest. We rose.

With the whine of the landing gear's retraction, he returned to his abnormal normalcy. "Fascinating stuff, though, chaos-complexity," he said. "Order in disorder. Disequilibrium as the source of life. Can you imagine it?"

"What?"

"God as flux? God as mutability?"

His pupils were dilated. Stoned from whatever he'd taken, I figured. For the next few minutes, neither of us spoke.

The captain turned off the seatbelt sign. The flight attendants wheeled the beverage cart down the aisle. Mickey flopped down his tray table and began to play solitaire with a deck of cards that, in my peripheral vision, I noticed were pornographic.

I dozed, woke up, fell into a deeper sleep. Somewhere during the flight, I heard Mickey and a flight attendant joking about Mr. Sandman....

IT TOOK TWO FLIGHT ATTENDANTS to rouse me. I looked around, lost at first. Mickey was gone. Up front, the last of the passengers were deplaning.

Inside the terminal, I wandered myself awake. At the pay phones, I fished out my calling card and punched in the numbers. Back in Colorado, our machine clicked on. "Hey," I said. "It's me. I'm at O'Hare. Doing all right, I guess—a little groggy.... Guy next to me on the flight here was a lunatic. And there were these kissin' cousins going to be on *Jerry Springer*. You want evidence that Western civilization's in sharp decline, just come to the airport.... Hey, Mo? I'm a little scared to be going back there. Lolly's my last link, you know? ... Well, okay. I'll call you tonight. Don't let the dogs drive you nuts." I stood there wondering what would come first: me saying it or the beep ending my message.

"I love you, Mo."

I love you, Lolly: I should have been saying it at the end of every one of those goddamn Sunday-evening calls. Should have been calling *her*. I love you: Why did that simple three-syllable sentence always get stuck in my throat? . . . Well, I was flying back there, wasn't I? She'd asked for Caelum, and here I was at fucking O'Hare instead of sleeping off my post-prom assignment. It was like what Dr. Patel told me that time: that "I love you" was just three meaningless words without the actions that went with them. Lolly's crippled tongue had said my name, or tried to, and I was halfway there.

I walked—up one concourse, down another, in and out of a dozen stores stocked with crap I didn't want. Walked past the smokers, sequestered like lepers in their Plexiglas pen, and a crazy-looking shoeshine guy, wearing a do-rag and muttering to himself at the base of his empty platform chair.

I bought a coffee and a *U.S.A. Today*. Sat and read about that Love Bug computer virus. It arrived via an e-mail titled "**I Love You.**" Opening its attachment, "**Love-Letter-for-You,**" was what infected you. Well, I thought, the diabolical prick who designed it understood technology *and* human psychology. I mean, something like that arrives, and you're *not* going to open it? It was both a virus and a worm, the article said; as it erased your files, it raided your address book, sending copies of itself to everyone on your e-mail list and spreading the havoc exponentially. Like HIV, I thought. Like that chaos-complexity stuff. Small disturbances, big repercussions. God, we were all so vulnerable.

Walking back, I passed that crazy shoeshine guy again. On impulse, I did an about-face, climbed up onto his platform, and sat. I was nothing more than a pair of shoes to him, and he went to work without so much as an upward glance. But as it turned out, he *hadn't* been mumbling to himself, as I'd assumed; he'd been rapping. He rapped under his breath while he shined my shoes. I caught a little of it: "*Calvin Klein no friend of mine, don't want nobody's name on my behind . . .*" When he finished, he rose from his stool. "Five dollar," he said, looking over my shoulder.

I handed him two fives. "One for the shine, the other for the performance," I said, at which point he *did* look at me. I figured he'd return my smile, but instead he nodded, blank-faced, stuffed the bills into his pocket, and gave me his back.

At the food court, I bought a turkey sandwich and another coffee. As I ate, an entourage caught my eye: four Buddhist monks, camped at the periphery of the food court seats, about thirty feet away. Shaved heads, maroon and pumpkin-colored robes. Each was smiling, even the one who slept. You'd think monks would be wearing sandals, wouldn't you? But these guys were wearing what I wear: Nike sneakers, Timberland boots. Two were horsing around with a Hacky Sack. Another was chatting quietly with a black woman in a Chicago Bulls sweatshirt.

I spotted a fifth monk, seated apart from the others. He was staring at something on his finger—studying it, or meditating on it, or whatever.

It moved.

Slowly, gently, the monk put his index fingers together, tip to tip, and it crossed the bridge they made, then traveled the back of the monk's hand and halfway up his arm. I got up. Got closer. Saw that it was a praying mantis. I watched that monk watch that mantis for . . . well, I don't know how long. But somehow, it made me feel better. Less anxious or whatever. Less alone.

THE FLIGHT TO CONNECTICUT WAS uneventful, and Bradley Airport looked and felt as glum as ever. I rented a Camry and picked up Interstate 91 going south. In Hartford, I exited onto I–84 and drove, with gathering dread, toward Three Rivers. Lolly'd been a life force my whole life. I didn't want even to *see* her diminishment, never mind have to *do* something about it. I wanted to be back in Colorado, facing nothing more than my computer monitor and three or four open bottles of beer.

En route, I passed billboards luring travelers to Wequonnoc Moon, the U.S. Army, the home cooking at Cracker Barrel, Jesus Christ. Weird how they all promised the same thing: rescue. Salvation from your dissatisfying life. "Begin the Quest!" one of those signs advised, but I didn't quite catch the quest for what. Smart advertising, whatever it was. A personal lord and savior, a casino jackpot, a Phoenician Yellow Mustang: everyone was out looking for something.

Right you are, Quirk. And what, pray tell, are you looking for?

Me? I don't know. To avoid the Love Bug virus, maybe?

Not something you're looking to escape, Quirk. Something you're looking for.

A little peace of mind, maybe? A full night's sleep? . . . Yeah, that'd be nice: eight uninterrupted hours of repose.

Don't play dead before you have to.

Approaching Three Rivers, things looked both the same (the dog's face painted on the rock ledge, the abandoned textile mills) and different (Wal-Mart, Staples, an Olive Garden restaurant). At the foot of the downtown bridge, they'd put up a sculpture: a Wequonnoc warrior, steroid-enhanced from the looks of him. For most of the twentieth century, Three Rivers had been in bed with the defense industry—the submarine base, Electric Boat. But the affair had fizzled when the Cold War ended, and now, for better or worse, the town was sleeping with the Indians. Or, as Lolly liked to grouse, "those phony-baloney one-eighth Indians. Those white one-sixteenth Wequonnocs."

I'd intended to drive out to the farm first, but changed my mind. I'd come all this way to see her, so I should go see her, right? I got to the hospital a little after six. They had a parking garage now—that was new. They'd redone the entrance: added an atrium, a gift boutique, a coffee bar. "*Courtesy of the Wequonnoc Nation,*" a banner proclaimed.

The receptionist told me Lolly was on the fourth floor. In the elevator, I could feel the beat of my heart.

At the desk, two nurses were conferring over a takeout menu. "Well, they wouldn't call it spicy tuna if it wasn't spicy, but you can probably order it milder," the frizzy-haired one said. Then, to me, "Can I help you, sir?"

"Louella Quirk?" I said.

"Oh, yes. I'm her shift nurse. Are you her nephew from California?"

"Colorado," I said. "How is she?"

"Well, according to her chart, she had some agitation earlier in the day, but she's been sleeping peacefully since I came on. Her vitals look good. I just took her temp and b.p. a few minutes ago. You can go on down. She's in 432, four rooms down on the left. I'm Valerie, by the way."

"Caelum."

"Hi. Hey, are you hungry? We were just about to order sushi." I shook my head and started down the corridor. Sushi? In blue-collar Three Rivers?

She was in a semiprivate, her bed the one near the window. I exchanged smiles and nods with the roommate and her visitor. Lolly's curtain was half drawn, her light dimmed. Her TV was on, moving images minus sound.

Her face looked lopsided, her mouth drooping open on the left side. Her coloring, usually burnished by the sun, was as gray as putty. There was dried blood at the point where the IV tube entered her hand. A sour smell hung in the air around her. When I kissed her forehead, she sighed in her sleep.

Valerie came in. "Aw, look at her," she whispered. "Sleeping like a baby." She checked her IV drip, plumped up her pillow, and left us.

A baby, I thought. Babies. Within the first few minutes of their lives, their mother had died, leaving them to be raised by a distant father and a no-nonsense prison matron of a grandmother. Daddy—

born second and assigned the burden of having killed his mother in the process—had drunk his life away. Lolly had soldiered on, worked hard, kept her spunk and her spirits up. She'd found love, too, whether people liked it or not. And now here she was, widowed and weakened, the rest of her life to be dictated by a damaged brain.

I kept a vigil by her bedside, feeling, in waves, both moved and bored. In the top drawer of the nightstand, I found the standard issue: tissues, lotion, a cellophane-wrapped comb. Lolly's short gray hair, usually permanent-waved and poufy, lay limp and oily. I pulled the wrapper off the comb. Tried to fix her hair a little. I didn't want to wake her if rest was what she needed, but I was hoping, too, that she *would* wake up. See me and know that I'd come. When I stopped combing, she did open her eyes. She stared at me for several seconds without recognition, then closed her eyes again. . . . Had she been awake? Had I just missed another chance to tell her I loved her?

Valerie reappeared, a cup of coffee in one hand, a cup of ice cream in the other. "Thought you might like a little something," she said. "I figured you for a chocolate man, but we have vanilla and strawberry, too."

"Chocolate's good," I said. "Thanks. She opened her eyes a few minutes ago. She looked right at me, but I don't think anything registered."

Valerie shrugged. "Hard to tell," she said.

I asked her how to activate the TV's closed-captioning, and as she did it for me, the *60 Minutes* stopwatch filled the screen. "Kind of fitting this show's coming on," I said. "It's her favorite."

"Oh, mine, too," Valerie said. "I love it when they nail the hypocrites."

I nodded toward Lolly. "She calls me every Sunday night after her supper, gives me all the updates. But as soon as that stopwatch starts ticking, she'll say, 'Well, gotta go, kiddo. My boyfriend's coming on.'"

Valerie smiled. "Who's her boyfriend?"

"Morley Safer."

She nodded. "Mine's Ed Bradley. I like his little earring."

I touched Lolly's shoulder. "Safer interviewed her once."

"Your aunt? What for?"

"This story they did called 'The Prison That Cures With Kindness.' Their researchers went looking for the correctional facility with the lowest recidivism rate in the country, and they came up with Bride Lake."

"The women's prison? When was this?"

"Long time ago. 'Seventy-eight, 'seventy-nine. The producers came up, dug around, and discovered Lolly. She was a guard there at the time, but she was also the granddaughter of the woman who'd established the place. See, before my great-grandmother came along, they used to just lock up the women with the men. The assumption was that they were throw-aways anyway."

"Oh, my God, that's horrible," Valerie said.

"But my great-grandmother had this idea that a separate facility run by women—plus fresh air, sunshine, farmwork, schoolwork—would rehabilitate. Community service, too. Giving back was part of her formula. And it worked, too, I guess. Sociologists, criminologists, shrinks: they came from all over to study her methods. Sigmund Freud visited once. That was in the *60 Minutes* story, I remember. There's this great picture of Freud and my great-grandmother strolling the grounds arm in arm.

"But anyway, they loved Lolly—the producers, the crew, Morley Safer. She'd never paid much attention to televison, so she wasn't intimidated by it. And that made her, whaddaya call it? Telegenic. And on top of that, Lolly's a great storyteller. She told Safer about the day Sophie Tucker came to visit an old vaudeville friend who was in for larceny and stayed on to do a show. And about the summer when the inmates served as surrogate mothers for a bunch of monkeys that were being fed experimental doses of lithium up the road at the state hospital. And the time when 'the gals' made hootch from the dried fruit platters the Baptist church ladies had given them for Christmas, and they were drunk on their asses when the state inspector dropped by for a visit."

Valerie laughed. Touched Lolly's hand.

"But like I said, Morley Safer got a kick out of Lolly. Sent his crew back to New York and stayed for supper. My aunt's companion fried some chicken and made peach cobbler, and Lolly told more stories. And somehow that night, he and Lolly discovered they shared a birthday, November the eighth. They've sent each other a birthday card ever since."

"Wow," Valerie said. "Well, now that I know I'm taking care of a TV star, I'll have to give her the VIP treatment."

I smiled, teared up a little. "I just want her to be okay," I said.

Valerie pulled a tissue from the little box on Lolly's tray table and handed it to me. "Sure you do."

I left the hospital sometime between eight and nine. There was a Taco Bell on West Main Street now; that was new. I pulled up to the drive-thru, got a couple of burritos. Ate as I drove. The endless day flew back at me in fragments: the post-prom, the monk and his praying mantis, the chaos theorist's jawing. God as mutability, I thought. God as flux. . . .

THE ROAD HOME WAS TRAFFICKY with cars heading to and from Wequonnoc Moon. I drove past its purple and green glow. Took the left onto Ice House Road, and then the right onto Bride Lake. Nearing the farm, I approached the prison compound. Braked. "Grandma's prison," Lolly always called it.

I put on my blinker. Slowed down, swung left, and headed up the dirt driveway to the farmhouse. My headlights caught a raccoon on the front porch, feasting out of the cat food dish. I cut the engine and got out of the car. "Get!" I shouted. Unintimidated, it sat up on its haunches and looked at me as if to say, *And who might you be?* It took its sweet time waddling down the stairs and into the darkness.

The storm windows were still in; the door latch was busted. I could take care of that stuff while I was here. The old tin coffeepot was where it always was. I reached in, and touched the front door key. In the foyer, I fumbled, my hand batting at the darkness until I felt the old-fashioned pull chain. I yanked it, squinted. . . . Things looked the same, pretty much—a little shabbier, maybe, a little more cluttery. Things smelled the same, too: musty carpet, cooking grease, a slight whiff of cat piss. I put down my travel bag and walked over to the large framed photograph that hung on the wall at the foot of the stairs. "Bride Lake Farm, Aerial View, August 1948."

God, this house, I thought. This abandoned Bride Lake life.

The place was radioactive with memories.

↠ *c h a p t e r   f o u r* ↞

MOTHER SAYS I'M NOT TO cross Bride Lake Road without permission, or dawdle near the ladies' prison fence, or walk past it to our south field where the corn maze is. But I've done all three this morning because I'm *mad* at Mother and really, *really* mad at Grandpa Quirk. He said I'm too young to run the cash register, and I'm *not*. In our arithmetic workbook, I zoom through the money pages and I'm always the first one done. "Well, I'm sorry, Davy Crockett, but this is our livelihood," Grandpa said. "No means no."

Mother said yes, we can go to the movies tomorrow if she finishes the priests' ironing, but no, we cannot see *I Was a Teenage Frankenstein*. "You're too young for those kind of pictures, Caelum. They could give you scary dreams."

I already *have* scary dreams, but Mother doesn't know. They're a secret.

October is busy at our farm: hay rides, pumpkins, the maze, the cider press. So many people come to Bride Lake Farm that we have to get extra helpers from the ladies' prison—not just Hennie, who takes care of Great-Grandma Quirk, but other ladies, too. Aunt Lolly picks them because she works at the prison. Most people need eight hours' sleep, but Aunt Lolly only needs five. Every day, she works at the farm, then takes her bath, puts on her uniform, and walks across the road to the prison. She doesn't get home until after my bedtime.

There's good and bad prisoners, Aunt Lolly says, and she knows the difference.

Chicago and Zinnia run the cider press. Chicago has big muscles. "Good luck if you met *her* in a dark alley," Grandpa said. Zinnia's fat, and she breathes real loud, and has orange hair. "Bleach," Aunt Lolly told Mother. "They snitch it from the laundry. Half the girls on the colored tier are strutting around like Rhonda Fleming." Mother said they'll be sorry when their hair starts falling out. Grandpa thinks all the colored people come from Hershey, Pennsylvania, and that's why some are dark chocolate, some are milk chocolate, and once in a while, one comes out white chocolate. They *don't* come from Pennsylvania, though. Colored people come from Africa. Mother says Grandpa Quirk's not as funny as he thinks he is.

In our parlor? We have this picture of our farm that some guy took from when he was up in his airplane. On account of, this other time, he had to emergency-land in our hay field. Grandpa had it blowed up and put in a frame. On the bottom, it says, "Bride Lake Farm, Aerial View, August 1948." In the picture, you can see the way Bride Lake Road cuts right across our farm. Our house and our barn and the apple orchard are on one side, and the pasture and the cornfields are on the other. The prison farm and Bride Lake are on our side, too—right in the middle. Grandpa says a long, long time ago, Bride Lake used to be part of *our* land. But then Grandpa Quirk's father died and his mother had to sell some of the farm to Connecticut. So that's when the prison got built. In the airplane picture, the cows look like ladybugs and the prison ladies look like fleas. There's different Alden Quirks, you know: Daddy is Alden Quirk the Third, Grandpa's Alden Quirk the Second, and Grandpa's father was just plain Alden. If my name was Alden instead of Caelum, I'd be Alden Quirk the Fourth. "Well, *someone* had to come along and break the curse," Daddy said. Then he told me not to tell Grandpa that he said it—that it was a secret between just me and him.

When Grandpa told me Bride Lake used to be ours instead of the prison's, I was *mad*. Aunt Lolly says there's perch in there, and bass, and crappies. Aunt Lolly takes the prison ladies fishing sometimes. "City girls," she said. "Tough as nails. But then they'll see some itty-bitty snapping turtle, or get a fish on their line, God forbid, and they turn to jelly. I've had to wade in after more dropped poles than I care to remember." Grandpa says, when he was a little kid, he used to get to fish at Bride Lake all the time because Great-Grandpa was the farm manager for the prison, and Great-Grandma was like the principal or something. Grandpa says he always used to try and catch this one largemouth bass, Big Wilma, but he never did. I wish *I* could fish there. I can't even go near the fence. If Big Wilma's still in there, I bet she's a monster.

You know how Bride Lake got called Bride Lake? Because a long, long time ago—when George Washington or Abraham Lincoln was president—this man and lady were getting married by the lake, and some other lady shot the bride in the head. Because they both loved the same man. The groom. Aunt Lolly says every once in a while, one of the prison ladies says she seen the ghost, walking out by the lake in her bride dress. "Nothing kills a nice quiet shift like one of those ghost sightings," Aunt Lolly told Mother. "Of course, most of the girls were brought up on superstitions. Burn your hair when it falls out, or your enemy will get ahold of it and make trouble. Don't look head-on at a gravestone, or someone you love will die. Don't let your feet get swept with a broom, or you'll end up in jail."

"I guess they all got their feet swept," Mother said.

I asked Hennie if she ever saw the ghost, and she said no. Chicago said no, too. Zinnia said she *might* have seen her one night, down near the root cellar, but she might have been dreaming.

This is how you make cider. First, Chicago cranks the crank and the press comes down and crushes the apples. Then the juice comes out and trickles down the trough and goes through the strainer. Then it runs into the big funnel, and out through the tube and into the glass jugs. Chicago scrapes the smushed apples into the slop barrel with a hoe, and dumps the new ones onto the pressing table, and they go *bumpity, bump, bump*, and they don't know they're about to get crushed to death.

Zinnia's job is bottling and capping the cider when it comes out of the tube. She has to switch the jugs fast, so that not much spills on the ground. Grandpa won't let *me* fill the cider jugs, because the only time I did it, I forgot to switch the tube and cider spilled all over the ground. Aunt Lolly says I'm *lucky* Grandpa won't let me fill the jugs. "The sugar from the spillage attracts bees," she said. "You want to get stung all day long, like poor Zinnia?"

Zinnia always wants to hug me and pat me because she has a boy my same age named Melvin. I said maybe some day Melvin could come play at our farm, and I could bring him to the maze and show him the shortcuts. Zinnia started crying. That's when I seen that she has freckles. All my Massachusetts cousins have freckles, but I never knew colored people got them.

I have chores, you know. Feed the chickens, bottle-feed the calves. My allowance is fifty cents. Plus, I earn more for extra jobs, like weeding and picking up the drops at the orchard. Grandpa gives me a nickel for every bushel basket I fill. And you know what? Brown apples and wormy apples are *good* for making cider, because it means the apples are nice and sweet. There's no worm guts in the cider, though, because of the strainer. When the slop barrel's full? Chicago has to roll it down the path and dump it underneath the barn, on top of the manure pile. There's this hole in the barn floor, and when you shovel out the manure, you throw it down the hole. And after, Grandpa uses it for fertilizer. He says apple slop sweetens the milk.

Zinnia and Chicago get to use our downstairs bathroom when they have to go, because we can trust them. They eat their lunch on our back porch—two sandwiches each, plus Coca-Colas and cake or pie for dessert. They told me our lunches are better than prison lunches because Hennie doesn't skimp on the meat or the cheese. Zinnia always gives Chicago one of her sandwiches, so Chicago eats three.

Chicago eats pie with her fingers, and then she sucks them clean instead of using her napkin.

You know what Zinnia's got? A tattoo that says, "Jesus

a

v

e

s." It starts on the palm of her hand and goes up her arm. She told me she made it with a safety pin and fountain pen ink, and it hurt but it was worth it. Sometimes, when she stares and stares at her tattoo, she can feel Jesus wrap his arms around her and calm her down. Mother says *I* better never try giving myself any tattoo, because my blood could get poisoned.

Zinnia hugs me different than Mother does. Mother hugs me stiff, and pats my back with these fast little pitty-pats, and I just stand there and wait for her to finish. But when Zinnia squeezes me, I squeeze back. Once, when she was hugging me, she started rocking back and forth and thinking I was Melvin. "How you eatin', Melvin? How your asthma? Your mama's main sufferation in life is missing you, baby boy." She was holding me so tight and so long that Chicago had to stop cranking and help me. "Come on now, Zinni," she said. "This boy ain't your boy. Let him go."

If you *had* poisoned blood, it might be good, because then bad people wouldn't come near you. "Get back!" you could say. "You want to be *poisoned*?"

Nobody even knows I'm down here at the corn maze, or that I took more stuff from the kitchen. It's not stealing, because Hennie would let me have it anyway. I took a chunk of the ham we had last night, and some icebox cookies, and some potatoes from the bin. This time I remembered to wrap the potatoes in aluminum foil like he wants. If he's not there, he said, I'm supposed to just leave it. Hide it in the baby buggy, under the baby.

The maze doesn't open until ten o'clock, and it's only eight o'clock, so the rope's hanging across the entrance, between the two saw-horses, and the "Keep Out" sign is up. One time? Teenagers snuck into the maze at night, and took the Quirk family's heads off and *smashed* them. Grandpa and me found them on Saturday morning, when we were putting out the free hot cocoa. "Goddamn juvenile delinquents," Grandpa said. He had to shovel the broken pumpkins into the back of the truck and hurry and pick out five new ones. And Aunt Lolly had to draw on all the new faces quick, before the customers came.

"Juvenile delinquents" means teenagers. One of them put a lady's bra on Mrs. Quirk, over her dress, and she looked weird with a bra on and no head. The pumpkins' insides looked like smashed brains.

When you figure out the maze and get to the middle, where the Quirk family is, that's when you get your free cocoa. It's on a table in two big thermos jugs, and there's cups and a ladle, and the sign says, "One cup per customer, <u>PLEASE</u>!" because some people are pigs. The Quirk Family is Mr. and Mrs. Quirk, their son and daughter, and their little baby in the baby buggy that used to be *my* baby buggy. We stuff them with newspapers and corn husks, and they wear our old clothes. This year, the boy's wearing my last year's dungarees, and my rippy shirt that I chewed a hole in the front of when I tried out for Little League, and my Davy Crockett coonskin cap. I didn't want my coonskin cap anymore after Grandpa told me the fur tail looked like it had the mange. I yanked it off and threw it in my toy chest. But Aunt Lolly sewed it back on for the Quirk boy. "First time I've had to thread a needle since Home Economics," she told Hennie and me. "Damn, I hated that class. My brother got to go to woodworking and make a knickknack shelf, and I had to do all that prissy sewing."

"Here, give me that, you ninny," Hennie said, but Aunt Lolly said no, no, now she was on a *mission*. She had to take lots of tries to get the thread through the needle. Each time, she stuck her tongue out and made cross-eyes, and me and Hennie laughed. Hennie and Aunt Lolly can be friends at our house, but not at the prison. If Hennie called Aunt Lolly a ninny over there, she'd get in trouble and have to go to this place called "the cooler." Which, I think, is like a freezer or something.

Sometimes, if Great-Grandma takes a long nap, Hennie makes me gingerbread. She's been working at our house for so long, she doesn't even need anyone to walk her over from the jail anymore. She just waves to the guard at the gate, and he waves back. I saw Hennie and Aunt Lolly kissing once, out on the sun porch. They didn't see me seeing them. On the lips.

You know what? The people that go into our maze are stupid. First, they run down all the dead ends and go, *Huh?* Then they go back on the same paths where they already went and don't even realize it. Some people get so mixed up, they end up back at the entrance. I'm not supposed to show anybody the shortcuts. "Folks *want* to be lost for a little while, Caelum," Grandpa Quirk said. "That's the fun of it. And anyway, nobody likes a know-it-all."

In the desk, out in the barn office, there's this map that Daddy drew. It shows what the maze looks like if you're a helicopter flying over it, or the geese. Daddy invented the maze, back when he was being good. He's the one who thought up the Quirk family, too, and the free hot cocoa. Mother makes it on the stove in two big pots, and then she pours it into the big jugs she got when she used to work at American Thermos. She quit there, though, because her boss was always yelling at everybody and he gave her an ulcer. Now Mother works at the bank, and she likes it better, except she has to wash her hands all the time because money's dirty and you never know where it's been. I licked a dollar once. Mother made me put Listerine in my mouth and not spit it out for a long time, and it *hurt*.

Sometimes my scary dreams are about Daddy, and sometimes they're about Mr. Zadzilko. Our school used to have a different janitor, Mr. Mpipi, but he got fired. And I was mad because Mr. Mpipi was *nice*. The teachers think Mr. Zadzilko's nice, too, because he brings them snapdragons and these stupid Polish doughnuts that his mother makes called *poonch-keys*. Mr. Zadzilko's *not* nice, though. When the teachers go to the toilet, he peeks at them through this secret hole.

Before Mr. Mpipi got fired, he came to our class once, and he told us about these people called the Bushmen that are his relatives or his ancestors or something. He showed us where they live on the world map—in Africa, near the bottom. You know what Bushmen hunt and eat? *Jackals*. And *desert rats*. And when they see a praying mantis, they think it's God!

Mr. Mpipi had our class all sit on the floor, even Miss Hogan. Us kids sat cross-legged, but Miss Hogan knelt on her knees and her skirt made a big circle around her. Mr. Mpipi told us a story about how Mantis made the moon by throwing fire into the night sky, and how he married a snake. And you know how Mantis travels around? Between the toes of an antelope, because that's his favorite animal. Mr. Mpipi talked Bushman talk, with these little clicky noises before the words. Everyone laughed, even Miss Hogan, and Mr. Mpipi laughed his high, squealy laugh, too. Mr. Mpipi is colored, I think, except he doesn't have chocolate skin. It's more like the color of those dried apricots Grandpa gets at Christmas.

After his visit, our class wrote Mr. Mpipi a thank-you letter on big easel paper, and we all signed it. And it made him so happy that he gave us a present: a praying mantis egg case. It was supposed to hatch in April, but it didn't. Then, after the assembly, Mr. Mpipi got fired. Miss Hogan was going to throw out the egg case, but I asked her if I could have it. She said yes, and I brought it home and put it on my windowsill.

I caught Mr. Zadzilko peeking. That's how I know about the hole. It's in the big second-floor closet, where the buckets and mops and the Spic And Span are. Miss Hogan wrote me a pass and sent me down to help him because I was the first one done with my Social Studies questions, and I had ants in my pants and kept bothering my neighbors. I opened the closet door and Mr. Zadzilko was peeking through the hole. He jumped when he saw me, and fixed his pants and his belt, and he was laughing like *heh heh heh*. "Look at this," he said. "Mop handle musta poked a hole in the wall. Gotta patch it when I get a free minute." He gave me a sponge and told me to wet it in the boys' room and then go downstairs and wipe the cafeteria tables.

And after, when the recess bell rang, I went back upstairs to return my sponge. Mr. Zadzilko wasn't there, so I turned a bucket upside down and climbed up and looked through the hole. And there was the principal, Miss Anderson, sitting on the toilet, smoking a cigarette. You could see her girdle.

I knew it was naughty to look, so I closed my eyes and got down off the bucket. And when I turned toward the door, Mr. Zadzilko was standing there.

"My, my, my," he said. "Aren't *you* the dirty boy."

He yanked the pull chain, and the closet light went on. Then he pulled the door closed behind him. He came over and sat down on the bucket, so that he was breathing right in my face. The hole was a secret between me and him, he said. If I said anything, he'd tell the teachers he caught me looking. "You were just curious," he said. "*I* understand that, but the teachers won't. They'll probably have you arrested. And everyone will know you're Dirty Boy."

He reached behind him and took a greasy paper bag off the shelf. He opened it and held it out to me. "Here," he said. "Help yourself." I reached in and pulled out one of those doughnut things his mother made.

"They're called *poonch-keys*," he said. "Take a bite. They're delicious."

I didn't want to, but I did.

"What are you, a little mouse nibbling on a crumb? Take a *big* bite."

So I did. The stuff inside looked like bloody nose.

"What kind did you get? Raspberry or prune?" I showed him where I'd bitten. "Oh, raspberry," he said. "That's my favorite, too. What are you shaking for, Dirty Boy?"

I tried to stop shaking, but I couldn't. He kept looking at me.

"You know what *poonch-key* means? In Polish?"

I shook my head.

"It means 'little package.' Because the doughnut makes a little package around the stuff that's inside, see?"

"Oh," I said. "Can I go now? It's recess."

"Like us men carry the stuff that's inside *us*. In our sacs. Get it?"

I didn't know what he was talking about, but I nodded.

"You don't *look* like you get it, Dirty Boy. If you get it, show me where your *poonch-key* is?"

"What?"

"Your 'little package.' Where is it? Point to it."

I could hear kids playing outside, but they sounded farther away than just the playground. I was trying not to cry.

Mr. Zadzilko made an O with his thumb and his pointing finger. "Here's the woman's hole, see?" he said. "Otherwise known as her snatch, or her pussy, or her bearded clam." He leaned closer and dropped his hand down. "And this, my dirty boy, is where your 'little package' is." He flicked his finger, hard, in the place where Mother says I shouldn't touch, and it *hurt*.

"It's recess," I said. "I'm supposed to go."

"Go, then," he said. "But just remember what happens to dirty boys with big mouths."

The hallway was empty. There was laughing coming out of the teacher's room. I went downstairs to the boys' room. I hadn't swallowed that bite he made me take; I'd hid it against my cheek. I spit it into the toilet and threw the rest of my *poonch-key* in after it. I kept flushing, and it kept swirling around and looking like it was going to go down, but then it would bob back up again. Then I thought, what if he's got a lookout hole in the boys' room, too? What if he's watching me flush his mother's stupid doughnut down the toilet? By the time I got out to the playground, I had a stomachache, and then the recess bell rang two seconds later, and we had to go in.

That night, I was lying in bed, thinking about Mr. Zadzilko, and Mother came in my room in the dark. "Caelum?" she said. "Are you asleep or awake?"

I didn't answer for a long time. Then I said, "Awake."

"I heard you crying. What were you crying about?"

I almost told her, but then I didn't. "I was thinking about Jesus dying on the cross," I said. "And it made me sad." I knew she'd like that answer.

Mother goes to mass every morning before work. That's why she can't get me ready for school. Aunt Lolly gets me ready, once she finishes morning milking. Except, if there's a problem, she calls me from the barn phone and I have to get myself ready, and not dawdle or I'll miss the bus. One time? Some of our cows got loose and started running up Bride Lake Road. Aunt Lolly had to go get them, because they could have got hit by a car, and she forgot to call me. And I started watching *Captain Kangaroo*, which I'm not supposed to watch TV in the morning. And then the bus came and I was still in my pajamas. Mother had to leave work, drive back to the farm, and then drive me to school. She was crying and yelling, because now Mr. McCully probably wouldn't pick her to be head teller, thanks to me. At the stop signs and red lights, she kept reaching over and whacking me. And by the time we got to school, we were both crying. I had to roll the window down and air out my eyes before I went in, because the school doesn't need to know about our private family business.

On Saturdays, Mother vacuum-cleans the priests' house for free and takes home their dirty clothes in pillowcases because Monsignor Guglielmo's helping her get annulled. Last year, when I made my First Communion, Monsignor gave me a Saint Christopher medal because Mother's always so helpful. All us kids got scapulars and little prayer books, but only *I* got a Saint Christopher medal. After Sunday dinner, Mother irons the priests' clean clothes and drives them back. And *if* she finishes in time, *then* we can go to the movies. My favorite movie is *Old Yeller*, except for the part where Travis had to shoot Old

Yeller because he got hydrophoby. Mother's favorite movie is *The Song of Bernadette*. She says Jesus sends messages to the boys he picks to become priests, and that I should always look and listen for signs.

"What kind of signs?" I said.

"It could be anything. A voice, a vision in the sky."

One time I saw a cloud that looked like a man with a big Jimmy Durante nose. When I sing "Inka Dinka Do" with my Jimmy Durante voice, the grown-ups always laugh. And at the end, I go, "Good night, Mrs. Calabash, wherever you are!" and they clap and tell me to do it again. Mother never laughs, though. She says that Jimmy Durante cloud was *not* a sign from Jesus. I told Mother the Bushmen think God is a praying mantis, and she said that was just plain silly.

Mother and I are Catholic, and Grandpa Quirk and Aunt Lolly are Protestant. One Sunday, when Mother was outside warming up our car for church, I heard Grandpa ask Aunt Lolly, "Have the cat lickers left yet?" On the way over to St. Anthony's, I asked Mother what cat lickers were. Her hands squeezed the steering wheel, and she took a puff of her cigarette and put it back in the ashtray. "Catholics," she said. "You and me. If Grampy Sullivan heard Grandpa Quirk call us 'cat lickers,' he'd be pretty gosh darn mad."

Aunt Lolly and Grandpa Quirk don't have to go to church unless they want to, and they don't have to eat Mrs. Paul's stupid fish sticks on Friday. Mother gets mad if I hold my nose when I eat my fish sticks. "Like a little fish with your ketchup?" Grandpa always says. When Mother's not looking, he sneaks me bites of meat.

My Grampy and Grammy Sullivan live in Buzzards Bay, Massachusetts, and so don't all my freckle-faced Sullivan cousins. When we go visit, Grampy Sullivan won't speak to Mother. It's because first, she didn't marry a cat licker, and then, she got a divorce. Whenever Mother walks into a room, Grampy Sullivan walks out. Mother says he's probably going to start speaking to her after she gets annulled. Poor Mother has to wait and wait and wait, like I had to wait until after Valentine's Day before I got my Christmas present from Daddy.

When I was little? I used to think Grandpa Quirk was Mother's father, but he's not. Grandpa Quirk is *Daddy and Aunt Lolly's* father. Aunt Lolly and Daddy are twins, except they don't look alike, the way the Birdsey twins in my grade do. Aunt Lolly's taller than Daddy, even though she's the girl. Plus, she's a little bit chubby and Daddy's skinny. He has black hair, and a bushy beard, and two missing front teeth that aren't going to grow back because they weren't his baby teeth. Daddy and Aunt Lolly's mother died in the middle of having Daddy, so Grandpa had to raise them by himself. And Great-Grandma Lydia was kind of like their grandmother *and* their mother. She wasn't crazy then. Aunt Lolly said Great-Grandma used to be very, very smart. Daddy said, "My sister came out first, so she grabbed all the smarts and left me all the stupids." He said he was the runt in a litter of two.

A lot of the kids in my class can't tell the Birdsey twins apart, except I can. Thomas has a little dot near his eyebrow and Dominick doesn't. Sometimes Thomas is a crybaby. They came over my house once. Dominick and I played *Whirlybirds*, on account of that's both of our favorite show. I was Chuck, and Dominick was P.T., and we jumped down from the loft onto the bales of hay, like we had to jump out of our helicopter just before it crashed. Thomas was too chicken to play *Whirlybirds*. He only wanted to play with the barn kittens and throw a stick for Queenie.

Queenie's our dog. She's brown and white, and has these little eyebrows that make her look sad even when she's happy. We got her from Jerry, the artificial insemination man. When Jerry comes to our farm, he brings this stuff called spunk that's from the best sires in the state. I asked Grandpa what spunk is and he said, "Male stuff." Jerry puts it in the cows' hineys with this big needle-looking thing. And later, the cows have calves that grow up to be good milkers. *If* they're girls. Grandpa writes a chalk mark on the barn wall every time a calf is born—X if it's a male, an O if it's a female. He says he'd be rich if he could only figure out how to milk a bull.

When I was a baby? It wasn't Grandpa and Aunt Lolly that did the milking. It was Grandpa and *Daddy*. Then Grandpa and Daddy had a big fight, and we had to move, and Daddy worked at this place that made helicopters. I don't remember any of that. All's *I* remember is Mother and me living at the farm without Daddy. I'm the only kid in my class whose parents got a divorce.

When I was in first grade, and Daddy was being good? Grandpa let him sleep on a cot in the milk house. He got to have Sunday dinner with us, too. Mother didn't want him to eat with us, but it wasn't her decision. It was *Grandpa's* decision. When Grandpa's foot got infected was when Daddy started being good. Grandpa couldn't milk, so Daddy came back and him and Lolly milked. Daddy was the one who taught me how to hang a spoon off my nose so it just stays there, and how to sing "Inka Dinka Do." At school, I did the spoon trick for our talent show, and everyone wanted me to teach them how to do it. At recess, kids kept chasing me and going, "Please, Caelum. *Please.*"

Daddy got the idea for the corn maze when he was staying in the milkhouse. At first, Grandpa said no—it wouldn't work. All people wanted was to drive out, buy their apples and pumpkins, and show their kids the cider press. And anyway, Grandpa said, what he needed come fall was silage, and what he *didn't* need was everyone in Three Rivers and their uncle tramping through his cornfields. Then he changed his mind and told Daddy he could try it. So Daddy drew that map, and when the corn was about a foot high, he put me on his lap and we tractored down the paths and dead-ends and loop-de-loops. And I was the one who held the map.

That first year, it was Daddy and me who stuffed the Quirk family. And it was Daddy, not Aunt Lolly, who drew on the faces. "Free cocoa?" Grandpa said. "I thought we were trying to *make* money, not *lose* it." But he changed his mind about that, too, and you know how much money the maze made us? Six hundred dollars! So Daddy got to eat Sunday dinner with us, whether Mother liked it or not.

One time, after Sunday dinner, Daddy made Mother cry. Lolly and

Grandpa took Great-Grandma for a car ride, so it was just the three of us. Mother told Daddy to leave, but I wanted him to stay and play with me, so she said he could. Daddy was being nice at first. He tried to help Mother by bringing the dishes out to the kitchen, but she said she didn't need any help. "If you two are going to play," she said, "then *play*."

Daddy read me the funny papers. Then we played tic-tac-toe. He wasn't paying attention, though. He kept tapping his foot and looking over at the record player cabinet. "Want to hear a record?" he said. I said yes, either *Bozo the Clown Under the Sea* or *Hopalong Cassidy and the Square Dance Holdup*. But Daddy said he felt like listening to music. "Where's your checker set at?" he said. "Go get it and we'll play some checkers."

At first, I thought the checkerboard was up in my room. Then I remembered it was in the pantry drawer. When I got to the bottom of the stairs, Daddy was standing at the record player cabinet. Except the door on the other side was open—the side where Grandpa's liquor's at. Daddy took a big swig out of one of Grandpa's bottles, and then another swig, and then he noticed me. He put the bottle back and cleared his throat. "They used to keep the records on this side," he said. "Guess I got mixed up. Got a little thirsty, too, but that's between me and you, buddy. Okay?" And I said okay.

Grandpa's good at checkers, but Daddy stunk. Plus, he was playing that Dean Martin music so loud, I couldn't concentrate. When Mother came back to the dining room to get the tablecloth, he said, "Rosemary Kathleen Sullivan, my wild Irish rose."

Mother didn't say anything. She bunched up the tablecloth kind of mad and tried to walk past Daddy, but he pushed his chair out so she couldn't get by. Then he touched her hiney.

"Don't!" she said. She got all red, and went the other way around the table, and banged open the kitchen door the way I'm not supposed to.

Daddy laughed and called into the kitchen. "Watch out, everyone! Rosemary's got her Irish up."

"It's your turn," I said. But instead of moving his man, he picked up one of mine and jumped a bunch of his own checkers. "You win," he said. "Go play." Over at the record player cabinet, he lifted the needle and dropped it down on that song about the moon hits your eye like a big pizza pie. He went into the kitchen, whistling.

"Because I don't *want* to dance with you, that's why!" Mother said. Then Daddy said something, and Mother said, "You think I can't smell it on you, Alden? You think I can't recognize a lost cause when he's standing in front of me?" Then there was some noises and a crash. The kitchen door banged open.

"Wanna play Crazy Eights?" I said.

At the parlor window, I watched him walk faster and faster, down the driveway and onto Bride Lake Road, taking swigs from Grandpa's bottle.

Mother was sitting on a kitchen chair, crying. She had one regular cheek and one all-red one. The broken pieces of our soup bowl were on the table next to her. "Lolly told me this tureen was one of Great-Grandma Quirk's wedding presents," she said.

"Oh. . . . You want a glass of water?"

"His wild Irish rose. That's a laugh! I was just the first girl he grabbed on the rebound." Then she looked at me. "Don't *you* ever be mean like Daddy."

"Want some water?" I said again.

She nodded. I got her the water and she took a little sip. She kept touching the broken soup bowl. "My hands were wet from the dishes," she said. "It slipped. It was an accident."

"Oh," I said. "Sorry."

She took another sip of her water. "How about a hug?" she said.

She put her arms around me. It was one of her stiff hugs, with the little pitty-pats on my back. "How come you never hug me back?" she said.

"I hug you back."

"No, you don't."

MISS HOGAN? AT MY SCHOOL? She used to be our second-grade teacher and now she's our third-grade teacher, too, on account of she switched grades. And I'm glad, because Miss Hogan's nice. Plus, she's pretty. She drives a green Studebaker and likes cats instead of dogs. This one time, Penny Balocki in our class was teasing me and saying that I love Miss Hogan and want to marry her. I don't, though. I like her, but I don't *love* her. And anyways, she's already *getting* married.

Miss Hogan's fiancé, Mr. Foster, used to play football at Fordham University, and now he's a cameraman at a television studio in New York City. Miss Hogan's favorite TV show is *I've Got a Secret* because that's the show where Mr. Foster works at. And you know what? When Mr. Foster visited us that time, Frieda Buntz raised her hand and said, "Can you and Miss Hogan kiss for us?" And she had to go stand in the cloakroom until recess.

One time, during vacation week, Mother let me stay up late and watch *I've Got a Secret*. One man's secret was that he got struck by lightning and didn't die. Another man had this long, long beard and his secret was that, at night, he slept with his whiskers *in*side the covers, not *out*side. They guessed the whiskers guy, but not the lightning guy. Last year, one of our best milkers got struck by lightning. Dolly, her name was. And you know what the vet said? That Dolly's heart *exploded*. Grandpa had to bulldoze her across the road and down into the gravel pit. All week long, vultures kept flying over our south field.

I've got a secret. Someone in our grade keeps spitting in the drinking fountain in the main hallway, and Miss Hogan thinks it's Thomas Birdsey, but it's not. It's me. Last week, our whole class wasn't allowed to get a drink until someone admitted they were the spitter. And everyone got madder and madder at Thomas because he wouldn't admit it. Even *I* was mad at him, because I was thirsty and I kind of forgot who the *real* secret spitter was. Then Thomas made a load in his pants, the way he used to in first grade, and the office made his mother come get him. Our whole classroom stunk, and Miss Hogan had to send for Mr. Zadzilko, and we all went outside and played dodgeball. Dominick Birdsey had to stop playing, though, because he was whipping the ball too hard and hitting people's faces. And after? When we came back in the building? Miss Hogan let us all get drinks. In the hallway, Mr. Zadzilko always looks at me, and I want to say, What are *you* looking at, Mr. Big Fat Glasses Face? I don't, though. I just look away.

You know what? I stole something once. Mother and I were at Lu's Luncheonette, buying Rolaids for Mother's ulcer. And while Mother and Lu were talking at the cash register, I just picked a Devil Dog off the rack and put it in my coat pocket. I *kind of* thought I was going to get caught, except I didn't. I don't even like Devil Dogs that much; I like Hostess cupcakes better. I didn't eat it. I just kept reaching inside my pocket and poking it with my finger. It got squishy, and the cellophane broke. And the next morning, I mailed it in the mailbox in front of our school.

Sometimes, when I try to hand in my paper early, Miss Hogan goes, "It's not a race, Caelum. Go back to your desk and check your work." If I check my work and I'm *still* waiting and waiting, that's when I have to take the pass and go help Mr. Zadzilko. After Mr. McCully picked Mother to be head teller, now she always has to stay late at the bank because of her extra responsibilities. She won't let me go on the bus, because Aunt Lolly's already working at the prison when I get home and Grandpa's getting ready for milking. But she doesn't pick me up until way after all the other kids go home. She had to talk to Miss Anderson about letting me stay and wait, and Miss Anderson lets me because Mother's divorced. Sometimes, I get to stay in our room with Miss Hogan, but sometimes I have to go be Mr. Zadzilko's helper.

He has me clap erasers, or empty the wastebaskets into the big barrel in the hallway, or wipe down blackboards with the big sponge. One time, after an assembly, I had to go to the auditorium and help him fold all the folding chairs. We stacked them on these flat carts that have wheels. You know where all the folding chairs go? Under the stage. This door I never even noticed before opens, and the chairs roll in on the carts and stay there until the next assembly.

After the United Nations assembly was when Mr. Mpipi got fired. After he did his dance. First, Miss Anderson gave a speech about the UN. Then the fourth graders sang "Around the World in Eighty Days." Then some lady who went on a trip to China showed us her China slides. Dominick Birdsey started tickling me, and Miss Hogan made us sit between her and Miss Anderson. The China lady talked so long that the projector melted one of her slides, and some of the sixth-graders started clapping.

Mr. Mpipi came on near the end. He walked out on the stage, and instead of his janitor clothes, he was wearing this big red cape and no shoes. He told everyone how the Bushmen hunted jackals, and prayed to their praying mantis god, and he talked their clicking talk. The sixth-graders started being rude. It's okay if you laugh *with* someone, but it's bad if you laugh *at* them. Mr. Mpipi thought everyone was laughing *with* him, so he started laughing, too—his squealy laugh— and that made things worse. Miss Anderson had to stand up and give the sixth-graders a dirty look.

Mr. Mpipi said he was going to show us two Bushman dances, the Dance of the Great Hunger and the Dance of Love. But he wasn't going to stop in between, he said. One dance was just going to turn into the other one. "Because what does all of us hunger *for?*" he asked. No one in the audience said anything. Mr. Mpipi waited, and then finally he said the answer himself. "We hunger for love!"

He untied his cape and dropped it on the floor, and all's he was wearing was this kind of diaper thing. I saw Miss Anderson and Miss Hogan look at each other, and Miss Anderson said, "Good God in Heaven." Mr. Mpipi was shouting and yipping and doing this weird, shaky dance. He had a big potbelly and a big behind, and the sixth-graders were laughing so hard, they were falling off their chairs. Then someone yelled, "Shake it, Sambo!" Mr. Mpipi kept dancing, so I don't think he even heard it, but Miss Andersen walked over and started flicking the auditorium lights on and off. Then she went up on the stage, handed Mr. Mpipi his cape, and said the assembly was over. "Everyone except the sixth-graders should proceed in an orderly fashion back to their rooms," she said.

Later, during silent reading, Miss Hogan had me bring a note down to Miss Anderson's office. Her door was closed, but I could hear Mr. Mpipi in there. He was saying, "But *why* I'm fired, Mrs. Principal? Please say the *why?*"

When the teachers are around, Mr. Zadzilko's all nice to me. He calls me his best helper, and his junior janitor, and stuff. When it's just him and me, he calls me "Dirty Boy," and he keeps flicking his finger at me down there. "That's to remind you that if you ever blab about certain secrets you and me got, I'll tell everyone that Little Dirty Boy likes to look at his teachers' twats." And I think that means their girdles.

I killed something once. One of our chickens—the brown speckled one with the broken beak and the pecked-at head. "Nervous Nellie," Grandpa always used to call her. He says a fox probably got her, but it didn't. The other chickens were out front, pecking at the dirt, and she was all by herself behind the barn. I never liked her—never liked to look at that broken beak. At first, I was just tossing pebbles to bother her. Then I tossed a rock. Then I *threw* a rock, hard as I could, and it bounced off the barn and beaned her on the head. It looked funny at first, the way she just dropped, but then I realized she was dead and I got sad. She had blood coming out her eye. When I picked her up, she felt limp, like the rag doll Great-Grandma Lydia always wants me to hold and kiss. "Hold my baby," she always says. "Kiss my Lillian." Mother says Great-Grandma Lydia has cracks in her brain, and that's what makes her crazy. The cracks are because she's so old. All day long, she laughs at nothing and wants me to kiss her dolly. When Nervous Nellie died? I said a Hail Mary for her and buried her under some mucky leaves by the brook. Mother says God has a different heaven for animals than the one for people, but there's no hell for animals, on account of animals don't commit sins.

If Daddy steps one foot onto our farm, Grandpa's getting him arrested for trespassing. Mother says I can't tell anyone at school because that's private information. Private information is like a secret, and trespassing's when you step on someone's private property and wreck things—like when those bad teenagers wrecked the Quirk family. At school, during morning exercises, we always say something about bad people who trespass against us. It's in either the Pledge of Allegiance or the Lord's Prayer. I always get those two mixed up. You know what? Miss Hogan's picked me to lead morning exercises twice this year, and some kids haven't even done it once.

"Tell him he can go to hell!" Grandpa said, that time the phone rang at supper, and Aunt Lolly answered it. It was Daddy.

"He just wants to apologize to you, Pop," Aunt Lolly said. "Why don't you let him apologize?" The phone in her hand was shaking, and Grandpa let out a big breath and got up from the table.

"Apologize for what?" I asked Mother, but she shushed me.

"Here, give me that thing," Grandpa said.

Mother leaned toward me and whispered. "For what he did when you two went downtown to buy your present."

"What is it, Alden?" Grandpa said. I could hear Daddy's little voice coming out of the telephone, except not what he was saying. "Yep," Grandpa kept saying. "Yep . . . Yep." Then he said, "You know how I end each day, Alden? I go upstairs. Kiss my poor, dear mother goodnight—make sure she's quiet and comfortable. Then I take my bath. Then, before I climb into bed, I get down on my two bad knees and pray to God that my beloved Catherine, who gave her life to bring you into this world, is resting peacefully in heaven. And do you want to know what else I pray for, Alden? I pray that your son doesn't grow up to be a no-good bum like his father."

Then I *could* hear what Daddy was saying. "But just *listen* to me. Okay, Pop? Can you please just *listen* to me?"

Grandpa said something about a broken record and hung up in the middle of Daddy's talking. He looked over at Aunt Lolly. "There," he said. "You *satisfied*?" Aunt Lolly didn't say anything, but she was almost-crying-looking.

And later? When Lolly and me were feeding the chickens? I said, "Do you love Daddy, even though he's bad?"

"He's *not* bad," she said. "He's just got his troubles, that's all. And of course I love him. He's my brother. You love him, too. Don't you?"

"I love him but I hate him," I said.

She shook her head. "Those two cancel each other out. You've got to choose one or the other."

I shrugged. Thought about it. "Love him, I guess."

Lolly smiled. Then she reached over, grabbed my nose, and gave it a little tug.

———

WHAT DADDY DID WHEN WE went downtown was: first, he got drunk, and then he broke the cigarette machine, and then he made that gas station lady dance with him. It was my fault, in a way, because I couldn't pee in the alley.

Grandpa had let Daddy borrow the truck, but Daddy and me were only supposed to go to Tepper's, pick me out my present, and then come right back.

On the way into town, it started snowing—little snowflakes, not the big fat ones. We were both pretty quiet for a while. Being alone with Daddy felt different than being with him when Grandpa and Aunt Lolly were there. Daddy said, "You know what I'm thinking of buying you? One of those genuine Davy Crockett coonskin caps. How would you like one of those?"

"Good," I said. I didn't really want another one, but I didn't want to say I didn't. I was a *little* scared, but not that much.

"You want to play Antarctica?" he said.

I didn't answer him because I didn't know what he was talking about. "Well?" he said. "Do you or don't you?"

I shrugged. "How do you play?"

He rolled down his window, then reached past me and rolled down mine. Cold air blasted in at us, and snow. "I don't suppose your mother ever allowed you the pleasure of spitting out the car window," Dad said. "But here in Antarctica, you can go right ahead and spit." So I did. Then we rolled our windows back up and played the radio loud. Antarctica was kind of fun, but not really. There was a parking place right in front of Tepper's.

The cash register lady said they didn't sell coonskin caps anymore, so Daddy said, "Let me speak to the owner." "No, sir," Mr. Tepper said. "Davy Crockett kind of came and went. How about a hula hoop?" I didn't really want one of those, either, but I picked out their last black one. "This thing's only two ninety-nine," Dad said. "Go ahead. Pick out something else." He didn't have enough money for ice skates, though, or this Cheyenne Bode rifle I kind of liked. So I got the hula hoop, some Dubble Bubble, and a Silly Putty egg. By the time we left Tepper's, the snow had started sticking. "Well, Merry Christmas in February," Daddy said. "Better late than never, right? You thirsty?"

The Cheery-O tavern had these two bartenders, Lucille and Fatty. Lucille asked Daddy what he wanted to wet his whistle, and Daddy said, "How 'bout a root beer for my buddy here, and I'll have a root beer without the root. And maybe you can get that good-for-nothing husband of yours to cook us up a couple of his fried egg sandwiches."

"Coming right up, Ace," Fatty said. Everyone at the Cheery-O was calling Daddy "Ace."

I ate my sandwich neat, but Daddy got yolk in his beard. He kept making me sing "Inka Dinka Do" for everybody. Then he started

playing cards and drinking these drinks called Wild Turkeys. Fatty
kept filling up my root beer mug without me even saying anything.
I had to show some man with watery eyes how, when you press Silly
Putty onto the funny papers and peel it off again, it makes a copy.
"The Japs must make this gunk," he said. "Because when you copy
it, the words come out Japanese."

"No, they don't," I said. "They're just backward." And the man
laughed and called over to Daddy. "Hey, Ace! There's no flies on this
one."

"No, but there's flies all over you, you piece a shit!" Daddy called
back. I thought the man was going to get mad, but he just laughed.
Everyone laughed.

At first, the Cheery-O was kind of fun, but then it got boring.
Daddy kept playing cards, and then Lucille yelled at me because I
was hula-hooping on my arm, and I started doing it faster and faster,
and it flew off and almost hit the bottles behind the bar. "One more
hand, Buddy," Daddy kept telling me. "This is my last hand." For a
long time, I just stood at the front window and watched the cars go
by, slipping and sliding in the snow.

"Okay, let's make like a tree and leave," Daddy finally said. We
were almost out the door when he grabbed my shoulder. "Hey, how
would you like to be my lookout?" he said. He got down on his hands
and knees and stuck his hand up inside the cigarette machine. My job
was to tell him if either Fatty or Lucille was looking. Then Daddy
said some bad words, and when he got up off the floor, his hand was
bleeding. When he kicked the front of the machine, the glass smashed.
"They're looking!" I said. We ran.

The problem was, all those root beers made me have to go. Daddy
took me to the alley between Loew's Poli and Mother's bank. "Go
piss down there," he said. "Go on. Hurry up." His blood was dripping on the snow.

"I can't," I said.

"Sure you can. No one's gonna see you. This is what guys *do* when they get caught short. It's what *I* do."

I started crying. "I want to, Daddy, but I *can't*."

He looked mixed up, not mad. "All right, all right. Come on, then."

Whenever Mother and I went in the Mama Mia Bakery, the Italian lady was nice. But she was mean to Daddy. "Drunk as a skunk, and with a little boy, no less! You ought to hang your head in shame!"

"He just needs to use your toilet," Daddy said.

"Get the hell out before I call the cops!"

Daddy said the Esso station would let us use their restroom, if his friend Shrimp was on and the boss wasn't around. Shrimp and Daddy were friends, from when Daddy used to work there, before he got fired.

"Harvey comes back from the bank and sees you here, he'll probably shitcan me," Shrimp said. The other mechanic stopped working and came over.

"Jesus Christ Almighty, Shrimp," Dad said. "You're gonna let the kid have an *accident?*" Shrimp gave Daddy the key, and Daddy unlocked the door. "I'll wait right out here," he said. "Make it snappy."

I was all shaking at first, and I got some on the seat and the floor. I kept peeing and peeing and peeing. The flusher didn't work. There were dirty words on the wall and someone had drawn a picture of a man's pee-pee. The sink had a spider in it. I put on the faucets full blast and watched it get caught in the tidal wave. It was dirty in there, but it was warm from this steamy radiator. I wanted to leave, and I didn't want to. I didn't like it when Daddy got drunk.

He *wasn't* waiting right outside. He was in where Shrimp and the other guy were fixing the cars. He was talking louder than everyone else. "What do you mean you don't want to dance with me, darlin'?" he said to some lady in a mink stole. "Sure you do!" He kept trying to waltz, and the woman kept trying not to, and when Shrimp tried to stop it, Daddy shoved him away. Then that Harvey guy got back from the bank.

It was a dirty fight. Three against one, plus Harvey kept hitting Daddy in the face with a bag of change. The lady's stole got ripped, and she got rippy stockings and a skinned knee. Dad's mouth was all bloody, and one of his front teeth was just hanging there. *Stop crying, kid*, everyone kept telling me. *It's okay. Stop crying.* And I wasn't even crying. I was just choking.

At the police station, we had to wait and wait. The blood on Daddy's hand and his mouth turned rusty-colored. He still had egg yolk in his beard. When he reached up and pulled on his hanging tooth, I looked away. "My name is mud," he kept saying. "Alden George Quirk the Third *Mud*."

"Yeah, but don't forget," I said. "You invented the maze."

And he laughed and said no, he didn't. All's he did was copy the idea from some farm he seen when he was hitchhiking through New Jersey. Then he touched my cheek with his sandpaper hands and told me I was his California kid. "How come I'm that?" I asked, but he didn't answer me.

Later, one of the policemen who arrested us at the Esso station came over and said they finally got ahold of Grandpa.

"What'd he say?" Daddy asked.

"That he can't come pick up the boy because you have his truck. But that's okay. We can run him back out there."

"What did he say about me?" Daddy said.

"That we should lock you up and let you dry out, same as we do with all the other bums."

The cruiser had a radio, and a siren, and chains on the tires because of the snow. The policeman told me to sit in the back. "Did I get arrested?" I said. He said I didn't because I didn't do anything wrong. "You know what you need for the ride back home?" he said. He pulled in front of the Mama Mia Bakery.

I don't think the Italian lady recognized me, because she was nice again. "Which would you like, sweetheart? A sugar cookie or a chocolate chip?" I took a chocolate chip and it was free. The policeman got a free cruller. He was going to pay for it, but the bakery lady said, "Oh, go on. Get out of here. Your money's no good in here." She said it nice, though. Not mean.

On the way home, I remembered about my hula hoop and my Silly Putty: I'd forgotten them back at the Cheery-O. I didn't eat my cookie. I just held it, all the way back. Even with the snow chains on, the police car kept wiggling back and forth on the snowy road. The cows were out in the pasture still, not in the barn. They had smoky breath and snow on their backs, and when I saw them, I started crying.

One time, I had a scary dream that Daddy was giving me a ride in a helicopter. We were flying over our farm, and he said, "Hang on. Something's wrong. We're going to crash!" And then I woke up.

In this other scary dream, Mr. Zadzilko grabbed me and put me in that dark space under the stage where the folding chairs go. He locked that little door and nobody knew I was there. When I tried to scream, nothing came out.

Mr. Zadzilko told me he killed a dog once, by tying a rope around the dog's neck and throwing the other end over a tree branch, and then yanking. "You oughta have seen the way that dog was dancing," he said. "You got a dog. Don't you, Dirty Boy?" he said.

I said no, I didn't.

"Yes, you do. He's brown and white. I seen him that time my mother and me drove out to your farm for cider. Maybe if Dirty Boy tells certain secrets, his dog will get the Stan Zadzilko rope treatment."

"How come you have a mother but no wife?" I said, and he got all red, and told me that was *his* business.

I DUCK UNDER THE KEEP-OUT rope and take the shortcut to the middle of the maze. That's where Daddy meets me. His tent's somewhere in the woods, past the gravel pit. Sometimes he's by himself and sometimes he's with that kerchief lady who always stares at me and smiles. He's trespassing.

I hide the ham and the cookies and potatoes in the baby carriage, under the Quirk baby, the way he says to do when he's not here. I'm *glad* he's not here this morning—him, and that lady, and his stupid jack-o-lantern missing teeth.

Back at the farm, there's trouble: a big fight, Hennie and Aunt Lolly on one side, and Zinnia and Chicago on the other. "One little raggedy-ass jug of cider—that's all I ever snitched from here, so help me Jesus!" Zinnia says. "So that later on down the line, I could sip me a little applejack."

"Then why's half a ham missing?" Hennie says. "Why is it that this morning a package of icebox cookies was unopened, and now it's half-gone?"

"I don't *know* about no icebox cookies!" Zinnia says. "Ax *him*!" Her finger's pointing at me.

"Caelum?" Aunt Lolly says. "Did you eat some of the cookies that were in the pantry?" I shake my head. And I'm not lying, either. I took them but I didn't eat them.

"Come on, Zinnia," Aunt Lolly says. "I'm escorting you back. You've broken a trust, so I can't have you working here anymore."

"Then take *me* back, too!" Chicago chimes in. "You can crank your own damn apples. Haul your own damn slop barrel down that hill."

"Don't you realize that it's a privilege to work here?" Hennie says.

"Privilege my black *be*-hind!" Chicago says. "What's so 'privilege' about me breaking my back all day for no pay?"

I *can't* tell Lolly and Hennie that it was me who took the food, because then Grandpa will find out Daddy's trespassing and get him arrested. And it's a secret. I *promised* him I wouldn't tell. And you know what? I think Lolly's wrong. I think I *can* love and hate Daddy. Because now Zinnia and Chicago are in trouble, just like Thomas Birdsey got in trouble that time when it was me who was the secret spitter. And tonight, if I die in my sleep like the prayer says, I'm probably going to hell because getting other people in trouble for something you did is, I think, a *mortal* sin, not a *venial* sin, and probably hell is going to have a hundred million Mr. Zadzilkos with devil horns.

BUT THAT NIGHT? WHEN I'M lying in bed, thinking about Mr. Zadzilko and getting scared again? I put my light on, and take my pen, and do what Zinnia did: I write "Jesus" on the palm of my hand, and the S in the middle of Jesus becomes the first S in "saves." It's not a tattoo, but maybe it'll work. I kept staring at it and staring at it, and saying, "Jesus . . . Jesus." I don't feel his arms around me, though; I don't feel anything. Maybe it's because I didn't prick myself with a pin, or because every time I say "Jesus," all's I can see is Mr. Mpipi, up on the stage, dancing his crazy dance.

On Monday morning, Miss Hogan makes an announcement. "We have to be extra tidy for the next several days," she says. "Poor Mr. Zadzilko's mother died over the weekend. He's going to be absent all week."

She shows us the sympathy card she's going to pass around and says to make sure we sign in cursive, in pen not pencil, and neat not sloppy. When the card gets to me, I write "Caelum Quirk," but Mr. Big Fat Glasses Face probably doesn't even know my name. All's he ever calls me is "Dirty Boy."

All day, I keep thinking about Mr. Zadzilko being absent. And after school—after I empty our wastebasket and wash our board and I'm *still* waiting for Mother—I go up to Miss Hogan's desk. "What is it, Caelum?" she says.

"I've got a secret."

"You do, do you? Would you like to tell me what it is?"

"Miss Anderson smokes," I say. "When she sits on the toilet. I seen her from Mr. Zadzilko's peeking hole."

For a long time she just looks at me—like I said it in Japanese or something. Then she gets up, takes my hand, and has me show her.

And you know what? The next morning, when I wake up? The egg case on my windowsill has hatched. There's tiny little praying mantises scrambling all over the sill, and on the floor, and even in my bed.

Hundreds of them.

Thousands.

Millions, maybe.

chapter five

LOLLY'S CAT WAS CAUTIOUS AT first, watching me from doorways, scooting from the rooms I entered. But half an hour into my homecoming, she sidled up to me, brushing against my pant leg. My aunt had given her some goofy name I couldn't remember. "Where is she, huh?" I said. "Is that what you're asking?"

In the pantry, I found a litter box in need of emptying, an empty bag of Meow Mix, and a note in Lolly's handwriting: "*Get cat food.*" There were a couple of tins of tuna in the cupboard. "Well, whatever your name is, you're in luck," I told the cat. With the first twist of the can opener, she began bellowing. We were probably going to be friends for life.

Thinking I should call Maureen, I flopped down on Lolly's sofa and grabbed the remote. *The Practice* was on. Okay, I thought. Not my favorite, but watchable. I stood up and brushed the grit off the sofa, sending cat fur flying. My aunt had many talents, but housekeeping wasn't one of them; that had always been Hennie's department. I pried off my shoes and put my feet up. Lolly's cat hopped aboard, walked up my leg, and nestled against my hipbone. Gotta call Maureen, I thought. Soon as the commercial comes on. . . .

WHAT? WHERE . . . ? I stumbled toward the ringing telephone, realizing where I was: back in Three Rivers, back at the farmhouse.

"Hey," I said. "I was going to call you. I must have conked out."

Except it wasn't Maureen. It was some doctor, talking about my aunt's stroke. Yeah, I *know* all this, I remember thinking. That's why I've come back. But somewhere in the middle of his monologue, it dawned on me that he was talking about a second stroke. Lolly hadn't survived this one, he said. They'd pronounced her dead ten minutes earlier.

I went outside. Sat on the cold stone porch step. The sun was rising, coral-colored, over the treeline. Higher in the sky, the moon was fading away.

I went back inside. Called Maureen and woke her out of a sound sleep.

"Caelum? What time is it?"

"I'm not sure. It's sunrise here. . . . She died, Mo."

I waited out the silence, the sigh. "How?"

"Another stroke."

"Oh, Cae. I'm so sorry. Are you at the hospital?"

I shook my head. "The farmhouse. I sat with her for a couple of hours last night, but then I came back here. They said when they checked her at four, she was stable. But then, twenty minutes later . . . Maureen, I don't feel sad. I don't feel anything. What's wrong with me?"

"Nothing, Cae," she said. "You just haven't been able to take it in yet. Absorb the shock of it." She said she'd talked to Lolly's doctor the day before, while I was en route to Connecticut. More of the test results had come back; the damage had been massive. "She might not have been able to walk, or talk, or even swallow food. Lolly would have *hated* living like that."

"They asked me did I want to come in and view the body. I said no. Is that something I'm *supposed* to do?"

"It's a personal decision, Cae. There's no 'supposed to.'"

"I should have stayed with her last night. Slept in the chair or whatever. God, I hate that she died alone."

Mo said should-haves weren't going to do Lolly *or* me any good.

"Last night? I got up and started combing her hair. More out of boredom than anything else, I guess. I'd just been sitting there, watching her sleep. And her hair was all smushed down and I found this comb in her drawer and . . . and when I *stopped* combing? She opened her eyes. Stared at me for a few seconds."

"Then she knew you'd come back."

"No. Uh-uh. Nothing registered."

"Maybe it did, Cae. Maybe knowing you were there, she could *let* herself die. The hospice team at Rivercrest always used to say that the dying—"

"Yeah, okay. Stop. I doubt it, but thanks."

"How did it feel?" she asked.

"What?"

"Touching her? Combing her hair?"

"It felt . . . it felt . . ." The question made my eyes sting and my throat constrict. Trying to stifle tears, I uttered a weird guttural noise that caught the cat's attention.

"It's okay to feel, Caelum," Mo said. "Just let yourself—"

"What's her cat's name, anyway?" I said, cutting her off. "I fed her tuna fish last night and now she's like my shadow."

"The black and white? Nancy Tucker."

"Oh, yeah. Nancy Tucker. Where'd that name come from?"

"Some folksinger Lolly likes," Mo said.

I stood there, nodding at the cat. *"Liked,"* I said.

Maureen asked me if I'd thought about what I needed to do that day. Should we go over stuff? Make a list? I told her what the hospital had said: that I had to let them know ASAP which funeral home they should contact to arrange for the transfer of the body. "I guess I'll tell them McKenna's," I said. "We used them when my mother died, and my grandfather. My father, too, I think. Or did we? Jesus, that's weird."

"What?"

"I can't remember my father's funeral."

"Well, you were so young."

"No, I wasn't. I was fourteen." For a second, I caught myself thinking I'd have to ask Lolly about it.

Maureen said I should tell the hospital to notify Gamboa and Sons.

"The Mexican funeral parlor? I don't think so, Mo. I doubt Lolly would have wanted a 'cat licker' sendoff."

"A what?"

"Nothing. Never mind."

Mo said Lolly had used Gamboa and Sons for Hennie's services—that Lolly and Victor Gamboa had been friends since the days when they'd worked together at the prison. "Lolly's preplanned and paid for her funeral, Cae. After Hennie's burial, she decided to do that. Which makes it easier, right? Now you won't have to second-guess what she would have wanted."

"Typical Lolly," I said. "Miss Practical. So what do you think? You going to try to get back here? Because I'll understand if you don't think you can—"

Sure she was coming, Mo said. She'd call Galaxy Travel as soon as they opened and let me know when she had the details. Now that she thought of it, she'd better call the kennel, too. "Sophie drove them crazy last time, and they were hinting about not taking her anymore. But under the circumstances . . . Maybe you should try to plan the wake for Wednesday and the funeral for Thursday," she said. "That way, if I can't get everything in place until—"

"Today is what day?" I asked.

"It's Monday, Caelum. Monday, the nineteenth."

"Monday. Yeah, that's right. I'm a little disoriented."

"Well, that's understandable. You were traveling all day yesterday. Plus, the time change. And you're probably overtired on top of that."

It *wasn't* those things, though. It was being back home: remembering, not remembering. How could I not recall my father's funeral? "I guess you better bring my suit," I said. "And those shiny loafers you had me get."

"Sure. Should we go over what you'll need to do today? Make that list?"

I grabbed a pen, a scrap of paper. "Yeah, okay. What?"

First, I should call the hospital and tell them about the funeral home—get that done. Then I'd need to make an appointment with Gamboa's to go over the details. "And you're going to have to make some phone calls. Let her friends know."

"How am I supposed to do that? She wasn't exactly the Rolodex type."

"Look in that little telephone table by the stairs. I bet she's got an address book in there, or numbers written inside the phone book. Call the people whose names you recognize, and ask them to call whoever else they think might want to know. And Ulysses. Call him. I guess you'll need to start thinking about what to tell him, job-status wise. Whether or not you're going to keep him on for a while to look after the property. You're her executor, right?"

"So she said."

"Then you can probably write checks from her estate—pay him that way—but I'm not sure. I guess you'd better try to get an appointment with her lawyer, too." Oh, great, I thought. Lolly's lawyer was Lena LoVecchio, the attorney who'd represented me on my assault charge against Paul Hay. Just what I wanted to do: revisit that whole mess. "I'm sure most of the legal stuff can be put on hold," Maureen said. "But there may be some short-term decisions to make, and while you're back there, you might as well—"

"Oh, man."

"What?"

"I suck at this kind of stuff. I'll probably screw everything up."

"No, you won't, Cae. People will help you. They'll *want* to help."

"And you're going to get here when?"

"Tomorrow, hopefully. *Tuesday*. Wednesday morning at the latest."

"Oh, man."

"Hey," she said. "You know what? After you call the hospital, why don't you go for a run? It'll help clear out the cobwebs, get rid of some of that tension. Then go back, take a nice hot shower and—"

"There's no shower here. Remember?"

"Oh, right. A nice hot bath, then. Even better. And eat breakfast, Caelum. You need to remember to eat."

"What else?" I said. "For this list?"

She said if she thought of anything else, she'd call me, but that she'd better get off. The dogs were chafing to go out.

I didn't want her to hang up. "Hey, I forgot to tell you. I saw Velvet before I left. At the airport. I guess she's on a cleaning crew?"

"Was," Mo said. "She called last night to tell me she quit. She saw you, too, she said. Oh, that reminds me: I better try and get ahold of her. She was going to meet me at school tomorrow to talk about reenrolling, but if I get a flight . . . okay, the dogs! I'll let you know when I'm coming. Call me if you need to. I love you, Caelum. I'll get there as soon as I can."

I DIDN'T RUN, AS MO suggested. I wandered, from room to room downstairs and then up to the second floor. At the top step, I looked down the hallway. Stood there, rocking on the balls of my feet. I couldn't do it.

From the house, I headed up the gravel road to the barn. Undid the latch, flipped on the overhead lights. Empty of cows, with its floor hosed and swept down to bald, cracked concrete, it was nothing but a glorified garage now—a parking place for the tractor and Lolly's truck. "Come, boss!" I shouted, calling in the ghost-cows for morning milking. "Here, boss! Come, boss!" My voice bounced around and rose to the empty loft.

At the height of things, Bride Lake Farms had milked a herd of sixty-five registered Holsteins. Every other day, the Hood Dairy truck would pull up, pump nine thousand pounds of raw milk out of the tank, and drive it off for processing. As a kid, one of my chores had been to take care of our personal milk supply: put out two big pans for the barn cats and carry six quarts back to the house whenever we got low. Damn, but that was good milk: icy cold, cream on the top. "You drank it unpasteurized?" Maureen asked once, when I was comparing farm milk to the watery gray skim milk we bought at the KwikStop. "Yeah, and look," I said. "I survived to tell you about it."

I walked over to Grandpa Quirk's beat-up wooden desk, still parked against the barn's south wall. It was covered now with half-empty cans of paint and turpentine. Back in the day, Grandpa had sat there, hunched over his bills and receipts and ratios. He'd hated that monthly math, I remembered, but God, he'd loved his milkers. Named them after movie stars: Maureen O'Hara, Sonja Henie, Dorothy Lamour. Whenever one of his girls started producing, he'd take three Polaroid pictures of her: a head shot, a body shot, and a closeup of her udder. He'd label them on the back, date them, and put them in his big tin box. Standing there, I recalled something I hadn't thought about in years: a game Grandpa and I had played. I'd pull one of the udder shots out of the box, hand it to him, and he'd look at it—study it at arm's length, hold it close, scratch his chin. Then he'd identify whose milk bag it was. He never got any wrong. Had there been some trick to it? Could Grandpa really recognize all those girls by their udders?

I spotted his cowshit shovel, still hanging from its same nail in the wall, identifiable by its chipped red handle. As a girl, Lolly'd painted it for her father as a birthday surprise, but she'd overturned the paint can in the process and gotten a surprise of her own: a spanking. Most, but not all, of that red paint had worn off the handle now. I lifted the shovel from the wall and tamped its blade against the cement floor. My fingers fit in the valleys Grandpa's grip had worn into the wood.

Or maybe *his* father's grip had made them. Who knew *how* old that damn shovel was? Four generations of Quirks had farmed here, if I remembered the history right. Five, if you counted me, which I didn't. I'd done my share of farmwork growing up—from junior high through grad school and beyond. But I'd never liked farming much—had never been interested in taking over. For the past several years, whenever Lolly mentioned my inheriting the farm, I'd cut her off. "Get out of here, you old coot," I'd say. "*You'll* outlive *me*." But she hadn't. And now, like it or not, this place was mine—the history and the burden of it.

Leaving the barn, I spotted Lolly's plaid jacket hanging from a hook—the one she was wearing the day she'd waved us off to Colorado. I reached out and grabbed the sleeve. Clutched it in my fist for a few seconds, and then let it go.

Most of the two dozen trees in the orchard looked blighted. Not long before we moved to Colorado, I'd helped Lolly cut down three or four of the dead ones. I saw her now, goggles on, chain saw in hand. "You're a maniac with that thing, old lady!" I'd yelled, over the buzz and the blade's bite, and she'd laughed and nodded like it was high praise. The apple house was in sorry shape, too—busted windows, half-collapsed roof. Well, what did it matter? The cider press was gone—sold to Olde Mistick Village years ago. There was nothing left in there that the rain could wreck. Let the bats and mice have it.

I headed back down, crossed Bride Lake Road, and started toward the cornfields on the far side of the prison. Walking along the road, I thought about how fucked up the layout was: a fifty-acre women's prison parked in the middle of a two-hundred-acre family farm. Lolly had filled me in on the history of the farm a few years back. Christmas day, it was—Maureen's and my first trip back home after we'd moved west. Mo and Hennie were in the kitchen, cleaning up, and Lolly and I had lingered at the dining room table, drinking brandy and passing around the old family pictures. I'd heard a lot of Lolly's Quirk family stories before, but that day, for some reason, I was more interested in them than usual. Why was that? Because I'd finally escaped Three Rivers? Because I'd reached my mid-forties? Whatever the reason, part of the pleasure that day was witnessing Lolly's pleasure in telling them to me.

The sale of land to the state had been a desperation move, Lolly'd said. The original Caelum was *Mac*Quirk, a native of Glasgow, Scotland. He'd married into manufacturing money and come to America to oversee his father-in-law's latest acquistion, the Three Rivers Bleaching Dyeing & Printing Company. But Caelum MacQuirk had failed at both textile mill management and marriage, Lolly said; he'd operated the company at greater and greater loss and fathered a child out of wedlock. To be rid of him, his father-in-law had bought him off, and with the money MacQuirk had purchased a two-hundred-and-fifty-acre tract of land along the southernmost boundary of Three Rivers. He'd married the child's mother and taken up farming, but had failed at that, too. "Hung himself," Lolly said, matter-of-factly. "Left his widow and son land-rich but cash-poor."

It would have made more sense for the widow Quirk to sell acreage at either the east or west end, but, according to Lolly, the state of Connecticut strong-armed her into selling them the tenderloin of the property, lake and all. Still, it had all worked out, in its own way. The deal they negotiated called for the widow's son, Alden—a recent graduate of Connecticut's agricultural college—to be installed as the new prison's farm manager.

"You remember my Grandma Lydia, don't you?" Lolly asked me. "Your *great*-grandmother?"

I nodded. "The tappy old lady with the rag doll."

"Well, she was a hell of a lot more than that. Back in her prime, Lydia Popper was a force to be reckoned with. Got her salt from *her* grandmother, she always used to say. She politicked for years until she wore down the state legislature and got 'em to buy the land and build her her ladies' jail. The cottage-and-farm plan, she called it.

Designed it, and ran the place for forty years. And raised a son all by her lonesome while she was doing it."

"Her son was Grandpa Quirk, right?"

"That's right. And then when *our* mother died delivering your dad and me, she had to step up to the plate and help raise us, too. She was in her sixties by then, and now here were these two babies to do for. She was smart, though. Got her prison gals to pitch in and help. Couple of 'em even wet-nursed us, my father told me."

"Nursed by convicted felons," I said. "Maybe that's why Daddy made all those trips to the pokey."

I'd expected my remark to draw a laugh from her, but it fell flat.

"Now, at first, Lydia balked at the idea of someone so young and untested as this wet-behind-the-ears college boy being put in charge of the farm operation, just because his mother had finagled him the position as part of the land purchase. See, Lydia'd promised those politicians up in Hartford that once it got going, the jail would pay for itself because of the farm production. What those gasbags up there cared most about was the business side of things, see? How it'd impact the state budget. Not whether or not a bunch of troubled girls got fixed. Got on with their lives. So the state gave her five years; if the place wasn't breaking even by then, they'd shut it down. Grandma knew that the whole ball of wax depended on the farm operation, okay? And she knew, too, that several of those politicians who'd opposed her were itching to see her fail. They didn't like the idea of a woman running things, see? Figured they'd give her just enough rope to hang herself. Lydia suspected they'd saddled her with this young Quirk fella to ensure her failure. Nothing she could do about it, though; it was part of the deal they'd struck with the widow.

"But Alden surprised Grandma. Turns out, young as he was, he was a damn good steward. Practical, shrewd. Worked like an ox. And he was good with the prison ladies, too. They liked him, so they worked their fannies off for him. Course, he was a good-looking son of a gun. I'm sure that didn't hurt. See? Here he is." She passed me a picture of a strapping young guy in overalls behind a team of plow horses. "You resemble him, don't you think?"

I shrugged.

"Well, if you can't see it, I sure as hell can. Your father resembled him, too. I got Popper looks, but your dad was all Quirk, same as you."

The robust farmer in the photograph looked nothing like my scrawny, straggly-haired father, and I told her so.

"Well, you gotta remember, kiddo. You only knew your dad after the booze got him. That goddamned war was what turned him alcoholic. Him *and* Ulysses, the two of 'em. They were high school buddies. Me, my brother, and Ulysses were all in the same class."

I said I hadn't realized that. Or if I'd known it, I'd forgotten it.

"Yup. The two of them, Ulysses and your dad, went down to the recruiting office and enlisted right after we graduated. I had wanted to go to college myself. To study anthropology—maybe go out west and work with the Indians. I used to find arrowheads out in the fields every once in a while—from when the Wequonnocs hunted out here, I guess—and that's what got me interested. Grandma Lydia was all for me going; she'd gone. Studied sociology. And little by little, me and her were wearing my father down on the subject. But after my brother enlisted, that was that. If Alden wasn't gonna stick around and help Pop with the farmwork, then I was gonna. Somebody had to. So I stayed put, and Alden went off to see the world and fight the Koreans."

"I never heard much about his war service," I said.

"Well, I never did either. After he came back, he wouldn't talk about it, not even to me. Whenever I'd ask him about it, he'd close up like a clam. Get huffy with me if I pursued it, so after a while I just shut my trap." I watched her eyes water up as she remembered it. "*Something* happened to him over there, because he came back different. Damaged, you know? And that was when he started drinking hard."

"No such thing as psychological counseling back then, I suppose."

"I don't know. But Alden wouldn't have signed up for it if there was. First month or so he was back, he mostly stayed cooped up in his room. And then when he did finally get out of the house, he mostly went off to the bars."

I opened my mouth to ask her some more, but Lolly shook her head and passed me another picture: her beloved grandmother, seated behind her desk at the prison, her young farm manager standing to her left like a sergeant-at-arms. "Look at the two of them with those matching Cheshire grins," I said. Lolly took back the photograph, squinted, and grinned herself.

"Little by little, he won her over, you see? She began to trust him. Rely on him. They swapped ideas, solved problems together. Became almost like business partners, I guess. And then, of course, it turned into a different kind of partnership. Lucky for us. Me and you wouldn't be sitting here if it hadn't." Observing that made her chuckle, and those watery blue eyes of hers recovered their sparkle. "To hear Grandma tell it, widow Quirk was fit to be tied. First the state of Connecticut steals her land away from her so they can build a prison. Then the prison matron steals her son out of the cradle. Course, nobody'd stolen anything. The state had paid her for that property fair and square, and Grandma and Grandpa just plain fell in love. I tell you, the gossips in town must have had a ball with *that* romance! Grandma was already in her forties—a confirmed old maid, or so everyone assumed until they got hitched. Married each other right down there by the lake, with all the prison girls in attendance. Nineteen eighteen it was. Grandma was forty-six and Grandpa was twenty-three. It was sad, though. We'd gotten tangled up in World War I by then, but Grandpa'd dodged *that* bullet—got a farm deferment from the government. Then he ups and dies of influenza. They'd been married for less than a year. When Grandma buried him, she was pregnant with my father."

"Alden Quirk the Second," I said.

"That's right. Alden Jr., speak of the devil." She passed me another picture: Grandpa Quirk, a boy in knickers, on the lap of a sober-faced Lydia.

"She looks more like his grandmother than his mother," I said.

Lolly nodded. "She'd started late, and then had to raise him by her lonesome. And then, like I said, after *our* mother died, she pretty much raised your father and me. It's funny, though: I heard her say more than once that making prisoners and little children toe the line was a cakewalk compared to dealing with her mother-in-law. Adelheid Quirk—Addie, they called her. Stubborn German girl. She was a pip, I guess."

"So Addie was your great-grandmother?" I asked.

"Right. On my father's side. Went to her grave blaming Grandma for her son's death. Thousands and thousands lost their lives during that flu epidemic, but she held Lydia P. Quirk personally responsible."

Walking along Bride Lake Road that morning, I smiled as I recalled that Christmas visit of ours three or four years ago: Aunt Lolly and me warmed by brandy and picture passing, by her desire to tell me the family stories and my desire to listen to them. "You gonna remember all this stuff?" she'd asked me that day. "You want a piece of paper to write it down?"

"Nah," I said, tapping my finger against the side of my head. "Got it all in here."

She nodded in approval, then called into the kitchen. "Hey, Hennie Penny. How about another slab of that apple crumb pie of yours?"

"Thought you said you were stuffed," Hennie called back.

"I was. But all this reminiscing's brought my appetite back." Turning to me, she asked if I wanted more pie, too, and I said I did. "Make that two pieces. And two cups of joe if there's any left."

From the kitchen, "Want ice cream on that pie?"

"Twist my arm," Lolly said.

A few minutes later, our wives had entered the dining room, plates of pie à la mode in one hand, coffee mugs in the other. "These two big lugs must've never heard of women's lib," Hennie had mock-complained. "Next time, we oughta burn our bras on the stove and make them get their own damn pie."

Mo had nodded in good-natured agreement.

———

I CAUGHT MYSELF DOING SOMETHING I'd often done as a kid: kicked a stone along the side of the road, trying to give it a ride all the way down to the cornfields. But I kicked it crooked and a little too hard, and it hopped into the poison ivy sprouting up along the roadside.

In that aerial-view photo back at the farmhouse, you could see that the prison property was wedge-shaped, as if Connecticut had come along and cut itself a big slab of Quirk family pie. Narrowest near the road, the prison compound fanned out from there, encompassing Bride Lake and, surrounding its shore in a semicircle, the six two-story brick dormitories that housed the inmates. "Cottages," they'd called them. Per Great-Grandma Lydia's orders, they were left un-locked, Lolly had told me, and because "the girls" *could* walk off the compound, few of them had. Behind the cottages had been the barns, coops, pastures, and fields that had made the prison self-sufficient and had provided surplus dairy and vegetables to the almshouse and the orphanage. The rear of the property was woods and, beyond that, an abrupt drop-off. A stone thrown from the cliff's edge would land in the town of New London.

A woman had thrown herself from that ledge once—a prisoner for whom Bride Lake had been a revolving door. I was in college at the time, and Mother had sent me a clipping about the suicide because the victim was someone I'd known as a boy. Zinnia, her name was. She'd worked for us during cider season. We'd been friends of a sort, Zinnia and me; she'd had a son my age and was always hugging me. Borrowing me, I realized now—borrowing my eight-year-old body. But at the time of Zinnia's death, I was nineteen or twenty, consumed by college work and college life, and grateful for both the reprieve from Three Rivers and the anonymity of Boston. I was momentarily sad to read my mother's news, I remember, and then the next moment I was over it. . . . I hadn't thought about Zinnia in years. Decades. But on that April day that Lolly died, I felt, again, Zinnia's fat, sun-warmed arms around me, and felt, along with her unequivocal embrace, the biting shame of my betrayal of her—my having let her take the rap for food I'd stolen.

Just past the curve in the road, the new high-tech complex came into view: a boxlike eyesore of a building, surrounded by chain link and crowned with spools of razor wire. "Makes me want to puke every time I come around the corner and see that goddamn thing, parked up there where the cow pasture used to be," Lolly had grumbled during one Sunday evening phone call. "It's like they're sticking their middle finger up at everything Grandma stood for."

"They" was the regime of Governor Roland T. Johnston, a law-and-order conservative from Waterford whom I'd had the pleasure of voting against before we moved out West. Johnston had come to power on the basis of his campaign promises to abolish the state income tax and put an end to the coddling of Connecticut's convicted felons. "Let every Willie and Wilma Horton in this state take note," I'd heard him say on TV the night he won. "The Carnival Cruise is over. The ship's been docked." Shortly after his inauguration, the custody staffs of the state's seven prisons were paramilitarized, Police Academy trained, and armed with Mace and billy clubs. For the first time in Bride Lake's history, male guards now roamed the compound, maintaining order largely by intimidation. Ground was broken on the state-of-the-art facility that would house the new, hard-core female inmate population, which, the governor maintained, had been the unfortunate byproduct of women's liberation.

"That's bullshit!" Lolly had declared. "There are some bad apples in the barrel over there—always have been. But it's not right, the way he's painting them all with the same brush. Most of the gals come in so beaten down by life that they're more dangerous to themselves than anyone else."

By the time the new "supermax" was open for business, Maureen and I were living out in Littleton, removed from state politics, but the age of Internet propaganda was upon us. "I had my friend Hilda write it down so you could take a look," Lolly phoned to tell me. "She's Miss Computer these days—Internet this, e-mail that. You got a pencil? It says double-ya, double-ya, double-ya, period, p-o, period, s-t-a-t-e, period, c-t, period, g-o-v. Whatever the hell that mumbo jumbo means. Hilda said to spell it out and you'd know."

By logging onto the Department of Correction's Web site, I was able to take a "virtual tour" of the new facility. During her forty-year tenure as superintendent of Bride Lake, Lydia Quirk had made fresh air and sunshine part of the equation by which female felons could heal themselves. But as the virtual tour proudly showed, the eight-by-ten-foot cells of the new high-tech prison had three-inch-wide window slits that didn't open or let in light. Air recirculated now, and the electronically controlled cell doors were popped once an hour so that inmates could take a five-minute rec break on the tier. "Recreation? That's a joke," Lolly had said. "These days, recreation means standing in line at the hot water pot with your Styrofoam cup and your ramen noodles. All that junk food and sitting around on their asses: they get as fat as pigs now. Half of them are on insulin, or Prozac, or blood pressure pills. Why bother to rehabilitate 'em when you can just drug 'em and fatten 'em up. Grandma would roll over in her grave."

Lolly went on and on during those Sunday night calls. "Uh-huh," I'd say, straining for patience. "Really? . . . Unbelievable." When I'd lived in Three Rivers, I'd invested in my aunt's outrage—had felt some of it myself because I knew how much she cared about those women in custody, and about how disheartened she'd become. But now, hundreds of miles away from her, I only half-listened. The trouble with Lolly, I told myself, was that she'd never escaped home port. It was too bad she *hadn't* gone to college. *Hadn't* traveled out West and worked on one of those reservations. But because she hadn't, she was hopelessly provincial and, well, *boring*. She *walked* to work, for Christ's sake. "Maureen's standing right here, waiting to talk to you," I'd say, waving Mo over to the phone. "Let me put her on." I'd have managed maybe five minutes of conversation, and Maureen would talk with her for the next twenty. Which was why, I guess, it was Mo who knew that the cat's name was Nancy Tucker. That Lolly had been taking an antidepressant since Hennie died and had prepaid for her own funeral at Gamboa's.

Had my long-distance disconnect from my aunt stemmed from indifference? Uh-uh. No way. It had stemmed from pain. Our move to Colorado had separated me from the one person I'd loved my whole life. The one family member who'd remained a constant after everyone else had either died or up and left me. But then *I'd* up and left—had put the Rocky Mountains between my aunt and myself in order to save face after my arrest and save my crumbling third marriage. And rather than own up to the pain of that separation, I had masked it. Hidden behind my guyness. Don't cry, we're told. Big boys don't cry. And so, on those Sunday nights when I'd hear the pain in her voice, or her old familiar chuckle, I'd safeguard myself against them. "No kidding," I'd say. "Wow. Well, here's Maureen." Oh, yeah, I was one armored and inoculated son of a bitch. Shit, when her companion died—the woman Lolly'd loved and lived with for thirty-something years—I hadn't even flown back for the funeral. But, it's like they say: hindsight's twenty-twenty. The night before? When she'd opened her eyes and stared right at me without registering who I was? Maybe that'd been some kind of karmic payback for the guy who'd never been honest with her about how much he missed her. How much, all his life, he had loved her. Well, I was facing the pain now, all right. Walking along that road and choking back sobs. Turning my face to the trees, so that people driving by wouldn't see that one of the big boys was crying. . . .

Approaching the prison's main entrance, I paused to look at the new sign they'd erected: my great-grandmother's name chiseled into a granite slab spanning two brick pillars. When the state opened the new facility in 1996, they renamed the compound Lydia P. Quirk Correctional Institution. Lolly had been invited, in her ancestor's honor, to assist with the ribbon-cutting. She'd declined via a bracing letter to the editor of the *Three Rivers Daily Record* in which she referred to the governor as "a hypocrite and a horse's back end." Protesting the forsaking of her grandmother's ideals, she'd written, "Lydia Quirk helped women get their dignity back. Associating her name with a place that beats women down is like spitting on her legacy."

"Ouch," I'd said, when she read me her letter over the phone. "You sure you want to burn your bridges while you're still working for the state?"

"Pass me the blowtorch," she'd said.

My eyes bounced from the sign to the gatehouse. Just outside, a uniformed guard stood smoking a cigarette and watching me. I waved. Ignoring the gesture, he just stood there, smoking and staring. "The goon squad," Lolly had dubbed the new regime.

Some of the inmates were already out in the west yard. A maintenance crew, from the looks of it—nine or ten women with shovels, hoes, and hedge cutters. Security risks, I figured, because they were wearing screaming orange jumpsuits. They were clearing brush and, by the looks of things, digging around for something. "Found another one!" I heard someone call, and a few of the others stopped working to go over and look.

Two male officers stood together, sipping coffees and supervising. "Morales!" one called. "Get your fat ass in gear! *Now!* You, too, Delmore!" Delmore must have said something he didn't like, because he shouted, "Yeah? Really? Then keep running your mouth, you stupid cow, because I'd just as soon march you off to seg as look at that pockmarked face of yours."

I shook my head. If this was the way they were treating them out in the yard when a pedestrian was in earshot, what was going on *inside* the place? That CO's attitude was the kind of thing that had chased most of the Bride Lake old timers into early retirement, according to Lolly. Not her, though. She'd stayed and fought, filing grievances against the younger guards who bullied some of the inmates and flirted openly with others. She'd blown the whistle on one officer who, for an entire eight-hour shift, had refused to issue toilet paper to a woman suffering from intestinal flu. She'd written up another whom she'd observed hanging himself with an imaginary noose when an inmate passed by him on the way to the chow hall—a woman who, the month before, had attempted suicide.

But Lolly had crossed a line when she complained to the deputy warden about the sexual shenanigans of a well-connected young CO named McManus. "Struts around like a rooster in the henhouse," she'd groused. "And that juvie he's got working for him is doing much more than washing and waxing floors, and everyone knows it." As a result of her complaint, Officer McManus was assigned a different helper—a Bride Lake lifer who'd killed her husband and was old enough to be his mother. That's about when the anonymous war against Lolly began.

A rubber dildo was left in her desk drawer. Lesbian pornography was taped to the inside of her locker door. At a staff training in Wethersfield, someone spray-painted the words *bull dyke* on her driver's-side door. Worst of all were the middle-of-the-night phone calls—whispered taunts that left Lolly and Hennie exhausted and frazzled. Still, my aunt was resolute. Or stubborn, depending on how you wanted to look at it. She had a goal in mind: to match her grandmother's forty-year service record at Bride Lake. Lolly'd begun working there on September 25, 1957. She planned to retire on September 25, 1997, and not one day earlier. "If those sons of bitches think they can wear *me* down, they've got another think coming," she told me. She took the phone off the hook. Took sleeping pills. Took Maalox for the ulcer she'd developed. She took no sick days, though. Shed no tears in front of them. Showed no signs of weakening in her obstinate resolve.

It was during this siege that Hennie's kidneys began to fail. Three mornings a week, Lolly drove her to the hospital for dialysis, cat napping or pacing in the waiting room during the three-hour procedures. On the good days, Hennie wouldn't hemorrhage in the truck on their way back home. Lolly would get her some lunch, get her to bed, and then put on her uniform and walk down the road to do battle with the coworkers who'd become her enemies. She'd return from work a little after eleven each evening, and the phone calls would begin. "I'm more fried than a hamburger," she admitted to me one Sunday evening. "But they might as well get it into their fat heads: they're stuck with me until September."

But in February, the warden called Lolly to his office suite and introduced her to the two state police detectives who had come to ask her some questions. A Bride Lake inmate had charged that Lolly had groped her during a strip search, inserting her fingers between the lips of her vagina and stroking her clitoris with her thumb. A second inmate corroborated the story and said Lolly had molested her, too—that, for my aunt, groping was business as usual. "They're junkies, both of those girls!" Lolly shouted at me over the phone. "Someone offered them something to say that stuff! Junkies will make a deal with the devil!"

"You need legal advice," I told her. "Why don't you call Lena LoVecchio and see what she says?"

"Too goddamned late for that," she snapped back.

For three hours, she said, those detectives had grilled her about the false accusations, and then about the history and the nature of her long-standing relationship with former Bride Lake inmate Hennie Moskowitz. "I told them my personal life was none of their goddamned business," she said. "But they kept chipping away and chipping away, and I let 'em get to me, goddamnit." The Department of Correction offered Lolly a choice: a discreet resignation, to be signed before she left the warden's office that afternoon, or a full-blown investigation, possibly followed by an arrest. She was exhausted. She was frightened. Hennie was so sick. Now she *did* cry in front of them. She tendered her resignation, effective on the first of March, six months and twenty-five days shy of her forty-year goal.

Lolly vetoed the idea of a testimonial dinner at which "those two-faced phonies from central office" might stand at a podium and praise her. She nixed the plans for a staff open house at which the guards she'd filed grievances against might stand around, having cake and coffee and smirking at her defeat. All she wanted on her last day on the job, she said, was permission to take her grandmother's sign with her.

The sign was a rustic pine board that had been presented to Lydia at the prison's dedication ceremonies in 1913. It had hung on the office wall behind her desk throughout her long tenure as Bride Lake's matron. Into the four-foot plank, Lydia's farm manager, later her husband Alden, had burned the one-sentence philosophy by which she operated Bride Lake: "A woman who surrenders her freedom need not surrender her dignity." "It was a personal gift from my grandfather to my grandmother," Lolly argued in her written request to the warden to take the sign. "And anyway, you've thrown out her values and her success rates. Why would you want it?"

When the warden denied Lolly's request on the grounds that the sign was state property, she petitioned Central Office. The commissioner upheld the denial. Lolly contacted the governor's office. Three unanswered inquiries later, one of Johnston's lackeys contacted her. Governor Johnston put implicit trust in the people he placed in positions of authority, she said, and made it his policy not to undermine that authority.

"Bull*shit*!" Lolly had responded, and at the end of her final shift, had unscrewed the sign from a corridor wall and taken it anyway, meeting and defeating the gaze of several junior officers who watched her but did not try to stop her. "Good thing for them," she told me later, "If they had, they'd have gotten clobbered with that board. I'd have broken noses if I had to."

Lolly hung the sign in the bedroom she shared with Hennie.

Hennie died in May.

I sent Maureen back East to the funeral instead of going myself.

And for the next two years, Sunday night after Sunday night, the phone would ring, and I'd guard myself against her frustration and her loneliness. Half-listen to her account of whatever latest stunt they were pulling over there at "Grandma's prison," then pass the phone to Maureen.

———————

AT THE WEST END OF the property, I tramped around in what had once been our cornfields. They were a fallow, neglected mess now, blanketed with dead leaves, weeds, and junk-food wrappers. I walked all the way back to the gravel pit, trying to pinpoint where, exactly, the maze had been. And in the middle of figuring it out, I was clobbered by the sudden remembrance of what, earlier that day, had eluded me: my father's wake. . . .

It *had* been at McKenna's Funeral Home: closed-casket, pitifully attended, and me standing there, wearing that itchy woolen suit they'd bought me for the occasion. I'd held my breath each time Mr. McKenna swung open the vestibule door, afraid that the next mourner might be someone from my school—someone who had connected me to that drunk in the newspaper—the fucking missing-toothed failure of a man who hadn't even managed to get himself out of the way of a moving train.

Then someone from school *had* come: Mr. Cyr, my freshman cross-country coach. He offered condolences to my mother, aunt, and grandfather. Then he put his hand on my shoulder and said he was sorry for my loss, and that he knew how it felt because he had lost his father when he was in high school, too. I nodded, mumbling uh-huhs and thank-yous without looking at him. His kindness filled me with contempt: for him, for my father, for myself. I quit cross-country the following week, although not in any aboveboard way. I just stopped showing up for practice. And when Mr. Cyr stopped me in the hall to ask me why, I lied. Told him my grandfather was short-handed and needed me for farm chores.

And I remembered something else about my father's wake—that weird disturbance near the end. I'd gone to the restroom, and when I opened the door to return to the viewing room, there she was: the kerchief woman. She was shaking badly, I remember. She said my name and reached toward me, like someone groping for something in the dark. And then my mother, in a voice louder than I had ever heard her use in public before, said, "Oh, good God Almighty! This isn't hard enough without *her* showing up here?" She rushed toward us, shouting, "Get away from my son! Don't you dare touch him! You get out of here! Now!"

Lolly and Hennie hurried Mother out of the room, and Grandpa and Mr. McKenna approached the kerchief woman, coaxing her away from me and out of the building. And then I was standing there, alone, looking back and forth between my father's coffin and the door through which the kerchief woman had just been given the bum's rush. . . .

What had ever become of that woman? I wondered.

Who had she been?

chapter six

I LIKED VICTOR GAMBOA, WHO was sympathetic without being smarmy. Cradling Lolly's file, he told me how much he'd enjoyed working with her when they were both second-shift COs. "She was always fair with the ladies, but she didn't put up with any of their monkey business either. What do they call it now? Tough love? I think your aunt invented it."

"Or inherited it," I said. "From what I've heard, that was her grandmother's style, too."

"Oh, the old lady? Yeah, she's a legend at that place. Or *was*, I should say. Different story over there these days."

"Tough love minus the love, right?"

He nodded. "We get a lot of the suicides."

Victor had photocopied Lolly's preference form, and we reviewed it together. She'd requested a nondenominational service, a cut-rate casket, and cremation. Her ashes were to be mixed with Hennie's ("blue jar in our bedroom") and spread on the farm. No obituary. ("You have to pay the paper for it now. Nuts to that!") No flowers. If people wanted, they could buy a book and donate it to the prison library. In the margin, she'd written, "The girls like murder mysteries, movie star biographies, and romance novels." Under "Music," she'd written, "Amazing Grace (my grandma's favorite hymn.)" We scheduled the wake for Wednesday evening, the funeral for Thursday morning.

The form had six slots for pallbearers. Lolly had written:

Caelum Quirk (nephew)   *Ulysses Pappanikou (employee)*
Grace Fletcher (friend)   *Hilda Malinowski (friend)*
Lena LoVecchio (lawyer)   *Carl Yastrzemski (ha ha ha)*

"Women pallbearers?" I said. "Is that okay?"

"Don't see why not, if that's what she wanted," Gamboa said. "You may have to get a stand-in for Yaz, though." As far as "Amazing Grace" was concerned, he said he had a recorded version he could pipe in, or he could call the soloist he sometimes used. "Or—" he said. He stopped himself.

"Or what?"

"Department of Correction's got bagpipers. They hire out, but they'll usually play gratis if it's one of their own. Of course, it'd have to be cleared by the higher-ups, which might be a problem. I know that, toward the end, there was no love lost between your aunt and the department."

"She had good reason to be bitter," I said. He nodded in agreement. I said the canned music would be fine.

He asked me if I'd bring over an outfit that Lolly could wear to her wake—that day, if possible, or the next morning. I could bring pictures, too, if I liked. Some families liked to display framed photos, or put together a collage of candids. "Celebrate the person's life," he said.

I nodded, my mind on something else. "You know what?" I said. "She gave them almost forty years. What the hell. Try for the bagpipes."

––––––

ULYSSES'S PHONE RANG AND RANG, unanswered.

Hilda Malinowski cried when I told her. Lolly and she had been friends since 1964, she said. She'd never been a pallbearer before, but if there was anyone she'd give it a try for, it was Lolly. She just hoped she was strong enough. She'd call Grace Fletcher for me, she said; Gracie was big-boned and she went to Curves, so she should be able to handle pallbearing.

Alice Levesque told me she knew *something* was up; Lolly hadn't looked right the last time at bridge club. "She played lousy, too. She was my partner, and I gave her the devil about it. Now I wish I'd kept my big mouth shut."

Millie Monk volunteered to make lemon squares, if we were having a get-together at the house after the funeral, which people would more or less expect, so she suggested I should. Lolly had always loved her lemon squares, she said. "She asked me for the recipe once, and I said, 'Who are you kidding? You wouldn't even know how to turn on the oven.' We always kidded each other like that, her and me. Jeepers creepers, I just can't believe she's gone."

Now that she thought about it, Millie said, maybe she'd come over to the house on Tuesday and tidy up a little. Run the vacuum. "Lolly was a sweetie pie, but she was never too zippedy-doo-da on the house-cleaning."

"Caelum Quirk! Long time no talk to," Lena LoVecchio said. "You haven't been swinging any more wrenches, have you?" I quieted her horsy laugh with the news about my aunt. "Jesus Christ! You're *kidding* me," she said. Lena told me she'd be *honored* to help carry Lolly's casket, and she'd be *happy* to meet with me while I was in town so that we could talk about the estate. Had I looked over her will? I told her Lolly had sent me a copy, but I'd never read it.

"Well, let's go over it together then. How does five o'clock tomorrow sound?" I told her I'd be there.

"Last time I saw Lolly was when I took her to a basketball game," she said. "The Lady Huskies versus the Lady Vols. Lolly wore her UConn sweatsuit and booed Pat Summit so loud, she drowned *me* out, which isn't easy to do. That's how I want to remember her: screaming her head off at Tennessee. Well, okay, I'll see you tomorrow."

"Tomorrow's Tuesday, right?" I asked.

She paused, momentarily taken aback. "Tuesday the twentieth," she said.

I tried Ulysses a few times more. No answer. Well, I might as well get this over with, I told myself, and headed up the stairs.

Lolly's bedroom—it had been her grandmother's originally, and then the room where she and Hennie slept—was at the far end of the hallway, adjacent to the sun porch. The bed was unmade, the blankets and sheets rucked up at the bottom. Nancy Tucker was curled up on Lolly's pillow. As I entered the room, the floorboards creaked and she opened her eyes and raised her head. Then she jumped from the bed and exited, bellowing down the hallway. "I miss her, too," I said.

There was clutter all around: on the night table, the chair, the bureau top. The hamper was open, more dirty laundry on the floor around it than in it. Above the bureau, on the wall, were Lolly's framed photographs: she and Hennie as younger women, arm in arm at some beach; a studio portrait of the two of them in middle age—some bank promotion, if I remembered right. They'd given me a copy of that picture, but I'd never framed it and put it out. There was a black-and-white photo of Grandpa, dark-haired and in a jacket and tie, holding some Farm Bureau award. Lolly'd put up two pictures of Great-Grandma Lydia: a formal portrait of her in an old-fashioned oval frame, and one of her at her desk down at the prison. There were several pictures of me—as a second-grader with missing front teeth, a high school kid, a college grad, a ridiculously young-looking groom at wedding number one.

The two photos that got to me the most that morning—put a lump in my throat and made me sit down on the bed—were the ones she'd hung in the middle of her montage: her own and her brother's high school graduation portraits. By the time they were both in their twenties, Daddy's alcoholism had begun to untwin them and, in their mid-thirties, that train speeding toward Boston had made the separation official. But there they both were again, on Lolly's wall—smiling seventeen-year-olds, hinged together in twin gold frames.

Riding atop Lolly's photo gallery, hung crookedly six inches below the crown molding, was Great-Grandma Lydia's wooden sign: "A woman who surrenders her freedom need not surrender her dignity." I reached up and touched it, inching it back and forth until it was straight.

I opened Lolly's closet door, looked through her bureau. The top right drawer brimmed with odds and ends: loose pictures, ancient elementary school report cards, a Camp Fire Girls medal, a Ted Williams baseball card from 1946. I removed the lid from a small white cardboard box—"Bill Savitt Jewelers, Peace of Mind Guaranteed." Inside were two envelopes, labeled in blue fountain pen ink: "Louella's first haircut, June 1, 1933" and "Alden's first haircut, June 1, 1933." I opened Lolly's envelope. The soft, dead golden tuft between my thumb and fingertips felt creepy and strange. How odd that families kept this kind of stuff, I thought. How strange that children grow up, grow old, and die, but their hair—dead cells, if I remembered from high school biology class—remains as is. I put the lock of Lolly's hair back in the envelope, tucked in the flap, and put it back in the box. Replaced the lid, closed the drawer. I didn't open the envelope containing my father's hair. Couldn't go there.

Wardrobe-wise, once you eliminated T-shirts, flannel shirts, jeans, and coveralls, there wasn't much to pick from. I chose the only thing Lolly had bothered to put on a hanger: the brown velour pantsuit she'd worn to Maureen's and my wedding. If I remembered right, she'd worn it that Christmas afternoon when we'd looked at the old pictures, too. It had a grease stain on the front—no one had ever accused Lolly of being a dainty eater. Maybe I should have it dry-cleaned, or maybe Gamboa's could camouflage it. It was either this pantsuit or her UConn Huskies sweatsuit, and I was pretty sure that outfit wouldn't fly with Hilda and Millie and the girls.

From Lolly's room, I wandered out to the sun porch. Cardboard cartons and wooden apple crates lined the floor. Stacks of ledgers and state reports, leather-bound albums and newspaper clipping files depressed the springs of the sofa bed. Two army-green filing cabinets, chock-full, stood against the west wall. Great-Grandma Lydia's prison archives mostly, I figured. Lolly had tried several times to get me to look at some of this stuff with her. It would take forever to sift through it and see what I should probably save. Alternatively, it would take twenty minutes to heave it all out the window and let it fall into a Dumpster below.

I picked up one of Lydia's musty-smelling diaries. Its rotting cloth covers exposed the cardboard beneath; its crumbly, age-browned pages were bound together with what looked like black shoelaces. I opened to a page dated September 17, 1886—a letter that had never been sent, I figured, addressed to a sister of hers named Lillian. "As ever, dear Sis, I struggle with two minds about Grandmother. Here, seated beside me, is the esteemed Elizabeth Hutchinson Popper, brave abolitionist, valiant battlefield nurse, and tireless champion of orphans and fallen women. But here also is the cold woman who has yet to remember her granddaughter's fifteenth birthday, now eleven days past. . . . Had Lizzy Popper been in charge during the time of the Biblical flood, she might have led all of God's creatures onto the ark, two by two, then closed the door against the torrent, and floated away, having forgotten her poor granddaughter at the pier!"

Well, it was interesting in its own way, except I wasn't that interested. Maybe some historical society would want it. Maybe not. When Maureen and I got back in summertime, I'd have to deal with all this stuff. I knew one thing: I wasn't going to ship it all out to Colorado. It would cost an arm and a leg to do that, and once it got there, where the hell would we put it all?

I walked up the hallway to Grandpa's room. It looked the same as it always had, except for the two missing drawers in his mahogany dresser.

At first, Alzheimer's had merely toyed with Grandpa's brain. There'd been an incident at CVS when the cashier, having pointed out that his coupon was from the previous week's circular, refused to give him the sale price on a jar of Metamucil. In response, Grandpa had called her a "dumb nigger" and stormed out of the store, product in hand, without benefit of a purchase receipt. Luckily, the cop who investigated had been, as a teenager, one of our farmhands. He and the store manager talked the cashier out of pursuing my grandfather's arrest for having used hate speech. Not long after that, we discovered that Grandpa—that most frugal of men—had sent two thousand dollars to an "astronomical consortium" for the purpose of having a star named after his long-deceased wife. The documentation for "the Catherine star" had rolled out of a dot matrix printer, and the Better Business Bureau said there was little they could do without a return address or phone number. In September of that same year, Grandpa drove to the Eastern States Exposition for the Holstein judging—something he'd done every year for decades. He had left the house at seven that morning. One of the fair's security guards had finally found him at ten p.m., asleep in a Port-a-Potty. He'd wandered the labyrinthine parking lot for hours, searching for a car he'd sold years before and later failing to remember what he was searching for, or where he was.

The mahogany dresser had lost those two drawers one afternoon when Grandpa had felt a chill. Hammer in hand, he'd converted them to kindling, added newspaper, and lit a cozy fire atop his braided rug. That had been the last straw for Hennie. She'd put her foot down—either Lolly was going to take hold of the situation, or she was moving out. Better that than die in a fire! And so Lolly had surrendered her father to Rivercrest Nursing Home.

The relocation had agitated Grandpa at first; he was baffled about why he was there and pissed as hell that an alarm would beep whenever he put on his coat and tried to walk out the front door. He'd had no idea that that alarm was triggered by the plastic bracelet around his ankle, or even that he was wearing a bracelet. Lolly visited Grandpa twice a day, at lunch and dinnertime, usually, figuring that if she bibbed and fed him herself, she wouldn't have to worry that he wasn't eating enough. I dragged myself there once or twice a week at first, less frequently as time went on. Entering his sour-smelling room, I'd often find him rifling through his dresser drawers, searching furiously for something he could never quite identify. Eventually, his restlessness subsided and he became sullen and withdrawn, sometimes rapping his knuckles against his skull in frustration. Toward the end, he sat listlessly, recognizing no one.

It was during that final phase of Grandpa Quirk's life that I met Maureen. A recent divorcée, she had just become Rivercrest's new second-shift nurse supervisor. Our first conversations centered around my grandfather. Who had he been before the onset of his disease? How had he made his living? Who and what had he loved? It moved me when she said that my answers to her questions would help her give him better care. I'd been divorced from Francesca for three years by then. I hadn't dated since, or wanted to. But Mo was as pretty as she was compassionate, and my visits to Grandpa Quirk increased. On the night I finally got up the nerve to ask her out, I felt the heat in my face when she said no. Too soon after her divorce, she said; she hoped I understood. "Of course, absolutely," I'd assured her, nodding my head up and down like freaking Howdy Doody. But a week later, Mo stopped me in the hall to ask if my offer was still good.

I picked her up at the end of her shift and took her to the only place in Three Rivers, other than the dives that my father used to haunt, that was open after eleven p.m. Over mugs of coffee in a booth at the Mama Mia Bakery, we talked about our lives—families, marriages and divorces, the way personal goals and actual outcomes could diverge. And we *laughed*: about my adventures working for the Buzzi family, about the funny things her patients sometimes said and did. God, that felt good. And when Alphonse came out from the back with a couple of just-made cinnamon doughnuts, it more or less sealed the deal—for me, anyway. Biting into that aromatic deep-fried dough, watching the way sugar clung to her lips as she ate hers: the warm deliciousness of that moment reawakened in me a hunger I hadn't felt in years. Two dates later, at her place, we made love. And afterward, when I was spent and sleepy, she told me in the pitch-dark that if part of what I was looking for was kids, I was going to have to keep looking because she couldn't have them. A nonissue, I assured her, with all the certainty of a guy still in his thirties—a guy whose childhood had been an unhappy one, and who didn't particularly want to be in charge of some theoretical future child's happiness.

We were married seven months after that first date of ours—a month or so after Grandpa's passing. November 8, 1988. Mo was twenty-nine and I was thirty-seven, a third-time groom in a charcoal gray suit with a red carnation pinned to my lapel. Lolly and Hennie were our witnesses. After the exchange of vows, the four of us went out to a nice restaurant and then returned to the farm. Hennie had baked that morning: a wedding cake for Mo and me and a birthday cake for Lolly. "Damn, Lolly," I said. "With everything else going on, I forgot about your birthday."

"Your father's birthday, too," she reminded me.

"Best Wishes Mr & Mrs Quirk," Mo's and my cake said. In Lolly's cake, Hennie had stuck candles and a little cardboard sign: "Good God in Heaven! Lolly's 57!" Fifty-seven, I remember thinking—if he had lived. Shoveling frosting and sponge cake into my mouth, I did the math. My father had been only thirty-three when he died. I had, by then, outlived him by four years. . . .

———————

I WALKED TENTATIVELY TOWARD THE stairs, stopping at the threshhold of the room I'd slept in as a kid, and later had returned to during bouts of marital troubles. Marital and *legal* troubles, the last time I'd had to come back home. I didn't particularly want to admit it, but I guess I'd been like my father in that respect: screw up, then come back home to regroup, to be good for a while. . . . My old room had been preserved as a museum of my boyhood. Red Sox and Harlem Globetrotters pennants on the wall, stacks of comic books and *Boy's Life*s still sitting on the pine shelf I'd made in seventh-grade shop class. The room had been a closet when the house was new, they'd told me, which was why it was windowless. I snapped on the overhead light. The twin bed pushed flush against the wall was covered with the same cowboys-and-Indians spread my mother had bought at the Durable Store, back when I'd watched *Wagon Train* and *Bonanza* each week without fail. To enter that claustrophobic former closet was to become, again, the boy whose father was a public nuisance, whose mother washed priests' dirty clothes and answered sass with a stinging slap across the face. This was *that* boy's room, and I backed out again. Escaped down the front stairs and out into the morning sunlight.

AFTER I DROPPED OFF LOLLY'S suit, I swung by the bakery to see Alphonse. "He's in back in his office," the counter girl said. "Supposedly doing his payroll, but he's probably looking at Internet porn." She had spiky red hair, a pierced eyebrow. Her nipples were poking out nicely from beneath the thermal undershirt she was wearing. This must have been the one Alphonse had been salivating about in his last few e-mails. "Make sure you knock first, or he'll bite your head off," she said.

"Or shoot me with his paintball gun," I said.

Instantly, I was her ally. "I know! Isn't that lame? He's like my father's age, and he's still playing army over at that stupid paintball place."

When I opened his office door *without* knocking, Alphonse hit the off button on his computer and popped out of his chair like a jack-in-the-box. "Quirky!" he said. "What the hell you doing here?"

"You know, if you don't shut that thing down properly, you'll shorten the life of your hard drive," I said.

"Yeah? Well, don't tell Bill Gates on me. So what's up, bro? You get homesick or something?"

He seemed genuinely sorry to hear about Lolly. "She used to come in here every once in a while," he said. "Her and her friend. What was her name?"

"Hennie."

"Yeah, that's right. They were a matched set, those two, huh? Always got the same thing: blueberry muffins, toasted, with butter—*not* margarine."

I smiled. "Gotta support the dairy farmers," I said.

"Hey, remember the summer when your aunt found those pot plants that you, me, and my brother were growing out behind your apple orchard?"

I rolled my eyes recalling the incident. "The three stooges," I said.

"And remember? She made us pull them up and burn them in front of her? And we all got stoned from the smoke—Lolly included."

"She didn't get stoned," I said.

"The fuck she didn't! I can still see her standing there, scowling at first and then with that goofy grin on her face. She was toasted."

"What *I* remember is that she didn't rat us out to my grandfather," I said. "Which is probably why we're still alive."

The comment dropped like a stone between us. One of the three of us *wasn't* still alive. Rocco had died of leukemia in 1981.

"Aunt Lolly, man," Alphonse said. "*A buon anima.*"

I asked him if he'd be one of her pallbearers.

"Sure I will," he said. "Absolutely. Whatever you need. Hey, you gonna feed people after the service? Because if you want, we can make up sandwiches and do some pastry platters. Coffee and setups, too. I'll get one of my girls to help out. What do you figure—somewhere around thirty or forty people?"

I shrugged. "What do I do—pay you by the head?"

"You don't pay me anything. This will be on me."

"No, no. I don't want you to—"

"Shut up, Quirky. Don't give me a hard time. Hey, you eat breakfast yet? Let me get you something." He disappeared out front and came back with bagels, cream cheese, and coffees.

We sat and ate together. Talked Red Sox. Talked basketball: how sweet it had been when UConn beat Duke in the championship game. "Jim Calhoun is *God*!" Al declared. "Takes those street kids and molds them into NBA players."

"With seven-figure incomes," I said. "You and I should be so lucky."

"Yeah, well, keep dreaming, Quirky. You never could play b'ball."

"Guilty as charged," I said, smiling. "Although, as I recall, you were more a master of the brick than the jump shot yourself."

I asked him how his quest for the holy grail was going—if any hot prospects had shown up on eBay or in the Yellow Mustang Registry.

"Nah, nothing lately. It's out there somewhere, though. One of these days, you wait and see. Some poor slob's gonna kick the bucket and they'll have an estate sale or something. And there it'll be: my 1965 Phoenician Yellow sweetheart, all two hundred eighty-nine cubes of her."

I took a sip of coffee. "Right," I said. "That'll probably happen right after monkeys fly out of your butt."

He nodded, deadpan. "Kinda redefines the concept of going apeshit, doesn't it?" I'd forgotten how funny Alphonse could be—how quick he was. Before his father had chained him to the bakery, he had talked about becoming a stand-up comic.

I asked him how his parents were doing. The Buzzis had always been good to me—treated me like family. In college, whenever they drove up to visit Rocco, Mrs. Buzzi always packed *two* care packages: one for him, one for me. Grinders heavy with meat and cheese and wrapped in tinfoil, Italian cookies, packs of gum, three-packs of underwear and athletic socks. My mother sent me clippings from the *Daily Record*—bad news, mostly, about kids I'd gone to school with. She was too nervous, she said, to drive in Boston traffic. "Here," Mrs.

Buzzi would say, shoving a ten-dollar bill at me at the end of their visit. And when I'd put up a show of resistance, she'd say, "Come on! Take it! Don't make me mad!" and stuff it into my shirt pocket.

Rocco's death had wiped out Mr. and Mrs. Buzzi. Of their two sons, he had been the favorite, the superstar: their college and law school graduate, their young lawyer with a fiancée in medical school. That Rocco's intended was an *Italian* girl had been the cherry atop the sundae. Alphonse, on the other hand, had been the family's baker-designee—the crab his parents had never let crawl out of the bucket. I'd stayed in touch with the Buzzis—called them from time to time, sent them cards, stopped in with a little something around the holidays. After they retired and moved down to Florida, I'd more or less let them go.

"I call them down in Boca maybe three, four times a week," Alphonse said. "Still fighting like Heckle and Jeckle, so I guess they're okay. Last week, Ma gets on the phone and she's honked off at my father. Hasn't spoken to him for two days because, when they were watching TV and the Victoria's Secret commercial came on, she told him to look away and he wouldn't." He launched into a dead-on imitation of his mother. "And you know what that louse had the nerve to say to me, Alphonso? That I was just *jealous*. Ha! That's a laugh! Why should I be jealous of a bunch of skinny *puttane* parading around in their underclothes?"

I laughed. "How old are they now?" I asked.

"Ma's seventy-eight, Pop's eighty-five. Of course, every time *he* gets on the phone, I get the third degree about the business. Has to point out all the things I'm doing wrong. We been selling these bagels for a couple years now, okay? Dunkin' Donuts sells bagels, Stop & Shop sells bagels, so *we* gotta sell them. My pop still hasn't forgiven me for it. 'You're running an *Italian* bakery, Alfonso. Since when does an Italian bakery sell Jew rolls?' 'Since I'm out of them by noontime,' I tell him. 'Yeah? Well you listen to me, Mr. Smarty Pants. When people come into an Italian bakery, they want rum cakes, *il pasta-*

ciotto, Napoleani.' Yeah, *his* generation maybe. But all those old spaghetti benders are either dead or down in Florida where *they* are."

"What this place needs is another miracle," I said, pointing toward Mrs. Buzzi's statue of the Blessed Virgin on top of the refrigerator. Back in the days when that statue had enjoyed more prominent placement in the window out front, a rusty red liquid of undetermined composition had, inexplicably, begun dripping from Mary's painted eyes. The Vietnam War had taken its toll by then, and when Mrs. Buzzi placed a white dishcloth beneath the statue, the "blood" stain that seeped into it had shaped itself into a map of that ravaged country. And so the Mama Mia, for a time, had become a tourist attraction, visited by the faithful and the media. Business had spiked as a result, particularly after *Good Morning America* came calling. A yellowing newspaper photo of then-host David Hartman, his arms around Mr. and Mrs. Buzzi, was still Scotch-taped to the back of the cash register out front. I'd spotted it on my way in.

"Hey, *tell* me about how I need a miracle," Alphonse sighed. "You know what the wholesalers are getting for almond paste these days?"

"Can't say that I've been keeping up with that one," I said.

"Yeah, and you don't *want* to know either. But hey, it's a mute point. The only Italian product we move these days are cannoli and sheet pizza."

"Moot point," I said.

"What?"

"It's moot point. You said mute point."

"Fuck you, Quirky. I already passed English, okay?"

"Just barely," I reminded him. "In summer school."

"And that was only because I used to bring doughnuts to class and crack up Miss Mish: remember her? She was pretty hot for a teacher, except for those sequoia legs. By the way, what do you think of these?"

"The bagels?" I said. "They're good."

He shrugged. "They're okay. Nothing to write home about. We get 'em from U.S. Foods and bake 'em frozen. Takes ten minutes, but they go out the door, you know? The thing my old man doesn't understand is that you gotta swim with the sharks these days. He never had to compete with the grocery chains and Dunkin' Donuts the way I do now. And if Krispy Kreme comes north? Orget-it fay. I'll just hang the white flag out front and lock the door."

"Orget-it fay?" I said.

"Yeah? What?"

"You're forty-five years old, Al. Stop talking pig Latin."

"Uck-you fay," he said.

I asked him if he wanted to go out that night. Get a bite to eat, have a couple of beers. "Can't," he said.

"Why not? You getting your bald spot Simonized?"

"Ha ha," he said. "What a wit. Don't forget, you got two more years on the odometer than I do. You look good, though. You still running?" I nodded. "Life treating you okay? Other than your aunt, I mean. You like it out there?" I nodded some more. Why go into it?

On our way out to the front, he stopped me so we could ogle his countergirl. "How'd you like to stick your dipstick into that?" he whispered.

"She's a woman, Al," I whispered back. "Not a Mustang."

"Yeah, but I don't hold it against her. I'd like to, though."

I asked him which he thought would come first: losing his virginity or getting his AARP membership card.

"Yeah, if only I was more like you," he said. "What wife are you on now—sixteen? Seventeen? I lost count." He stuck his middle finger in my face, then jabbed me in the breastbone with it. "Gotcha," he said.

WITH NOTHING BETTER TO DO, I drove over to the mall and walked around. The sound system was playing that Cher song you couldn't get away from—the one where she sings that part with her techno-electro voice: *"Do you believe in life after love, after love, after love, after love . . ."* Cher, man. You had to give her credit for career survival. She'd been around since the days when Lyndon Johnson was president and Alphonse Buzzi's Phoenician Yellow Mustang was rolling off the assembly line. If there was a nuclear holocaust, there'd probably be two surviving life forms: cockroaches and Cher. *"Do you believe in life after love, after love, after love, after love . . ."* Hey, more power to her. I just wished they'd give that fucking song a rest.

I bought a newspaper and sat down in the food court to read it. The front page had stories about Kosovo, the casino, the Love Bug virus. In the second section, there was an article about a project at the prison. That morning? When I'd walked past and seen the inmates out there, digging around for something? Apparently, they'd been unearthing graves. Baby graves, identifiable by flat stone markers, some with initials carved into them, some not. A surveyor had come upon what had been, in the early days of the prison, a cemetery for the inmates' infants. Back then, it said, women had gone to prison for something called "being in manifest danger of falling into vice." Translation: they'd gotten knocked up. Raped, some of them, no doubt. Talk about blaming the victim. . . .

Two local ministers were leading the women in the recovery project, the article said, and the administration was cooperating. They weren't sure yet what they were going to do once all the graves were recovered, but a couple of suggestions were on the table: a healing ceremony, a little meditation park where inmates with good behavior records might be allowed to go. One of the women interviewed, identified only as Lanisha, said she felt the infants' souls knew they were there, looking for them. Another, Sandy, said it was hell being away from her own three kids while she served her sentence. "These babies were suffering back then, and my babies are suffering now. There's no one in this world can take care of my kids as good as I can." It got to me, that article. For a few seconds, I was on the verge of tears over those long-buried babies. When it passed, I looked around to make sure nobody'd been watching me. Then I got up and threw the paper and my half-drunk coffee into the trash.

On my way back to the farm, I picked up a six-pack, a Whopper at BK, and cat food for Nancy Tucker. Passing the prison yard, I braked. Looked out at the field where I'd seen those women digging. There was no one out there now. I counted the ones I could see: eleven unearthed grave markers.

Maureen had left me a long, rambling phone message. The travel agency had had a hard time getting her a flight. She couldn't get out of Denver until Tuesday night at 7:00 p.m., which meant she wouldn't get into Hartford until 1:15 a.m. Wednesday morning. She'd probably just go in to school Tuesday, since her flight was so late. I could reach her there until two o'clock or so, but then she'd have to go back to the house, pick up the dogs, and bring them to the kennel. At least this way, she wouldn't have to cancel out on Velvet; she hadn't been able to get hold of her to say she was going to be away. She'd been thinking about me all day, she said; she hoped I wasn't feeling overwhelmed. She was sorry she'd be getting in at such a hideous hour. She loved me. She'd see me soon.

That night, woozy from beer, I let myself fall asleep on the couch again rather than head upstairs. I got up in the middle of the night, peed, got up again, peed again. At dawn, I awoke from a dream. My grandfather and I were in a rowboat on a lake that may or may not have been Bride Lake. There were graves along the shore, and I was a boy again, sitting on the seat nearest the bow. Grandpa was in the middle of the boat, rowing in long, steady strokes. "Don't cry," he said. "Be brave. She's all right."

"Who?" I asked. "Mother?"

"Maureen," he said. And I saw in the water's reflection that I was not a boy but a grown man.

ULYSSES CAME BY THE HOUSE the following morning. He looked scrawnier than I remembered. Grubbier, too. His eyes were bloodshot, his pupils jumpy. When I handed him a cup of coffee, he took it with trembling hands.

He already knew about Lolly, he said. He'd walked to the hospital the morning before and identified himself as the man who'd found her and called 911. "The woman at the visitors' desk was full of herself. Wouldn't give me the room number. Kept stalling, calling this one and that one. Then finally she just told me that Lolly had died. I was afraid I was going to break down in front of her. So I left. Walked down to the Indian Leap and tied one on."

He was okay, though, he said. He'd just come from an AA meeting. It happened now and again, him falling off the wagon, but then he'd get himself to a meeting and climb back on. "Lolly was always good about it when I messed up," he said. "She'd get mad at first— say that was it, she was done with me. But then she'd calm down again. She always took me back."

I suddenly realized *why* she had, despite the fact that she'd nicknamed him "Useless" and was forever complaining about what a lousy worker he was. Ulysses was a drunk like my father and had been my father's friend. Over the years, he had become her brother Alden's surrogate.

He fished into his pocket and took out his key to the farmhouse. Placed it on the table. "Why don't you keep it?" I said. "I'm just here for the next few days, and then I have to get back to Colorado. Probably won't come back here until the start of summer. And until then, I'm going to need someone to look after the place, make sure everything's okay. You interested in the job?"

He looked away and nodded.

"I'm seeing her lawyer while I'm here. She can help me figure out how to pay you. So I'll have to get back to you about that. How did Lolly pay you?"

"By the hour," he said. "Ten bucks per."

I nodded. "Fair enough. Just keep track of your time."

"What about Nancy Tucker?" he said.

"Well, I guess you'll have to feed her, empty her litter box."

He nodded. "I got catnip growin' wild in back of my place. I could bring her some of that when I come over."

I thanked him for helping Lolly. "She was good people," he said. He swallowed the rest of his coffee, stood, rinsed his cup in the sink. Without another word, he started for the back door.

"One more thing," I said. "Lolly planned out her funeral before she died. She wanted you to be one of her pallbearers."

He turned and faced me. "She did?"

I nodded. "Do you think you could do that for her?"

Tears came to his eyes. "I'd like to," he said. "But I don't have no good clothes." I reached for my wallet, then stopped myself. It wasn't going to do either of us any good if he drank up his clothing allowance.

"Come on," I said.

At Wal-Mart, I bought him a pair of navy blue pants, a boxed shirt and tie set, socks, underwear, and a cheap pair of black tie shoes. A chili dog, too, and a large Dr Pepper. "Now I'm good to go," he said.

———

MY MOTHER'S BEDROOM WAS AS I remembered it: pale yellow walls, lace curtains. Her dust-covered Sunday missal still sat on her nightstand.

I walked up to the crucifix on the wall opposite her bed. Mother's crucifix had been blessed by Pope Paul and given to her by her father, Grampy Sullivan, when, on his deathbed, he had at last made amends with the only one of his six daughters who had married a Protestant, and the only one who'd ever gotten a divorce. A chain smoker, Mother had died of lung cancer a few years later—the year she was fifty-five and I was thirty. On the morning of her final day, she'd asked me in a whispery voice to lift the crucifix off the wall and bring it to her. I'd done it and she'd cradled the cross in her arms, as tenderly as if it were an infant, while I stood and watched in envy.

I had never quite loved my mother the way other sons—the Buzzi brothers, for example—seemed to love theirs. Growing up, whenever Mother had held out her arms for one of those hugs, it was almost as if there was something parked between us. Something intangible but nevertheless real, I didn't know what. . . . I'd stayed with her at the end, though, from early morning until late that night. People had come in and out all day, whispering: Lolly, Hennie, some of the nuns Mother had befriended, the priest who mumbled her last rites and, with his thumb, anointed her by drawing an oily cross on her forehead. Back in catechism class when I was a kid, they'd made us memorize the sacraments, and those seven "visible forms of invisible grace" had remained stuck in my brain: baptism, confirmation, penance, Holy Eucharist, Holy Orders, Holy Matrimony, and, at every good Catholic's final curtain, extreme unction. "Thanks a lot, Father," I'd said when that priest had finished and started for the door. Slipping him a twenty, I'd added, "Here's a little something for your trouble." For your holy hocus-pocus, I'd thought but not said. It was weird, though. Even with the lights dimmed and the window shades half-drawn, that cross on Mother's forehead, for the next several hours, had glistened eerily. . . . It was just the two of us at the end, and I witnessed, clearly and unmistakably, when life left my mother. One moment, she'd been a living, suffering woman; the next moment, her body was nothing more than an empty vessel. Later, after the McKennas had retrieved the corpse and Hennie had stripped the bed, I'd returned to Mother's room. Her crucifix lay against the bare uncovered mattress. I picked it up, kissed Jesus' feet, and hung it back on the wall. I made the gesture for her, not for her god or for myself. I was a twice-divorced thirty-year-old, teaching Twain and Thoreau to indifferent high school students by day and, by night, going home to my life of quiet desperation and one or two too many Michelobs. I'd long since become skeptical about an allegedly merciful God who doled out cosmic justice according to some mysterious game plan that none of us could fathom.

———

THE DOORBELL RANG. I LEFT my mother's room, went downstairs, and opened the door. The woman on the other side looked vaguely familiar. "Millie Monk," she said. "Here's the lemon squares."

I thanked her. Took the box she held out and stood there waiting for her to go. She reminded me that she'd come to do some vacuuming and tidying up. "No, really, I can do it," I insisted. Millie was insistent, too.

"You put these on top the Frigidaire and then go relax," she told me. "Put your feet up and watch some TV so I can get busy."

I did as I was told, channel-surfing in the den while she vacuumed the rest of the downstairs. I'd just switched to CNN when the vacuum cleaner's whirr turned the corner and entered the room. I got up, went into the kitchen. Figured maybe she'd like some tea.

The vacuum stopped. She called out to me over the sound of tap water rattling the bottom of the teakettle. "What'd you say?" I called back.

"Something bad's happening," she said. "Out in Colorado. Do you live anywhere near Littleton?"

"Littleton?" I said. "That's right . . . that's where . . ." By then I had made it back to the den.

I stood there, stupefied. Why was Columbine High on TV? Why was Pat Ireland crawling out onto the library's window ledge? Shot? What did they mean, he'd been shot?

"You're looking at live pictures from Littleton, Colorado, where the local high school is under attack by as few as two or as many as six shooters," the news anchor said.

Patrick dangled, then fell from the ledge, landing in the arms of helmeted men on the roof of a truck.

What the—? In the kitchen, the teakettle screamed.

I'll probably just go in to school tomorrow, since my flight's so late.

"Oh, no! Oh, please, God. No!"

→→chapter seven ←←

I KEPT DIALING HOME, PACING, trying friends' and other teachers' numbers, trying home again. I cursed myself for telling her a while back that we didn't need cell phones. When the phone rang, I lunged. "Maureen?"

But it was Alphonse. He'd just heard about it on the radio. "I can't get ahold of her!" I shouted. "I've been calling for over an hour! I get halfway through the number and the busy signal cuts in!"

"Okay, take it easy, Quirks. What do you need?"

"To hear her voice. To see her."

He was at the farmhouse ten minutes later. He drove me to Bradley Airport, got me an emergency ticket to Denver with a connecting flight in Chicago, delivered me to the right gate, and waited with me. It was seven p.m.——five o'clock in Colorado. Six hours since they'd opened fire.

This was what I knew: there were dead bodies outside and inside the school; some of the injured were undergoing emergency surgery; bombs had gone off; the shooters—thought to be students—had fired back at the police from inside the library. I kept seeing what I'd seen on the news before we left for the airport: Columbine kids, a lot of them recognizable, streaming out of the building with their hands on their heads like captured criminals. Students had done this? I couldn't wrap my head around it.

"Still no answer?" Alphonse asked. I shook my head and handed him back his cell phone. "The library's *up*stairs," I said. "And the clinic where she works is *down*stairs, in another part of the building. So she was probably nowhere near the gunfire. Right?"

"Right," he said.

"Did I already say that?"

"Yeah. Hey, you know what, Caelum? How about I go get you a sandwich or something? Because at this hour, all's they're probably going to give you on the plane is a soda and one of those little things of peanuts."

"Pretzels," I said.

"What?"

"They don't give you peanuts anymore. They give you pretzels." I unfolded the paper where I'd jotted down the numbers for the hospitals: Littleton Adventist, Denver Health, St. Anthony's, Lutheran Medical. Held out my hand for his cell phone again.

"Probably all that peanut allergy stuff that everyone's so hopped up about now. Down at the bakery? We got about sixty different regulations from the state about product that has peanuts in it. Man, I make a batch of peanut butter cookies and I gotta fuckin' *sequester* 'em."

Most of the hospital lines were still busy, but when I dialed the number for Swedish Medical Center, it was silent for a few seconds and then, miraculously, I got a ring.

"It's like a status thing, you know? 'My kid's special because he's got a peanut allergy.' I'm surprised they don't have a bumper sticker for it."

"Al, *stop!*" I said.

The operator passed me on to the crisis spokeswoman, who was polite at first, then less so. "Okay, look," I said. "I can appreciate you're not releasing any names yet. I understand that. But *I'm* giving *you* her name. All you have to do is look at your list, or your computer screen or whatever, and tell me she's *not* there." She gave me some line about following her protocols, and we went at it for a few more rounds, but she wasn't going to budge. With my fingernail, I pushed the little end call button and handed the phone back to Alphonse.

He kept steepling his fingers, cracking his knuckles. "You sure you don't want to eat something, Quirky? What about a hot dog?"

"What about the car I rented?" I said.

"What about it?"

"I didn't return it."

He stared at me in disbelief, then reached into his jacket pocket and produced the paperwork and the key I'd given him. "We worked that out. Remember? I'm going to drive it back up here midday tomorrow. Have one of my workers follow me up and give me a lift back."

I nodded. "I already knew that, right?"

He nodded. "How about a couple of candy bars?"

"Alphonse, I can't eat, okay?" I snapped. "My stomach's in fucking knots." As we sat there, across from each other, I suddenly realized he was still in his baker's clothes: black-and-white checked pants, Mama Mia T-shirt, stained apron. He had flour in his eyebrows, bags under his eyes. "Thanks, man," I said.

"For what?"

"Getting me here. Keeping me glued together."

"What? You didn't do the same thing for me, when my brother was down at Yale–New Haven?" I nodded. Flashed on Rocco in his hospital bed. In his coffin, Red Sox button pinned to his suit jacket lapel, rosary beads twisted around his hand. "Do you think I did the right thing?" I said.

"About what?"

"My aunt's funeral. They said they could keep the body refrigerated. Postpone the service until I could get back here and—"

He shook his head. "Better this way, Quirky. The last thing you need is stuff hanging over your head at this end. Not with what's going on out there. Don't worry. Me and the old ladies'll give her a good send-off."

"What if she's dead?" I said.

He cocked his head, gave me a slight smile. "She *is* dead, man."

"I mean Maureen."

He opened his mouth to answer me, then closed it again. When he finally spoke, it was to ask me what time my plane arrived in Denver.

"Ten fifty-five," I said. "Provided I get the hell out of Hartford."

"Ten fifty-five our time?"

"Colorado time," I said.

He nodded. "How about some nuts? What do you like? Cashews? Peanuts? You like those smoked almonds if they have them?"

I held out my hand. He handed me his phone. "I don't care if you want them or not," he mumbled, rising from his chair. "I'm getting you some nuts. Just shut up and put 'em in your pocket."

I dialed our number. Got what I'd gotten for hours: the four rings, the click of our machine, my voice, the beep.

THE FLIGHT TO CHICAGO WAS uneventfully torturous. The seat next to mine was empty—that was a relief—but it was hell to just sit there, strapped in, waiting for time and distance to pass. I thought about that *other* night: the worst night of our marriage, when I'd confronted her about Paul Hay, and then hurt her wrist, and she'd gone out on those icy roads and totaled her car. She could have died that night. . . . Steer *toward* the skid. She knew that, but she'd panicked, jerked the wheel the other way, and gone skidding toward that tree. "Almost in slow motion," she'd said later. That's what flying back felt like: being in the middle of a slow-motion skid, waiting for the crash.

The captain came over the intercom to tell us we'd reached cruising altitude. The flight attendants wheeled down the aisle with the beverage cart. The little TV screens descended. I left the earphones in the seat pocket and sat there, staring at Kramer and Jerry's moving lips, penguins hopping into and out of icy blue water, a Belgian chocolatier decorating petits fours. "Hey," I said to a passing flight attendant. "Do these things work?"

"The in-flight phones? Yes, sir." She pushed the button and the receiver popped free from its holder. "Just follow the instructions."

"I wouldn't if I were you," someone said. "They gouge you on those calls." I looked across the aisle. Nodded to the guy who was talking.

"Yeah, well . . ." I said. I punched in my credit card number, waited. One ring, two, three, four. *"Hey, how's it going? You've reached the Quirks. We're not home right now, but you can leave a message after the beep."*

"Mo, where are you?" I said. "I'm in a plane. I'm coming home."

I ate Al's almonds. Looked out the window at nothing. Cross-hatched over the faces in the complimentary magazine. I thought about how fucked-up this was: the person on the plane is the one whose life is supposed to be at risk, not the person who stayed home. I wrote her name, over and over, in the margins: *Maureen, Maureen, Maureen* . . . I had never realized how much I loved her. Needed her. How over my own life was going to be, if she was dead.

O'HARE OVERWHELMED ME. I KNEW I had to get to Concourse G, but I couldn't figure out how, and when people tried to direct me, I watched their mouths move but couldn't make sense of what they were saying. Finally, on the verge of panic, I approached an airline employee—a black woman with copper-colored hair. "I'm lost . . ." I babbled. "My wife . . . a shooting at our school."

"The one in Colorado that's been on the news? Lemme see your boarding pass." She took it from my shaking hand. "Okay, this is Terminal *Two.* You gots to get to Terminal *Three.* That's where Concourse G's at."

I burst into tears.

She stared at me for a moment, then shouted over her shoulder.

"Hey, Reggie! I'm going on break now!" She took my hand; hers was rough and plump. "Come on, baby," she said. "I'll take you there."

The waiting area for gate G–16 had a TV. Now CNN was saying the shootings may have been committed by students who belonged to a cult called the Trenchcoat Mafia. I shook my head. Those Trench-coat Mafia kids had graduated the year before. And anyway, they were ironists, not killers. What the hell was going on? Eric Harris's and Dylan Klebold's yearbook photos filled the screen. "Once again, we want to emphasize that these are *alleged* suspects," the anchor-woman said. "What we do know is that officers from the Jefferson County Sheriff's Office have entered the boys' homes with search warrants, and it is believed, although not yet verified by the authori-ties, that the bodies of Klebold and Harris were amongst those in the library. At the very least, they are persons of interest."

My mind ricocheted. Blackjack Pizza, the after-prom party, *Sieg heil!* . . .

I sensed the people around me were staring at me before I knew why. Then I heard moaning and realized it was coming from me.

I DON'T REMEMBER MUCH ABOUT the flight from Chicago to Denver. We landed a little after eleven, and I ran through the air-port, ran to my car. Floored it most of the way home.

The house was dark. When I pulled into the driveway, Sophie and Chet began barking frantically. I got the door open, and they jumped on me in lunatic greeting, then bounded past me to the outside. There was dog crap on the living room rug, a puddle of pee on the slate in the front hallway. They hadn't been let out since morning.

"Maureen?" I called. "Mo?" I took the stairs two at a time. The bed was made. Her little suitcase was packed for the trip to Connecti-cut. I looked at her jeans, folded on the chair beside our bed, and a chill ran through me. Downstairs, Chet and Sophie were barking to be let back in.

There were eighteen phone messages, half of them from me. Her stepmother, Evelyn, had called, and later, her father. "We're starting to worry about you, Maureen," he said. "Give us a call." As if, suddenly, her safety mattered to him. As if *he* had never put her at risk. . . .

There was a message from Elise, the secretary at the school clinic. "I guess if you're not answering, you're probably still over at Leawood."

Leawood Elementary School! The TV news had shown footage of evacuated students and staff reuniting with their families there. I threw some food into the dogs' bowls and grabbed my keys. Elise's message had come midway through the sequence, which meant she'd left it hours earlier. It was late. Most, if not all, of the kids would have been picked up by now. But maybe, for some reason, Maureen was still there. Or, if not, maybe someone knew where she was. I'd start at Leawood, then drive from hospital to hospital if I had to. Be there, I kept saying. Please be there, Mo. Please be all right.

The eight or nine cars leading up to the school were parked helter skelter, a few on the sidewalk, one abandoned in the middle of the street. Parents must have pulled up, thrown open their car doors, and run for their kids. A cop was posted at the entrance. "Yes, sir, can I help you?"

I blurted that I'd been away, that I was trying to find my wife.

"Are you a parent of one of the Columbine students, sir?"

"I teach there," I said. "My wife's one of the school nurses. Do you know if there were shots fired anywhere near the medical clinic?"

He said he'd heard all kinds of rumors about the boys' movement inside the school, but that that was all they were: rumors. He took my driver's license and wrote down my information on his clipboard. "It was bedlam here earlier," he said. "It's quiet now, though. Too quiet. Looks bad for the families still waiting. There's eleven or twelve still unaccounted for, and there's bodies inside the school, so it's a matter of matching them up. 'Course, some of the kids may show up yet. If you're sitting there waiting, you gotta hang onto some hope, I guess. You have kids?"

I shook my head.

"Me neither. The wife and I wanted kids, but it just never happened. You can go ahead in. They're in the gym, all the way down past the showcase. There's lists posted on the wall."

"Lists?"

"Of the survivors."

I walked warily down the hallway, my footsteps slowing as I neared the gym. Let her be here, let her be here. Let her be on that list. . . .

She was seated by herself, cross-legged on a gym mat, a blanket around her shoulders, a pile of Styrofoam coffee cup spirals in front of her. "Hey," I said. She looked up at me, emotionless for several seconds, as if she didn't quite recognize me. Then her face contorted. I dropped to my knees and wrapped my arms around her. Rocked her back and forth, back and forth. She was here, not dead, not shot. Her hair smelled smoky, and faintly of gasoline. Her whole body sobbed. She cried herself limp.

"I wrote you a note," she said. "On the wood inside the cabinet."

"What cabinet, Mo? I don't—"

"Velvet's dead."

At first, it didn't register. "Velvet?" Then I remembered: she was going to meet Maureen at school that morning, to talk about re-enrolling.

"I went to call you, to see how things were going, and then there was this explosion and the whole library—"

"Oh, Jesus! You were in the library?"

She flinched. Made fists. "The coroner was here earlier," she said. "She passed out forms. She wanted names and addresses, descriptions of their clothing, distinguishing marks or features, whether or not they had drivers' licenses. Because of the fingerprints, I guess."

Her crew cut, I thought. Her tattoo. "She said she might need dental records, too. Dental records: that's when we knew."

"Knew?"

"That they were dead. And I couldn't even . . . I couldn't . . ." She began to cry again. "She called me Mom, and I couldn't even give them her address."

"Come on," I said. "Let me take you home."

"I can't go home!" she snapped. "I'm her mom!"

I opened my mouth to argue the point, then shut it again. I took her hands in mine and squeezed them. She didn't squeeze back.

A short time later, a middle-aged man with a droopy mustache entered the gym. "That's the district attorney," Maureen said. "He was here before, when the coroner was here." He mounted the stage, and the thirty or forty of us, scattered throughout the gym, approached.

He said he understood that waiting was pure hell—his heart went out to each and every one there because he had teenagers, too. But he wanted us to know that, for safety reasons, the building had been secured for the night and the exhausted investigation teams had been sent home to get a few hours' sleep. "We've made the decision to resume at six thirty a.m.," he said. "And at that point we'll continue with the identification of—"

"The hell with that!" someone shouted. "Our kids are in there!"

"Sir, I know, but there are still live explosives inside the school. How many, and where, we just can't say yet. A short while ago, a bomb detonated as the technicians were removing it from the building. Now, no one was hurt, but it's been a very long, very difficult day for all of us. Nerves are frazzled, people are dog-tired. We just don't want that fatigue to turn into more tragedy."

"I need to get to my daughter," a woman wailed. "Dead or alive, she needs to know she's not alone in that place."

"Ma'am, I understand what you're saying, but the entire school is a crime scene," the D.A. said. "Evidence has to be gathered and labeled, procedures have to be followed. Victims have to be identified, bodies removed and autopsied before they can be released to their families. Those of you who've followed the JonBenet Ramsey case can appreciate that when evidence is compromised——"

"We don't care about evidence!" a man retorted. "We care about getting our kids the hell out of there! And don't give me that 'I've got kids, too' bullshit, because your kids are safe at home tonight, and ours . . ." His reprimand broke down into sobs that echoed through the cavernous gym.

A woman announced fiercely that until she saw her son's body, she refused to give up hope. We should prepare ourselves for miracles, she advised. No one responded. Someone asked when the names of the dead would be released.

"As soon as the coroner feels she's gotten absolutely positive IDs for the twelve that are still in the library," the D.A. said.

"Does that number include the two little bastards that did this?"

The D.A. nodded. "I'm guessing midday tomorrow we'll have the final list. We'll release it to you folks first, of course, and then to the press. And while I'm on the subject of the press, I want to advise you that talking to them at this point in time might not be in your own or the children's best interests. Now you're welcome to stay the night here, and if you do, I'm sure the volunteers will make you as comfortable as possible. But if I could, I'd like to suggest— since nothing more's going to be released until late morning at the earliest—that you all go home, say some prayers if you're so in-clined, and try to get some sleep. Let's meet back here at noon, and I think I can promise you by then that I'll have the names for you. And I also want to promise you . . ." He faltered, struggled to regain his composure. "I want to promise . . . promise you that . . . we are going to treat your children like they are our own."

Maureen slumped against me. "Take me home," she said.

IT WAS A BRUTAL NIGHT. She wandered from room to room, cried, cursed the killers. She couldn't tell me about it yet, she said, but she kept seeing it, over and over. Seeing what, I wondered, but I didn't push her. In bed, she needed the light on. She kept bolting upright. "What was that?"

Somewhere after three in the morning, I convinced her to drink a glass of wine and swallow a couple of Tylenol PMs. They knocked her out, but her sleep was fitful. She kept clenching, whimpering. I finally dozed off myself, awakening from a leaden sleep at dawn. Maureen's side of the bed was empty. I found her asleep on the floor, between the dogs. Her splayed hand, resting on Sophie's side, rose and fell with each breath that dog drew.

She managed to get down a little breakfast—half a piece of toast, half a cup of coffee. I drew her a bath. She wanted me to stay in the bathroom with her, but when I soaped up a washcloth and tried to wash her back, she flinched. "Don't touch me!" she snapped. Then she apologized.

"You want me to leave?"

"No, stay. I just don't want you to touch me."

And so I sat there, watching her wash herself. Watching her fall back into whatever it was she had lived through the day before. Watching the way her shivering shivered the bathwater.

The news was reporting that Dave Sanders had died. Shot in the science corridor while shepherding kids to safety, he'd staggered into one of the classrooms, collapsed face-first, and bled to death during the hours it took the SWAT team to take back the school and get to him. I needed to react, but she was watching me. She'd been through enough without my breaking down in front of her about Dave. "I'm taking the dogs out," I said, nudging them from their naps with the toe of my shoe.

I walked around in the backyard, crying for Dave—thinking about the lunches we'd shared, the duties. He'd befriended me my first year at Columbine—one of the few who'd taken the time to welcome a newcomer. In return, I'd started going to some of the girls' basketball games, running the clock for him during some of the home contests. He was a good coach—a teaching coach who used the kids' mistakes as learning opportunities. I thought about that ugly orange tie he wore on game days to inspire his girls. It was typical that, when the shooting had started, he'd tried to get the kids to safety rather than running for cover himself. . . . Maureen was at the kitchen window, watching me, and so I bit my lip. Whistled for the dogs and rough-housed with them when they came running. I had no right to this playful romp, and no right to cry in front of Maureen.

When I came back in, she asked me if Dave Sanders had children.

"Daughters," I said. "And grandkids, I think. Babies."

She nodded. "*I* should have died," she said. "Not him."

"Don't say that."

"Why not? I'm nobody's parent. I'm expendable."

"You know something?" I said. "Until yesterday, I don't think I ever fully appreciated what crap my life would be without you. I was so scared, Mo. You're *not* expendable. *I* need you."

I opened my arms to her, but instead of coming to me, she sat down on the kitchen stool and stared at nothing, her face unreadable. "The summer I was eleven?" she said. "After my father moved out? I had this friend, Francine Peccini, and she invited me to go with her to the convent where her church was. The Church of the Divine Savior, it was called. Her mother was the church secretary, and Francine used to go over there mornings and help at the convent. Dust, do dishes, fold laundry. And one day she asked me to go with her. My mother never had much use for Catholics, but she was so distracted by the separation that she said okay, I could go. . . . And I *liked* the nuns. They were nice, and sort of mysterious. At lunchtime, we'd stop our work and eat with them. And after lunch, we'd say the rosary. At first I didn't know the words to the Hail Mary, but then, they got repeated so much that I did. . . . And in the afternoon, we went back to Francine's house, and she and I went up to her room and pretended we were nuns. Sisters of Mercy. We put bath towels on our heads for veils, and stapled them to these oaktag things we cut out. What are they called? Those stiff things around their faces?"

"Wimples," I said. Why was she telling me all this?

She nodded. "Wimples. And on weekends? When I used to have to go over to my father's? In his car on the way over, I used to say it to myself: '*Hail Mary, full of grace, the Lord is with thee . . .*' And at night, when he'd come into my room and . . . and . . . I'd say it then, too, over and over, until he was finished and got up and left. . . . And yesterday? When I thought those boys were going to find me and kill me? I said the Hail Mary, over and over and over. The words came back to me from that summer when I was eleven. 'Hail Mary, full of grace. The Lord is with thee. Blessed art thou amongst women, and blessed is the fruit of thy womb, Jesus. Holy Mary, mother of God, pray for us sinners, now and at the hour of our death.' . . . Okay, here it is, I kept thinking: the hour of my death, because they're going to find me and kill me. And that was when I got the idea to write you a note, Caelum. On the wall of the cabinet I was hiding in. I managed to inch the pen out of my pocket without hitting the door, and I wrote, in the dark, with my hand squeezed between my knees . . . and I kept thinking, they're going to find me in here, and shoot me, and later on, someone will find my body and . . . and Caelum will suffer, grieve for me, and then he'll move on. Find someone else, marry her. And Sophie and Chet will get old and die. And then Caelum will get old, too, and maybe he'll die without ever knowing I had written him the note."

Should I go to her? Hold her? Keep my distance? I didn't know *what* she needed. "What did it say, Mo?" I asked.

She looked at me, as if she'd forgotten I was in the room. "What?"

"What did your note say? What did you write to me?"

"That I loved you more than I ever loved anyone else in my life, and I hoped you could forgive me for the mistakes I made. . . . And that, if Velvet survived and I didn't, I hoped you could forgive her for the things she did, and look after her. Make sure she was okay."

Before I could respond, the phone rang. "Don't answer it!" Maureen said. But I told her I'd better—that it might be the investigators.

It was her father. "No, no, she's pretty shaken up, but she's all right." I pointed to the receiver and lip-synched the words: *your father.*

Mo shook her head vehemently and hurried out of the room.

"Well, actually, she's sleeping right now," I said. "She had a bad night."

———————————

LATER THAT MORNING, TWO DETECTIVES came to the house—Sergeant Cox, a small blonde in her early forties, and an earnest younger guy, Asian-American, Detective Chin. They didn't want coffee, but Detective Chin took a glass of water. The four of us sat in the living room. Sergeant Cox did most of the questioning. She was gentle, coaxing. She seemed to have a calming effect on Mo. That was how I learned what had happened to her the day before.

Expecting Velvet to stop by the clinic later that morning, Maureen had gone to the guidance office and spoken to Ivy Shapiro, her counselor, about the possibility of Velvet's coming back to school. Ivy had said she was all for it, but that Velvet would have to petition for readmittance. That meant filling out some paperwork and writing a one-paragraph statement about her intent. Columbine wanted to encourage returnees, Ivy explained, but also to send them the message that school was not a revolving door. She typed Velvet's name into her computer. "Looks like she never handed in her textbooks from last year," she told Mo. "She'll have to return them before we can issue her a schedule. And it says here that she owes library fines, too. She'll need to take care of those."

It was hectic at the clinic, as it always is during fifth hour, Mo said: kids coming in to take their medications, pick up forms, drop off doctors' notes. A freshman boy was icing the ankle he'd sprained in gym. A junior girl with chills and a temp sat wrapped in a blanket, waiting for her father to pick her up. Velvet arrived in the midst of the hubbub. Her clothes were subdued—jeans and a sweater. She had rinsed the blue dye out of her crew cut. Kids stared nonetheless. Snickered. Mo said she was afraid Velvet might lose her temper, or worse, lose her nerve and abort her plan to reenroll.

"I brought 'em," Velvet said, when Mo relayed Ivy's message about returning her textbooks. She overturned her backpack and several heavy books clunked out onto Mo's desk. "Oh, yeah, I found this, too," she mumbled. Eyes averted, she slid my signed copy of *To Kill a Mockingbird* toward Maureen.

Mo said she took a breath, tried not to show too much of a reaction. "Great," she said. "Mr. Quirk will be glad to get it back. He had to fly home to Connecticut because of a death in his family, but when I talk to him, I'll tell him you found it."

"Whatever," Velvet said.

A girl laughed out loud. "*Her?*"

Mo said her colleague, Sandy Hailey, saw what was happening and tried to short-circuit the ridiculing without drawing attention to it. "Why don't you take your break now, Mrs. Quirk?" she said. "I can hold down the fort here, and then later on, you can spell me." Ordinarily, Maureen didn't take a break during fifth hour, but she mouthed a silent thank-you to Sandy and grabbed her purse. She suggested to Velvet that they head upstairs to the library, where they could fill out the readmission materials and pay the book fines.

Louise Rogers was working the circulation desk. She typed Velvet's name into the computer. "Wow," she said. "Says here you owe us twenty-nine dollars and sixty cents. I believe that makes you this year's grand champion." Maureen said she smiled at the joke; Velvet scowled. "Tell you what," Louise said. "Why don't we just round this off to twenty dollars and call it even?" Maureen thanked her and took out her wallet. Velvet fished into her pocket and slammed a fistful of loose change onto the desk. "She comes off so *hostile*," Mo told the investigators. She promised herself she'd address the subject with Velvet—maybe sit out in the sun with her for a little while after they'd finished the forms. She'd treat her to lunch. Get yogurts or sandwiches in the cafeteria and take them outside.

Mo asked Velvet where she wanted to sit, and she pointed to a remote table behind the rows of bookshelves on the far side of the room. Maureen told Velvet she needed to call me to see how things were going, but that she'd be right back. "Why don't you get started on your statement?" she said.

"What should I put?" Velvet wanted to know. Maureen told her to just be honest. "Okay then, I'll say, 'This school still blows dead moose cocks, but *Springer* and *Sally Jessy* are all reruns.'" Mo looked at her, not smiling. "Jesus Christ, Mom. I was only *kidding.*"

Maureen asked Louise if she could use the library phone to make a credit card call. "Sure thing," Louise said. "You want to use the one in the break room? Less noise, more privacy."

"Great," Mo said. She looked back to see if Velvet had gotten to work, but her view was blocked by the bookshelves.

Unused to credit card calling, Mo kept screwing up and having to start over. And when the phone finally did ring, an unfamiliar voice picked up. "Oh, sorry," she said. "I must have dialed the wrong number." She hung up and called the operator so she wouldn't have to pay for her mistake.

It was a wall phone, Mo told the investigators. She was standing beside it, shoulders against the cinderblock wall, so she both heard and felt the vibration of the first blast. What was *that?* she wondered. Construction? The operator came on. "What number were you trying to call, ma'am?" she asked.

There was a second blast. Maureen faltered. Then, refocusing, she recalled Lolly's phone number and recited it. The science labs were just down the hall; maybe there'd been a chemical explosion. If so, someone might be hurt. Another, louder explosion shook the floor.

Louise and an elderly library aide threw open the break room door and rushed past her toward the television studio. "Someone's got a gun!" Louise screamed. "He's shooting out in the hallway! Hide!"

No, it's a chemical explosion, Maureen thought. She'd better get down there, see if anyone needed medical assistance. "Would you like me to dial that number for you, ma'am?" the operator asked. Mo hung up.

She opened the door to the library. There was an acrid smell, smoke pouring in from the hallway. The fire alarm began to blare. Strobe lights started winking on and off. One of the art teachers—the pretty blond one, Mo couldn't remember her name—was at the circulation desk, seven or eight feet away. She was breathless, speaking rapid-fire into the phone. "Yes, I am a teacher at Columbine High School! There is a student here with a gun! He has shot out a window. And the school is in a panic, and I'm in the library. I've got students down. UNDER THE TABLES, KIDS! HEADS UNDER THE TABLES!"

At the break room doorway, Maureen stood, stunned. A boy was crouched behind the photocopier, hiding in plain sight. Another boy sat at a computer station, dazed. Most did what they were told, sliding from their chairs to the floor, huddling together beneath the tables. Like faces in a dream, Maureen recognized, among the strewn backpacks and spilled note cards, kids she knew: Josh, Valeen, Kristin, Kyle. She had to get to Velvet—grab her and pull her to safety. But, as if in a dream, she couldn't make her feet move. Velvet was all the way across the room, and Mo was too afraid. Make this be a horrible dream, she thought. Make this not be happening.

The art teacher, still on the phone, dropped out of sight behind the desk. "Okay, I'm in the library," Maureen heard her say. "He's upstairs. He's right out here. . . . He's outside this hall. Okay. . . . Oh, God. Oh, God. Kids, just stay down!" In the hallway, there were several more blasts. *"Woo-hoo!"* someone shouted. "I'm on the floor. . . . In the library, and I have every student in the library on the floor and . . . . YOU GUYS STAY ON THE FLOOR!"

Maureen said she saw them enter, carrying duffel bags, the tall one in a long black coat, the shorter one in a white T-shirt and cargo pants tucked inside his boots. He was gripping a shotgun. He looked at her, grinning. Eric, his name was. Luvox, 75 milligrams at lunchtime. "Get up!" he shouted. "All the jocks stand up! We're going to kill every single one of you!"

"Anyone with a white hat, stand up!" the other one shouted. "Are you guys scared? Well, don't be, because you're all going to die anyway!"

Maureen backed into the break room, pulling the door closed behind her. She was afraid to shut it tight—afraid the click of the lock might draw their attention. Draw their gunfire.

She heard screaming, pleas, the crack of gunfire, shattering glass. "How about you, big boy? You want to get shot today? . . . Hey, you? Peekaboo!"

Bam! A flash. *Bam!* Another flash.

Trembling violently, she was barely able to control her hands, she said, but she managed somehow to open the door of an under-the-counter cabinet and dump its contents to the floor. Bulletin board decorations, she remembered now; cardboard Pilgrims and turkeys, shamrocks, Valentine's cupids. She removed the cabinet's adjustable shelf. She meant to place it quietly on the counter, but one end dropped with a bang. Oh, God! she thought. Oh, God! Let them not have heard!

On her hands and knees, she crawled into the open space. Her skull was pressed against the ceiling of the tight enclosure, her knees jammed against the wall. With her fingernails, she clawed at the door from inside. It wouldn't close all the way, and she was terrified that half-inch opening would lead them to her.

Over the alarm, she could hear their taunts, the ridiculing of their victims before the shotgun blasts. It was as if each of the shots passed through her, she said. She knew they'd find her. She was sure she was going to die—that this cabinet would be her coffin.

The air carried the stink of gunpowder and gasoline. Crying would cleanse her burning eyes, but she was too afraid to give in to tears—afraid it might attract their attention. Then the break room door banged open, and she thought, *This is it*. There was a spray of gunfire, the sound of things shattering and splintering on the other side of the room, and then on her side, above her. "Let's go down to the commons!" one of them called, and the other, the one closest to her, said he had one more thing to do. Kill *me*, she thought: he's going to kill me, and then they'll leave. There was a loud crash that sounded like furniture being smashed. After that, for a long time, she heard only the fire alarm's drone.

Had they killed all of the students? Should she take a chance—crawl out of the cabinet and see? Go to Velvet? Try to save herself? But if she ran for it, which way would she go when she didn't know where they were? "Let's go down to the commons": it could be a trick to lure her out of hiding.

Her back ached. The blood pounded in her head. Her legs and feet were numb. Would they work if she climbed out and tried to run? She felt the smooth face of her wristwatch but couldn't read it in the dark. She couldn't tell how much time had passed.

She heard helicopters above. Life Flight for the injured? A news crew? Later, she heard voices in the outer room. Had the police gotten there? Had the boys come back? She heard someone count, "One, two, three!" Then gunfire, a single shot. Maybe two. She waited. Recited the Hail Mary, over and over, counting the decades on her fingers. She wrote me her note.

"What did the note to your husband say, Mrs. Quirk?" Sergeant Cox asked softly. "What was the gist of it?"

Mo's answer was barely audible, and she did not look at me when she said it. "The gist of it? Good-bye."

Much later, she said, she heard more glass smashing out in the library.

"That might have been when Pat Ireland knocked out the window and crawled out onto the ledge," I suggested.

"That would have been about two thirty," Officer Chin said.

I nodded. "Four thirty in Connecticut, where I was," I said. "That's when I first knew something was wrong. I turned on CNN and they were showing it live: Pat dangling out there on the ledge, then falling into the arms of the rescue workers."

"Then what, Mrs. Quirk?" Sergeant Cox said. "After you heard the breaking glass?"

"I heard Louise's voice."

"The librarian?"

Maureen nodded. "She was speaking to someone. A man. I heard her telling him that I'd been in the break room when she and her aide went to hide. And the man called out to me. He said the building had been secured and that if I was able, I should come into view. 'It's all right, Mrs. Quirk,' I heard Louise say. And so I opened the cabinet door a little more and saw the man—a member of the SWAT team, I guess he was. He was wearing a helmet and big, thick glasses—safety glasses, I guess. And then I saw Louise, and the art teacher who had called 911. And so I swung the door open and got out. And the man had each of us, one by one, place our hands on his shoulders and follow him out of the library. He told us not to look at anything around us—to look just at the back of his helmet—and so that was pretty much what I did. I saw a little. There was glass all over the floor, and it crunched underneath my shoes, and I saw that the carpet had gotten scorched. And, out of the corner of my eye, I saw one of the students, sitting at a computer. He must be dead, I figured. Why else would he be just sitting there? His computer was still on. I didn't look at anything else. A part of me wanted to ask the SWAT man if we could go to Velvet's table, but I was too afraid. I didn't want to see her dead, and I didn't want to make the man mad.

"And then, out in the hallway, another of the SWAT guys had to frisk us. He was apologetic, but we were saying, 'That's okay! That's okay! We understand!' He frisked me first, and while he was frisking the others, I noticed bullet holes in the wall and dents in the lockers, from where the bullets had hit. And there were black scorch marks on the wall and the ceiling, from the bombs, I guess. And bullet casings all over the floor. The officer had us write down our names, addresses, and phone numbers in a little notebook. He told us the police would question us later, but that right now we needed to go down the stairs and walk directly out of the building. He said there'd be officers just outside who would escort us safely off the school property. And then I remembered my purse. It was still inside the break room. I didn't want to go back in there, but I needed my purse, so I asked the man if he could get it for me. He said no, no, my purse was evidence—that the library was a crime scene and everything in it was evidence. And I said, 'Well, but my car keys are in my purse.' And he said all the cars in the parking lots were part of a crime scene, too, and that no one was going to be able to claim their cars for a while. 'Just go down the stairs and out the building,' he said. He sounded a little mad, a little impatient, and it scared me. So that was what we did, the four of us—Louise, her aide, the art teacher, and me. And when we got to the bottom of the stairs, I stopped to look around the cafeteria. The ceiling sprinklers were on, and the kids' backpacks were all over the floor, floating in water. And there was a kind of burnt chemical smell in the air. And then the fire alarm shut off. It had been going for hours, and suddenly it was quiet. You know when people say, 'The silence was deafening'? That's what it was like. All you could hear was the sound of the sprinklers. It was like a light rain, like it was raining inside the cafeteria. The sprinklers. And . . . and what sounded like birds chirping."

"Birds?" Sergeant Cox asked.

"I know it *wasn't* birds," Maureen said. "But that's what it sounded like."

"Cell phones," Detective Chin said.

The three of us looked over at him. His water glass was empty. He'd hardly said a word. "Cell phones," he said again. "Ringing in the students' backpacks. Parents trying to reach their kids."

Sergeant Cox asked Maureen if she and the others were escorted off the school grounds once she was outside. Mo nodded. "The four of us got into a cruiser, and they drove us to Clement Park. There were people everywhere—parents, kids. Everyone was crying, hugging each other. Two or three of the kids were hysterical. I didn't speak to anyone. I just kept walking, through the park. And then, at the other end, I saw the library and said to myself that I'd go in there."

"The public library?"

"Yes. So I went in, and went to the women's room. And I started seeing and hearing everything I'd seen and heard that morning, when those boys . . . walked in and started laughing and yelling. . . . And I thought I was going to have to throw up, but I was too afraid to close the stall. I didn't want to be closed in, even if I was going to vomit. And then I did vomit, with the door open. And later, I heard that people were meeting their kids at Leawood, so I walked to Leawood, and I thought, I'll walk in and Velvet will be there, or *I'll* be there and she'll walk in and see me. But . . ."

———

A LITTLE BEFORE NOON, MAUREEN and I drove over to Leawood Elementary School. Most of the family members who'd been there the night before had made it back. The D.A. arrived at about twelve fifteen. True to his word, he had a list. He said he would read the names of *all* the deceased—those who had died outside and inside the school. As he read from his list, fathers and mothers clamped their eyes shut, nodding in anguished resignation, but no one screamed out. No one wailed.

"Lauren Townsend, Rachel Scott, Kyle Velasquez, John Tomlin,

Cassie Bernal, Daniel Mauser, Daniel Rohrbaugh, Corey DePooter, Isaiah Shoels, Steven Curnow, Kelly Fleming, Matthew Kechter, William 'Dave' Sanders, Dylan Klebold, and Eric Harris."

Maureen and I looked at each other. We approached the D.A. Waited while several of the others asked him questions about the removal and reclaiming of their sons' and daughters' bodies. At last, he turned to us.

"What about Velvet Hoon?" Maureen asked.

He looked again at his list. Shook his head. "Is she your daughter?"

I told him she was an emancipated minor, a former student.

"She was there," Maureen said. "In the library."

He consulted his list again, twisted the hairs of his mustache. "Ma'am, at this point in time, we've examined every square inch of that school," he said. "If her name's not on this list, then she got out."

→→ *c h a p t e r   e i g h t* ←←

EXCERPTS FROM DYLAN KLEBOLD'S JOURNAL, 1997:

*"Fact: People are so unaware . . . well, Ignorance is bliss I guess. . . .
I swear—like I'm an outcast, & everyone is conspiring against me . . .
The lonely man strikes with absolute rage."*

Excerpts from Eric Harris's journal, 1998:

*"I will sooner die than betray my own thoughts, but before I leave this
worthless place, I will kill whoever I deem unfit. . . . I want to burn
the world, I want to kill everyone except about 5 people. . . . I'm full
of hate and I love it."*

Posting on Eric Harris's AOL Web site, 1998:

*"YOU KNOW WHAT I HATE!!!? Cuuuuuuuuhntryyyyyyyyyyy
music!!! . . .*

*YOU KNOW WHAT I HATE!!!? People who say that wrestling
is real!! . . . YOU KNOW WHAT I HATE!!!? People who use the
same word over and over again! Read a fucking book or two, increase your vo-cab-u-lary fucking idiots. . . . YOU KNOW WHAT*

I HATE!!!? STUPID PEOPLE!!! Why must so many people be so stupid!!? . . . YOU KNOW WHAT I HATE!!!? When people mispronounce words! And they don't even know it to, like acrosT, or eXpreso, pacific (specific), or 2 pAck. Learn to speak correctly you morons. . . . YOU KNOW WHAT I HATE!!!? STAR WARS FANS!!! GET A FasaaaaaRIGGIN LIFE YOU BORING GEEEEEKS! . . . My belief is that if I say something, it goes. I am the law, if you don't like it, you die. If I don't like you or I don't like what you want me to do, you die. If I do something incorrect, oh fucking well, you die. Dead people can't do many things like argue, whine, bitch, complain, narc, rat out, criticize, or even fucking talk. So that's the only way to solve arguments with all you fuckheads out there. I just kill! . . . Feel no remorse, no sense of shame. . . . I will rig up explosives all over a town and detonate each one of them at will af- ter I mow down a whole fucking area full of you snotty ass rich mother fucking high strung godlike attitude having worthless piece of shit whores. I don't care if I live or die in the shoot-out. All I want to do is kill and injure as many of you as I can, especially a few people. Like Brooks Brown.[1] . . . From now on, I don't give a fuck what almost any of you mutha fuckas have to say, unless I respect you which is highly unlikely, but for those of you who happen to know me and know that I respect you, may peace be with you and don't be in my line of fire. For the rest of you, you all better hide in your house because im comin for EVERYONE soon and I WILL be armed to the fucking teeth and I WILL shoot to kill and I WILL fucking KILL EVERYTHING! No I am not crazy, crazy is just a word, to me it has no meaning, everyone is different, but most of you fuckheads out there in society, going to your everyday fucking jobs and doing your everyday routine shitty things, I say fuck you and die. If you got a problem with my thoughts, come tell me and I'll kill you, because . . . god damnit, DEAD PEOPLE DON"T ARGUE!"

---

[1] A former friend with whom Harris had a falling out

Excerpt from a "mea culpa" school essay by Eric Harris, describing what he learned after he and Dylan Klebold were arrested for breaking into and stealing equipment from a parked van on January 30, 1998. Shortly after the theft, Harris and Klebold were approached and later brought into custody by Officer Tim Walsh of the Jefferson County Sheriff's Office, who was on patrol and noticed the boys, parked not far from the break-in, examining the stolen goods.

> *"After a very unique experience in a real live police station being a real live criminal, I had lots of time to think about what I did. . . . As I waited, I cried, I hurt, and I felt like hell. . . . My parents lost all respect and trust in me and I am still slowly regaining it. That experience showed me that no matter what crime you think of committing, you will get caught, that you must, absolutely must, think things through before you act, and that just because you can do something doesn't mean you should. To this day I still do not have a hard realistic reason why we broke into that car, but since we did, we have been set on a track that makes it mandatory for me to be a literal angel until March of 1999."*

Excerpt from Eric Harris's journal describing his private reaction to the van break-in:

> *"Isn't America supposed to be the land of the free? How come if I'm free, I can't deprive a stupid fucking dumbshit from his possessions if he leaves them sitting in the front seat of his fucking van out in plain sight and in the middle of fucking nowhere on a Fri-fucking-day night? NATURAL SELECTION. Fucker should be shot."*

Videotaped boast of Eric Harris:

> *"I could convince them that I'm going to climb Mount Everest, or I have a twin brother growing out of my back. I can make you believe anything."*

Excerpt from Eric Harris's journal entry dated April 26, 1998:

"Once the first wave starts to go off and the chaos begins, V opens fire and I start lobbin' the firebombs. Then I open fire, V starts lobbin' more crickets. Then if we can go upstairs and go to each classroom we can pick off fuckers at our will. If we still can we will hijack some awesome car, and drive off to the neighborhood of our choice and start torching houses with Molotov cocktails. By that time cops will be all over us and we start to kill them too! We use bombs, fire bombs, and anything we fucking can to kill and damage as much as we fucking can. . . . I want to leave a lasting impression on the world."

Excerpt from Eric Harris's journal on the December 1998 day fellow Columbine student Robyn Anderson purchased weapons for Klebold and Harris at a gun show:

"We . . . have . . . GUNS! We fucking got em, you sons of bitches! HA! HA HA HA! Neener! Booga Booga. Heh. It's all over now. This caps it off, the point of no return."

Excerpt from Dylan Klebold's February 1999 creative writing class assignment, a short story about an assassin who kills unsuspecting victims as they emerge from a bar:

"I not only saw in his face, but also felt emanating from him power, complacence, closure, and godliness. . . . The man smiled, and in that instant, through no endeavor of my own, I understood his actions."

Dialogue voiced by Eric Harris in a late 1998 video, in which he plays the part of a professional hit man for "Trenchcoat Mafia Protection Services." The video was submitted in fulfillment of an assignment for Harris's Government and Economics class, in which students were to design and promote a product or service:

"If you ever touch him again, I will frickin' kill you! I'll pull out my shotgun and blow your goddamn head off! Do you understand, you worthless . . . piece . . . of crap?"

Dialogue voiced by Dylan Klebold, in the "Trenchcoat Mafia Protection Services" video:

"If you bother him again, I will rip off your goddamn head and shove it so far up your friggin' ass, you'll be coughing up dandruff for four frickin' months!"

Scrawled by Eric Harris in a fellow student's yearbook:

"I hate everything unless I say otherwise, hey don't follow your dreams or your goals or any of that bullshit, follow your fucking animal instincts, if it moves kill it, if it doesn't, burn it. Kein mitleid!!!"[2]

Dylan Klebold, asking the traditional questions at the Klebold family's seder, Passover 1999, as is customary for the youngest at the table:

"Why is this night different from all other nights? Why do we eat only matzoh on Pesach? Why do we eat bitter herbs at our Seder? Why do we dip our foods twice tonight? Why do we lean on a pillow tonight?"[3]

Exclamation of Dylan Klebold and Eric Harris when they got strikes in bowling class:

"Sieg Heil!"

[2] No Mercy
[3] The Klebold family observed both Jewish and Christian customs.

Sardonic off-camera comment of Eric Harris during videotaped shooting practice at Rampart Range, March of 1999. A closeup shows a shooter's hand, bloody from shotgun kickback.

"Guns are bad. When you saw them off and make them illegal, bad things happen."

Comment by Dylan Klebold during the videotaped shooting practice at Rampart Range. A closeup shows a bullet-shattered bowling pin.

"Imagine that is someone's fucking brain."

From Eric Harris's journal, April 3, 1999:

"Months have passed. It's the first Friday night in the final month. Much shit has happened. VoDKa has a TEC–9, we test fired all our babies, we have 6 time clocks ready, 39 crickets, 24 pipe bombs, and the napalm is under construction. . . . Feels like a goddamn movie sometimes. I wanna try to put some bombs and mines around this town too, maybe. Get a few extra frags on the scoreboard. I hate you people for leaving me out of so many fun things. And no, don't fucking say 'Well that's your fault' because it isn't, you people had my phone #, and I asked and all, but no no no don't let the weird looking Eric KID come along. Ooh fucking nooo . . ."

Dylan Klebold's last journal entry, April 18, 1999:

"About 26.5 hours from now, the judgment will begin. Difficult but not impossible, necessary, nerve-wracking and fun. What fun is life without a little death? It's interesting, when I'm in my human form, knowing I'm going to die. Everything has a touch of triviality to it."

From Eric Harris's journal:

"It's my fault! Not my parents, not my brother, not my friends, not my favorite bands, not computer games, not the media, it's mine."

Scrawled on the page for Mother's Day 1999 in Eric Harris's academic day planner:

"Good wombs have born bad sons."

April 20, 1999, itinerary written in Eric Harris's day planner:

5:00	*Get up*
6:00	*meet at KS*
7:00	*go to Reb's house*
7:15	*he leaves to fill propane*
	I leave to fill gas
8:30	*Meet back at his house*
9:00	*made d. bag set up car*
9:30	*practice gearups*
	Chill
10:30	*set up 4 things*
11:	*go to school*
11:10	*set up duffel bags*
11:12	*wait near cars, gear up*
11:16	*HAHAHA*

Final entry in Dylan Klebold's math notebook:

Walk in, set bombs at 11:09, for 11:17
Leave,
Drive to Clemete Park. Gear up.
Get back by 11:15

> *Park cars. Set car bombs for 11:18*
> *Get out, go to outside hill, wait.*
> *When first bombs go off, attack.*
> *have fun!*

Eric Harris's laughing advice to classmate Brooks Brown outside Columbine High School, shortly before the shooting began, April 20, 1999:

> *"Brooks, I like you now. Get out of here. Go home."*

As Harris and Klebold, wearing black trench coats and carrying a backpack and duffel bag, stand together at the top of Columbine High School's west exterior, the order by one to the other to begin shooting, as reported by a witness, 11:19 a.m., April 20, 1999:

> *"Go! Go!"*

Klebold or Harris, between 11:19 and 11:23 a.m., during which time they killed students Rachel Scott and Daniel Rohrbough and injured students Richard Castaldo, Sean Graves, Lance Kirklin, Ann Marie Hochalter, Mark Taylor, and Michael Johnson outside the school, as reported by a witness:

> *"This is what we always wanted to do! This is awesome!"*

Klebold or Harris, before entering the school library, 11:29 a.m., as reported by a witness:

> *"Are you still with me? We're going to do this, right?"*

Written on pipe bombs thrown inside the school:

"VoDKa Vengeance"

Miscellaneous taunts of Klebold and Harris, laughing and shouting in the library while killing students Kyle Velasquez, Steve Curnow, Cassie Bernal, Isaiah Shoels, Matt Kechter, John Tomlin, Lauren Townsend, Kelly Fleming, Danny Mauser, and Corey DePooter, and injuring students Evan Todd, Dan Steepleton, Makai Hall, Patrick Ireland, Kasey Ruegsegger, Mark Kintgen, Valeen Schnurr, Lisa Kreutz, Nicole Nowlen, Jeanna Park, Jennifer Doyle, and Austin Eubanks, as reported by witnesses and recorded on a 911 call, 11:29 to 11:36 a.m.:

> *"Get up! Are you guys scared? Well, don't be, because you're all going to die anyway. . . . Everyone wearing a white hat, stand up! All the jocks stand up! We're going to kill every single one of you! . . . Yahoo! . . . Hey, I think I got a nigger here. I always wondered what nigger brains looked like. . . . How about you, big boy? You want to get shot today? . . . Why should you live? . . . Do you believe in God?[4] Why? . . . You think you look cool? You're a fucking geek. . . . Hey, fat boy. You're pathetic. . . . Peek-a-boo! . . . Look at that head blow up. I didn't know brains could fly."*

Klebold's answer to a student hiding beneath a library table, after the student asked Klebold what he was doing:

> *"Oh, just killing people."[5]*

Voices in unison, heard by a library witness shortly before Harris's and Klebold's suicides:

> *"One! Two! Three!"*

[4] Asked in response to a student's pleas, "Oh, God. Oh, God."

[5] This student, a friend of Klebold's, then asked if he was going to be killed. Klebold told him to leave the library immediately, which he did.

Excerpts from three videocassettes left behind by Eric Harris and Dylan Klebold, recorded during several sessions in March and April of 1999, mostly in the Harris family's basement. The last segment was taped on the morning of April 20, 1999, shortly before the two left Harris's home to begin their rampage.

HARRIS: *"There is nothing that anyone could have done to prevent this. No one is to blame except me and VoDKa."*

KLEBOLD: *"War is war."*

KLEBOLD: *"I hope we kill 250 of you."*

KLEBOLD: *"I think this is going to be the most nerve-racking fifteen minutes of my life, after the bombs are set and we're waiting to charge through the school. Seconds will be like hours. I can't wait. I'll be shaking like a leaf."*

HARRIS: *"It's going to be like fucking Doom.[6] Tick, tick, tick, tick. . . . Ha! That fucking shotgun is straight out of Doom!"*

KLEBOLD: *"People have no clue."*

HARRIS: *"We're going to kick-start a revolution."*

HARRIS: *"We're gonna come back as ghosts and haunt the survivors. Create flashbacks from what we do and drive them insane."*

HARRIS: *"More rage. More rage. Keep building on it."*

HARRIS: *"Isn't it fun to get the respect that we're going to deserve?"*

KLEBOLD: *"If you could see all the anger I've stored over the past four fucking years. . . . Being shy didn't help. I'm going to kill you all. You've been giving us shit for years. . . . You're fucking going to pay for all the shit. We don't give a shit because we're going to die doing it."*

---

[6] A video game in which the winner is the player with the highest body count.

HARRIS: *"We are but aren't psycho."*

KLEBOLD: *"It's humanity. Look what you made. You're fucking shit, you humans, and you deserve to die."*

KLEBOLD: *"Fuck you, Walsh!"*[7]

HARRIS: *"My parents are the best fucking parents I have ever known. My dad is great. I wish I was a fucking sociopath so I don't have any remorse, but I do. This is going to tear them apart. They will never forget it. I really am sorry about all this. . . . It fucking sucks to do this to them."*

KLEBOLD: *"'I love Jesus. I love Jesus.' . . . Shut the fuck up!"*

HARRIS: *"I would shoot you in the motherfucking head! Go, Romans! Thank God they crucified that asshole."*

KLEBOLD: *"Go, Romans! Go, Romans! Yeah! Whooo!"*

KLEBOLD: *"I'm sorry I have so much rage."*

HARRIS: *"I just want to apologize to you guys for any crap. To everyone I love, I'm really sorry about all of this. I know my mom and dad will be just fucking shocked beyond belief."*

KLEBOLD: *"Hey, Mom. Gotta go. It's about half an hour before our little judgment day. I just wanted to apologize to you guys for any crap this might instigate. . . . Just know that I'm going to a better place than here. I didn't like life too much, and I know I'll be happier wherever the fuck I go. So, I'm gone."*

KLEBOLD: *"We did what we had to do."*

HARRIS: *"That's it. Good-bye."*

---

[7] Jefferson County Sheriff's officer Tim Walsh, who apprehended Klebold and Harris after the 1998 van break-in.

→→ *chapter nine* ←←

BY WEDNESDAY AFTERNOON, MAUREEN SEEMED better. Shaken, still, but functioning. Putting one foot in front of the other. She braided her hair, put on makeup, folded some laundry. The dogs were a comfort to her. Sophie, in particular, seemed to sense she was needed. She stuck close, following Mo from room to room. As for me, I watched.

She kept looking at the phone, wandering over to the windows. When she asked if I thought we should file a missing person report on Velvet, I shook my head. "Give her time," I said. "She'll surface as soon as she's ready."

"Maybe she thinks I'm dead."

I tried to stifle the shudder that passed through me. "Well, you're not, Mo. You survived. And Velvet's a survivor, too. Look at everything that kid's lived through already. Wherever she is, she's okay."

When she turned from the window to face me, her body was outlined in daylight, her face in shadow. "You weren't there," she said.

———

THE SIX P.M. NEWS SHOWED people gathering, impromptu, at Clement Park. "There is a need for this Columbine community to grieve together, to be there for one another," the sober young reporter said. "This is Rob Gagnon, Eyewitness News."

Maureen went to the closet and got our jackets. "We need to go over there," she said.

"Mo, I think you need to stay home. Rest. Absorb the shock of what you've been through."

"But what if she's over there? What if she's wandering around, looking for me?"

I shook my head. "She'd call you. She wouldn't——"

"She writes phone numbers down on her hand, okay? And even if she *does* have our number, she might not be anywhere near a phone. She might not even be thinking straight." She punched her fists into the sleeves of her jacket. "You don't want to go? Fine, Caelum. Don't go. But don't you tell me what *I* need. Because what *I* need is to find that kid and make sure she's okay."

And so we went.

Mercifully, the cops had established a boundary for the media. I took hold of Maureen's arm and walked her past the satellite trucks and TV crews. "Sir? Ma'am?" someone behind us called. "Can we talk to you for a minute?"

"No, thank you," I called back over my shoulder. If they got wind of Mo's ordeal, it'd be like dogs on raw meat. I could at least spare her that much. I took hold of her hand, gave it a squeeze. "The less you say about what happened to you yesterday, the better," I said.

———————

A COUPLE HUNDRED MOURNERS HAD come—students, teachers, ashen-faced moms and dads. I spotted Jon and Jay, the custodians who'd heard the gunfire outside and helped Dave Sanders hustle kids out of the cafeteria. I saw Mrs. Jett, the detention room monitor, in the crowd, and Henry Blakely, the history teacher who'd walked out in a huff during our meeting about Velvet. Passing behind Henry, I heard him tell someone he'd planned to retire a few years down the line but, after this, he might just "pack it in."

Mo and I spoke with Jennifer Kirby, Andy's wife. Andy was home with a migraine, she said; it had started that morning and lasted all day. "And, oh my God, Maureen, I heard about what happened to *you*. How are you *doing*?"

Mo's eyes jumped from face to face in the crowd. She didn't seem to hear the question.

"Maureen?" I said.

"What?"

"Jen just asked you how you were doing."

"Me?" She looked from me to Jennifer. "I'm okay. Why?"

Someone had nailed a homemade poster to a tree—multicolored block letters that insisted "Columbine Is LOVE!!" At the base of the tree, kids had placed their tributes: cellophane-wrapped supermarket bouquets, handwritten poems torn from spiral notebooks, sports jerseys, teddy bears, snapshots in Ziploc bags. Photocopied pictures of the dead, tacked to the tree, fluttered in a damp, chilly wind. The day before had been springlike, they said. Go-outside-without-a-jacket weather. But here, again, was winter.

Maureen exchanged bear hugs with several of her health clinic regulars. The needy ones would be needier now than ever—oblivious to what *she'd* gone through. They'd use her up if she let them. To my surprise, I got hugged, too—approached and embraced by kids who'd earned A's in my classes, kids who'd flunked, kids whose names I couldn't even remember. *Long* hugs, these were—longer than felt comfortable. Okay, that's enough, my body kept trying to say to them, but no one seemed to want to let go.

As dusk turned to dark, a white-haired woman, too old to be the parent of high school kids, circulated through the crowd, passing out candles from a cardboard box. Thin white tapers, these were, with little cardboard skirts to catch the drips. "Get yours lit, then light someone else's!" she called. "Our Lord and Savior Jesus Christ wants us to lead each other out of the darkness!"

I watched Maureen and the three or four kids huddled around her take candles. A tall, skinny boy in baggy jeans produced a lighter, and the flame passed from wick to wick. Maybe there was something to this "power of prayer" stuff, and maybe there wasn't. It wasn't like *I* had any of the answers. But I resented the white-haired woman, shilling for God among the walking wounded. And when she approached me, candle in hand, I shook my head.

"You sure?" she said. "Better to light a candle than to curse the darkness." Her demeanor was grandmotherly, but her eyes were my mother's eyes that Sunday morning when I'd refused to get in the car and go to mass with her. I was fourteen, fed up with her Holy Roller bit. "Because I'm an *atheist*, that's why," I'd said, though I wasn't, and she'd reared back and delivered a slap across my face that still stung, years later, in Littleton. The candle floated between the woman and me. I held her gaze.

"Well, suit yourself," she said, and moved on. I looked back at Mo. At the center of her little group of students, she seemed to be someplace else.

It began to sleet. Umbrellas popped open, sweatshirt hoods came up. "It's awful, isn't it, Mr. Quirk?" someone said.

I turned to face a gray-bearded guy in a warmup jacket and a Rockies cap. As we shook hands, he reminded me we'd met a few years back, at parent-teacher conferences. His daughter, Megan, had been in my class. "Megan Kromie?" he said. "Tall redhead?"

"Oh, yes, Megan," I said. There'd been so many Megans. "How is she?"

"Fine. Great. Loves UC Santa Cruz. Of course, she's heartbroken about what's happened here. She played for Coach Sanders." I nodded, blinking back sudden tears.

"Were you anywhere near the line of fire yesterday?" he asked.

I shook my head. "My wife was, though. She was in the library, helping a student, when it started." Belatedly, I remembered my advice to Mo not to mention her ordeal, lest the media get ahold of her.

"But she got out okay?" Megan's father asked.

"She hid."

He winced, shook his head. When he asked how she was holding up, I looked over at her. She'd forgotten to hold her candle upright; cocked at a diagonal, its wax drip-drip-dripped onto the ground. Why was she staring up at the trees? "She'll be okay," I said.

He nodded. "And how are *you* doing?"

"Me? I'm all right."

"Really?"

I looked away from him, then looked back. When I opened my mouth, it was to tell him about Velvet's disappearance. But instead, I began speaking about Eric and Dylan. "I was waiting for my pizza, and the three of us were talking about mundane, everyday things: the prom, their plans after graduation, Dylan's fantasy baseball picks. I mean, how can they work their shift on a Friday night, sit in class on Monday, and, the next day, bring shotguns to school and murder thirteen people?"

"The banality of evil," Megan's father said.

"What?"

"I'm sorry. You made me think about something I read once, about the Nazis who ran the death camps. The way they could dissociate: sip wine with dinner, chuckle at radio comedies, tuck their kids into bed, and kiss their wives good night. Then get up in the morning and murder thousands more Jews."

I flashed on Eric and Dylan at the after-prom party, *Sieg Heil*ing in celebration of the free passes they'd won to Rock'n'Bowl. Had they realized they were never going to use them?

"I suppose it doesn't even apply, really: the 'banality of evil' principle. Those boys were obviously sick—psychopathic or sociopathic, I'd venture to say, although it's not really fair of me to diagnose them. Eichmann and the others were . . . well, good bureaucrats."

"Are you a psychiatrist or something?" I asked.

"A psychologist," he said. "And a minister."

"So you see it as evil, what they did?"

"Mr. Quirk, I'm as rocked off course and confused by all this as everyone else. I don't know *what* to think." Sleet spattered the brim of his Rockies cap and the back of the hand he held up to protect his candle flame. "Anyway, several of us are putting together a grief counseling session for tomorrow afternoon. It's at the Community Church on West Bowles, one p.m. We have guidance people from several of the schools coming, and someone from the university who's going to talk about posttraumatic stress. But the main purpose is to just get people talking about what they went through, and how they're feeling. The worst thing we can do at this point is isolate ourselves from each other. Why don't you come and bring your wife?"

I told him I'd see if I could get her there.

"Good. Great. Hey, could you use a hug?" He took a step forward, his arms parentheses spread wide, but he seemed to read my hesitation and squeezed my shoulder instead. "Okay, then. Hope to see you there tomorrow, Mr. Quirk. God bless."

"Say hello to Megan," I said.

"She learned a lot from you, you know."

Doubtful, I thought. But I wished to Christ I could remember her face.

Maureen was standing alone now, looking forlorn. Looking up, still, from tree to tree. What did she think: that Velvet was hiding in one of them? "Hey," I said, approaching her. When I put my arm around her, I felt how badly she was trembling.

"We're not safe," she whispered.

"What?"

"They're here."

They? "Velvet, you mean?"

She shook her head. "Their accomplices."

"Babe, the police said there *might* have been accomplices, but probably not. They're trying to rule that out."

"They're here," she repeated. "They're getting ready to finish the job." By the time I got her back to the car, the sleet had turned to snow.

THE DOGS GREETED US AT the door with swishing tails and swaying behinds. The light on our machine blinked red. I took a breath, hit the button.

"Hey, guys, it's Alphonse. Just wanted to let you know Lolly's funeral went off without a hitch. Bagpipers and all. The get-together afterward, too. Everyone says to say they're thinking of you. I been watching all the Columbine stuff on CNN. Jesus Christ Almighty, those kids were sick fucks, huh? Whoops, excuse my language. Hang in there, you two. Talk to you later."

"She'll call, Maureen," I said. "I bet we hear from her tomorrow."

"I'm going to bed," she said.

I got the dogs in, poured her a good-sized glass of red wine, and brought it up to her. Handed her a pair of Tylenol PMs. She took them, took a sip of her wine. She'd gotten into bed without undressing.

"I don't think I'm going to be able to sleep tonight," she said.

"You want another Tylenol?"

"I shouldn't take three," she said. She took another gulp of wine. "Yeah, all right. I guess it wouldn't hurt."

Ten minutes later, she was out.

Unable to sleep myself, I went back downstairs. I poured myself a glass of wine and walked, in the dark, from room to room. At the doorway to my study, I flipped on the light and stared at the stuff spread out on my work table—a set of *Hamlet* tests from my seniors, an American lit anthology opened to Robert Frost, a stack of ungraded research papers from my second-hour sophomores. It seemed inconsequential and beside-the-fact now: all this busy work the kids and I had generated in the days before they opened fire.

I flipped through the research papers. Some were laser-printed, spiffed up with colorful plastic covers; others were stapled, unadorned. I'd let them choose their own subjects, and they'd gone every which way. "Wiccan Beliefs and Practices," "Anorexia Nervosa in Adolescent Girls," "Bill Gates," "Black Holes." I picked up the latter paper and read the first sentence: "A black hole is a concentrated region of space-time with a gravitational pull so intense that nothing can escape from it, not even light."

I killed the rest of the wine and teetered back upstairs, somewhere between two and three. The dogs were asleep on the floor on Maureen's side. I took a piss, crawled under the covers, and realized I'd forgotten to turn off the bathroom light. But instead of getting up and turning it off, I started thinking about that woman at Clement Park—her and her candles. I'd already forgotten her face—had turned her into Barbara Bush. If my mother had lived, she'd be white-haired by now, too.

"You weren't there," Maureen had said to me, and it was true. As scared as I'd been for her safety—as much of a nightmare as that endless trip back from Connecticut had been—it was *she* who'd had to hide for hours in the pitch-blackness of that cabinet, listening to the death screams, waiting for them to find and kill her, too. And I *didn't* know what that felt like. Didn't want to. She'd recited the Hail Mary, over and over in the dark, she said—*Pray for us sinners, now and at the hour of our death*—and, later, had crawled out of that cabinet like a newborn, into the light and the chaos they'd made. But she'd lived. Here she was, next to me, breathing in, breathing out.

My sobs came out of nowhere, and I clenched my body, as best I could, to squelch them. Shaking the bed would wake her up, and there was nothing she needed more than sleep. After I got hold of myself again, I leaned on my elbow and shifted toward her. By the bathroom light, I watched her sleep.

She sighed a few times, whimpered a little. I leaned forward and brushed my lips against her cheek. Her eyes were shifting rapidly beneath the lids. . . . Get up, I kept telling myself. Turn the light off. She'll sleep better in the dark. But I kept not doing it. Kept dozing, coming to, dozing again.

Fuck it, I thought. Let there be light.

→→ *chapter ten* ←←

ON THURSDAY, THE SNOW FELL. The coroner released the bodies to the mortuaries. Janet Reno flew in from Washington to tour the crime scene.

In the morning, Maureen had agreed to let me take her to the grief counseling session at the church, but at lunchtime, sitting before her untouched soup and crackers, she balked. "What if Velvet calls?"

"She'll leave a message."

"She needs to talk to *me*, Caelum. Not to our answering machine."

"And what about you?" I said. "What do *you* need?"

"To stay home and rest. Isn't that what you told me yesterday? So I don't know why, today, you're pushing me to go to this thing."

I wasn't sure, either, but it had something to do with Megan's father. "This guy I talked to last night? One of the organizers? He said the one thing we need to do is—"

"What *we* need, Caelum?" she snapped. "You were in airports. You were on a plane. And wherever this organizer was, he wasn't hiding inside a cabinet, listening to kids beg for their lives. So don't tell me what *we* need, okay? I'm not going, so stop pressuring me."

"I'm not. All I'm saying is—"

"Stop it! Stop it!" Her fists pounded the tabletop. Her soup jumped. The dogs, aroused from their naps, looked from Mo to me.

And so I conceded—ran water for tea while she sat at the table, crushing crackers into powder and imagining, aloud, scenarios by which she could have saved those kids' lives. Maybe if she'd tried reasoning with them. Negotiating. Reminding them about how much their parents would suffer.

"They would have shot you rather than listen to that," I said.

She stared at me for several seconds, then looked away, mumbling something about overpowering them.

"Overpower them how?"

"I don't know. Hit them with a chair or a desk drawer or something."

"Maureen, you're what? Five-four? Klebold must have gone six-three, six-four. You would've had to *stand* on a chair before you hit him with one. And what was his buddy going to do? Stand there and wait his turn while Wonder Woman—"

"Don't make fun of me!"

"I'm not, babe. I'm sorry. I just . . . look, you have to give yourself a break here. You did the only thing you *could* do. You survived."

She began to cry. "Where *is* she?"

I sat down beside her. Took both her hands in mine. "Maureen, this is what Velvet *does* when her life gets crazy. She disappears. But sooner or later, she's going to come out of hiding, and when she does, she'll pick up the phone. Or ring our doorbell. Or come walking out of the woods and into the backyard like she did last Saturday. And until then—"

She withdrew her hands. "Okay. I'll *go* to your stupid meeting."

"It's not my meeting, Mo."

"Then whoever's it is!"

She stood so abruptly, her chair fell backward and clattered against the floor. Then she, too, was on the floor, crawling beneath the table. She sat crouched, her hands on her head, her head between her knees.

At first, I just stood there, unsure of what to do. Then I knelt down next to her. Spoke with as much calm as I could manage. "The chair fell, Mo. It was just the chair." When I reached out to touch her shoulder, she batted my hand away. Sophie and Chet stood like sentries on either side of her, low growls rumbling in their throats.

A minute or two later, Maureen was on her feet and heading for the stairs. When she came back down, she had put her hair in a ponytail and changed her blouse. "Come on," she said. "Let's go."

THE PARKING LOT WAS FULL to overflowing. On our way inside, I overheard two older women. "I'm not even sure why I wanted to come to this," one of them said. "Just to be sad with other people, I guess."

At the steps leading down to the basement hall, we were approached by Lindsay Peek, a sophomore, one of my honors kids. One of Mo's clinic regulars, too. Lindsay was painfully shy. Chewed the ends of her hair during tests. Her handwriting was so neat and regimented, it looked machine-generated. She spoke to Maureen, not me. "My mother made me come to this, but she had to go to work." There was panic in her darting eyes.

Go away, I wanted to say; leave her alone.

"You want to sit with Mr. Quirk and me?" Maureen asked. Lindsay nodded. She opened her mouth to say something, then closed it again.

"What is it, hon?" Maureen asked.

"I saw you. When you came in with that girl."

I didn't understand what she meant, but Maureen did. She touched her arm. "You were in the library, Lindsay?"

She squinted. Her eyebrows, bare in spots, were studded with scabs.

"Linds?"

"My mother said I have to work this summer? Because I turned sixteen and she doesn't want me hanging around the house all day? And so, last week, she drove me around to all these places and made me go in and get applications. And then, Monday night, she came into my room and started screaming about how I was stalling on doing them because I was so lazy. And so, on Tuesday, at lunch, I went to the library. . . . And I was filling them out. And it was weird because you had to put down references? And I had just written 'Maureen Quirk,' and then I looked up and there you were. You and that weird girl. . . . They're not going to make us talk at this thing, are they? Call on us or whatever? Because I don't want to talk about it."

"No, neither do I," Maureen said.

They clasped hands, and I followed them inside.

REVEREND JUDY CLUKEY WAS A plump, reassuring Mrs. Santa Claus type. As pastor of the host church, she welcomed everyone who had come and introduced her fellow members of the faith community: Reverend Sands of South Fellowship, Rabbi Effron from B'nai Chaim, Pastor Benson of Faith Lutheran in Castle Rock, Reverend Kromie of the Unitarian Universalist Church. Father Duplice from Pax Christi had wanted to come, too, she said, but he'd had knee replacement surgery the week before and couldn't yet handle stairs. Several of the clergy spoke briefly about services and programs planned at their houses of worship in the coming days.

"Now I've been asked to explain the seating for today's session," Reverend Clukey said. We probably noticed that the folding chairs had been arranged in three concentric circles. The innermost circle was reserved for witnesses to the killings, and for those who themselves had been fired upon. The next, larger circle was for students and staff members who'd been at school but had not personally witnessed the violence. The outer circle was for the rest of us. "Now our thinking in seating you this way," she said, "is that what happened at

Columbine two days ago was the emotional equivalent of a terrible earthquake. Nine-point-eight on the Richter scale of our hearts and minds. Am I right?"

Around the room, adults and kids nodded glumly.

"And it's shaken us badly, this . . . upheaval. As individuals, as a community, as a nation. We're frightened and confused. How can our children have been taken from us? How can the friends we've gone to grade school, and dance class, and football games with no longer be among us? The ground seems to have cracked open, and it feels as if we're standing at the crumbling edge of some terrible abyss."

Heads hung low; people dabbed at their eyes, looked out at nothing.

"Now some of us here today found ourselves, two days ago, at the epicenter of this emotional earthquake." I glanced at Maureen, standing a few feet away. She was listening intently, hungrily. Beside her, Lindsay Peek looked dazed. "And *these* are the people we most want to reach out to today with our love and our support. Because loving one another may be the key to stepping back from the edge of this abyss, no matter where fate, or the Good Lord, or happenstance placed us on Tuesday at 11:19 a.m. when those two lost souls opened fire. We need to stare back, without blinking, at the depravity of those boys' actions and realize that our love is more powerful than their hatred."

Sobs broke out around the room. "Amen," someone said.

"And so we invite those of you who were in the line of fire on Tuesday to please come forward and take seats at the center of this room. Because we love you. And because we want to listen to you—to bear witness. You're the ones who've been given the heaviest crosses to bear, and we want to help you carry them. So please, everyone. Come. Sit."

The crowd shifted. A dozen kids and half as many adults moved toward the center seats, some without hesitation, others more tentatively. Maureen dug her nails into my arm. "I'm not going up there," she whispered. I looked from the fear in her eyes to the fear in Lindsay's. Nodded. Led them, against the flow of bodies, to the back wall. Up front, five or six chairs remained unclaimed.

Reverend Benson, the Lutheran minister, took the floor. Back during World War I, he said, there'd been a saying: "In the foxholes, there are no atheists." "And so, let's begin today's meeting by clasping hands, closing our eyes, and reciting, together, the Lord's Prayer. And if you're a nonbeliever, or if right now you're too angry at God to pray to Him, we respect your silence. But do close your eyes and hold the hand of the person next to you, so that you might feel, if not the Lord's mercy, then the solidarity of our community."

Our Father, Who art in Heaven, hallowed be thy name. . . . There were a couple hundred people in that room. Most of us, myself included, held hands as he requested. Moved our lips. But very few of us—not Maureen or Lindsay, no one in the first circle, that I could see—felt inclined to close our eyes. *Forgive us our trespasses as we forgive those who trespass against us. . . .* Eyes open, I saw my mother, kneeling next to me at St. Anthony's, her mantilla covering her head, her eyes closed in fervent faith. What had Mother been praying for all those Sundays? Her father's forgiveness? Her husband's soul? . . . I saw Eric Harris, leaning against the counter at Blackjack Pizza, staring at his spinning cell phone. Saw them both, in their aprons, their T-shirts and cargo shorts, traveling incognito as kids with part-time jobs and plans beyond high school. . . . The minister's voice boomed toward the end—the line about our deliverance from evil. Had they been evil monsters? Lost souls? Psychopaths? All or none of the above? And what about their parents? Their older brothers? How, for the rest of their lives, were *they* supposed to walk in the world? What kind of black hole had *they* been sucked into?

In my peripheral vision, I noticed Maureen's fidgeting hands. Looked to my left and watched her. With the thumb and index finger of her right hand, she was twisting the wedding ring on her left.

Around, around, around, around. She probably didn't even realize she was doing it. By the time I refocused, Ivy Shapiro was addressing the group. Although classes for Columbine students would not resume for another week and a half, she said, she and the other counselors would be on call immediately. She gave telephone numbers, e-mail addresses. They'd be happy to talk to whoever wanted to talk, happy to schedule appointments and accommodate walk-ins. "So let's all talk about it, kids," Ivy said. "As much as possible. You don't need to suffer in silence."

Three women from St. Frances Cabrini spoke next. The grief committee, they called themselves. They draped hand-crocheted prayer shawls onto the shoulders of the folks in the first circle. "Wear them whenever it's starting to overwhelm you," their spokeswoman advised. "Put them on and feel God's loving arms around you." Beside me, Maureen let out an unnerving chuckle.

When Reverend Clukey introduced Megan's father, he stepped to the center of the first circle. He was wearing jeans and hiking boots; his clerical collar peeked above his Columbine Rebels sweatshirt. He said some people knew him as Pastor Kromie, others as Dr. Kromie, but he invited us to think of him, if we liked, as just plain Pete. He said he had a confession to make: that although, as both therapist and minister, he had counseled many grieving families, he had never before dealt with a grief this widespread and profound. And so he felt inadequate. At a loss. He needed our help. "A lot of you have had the impulse to come here today—there are more people than there are chairs. And I think this says that we need *something* from one another. But what? In the coming days, I suspect, our needs may be different than they are today, forty-eight hours after this terrible tragedy. Grief is a process—an evolution. But what do we need at *this* moment?" His eyes circled the room, scanning faces in the front, the middle, the back. "To vent? Is that what we need today? To cry and hold each other? To ask the questions 'Why?' and 'Why us?' and

'How could a hatred so deep and disconnected from everything we value have taken root here in Littleton?' Maybe we can figure out, together, what we need this meeting to be."

He seemed to be looking at me when he said it. I nodded back. Looked over at Mo. She was twisting her ring again.

Pastor Pete invited audience members to talk about what they were feeling, or what they had experienced. Few did—no one in the shell-shocked first circle. A girl in the second circle said she'd been trapped in her art class for two hours before she got out of the building. "I prayed the whole time," she said. "And My Lord and Savior Jesus Christ saved my life."

"Jesus saved me, too," a tall, skinny boy in the back agreed. "I woke up with a sore throat, and my mother called me in sick."

A girl in the middle circle popped out of her seat. "So if Jesus is so great, why didn't he save my friend Kyle then? Or Cassie? Or Rachel Scott, who would never even hurt a mosquito?" She glared accusingly at the sore-throat kid, waiting for an answer.

"I don't know," he said.

"None of us does," Pete told him. "We're all struggling with that one."

A girl who'd been trapped in her science class said she called her mother on her cell phone, and that her mother had stayed on the line with her through the whole ordeal. "If she hadn't," she said, "I probably would have gone crazy. I just wanted to say that I love my mom so much."

Maureen let go an impatient sigh. Her shoulder-length hair was down now, her fingers fidgeting with the purple elastic that had held her ponytail in place. She'd put it around her fingers and kept stretching it and letting go, letting it snap against her knuckles.

A hand went up in the second circle. When Pete nodded, a young guy in his twenties—shaved head, earring in one ear—stood and addressed the crowd in a shaky voice. He said he'd been subbing at the school and was on his break when he got wind of what was happening. He'd locked himself in a stall in the staff bathroom and had heard one of them laughing out in the hallway, banging on doors and shouting, "I know you're in there!" The night before, he said, his girlfriend had told him she was pregnant, and he wasn't exactly thrilled about it. But now he was glad about the baby, and he and his girlfriend had decided to get married. He was going to try and be the best husband and father he could be. I was unnerved by Maureen's one-note chuckle. "Give me a break," she mumbled, more to herself than me.

People spoke, others listened. There was no give and take, no response, beyond grateful nods from Pastor Pete. It was like that AA meeting I'd gone to that time, back in Three Rivers. I'd told Dr. Patel, the marriage counselor, about my father's alcoholism, and about the way I'd get wasted on weekends sometimes, and drink when I couldn't sleep. She'd urged me to go to a meeting—try it out—and so I had. Once. It creeped me out: all that handholding and surrendering to a Higher Power. All those heartfelt confessions and nobody saying anything in response. It just wasn't for me, and anyway, those people were a lot more far gone than I was. More in my father's league than mine. I just cut back a little. Less beer and liquor, more jogging. I was fine.

"I keep seeing them," Sylvia Ritter was saying. "One of them, anyway." She was the first person in the fishbowl up front to speak—the only person, as it played out. A biology teacher nearing retirement, Sylvia told the crowd she'd gone out in the hallway when she heard the second explosion, and that Dave Sanders had run past her, shouting for her to get back in her classroom, get the kids away from the door, and lock it. "And that's when I looked down the hallway, and I saw one of them. Down near the library. I don't know which one. I didn't see a face, just a raised rifle, or a shotgun, or whatever it was; I don't know about guns." She stopped to compose herself, and when she spoke again, it was about how, the week before, she'd seen Dave Sanders in the office. She had asked him about his new granddaughter, and he'd taken out his wallet and shown her the baby's picture. "That's when they must have shot him, I think. Right after he warned me to go back in my classroom and lock the door."

Beside me, Maureen seemed to be gulping back tears. I reached over and started rubbing her back, but she shook her head no. She'd put her hair back in the ponytail.

A tall girl standing in back said she didn't want to talk about her experience on Tuesday. She just wanted to say that Coach Sanders had been an awesome coach and she was never going to forget him.

Two freshmen girls asked if they could sing the Mariah Carey song "Hero" and dedicate it to the kids who'd died. "That would be fine," Pastor Pete said, and they launched into their heartfelt, off-key a capella tribute. That was what got to me more than anything at the grief meeting, I think. Those poor, scrawny girls singing that shitty song, badly. Them, and the substitute—the father-to-be. Maureen rocked her head back and forth during the singing. She seemed both bored and nervous. She kept looking over at the wall clock.

Near the end of the program, Reverend Clukey introduced Dr. Bethany Cake, a University of Denver professor whose area of expertise was trauma. "Dr. Cake is here to share information that can help us understand what we're going through, and how best to deal with the days and weeks to come. And may I add that she's been good enough to come on very short notice. One of her colleagues was scheduled to speak to us, but he was called unexpectedly to the governor's office this morning, to help plan the memorial service that's being planned for Sunday. So we're grateful Dr. Cake could make it. Bethany?"

A small, dark-haired woman in her early forties made her way to the center of the circle. She was gripping the neck of an overhead projector in one hand, a laptop computer in the other. An extension cord was lassoed around her shoulder. "I've brought a PowerPoint presentation," she said, beginning the setup of her equipment. "Someone want to douse the lights?"

People mumbled, shifted uncomfortably. "Can we leave the lights on?" someone called. Dr. Cake didn't seem to hear the request.

Reading the crowd's discomfort, Pastor Pete stood. "Dr. Cake? I'm wondering, since this room doesn't particularly lend itself to this kind of presentation, if you could maybe summarize your material and then open up the floor to questions?"

She stared back at him for a few uneasy seconds. "I can project it onto that wall there," she said. "And sure, I can *do* a q & a, as long as everyone realizes that I'm a researcher, not a clinician." And so there was an awkward shifting of chairs and a compromise: a dimming of *some* of the lights.

Dr. Cake began by laser-pointing to a list of responses to what she termed "the traumatic event." I pulled out the small notepad and pen I'd shoved in my pocket before we left and jotted down "hypervigilance, flashbacks, survivor guilt, psychic numbness, palpitations, hypersensitivity to noise, hypersensitivity to injustice."

"Now these are all normal *initial* responses," Dr. Cake said. "So if you're experiencing some of them at this point, all it means is that you're processing. Working through your anxiety. You've all heard of the mind-body connection, right?"

There was a collective nodding of heads.

"Each of us has a kind of thermostat that coordinates environmental stimuli with encephalic activities and endogenous activities."

From the sidelines, Pastor Pete said, "In other words, what our brain does and what our body does with the stimuli we take in."

Trauma could throw our thermostats out of kilter, Dr. Cake explained. So maybe we were feeling extremely jumpy, or uncharacteristically angry, or emotionally numb. Maybe there were blank spots when we tried to remember what we'd been through. The good news was that most people's thermostats would self-adjust, and these responses would subside over the next few weeks. "It's only when they persist, or evolve, that there's clinical concern."

"Persist for how long?" someone asked.

"Rule of thumb? Beyond four to six weeks," she said. "But I'd appreciate it if you hold your questions until the end."

"Miss Warmth," I wrote on my pad. When I showed Mo, she looked at me, confused, as if I'd written something cryptic. Lindsay was chewing on her hair.

Posttraumatic stress disorder would result if the individual's central nervous system was impacted significantly at the time of the event, Dr. Cake said. And that impact would only reveal itself over time through "the three Es."

The words *environmental*, *encephalic*, and *endogenous* appeared on the wall, in a diagram with arrows going this way and that. I copied it onto my pad without knowing what the hell it meant. Too technical, I thought; she's talking to sufferers, not psych majors.

She spoke about triggers—sights, sounds, smells, tactile sensations that might induce a flashback. Or a panic episode. Or psychic numbness. "How many of you heard gunshots on Tuesday?"

Hands went up around the room.

"Okay. So let's say there's a loud clap during a thunderstorm. Or you're at a party and a balloon pops. Bang! Not out of the ordinary, right? But sensory cues that wouldn't ordinarily disturb anyone may now become triggers. Cause a flashback, say. Which is stressful, sure, but not really a clinical problem at this stage of the game. But if you're *still* getting hijacked by sensory stimuli six months from now, then you've probably gotten stuck. And each time a flashback occurs, it *re*traumatizes you. We see it in the research on rape victims. In their flashbacks, they get re-raped. Veterans, too, especially Vietnam vets. They go back, again and again, to the war zone."

Maureen reached over and took my pad and pencil. *This woman is making me nervous*, she wrote.

Want to go? I wrote back.

She shook her head.

Hands shot up, and to her credit, Dr. Cake relaxed her no-questions-until-the-end rule. "Yes?" she said, calling on a woman in the second circle.

"So why do some people get stuck, and others don't?"

Our central nervous systems were all different, she said. And there was *some* evidence that some people were more genetically predisposed to PTSD than other people. "And it can depend, too, on whether or not you experienced trauma during childhood."

A girl raised her hand. "So can this PSTD or whatever be cured?"

"P*TS*D," Dr. Cake said. "Yes. Particularly if it's treated successfully during the acute, rather than the chronic, stage. And what can't be cured can often be managed, the way diabetics monitor and manage *their* disease." She rambled on, oblivious to the fact that she seemed to have put the first circle in a trance. I zoned out for a while myself, suddenly aware of how exhausted I was. Worried about Mo, I hadn't slept for shit the night before. With my pen, I made crosshatchings over the notes I'd taken. Whatever it was that we needed, it wasn't a bunch of clinical information about what might happen to people's heads four to six weeks down the line. . . . Were they going to make the kids finish the school year, given the circumstances? If not, maybe Maureen and I could get back to Connecticut a little earlier. Get away. Start figuring out what to do about Lolly's house and the farm property. It was going to be a lot of work, clearing out that place, whether we decided to sell it or rent it out. There was going to be a lot of emotional baggage, too. But it'd be nothing compared to this. And the distraction might be good for Mo. Maybe we could put the dogs in the backseat and drive back there instead of flying. Meander a little. Take the scenic route. . . . When I tuned back in, Dr. Cake was talking about physical ailments: ringing in the ears, tingling sensations, lack of bladder control, sexual dysfunction.

"And these would be psychosomatic rather than real?" someone asked.

"Well, they're *very* real to the sufferer. People with PTSD will sometimes go from doctor to doctor to doctor to get to the bottom of their physical ailments. But the origin of their pain is in their mind, not their body."

"But we don't want to put the cart before the horse," Pete said. "As Bethany said earlier, many of you—the *majority*—will wrestle with some symptoms in the short term, but they'll subside."

"That's right," Cake said. "But there could be a high price to pay for ignoring treatment. That's all I'm saying." God, this woman is terrible, I thought. They should unplug her projector and get her the hell out of there.

A boy in the second circle raised his hand. "You said something before about 'psychic numbness'? Is that like when the person acts like a space cadet?"

This drew a smile from Cake—the first she'd displayed. "Well, that's one way of putting it," she said.

"Because I was in trig when it started? And I got out okay? But my little brother was in the cafeteria. And after they left the library and came downstairs to the caf—"

"After *who* left the library?" Dr. Cake asked.

"You know."

"The killers?"

He looked nervously at the people around him, then nodded.

"Do you know their names?"

He nodded again.

"Then why don't you say their names?"

He shook his head. "I don't want to."

"Why not?"

Hey, lady, I thought. You're a researcher, not a shrink. Remember?

"Because I just don't *want* to," the boy said.

"Okay. Go on, then. There were explosions. There was gunfire. And then they came down to the cafeteria where your brother was."

The boy nodded. "And he and these two other kids he was hiding under a table with decided to make a run for it? But they saw them and started chasing them down the hallway. Firing at them. Ethan said he could hear bullets flying past him, and over his head. Making this whistling noise and, like, skidding along the walls. He thought he was going to get hit, you know? But he just kept going, and then he cut through the auditorium and got outside. . . . And after? When my parents picked us both up at Leawood? All's *I* wanted to do was go home. But Ethan wanted to go to McDonald's and get a Quarter Pounder with cheese. He had this craving, like."

"Probably more for normalcy than hamburgers," Dr. Cake noted. Inexplicably, Maureen let out a laugh.

"So that's what we did," the boy said. "It was kind of weird, you know? After everything that happened, we go to Mickey D's? . . . But anyways, he seemed okay that night. Watching the news, talking on the phone to our grandparents and our cousins. He was kind of getting into being an eyewitness or whatever. But then yesterday? And today? He just keeps staring out at nothing, and it's like 'Yoo-hoo? Earth to Ethan?' And he wouldn't come to this thing today. My parents wanted him to, and I wanted him to, but he was all like, 'What? Nah, I'm too tired. I don't need to. I don't even remember a lot of it.' And I was just wondering: is that that psychic numbness stuff?"

Dr. Cake said it wasn't appropriate for her to comment on his brother's responses specifically. What she could say was that, in the wake of trauma, the brain sometimes acts protectively by blanking out the terrible memory. "Which is okay in the short run. But if psychic numbing—'emotional amnesia,' it's also called—if this persists, then the patient can't confront the feelings and the fears. And, over time, that avoidance can do damage."

"Think of it in terms of the hard drive on your computer," Pastor Pete added. "The memories are *in* there. Stored. But they're not being accessed."

"Actually, let me take that metaphor a step further," Dr. Cake said.

"Psychic numbing can act like a computer *virus*. Because those unaccessed memories are in there, doing their damage, undetected. And then, one day, nothing works."

On my pad, I wrote "Love Bug." Had it only been a couple of days ago when I'd read about that computer virus sweeping the country? Jesus, it seemed more like two or three *months* ago. Back when we were naïve about what a couple of high school kids could do—when we thought an erased hard drive was a tragedy. An elderly aunt's stroke. Was this how Maureen and I were going to organize our lives from now on: before and after they opened fire?

"I'm not trying to put you on the spot," Dr. Cake said. She was back at the boy whose brother had gone into emotional retreat. Back to trying to get the poor kid to speak their names. "I just want to make the point that it's important for us to—"

"Dylan Klebold!" the kid blurted. "Eric Harris!" He began to cry.

"Cock-sucking mother*fuckers*!" someone else shouted. A collective flinch traveled around the room. There was nervous laughter, grumbling, whimpering. My eyes lit on a big, red-faced kid in the middle circle. Steve something, a halfback on the football team. The kids seated around him in the second circle—teammates in matching Rebels jerseys—tried to pull him back down in his seat, but he shook them off, bolting for the exit. The slam of the door made Maureen gasp and grab my arm. Like gunfire, I realized. Oh God, Mo.

From another part of the room, a gray-haired couple stood and made for the door, too. "I want to apologize for my son," the man said. "They killed his buddy. His best friend since second grade. They were going to go camping together this coming weekend. And that's not his usual vocabulary, either."

After they left, Pastor Pete turned to his teammates. "What's his name?"

"Steve," one of them said.

"Well, when you see him, you tell Steve not to be embarrassed about what just happened. Tell him his outburst was a *healthy* reaction. Okay? One of you want to tell me why?"

We all waited, but Steve's friends volunteered nothing more. Ivy Shapiro stood up. "Because he got it out," she said.

"Got what out?" Pete asked.

"His anger."

"Right. And not only did he get it out, but he directed it at the appropriate parties. Not his parents, or his teachers, or himself. He directed it at the two people who murdered his best friend. How many of you feel angry at Harris and Klebold?"

The majority of people, kids and adults, raised their hands. I did. Maureen did. Lindsay's hands stayed in her lap.

"Then you need to *express* that anger. Get it out on the table, rather than letting it fester. Direct it where it belongs."

One of the football kids stood. "I think it sucks that they killed themselves," he said. "They should have gone to trial, gotten convicted, and fried in the chair."

"Faced a firing squad," someone muttered.

"Hung from a fuckin' tree."

A girl in the first circle stood and gathered her things. "Sorry," she said. "I can't take this." She followed Steve out the door.

A squat, muscular boy—a wrestling team standout whose name I've forgotten—rose from his chair. "Know what I would have done to them?" he said. "I was thinking about this last night. I would have skipped all that trial stuff and gotten two pieces of rope, okay? Tied one end to their ankles and the other end to the bumper of my truck. Then I would've gotten in and put the pedal to the metal, okay? Cranked that sucker to ninety, a hundred miles an hour and enjoyed the screaming. Worn their backs down to the spinal cord, then ripped 'em out and stuffed them down their throats. That's what *I* would have done."

His comment drew revulsion and applause. He looked around the room, pleased with himself. Pastor Pete looked glum but said nothing. Dr. Cake looked confused. She hurried through the rest of her presentation, laser-pointing to PTSD Web sites we could visit, articles and books we could read, clinic numbers we could call.

Passing Pete on the way out, I said, "Well, you said they could vent. They vented."

He nodded sadly. Apologized for the way things had gone, and for Cake's insensitivity. He said the guy who was supposed to have come was terrific. "How's your wife doing?" he asked. His eyes followed mine to Maureen, walking five or ten steps ahead with Lindsay Peek. I looked back at him and shrugged.

We gave Lindsay a ride home. The driveway was empty, the house was dark. Her mother got out of work at six, she said. Reluctant to leave her alone, Maureen suggested the three of us go someplace and get an ice cream. Lindsay said she'd be okay. *Oprah* was on. She'd go in and watch *Oprah*.

"Lindsay?" I said. "The girl Mrs. Quirk was with when she came into the library? Velvet? Did you see what happened to her in there?"

She nodded. "I could see her from where I was. Most of us were under the tables with other people, but there was no one else under hers. Just her."

"Did they say anything to her?" I asked.

"The tall one did. He called her a name. I don't want to repeat it. It wasn't very nice. . . . He asked her if she believed in God. They were both asking kids that. Then they'd laugh at their answers and shoot them."

Maureen put her fist to her mouth. She looked away from Lindsay.

"What did Velvet say when he asked her?" I asked.

"I don't know. I couldn't hear that good, because of the alarm, and kids crying and everything. And then, I think it was right after that, the short one jumped up onto a bookcase."

"Eric?"

She nodded. "He was screaming and swearing. Shaking books off the shelves. And then they left. . . . That's when kids started getting out from under the tables and going down that little hallway and out the side door. I was scared to get up at first. Scared to look at everything. But then these kids near me got up and I just followed them."

"Did you see her later on? Outside?"

"That girl?" She shook her head. "No, wait. I did. She was walking toward the park."

"Was she with anyone else?" Maureen asked.

Lindsay shook her head. "By herself. She was crying."

On the way home, the car radio said Janet Reno's tour of the school had been canceled when another live bomb was discovered among the debris and floating book bags in the cafeteria. The Education Commissioner's prerecorded voice announced that Columbine High would remain closed indefinitely. We would complete the last eighteen days of the school year at nearby Chatfield High. Double sessions: the Chatfield kids in the morning, our kids in the afternoon, from one to five. "Well," I said. "I guess we can limp through anything for eighteen days."

Maureen said the Chatfield nurses would probably work both sessions, or maybe split the schedule with Sandy Hailey, Columbine's full-time nurse. "They won't need me," she said.

"Mo, they're not going to cut your position with eighteen days left. You'll still be half-time. Go in for a couple of hours."

She shook her head. "No, they won't want both Sandy and me."

I wasn't sure what she was saying. "Do you *want* to go back to work?"

She stared ahead.

The dogs bolted past us to the outside. The message machine was blinking. We both stood there, staring at it. I pressed the button.

"Maureen? Sweetheart? It's your father. We've been thinking about you. Wondering how you're doing after your ordeal. Worrying about you. Evelyn and I are planning to drive down to visit you in a few days. On Sunday, unless you call and tell us otherwise. Until then, if there's anything you need—" The message seemed to have ended, but there were four or five seconds of silence, no beep. Then, belatedly, "I love you, Maureen. Very, very much."

Mo burst into sobs. I think she may have been waiting a lifetime to hear those words. But look what it had cost her.

The second caller was speaking so softly that I missed the first few words of her message. "It's Velvet!" Maureen said. I hit replay.

"Hi, Mom. . . . It was pretty bad, huh? Those fuckers. . . . I looked for you after I got outside. I wasn't sure where you were, and I was scared that maybe . . . but I know you got out okay, because I seen the list and you weren't on it. . . . I'm okay, I guess. I'm gonna split. I just wanted to say good-bye to my mom. And thanks for, you know, hanging with me. I'm not sure where I'm going. Just away from this fuckin' place. This guy I met's giving me a ride. He may be going to Vegas, or California, or maybe even down to Mexico. It depends. Maybe I'll call you when I get someplace. Just to see how you're doing. How my mom's making out. . . . Oh, and tell Mr. Quirk—"

Beep. End of message.

chapter eleven

I WENT BY MYSELF TO the funerals.

John Tomlin's, on Friday, was the first. His girlfriend spoke of his infectious grin. His minister warned of the devil. "Satan loves this," he said. "He wants us to be overwhelmed by the evil and the fear. He wants us to return evil for evil."

On Saturday, Rachel Scott's mourners, myself among them, queued up to sign her off-white casket with marker pens. Two people from the front, I could read the messages. "Honey, you are everything a mother could ask the Lord for in a daughter." "Sweet Rachel, we love you." "I promise to finish the dreams we had together." My hands began to shake. How could I hold a pen? What could I write? I had no words for Rachel—nothing to counteract the senseless shame of that sweet kid's being inside that polished box. And so I left the line, left the church, and drove home. I must have, because one minute I was sitting behind the wheel in the church parking lot, and the next I was walking through our backdoor, moving toward the ringing kitchen phone.

It was my father-in-law. "Apparently, half of Colorado is going to that memorial service tomorrow. Evelyn has to show a house at nine. She'd reschedule, but it's a VIP client—the new cohost for *Good Morning, Denver*. The soonest we could get on the road would be ten, ten thirty, and by then, traffic's going to be a nightmare."

Right, I felt like saying. Your daughter's falling apart at the seams, but we'd hate to see you and the Barracuda inconvenienced by a little bumper-to-bumper. And besides: letting her down? It's not like you haven't established plenty of precedent. "No, I understand," I said. "Maureen will, too."

I hung up feeling pissed but relieved. I'd come face to face with Daddy Dearest twice since Mo and I had been together, both times in neutral places—high-end restaurants he and Evelyn had suggested. Both times, I'd sat there, chewing and swallowing food I wasn't going to pay for, answering patronizing questions about my teaching, and itching to confront him about it: *Masturbate in front of your eleven-year-old-daughter? Mess with her head like that?* . . . Arthur Ekhardt and his charity golf tournaments, his Italian silk suits. Hey, my father may have been a drunken failure, but at least he'd never . . . I mean, why would she even *want* him in her life? That's what I didn't get.

In lieu of themselves, my in-laws sent, later that afternoon, a huge cellophane-wrapped basket filled with gourmet cookies, candies, coffees, and teas. There was a pricey bottle of pinot in there, too, and a copy of *Chicken Soup for the Grieving Soul* or some such crap. The card's inscription—"Thinking of you both. Love, Evelyn and Dad"—was written in someone else's handwriting.

"That was really nice of them," Maureen said.

"Yeah," I said. "Couple of sweethearts."

"Caelum, don't."

"Don't what?"

By way of an answer, she walked out of the room.

Insomnia-wise, she and I had been taking shifts all week. Neither of us could concentrate enough to read. That night, she lay in bed, staring at nothing while, lying next to her, I catnapped my way through the last innings of a Rockies game and *Walker, Texas Ranger*. She tapped me awake a little before eleven. "Hmmph? What?"

"Did you lock the doors before you came up?"

"Yeah."

"The second time, I mean? After you let Sophie out?"

"Yeah. . . . I'm pretty sure."

"Could you check?"

I sighed. Swung my feet to the floor and sat there. Got up, headed down. I tried not to think about it: her hiding inside that cabinet, listening to the gunfire, the kids wailing and pleading. Well, I was awake *now*, goddamnit. Up for my two-to-three-hour vigil.

I checked the front and backdoors, the door leading in from the garage. I thought about that note she'd left me. In the dark, on the inside of the cabinet. She'd worried no one would find it—that I'd never know she'd written me a good-bye. Maybe after all the investigators left and we could take back the school, I'd go up there, into the break room. Crawl inside that cabinet and sandpaper over it. Because she'd survived, right? She was upstairs. She was safe.

I went to the bottom of the stairs and called up. "All set!"

No response.

"Maureen?"

"I just took two more Tylenol PMs."

"Yeah? Okay then. Give 'em time to work. Be up in a few minutes."

Silence.

I stood at our front window for a while, rocking on the balls of my feet and staring out at the stillness. Asked myself: What are you afraid of?

That she won't come back. Be Maureen anymore.

But they said the symptoms would subside.

For *most* people. What if she's not one of them?

Relax. One day at a time.

Fuck you, one day at a time. Every day I'm walking on eggs, waiting for her to freak out. Going to kids' funerals, seeing the horror of it in their parents' faces. And every night, I'm up for the count, trying not think of what they would've done to her if they'd found her in there.

Satan wants *you to be overwhelmed by the evil and the fear.*

Yeah, and Santa wants me to leave milk and cookies by the fireplace. Shut up. Get fucked. I'm going to go watch TV.

The news was on: the investigation, their yearbook photos, workers assembling the stage for the next day's memorial. The big guys would be there: the governor, the Gores, Colin Powell. Thirty to forty thousand people in that movie theater parking lot? I couldn't even picture it. A pretty blond reporter at a highway rest stop was asking out-of-staters why they were making the pilgrimage. "We just want to be there for the families," a big guy in a fishing hat said. "Because we're *all* Columbine."

Yeah? That right, buddy? Any of *your* kids in a coffin? Is *your* wife flinching every time you move to touch her?

I'd exiled the unopened gift basket to the mudroom. Now I carried it to the kitchen, slit the cellophane with a steak knife, and reached in for the wine. Uncorked it, poured a juice glass full. Stood there in the moonlight, in my skivvies, and raised a toast to my father-in-law. *Cheers, you sick fuck. CEO child molester.* I downed the glass, poured a second. Carried it, and the bottle, and an almost-empty box of Cheez-Its back into the living room.

Drank, ate. Surfed past *Saturday Night Live*, the Bowflex guy, Steve McQueen in *Bullitt*. I licked my fingers and stuck them into the cheese dust at the bottom of the box. Sucked my fingertips, drank some more. . . . Maybe I'd go over there tomorrow, join the throng. Or stay home. Be with her. She sure as hell couldn't go—not with that size crowd. Over at Clement Park, she'd imagined snipers in the trees.

On MTV, black girls in thongs were shaking their booties behind a gold-toothed rapper. VH–1 was playing a video by that group Dylan's son was in. Handsome kid—must take after his mother. Bobby'd never been too pretty to begin with, and middle age hadn't improved the situation any. . . . Maybe I'd call Andy and Jen Kirby in the morning, see if they were going. Hitch a ride with them. Or not. Stay home. Watch it on TV if she wanted to.

I felt the memory of that marker pen in my hand. *Sweet Rachel, forgive us. We hadn't realized they were monsters.* . . .

I found an old Celtics-Lakers game on ESPN Classic. Okay, now we were talking. I turned the volume down to zero. Pushed the recliner back. Nineteen eighty-four or eighty-five, it looked like. Bird and Magic in their prime, all motion, no sound. I reached for the wine.

Scoreboard says 99 to 99, twenty-seven seconds left. Worthy gets it to Magic, who pump-fakes once, twice, then drives to the basket. Takes a gravity-defying leap and stuffs it, one-handed.

Balletic, I hear Francesca say. Close my eyes and see her, sitting next to me at Madison Square Garden. She's wearing that red sweater, the one that hugs her tits and bares her shoulders. . . .

Someone at the publishing house hadn't been able to use their Knicks tickets, and she'd bought them to surprise me. Knicks-Bulls. She'd never been to an NBA game before, or even a high school game. Not much hoop action at Miss Porter's School for Girls. "I thought I'd be bored, but I'm fascinated. Their movements are . . . *balletic.*" And I'd rolled my eyes and laughed. Leaned over and kissed her.

Near the beginning, this was. Winter of '84, when she was editing my novel and I was taking the 5:07 train down to Manhattan every Friday afternoon. Rushing from Grand Central over to her little apartment on Ninth Avenue. The first one. The one with the cockroaches and the waterbed. . . .

Four seconds left, 101 to 99. Parish passes to Bird, who trips, stumbles forward, shoots anyway. Swish. You forget how fucking unbelievable Bird was. Game goes into overtime.

Weird the way all that happened: Francesca and me. I'd started writing my novel the year Patti and I got married, and finished it eight years later—the year she left me to go to business school. "Move back here with Hennie and me," Lolly had said. "We can always use another hand and set another supper plate." It was like that kids' game, Red Light, where, if they see you moving forward, they send you back to the starting line. So I'd boxed up my stuff and moved back to my windowless bedroom with the cowboys-and-Indians bedspread. I didn't have a wife anymore, or an apartment. Didn't have a title for my novel, or a clue about why I'd written it, or how to get it published. So it just sat there in a box on the top of my bureau—the one I'd used as a kid. A nameless 457-page story that I didn't know what to do with. Was it any good? Could someone whose wife had left him because he was "too aloof" and "just not that interesting" write something anyone would *want* to read? I asked the dusty Magic Eight-Ball that still sat on the bookshelf in that second-floor bedroom I thought I had escaped forever. Shook it and tipped it over. The answer floated into view. *It is highly doubtful.*

And then? At school? In one of my C-level classes? This sullen, seedy kid, Michael Mull—a druggie, everyone said. His attendance had been spotty from the start, but then he'd stopped coming altogether. Days in a row, then weeks. One day, one of my talkers, Missy Gingras, rushes through her test as usual, comes up to my desk, and hands me her paper and a note: "Can I switch seats with the absent boy?" Now, I know why she wants to switch: because Michael Mull's desk is next to her girlfriend Joline's, and Joline's another yapper. So I shake my head, and Missy goes back to her seat and pouts.

But that note: I keep looking at it. "Can I switch seats with the absent boy?" There's a pad of late passes on my desk, and I rip one off and turn it over. Write: "The Absent Boy." Write it again, upper-case. "THE ABSENT BOY." Put the paper in my pocket. And that night, while I'm correcting those tests at the dining room table, Hennie sticks her head in the doorway. "Doing a load of laundry, Caelum. You got any darks?"

"Yeah. I'll go up and get them."

Upstairs, I bundle my clothes, check the pants pockets. In the khakis I've worn that day, I find the paper. I'd already forgotten about it. I flatten it out, place it on top of my manuscript. *The Absent Boy.* My novel's got a name.

The next week, on a field trip to New York, while my students are wandering the great halls of the Metropolitan Museum and sneaking out to the front steps to smoke, I get an idea. I find a phone booth just outside the rest rooms on the bottom floor, look up "publishers" in the phone book, and tear out the pages. I didn't know anything about publishing protocol or literary agents, but now I had three or four tissue-paper pages of addresses.

That weekend, I had the photocopy place make me six copies of *The Absent Boy.* Stuffed them into oversized envelopes and sent them off to the six publishers whose names I'd circled. No cover letters, no editors' names or return postage enclosed. Just my novel and an index card with my return address paper-clipped to page 1.

For the next few weeks, every time Lolly's phone rang, I suspected it might be a publisher. A month went by. Two months.

Turns out, Michael Mull was dead. Murdered. His body was discovered behind a shed out near Pachaug Pond, his skull smashed in with a rock. The morning it was in the paper, the vice principal came on the PA and led us in a ten-second "moment of silence" for Michael. The month before, a pretty senior girl—National Merit Scholar, Thanksgiving food drive coordinator, homecoming princess—had been killed in a car accident. There'd been a special assembly, a tree planting, a scholarship fund set up in her memory. The day of her funeral, the kids had been allowed to come in late without a note. But no one mourned for Michael Mull. "Who?" my homeroom kids buzzed. "What did he look like?"

I went to the wake, a sorry little gathering—ten or eleven people, counting the Ozarks-looking aunt and uncle he lived with, and me. "He *loved* this goddamned snake," the uncle told me, handing me a creepy Polaroid of Michael, shirtless, his torso emaciated, his boa constrictor draped around his neck like a winter scarf. "We gotta get rid of it, though. Her and me can't be running and buying mice all the time. You like snakes?"

At the six-month mark, three of the six copies I'd sent out had drifted back, one with a snotty Xeroxed note about how much money unsolicited manuscripts without SASEs cost publishers. SASEs? It took me a week and a magazine, *Writer's Digest*, to crack the code.

The police arrested the killer, a forty-year-old speed freak who claimed Michael had cheated him on a drug deal. *The Absent Boy* was about the abduction of a four-year-old boy, not the murder of a teenage druggie. My story and Michael Mull's story weren't alike at all. But with each passing month, each returned manuscript, the title took on deeper resonance for me. At the one year mark, I admitted to myself that the book was stillborn—as dead as Michael—and that I'd been an asshole to fantasize about ever being a published writer.

Then it was August 26, 1983. I'd spent the morning haying with Lolly, and had planned to spend the afternoon over at school, getting my classroom ready for opening day. But while Lolly, Hennie, and I were eating lunch, the doorbell rang. The divorce papers had arrived from Patti's lawyer. I never made it over to school. By midafternoon, I was still lying upstairs on my bed with that unopened package of legal papers sitting on my stomach. Thinking: Well, she was right. We'd gotten married too early and grown in different directions. I *was* aloof. I *was* boring. And in the middle of my pity party, Lolly called up the stairwell. "Caelum? Phone!"

It was Enid Markey, a senior editor at Simon & Schuster. Said she usually only read books that were represented by agents, but that one of their summer interns had been assigned the slush pile and had discovered *The Absent Boy*. The manuscript had made its way from office to office and had, the day before, landed on her desk.

"What's the slush pile?" I said. It was pretty much what I thought.

Enid said she'd read through the night, intrigued by the first chapter, enthralled by what came after. That was the word she used: enthralled. Introducing readers to a talented new writer was the part of her job she most enjoyed, she said. The book's flaws were entirely fixable. Simon & Schuster would be delighted to publish *The Absent Boy*. "I'm assigning you to a wonderful young associate editor, Francesca LaBarre. Arrived last year, summa cum laude from Bryn Mawr. She's brilliant!"

And she was. Beautiful, too. Not fat, but fleshy. Different from Patti in every other way, too: self-assured, temperamental, sexy. She signaled me that very first meeting, up there in her cramped little office on the twelfth floor. Pulled my chair next to hers so that we could go through the text together, and while she was making her points, asking her questions, our shoulders kept colliding. I'd go to turn a page, and she'd stop me. Put her hand on top of mine, her fingertips resting in the spaces between my knuckles. I mean, in terms of pheromones, they were going off like the Fourth of July. After our second meeting, she took me to lunch at a place just down the street from her apartment. "You want to come up?" she asked. . . . You always hear how, what men want is release and what women want is intimacy. Not Francesca. She preferred coming to cuddling. Made love the way she tackled text and the way she ate: with an urgent and ravenous appetite.

God, that one time? I get off the train at Grand Central, get over to her place. She buzzes me up, and I'm barely in the door before we're going at it. Her, with her skirt hiked up and her shoulder blades banging against the wall and me, with my pants down at my ankles and my sports jacket still on—the one I wore teaching that day—thrusting *in*to her, and *in*to her, and *in*to her. . . .

I popped a boner thinking about it.

And God, New York, man: that was part of it, too. Those art house movies she liked, the galleries and used bookstores. That little Italian restaurant on Mulberry Street with the big olive jars in the windows, and that same waiter we always had. What was his name? . . . Manhattan was like the antidote for Three Rivers, Francesca the antidote to

Patti, my high school sweetheart, my prim, inhibited Irish-Catholic wife who used to have to undress in the dark. Who'd had her first orgasm maybe two, three years into our marriage. When I was writing my novel, I'd hand Patti a new chapter to read, and she'd read it and hand it back to me, nervously. "It's good," she'd say.

"That's it? It's good."

"I work in a *bank*, Caelum. What do you *want* me to say?"

As opposed to Francesca, who understood the nuances of my story better than I did. Who could finesse a sentence, change a verb, and make a whole paragraph sing. She was as brilliant an editor as Enid had promised. Helped me make a much better book. And Jesus, the fringe benefits. . . .

It got so we could synchronize it. Get there together. She was the only one of the three of them that I could do that with. I told Alphonse Buzzi about it, and he said, "Oh, man, you gotta *marry* that." And I had. Met her the first of September, married her the first of February.

"Married? *Already?*" Lolly shouted into the phone. "Good God almighty, you work quick! You moving to New York, or is she moving here?"

"Neither one for now," I said.

Then Enid gets uterine cancer and joins the fucking Hemlock Society. Francesca gets a better offer at Random House. The new regime sweeps in, cancels my contract. "It's a fine book in many ways, Mr. Quirk," the new senior editor tells me. "It's just not a home run."

I'm sitting across from her, thinking I wish I could say it. Then I *do* say it. "You know, you got a pretty heavy mustache for a woman."

Francesca tried selling *The Absent Boy* at Random House, although how *hard* she tried I never really knew. She kept telling me I needed an agent, so I got an agent. The first time we ate lunch together, Lon said my writing read like a hybrid of poetry and prose, and that the ending of the novel, jaded as he was, had made him cry. His plan was to get two houses interested, have them fight it out in an auction situation. "The whores out in Hollywood are going to give you *blow jobs* to get ahold of this story." Then this Kevin Costner movie comes out, and it's about the abduction of a little boy. Goes belly-up at the box office. By the end of the second year, Lon wasn't even returning my phone calls.

"Take a leave of absence from teaching and start something new," Francesca advised. "Move in with me." Instead, I carried my galleys up to Lolly's attic and took a second job, teaching a lit course over at Oceanside Community College. Going into New York every weekend got old. Too many student papers to get through, too little of Francesca's attention when I did take the train down. And God forbid *she* should get on one. Get herself up to Connecticut on a Friday night and be with her husband. . . . Hey, it was a mismatch from the beginning. The foreign service diplomat's daughter and the son of a drunk. The weekend marriage. Wasn't going to work. She took her appetites elsewhere and claimed *I* was the problem. . . . *Emotional castrato*: she couldn't just insult me. Had to give it that finishing-school twist. Had to take her house key and scratch it onto my fucking computer monitor. . . . But it was good before it got bad. *Great* at the beginning. Weed and waterbed sex, that floor-to-ceiling mirror propped in the corner of her bedroom wall so we could watch ourselves. . . .

I took another sip of wine. Took matters into my own hand. Hey, why not? Expedient. Uncomplicated. Might even help me get some sleep. It wasn't like I could go upstairs and ask *her* for it. Not then, and probably not for quite a while. It was like she was radioactive or something. Like she was that scared little eleven-year-old over at her father's house. . . .

So I jacked a little faster, conjuring Francesca's breasts—the heft of them in my hands, those areolas dark as wine. I stroked to the rise and fall of her waterbed. Made my finger do that little flicking thing she'd do with her tongue. Thought about how she'd laugh as I came. Taste it. Welcome it. With my free hand, I groped for something, anything. Grabbed the Cheez-It box and let go in that. . . .

I cleared my throat, tucked myself back inside my boxers. What was that old Joni Mitchell lyric? "After the rush, when you come back down. . . ." Upstairs, the toilet flushed. Selfish prick, I thought. Absent Boy. . . .

Gualtiero: that was that waiter's name.

I sure as hell hoped she wasn't up there taking more Tylenol. I had to get her to a doctor. Get her some *real* sleeping pills, rather than screwing around with over-the-counter shit. I'd call Monday morning, get her an appointment. Maybe if she could start sleeping through the night again, I could, too. Shit, man, half of Arapahoe County must be taking sleeping pills.

I killed the last of the wine. Reclined my chair the rest of the way. The Lakers-Celtics game went into double overtime. . . .

I woke up at dawn. The dogs were sniffing my feet. The TV was still on: bass fishing now. I righted the recliner, got up. Stepped on the Cheez-It box. Collapsed and folded it as tight as it would go, then stuffed it into the garbage. With my entourage, I stumbled barefoot to the backdoor. The dogs rushed out, the cold air rushed in. If I wanted to find out who won that game, I'd have to do a freakin' Internet search. I had a bitch of a headache.

"*FORBID* YOU?" I SAID. "MAUREEN, when have I ever *forbidden* you from doing anything? I'm just making the point that, when we went over to Clement Park Wednesday night, the crowd freaked you out. And the thing at the church. You said being in that packed room made you nervous. Made your heart race."

"I was preoccupied about Velvet," she said. "Now I'll be able to focus."

"This crowd's going to be *a hundred* times bigger. That's all I'm saying. But *forbid* you? Come on, Mo. Get real."

She insisted she could handle it. She'd had a four-hour stretch of uninterrupted sleep, she said, and was feeling better. More in control.

She'd take *comfort* in the anonymity of a big crowd. Nobody would know where she'd been during the shootings. What she'd seen and heard. This wouldn't be anything like that church meeting, where she'd been afraid they were going to call on her and make her speak.

"Okay," I said. "We'll give it a try."

We left the house an hour before the program was scheduled to start, but they'd blocked off several of the streets and I had to park almost a mile away from Bowles Crossing, where the service was. The rain began when we were halfway there. I had Maureen get under the awning of a coffee shop. "Go inside and get a coffee if you get cold," I said. I jogged back to the car, got my big umbrella, and made it back in under fifteen minutes.

She wasn't out there. Wasn't inside either. I ran down to the cross street. No sign of her. With my heart pounding, I went back inside the coffee shop. Approached the skinny, aproned guy behind the counter. "You see a woman come in here? Jean jacket and a turquoise skirt? Reddish-brown hair?"

"She's in the back with Andrea. She came in here and she was like whimpering or something. And then she comes behind the counter, starts opening the cabinet doors like she's looking for something. And we're like, 'What's the matter, lady? What's wrong with you?'"

She was seated at a tiny table in a room jam-packed with boxes. There was a steaming, oversized cup of coffee on the table. A punk-rock-looking woman, early twenties, was holding Mo's hand, stroking it.

"Hey?" I said.

Mo looked up at me. Didn't smile.

"We didn't know whether to call nine-one-one or not," the woman said.

"No, we're good," I said. "Thanks for your concern. What do we owe you for the coffee?"

She shook her head. Repositioned herself in the doorway. "Ma'am, do you want to go with this gentleman? Or would you rather stay here and have us call someone?"

"Hey, I'm her *husband*," I said.

She looked me in the eye, nostrils flaring. "I volunteer at a women's shelter. I know a lot about husbands."

We stood there, glaring at each other. "Not that it's any of your business," I said. "But this isn't about me. It's about Columbine High School."

"Oh," she said. She dropped her defensive stance and stood aside.

We walked out front, ignoring the stares as best we could. Outside, I started her in the direction of our car. "No!" she said, pulling away. She'd panicked, but she was okay now. She was going to the memorial service. "Where *were* you?" she demanded.

"Maureen, you know where I was. I went to get the umbrella. I got back here as fast as I could."

A few hundred silent steps later, she told me what had happened. Two teenage boys—one tall, the other short—had sauntered past the coffee shop, laughing and talking loudly. "I got confused," she said. "I thought they were alive again. I thought I was back in the library."

"Oh, Mo," I said. "Oh, Jesus, Mo."

———

HUDDLED UNDER UMBRELLAS AND JACKET hoods, the bereaved and the curious filled the three-acre parking lot. The overflow crowd was out in the street, on the rooftops of nearby stores and restaurants. Seventy thousand, the paper said the next day—twice what they'd expected. As Maureen and I approached the periphery, music was playing—guitars, undecipherable lyrics. Silver and blue balloons, hundreds of them, lifted into the drizzly sky.

We were way the hell away from the stage, but they'd set up big video screens. Denver's archbishop assured us that love was stronger than death. The rabbi from Beth Shalom told us our grief should in-

spire us to greater awareness of the humanity in all. All? I wondered.
Even those two?

As the governor read the names of the victims, a fluttering white
dove was released for each. Eric's and Dylan's names were omit-
ted. No doves for them. Watching one of those birds soar on the big
screen sent me back to Three Rivers—to that stained glass window
at St. Anthony's. The Holy Trinity, the three-in-one: I'd stare at
them every Sunday when I was a kid, trying to figure it out. God the
Father and God the Son I could understand, no problem. But God the
Holy Ghost? A white bird with a halo? My friend Jimmy Jacobson
had a bird—a cockatiel—and it'd crap all over the bottom of its cage.
Latch on to your finger with its toenail beak, and it would *hurt*. "Is it
a bird or is it a ghost?" I'd ask my mother.

"God is a mystery," she'd say. As if *that* was a satisfactory answer.

Amy Grant sang a Christian song. Billy Graham's son said a prayer.
Al Gore approached the podium, looking somber and stately. "What
say we into the open muzzle of this tragedy, cocked and aimed at our
hearts?" he asked. The answer to that question shaped the rest of his
remarks, but I can't remember what he said.

Jack Eams, a coach and assistant principal, was one of the last speakers to be introduced. He'd played pro football for a few seasons back
in the sixties—the Vikings, if I remembered right. A silver-haired
bulldog in a tan suit, he approached the podium, gripped it on either
side, and leaned into the mic. "Raise your hand if you go to Columbine High," he said. He scanned the crowd, nodding at the waving
hands. "I want to talk to *you* kids specifically, okay? Remind you that
what happened last Tuesday does not define who we are, okay?" His
delivery seemed out of sync with the rest of the service—more half-
time pep talk than tribute. "Because Columbine's not about hatred,
okay? Columbine's about love. Columbine *is* love. And I want you to
repeat those words after me, and I want everyone else here today to
say them along with you. Okay? You ready? Columbine is love."

"Columbine is love," the crowd murmured.

"Louder! Columbine is love!"

"Columbine is love." I couldn't say it. Neither could Maureen.

"I can't hear you! Columbine is love!"

"Columbine is love!"

"This is total bullshit," someone near us said.

"Yeah," another voice agreed. "When the white hats spit on me in the hallway, I can really feel the love."

I turned around to see a quartet of Goth-looking kids—three skinny boys and a fat girl with eggplant-purple hair and fingernails. The kid with the goatee said, "How about when that Snapple bottle hit me in the face and Eams goes, 'Wear different clothes and they won't target you'? And I'm like, 'Yeah, but how come the jocks *get* to target people?'"

"Because they're the crown princes of Columbine!" the girl trilled, in mock adulation.

"Hey!" a beefy-faced guy near us said. "Would you kids mind shutting your mouths and showing a little respect?"

Maureen turned and faced him. "They're right, though," she said. "The APs look the other way at the bullying. You know what a 'twister' is? When they pinch your skin between their fingers and give it a twist. Makes a nasty little contusion. You know what 'bowling' is? They pour baby oil on the floor, then grab some poor freshman and send him flying down the corridor. They shoved one boy so hard, he fell and broke his wrist."

"Yeah, and how do you know all this?" the guy said.

"Because I'm a school nurse."

"Yeah? Well, my kid graduated from Columbine. Played football, wrestled, and he threw the shotput. And he never bullied anybody."

"As far as *you* know," Mo retorted. When I glanced over at the Goth kids, I saw their backs retreating into the crowd.

"Hey, Maureen?" I said. "This isn't really the time to—"

Mo turned to the guy's wife. "They bully the girls, too. Block their path when they're trying to get to class. Slam them against the lock-

ers if they have the nerve to talk back. And they get away with it."
She waved a hand at Eams's face on the big screen. "I've been to him
about the injuries. I've been to all of the APs, and I guess I should
have kept going. Because maybe if they'd bothered to *address* the bullying, instead of—"

She was drowned out by the roar of the F–16 fighter jets—four of
them, flying in formation above us to honor the dead. Frightened by
the noise, Maureen positioned her body against mine. She was trembling badly. "I need to go now," she said.

Neither of us said anything on the walk back to the car, and when
we got near that coffee shop, we crossed the street and walked on the
other side.

Back in our driveway, I cut the engine and turned to her. "Can I
say something?" I asked. She looked at me. Waited.

"That 'Columbine is love' stuff? That's a stretch, granted. But the
equation's a little more complicated than what you were saying back
there. Lots of high school kids get bullied, but they don't bring guns
and bombs to school and start wasting everyone."

"So we're all exonerated, Caelum? Gee, that's convenient." She
got out of the car. Slammed the door. I sat there, watching her jam her
key at our front door lock until she got in. Sat there, thinking about
that time Rhonda Baxter had had me read Klebold's short story—the
one where the mysterious assassin in the black coat murders "jocks
and college preps" as they leave a bar. A lot of the boys write this
stuff, I'd told Rhonda. Testosterone, too many video games. Nothing
that getting a girlfriend wouldn't cure.

THERE WERE FOUR FUNERALS ON Monday, three on
Tuesday, one each on Wednesday and Thursday. The pastor at Grace
Presbyterian told us it was typical that Danny Rohrbough had held
the door open for others to escape when the shooting began. He
might have lived if he'd been more selfish, but that was Danny for

you. The youth minister at West Bowles Community told us there'd been a wedding in heaven; Christ was the groom, Cassie Bernal the bride. Corey DePooter's tribute video ended with the words, "Gone fishing."

At St. Frances Cabrini, Father Leone asked Matt Kechter's teammates to stand, and when they did, he turned to the victim's younger brother. "Adam, look at Matt's football team over there. These guys are your big brothers. In the coming days and weeks, they will be there for you." I spotted the red-haired boy—the one who'd caused the outburst at the grief counseling meeting. He looked over at Matt's little brother. Nodded. Gave him a thumbs-up.

Dave Sanders's funeral was both the hardest and the least hard to attend. I'd known Dave better than I'd known any of the kids, and differently. He was a colleague, a contemporary. But Dave had lived three times as long as those kids. He'd had forty-seven years to make his mark, learn from his mistakes. A dozen or more people approached that podium at Trinity Christian to speak about Dave: thank him for his teaching, his coaching, his having been like a second father, his bravery that day. At the end, we all passed by his open casket. I was glad the family'd decided to bury him in his orange basketball tie, his good luck "game day" tie—the one we used to tease him about.

Isaiah Shoels's funeral was the last, and one of the biggest. They'd dressed Isaiah in the cap and gown he would have worn in May and laid him to rest with gospel music, blue-and-white balloons, and calls to end racism. "I was ten years old when my father was gunned down by senseless violence," Martin Luther King III told the five hundred or more of us who had come. "There is still something gravely wrong with our nation when two young men who worshipped Adolf Hitler go on a killing spree on his birthday."

When I got home from Isaiah's service, there was a car parked in front of the house—a silvery blue Mercedes. Couldn't be local detectives. Did FBI agents drive cars like this? Then, fuck, I realized who it was. I walked around back and came in through the garage, where Sophie and Chet had been exiled. The Barracuda was afraid of dogs.

There was a bouquet on the kitchen counter, a stack of drawings, a note in a kid's deliberate cursive. "Dear Aunt Maureen, I heard you were sad. I hope these pictures make you happy! I LOVE You!!! Love, Amber." When we'd first moved out there, Mo and her niece had hit it off, but Cheryl, the half sister, had withheld Amber—had decreed she'd be much too shy to stay overnight at our place, or for us to take her anywhere. She was four then, nine now. Big-time into glitter, from the looks of it. Everything in her drawings sparkled: the princesses' crowns, the mermaids' bras and fishtails, the dragonfly's wings, the tips of the praying mantis's antennae.

Their voices were in the living room. "Of course, it's entirely up to you," Evelyn was saying. "But I think it would be an *important* interview."

I stood in the doorway, unnoticed. Maureen was slumped on the sofa, clutching a pillow. She looked close to tears. "What interview?" I asked.

"Well, look who's here!" Arthur said, as if it was a big surprise that I'd shown up at my own house. He stood, walked toward me, pumped my hand like we were pals. "Long time no see."

Evelyn approached, too. Took my hands in hers and offered her cheek for kissing. "Maureen says you were at one of the children's funerals." She was whispering, like it was a secret. "How was it?"

"Brutal," I said. "They've all been brutal. What interview?"

"Oh. Well, Todd Purvis, the new coanchor on *Good Morning, Denver*, is a client of mine. I was telling him about Maureen's terrible ordeal, and he wanted me to ask her if she'd consider—"

"No," I said.

She smiled patiently. "Well, Caelum, if you'd let me finish."

I turned to Mo. "You're not interested in this, are you?" She looked down at the rug and shook her head.

But we didn't call Evelyn the Barracuda for nothing. "I just want to assure you both, before Maureen makes her decision, that Todd is a serious journalist. I never would have broached the subject otherwise. He's worked at CNN, CBS News. He started out as a researcher for MacNeil/Lehrer while he was still a student at Columbia."

"His résumé's not the point," I said. "She's not interested."

"It wouldn't have to be this week. Would it, darling?" Arthur asked.

"No, of course not. It could be next week, the week after. Whenever Maureen felt she was ready." She took a seat beside Mo. Took her hand. "And Todd said they could come out and tape it here, rather than at the studio, if that was more comfortable for you. He's really a wonderful man, Maureen. Very smart, very sensitive."

"And an exclusive like this would put him on the map in a new market, right?" I said. "So that'd be a feather in *your* cap. "

We sat there, looking at each other. "Ouch," she said.

Mo turned to her father. "What do you think, Daddy?"

Shit! Don't weaken, Mo. Screw these jackals.

Arthur smiled, stood up. "Well, sweetheart, I think you should listen to what this Purvis fellow has to say, and then do whatever you decide is best. And I also think I'd like a drink. Caelum, how are you fixed for scotch?" And with that, he walked past me and into the kitchen.

I poured us each a drink from my special-occasion bottle of Glenlivet. Mumbled some thanks for that fancy basket they'd sent. "So," he said. "Now that we're out of earshot, how is she?"

"Stricken," I said.

"Well, that's to be expected. It only happened a week ago."

"Nine days ago," I said.

He nodded. "Hell of a thing that you were back East, burying your relative. Uncle, was it?"

"Aunt."

"And then you have to rush back here to all this."

"Not knowing if she was alive or dead," I said. "That was the hard part." I took a sip of scotch. "In a way, she's neither."

He cocked his head. We looked each other in the eye.

"It's like, what she went through . . . and hey, I can't even *fathom* all she went through. I don't even *want* to go there, you know? But it's like . . . like that day stranded her on this . . . this small, lonely island." What was I doing? Why was I trusting him? "And I can see her, you know? I can call to her. But I can't reach her. Can't rescue her because . . . because the water between us is thick with sharks. Thick with the blood of those kids."

For the next few seconds, we held each other's gaze, and I thought, He *gets* it—Arthur, of all people. But when he opened his mouth, it was to suggest I was being, maybe, a little melodramatic. "I know my daughter, and she has an inner strength that will serve her," he assured me. "Just as it has during other difficult times in her life."

"Such as?" I said. Go ahead, I thought. Admit what you did.

"Well, when she and her sailor split up. And of course, they'd accrued all that debt on top of it. That complicated matters. But you know how difficult divorce is, right? Weren't you divorced?"

"Twice," I said.

He nodded. We sipped our scotches. On the other side of the door, the dogs were whimpering and scratching to be let back in.

"She lost her way in high school for a while," he said. "Made some bad choices, did some things she shouldn't have. But she came to her senses. Entered that nursing program at the university and straightened herself out. When she graduated, she got one of the nursing school's biggest awards."

"What about when you and her mother split up?" I said. "That was another tough time for her, wasn't it?"

"Patricia and I saved our acrimony for the lawyers' meetings," he said. "We spared Maureen that."

"That's not how she remembers it," I said. "The separation. Those weekends at your place. She was what? Eleven? Sixth grade?"

"Seventh," he said.

"No, sixth. According to her. She's told me about those weekends."

He looked away, then looked back. Watched me over the rim of his glass as he sipped his drink. "Well, that's ancient history," he said. "But my point is, Maureen's a strong person. A *resilient* person. She'll land on her feet." He touched the bottle. "May I?"

"Be my guest."

He poured himself two or three fingers more—with a bit of a tremor in his hand, I noticed. I took some small, cheap satisfaction in that. That's right, you son of a bitch. I know your dirty little secret, and it's not necessarily safe with me. I smiled. He smiled, sipped. It seemed like a good time to negotiate.

"Tell your wife to back off about that interview," I said. "Because there's no way in hell I'm going to let her get exploited like that."

"You think that's the motivation, do you?"

"I think profit's the motivation, and Maureen's the means to an end."

He was still smiling. "That's pretty harsh, isn't it? I didn't realize you were such a cynic." He reached inside his sports coat and pulled out a brochure. Handed it to me. I was staring at Mickey and Minnie Mouse in sailing garb.

"Disney cruise?" I said.

"It was Cheryl's idea, actually. You've met our daughter Cheryl, haven't you?" I shook my head. "Evelyn and I wanted to treat you and Maureen to a getaway of some kind—an escape from all this ugliness. But we were thinking more along the lines of plane tickets to London or Paris. Then Cheryl suggested this: after the terrible ordeal Maureen's been through, a voyage back to innocence. She and Barry took their little one on this cruise, and they had a ball. Stage shows, snorkeling. And I want you to know, we're covering everything, including your flights to and from port. Time-wise, it's open-ended. You just call our travel agent when you're ready. Misty, her name is. Her card's stapled to the inside of the pocket. She'll book everything, whenever you give her the word. And I've told her to get you an out-side cabin. They cost a little more, but they have portholes. Reminds you you're on a ship, not at a hotel."

"Arthur, how can you not understand?"

"Understand what?"

"What happened to your daughter is a lot worse than a divorce. Or a big MasterCard bill. It's not something Mickey Mouse can fix."

And how the fuck can you be mourning her innocence, after what you did? I was a couple more sips of scotch away from saying it, instead of just thinking it. And once I said it—once it was out on the table—I might clock the son of a bitch. Pick up that scotch bottle and use it on him. I could feel my engines revving.

So instead, I went to the door and opened it. The dogs bounded in, rushed past us and into the living room. Evelyn let out a satisfying little shriek. Five minutes later, they were in their Mercedes and on their way.

I taped Amber's pictures to the door of our refrigerator. Made us cheese omelets for supper.

"Thanks, Cae," Mo said.

"Yeah, I'm a whiz with eggs, aren't I?"

"I mean, for not letting her push me into doing that interview."

"No problem," I said. I showed her the Disney cruise brochure.

She read through it, shaking her head. "They'd probably have to straitjacket me by the second day. Put me in a padded cabin."

"Yeah, and all the psych aides would be Disney characters." I got up to clear the table. Stopped to look at her. "Hey," I said.

"What?"

"You smiled."

Later, undressing for bed, I noticed glitter on the tops of my shoes. Bent down to brush it off, then stopped. Left it there. When I closed my eyes, I saw Velvet Hoon—that glittery eye shadow she'd wear sometimes, the sparkles in her blue crew cut. Velvet was long gone from Littleton by now, I figured. Maybe she was the smart one.

⤛ *chapter twelve* ⤜

THE YEAR MAUREEN AND I started at Columbine was also the year that an extensive remodeling of the school was completed. The sunlit commons area was new, and directly above it, the library and media center. To accommodate the expansion, construction workers had bulldozed the existing student parking lot, lowering it by eight feet. But rather than truck away the excavated earth, they'd mounded it behind the school, creating what the kids soon dubbed "Rebel Hill." That first year, Andy Kirby and I made the mound part of the training course for our cross-country kids. It was steep enough to sled down in winter, and private enough on its far side for kids to toke up or make out. From the crest, you could see all the way to Boulder. In the aftermath of the killings, mourners trudged to the top of Rebel Hill to visit the crosses.

Maureen saw three doctors that first month. Dr. Strickland, a pretty, young M.D. at the open-on-weekends clinic, was sympathetic when Mo discussed her anxiety about going back to work. But the waiting room was full, and the clinic was "down a doc," as Dr. Strickland put it.

"How are you sleeping?" she asked.

Mo told her she couldn't get more than two or three hours at a time.

"Do you *have* to finish the school year? Is it a contractual thing?"

Mo gave me the look: *you* answer her. "We both feel it's better if she tries to confront her fears instead of giving in to them," I said. The doctor's eyes jumped back and forth between us.

There was a soft knock, a nurse in the doorway. "I've got a broken nose in room D," she said. "Hemorrhaging pretty badly."

Dr. Strickland said she'd be right there. She scrawled two prescriptions for Maureen: Restoril for sleep—one at bedtime, a second if she woke up in the middle of the night—and Xanax to "take the edge off" during the day. Ten tablets of each. "To tide you over until you see your regular doctor," she said.

It was Brian Anderson, a junior at Columbine, who'd contacted Greg Zanis about the crosses. Zanis, a carpenter from Illinois, had made it his mission to build and plant crucifixes to commemorate the lives of murder victims. Whether by fate or accident or the hand of God, Brian Anderson had been spared twice on the morning of the murders—first at the west entryway when Eric Harris fired at him and Patti Nielson, the teacher on hall duty, and minutes later in the library, where Brian and Patti, both wounded by shrapnel, had run for safety. Zanis promised Brian he'd come. A few days later, he and his son drove the sixteen hours to Littleton. Brian was waiting for them on Rebel Hill. Without fanfare or media attention, they erected the crosses—fifteen of them, not thirteen. Then Zanis and his boy got back in their truck and headed home.

Maureen's Xanax ran out on day three of her five-day supply, but luckily, Dr. Quinones had a cancellation. "At your checkup last February, you weighed a hundred and ten," he noted. "That's an ideal weight for you, Maureen. I'm concerned that you're down to ninety-six."

"She won't eat," I said.

"I *can't* eat, okay?" Mo snapped. "I'm nauseous all the time. And it doesn't help that you're always nagging me about eating."

Dr. Quinones asked her if she'd gotten her period that month.

"I'm not pregnant, if that's what you mean," she scoffed.

He shuffled through the papers in Mo's folder. "Oh, yes, yes. Tubal ligation. I'd forgotten. So what do you feel is making you nauseous?"

"I don't know. Living?"

Quinones's gaze turned from Mo to me, then back again. He sat down beside her, lowered his voice. "Are you having thoughts about suicide?"

She shook her head.

"Feeling depressed?"

"Afraid," she said. "I'm always afraid."

I told Quinones she was nervous about returning to school. "I keep trying to tell her it'll be good for her, you know? See the kids. Focus on the day-to-day stuff."

"Sixteen days left to go, is it?" the doctor asked. The Quinoneses had twins at Columbine—sophomores, a boy and a girl. They were both in my honors class.

"Eighteen," I said. "But Chatfield's going to be a whole different environment. It's not like she's going to have to walk back into—"

"Yesterday?" she blurted. "We were just driving *past* Chatfield, and I had a flashback."

"A short one, though," I said. "Less than a minute, and she was back."

"Right, Caelum, and for the rest of the day, I was scared to death that I was going to get another one." She turned to the doctor. "He doesn't realize how they wipe me out."

"Yes I do, Mo. Sure I do."

"We had to go to the superintendent's office?" she said. "To get our pictures taken for the security badges they're making us wear. And first of all, I was a nervous wreck because it was so crowded. Then everyone kept coming up to me, asking about it. And I got so flustered. I couldn't remember anyone's name—people I've worked with for years now—and I kept saying, 'I'm sorry. I just can't talk about it.' And they kept talking anyway. And I wanted to scream, 'Shut up! Just shut up!'"

"I tried to run interference for her," I said. "But, you know. Word's gotten out about where she was. People mean well, but—"

"And then in line? For the ID pictures? That flash kept going off, and it was making me nervous. I can't explain it, but I was afraid to have my picture taken—have that thing flash in my face. And I had to keep leaving the line and rushing to the rest room because I thought I was going to vomit."

"Did you?" Quinones asked.

"No. I got a splitting headache, though. It lasted for the rest of the day."

"But, Doc," I said. "Don't you think if she confronts it—gets through those first couple of days at Chatfield—she'll be better off in the long run? Not have it hanging over her all summer?"

Instead of answering me, Quinones asked if I wouldn't mind stepping out to the waiting room so that he could chat one-to-one with Maureen. It took me back a little. What did he have to tell her that he couldn't say in front of me? "What do you think, Mo?" I said. "Would you prefer I stay?"

She shook her head.

So I left. Sat out with the stale *Newsweek*s and *Entertainment Weekly*s for a good fifteen minutes, and when finally I was called in from exile, Quinones told me that Maureen had decided to take a leave of absence for the remainder of the school year. He endorsed that decision, he said, and would write the school board a letter that it was medically advisable. He said Maureen also needed me to know that, although she certainly appreciated all I was doing to help her recover, she sometimes found my efforts and my advice overwhelming.

When I looked over at her, she looked down. Spoke to her fidgeting hands. "You hover," she said.

"Hover?"

"You don't need to follow me around from room to room, okay? Ask me twenty times an hour if there's anything you can get for me. Because there's nothing you could go and get me that's going to make it go away."

"I know that, Mo. All I'm trying to do is—"

"And I don't need you to keep telling me that going back to work will be good for me." Here, she finally did look at me. "Because you don't know what's good for me any more than I do, Caelum. So stop acting like you've read the instructional manual on what I need." I suddenly noticed the box of tissues on her lap. She must have been crying before, but now she was dry-eyed and pissed off. Her chest was heaving like she was short of breath.

Apropos of nothing, I told the doctor I'd been in Connecticut during the shootings. It came out like a confession. *Bless me, Doctor, for I have sinned.*

He said something about crises always coming at inconvenient times.

"And in my own defense?" I said. "Yesterday? When we were grocery shopping? We couldn't find the bread crumbs, okay? Thought maybe we'd already passed them. So I backtracked. Left her alone for maybe three or four minutes at the most. And when I got back to her, she was freaking out."

"Freaking out how?" Quinones asked.

"Crying, muttering. This kid stocking shelves is just standing there, staring at her. So I get her calmed down, right? And when I do, she starts reaming me out for leaving her alone. And now I hear she doesn't want me to *hover?*" When I looked over at her, I realized, suddenly, how hollow-cheeked she'd gotten. How gray she looked. "She's right, though," I said. "There *is* no step-by-step to follow with something like this. Because what happened to her was so . . ." Defeat overtook my defensiveness. I was suddenly so tired. "Maureen," I said. "What you went through overwhelms me. And I'm so, so sorry it happened to you. And that I wasn't there to . . . and all I want . . . all

I'm trying to do—and hey, I guess I'm doing a lousy job of it—but Mo, I'm just trying to be part of the solution, you know? Not part of the problem."

She nodded. Didn't look at me. Didn't smile.

Quinones reached over and cupped my shoulder. "You *are* part of the solution, Caelum. An important part. She just needs a little more breathing room. And a little more time to heal before she tries going back to work."

He handed her a slip of paper on which he'd written the name and number of a psychiatrist he recommended, Dr. Sandra Cid. "She and I were in med school together," he said. "I think she can help you. Will you call her?"

Mo said she would.

"And in the meantime, I want you to begin to take charge, like we talked about. Plenty of rest. A little bit of exercise and fresh air to fight the lassitude." He produced a sample four-pack of Boost. "And two cans of this a day, minimum. In *addition* to your meals, not instead of them. Agreed?"

She nodded.

"Okay, then. Good. Are we done?"

"What about my prescriptions?" Maureen said.

"Oh, right. We were going to get back to that, weren't we? You feel it's helped you?"

She nodded. "I'm sleeping better with the Restoril. Not great, but better. And the Xanax *really* helps."

"All right, then. Dr. Cid may want to try you on something else after she's assessed things, but we can stay with these for the time being. The sleep medication's fine. And the Xanax: you've been taking two a day?" Three a day, I thought to myself, but I kept my mouth shut. "Why don't I write you scripts for thirty of each, and we'll see where we are in two weeks? Make an appointment with Blanca on the way out." He stood, opened the door for us. "Hang in there, you two. And Maureen? You're a very brave woman."

Skip the platitudes, I wanted to say. Instead, I thanked him, pumped his hand. When he went to hug Maureen, she took a backward step.

Blanca Quinones was the doctor's wife as well as his receptionist. I asked her how the kids were doing. "Catalina's chafing at the bit to go back, be with her friends," she said. "Miss Social Butterfly. But she thinks it's an outrage they have to finish the year at Chatfield, their biggest sports rival."

"Yea rah rah," Maureen mumbled. She released a weird little laugh.

"How about Clemente?" I said. Catalina was your classic over-achiever; her brother was quieter, more of a loner.

"Clemente doesn't say much. Stays up in his room and reads, plays his video games. I think he's anxious about going back. Last couple days, he's been asking me about home-schooling."

"Where were they?" I asked. We all did that now: spoke in short-hand about April the twentieth.

"Catalina was in gym, so she got right out. Clemente was in biol-ogy. Two doors down from where Mr. Sanders was. Thank God he didn't have to see that. He kept calling me, so I knew he was okay. Thank God for cell phones. I tell you, though. It wasn't until I saw him for myself, sitting on that stage over at Leawood School . . ." Her eyes filled with tears. "I'm sorry. I still get so emotional."

Maureen sighed impatiently. "Is there a co-pay for today?" she said.

We stopped at the pharmacy on the way home. I went in; she stayed slumped in the car with the doors locked. I got her prescription, a case of Boost. At the register, there was a display of Panda licorice, the kind she likes. You don't see it that many places, so I thought I'd surprise her. But back in the car, she made no mention of it. Fished through the bag and found the Xanax. Popped the cap, placed one on her tongue, and swallowed. "Aren't you supposed to take those one in the morning, one at night?" I said.

"So?" she said.

"So it's two in the afternoon. They're not M&Ms."

"This is just what I mean by hovering."

NEXT MORNING, THE HEADLINE IN the *Rocky Mountain News* said, "Dad Cuts Down Killers' Crosses." The reporters had caught up with Zanis, the press-shy carpenter. He said he'd included Dylan and Eric in his tribute because they'd had family, too—parents who suffered and grieved for *their* lost children, no matter the terrible circumstances. But Danny Rohrbough's dad wasn't having it. With his slain son's grandfather and stepfather, he'd climbed Rebel Hill, knocked down the killers' crosses, and carried them away. "Took them to a better place," was the way he'd put it.

"You see this?" I asked her, holding up the article.

She squinted at it. Walked out of the kitchen and back upstairs. She'd had two or three bites of an English muffin, a little juice, and, at best, a third of a can of Boost. The afternoon before, she'd called Dr. Cid and gotten her answering service. "No, no message," I'd heard her say.

I read the rest of the article. Sat there, wondering if the Harrises and the Klebolds had read it, too. Bad as it was for the other parents, it had to be even more of a nightmare, in some ways, for them.

Oh, yeah? Then maybe they should have paid more attention to what their kids were up to. There had to be all kinds of warning signs.

But didn't Zanis have a point? Weren't Eric and Dylan victims, too?

Of?

Mental illness? Video games? Who knew? And let's face it, we *did* sometimes look away from the bullying. Let it go when the athletes cut the cafeteria line. Gave the wiseguys in the hallway a dirty look but kept going. You've got to choose your battles, I used to tell myself. You're a teacher, not a security guard. But maybe if . . .

Bullshit. You said it yourself: kids get picked on all the time. But most of them don't bring shotguns and propane bombs to school.

I don't know. Maybe it was inevitable. Maybe it all comes down to
. . . what'd he call it? That guy on the plane? Sensitive dependence
on initial conditions?

Oh, this ought to be good. Go on.

I don't know. But maybe . . . if a butterfly's wings can perturb the
air and trigger a tornado half a world away, then maybe a spanking, or
some small slight by a kindergarten teacher, or something a grandpar-
ent did could set something in motion. Travel through time and . . .

And what?

Trigger a massacre.

*So they're off the hook then? Harris and Klebold and their parents? It
was all just inevitable? It was chaos's fault? That's total bullshit. And if
I remember right, didn't that jerk on the plane claim that chaos bred life?
Tell that to the parents of those kids they killed. Tell it to Dave Sanders's
widow. Hey, tell it to her up there! Because if she never gets over this, then
they've taken her life, too. Haven't they? So maybe, instead of making excuses for them, you should have grabbed a hammer and marched up Rebel
Hill. Taken a few swings at those goddamned crosses yourself. It's not like
there isn't precedent. Not like you haven't swung a hammer before.*

It was a pipe wrench.

*So what? Same difference. Wouldn't it have felt good to destroy those
things? Wouldn't it have felt like you were doing some*thing?

I got up from the table. Brought the newspaper into the study and
put it on the pile. Newspapers, magazine articles, computer printouts:
I wasn't sure why I was saving everything. Maybe some day down
the line, I'd go through it all and it would make sense. Maybe not.
Maybe I should take it all outside and put a match to it. Watch all
those pictures and words go up in flame.

I went upstairs. She was taking a bath. Her Xanax was on her nightstand. I popped the lid, spilled the tablets onto my palm. Twenty-
six. Don't dog her, I reminded myself. Don't mention the pills, or
the Boost, or this Dr. Cid. Let her be in charge of it. Let her come
around.

THE NIGHT BEFORE SCHOOL RESUMED, I spent more hours awake than asleep. Although I'd been thousands of miles away on the morning of the murders, I could, during that long night, "see" the unfolding events as if, in my head, a camera had captured the morning like grainy surveillance video. Spliced together from articles and rumors, from TV reports and the things Maureen had said, it played soundlessly, over and over, and I tossed and turned and watched in dread. . . .

Eric's gray Honda pulls in, comes to a stop in the juniors' parking lot. Dylan's old black BMW follows, proceeds to the west-side senior lot. Their cars flank the front and side entrances to the cafeteria. Their long black trench coats hide the shoulder straps they've cinched to themselves, their ammunition belts and holstered firearms. Each hefts a duffel bag that holds one of the propane bombs they've timed to explode during "A" lunch. I can read the sense of purpose on their faces. The wait is almost over. They're about to answer the hundreds of injustices they've suffered in silence. People are going to be sorry they fucked with them. . . . Inside, Maureen and Velvet leave the clinic, move down the corridor toward the commons, climb the stairs to the library. . . . Eric and Dylan wait at the top of the outside stairs. They're ready. Psyched to shoot survivors as they flee the cafeteria explosions. But something's wrong. Nothing explodes. No one's fleeing. Eric stares at Rachel Scott and Richard Castaldo, eating their lunch on the grassy bank near the stairs. He raises his rifle. . . . In the caf, Dave Sanders directs kids away from the windows, herds them up the stairs to the library hallway. . . . In the upper west hallway, Brian Anderson runs toward the double glass exit doors. Patti Nielson is there, frowning at the two boys outside at the top of the stairs. They're wearing costumes of some kind—one's in a long black trench coat, the other is dressed like a militiaman. Fed up with these silly senior pranks, she moves to the door to tell them to knock it off. Eric sees Patti, smiles, takes aim. Glass and metal fly around her and Brian. . . . Outside, near the west entrance, Eric

*spots the patrol car, lights flashing, in the lot below. From inside the shat-
tered doorway, he aims, fires. The officer fires back. Rachel Scott is dead,
Richard Castaldo badly wounded. Danny Rohrbough lies facedown at the
base of the stairs. Eric and Dylan enter the building. . . .*

My "tape" stopped there. Rewound. *Eric arrives in the parking lot.
Dylan follows. . . .* My mind wouldn't let me see them shoot Dave
Sanders, or the kids in the library, or Maureen, on her hands and
knees, crawling inside that cabinet.

In the morning, I filled the sink bowl with cold water. Stuck my
face in. Came up for air. Bags under my bloodshot eyes, a twitch in
my left eyelid: my face was wearing what a tough night it had been.
Later, I shaved. Gelled my hair a little. My hands shook when I tried
to get the Visine in. Visine tears dribbled down my cheeks instead of
landing where they were supposed to. Maureen walked in, her hair
askew. It was past noon, and she was still in her pajamas. She'd spent
the morning watching some old black-and-white Bette Davis movie
on TV. Staring at it, anyway. When I'd asked her what it was about,
she couldn't tell me.

"Good luck," she said.

"Thanks. You sure you're going to be okay here by yourself? Because you could always call—"

"I'll be okay," she said.

"I made you a sandwich. It's in the fridge. Try to remember to call
that shrink, okay?" I waited for a response that didn't come. "Well,"
I said. "At least while I'm at school, I won't be hovering. Right?"

She gave me a look: *I have no idea what you mean.*

I FELT A LITTLE NAUSEOUS driving there. Lack of sleep
didn't help. And the fact that, at the red lights, that "tape" was still
playing in my brain. The schedule felt way out of whack: hang around
the house all morning, then get to work for one p.m. And parking was
a pain. The Chatfield teachers were done at noon, but a lot of them

had hung around. Several of us had to jump the berm and park on the lawn. And checking in with the security cop: that felt strange. Having him check through my briefcase, look back and forth between my ID badge and me. I couldn't see why the faculty had to be treated like prospective bombers.

My first class was my American lit sophomores—the honors kids. We were all feeling like strangers in a strange land, I think, but I couldn't really address it while Mrs. Boyle was still in the room. Mrs. Boyle was the teacher whose classroom I was borrowing, and she was taking her sweet time getting her stuff together and leaving us alone. She was nice enough—had cleaned out one of her desk drawers for me and put up a bulletin board: "Welcome, Columbine. Chatfield stands with you." Thirteen silver balloons thumbtacked to a blue background. But as far as blackboard space? She'd hogged over half of it and taken colored chalk and written, "Please SAVE! Please SAVE!" around the edges. So, you know, it didn't leave a whole lot of space for me. And I like to sprawl a little when I'm using the board. When the kids get going during a discussion. You write down a little something of what each of them says. Legitimizes their comments, you know? Gets more kids participating. Now that I think of it, Mrs. Boyle *looked* like she'd been boiled: pink complexion, kind of sweaty. *"Adios,"* I said when she finally headed out the door. Her hand appeared over her shoulder and waved bye-bye. The sound of that door catch was music to my ears.

I looked out at the kids. Smiled. Said it was good to see everybody. They were wearing their security badges, too—hung like pendants around their necks, per order of the superintendent's office. Poor Lindsay Peek looked miserable—more gaunt than Maureen. She probably should have stayed home for the rest of the year, too. Had her work sent to her.

"So," I said. "Day one of our last eighteen. What do you guys want to do today?" No one responded. "You want to talk about it? *Not* talk about it?"

"Not talk about it," one of the boys in back said. It dawned on me that they'd taken seats in approximately the same places where they'd sat in my classroom.

"Then shall we just get back to the book we were reading?" I asked.

"I don't know. What book were we reading?" Katrina said. A few kids laughed, several smiled. All year, she'd been the class smart-ass—never as funny as she thought she was. But I decided to play along.

"What book?" I groaned. "Only Nobel Prize winner John Steinbeck's masterwork. How many of you have finished it?" About half the kids raised their hands. Several of the others reminded me that the police hadn't let them retrieve their backpacks from the crime scene. Luzanne Bowers, a cop's kid, said her dad had told her nobody was going to get their stuff back until July.

"I finished it," Travis said. "What was up with that ending? Her baby dies, so they put it in a box and send it down the river?"

"Like Moses. Right, Mr. Quirk?" Luzanne asked. "One of those biblical illusions we were talking about before?"

I nodded. "*All*usions," I said. I wrote the word on the board.

"Yeah, but why did she breast-feed that starving dude?"

"Duh-uh," Katrina said. "Because he was *starving*."

"Yeah, but come on. That was gross."

"Not as gross as going to school at Chatfield," Charissa said. Several kids mumbled in agreement.

"Hey, it's not all bad," Malcolm said. "We get to sleep in in the morning. And has anyone checked out their vending machines? They got Yoo-Hoo!"

Lynette said she hated that the media was there. "Can't they just leave us alone on our first day back?" I suggested that their first day back *was* the story. Catalina Quinones said she saw Katie Couric out front—off-camera, eating a yogurt like a normal person. When she waved, Katie had waved back.

"Big hairy deal," Alex said.

"Well, maybe it is for me, since I want to be a TV journalist," Catalina retorted. Delbert said he'd seen "that CNN dude. One of the main ones. I forget his name." Charissa complained that she couldn't ever turn on TV anymore without seeing Mr. DeAngelis being interviewed by somebody. If we asked her, she said, he should remember he was a high school principal, not some big TV star. Plus, he had a big, fat pumpkin head. She just wanted to say that, too.

"Can I say something?" Jenny Henderson asked. She looked upset. Looked over at the silver balloons on Mrs. Boyle's bulletin board. "Lauren Townsend lived on my street? And I always . . . she was like a role model for me? Because she was so smart? But she was like really, really nice, too." The rest of us looked at her. Waited. "That's all I wanted to say. Just that Lauren was an awesome person."

"Thanks, Jen," I said.

Kyle Velasquez had rocked, too, Charlie told us. He and Kyle had bet ten dollars on the Super Bowl in January and Kyle had won. They'd gone to DQ and Charlie had paid off his bet in Blizzards. "Dude, trust me," Charlie told us. "That dude could eat ice cream!"

Melanie said she'd been in the lunch line once and didn't have enough money. "And the cafeteria lady had already rung me up and she was all like, 'Well, what did you *take* that for if you can't pay for it?' And then this kid behind me? He tapped me on the shoulder and handed me a dollar. He didn't even know me or anything. I didn't know his name. And then? After everything happened? . . . It was that kid, Danny Mauser."

I nodded. Smiled. "Anyone else?"

Delbert's hand went up. "How's Mrs. Quirk?"

The question rattled me. I felt my face redden.

"How is she? She's fine. Why?"

"She was in the library. Right?"

Involuntarily, I looked over at Lindsay. She was staring straight ahead. Chewing on her hair. I looked back at Delbert. "She was, yes," I said. "She's okay, though. She'll be back next year."

"My friend Eli was in the library," Annie said. "He's changing schools." I saw four or five kids sneak peeks at Lindsay. From the looks of it, some of them knew where she'd been, some didn't.

Clemente Quinones's hand shot into the air. It surprised me; unlike his sister, he rarely spoke in class. "In the book?" he said. "When Rose of Sharon bares her breast? Isn't that from the Bible, too?"

"No, it's from *Playboy*," Katrina quipped.

I gave her a look, but Clemente ignored her. "Isn't it like 'the milk of human kindness' or whatever?" he said.

"Well, that phrase is from Shakespeare," I said. "*Macbeth*. You guys will read it next year. But you're right, Clemente. That's exactly what Rose of Sharon is offering the starving man. Think about it. Her husband's ditched her, her baby's just died. But she unbuttons her dress and offers a stranger the milk of human kindness. The gift of hope."

On the other side of the room, Lindsay Peek burst into tears.

It was Jesse who went to her. Put her arm around her. Lindsay clung to her like she was drowning. She was shaking violently. Making a gurgling sound.

"Linds?" I said. "Do you need a pass to the nurse?" She didn't answer.

My mind raced. *Panic attack*, I thought. *She can't go to the nurse. She can't move.* "Could someone please go and get the nurse?"

Delbert stood and started toward the door. "Where's her office at?"

I searched from face to frightened face. None of us knew.

chapter thirteen

I GOT HOME A LITTLE after six. Got the dogs exercised and
fed. Broiled some chicken, made a salad. I had to call her three different times before she got herself downstairs and to the table. Her
eyes were puffy, her hair uncombed. "Well," I said. "One day down,
seventeen to go." She looked at me, puzzled. "School," I said.

"Oh. Right."

I waited for her to ask me about it—about the kids—but she just
sat there, looking sad and stoned. "You should eat," I said.

She took a bite.

"Lindsay Peek had a tough time today."

"Did she? That's too bad." End of subject.

"So how'd it go here? What did you do all afternoon?" I waited.
"Mo?"

"What?"

"What did you do this afternoon?"

She shrugged.

"No panic or anything?"

She shook her head. "Someone came here," she said.

"Who?"

The fork shook in her hand, the tines clinking against her plate.
"Would you please stop doing that?" she said.

"Doing what?"

"Making that tapping noise. It's driving me crazy." I pointed to her plate. Showed her that she was making the noise. "Oh," she said. Put down her fork.

"Who came here?" I said.

She looked up. Looked away. "What? Oh. No one."

I took a bite, watched her. "So which is it? Someone came, or nobody came?" She remembered now, she said: she'd taken a nap and *dreamed* someone was at the door. She picked up her napkin and started shredding it.

I told her I'd tried calling a couple of times but kept getting a busy signal. Who was she talking to? No one, she said; she'd taken the phone off the hook. "And then later? After my nap? As soon as I hung it back up, it started ringing. For some reason, I thought it was going to be Velvet, so I answered it. But it was what's-his-name."

"What's-his-name?"

"From Connecticut. The baker."

"Alphonse?" Jesus, she couldn't remember my best friend's name?

"He said to tell you the police were out at Lolly's. They caught some kids fooling around down at the apple house."

"Oh, great," I said. "Just what I needed. The rest of that roof could come down any time. Hurt someone, and the next thing you know, their parents would be suing us. What else did he say?"

"Who?"

"Alphonse."

"I couldn't find a pen," she said. "We never have enough pens in this house." She stood up and, teetering, carried her meal to the sink. With her hand, she pushed it into the drain. Hit the garbage disposal switch. "Put the faucet on," I reminded her. Waited. "Hey, wake up! Put the faucet on!"

She pivoted. Screamed, "Don't yell at me!"

"I'm not. I . . . you run it without the water on, the motor burns out."

"I know that! I forgot!"

Well, it was as good a time as any, I figured. "How many of those tranquilizers you take today?"

Two, she said. Why?

"Because ever since I got home, you've been acting so tranquil, I'm wondering if you have a pulse. And by the way, it's you who's yelling, not me. How many'd you really take?"

She reminded me that she was a nurse with pharmacological training. Only trouble was, she had a little trouble pronouncing "pharmacological."

"You call that shrink yet?"

She stared at me for several seconds. "He's going to e-mail you."

"He? I thought Dr. Cid was a she."

"Alphonse." She said she was going to bed.

"Yeah? Why's that?" I called after her. "So you can go up there, take another couple of those goofballs?"

I hadn't checked my e-mail since before the killings. Hadn't even turned the computer on. There were thirty-something unopened messages, most of them spam. The "I Love You" message was there: that computer virus I'd read about and I remembered, luckily, not to open it. There were three or four missives from my cyberbuddies—postings about our greatest-records-of-the-rock-era lists. I'd missed the deadline. Well, so what? It all seemed so stupid to me now: bunch of bored baby boomers trying to recapture their rock'n'roll youth. I block-deleted everything but Alphonse's message.

From: studlysicilian@snet.net
To: caelumq@aol.com
Sent: Monday, May 3, 1999
Subject: Farm Trouble

QUIRKY—JErry martineau called me @ the bakery this a.m. Wanted your #. Called back this afternoon. Sez a woman answered, but when he told her it was the Three Rivers P.D. she hung

up on him, then alls he got was busy signals.
Needs YOU to call HIM about something that
happened out at your aunts place. They got a
call last nite @ the station, had to send a
cruiser out there. Your guy Ulisees (or however the fk u spell his name) caught some kids
partying down @ that little building where the
orchard was. He called the cops but then decided to take matters into his own hand, Went
after 'em with a 2-by-4. Jerry sez he was shit-
faced. Swung and missed, but one of the kids
shoved him & he fell back on the cement floor &
cut his head open. Kids were gone by the time
the cops got there. They called the EMTs, got
him to the hospital & stitched him up. Martineau sez he's ok, no concusion but he's worried the kids will come back and U. will do
something stupid. Sorry to add to your shit
but i thought you better know. Let me know
if you want me to do anything. Hey, Maureen
sounded kind of out of it when i called. (Hope
she's not reading this.) She alright? Anyways,
call Martineau. Later.

   Alphonse

   P.S. eBay had a 65 'Stang listed last week.
Had the 4-barrel & the sweet 289 but it was a
white ragtop. i was gonna bid, but came to my
sensses. And anyways, the seller was all the
way out in North Dafuckin'kota. My sweet Phoenician Yellow's out there somewheres. Patients
is a virtue, right Q? Didn't you always used
to say that? Or was that my mother. i get you
2 mixed up because you both wear your nylons
rolled down to your ankles when it get's hot,
ha ha. Speaking of, Ma called last nite to
complain about my pop because after there
bocce game, he & his cronies went to Hooters
for lunch. i said Ma, once a dog always a dog
and she goes That's not funny Alphonso, and if

```
I ever hear that you've been to one of those
places, I'll get on a plane and go up there
and swat you a good one. Good ole Ma. She
was asking how you were doing. Sez her & her
rosary circle are saying novenas for everyone
out in Littleton. So your all set!
```

I had to smile, thinking of Mr. and Mrs. Buzzi driving each other crazy down there in retirement heaven, same as they had at the Mama Mia all those years. Mrs. B must be approaching her one millionth novena by now—ought to get some kind of citation from the Vatican. I was working at the bakery when they voted in the Polish pope. She wasn't too happy at first because they hadn't picked an Italian, but within a month, she was gaga over the guy. Had his picture up all over the place at the bakery. And when he got shot? Man, the only time I ever saw Mrs. B in worse shape was when Rocco was dying. . . . So Ulysses was drinking again? I pictured him sitting forlornly at Lolly's kitchen table a few weeks before, making his bullshit promises that he'd stay sober in exchange for the faith I was putting in him. Well, so much for the word of a lush. . . . And Maureen. Jesus Christ. Martineau calls on police business and she hangs up on him? I had to get her to that shrink—pick her up and carry her there if I had to. Had to count those pills before I went to sleep. Those things were just supposed to chill her out a little, help her get to sleep. Not turn her into something out of *Night of the Living Dead*.

The dispatcher told me Captain Martineau was gone for the day. Would I like to speak to an officer on duty?

"Captain?" I said. "When did Jerry make captain?"

"First of the year, sir." She said she wasn't authorized to give out Captain Martineau's home number. Did I wish to speak to an officer, or would I like the captain's voice mail? Neither, I told her. Hung up and found his home number in the Internet white pages.

"I'll see if he can come to the phone," his wife said. "Who should I say is calling?"

"Tell him it's one of the Four Horsemen."

"Excuse me?" His first wife, Connie, would've gotten it; she and Jerry had been together since high school. But this was wife number two, the assistant city planner he'd had the affair with.

"One of the Four Horsemen," I repeated. "He'll know what I mean." As in: he had a history before you came along, darlin'. I'd run into Connie in the dairy section of Big Y once. Her bitterness could have curdled the milk.

Back in high school, Martineau and I had had two things in common: we both ran cross-country and track, and we both had fathers who'd committed suicide. (Not that either of us ever spoke about it.) Senior year, at the state meet, Jerry, Ralph Brazicki, Dominick Birdsey, and I broke the record in the four by eight hundred. The sports writer for the *Daily Record* dubbed us "the Four Horsemen," and then everyone started calling us that. Last I knew, we still held the state record: 7:55. But "last I knew" was before we moved to Littleton.

"Hello?"

"So what do you say, Captain Martineau?" I began. "You want to get ahold of Birdsey and Brazicki, see if we can still pass off the baton without dropping it?" He laughed. Said these days he'd have to run with a wheelbarrow in front of him to carry his gut. I congratulated him on his promotion; he said he wasn't sure if congrats or condolences were in order. "No, really," I said. "You've given that town a lot of good years. You deserve it."

Martineau said my "buddy over at the bakery" had filled him in about my connection to Columbine. "You work in law enforcement for as long as I have, and you think you've seen it all," he said. "Then something like this happens. I tell you one thing: I don't envy that sheriff's department out there. Investigation's gotta be brutal, and then, on top of that, you got the press and the FBI and the politicians breathing down your neck. Not to mention a bunch of heartbroken parents. How's the wife doing?"

I clenched. "My wife? She's hanging in there. Thanks for asking."

"That her I spoke to briefly when I called today?"

"Uh, no," I said. "No, she was out all day. Must have been the woman who cleans our house. She's a little self-conscious about her English."

"Is she?"

"Yeah. She is. Mexican. Lot of Mexicans out here."

"Here, too," he said. "More and more. Come up to work at the casino. Mexicans, Haitians, Malaysians. It's like the UN around here now. So I guess you heard you had some drop-in visitors out at your aunt's place."

"And that my caretaker took matters into his own hands and ended up in the hospital."

Could have been worse, Jerry said.

"You catch the little shitheads?"

Not yet, he said. But his guys were making some inquiries, keeping their eyes open. Meanwhile, he wanted to avoid another confrontation. "We've had dealings with Mr. Pappanikou from time to time. He's fine when he's sober, but when he's not, that's a different story. And my philosophy is: Let's prevent something from happening if we can, rather than cleaning up the mess *after* it's happened. Last thing we want is for him to catch those kids out there again when he's three sheets to the wind. Grab a shotgun, do something stupid."

My mind flew to those CNN pictures of Rachel and Danny, lying dead outside the school. "Jesus, no," I said. "Look, I'm planning to get back this summer. Tear down their little clubhouse."

"He have a key to the farmhouse?"

I said he did—that he went over and checked on things for me.

"But that's it? You didn't give him permission to stay there? Because, according to my guys, that seems to be what he's doing. And if he's stumbling around drunk in there, he could start a fire, fall down the cellar stairs. I don't mean to mind your business for you, Caelum, but I think you better get someone else to keep an eye on things for you."

I told him I'd get ahold of Alphonse, have him go out to Ulysses's place and get the keys from him.

"Well, you better tell him to wait till the weekend," Jerry said. "I called in a favor from Bev Archibald over at Social Services, and she got Ulysses into Broadbrook on a five-day. Dry him out a little."

"That's above and beyond the call," I said. "Thanks."

"Well, there's a connection there. He and my dad went to high school together. Went down and enlisted right after high school. Fought in the Korean War."

"My father, too," I said.

"Yeah, that's right, isn't it? Who knows? Maybe Korea's what messed all three of them up." And there it was: the first mention either of us had ever made about our fathers' having killed themselves.

"Yeah, well . . ." I said.

Jerry said I should give him a call when I got into town. "Maybe you and me and the wives can get together, go out to dinner or something."

Doubtful, I thought, unless she begins to pull out of it. "Sounds good," I said. "Or maybe you and I could do some laps around the track. How's our state record holding up?"

"It's not. Team from Storrs finally beat our time by one second. But we were on the books for what? Twenty-six years? Not too shabby."

I asked him if he ever heard from Brazicki or Birdsey.

"Birdsey I see from time to time. Not too often. Probably too busy counting his casino millions. He's a good guy, though. Writes us a nice check every year for the Policemen's Benevolent fund. You know his brother died?"

I told him my aunt had sent me the clipping. "Drowned, right?"

"Yeah, that was a tough one. . . . I tell you one thing about that casino, though. They get some damn good entertainment down there. The wife and I have seen Travis Tritt, Dolly Parton, the Oakridge Boys."

"So I take it your heavy metal days are over?"

"Yeah, and come to think of it, you never did give me back that Iron Butterfly album you borrowed."

I laughed. Told him I was pretty sure the statute of limitations was up on that one.

"You know Brazicki became a priest?"

"Ralphie? You're shitting me. I thought he was one of the evil capitalists at Aetna."

"He was. Got the calling after Betsy died. Resigned, sold the house, the boat, their place at the Cape. His kids weren't too happy about it, but what the hell. They're both grown and married. He's a prison chaplain. Says the inmates are a piece of cake compared to the sharks he used to have to deal with in business."

"Father Brazicki," I said. "Well, what the fuck. He and I bought our first Trojans together at Liggett's Drugstore. The afternoon of Kitty Vinsonhaler's skinny-dipping party."

"The one her parents came home in the middle of?" Martineau said. "Don't remind me."

"Yeah, that'd make a great story down at the station," I said. "You scaling that fence butt-naked with Mr. Vinsonhaler in hot pursuit."

"Not to change the subject," he said, "but I don't think you ever gave me back my Grand Funk Railroad record, either."

After I hung up, I thought about the three of them: Jerry's dad, my dad, Ulysses. "Messed up" was right. Mr. Martineau had put a gun to his head and Daddy had put himself in front of a moving train. Ulysses was taking the slow boat, but he was killing himself, same as the other two. His liver was probably liverwurst at this point. . . . I'd asked Mother about my father's Korean War experiences a couple of times. Lolly, too. Both had said they didn't know much themselves— that Daddy had always kept it to himself. . . . Anyway, I was lucky nothing worse had happened in that dustup between Ulysses and those kids. I couldn't have taken another shooting. Maybe I shouldn't wait until I got back. I could hire someone to tear down the apple house. Someone who might haul it away in exchange for the scrap lumber and the window casings. I could remove the floor myself. It'd feel good to swing a sledgehammer, take out my frustrations on a slab of concrete.

No, she was out. Must have been the woman who cleans our house. She's self-conscious about her English. Now why had I lied like that?

Because she's becoming an embarrassment.

No, she's not. I'm going to get her to that shrink. She'll pull out of it.

Right. And Mrs. Buzzi's novenas ought to be kicking in any minute, too. You two are going to live happily ever after, rise right up to heaven at the end of it all. Right?

The phone rang. Was it Martineau calling back? Velvet Hoon?

But it was Sergeant Cox, one of the investigators who'd interviewed Maureen a few weeks earlier in our living room. She said she was sorry to be calling back so late, but they were trying to firm up their schedule with the eyewitnesses. Had Mrs. Quirk and I had a chance to discuss their request?

"What request?" I said.

There was a pause. "She didn't tell you about it?"

Cox said she and Detective Chin had stopped by the house that afternoon. They'd explained to Mo that they'd been assigned to a team that was reconstructing a minute-by-minute time line of the events at the school, from 11:10 a.m., when Harris and Klebold arrived on campus, until the last person was evacuated from the building. "So basically, what we're doing is piecing together a jigsaw puzzle from the evidence and the eyewitnesses. Or, in your wife's case and a few of the others, *ear*witnesses. What we're asking people to do is return with us to the school, pinpoint their exact location, and share their memories with us, as specifically as possible." Memory could be unreliable, she said; the more people they could gather information from, the more accurate a composite picture they could develop.

"And you're saying she'd have to go back in there?"

"Yes, sir. In Mrs. Quirk's case, what we'll do, what *I'll* do, probably—most women and girls seem to feel more at ease with another female—so what I'll do is get down on the floor with her. Have her get inside the cabinet and close the door. And then, while we're sitting there, I'll interview her. Record her recollections. We find that on-site interviews are effective in—"

"Is it cleaned up?"

"The crime scene? No, sir. Everything has to be left as is while the investigation is ongoing. With the exception of the bodies. We've put cards down where the victims were."

"But the blood, and the bullets and the glass . . ."

"Yes, sir. While the investigation's under way."

"How many takers have you gotten for these interviews?"

She said there were a few more people they still needed to reach, and a few that felt they had to decline, but that most of the eyewitnesses had agreed to assist them. "The kids have been super," she said. "And we do appreciate that this is a lot to ask of people who've been through so much already. We'd spare folks if we could, but this is extremely important to our investigation. I can't overemphasize how much."

"What did she say? When you asked her?"

"Mrs. Quirk? Well, actually, sir, she seemed troubled."

"As in distracted? Unfocused?"

"No, sir. Actually, she became quite agitated and told us to leave." And then, I figured, she must have gone upstairs and popped two or three more Xanax. "Which is actually another reason why I'm calling this evening instead of waiting until morning," Sergeant Cox said. "I wanted to find out how she's doing. I'm a little surprised she didn't tell you we'd stopped by."

I told Cox I'd talk it over with Maureen. Told myself there was no way in hell I was going to allow her to go back there. Fuck their investigation.

Cox said the on-site interviews would take a week or more. She could put Maureen at the end of the schedule, and we could see how things went. I agreed to that, but made sure she knew that there was no commitment.

I poured myself a scotch—a generous one. Went up there. Leaned against the door frame and watched her sleep. I found the prescription bottle hidden in her beaded purse—the fancy one she carried for dress-up occasions. I spilled the tablets into my cupped palm. Nineteen. She'd taken seven that day.

———

CALL SERGEANT COX'S REQUEST a double-edged sword. Maureen was terrified by the possibility of having to return to the library and crawl back inside that cabinet. But her terror was what finally motivated her to call Dr. Sandra Cid.

Her office was in a high-rise in downtown Denver. We had trouble finding it, and then, once we did, trouble finding parking. We had an argument at the elevators in the lobby. "But we're *late*," I reminded her, and *she* reminded *me* that she couldn't handle enclosed spaces. "Come on then!" I said, and slammed open the door to the stairwell. I started up the seven flights, two stairs at a time, with her shoes click-clacking behind me. There were windows at the landings and, late or not, Mo stopped at each of them. To gather herself, I realized later. To assure herself that, outside this metal and cinder-block chimney she was climbing, there was a world of daylight and normalcy. By the time I reached the seventh floor, my heart was jackhammering. Maureen was a mess. This Dr. Cid had *better* be good, I thought.

She was soft-spoken and plump—one of those sixty-something women with the dyed black hair, the colorful suits and scarves. Mexican, maybe? Puerto Rican? She poured us each a paper cone of water from her water cooler and invited Mo into the inner sanctum.

The walls of her waiting room were decorated with framed color photographs—seascapes, most of them, pencil-signed by an Edgardo

Cid. Her husband, I figured. Ten minutes after they'd disappeared, Dr. Cid reappeared at the doorway. "Mr. Quirk?"

"Caelum," I said.

"So noted. Maureen is feeling anxious. She'd like it if you could join us."

"Sure," I said, springing like a jack-in-the-box from my chair. "Whatever she needs." My anger about the elevators had dissipated like fog.

Mo was trembling badly. I sat beside her on a sea-green couch and took her hand, stroked the back of it. "Sorry I was a jerk before," I murmured.

"You were frustrated," she said. "Hey, I'm frustrating."

Dr. Cid waited for an opening. "Maureen was just sharing with me that, in addition to the fear that's always with her, and the sadness about the children, she wrestles with constant anger, too."

I nodded. Waited.

Mo turned to me. "I have to tell you something. Yesterday? When I let the dogs back in? Chet had been digging, and he tracked mud all over the house. And I got so mad, I grabbed the yardstick and . . . started beating him. I couldn't stop. Then the yardstick broke, and I beat him some more with the broken piece. And he snapped at me. Bared his teeth."

I told Dr. Cid it was completely out of character—that Maureen was the type who shooed flies out the window rather than use the fly swatter.

Dr. Cid asked Mo if she could identify the source of her anger.

Me, I thought. She's always mad at me.

"Them."

"The murderers?"

"They stole my life." She glanced at me. "*Our* lives."

I said what I'd been saying for three weeks: that it was temporary. That it took time. That she was going to get her bearings.

"Will I, Caelum? And how do you know that? Did you gaze into your crystal ball?" The doctor looked back and forth between us.

"That's new, too," I said. "*I* used to be the smart-ass."

Dr. Cid offered me a smile. "Sarcasm is a suit of armor," she said. She asked Maureen if she would please describe a typical day.

"A 'typical' day?"

"Since the trauma, I mean. Walk me through it. You wake up in the morning and . . . ?"

"And I lie there. Not wanting to get out of bed."

"Why not?"

"Because I don't want to face whatever's going to clobber me. A flashback, or a memory, or some horrible new thing about it in the newspaper. And then . . . and then I tell myself, 'Okay, maybe today's the day you're going to get up, get dressed, and not let it overwhelm you. Maybe today's the day you start moving past it.'"

It was the first I'd heard of these pep talks. "That's good, Mo," I said. "See? You're beginning to fight it."

Dr. Cid asked if she could interject. "It sounds to me, Maureen, that even before your feet touch the floor, you're putting enormous pressure on yourself. Setting yourself up for failure, I think, because trauma is not really something you can wish away with 'maybes.' You have to learn how to manage it. Develop coping strategies you can use when these difficult moments present themselves. *That's* how you're going to heal, Maureen. But please, go on. What happens when you get out of bed?"

Maureen sighed. "I get up. Go into the bathroom. And I'll be washing my face, or brushing my teeth and . . . I'll start remembering things."

"Such as?"

"Gunfire. Breaking glass."

"So it's mostly sounds you remember?"

"Smells, too," I said. "The other day? The bottom of one of our garbage barrels had rotted out? So I said, 'Come on. Let's drive over to Home Depot, get another barrel.' And she didn't want to go, but I was like, 'Just take a ride with me. You can't stay cooped up in here.' And so we went. And while we were looking for the garbage barrels, we passed the lumber section. And the smell of the lumber, the raw wood . . ."

"It smelled like the inside of the cabinet," she said.

"She got nauseous. Dizzy."

"And for the rest of the day, I had a bad headache. And I felt so . . ."

"Anxious?"

Mo shook her head. "Defeated. I mean, Home Depot has nothing to do with what I went through, but it's like . . . everything's a land-mine field. Which is *why* I don't want to leave the house."

"But there are trip wires there, too," I said.

Dr. Cid asked Mo to describe some of the other auditory memories that made her feel defeated.

She closed her eyes. I watched her hands dance and fidget in her lap. "Their laughing and whooping while they were shooting them. . . . The way the kids were wailing. Begging for their lives." She was struggling. Being so brave. "And the fire alarm. It just kept scream-ing, you know? All the time I was hiding inside the . . . I remember thinking at one point, well, if they find me and kill me, I won't have to hear that alarm anymore."

We sat there in silence, the three of us.

It was Dr. Cid who finally spoke. "Maureen, when you remember these terrible sounds, what effect does it have on you?"

"It's like . . . there's this wave coming toward me, but there's nothing I can do about it. And then it reaches me, crashes over me and . . . and I'm done for another day. I just give up. Give in to it. Because how do you stop a wave?"

"You don't," Dr. Cid said. "And you're wise to recognize your powerlessness to do so. But what you *can* do is learn how to *negotiate* this wave. Work within the context of its inevitability." When she was a little girl living in Cuba, she said, her older brothers taught her how to manage the surf. She learned that, as a wave approached, she needed, first of all, to calculate whether it was going to break over her, or pass by her and *then* crest. If the latter was the case, she could spring upward and bob above the swell. Or, she could make her body rigid and lean into the curl. Ride the wave in to the shore, and then stand, adjust her swimsuit, and return again to deeper water. But if the wave was about to break against her, she said, the best plan was to face it head-on. Take a gulp of air and stick her head right into it. Better that than to be battered by it, lifted off her feet and sent tumbling and choking on sea water.

Maureen rolled her eyes. "Well, if I ever go swimming in Cuba, I guess I'll know what to do."

"Mo, stop it," I said. "She means—"

But Dr. Cid put her hand up like a traffic cop. "Maureen's an intelligent woman," she said. "I think she understands the metaphor. And if she needs to resist it, that's okay, too."

We had been booked for a double session, and near the end of those hundred minutes, Dr. Cid shared her conclusions with us. Maureen's symptoms indicated that she was certainly suffering from acute-phase posttraumatic stress disorder. If they were to continue working together, her goal would be to help Maureen manage her stressors so that she could avoid advancing to chronic PTSD. "This needn't be a life sentence," she said. "For either of you."

I asked her to describe what Mo's treatment would be like.

"A mix," she said. "Talk therapy, instruction in relaxation techniques, medication. And perhaps, down the line, a session or two with an Ericksonian hypnotherapist."

Maureen shook her head emphatically. "I am *not* having anyone hypnotize me."

"So noted," Dr. Cid said. "But that's a common misconception about hypnosis: that someone else does it *to* you. In actuality, all hypnosis is self-hypnosis. Now let's talk about medication."

I was blunt. Told the doctor I thought Mo was taking too much Xanax.

"But they *help* me," Mo insisted. She was on the verge of tears.

"In the short run, yes," Dr. Cid said. "Because numbness is preferable to confronting the fear, and the anger, and the ferocious memories. But in the long run, they could do quite a lot of harm. Numbness will arrest your ability to get past your illness to the other side. The truth is, Maureen, you've been misprescribed. Xanax can be useful in treating *chronic* sufferes of PTSD. But at this stage, one of the SSRIs would be a much better choice for you."

Maureen crossed her arms over her chest and sighed in disgust. I asked the doctor what SSRIs were.

"Selective seratonin reuptake inhibitors. Quite a mouthful, isn't it? They're in the family of antidepressants—not magic pills, certainly, but they should help to quell Maureen's flashbacks, and make her memories less debilitating. That 'wave' will most likely shrink to a less daunting size. And, unlike the Xanax she's taking, these medications are nonaddictive." She turned to Mo. "Maureen? I'd like to start you on Zoloft. Twenty-five milligrams a day for the first week, fifty for the second. We can go up to two hundred a day if we need to, but I'd prefer to err on the side of caution for now. You'll need to be patient, though. This medication will take a while to build up in your system, so you won't feel the benefits immediately. Understand?"

Mo scowled, said nothing.

"When *will* it kick in?" I asked.

"Two to three weeks, and she'll start feeling the benefits. Oh, and about the police investigation? Going back into the school and getting inside that cabinet? Absolutely not. It may be helpful to them, but it could be very harmful to Maureen. It could very likely retraumatize her. Whether or not Maureen chooses to work with me, I'll be happy to write a letter to that effect, based on our conversation today.

Just call the office tomorrow and leave me a name and address so I'll know where to send it."

I wrote her a check; she handed me a receipt. She said the insurance companies were sometimes reluctant to reimburse for PTSD, but that given the high profile of the Columbine shootings, she imagined it would not be a problem. She reached behind her and patted her desktop until her hand located her appointment book. "Shall we schedule our next session then, or would you rather go home and talk it over?"

Simultaneously, Mo said, "Talk it over," and I said, "Schedule it."

We left with the Zoloft prescription and instructions on how to wean her off the Xanax. Descending the seven flights of stairs to the lobby, we said nothing to each other. We were silent, too, in the parking garage, and in the line of traffic that inched toward the highway entrance ramp. It wasn't until I'd accelerated to sixty-five or seventy, that I turned to her. "I feel hopeful," I said. "She really knows her stuff."

"She's a quack," Maureen said.

"No, she's not. Why do you say that?"

"That whole thing about riding the waves in Cuba," she said. "I felt like saying, 'What about undertow, you stupid idiot? What if a wave sucks you under?' . . . And hypnosis. Why not voodoo? Maybe I could chant some spells and drink chicken blood."

"Uh-uh," I said. "You're way off on this."

"Why? Because I'm crazy?"

"No one's saying you're crazy, Maureen."

"That's grounds for a divorce, right? When your wife's insane."

The hope I'd been feeling drained out of me like engine oil. I let a mile or two go by. "What's this really about?" I said. "The fact that she's taking you off the Xanax?"

"Fuck you, Caleum," she said. "Fuck . . . *you*."

From: studlysicilian@snet.net
To: caelumq@aol.com
Sent: Monday, May 14, 1999
Subject: That cat is PSYCO!!!

QUIRKY: The good news is that i'm not going to
sue you. The bad news is that i could. First
i went over and got the keys from Ullises. He
was crying, shaking like a leaf and going on
and on about how you trusted him and he let
you down. i didn't know what to say so i said
he could stop by the bakery and we'd give him
coffee on the house whenevr he wanted it. Then
i went over to your aunts to get the cat. My
afternoon counter girl Yvette—you met her, the
freaky-lookin one with the nice boobies (36-Ds
I'd guesstimate). Her and her mother rescue
cats. They already got like 12 of them but she
said she'd take it. So i go out to your aunt's
and first of all i can't find the stupid cat.
Then i find it but i can't catch it. Then finally i corner it out on that closed-in porch
where all the file cabinets are. Grab the
thing by the scruff of the neck and it starts
fightin back like Mike Tyson. Scratched me up
bad. Then i'm driving over to Yvettes trailer
park and the cats howling so loud i can't even
hear myself think. So we stop at a light and
it finally shuts up and so i go Nice kitty. And
the fucker takes a leap, sinks all 4s into
my leg and bites me on the knee. When we get
there, Yvette's mother goes Oh, poor thing was
just scared, and i'm thinking here I am practically having to go to the emergency room
and that cat's the poor thing??! So you owe
me bigtime Quirky. And now at the bakery they
keep putting that Ted Nugent song YOU GIVE ME
CAT SCRATCH FEVER on the tape player and i
go ha ha very funny, keep it up and I'll fire
all your asses. But anyway Lollys cat is taken

care of and I got the keys. Anything else you
need?
  Alph

The kids and I limped through the rest of the school year. I didn't
give exams. And because my grade book was still locked up at Columbine, I had them write down the grades they thought they de-
served, and those were pretty much the grades I gave them. (Well, I
adjusted for inflation in the case of three or four optimists.) Lindsay
Peek never returned after that first day. Rather than give her an incomplete, I gave her a B and let it go at that. On the last day, after the
kids left, I filled a couple of cardboard cartons with my stuff. Grabbed
Mrs. Boyle's bottle of Fantastik and cleaned all her desktops for her.
I'd gotten her a box of chocolates, too. Left them on her desk, with a
note thanking her for sharing her space with me. She'd been a pain in
the ass about leaving promptly, but she was a nice lady. Baked cookies
for the kids and me. Twice.

Graduation at the Amphitheater was a tearjerker—and, of course,
a media event. No avoiding it. Isaiah Shoels's family didn't go to the
ceremony, but the Townsends were there. Lauren's older brothers and
sisters accepted her diploma. Dylan and Eric would have graduated,
too, but there was no mention of them. I choked up when the kids
who'd been injured received their diplomas: Jeanna Park with her arm
in a sling that matched her graduation gown, Lisa Kreutz in her wheelchair. Val Schnurr had taken nine bullets, but you'd have never guessed
it from her triumphant walk across that stage.

It was customary for a lot of the Columbine faculty to go out together after graduation—go to a bar and toast the school year just
ended and the beginning of summer vacation. But that night, no
one even mentioned going out. We all just got in our cars and went
home.

The downstairs lights were off, the dogs wandering around outside
like orphans. I figured she must have forgotten they were still out

when she went to bed. The downstairs TV was on, and so was one of the burners on the stove—a blue ring of flame heating nothing. The message machine was blinking.

Beep. "Hello? Mr. Quirk? This is Ulysses Pappinikou calling. I got your number from the guy at the bakery. I just wanted to tell ya that if you can find it in your heart to—"

I hit "skip." Didn't have the strength.

Beep. "Hi, there! This is Cyndi Pixley from Century Twenty-One returning Maureen Quirk's call? Sure, I'd love to come out there and do a walk-through and an appraisal. You just call me tomorrow, and we'll set up a time. And thanks! Can't wait to meet you!" I recognized the name—Cyndi Pixley's perky face showed up every week in the real estate circular. Mo had called her?

Beep. "Hi, Ma. It's Velvet. Just thought I'd call and see how you were doin'. I'm in Louisiana. This town called Slidell. It's near New Orleans. I got a job cleaning rooms at this skeezy motel. It's—what? Wait a second, Mom, okay? . . . KEITH, PEACE *OUT*! I'M ON THE FUCKIN' PHONE! . . . What? . . . Okay. Okay, I'm sorry. I'm *sorry*, Keith. Hey, Ma? I gotta go."

Beep.

Well, whoever Keith was, he sounded like a creep. I went upstairs. She was in the bathroom, in her pajamas. She was studying her face in the mirror—opening and closing her mouth like a fish.

"Hey," I said.

The prescription vial she'd been holding went flying. Pills rolled everywhere. "Jesus Christ! Don't sneak up on me like that!"

"I wasn't sneaking."

"My nerves aren't bad enough, Caelum? Is that it? You have to—"

"Mo, come on. I—"

"Asshole!" She was on her knees, snatching up the pills she'd spilled. I bent to help her. "No!" she said. "*I'll* get them! Just get out!"

But I was already holding a Xanax between my thumb and index finger. "You're not supposed to be taking these anymore," I said. I grabbed her wrist and pried her fingers apart. When the vial dropped from her hand, I snatched it before she could. Read the label. "Who's Dr. Radwill?" I said.

———

THE NEXT MORNING, SHE WAS sullen—and pissed as hell that I'd flushed her new supply down the toilet.

"You have no idea what this is like for me," she said.

"No, Maureen, I guess I don't. But that doesn't mean I'm going to stand aside and let you develop a drug addiction."

She told me I could go to hell.

"I'm not going anywhere," I said. "And what's this Cyndi Pixley stuff?"

She said she'd called Cyndi Pixley after Sergeant Cox and Detective Chin's latest drop-by. Even after that letter from Dr. Cid, they were still putting pressure on her about that interview. Maybe if we moved away, she'd feel safer, less assaulted by it, day after day after day. She was pretty sure she would. The farmhouse was just sitting there, right? What was keeping us here?

"Our jobs," I said. "Our house. Our friends."

"What friends?"

I ignored the whack. "How about your family, then?" I said. "We moved back here so you could be nearer to your family."

"My *father*," she said. "And he doesn't give a shit about me."

She played Velvet Hoon's message over and over. "Why Louisiana?" she said. "And who's Keith? She sounds afraid of him."

"Velvet's not your responsibility," I reminded her. "*You're* your responsibility."

"You know what I wish? That they had spared one of those kids' lives and killed me instead."

I grabbed my car keys. "I can't listen to this," I said.

"Why not? Because that's what you wish, too?"

A better man would have stayed and comforted her. Instead, I slammed the door. Revved the engine to drown out the sound of her sobbing in there. If I didn't get the fuck away, my head was going to explode.

I drove around for a couple of hours, burning up half a tank of gas and thinking about the irony of it: me arguing in favor of staying put, and her arguing that we should move back to Connecticut. But that farm without Lolly was . . . what? A bunch of bad memories and a house full of junk. One headache after another, starting with that goddamned apple house.

Filling up at the Mobil station, I watched a cabbage butterfly flutter above a pot of yellow marigolds, then light on one of the flowers and flap its wings. Looked innocent enough, but maybe it was starting a domino effect—triggering a disaster in some other part of the world. . . . Maybe I'd sell the farm. Be rid of the burden of it.

A big-ass Jeep pulled up to the pump next to mine, blasting rap. Guy cut the engine, climbed out. One of those twenty-something guys with the requisite shaved head and earring, the tattooed fore-arms. I was trying to remember where I knew him from when he caught me looking. "What's up?" he said.

"What's up?" I said. Then I remembered. He'd stood and spoken at Pastor Pete's grief counseling session. The substitute—the guy whose girlfriend had gotten pregnant. When the shooting started, he'd hidden in a stall in the staff bathroom. They'd banged open the door, rapped on the stall. "Yoo hoo! We know you're in there!" At the grief meeting, he said he'd been unhappy about the baby at first, but then glad about it. Said he was going to be the best father he could be.

When I asked him how the pregnancy was going, he looked a little taken aback. "The grief counseling session at the church," I ex-plained.

"Oh. Right. She's starting to show." My pump clicked off. I hung up the nozzle, screwed my gas cap back on. "You have kids?" he asked.

I shook my head.

"I'm scared," he said.

It wasn't the kind of thing you usually confessed to someone at the gas station, but what happened at Columbine had changed all of the rules. Turned everything upside down. I mean, look at me, telling Maureen we should stay in Colorado.

"Scared of what?" I said.

"Being a dad."

"Not that I'm an expert," I said. "But I think most prospective parents—"

He cut me off. "From what I read, they came from good homes. Had decent parents, enough money. Paper said the Klebolds had a swimming pool, a tennis court, a basketball court." I nodded. Watched that cabbage butterfly float above his head, then land on his shoulder. "I mean, don't get me wrong. It's cool to think about having a son. Taking him fishing, taking him to his first Nuggets game. But what if it's born with all its fingers and toes, and her and I give him a good life, and, in spite of all that, he turns out to be . . . "

"A monster?"

He nodded. Noticed the butterfly and shooed it away.

"I guess you just do your best," I said. "And realize that the rest is a crap shoot. But for what it's worth, I've been teaching high school for a long time. Worked with a lot of untroubled kids and a lot of troubled ones. Those two were the only two monsters I ever came across. So the odds are with you."

He nodded pensively.

"Let me ask you something," I said. "When you went in that day? Who were you subbing for?"

He shrugged. "Some English teacher. He had a death in the family. Name began with a Q, I think."

CYNDI PIXLEY LISTED OUR HOUSE at one eighty-nine, nine, but warned us we'd most likely have to come down. People with kids weren't exactly champing at the bit to buy property in Littleton. She advertised it as "a charming cottage with warmth and flair—ideal for empty-nesters!"

The Paisleys—empty-nesters, sure enough—offered us one eighty-five, with two stipulations: that we leave behind our "window treatments" and postpone the closing until they could sell their home in Arkansas. We agreed. And they agreed to *our* only stipulation—Maureen's, actually. For a year after they took occupancy, they were to post at both the front and back doors our new address and phone number. In the unlikely event Velvet returned to Littleton and came looking for us, Maureen wanted her to know where we could be found.

We quit our jobs, gave our plants to the Kirbys, and brought three carloads over to Goodwill. Dr. Cid called some East Coast colleagues, who called colleagues of theirs. At their fourth and final session, Maureen was given the names and numbers of doctors in Connecticut who could help her with her recovery. "Moving away won't be enough," Dr. Cid warned Mo. "The fear and the anger will travel right along with you. You have to keep working hard." Maureen had been taking Zoloft for about a month by then—with little to no effect, she claimed. The Xanax had made her feel much better.

Three nights before we departed, Maureen's father insisted on hosting a farewell dinner for his "little girl" at his and Evelyn's favorite steak house in Denver. Cheryl, her husband Barry, and their daughter Amber were to have joined us, but they begged off at the last minute. Arthur was put out that Maureen ordered only salad and a cup of tea. "Every party needs a pooper, that's why we invited you," he sang, somewhere between his second and third Macallan. The Barracuda said it was "just plain silly" of us not to have consulted her before listing our house; she did business with Denver-area realtors all the time and, as a professional courtesy, could have most likely saved us the realtor's commission. "Which would be a bigger deal for you than it is for us," I told her, more to knock her off her high horse than anything else. She whacked me right back, though—said she didn't realize schoolteachers had so much money to burn. Arthur reminded us three different times that his travel agent, Misty, was standing by to hear from us about the Disney cruise. When we got up to leave, he took Mo's hand in his and kissed it, as if he were some genteel country gentleman instead of the scumbag he really was.

"Well, that's over with," I said, in the car on the way home.

"Thank God," she said, her voice full of tears. "I wish we'd never moved back here."

Our vet gave Sophie and Chet treats, good-bye kisses, and dog-chew tranquilizers for the long ride home. We put the Rockies to our backs and left Littleton in the predawn darkness on a Monday morning during the third week of July. Drove across the flat green belly of Kansas and into Missouri, listening to country music, books on tape, evangelists' warnings of coming doom. We stayed that first night in St. Louis, at a motel that allowed dogs. (If you're ever at a restaurant there and see crab cakes on the menu? Take my advice: order something else, unless you want to get up close and personal with your Holiday Inn toilet bowl.) We got off to a later-than-expected start on the second day—made it as far as Cleveland. Mo and the dogs flopped back on the motel beds, and I hightailed it over to the Rock'n'Roll Hall of Fame. Got in an hour or so before they closed for the day. Next day, we drove horizonally across Pennsylvania and into upstate New York. We hit Springfield, Massachusetts, during the five o'clock rush hour. Stopped for supper at a Friendly's in Hartford. It was a little before nine p.m. by the time I drove through downtown Three Rivers, crossed the viaduct, passed the casino, and took the right onto Ice House, the left onto Bride Lake. Great-Grandma's prison was in silhouette, a blood orange sunset behind it. *Red sky at morning, sailors take warning,* I heard Aunt Lolly say. Heard my mother, singing in church. *Praise the Holy Trinity, undivided unity . . .* Heard my father, in love or in ridicule: *Rosemary Kathleen Sullivan, my wild Irish rose.* I heard the smash of Great-Grandma's soup tureen out in the kitchen and saw, again, from my post at the parlor window, my father storming away from us, Grandpa's liquor bottle in hand. Why was it that I had loved him, the parent who'd cut me loose, more than her, the parent who'd stayed? It was a question I'd carried into middle age. Maybe now that I was back home again, I'd finally figure that one out. Or maybe I'd finally just let it go and get on with it.

I put my blinker on. Drove up the gravel driveway to the house and all its ghosts. The Rocky Mountains were far, far away now, and Columbine High School was part of our past. For better or worse, I had come back home, with my barking dogs in the backseat and my sleeping, stricken wife beside me.

PART TWO

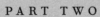

Mantis

→ chapter fourteen ←

BIOGRAPHY QUESTIONNAIRE—SECTION A
Instructions: The following questions concern background information prior to your traumatic event. Please read each question carefully and answer as accurately as you can remember. Do not skip any questions.

Name: *Maureen Quirk*

Present age: *41*

Date of birth: *March 26, 1959*

Place of birth: *Syracuse, N.Y.*
　　　　　　　City and State or Country

When did the traumatic event occur?

_____ Less than two weeks ago

_____ Two weeks to one month ago

_____ One to three months ago

_____ Three to six months ago

_____ Six months to one year ago

__X__ One year to eighteen months ago

_____ Eighteen months to two years ago

_____ Longer than two years ago

Race or ethnicity

_____ American Indian or Alaskan Native

_____ Asian or Pacific-Island American
_____ Mexican-American
_____ Black
__X__ White

How many brothers and sisters do you have?
_____ Brothers
__1__ Sisters *(half sister)*
_____ None

Were you the oldest child, youngest child, or in between?
__X__ Oldest *(Never lived with my half sister—pretty much an only child)*
The _____ oldest of _____
_____ Youngest

What was the size of the city or town in which you lived?
_____ Under 5,000
_____ 5,000–25,000
__X__ 25,000–100,000 *We lived in several places while I was growing up, mostly suburbs of larger cities (father in business)*
_____ 249,999–One Million+

How much schooling have you had?
_____ Completed grade school or less
_____ Some high school
_____ Completed high school
_____ Some college
_____ Completed college
_____ Some post-graduate work
__X__ Completed postgraduate work *(Nursing administration)*
_____ Completed Ph.D.

Through high school, how many different towns or cities
did you live in? __6 *or* 7__

What is your present employment status?
_____ Employed full-time
_____ Employed part-time (and want it this way)
_____ Employed part-time (but don't like it this way)
_____ Unemployed (but actively looking for a job)

__X___ Unemployed (and not looking for a job) *Not yet—want to work when I feel more in control and I'm not in so much physical pain*
_____ Laid off

What is your approximate annual income before taxes?
_____ $0–$10,000
__X__ $10,000–$25,000 *(was)*
_____ $25,000–$50,000
_____ $50,000–$100,000
_____ More than $100,000

Were you married at the time of the traumatic event?
__X__ Yes
_____ No

If yes to the above, how long had you been married? __*12 years*__

Did you have any children at the time the traumatic event occurred?
_____ Yes
__X__ No

What is your present marital status?
_____ Single
_____ Married (never divorced)
__X__ Married (previously divorced)
_____ Married (previously widowed)
_____ Separated
_____ Divorced and still single
_____ Divorced, living with partner
_____ Living with partner
_____ Common law marriage
Present number of children: __*0*__

BIOGRAPHY QUESTIONNAIRE—SECTION B
Instructions: Check those problems (if any) which happened to you **prior to** your having experienced the traumatic event.

_____ Sexual abuse
__X__ Physical abuse *(first husband—only twice)*

__X__ Verbal abuse *first husband—when he was drinking*

__X__ Truancy ("cut" school more than 5 days a year)
Ran away with boyfriend

_____ Expulsion or suspension from school
(senior yr. h.s. gone for 1 week)

_____ Delinquency (arrested or appeared in Juvenile Court)

_____ Running away from home on more than one occasion
(just that one time)

_____ Persistent lying

__X__ Frequent sexual intercourse in casual relationships
(In high school, college)

__X__ Getting drunk or using drugs regularly
in h.s.—much less in college

__X__ Thefts (stealing for fun) *freshman year of h.s. (shoplifting)*

_____ Vandalism (for fun)

_____ Poor grades in school

_____ Frequent violation of rules at home, school, or work

_____ Initiation of fights

_____ Walking off jobs because you got angry

_____ Being negligent as a parent

_____ Engaging in illegal occupations

__X__ Being reckless and getting into trouble because of it
(somewhat in h.s.)

_____ Moving frequently without prior planning

_____ Persistent conning, manipulating, or exploiting others for
personal gain

_____ Experiencing conflicts with authority figures
(e.g., boss, teacher, police)

_____ Expectation of trickery or harm from others

_____ Continually being on the lookout for signs of threat

__X__ A need to be guarded or secretive in your affairs *(somewhat)*

_____ Tendency to avoid accepting blame when warranted

__X__ Tendency to question the loyalty of others

_____ Tendency to be overly concerned with people's hidden
motives and the special meanings of their words

_____ Tendency to be overly jealous

_____ Tendency to be easily slighted and quick to take offense

_____ Tendency to exaggerate problems ("making mountains out of
molehills")

_____ Tendency to be ready to counterattack when threat was
perceived

_X_ Often found yourself unable to relax

_____ Tendency to give the appearance to others
of being "cold" (unemotional)

_____ Tendency to take pride in being objective, rational,
unemotional

_X_ Tendency to lack a sense of humor *(so I've been told)*

_____ Found it hard to experience passive, soft, tender
and sentimental feelings

_____ Feeling you were a person of unusual importance or
uniqueness and capable of doing truly great things in life

_____ Feeling or thinking that you could achieve unlimited success,
power, accomplishment, beauty, and wealth

_X_ Tendency to feel that your "looks" were especially important
to your success with others *But never really satisfied with my*
appearance

_____ Tendency to find it "hard" or "stupid" to sympathize with
others when they were in periods of distress

_X_ Tendency to feel it was okay to take advantage of others if it
was in your interest in terms of personal gain
—*To some extent in h.s. (with boys)*

SYMPTOM INVENTORY CHECKLIST

In the following list, please mark an **X** to show the degree to which you have experienced each item listed **following** the accident or traumatic incident. Also, please mark an **O** to show the degree to which you experienced that item **before** the accident or traumatic event.

	Never	Seldom	Sometimes	Often	Very Often
1. Heart beating fast		O		X	
2. Difficulties in breathing	O		X		
3. Trembling, shaking of the hands or body	O			X	
4. Nausea		O	X		
5. Vomiting		O	X		
6. Diarrhea		OX			
7. Dizziness	O	X			
8. Lightheadedness or unsteadiness	O	X			
9. Hot flashes or flushing	O	X *(if having flashback)*			
10. Tingling sensations in arms or legs	O			X	
11. Headaches		O			X

	Never	Seldom	Sometimes	Often	Very Often
12. Physical pain	O				X
13. Nervousness (stress, anxiety)		O			X
14. Blurred vision	XO				
15. Ringing in the ears	O			X	
16. Problems sleeping		O		X	
17. Nightmares		O	X		
18. Extreme sensitivity to noise	O				X
19. Irritability		O		X	
20. Outbursts of anger		O		X	
21. Lack of interest in sex			O		X
22. Excessive sweating	O		X		
23. Feeling that my personality has changed	O				X
24. Marriage problems			O	X	
25. Lack of interest in life (family, social/recreational activities)	O		X		

	Never	Seldom	Sometimes	Often	Very Often
26. Feeling detached from others	O		X		
27. Depression				O	X
28. Feeling faint	O	X			
29. Being told by others that I have changed	O				X
30. Crying spells			O	X	
31. Not able to express or show my feelings			OX		
32. Unable to remember recent events		O	X		
33. Thoughts of death		O		X	
34. Thoughts of suicide		O	X		
35. Thoughts about accidents		O	X		
36. Thoughts about injury		O		X	
37. Feelings of worthlessness		O		X	
38. Low energy level	O			X	

	Never	Seldom	Sometimes	Often	Very Often
39. Slowness in thought or movement	O		X		
40. Difficulties in concentrating	O			X	
41. Tiredness, fatigue, weakness		O		X	
42. Restlessness		O		X	
43. Muscle aches	O			X	
44. Problems at work			O *(Not working currently)*		
45. Feelings that familiar things seems strange or unreal	O		X		
46. Difficulties in decision-making		O		X	
47. Feeling "blue" or "down in the dumps"			O		X
48. Feelings of terror or panic		O		X	
49. Feeling unreal or like another person	O		X		

	Never	Seldom	Sometimes	Often	Very Often

50. Avoidances of
places that are not
related but remind
me of the traumatic
incident

X (Often)

51. Avoidance of places related
to the traumatic incident

We moved (Often)

52. Thinking about the
traumatic incident

X (Often)

53. Anger toward self or
others for their part in
the traumatic incident

X (Very Often)

54. Guilt feelings for or about
the traumatic incident

X (Very Often)

55. Sensations as if the
traumatic incident were
happening again (flashback)

X (Much less than before) (Very Often)

Is there anything else you wish to add to this inventory?
I have pain (severe sometimes) in my back, knees, and on the top of my head. Have had MRIs done but doctors say there's nothing physically wrong. I strongly disagree!

→ chapter fifteen ←

THE OTHER DAY, WHILE CLEANING out a bureau drawer, I found the pocket calendar I had kept and carried back in 1999. I've learned to do that now, in the aftermath of everything that's happened: assign myself small tasks that I'm likely to finish before the feeling of futility overtakes me. These days, I'll tackle a drawer, not a whole bureau. Call back a creditor, and let the rest of them take a number. When that little calendar presented itself, I sat back on the bed and leafed through it to the April pages. Saturday the seventeenth: the day Ulysses Pappanikou had found Lolly wandering in the yard, talking gibberish. But what I'd written was "Change oil and filter" and "post-prom party—be there @ 11:00 p.m." Tuesday, April twentieth—the day that changed our lives—is blank. So are most of the pages after it. One exception is July the twenty-ninth.

She and I were on the road that day, heading back to Connecticut with the dogs. We'd gotten an early start, then stopped midmorning for breakfast at a Cracker Barrel restaurant in upstate New York. I'd parked at the edge of the lot so the dogs could do their business. Thrown a tennis ball a dozen or so times, so they could chase after it, get a little exercise. (Watching Sophie run in that parking lot—that was the first time I noticed the weakness in her back legs.) Inside, I'd ordered eggs and grits. "This wallpaper paste's not half bad," I'd told

Mo, shoveling in a forkful of grits. "Of course, you could ladle gravy over boiled sneakers and they'd taste good."

I can still see her, sitting across from me in that booth, poking at her poached egg. She had no idea I'd just spoken. Psychic numbness, it's called. Wherever she was, it wasn't at the Cracker Barrel.

Later, waiting in line at the register, I watched her wander, disengaged, among the normal gift-shop customers—all those folks who had the luxury of not being able to recall what they'd been doing back on April the twentieth. "You ready?" I asked, itchy to make more miles. She said she'd better use the rest room first. Glancing over at the line of ten or eleven women she could have already been in the middle of, I nodded. Managed a smile. I told her I'd wait for her outside.

The porch had for-sale rocking chairs. I sat on one and pulled out my pocket calendar. Rocked and wrote.

THURSDAY, JULY 29, 1999

Game plan for August:

1. Get moved in
2. Get her a shrink
3. Look for teaching job
4. See financial planner about house sale $—maybe beef up our IRAs?
5. Tear down apple house
6. Scrape, paint farmhouse (maybe)
7. See lawyer about probate stuff
8. Set up home office—maybe sunporch upstairs? If so, figure out what to do with Great Grandma's boxes, papers, etc. Dump or donate??

That was seven years ago. I had Sophie put to sleep in 2002; her hip dysplasia had gotten so bad, she couldn't even walk across the kitchen floor. The following year, Chet had barreled down the driveway in pursuit of a squirrel and gotten himself killed by a passing oil truck. Today, the apple house is still standing, although it's listing badly to one side, and most of the roof's fallen in. The farmhouse's exterior remains unscraped, unpainted. Inside, on the upstairs sunporch, Great-Grandma Lydia's boxes, ledgers, and filing cabinets full of prison business still occupy the space. The Connecticut State Library didn't want them, and the Three Rivers Historical Society said they didn't have the room. I quit calling places after that, but I could never quite haul it all to the dump. Like I said, I can handle small projects. The bigger ones overwhelm me. . . .

The closest thing I have to a home office is the dining room. My books are stuffed to overflowing in the china closet and stacked in columns on the mahogany buffet. There are plastic bins on the floor marked "Teaching Stuff," "Colorado," "Farm," "Financial." I use Great-Grandma's dining room table for a desk; its surface is littered with bills, office supplies, reams of computer paper. One cardboard carton brims with Columbine articles and printouts, another is marked "Maureen—Legal." Over the years, rather than go through stuff and throw out what I might not need, I've added table leaves. My computer sits on the dining room table, too. I set it up there the week we moved back—temporarily, I'd thought, but that's where it's stayed. Sometime during our first year back, I pushed the table up against the wall so we wouldn't keep tripping on the wires and cords, or that cinder-block-sized backup battery. The dining room's overhead fixture is ugly, but it sheds some decent light, and, hey, it wasn't like she and I were going to be throwing any dinner parties. Outside of Alphonse and the occasional duos of Jehovah's Witnesses or Latter-Day Saints, I can't remember us ever having company.

The money we got from the sale of our Colorado house is gone now. Capital gains tax took a chunk of it, and Mo's medical bills and lawyers' fees ate up the rest. The farm property's assessed at a million six, but because of an agreement Lolly signed with the Farm Bureau back in 1987, we can't sell it to anyone who's not going to farm it. And these days, small dairy farms have gone the way of the dodo bird and the eight-track tape player. Everything's geared to the big guys now—the agribusinesses. So, like Caelum MacQuirk's widow, the infamous Addie, we're land rich but cash poor. And if the Seaberrys go through with the civil suit they've threatened, we could lose the property, too. "Be optimistic," our attorney says. "People's anger subsides after a while, and threats about lawsuits fade away." He means well, but it's painful to have to listen to a lecture about human nature from someone who was born during the disco era. His name's Brandon, for Christ's sake. Looks like he started shaving the day before yesterday. But anyway, if they do go forward with it and win, they could take the house, the farm, basically everything we've got left. The problem is, when Lolly was making out her will, she called and asked me if I wanted the farm put in just my name, or both our names. "Both," I'd said. It was an act of faith, you know? Maureen and I had just reconciled. But that's the problem. Maureen's name on Lolly's will makes us vulnerable.

But anyway, I sat on our bed that day and tried to decide whether to keep that 1999 pocket calendar or toss it. Then, without seeming to direct the operation, I watched my hands pull it apart, tear up the pages, and throw those torn bits of paper into the toilet. Watched my piss hit them. Watched them swirl down the hole.

———

APRIL 20, 1999. IN THE days, weeks, months, and years, now, since they opened fire, I have searched wherever I could for the whys, hows, and whether-or-nots of Eric Harris and Dylan Klebold's rampage. They had been my students first, but I became theirs, stalking them so that I might rescue my wife from the aftermath of what they'd done. On that day, Maureen had escaped execution by opening a cabinet door and entering a maze—a many-corridored prison whose four outer walls were fear, anger, guilt, and grief. And because I was powerless to retrieve her—because I, too, entered the labyrinth and became lost—my only option was to find its center, confront the two-headed monster who waited for me there, and murder it. Murder the murderers, who had already murdered themselves. You see what a puzzler it was? What a network of dead ends? Like I said, I was lost.

On what they called their "little Judgment Day," Dylan had armed himself with a TEC–9 nine-millimeter semi-automatic handgun with shoulder strap and a Stevens twelve-gauge shotgun, its double barrel cut down to twenty-three inches. Eric's weapons of choice were a Hi-Point nine-millimeter carbine rifle on a strap and a Savage Springfield twelve-gauge pump-action shotgun. Because he had stunted its barrel, the kickback when he fired it at his victims in the library had been powerful enough to break his nose. He didn't seem to be in pain, one eyewitness noted; he had kept smiling, and the gush from his nostrils made it look as if he'd been drinking his victims' blood. By the time it was over, Eric had fired the nine-millimeter rifle ninety-six times—thirteen shots in the library, thirty-six inside the rest of the school, and forty-seven outside. Dylan had fired the TEC–9 fifty-five times: twenty-one inside the library, thirty-one inside the rest of the school, and three times outside.

They had taped match-strikers to their arms for quicker lighting of the bombs they carried. Dylan wore a black glove on his left hand; Eric wore its twin on his right. Both wore utility belts, their pouches filled with shotgun shells. They'd tucked the legs of their cargo pants into their boots, Nazi-style, and had stuffed their pockets with CO_2 bombs and clips of nine-millimeter bullets. Both boys were armed with knives, but neither used them. They carried their bombs in a duffel bag and a backpack. Thirty of these exploded: thirteen outside, five in the library, six in classrooms and hallways where the boys

wandered, and six in the cafeteria. Forty-six bombs did not explode:
two outside, twenty-six in the library, fourteen in the hallways and
classrooms, and four in the cafeteria. Twelve unexploded bombs, including the components for a car bomb, were found in Dylan's black
BMW. One unexploded bomb was discovered in Eric's gray Honda
Prelude. The bombs in the cafeteria included two twenty-pound propane tank bombs, which failed to detonate.

They had planned for a much higher body count—higher, they
hoped, than Oklahoma City. Their goal was two hundred and fifty
casualties—the number they'd need to out-McVeigh McVeigh.
Having studied the traffic flow in the cafeteria, they'd set the timers
on the propane bombs for 11:16, when the maximum number of
students would be gathered: five hundred or more, at the tables, in
the lines. The fireball would race through the room, eating oxygen.
They'd be waiting, geared up outside on the hill, and would pick off
the ones who got out alive. Some of their friends would have to die,
but war was war. Sorry, guys. Nothing personal.

For a while, I clung to the editorialists' oversimplifications: the
cause-and-effect of school bullying, violent video games, nihilistic
song lyrics. Maybe overly permissive parenting was to blame. Or
America's rampant, godless consumerism. Or the kickback effect
that anti-depressants can have on children. Or the sorry fact that an
eighteen-year-old girl, accompanied by her underage friends, could
stroll into a weekend gun show and buy two shotguns and a nine-
millimeter carbine rifle without a permit or a background check. The
problem was, I couldn't follow the thread between those causes, alone
or in concert, and the grim realities of Maureen's post-Columbine
existence. Back in Connecticut, her weight dropped to a dangerous
eighty-six pounds. Her hair fell out in clumps. She couldn't work,
couldn't complete household chores, couldn't remember where she'd
put things. She complained incessantly about the chronic pain in her
back and knees, and at the top of her head. In one of Mo's nightmares, Dylan and Eric took turns shooting me in the head, splatter-

ing her with my blood and brains. In another—a dream she dreamed twice—she was trapped in the backseat of a black car. Dylan was at the wheel, taking the hairpin turns of a narrow mountain road at suicidal speeds.

I've searched for answers in churches, and in the offices of my wife's psychiatrists, psychologists, and psychiatric social workers. I've stalked the monster during long, meditative runs on country roads, at the bottoms of wine and scotch bottles, and over the Internet, that labyrinth inside the labyrinth.

Google "Klebold Harris," and you get 135,700 hits. From there, you can lose yourself in the hundreds of pages of the Jefferson County Sheriff's Department's report, or among the myriad criticisms of those official findings. You can listen to the 911 calls, print out the autopsy pictures, take a virtual tour of what the library looked like after the shootings. You can click on the killers' school essays and journal entries, Dylan's elementary school pictures, Eric's Web-site spewings, his pencil sketches of superheroes and minotaurs. You can visit the site where bloggers conjecture about whether Dylan put the gun to his own head or Eric killed him, and whether or not the boys—ridiculed at school as "fags" and "homos"—were, in fact, lovers. And if you have a particularly strong stomach, you can check out the "tribute" Web sites. Built by romantic young women and men who seem to have crushes on the killers, these recast them as misunderstood tragic heroes whose smiling, soft-focus studio portraits stare back at you while sappy pop songs play through your computer speakers.

Because they'd been vicious videographers, Eric and Dylan bequeathed to the police, their parents, and the rest of us several hours' worth of VHS evidence that they'd been hiding in plain sight all along—that we might have stopped them if we hadn't all been so blind. And because individuals and organizations went to court to ensure your right to see it, you can download and watch some of this in-your-face evidence. You can view, for instance, their performances as "Trenchcoat Mafia Protection Services" hit men. Produced for a class assignment, the video shows them first intimidating and then executing unsuspecting bullies. You can watch their shooting practice out at Rampart Range. In that one, they get acquainted with the TEC–9 pistol, the carbine rifle, and the sawed-off shotguns they've gotten hold of with the help of Robyn Anderson and Mark Manes. Manes practice-shoots in this video, too—he, and his girlfriend, and Phil Duran, Eric and Dylan's Blackjack Pizza coworker. It was Duran who introduced them to Manes, and Manes who, for five hundred dollars, sold them the TEC–9 Dylan later used during the massacre. While examining a bowling pin they've just shot up, Dylan muses about the damage a shotgun shell will do to someone's brain.

My pattern was to get Maureen up to bed first, then come back downstairs, pour myself a couple of inches of scotch, and go on-line—cybersearch for an hour or two, often longer, sometimes *much* longer. Occasionally, I'd be on that thing until the sun came up. On the night I downloaded the Rampart Ridge video, I watched it twice, then got up, went outside, and stared up at the indifferent moon, the clouds drifting in front of it. Stared for a while at the halogen glow from the women's prison. I recalled the sight of Lolly, in her uniform, walking down Bride Lake Road on her way to work. That purposeful gait of hers, her arms swinging at her sides. She'd been the most reliable person of my whole life—just about the *only* reliable person—and, once again, I felt the sharp pang of having lost her at the point I needed her most. Then I went back inside and poured myself another drink. Googled "chaos theory" and got fifteen million hits. I clicked on a random one and scrolled down. *Explosive bifurcation is the sudden transition that wrenches the system out of one order, and into another.* Well, they had that right: there was our life before April the twentieth, and our life after it.

I Googled "chaos theory Harris Klebold." Zilch.

Googled "chaos theory Colorado State" and got the curriculum vita and the university office number of Mickey Schmidt, my seatmate on that flight that had brought the two of us out of the Rockies and east——me to my dying aunt and Mickey to Wequonnoc Moon Casino, where he planned to beat the house by applying chaos-complexity theory. Maybe Mickey could guide me through the explosive bifurcation of it all——point me in some direction that might lead us out of the maze. It was December 31, 1999, somewhere after 11:00 p.m. Y2K was upon us, and it was semester break besides. College professors would be away from their offices for weeks. I picked up the phone and called him anyway, and guess what? He answered.

"*Who'd* you say this is?"

"Caelum Quirk. The guy on the plane. We talked about chaos theory. You said you were writing a book for gamblers."

He told me he thought I'd called the wrong guy.

"No, I didn't, man. Your picture's on the faculty Web site."

"Look," he said. "*I'm* busy, and *you're* drunk."

"You told me you were afraid to fly," I said. "You asked me to hold your hand during takeoff."

"And did you?"

"I . . ."

"No," he said. "You didn't. You had me grip the armrest instead. You couldn't do that one small thing."

He hung up before I could get to my questions about Columbine. And so, in the waning minutes of the twentieth century, I finished my drink and poured another. Shut down the computer, rested my cheek against the keyboard, and started sobbing like a baby. I cried so loudly that it woke her up. She came down the stairs. Sat down next to me and touched my cheek. Stroked it, over and over.

"Everything's all right," she lied.

The overhead light shone on her bald patches. The pajamas she wore night and day were stained with food, missing a button. "No, it's not," I said.

"I'm going to get better, Caelum," she said. "I *am*. I promise." And by the time I stopped crying, it was January. A new year, a new century. Outside, the snow was filling up our fallow fields.

I DON'T KNOW. MAYBE WE'RE all chaos theorists. Lovers of pattern and predictability, we're scared shitless of explosive change. But we're fascinated by it, too. Drawn to it. Travelers tap their brakes to ogle the mutilation and mangled metal on the side of the interstate, and the traffic backs up for miles. Hijacked planes crash into skyscrapers, breached levees drown a city, and CNN and the networks rush to the scene so that we can all sit in front of our TVs and feast on the footage. Stare, stunned, at the pandemonium—the devils let loose from their cages. "There but for the grace of God," the faithful say. "It's not for us to know His plan."

Which, I've concluded, is bullshit. Big G, little g: doesn't matter. There *is* no mysterious Master Planner, no one up there who can see the big picture—the order in the disorder. Religion's just a well-oiled, profit-driven denial of the randomness of it all. That's what I've come to believe. Because if some merciful Lord and Master Puppeteer were up there pulling the strings, then why did my wife have to crouch in the dark inside a cabinet that day, listen to all that murder, and survive, only to become her frail, bitter, self-absorbed *un*self? O come all ye faithful and tell me why, in the heat of the moment back in 1980, your all-seeing, all-knowing, Intelligent Designer would *not* have spared us those two collisions of sperm and egg, those divisions and multiplications of cells that became Eric and Dylan. Tell me why, if a benign god's at the control panel, those two kids had to exist, hook up, and stoke each other's mind-poisoned rage.

Not available for downloading are Eric and Dylan's "basement tapes"—the smug, ridiculing rants they recorded late at night, mostly in the Harrises' basement, and left behind for the cops to find and confiscate. Too disturbing for public consumption, a judge ruled. Too much danger of copycat crimes. *I've* seen them, though—the basement tapes. Some of them. It happened more or less by accident.

"Good news!" Cyndi Pixley told me over the phone that December day. "The Paisleys sold their house, so we can go ahead and schedule the closing on your place. How soon do you think you could make it back?"

I hired one of Alphonse's counter girls to stay at the farmhouse with Maureen and flew back to Littleton. And after the Paisleys and I had signed all the paperwork and shaken hands, Cyndi Pixley, whose husband was a cop, casually mentioned that the sheriff's office was showing the basement tapes to the media that afternoon. "Where?" I said.

"The Dakota building, I think Ron said."

"When?"

"One o'clock?"

I looked at my watch. It was twelve forty-three. I ran.

At the door to the screening room, a woman cop stopped me and asked to see my press credentials. "I don't have any," I said.

"Then I'm afraid I can't let you in, sir."

"Oh, I'm going in," I said. "I was one of their teachers at Columbine."

"Well, sir, this viewing is only for—"

"My wife was one of their victims," I said.

"Sir, there were thirteen victims: twelve students and a male teacher."

I nodded. "Dave and I used to eat lunch together in the faculty room. My wife is one of their collateral victims."

"But like I've told you, this screening is strictly for—"

"She can't sleep. Can't concentrate. Can't work."

"Sir, I'm sorry, but I have my orders."

"The investigation you guys did? Where you had everyone go back in the library and get into their same positions? Man, that request did her in. The thought of having to see the bloodstains, the dead kids' names on cards."

"She was in the vicinity of the library then?"

I nodded.

"Sir, these tapes are very disturbing."

"She's lost," I said. "*I'm* lost."

We stared at each other for the next several seconds, neither of us looking away. Then she took a step back and swung the door open wide. There was one seat left, at the end of the second to last row, against the wall. "Morgan McKinley, *Chicago Sun-Times*," the guy next to me said. I looked at the hand he was extending, then shook it. "Yup," I said. "Good. Great."

"Where you here from?" he asked. To my relief, the officer up front stopped talking, and the room went dark before I could answer him.

The tapes resurrect them. In the first one, they talk about what they'll do "next month," so it's March. Lolly's alive, the blood still flowing to her brain. Maureen's mentally healthy—in charge of herself and the kids in her care. It's late at night, long after Eric's parents have gone to sleep upstairs. Looking into the lens of a camera they've borrowed from school, they address the cops, their parents, the classmates they hate, the rest of us. Their shotguns are in their laps. They swig from a bottle of Jack Daniel's and reveal their plans and preparations, their philosophies. They're "evolved," they tell us. "Above human." Theirs is a two-man war against everyone. They sound so fucked-up full of themselves, so pathetically juvenile, that it's hard to believe they'll cause this much pain. "We need to kick-start the revolution here," Eric says. "We need to get a chain reaction going." He stands and opens his trench coat, the better to display his gear. "What you will find on my body in April," he says.

"You're fucking going to pay for this shit," Dylan warns us. "We don't give a shit because we're going to die doing it."

They knew we'd be watching these tapes after they'd killed the others, then themselves. Their suicides had been a part of the plan. They laugh, imagining themselves as "ghosts" who will trigger flashbacks in the survivors' brains. Make them go insane.

That was when it hit me, with the full-force pain of a kick to the groin. They had foreseen Maureen's struggle. Orchestrated it. I'd gone looking for the monster and found it in the darkened room of a municipal building, on a television monitor hooked to a videocassette player inside which tape spooled from left to right. My heart pumped wildly, and the fight-or-flight adrenaline surge I'd felt that morning out at Paul Hay's house was with me again. But there was no pipe wrench in my hand this time, and it was futile to fight videotaped ghosts. I did the only other thing I could do. I fled. Jumped from my chair, pushed past the people standing in back, banged open the door, and ran, stumbling, down the well-lit hallway. And when a men's room door presented itself, I shoved it open, whacked open a stall door, and emptied my gut into a toilet.

On the direct flight back to Connecticut, the seat next to me was empty. I decided I wouldn't tell her—could never tell her—that I'd seen those tapes.

ON THAT MILLENNIAL NIGHT WHEN Maureen came downstairs to stroke my face and quiet my sobs, she had promised me she would get better. And she had, too. Little by little, small gain by small gain. At least it seemed so.

She started getting dressed in the morning. Started walking the dogs after breakfast. And because the exercise energized her, she began eating more. "Caelum, come here," she said one morning, and I followed her voice into the bathroom. She was standing on the scale, smiling shyly. "Ninety-seven? That's great, Mo!" I put my arms around her and pulled her close.

"Ow, ow," she said. "You're hurting my back."

She began taking vitamins, taking the car for short runs to the grocery store. She went to the little IGA on Orchard Street, not the Super Big Y, where, she said, the lights were too bright, the array too overwhelming. When her bald patches grew in, the stylist talked her into having the rest of her hair cut off to match that inch or so of new growth. "Looks cute," I told her. And it did, too, in a boyish, Peter Pan kind of way. Despite her weight gain, she still wasn't menstruating, far as I knew. Sex? We didn't go there. I was pretty sure she didn't want to be touched, and my desire to touch her had waned, anyway. I got that need taken care of in another lost corridor of the Internet.

It took us a year, year and a half, to work our way down the list of psych referrals Dr. Cid had given us before we left Colorado. Dr. Burrage just plain didn't get it, she said. Dr. Darrow's flat affect unnerved her. The drive down I–95 to Dr. Kersh's office was too nerve-racking. "But you're not driving," I said. "*I'm* driving."

"Zigzagging in and out of lanes, passing every single truck you see. By the time I get to his office, I'm a nervous wreck, and then I've got to sit there for fifty minutes and look at that lazy eye of his. Therapy's supposed to make you feel better, not worse."

Dr. Bain gave her homework: a ten-page form that she kept sighing and crying over as she filled it out. I saw the form poking out of her purse the morning of her appointment. She was upstairs; the shower was running. I guess I shouldn't have, not without asking her, but I pulled it out and read it. The symptom checklist got to me: her suffering, spelled out in all those X's and O's. Her answers on the bio contained some surprises. She'd told me her first husband had sometimes been "a bully," but I didn't know he'd hit her. And the high school stuff: she'd run away with a boyfriend? Shoplifted? I noted that she'd left "sexual abuse" unchecked—had given her father another free pass.

But Bain must have been on to something regarding "Daddy," because after their fourth session, Mo said she wasn't going back. "Because he's fixated on my parents," she said, when I asked her why not. "My mother's dead and Daddy's basically out of my life. What's the point?"

"Well, I think—"

"I was *there* that day. I heard those kids being murdered. *That's* the point. Not what my parents did or didn't do."

"But maybe there's some connection between your reactions to what happened that day and your reaction to what your father did when—"

"Shut up!" she screamed. "My father never touched me!"

Dr. Bromley's office had an odor that made her feel nauseous. Dr. Adamcewicz was condescending. And if stupid, frog-eyed Dr. Mancuso thought he was going to put her in a trance and guide her back to that library, he could go to hell.

I pointed out that we'd reached the end of Dr. Cid's referral list.

"Good!" she said. "Great! Then I'm done with shrinks!" Her brain wasn't the problem, anyway, she told me; her body was. If she could just be free of the pain in her back and knees, the pressure she felt at the top of her head, she could sleep through the night. Have a life again. Go back to *work*.

Her bringing in a paycheck would have helped, I had to admit. The month we moved back, JFK, my old high school, had been advertising for an English teacher. I'd applied for the position but hadn't even gotten an interview. Nineteen years of service? Yeah, so what? A few months later, Kristen Murphy—my former *student* teacher, for Christ's sake—was getting ready to go on maternity leave. I asked to be considered for the long-term sub's job but wasn't. That's when the lightbulb finally came on. I'd done my penance and gotten that assault charge expunged from my record, but it had never been expunged from the superintendent's memory. They were done with me.

What I did was stitch together an income. I took an adjunct teaching job at Oceanside Community College: two back-to-back evening courses. Basic English, thirty-five hundred bucks per, no health insurance. Steve Grabarek gave me ten or twelve hours a week at his sawmill. I pinch-hit weekends for Alphonse's nighttime baker. So I was doing a little of everything, but what I *wasn't* doing was making enough to meet our monthly expenses and pay her doctor bills. Once the probate stuff was settled, we'd be able to get at the money in Lolly's bank account and pay down our Visa bill. Until then, I had to keep dipping into our house sale money. It was hard not to pressure her, you know? She was an RN, and places needed nurses. But she couldn't handle a job yet. We both knew that.

She saw an osteopath, two neurologists, a chiropractor, and three GPs about her chronic pain. Well, five GPs, but at the time I only knew about three. Dr. MacKinnon suspected it might be Lyme disease, but the test came back negative. Dr. Mosher ordered a bunch of tests, reviewed the results, and concluded that Mo's pain was psychosomatic. She dismissed him as a quack. Dr. Russo ordered retests of some of the ones she'd already had, plus a CAT scan and an MRI. When all the data was in, the three of us sat down for a powwow. "Mrs. Quirk, I imagine it must have been a terribly tight squeeze inside that cabinet," Russo said. "How long did you say you were hiding in there? Four hours? In the fetal position, right?"

Mo nodded glumly.

"So what I'm thinking is, there had to have been enormous pressure at just the points where you're feeling this persistent pain."

"Are you saying it did nerve damage or something?" I asked.

"No evidence of that." He turned back to Mo. "Your pain is real, Mrs. Quirk. I understand that. But I'm ninety-nine and forty-four one hundredths percent sure the cause is psychological. Now there's a Dr. Mario Mancuso down in New Haven who's done some wonderful work with Ericksonian hypnosis and . . ." His eyes followed her out of the room.

Mo felt more simpatico with Dr. Pelletier, a general practitioner in his seventies whom she knew from her days as nurse supervisor at Rivercrest Nursing Home, and who, without ordering tests, prescribed the "muscle relaxer" Valium to address both her pain and the insomnia it caused.

I kept my mouth shut for a while. Kept watch. Kept counting her remaining tablets each morning when she walked the dogs. More and more, I didn't like the math. She seemed dazed sometimes. Was it psychic numbness or was she overdoing the Valium?

"Look, they *help* me, okay?" she insisted. "Why is that a problem?"

"Because the bottle says three a day tops, and they're disappearing faster than that." If I wanted to act like a prison guard, she said, then I should go next door where the *real* drug addicts were. Because she *wasn't* one, and she resented being treated as if she were. She was a nurse, remember? She knew a hell of a lot more about medications than I did.

The next day, while she was out, I called Pelletier's office. No, I told the receptionist, I *didn't* want a call-back; I'd hold. I stood there, waiting, shaking her pill vial like a castanet. "*Mister* Quirk," he finally said, like I was one more pain in the ass he had to tolerate in the middle of his busy day.

I blurted it out. "Valium's addictive, right?"

He said all minor tranquilizers had the potential to become habit-forming; the risks had to be weighed against the benefits. "Valium got a bad rap after that Hollywood book came out back in the seventies. I forget the title—something about dancing. But I've been prescribing it without a problem for years now. To *hundreds* of patients. Your wife says her pain has lessened, her sleep patterns have regulated. And she understands this is a short-term, not a long-term, solution. Now is there anything else I can do for you?"

"Guess not," I said.

"Good. Stop worrying. She'll be fine."

But Dr. Pelletier didn't know that Dr. Yarnall up in Plainfield was also writing her scripts for Valium, or that Dr. Drake down in New London was supplying her with Ativan. I didn't know this either, until that afternoon down at the bakery. I was helping Alphonse with a big special order: fifteen dozen pastries for some ballroom lecture event up at UConn. "Hey, Quirky! It's for you!" Al called, and I put down the frosting knife and walked over to the wall phone. Jerry Martineau was on the other end. One of his detectives had brought Maureen in, he said. I'd better get down to the station ASAP.

"She's been doctor-shopping," Jerry said. We were seated side by side on a long wooden bench in the hallway of the station house, speaking in hushed voices. "And this afternoon the computer system caught up with her."

I nodded. "So I take it you're arresting her. I better get her a lawyer, right?" Jerry shook his head. He said he understood she'd been to hell and back because of what happened "out there." So when Detective Meehan brought her in, he told him he'd handle this one personally. He'd made some calls, pulled in a favor from the controlled substance guys—not that *that* was for publication. Maureen and he had had a long talk, he said, and she'd made him two promises: she was going to get back into counseling and she was going to start going to meetings.

"What kind of meetings?" I asked.

"Narcotics Anonymous. And I need *you* to make sure she keeps her promises. Okay?" I nodded. "Okay. Good. Now what do you think? You want to take her home or get her into a treatment place? Because, depending on how much of that shit she's gotten hooked on, the next couple days might not be too pretty."

I told him I'd take her home.

"Okay then. Your call, Caelum. I'll go get her."

While I waited on that scarred old wooden bench, I wondered if it was the same one I'd sat on all those years ago, on that snowy day when my father and I had gone downtown to buy me a Davy Crockett coonskin cap and we'd ended up, side by side, in this same friggin' station house hallway. I closed my eyes and saw him again: his front tooth dangling, his shirt stained with blood and egg yolk. *Don't you ever be like me, buddy,* I heard him say. *Because my name is mud. Alden George Quirk the Third MUD!*

Maureen and Jerry approached from the opposite end of the corridor. It hit me: she *looked* like an addict—scrawny and scared, with those jumpy eyes. She walked up to me and, without a word, rested her forehead against my chest. My hand hovered an inch or so away from the small of her back, but I couldn't bring myself to place it there. Not with Jerry standing there, watching us. I felt grateful to him, but resentful, too. "Let's go home," I said.

In the car, she kept thanking me for my loyalty and begging me not to leave her. She was *relieved* she'd been found out, she said. As horrible as this day had been, it had given her the motivation she needed. She was going to get better. I'd see.

"Good," I said. "Because I'm not even sure who you are anymore. I miss the woman I married. The woman that sat across from me in the bakery on our first date. Where did *she* go?" Neither of us said anything more, but we were both in tears.

The dogs managed what I couldn't: a welcome-home party. They barked and sashayed, nuzzled her. "I don't want to have to pull this whole place apart," I said. "So why don't you get up off your knees and show me where you've stashed it all?" She nodded obediently and got back on her feet.

Her prescription from Dr. Pelletier—the only one I'd known about—was in the medicine cabinet. She handed it over. She'd hidden the pills from Dr. Yarnall inside a package of tampons. The generic mail-order meds were in her closet, tucked in the toes of her winter boots. She smiled and said she was glad all the sneaky stuff was over. "What about the Ativan?" I said.

"The Ativan?"

I consulted the notes I'd taken during my conversation with Jerry. "The shit you conned some Dr. Drake into giving you," I said.

She nodded, defeated. I followed her back downstairs and into the pantry. Standing on the stool, she stretched her arm to the top shelf and groped behind some of Hennie's old cookbooks. "Here," she said.

"And that's all of it?" She said it was, but, hey, you take an addict's word with a grain of salt.

Her contrition lasted until about nine that evening, at which point her panic went into overdrive and she went on the attack. "What about *you?*" she screamed. "You drink too much, and you're on that goddamned computer all the time! Those are addictions, too, aren't they? What's the difference?"

"I didn't get my ass hauled into the police station today. *That's* the difference. Do you know how close you came to getting arrested?"

"Oh, shut up. You and your bullshit self-righteousness. Why don't you pour a drink and toast yourself for being so superior? Fucking hypocrite!"

I went to the liquor cabinet, uncapped and uncorked every bottle that was in there, and brought them all to the sink. Then I pulled her confiscated meds out of my jeans pockets, uncapped the vials, and poured them down the drain. Poured my scotch and vodka and wine over them. When she lunged for the few pills that hadn't made it down the pipe, I grabbed her from behind and pulled her away. She took several half-hearted whacks at me, but I blocked them. In the scuffle, we both tumbled onto the floor. The dogs stood over us, barking crazily. Maureen got herself up and, from the doorway, glared at me. "I need help!" she screamed. "Help me!"

"What the fuck do you think I'm *trying* to do?" I screamed back.

We were up most of that night, her pacing through the house, ranting half the time, sobbing and whimpering the other half. At one point, she said she wished they'd found her that day and killed her, too. "Well, they didn't," I said. "You came out of there alive. So goddamn deal with it."

I made pots of coffee, mugs of tea, trying to stay awake and alert, trying to outlast her. She finally conked out, splayed the wrong way across our bed, somewhere after three in the morning. I covered her with a quilt, then flopped into the chair by our bed and fell into a deep sleep myself. I awakened with a start to a clanging sound. She wasn't in bed, or in any of the upstairs rooms. I ran downstairs and headed to the kitchen, where the noise was coming from. From the doorway, I took it in: my toolbox, the wrenches, the hammer wrapped up in a dishtowel. She'd tried but failed to disassemble the drain pipe. Now she was standing at the sink, slamming her hand, over and over, against the drain. Hoping against hope, I realized, that she might jam her hand down far enough and retrieve a pain pill or two that had survived the dousing.

Her desperation gave her a broken finger, a sprained wrist, and five badly skinned knuckles, but none of those lost pills.

———

HER NARCANON MEETINGS WERE IN the basement of the Episcopal church at the corner of Sexton and Bohara. Night driving made her uneasy, especially in that area of town, so every Tuesday, Thursday, and Saturday evening, I'd drive her over there, then drive back home. Get in the car and go pick her up an hour and a half later. "So how'd it go?" I'd ask.

She'd shrug.

"These meetings helping you?"

She'd shrug again.

Her sponsor, Gillian, was laconic-bordering-on-hostile. She usually called at dinnertime. "It's the Ice Queen," I'd say, my hand over the mouthpiece, and Maureen would rise from the table, take the cordless from me, and leave the room. Leave me sitting there with my meal and myself. "Maybe you could ask her to call a little later?" I suggested one night.

"Why?"

"Because this is *our* time. And because I hate to see you have to get halfway through your dinner and then come back to it after it's gone stone cold." Maureen said Gillian worked full time and had a family. She called when she could. These conversations were more important than whether or not she ate hot food.

I ran into Jerry Martineau at Target. Yes, she was going to meetings,

I reported. No, she hadn't gotten back into counseling just yet, but we were working on that, too.

That night, I sat in bed with her, leafing through the Yellow Pages.

"What about Dr. Patel?" I said. "You liked her."

She reminded me that Dr. Patel was a couples counselor.

"That's what *we* went to her for. Doesn't mean that's all she does."

I called and left a message; Dr. P called back. Yes, yes, she said. Many of her patients over the years—the majority of her forensic patients, actually—suffered from posttraumatic stress disorder. So while she couldn't claim to be an expert, she was certainly familiar with this malady and its treatments. And it would be lovely to work with Maureen again. "And so, very good, we will meet next Wednesday at four p.m. Yes, yes."

She had relocated her practice to a warren of duplex two-stories in the Industrial Park—medical and dental offices, for the most part. The brick walkway leading to her door was lined with waist-high Indian statuary—Hindu gods and goddesses whose serene smiles and bared breasts belied the damp chill of the gray March day. The waiting room was narrow and nondescript. We were hanging up our coats when the inner office door swung open, and Dr. Patel emerged in a sari of brilliant blues and greens. "Ah, yes, the Quirks. Come in, come in." She seemed genuinely happy to see us, but of course, she didn't know who we'd become.

Her office walls were painted a sunny yellow; the furniture, soft and comforting, was kiwi green. Mo and I sat on the sofa, and I was suddenly aware of how drab and monochromatic we were: she in her baggy gray sweater and black jeans, me in gray jeans and a gray UConn sweatshirt. The table between us held a small stack of magazines, a bubbling dish fountain. A terrarium, filled with lush, moist plants, was home to a fat leopard frog, turquoise and black.

She fed us first: slices of mango on a pale green dish, a small bowl of cashews, a larger bowl, royal blue and white, that brimmed with strawberries. "It's robbery, the price they ask for fruit out of season," she said. "But March is such a long and dreary month. One must treat oneself to small indulgences, yes?" I nodded. Popped a strawberry in my mouth. It was so delicious that I ate another, a third, a fourth. Maureen bit into a single cashew.

I told Dr. P about our lives in Littleton: our home, our jobs, Mo's attempts to reestablish a connection with her father and his family, the shootings and their aftermath. "You want to tell her about the pills?" I asked Mo. She shook her head, so I told her. I was aware, as I spoke, that Dr. Patel was both listening to me and observing Maureen.

"Most helpful, Mr. Caelum," she said. "Very, very useful information. And now, shall we hear from Saint Augustine?"

I shrugged. "Why not?" I said.

Dr. P read from a blood-red leather book. "*My soul was a burden, bruised and bleeding. It was tired of the man who carried it, but I found no place to set it down to rest. Neither the charm of the countryside nor the sweet scents of a garden could soothe it. It found no peace in song or laughter, none in the company of friends at table or in the pleasures of love, none even in books or poetry. . . . Where could my heart find refuge from itself? Where could I go, yet leave myself behind?*"

She closed the book, then reached across the table and took Maureen's hand in hers. "Does that passage speak to you?" she asked. Mo nodded and began to cry. "And so, Mr. Caelum, good-bye."

Because the passage had spoken to me, too, it took me a few seconds to react. "Oh," I said. "You want me to leave?"

"I do. Yes, yes." She handed me a couple of the magazines on the table: the *Sun*, *Parabola*. "So we shall see you in, oh, thirty minutes."

"Yeah, okay. Sure." I stood. Began backing out of the room. I was reluctant, suddenly, to leave a place so full of color: the warm yellow walls, Dr. Patel's peacock blue sari, the orange flesh of the mango, and those strawberries, like fat, edible jewels.

Rather than cool my jets in the waiting room, I left. Put the key in the ignition, started the car, and drove around until I found a florist. I bought Maureen a bouquet: red carnations, blue delphinium, and a single Stargazer lily. The aroma of its fleshy bloom filled the car.

"Where'd you go?" she asked.

"Here." I handed her the bouquet.

She smiled, smelled the lily. When we got home, she put the flowers in a vase and carried them up to the bedroom. It had been Lolly and Hennie's, and now it was ours. I lit two candles. Put one on her bureau and one in the window. "I love you," I said.

"I love you, too."

That night, for the first time in two years, we risked intimacy.

chapter sixteen

WHEN MORGAN SEABERRY WAS IN utero, his mother had been sick as a dog. Morgan's older brother, Jesse, was three at the time. Studying the murky ultrasound photos of his brother-to-be, he had wondered aloud if, in the event that they didn't like the baby after it arrived, they could give it back. "That's not how it works, buddy," his dad had told Jesse. "And it's a 'he,' not an 'it.' You're going to have a little brother." This was Carole Seaberry's third pregnancy. There'd been a miscarriage between Jesse and Morgan.

Morgan was born two weeks before his due date, on Labor Day of 1987. It was a relatively easy delivery, compared to Jesse's: two hours in the birthing room at Rockville Hospital, as opposed to fourteen. Mike Seaberry had meant to clear out and wallpaper the spare room that summer, but it had been crazy at work (Mike was in Human Resources at the University of Connecticut), and he just plain hadn't gotten around to it. So he'd pasted and put up the paper—a repeating circus theme—while three-day-old Morgan sat contentedly in his infant seat on the just-carpeted floor. "That's the image that comes to me whenever I think about him," Mike Seaberry was quoted as saying in "A Victim's Victims," which appeared as a lengthy Annals of Justice article in the *New Yorker* the week before Maureen's sentencing. "Good-natured right from the beginning."

Morgan had been an easy baby, his mother said—and a funny one.

So much so that the Seaberrys bought a camcorder they couldn't really afford because they wanted to capture for posterity their younger son's comical antics: his impromptu dances and Pampers-padded pratfalls, his inverting of the dog's water dish and wearing it as a hat. Rosalie Rand, the author of "A Victim's Victims," was shown some of these videos. She wrote of them: "Jesse leaps and flies between the camera and his little brother, trying hard to upstage him, but Morgan is clearly the star of the show."

"He was very creative," Morgan's teacher, Mrs. Leggett, recalled. "And such a sweet boy, too. Never a tattletale. And so considerate of others. When we played 'dog and bone' or sang 'Farmer in the Dell,' Morgan would always go out of his way to choose the children least likely to be picked by the others."

In 1996, twelve-year-old Jesse was "identified" and medicated (ADHD, Ritalin) and Morgan, a fourth-grader, won three awards. *Weekly Reader* magazine cited him for his poem about endangered Bengal tigers. His fire prevention poster was Vernon, Connecticut's entry in the statewide competition that year. In May, Morgan was named Vernon's Student of the Month. The Seaberrys videotaped the presentation of his award at the school board meeting, capturing, simultaneously, Morgan's comical acceptance speech and, behind him in the audience, his brother Jesse's obstinate concentration on Simon, the noisy handheld electronic game he was playing as an alternative to watching his brother's latest triumph.

Mike and Carole Seaberry's abrupt separation in 1997 had been unanticipated by their children, and, until seventy-two hours earlier, by Carole. There were three Seaberry siblings now; Jesse was fifteen, Morgan was eleven, and little Alyssa was five. Mike, who later married Ellen Makris, the young associate professor of Romance languages with whom he'd begun an affair, remained in Connecticut. (He'd been promoted twice and was now UConn's Human Services *director.*) Against her estranged husband's wishes, Carole relocated with the kids to Red Bank, New Jersey, the town where her parents lived. The divorce became final the following year, at which time Carole dropped the surname Seaberry and became, again, Carole Alderman.

It was after the move to Red Bank that Jesse Seaberry's downward spiral gained momentum. He'd had few friends back in Vernon, but now he had none, except for the forty-seven-year-old arcade operator at Monmouth Beach who hired Jesse as a janitor and roving change-maker, and who paid him in whiskey, weed, and fistfuls of quarters. In October Carole was notified that Jesse, who'd been leaving the house at 7:15 each morning, ostensibly to catch the school bus, had missed nineteen consecutive days of school. They *had* contacted her, the attendance officer insisted. Three times. Had Jesse been intercepting their messages? Shaken, Carole swallowed her pride and called her ex for backup. Mike had driven to New Jersey two days later to give his son "a reality check." Jesse had refused to come out of his room, and the one-hour standoff ended only when Mike threatened to break the lock on Jesse's bedroom door, remove the door, and drive it, Jesse's computer, his PlayStation, and his CD and video game collections back to Connecticut. The lock clicked, the door opened, and Jesse emerged, stinking of pot and body odor. He was shirtless, and the ripped, dirty jeans he was wearing rode four or five inches below his underwear. Across his bony chest he'd Magic Markered the words *Satin Rocks*. Halfway through Mike's harangue, he had pointed at his son's chest and asked, "What's *that* about? 'Satin rocks?' What the hell does that mean?"

"It's *Satan* rocks!" Jesse had retorted. "You work at a college, and you can't even read?" Mike had laughed in his son's face and said that if Jesse was going to worship the devil, the least he could do was learn how to spell his name. Then Jesse had called his father an "a-hole," and Mike had lost it and backhanded him, accidentally chipping his son's front tooth with the big, clunky college ring he still wore (Rutgers, class of 1978; he'd been a senior when Carole was a sophomore). In "A Victim's Victims" Mike identified this as a critical juncture in

Jesse's life—the point at which he should have overruled his ex-wife and taken his at-risk son back to Connecticut where, under a father's firm hand, Jesse might have turned back from the road he had started down. Carole Alderman told Rosalie Rand that yes, it was true that Mike had made the offer to intervene with Jesse during that visit, but, in her opinion, the proposal had been made halfheartedly. And if Mike had wanted so badly to be a responsible parent, why had he abdicated and set up housekeeping elsewhere?

Morgan, too, had had a bumpy transition to Red Bank. One of his new classmates had taken an immediate, illogical dislike to Morgan and began ridiculing him relentlessly, insisting that Morgan was a girl's name, hence Morgan must be gay. Morgan had tried to ignore his tormenter, who lisped and flapped a limp wrist at him in the hall-way for the amusement of his buddies. Then, one day in the cafeteria line, Morgan had lost his temper and whacked the bully in the face with his lunch tray, giving him a very public bloody nose. Morgan's victim was sent to the nurse, and Morgan was sent to the office—for disciplining this time, rather than for an award. But Morgan, being Morgan, had turned things around. While waiting for Mr. Wengel, the assistant principal, he passed the time by entertaining the school secretaries with jokes and impressions of Presidents Clinton, Reagan, and Nixon. When Mr. Wengel returned from his meeting, he'd asked what all the laughing was about, and the secretaries had made Morgan repeat his routines. By the time Mr. Wengel notified Morgan's mother to report the lunchroom incident, he began the conversation with, "Ma'am, I'm calling about a problem, but first of all, let me tell you that's quite a kid you have there." Recalling the incident, his mother, smiling through her tears, had told Rosalie Rand that Morgan could have taught Dale Carnegie a thing or two about how to win friends and influence people.

Out of financial necessity, Carole Alderman had surrendered her status as a stay-at-home mother and become, first, a graduate stu-dent (her parents paid for her coursework and pitched in with the kids) and, later, a paralegal for the Perth Amboy Housing Authority. She'd been on the job a scant six weeks when she fingered a lump in her breast. There were tests, a mastectomy, difficult post-op radiation treatments. The Housing Authority, considering Carole had just barely begun her career there, had been great about it. Her insurance had covered everything, and they'd held her job open during her three-month recuperation. Her coworkers had even thrown her a small welcome-back party. Amidst the cake-eating and well-wishing, Carole had given an impromptu speech, addressing cancer itself— warning the disease that, if it thought it was going to beat *her*, it had better think again, because she had kids to raise and worthwhile work to do. Everyone in the break room had put down their plates and applauded. And Carole's defiance of the disease seemed to have worked, too; every half-year since, her tests had come back negative. Her kids had been terrifically supportive during her ordeal, too, she told Rosalie Rand; all three of them, Jesse included, had locked arms and accompanied her during her first postradiation Walk for Life. Mike had driven down, too, at Morgan's secret request. It had floored her: Morgan's doing that and Mike's having made that effort. They were a family again, for an afternoon, at least, and for an evening. The five of them had gone to dinner at the Olive Garden, and, well, if Carole's cancer ever *did* return, at least she could say she'd had that night, when they'd laughed and eaten all those different kinds of pasta and had gotten silly enough to play chew-and-show with the tiramisu, even Carole, wearing her paisley head scarf and prosthetic breast.

Carole had dated a little before she'd gotten sick, but postmastectomy she did not. She felt self-conscious about her absent breast, and on top of that she had gained weight, thanks in large part to the stress brought on by Jesse's various dramas. And kids were a liability to a woman trying to date; she loved her children more than she could say, but what man in his right mind would want to date someone who had a Lane Bryant wardrobe, a single breast, and three children, one of whom had a drug problem? No, she had faced it:

she was going to remain single, and so be it. As much as she'd like to claim otherwise, she loved Mike and only Mike, the man with whom she'd created four children, three of whom still walked the earth. She pictured that love as a perpetual flame, like the one Jackie Kennedy had designated for the grave of her slain husband. President Kennedy: *another* husband who had stomped on his marriage vow. No, Carole would always love Mike, she admitted to Rosalie Rand, but she remained bitter about his betrayal.

Jesse, like his mother, harbored a powerful resentment of his father and refused to have anything to do with him, not even that Saturday night when Mike drove down from Connecticut on a moment's notice—the night when Jesse was arrested for possession of crystal meth and needed, if not his dad, then the lawyer and the bail bondsman his dad had gotten him. Not even the night when Mike arrived, white as a ghost, and stood at Jesse's bedside in the emergency room, sobbing and apologizing. He'd driven like a bat out of hell down I–95 after Carole had called to tell him Jesse had tried to end his life by hanging himself with his belt in that filthy apartment where he lived with the woman who owned all those cats. "You're the invisible man. I don't even see you standing there," Jesse had told his father, slurring his words, and then falling into a deep, tranquilized sleep.

Conversely, Morgan and Alyssa visited their dad and his fun young wife, Ellen, for a one-month vacation every July. In 2001, Mike and Ellen took the kids to Disney World; the following year, the four of them went to a dude ranch in Wyoming. Morgan, who, after his move to New Jersey, had remained a loyal fan of UConn basketball, was also allowed to fly back twice a year by himself to Connecticut. (Carole would not even *discuss* Thanksgiving or Christmas.) Morgan arrived at Bradley Airport each October for "Midnight Madness," the official kickoff of the Huskies' season, and then again in March, when he and his dad would drive down together to Madison Square Garden for the Big East championship. Because of Mike Seaberry's status at UConn, Morgan got to pin a badge to his shirt pocket and attend press conferences and Husky Hospitality Receptions, where he could stare up at, and even converse a little with, the players. He would bring his Sharpie pen and his memorabilia to these gatherings, and so he became the proud owner of autographed cards, mini-basketballs, team pictures, and posters from the likes of Ray Allen, Kevin Ollie, and Rip Hamilton, each of whom had gone on to successful careers in the NBA. Jesse, home from rehab in 2002, had hacked his way past the password of his mother's computer and offered his brother's signed sports memorabilia collection for quick sale on eBay. He'd gotten three hundred and twelve dollars for it, most of which he later shot into his arm. Carole, who had learned from the other addicts' parents in her therapy group that enabling only made matters worse, urged Morgan to press charges against his older brother. But Morgan was resolute in his refusal to do so. Despite everything, he still loved and looked up to his big brother as he always had, and still kept his favorite photo on his bedroom bureau: the one Mike had snapped of his sons, ages five and nine, on the Ferris wheel at the Woodstock Fair. In the photo, the brothers sit, hip to hip, wearing UConn T-shirts and those trendy bi-level hairstyles that, back during the Depression, had been called bowl cuts. Arms around each other, the brothers laugh, open-mouthed, Jesse with his surfboard-sized second teeth and Morgan still in his baby teeth. The crossbar has been snapped safely shut, and the hairy hand on the left side of the picture grips the lever that is about to propel the wheel forward. The brothers anticipate their exciting and terrifying ascent.

In his junior year of high school, Morgan was named a soccer team tri-captain, and he was the track team's best hurdler. He had decided not to participate in a winter sport, so that he could take part in the Drama Club's production of *Of Mice and Men*. Mrs. McCloskey cast him against type in the role of Curly, the sadistic nemesis of George and Lenny, the leads, and audiences were impressed that such a nice kid could play a creep so convincingly. Morgan was a class officer that year, too—treasurer—and, in May, was named to the king's court at the junior prom. (His date, Emily Nickerson, was prom queen, and Emily's mother, who was vice-president of the PTO, had confided to Carole Alderman that Morgan had only missed being king by three votes.) That same spring, Morgan was inducted into the National Honor Society. He held membership in the Politics Club, the Latin Club, the Hunger Relief Committee, and the Gay-Straight Alliance, which had successfully lobbied for the right of two senior girls, avowed lesbians, to attend the senior prom as a tuxedoed couple. Morgan's SAT score that spring was an impressive 1540, up eighty points from his PSAT score earler that year.

Carole Alderman told Rosalie Rand that her two younger children "validated" her. Her husband might have left her, and her firstborn might be beyond saving, but she must have done *something* right, because her daughter, Alyssa, was the sweetest, most helpful girl in the world, and her son, Morgan Alderman Seaberry, had been listed in the 2002–3 volume of *Who's Who in American High Schools*. His, she knew, would be a limitless future.

With that in mind, Carole had begun planning a college application strategy for her highest-achieving child. Rutgers would be Morgan's "safety" school, Brown and Princeton his "reach" schools. He'd likely get into some or all of the following: NYU, Wesleyan, Georgetown, and Cornell. Carole went online and took the virtual tours of several of these campuses. But Morgan, since his move to Red Bank, had had his heart set on attending a school not on his mother's list: UConn, where he might sit in the student section at Huskies games and hang out at his dad's on weekends. Carole objected rigorously, despite the fact that her ex-husband's affiliation with the school meant a free ride, tuition-wise. "Party school!" she'd argued. "You're Ivy League material!" She and Morgan had quarreled about this, Carole Alderman told Rosalie Rand, but that had been the *only* time, really, when she and her younger son had ever disagreed about *anything*. In the end, Carole had agreed, begrudgingly, to accompany Morgan to a UConn Open House during Columbus Day weekend. The foliage would be at or near its peak, she figured, and she could visit her old Connecticut friends who were undertaking the college selection process with *their* kids. That would be fun. And whatever arguments the presenters might use to sell Morgan on UConn, she could debunk these, point by point, as she walked alongside him.

But there was a complication: Jesse, recently released from the halfway house, was working at a chicken farm and living back at home, rent-free—just for the time being. Carole was not about to enable him long-term. Nor was she going to trust him in her house by himself for a three-day weekend. The last time she'd done that, she'd ended up with a two-hundred-dollar cable bill because of the smut he'd watched on pay-per-view. Well, live and learn, she'd told herself. This time, she had made his living there conditional on his coming along with them to Connecticut for the open-house weekend.

Mike and Ellen, who were delighted at the prospect that Morgan might matriculate at UConn, had invited them all to stay at their beautiful new four-thousand-square-foot home in Glastonbury. Carole had put her foot down and said she could absolutely *not* stay in that woman's house, no matter how modern and cool and twenty-first-century it would be to become friends with the person who had stolen her husband away from his children. Instead, she had booked two rooms at the Comfort Inn a few miles south of UConn on Route 32. She and Alyssa could stay in one room, Carole told the kids, and Jesse and Morgan could double up in the other. "The motel is right near a mall!" she'd said, by way of counteracting Morgan and Alyssa's disappointment about this alternate arrangement. "And it's directly across from a McDonald's! We can have breakfast there!" Jesse had raised vehement objections to being dragged along to some "stupid college propaganda thing" for the benefit of "Mr. Wonderful," but was nevertheless on board for staying any place where he wouldn't have to see his father, who, he firmly believed, had wrecked his life.

UNDER DR. PATEL'S GUIDANCE, MAUREEN devised a list of personal goals by which she might, by increments, reengage with the world. She posted these—there were nine—on the inside of our bedroom closet door. One by one, she began checking them off. She planted and maintained a flower garden that summer. She bought a digital camera and taught herself how to use it. She joined Curves for Women and exercised there four mornings a week. At Curves, she ran into her old friend, Jackie Molinari. Mo and Jackie had been nurses together at Rivercrest. Mo called me on her cell phone (she had a cell phone now) to tell me she and Jackie were going out for breakfast. "Great," I said. "Awesome. Gotta go." I was in the middle of my quick-change routine: shuck my bakery clothes, shower away the smell of grease, climb into my teaching khakis, and get the hell down to the community college, a forty-minute commute. My Oceanside students were, for the most part, sincere but obtuse. That week, we were struggling through essays by Montaigne, Emerson, and Joan Didion. Tired of circling the endless errors on their papers, I was also planning to give them a usage lesson on *its* and *it's*; *your* and *you're*; *there*, *their*, and *they're*. In teaching, you have to begin where they are, you know?

Maureen began to read again—number five on her list of resolves. Before her posttraumatic stress, she'd been an avid reader—novels, mostly. Right after the killings, she'd *try* to read, but would stare at the words, unable to make sense of them. Later, after her comprehension skills returned, she had struggled to recall, from one page to the next, what had happened. Descriptions of violence short-circuited her. (For the same reason, she avoided television.) Books had become one more source of frustration and fear, so she'd stopped opening them. Now, with Dr. Patel's coaxing, she tried again and found that the pleasure of reading had returned to her. She got herself a library card and checked out a book a week, sometimes two. That was cool. But then she signed up for the Preferred Readers program at the bookstore in the mall and began ordering stuff on Amazon.

I had to put the brakes on her book *buying*. Dr. Patel had adjusted her fee because we were paying her out of pocket, but sixty a session twice a week still added up. Sixty a session was what we were paying the chiropractor, too, to alleviate her back pain, which, I was pretty sure, was in her head, not her spine. Sophie's hip dysplasia had been diagnosed by then; the vet bills, plus her medication, were averaging about a hundred and a half a month. On top of that, Mo's Accord started acting its age. She freaked one afternoon when it quit on her while she was driving back from the IGA, and a guy who she said looked like pockmarked Richard Speck, that nurse killer from way back when, stopped to offer assistance. My Tercel was three years newer, so we switched cars. The Accord died on me once, too. I was driving back from Oceanside, traveling fifty-five or sixty maybe, and the engine just stopped. God, you ought to have heard all the honking and brake squealing, seen all those raised middle fingers. That commute back from school was a bitch, anyway: me fighting sleep after a night's worth of doughnut-making and a morning's worth of teaching, and cars and buses are whizzing past me on the right *and* on the left, everyone itching to get to the casino so they could hand over their money to the Indians.

"Risk new friendships" was number seven on Maureen's list. Her first year of NarcAnon, she automatically said no whenever anyone at the meetings invited her to go out for coffee afterward. But Dr. Patel nudged her to respond to some of these overtures—the ones from people to whom Mo was drawn. That was how she became friends with Althea, the watercolorist, and Nehemiah, who was HIV-positive and ate macrobiotic, and Tricia, who worked for a caterer and was "a riot." Mo spoke often about this trio, although I never met them, or knew what they looked like, or what their last names were. One Saturday night, the four of them drove down together to Madison. Amy Tan was giving a reading at R. J. Julia. I'd read Tan and wasn't working that night. I would have liked to have gone, too, but I wasn't on the guest list. Mo came back after eleven, aglow, clutching her signed copy of *The Bonesetter's Daughter*. The reading had been great, she said; Amy Tan had been charming and funny, and Mo had even gotten to pat her adorable little dog.

"You know something?" I said. "NarcAnon's like your netherworld."

She had gotten into bed a few minutes earlier and was already on page 9 of *The Bonesetter's Daughter*. "My netherworld?"

Having gotten her attention, I extended the simile. "Yeah, and these mysterious addicts you hang with: they're like hobbits or something."

She closed her book, placed it on her nightstand, and turned off her light. Her disembodied voice mumbled that I should get some sleep.

"You know what's hard?" I said. My eyes had adjusted, and I was looking at her back, her blanket-covered head.

She didn't answer.

"About your NarcAnon buddies? And your list of goals? It's always about *you*. What's good for *you*. Never, you know, about what's good for *us*. I mean, nine goals, and I'm not in *any* of them?"

"Caelum, you're in all of them," she said. "If I can get better, *we* can get better. And I'm making gains—you know I am. But I need you to be patient."

"You," I said. "You, you, you, you, you."

The next day, when she returned from her appointment with Dr. Patel, she informed me that I needed to stop referring to her friends as hobbits.

Oh? Why was that? I asked her.

"Because it trivializes them. It minimalizes their struggle to maintain sobriety, and my struggle, too. Those meetings have taught me what bravery is, okay? I had a long talk about it today with Beena and—"

"Beena? You two are on a first-name basis now? Gee, maybe Beena can hang with you and your posse next time Amy Tan and her dog are in town."

I know, I know. A case could be made that I was being a jealous jerk. I was drinking again—not that that justified anything. That night when I'd dumped all her pills and all my alcohol down the sink? I'd abstained for several months after that. But I'd started up again. It had begun with a beer or two while Alphonse and I were watching a game, a glass of wine with dinner. Then two or three glasses. Then a stop-off at the package store and a right turn toward the hard liquor wall. It wasn't like I was stumbling around drunk or anything. Not like I was turning into my father. But between the Mama Mia and the teaching and paper-grading, I was averaging sixty, seventy hours a week, just so we could tread water. I'd get home from Oceanside, and I'd be both exhausted and keyed up. So I'd pour myself a drink or two to take the edge off. Mellow out a little. Because in the next seven hours, I'd have to squeeze in sleeping, eating, and getting through my students' papers, then head over to the bakery and start churning out product. I was careful not to pressure her about getting back to work; I knew she wasn't ready. But it wasn't easy working days and nights. A couple of drinks made it a little easier.

In the plus column, we had a sex life again. Sunday mornings, mostly. No teaching or baking or NarcAnon on Sundays. The dogs would start bugging me around sunrise, so I'd stumble out of bed and down the stairs. Let them out, let them back in and feed them. Brew us coffee. I'd come back upstairs, mugs in hand, and she'd have gotten ready for me: hair combed, teeth brushed, and naked under the covers. So it was nice, those Sunday mornings. Different, though. A little too deliberate. And there was the orgasm issue. Before, she'd been able to get off pretty regularly. Now, it took her a lot longer, and a lot of those Sunday mornings, she couldn't get there. I mean, after a while I'd be getting carpal tunnel and/or tongue fatigue, you know? Then she'd push my hand or my head away and stick me inside of her, and I'd have such a case of blue balls by then, I'd be done in seconds. "Aah, oh, I love you," she'd go, and it would remind me of that restaurant scene in *When Harry Met Sally*, when Sally demonstrates to Billy Crystal how good women are at faking it. . . . What was that actress's name? The one who played Sally? The one who, in real life, cheated on Dennis Quaid with that other actor. The Gladiator. Couldn't remember his name, either.

So what does that tell you, Sherlock? I asked myself at the bakery one night, when I was thinking about all this.

Tells me I identify with the wronged husband.

Right you are!

You can do that, you know, if you work the graveyard shift solo: have conversations with yourself. It's not like the doughnuts are going to talk to you.

From: studlysicilian@snet.net
To: caelumq@aol.com
Sent: Wednesday, March 3, 2003
Subject: That explains it

A new Sex Institute of America study shows that a woman's sexual attraction to a man varies according to her menstrual cycle. When she is ovulating, she is attracted to rugged, virile males. But when she has PMS, she pre-fers a man who has a scissors sunk in his head, a live bat jammed up his ass, and is strapped into a recliner that's going up in flames.

From: caelumq@aol.com
To: studlysicilian@snet.net
Sent: Wednesday, March 3, 2003
Subject: That explains it

Amazing how you got to be such an expert on women, considering the only ones you've ever had are your Sexy Cindy blow up doll and Fanny Five Fingers.

From: studlysicilian@snet.net
To: caelumq@aol.com
Sent: Wednesday, March 3, 2003
Subject: That explains it

U forgot about the time Heather Locklear came
into the bakery craving an oversize
cruller.
   Hey can u wrk for me Sat. afternoon? Thinkin
about drivin down to NYC for the auto show.
Kinda wanna see that McLaren.

From: caelumq@aol.com
To: studlysicilian@snet.net
Sent: Wednesday, March 3, 2003
Subject: That explains it

Can't. Maureen and I have an appointment with
her shrink.

From: studlysicilian@snet.net
To: caelumq@aol.com
Sent: Wednesday, March 3, 2003
Subject: That explains it

Uh oh. Sounds like your in the dog house.

From: caelumq@aol.com
To: studlysicilian@snet.net
Sent: Wednesday, March 3, 2003
Subject: That explains it

It's "YOU'RE in the dog house." As in "YOU ARE
in the dog house."

From: studlysicilian@snet.net
To: caelumq@aol.com
Sent: Wednesday, March 3, 2003
Subject: That explains it

Yeah but Quirky, who besides you gives a rats
ass?

Alphonse had been right: I *was* in the doghouse, which was why
Dr. Patel had called the summit. Earlier that week, I'd cut my finger,
gone looking for a Band-Aid, and found, at the back of Mo's nightstand drawer, an unrecognizable white box. Inside the box was a
flashlight-looking gizmo. Plastic, putty-colored, battery-operated. I
turned it on, and that's when it dawned on me: she'd gotten herself a
vibrator.

I let it massage the palm of my hand, the stretch of skin between
my thumb and index finger. *This* was going to do it for her, when I
couldn't? Out of nowhere, I heard Paul Hay's wife's friend that night
she called to clue me in on Mo's affair. Saw Paul Hay come flying at
me that morning when I'd gone out to his house, busted his Andersen windows, and almost busted in his skull. Not that they were in
the same ballpark or anything, but Mo'd had her trauma and I'd had
mine. We both had our triggers.

I went downstairs and presented the evidence. Pointed it at her and
flipped the switch. "So who do you fantasize about when you're using
this thing?" I said. "Brad Pitt? Batman? You want me to wear tights
or something?"

It wasn't like that, she said. "Beena suggested—"

"Beena? You fantasize about your *shrink*?"

She asked me to please stop being a jerk.

But at that moment, I *felt* like being one. Felt justified. "I mean, it
can't be me you're fantasizing about, because, hey, you've got direct
access there. Not that *that's* doing much for you. So who is it? Tom
Cruise? Paul Hay?"

———————

DR. PATEL HANDED US CUPS of licoricy-smelling tea. Her
sari that day was purple—a shimmery, iridescent material draped

over a pale blue shirt. She was smiling as serenely as Buddha. "I'll get right to the point, Mr. Caelum," she said. "It is I who encouraged Maureen to experiment with a marital aid."

"Oh," I said. "Yeah?" Some of my tea spilled into the saucer.

"And it appears you are uncomfortable with that?"

I shifted from one butt cheek to the other. "Uncomfortable? No, I wouldn't say that."

Maureen, seated beside me, snorted quietly.

"What? I'm *not*. I just . . . I guess I just don't understand why . . . "

"Go on," Dr. Patel said.

"No. Never mind."

"Very well, then. May I ask you a question?"

"Shoot."

"Do you masturbate?"

I felt my ears blush. "Do *I*? Not with something that requires double-A batteries." She kept looking at me, not smiling. If you'd given me a choice at that moment—either stay seated there or go get a root canal—I'd have hightailed it to the dentist's. "Occasionally," I said. "I don't think there are too many guys who don't."

"Nor too many women," she said. "May I share some information with you about Maureen's sexual history?"

I glanced over at Mo. She'd pulled the sleeves of her sweater over her hands and was staring straight ahead. "I don't know. What about doctor-patient confidentiality?"

"Oh, Mr. Caelum, I assure you that my ethics are quite intact."

"Oh," I said. "Right. Well, if it's the stuff about what her father did when she was little, I already know about all that."

"Yes, I know you do. And wasn't that both an act of courage and, more significantly, an act of *intimacy* when Maureen took you into her confidence about such a painful subject?"

I said I'd never thought of it as intimacy, but that, yes, I could see what she meant. I reached over and kneaded Mo's shoulder a little. Figured I'd pick up a few points for that.

"Perhaps you are unaware, Mr. Caelum, that, until very recently, Maureen had never masturbated? That she had always put men in charge of her sexual release?" I could see that, beneath those sweater sleeves, Mo was making and unmaking fists.

"And that's bad?" I said.

Dr. P gave me a smile. "Not bad, but, perhaps, limiting. In that it puts her in a recessive position. A position of powerlessness."

I smiled back at her. "And all this time, I thought you two were working on what happened to her back in Colorado."

"And so we have been. But in our work together, Maureen has discovered a connection between the two traumatic events, so many years apart. The terrible trauma she experienced that day at the school reawakened in her the earlier trauma her father visited upon her— another violation of her safety, albeit one that was far more private, and, of course, of a different magnitude. And one which, Maureen now realizes, she had never fully dealt with. And so, after the shootings, she became doubly vulnerable. She was both the woman hiding in the cupboard and the little girl being forced to witness her father's puzzling and frightening behavior. She was, in both instances, powerless and afraid. Which is why, perhaps, following the shootings, her posttraumatic stress advanced from the acute to the chronic stage. And why Maureen sought to numb her terrible pain with more and more medicine until that became a problem, too. Do you see all of the ways in which these things became intertwined?"

"What I see is my hands around her father's neck," I said. From the corner of my eye, I saw Maureen flinch.

Dr. Patel put down her teacup. She said mine was an understandable reaction, but not a very useful one. "Mr. Caelum, Maureen's father betrayed her in a deep and damaging way. As did the two troubled boys. But she does not need retribution. She needs tenderness. Gentleness. Intimacy. Which brings us back to the reason I've asked you to come here today. Given Maureen's history—her unhealthy initiation to sex and her equally unhealthy promiscuity during her teenage years—I have advised her that, if she embraced the practice of pleasuring herself, she might, first of all, enjoy the sensations in and of themselves, but also, that she might begin to feel she has some control over her life. Her sexual life, yes, but also her life in more general terms. And if she can bring herself to a position of greater empowerment, then, perhaps, she can feel more open to the idea of *shared* intimacy. And by this, I mean intimacy in the broader sense, of course, not just as it is expressed in the bedroom. But in terms of sexual intimacy, I have suggested to Maureen that masturbation might lessen some of the pressure she feels about climaxing when you and she are intimate. And so, you see, this practice, rather than distancing you from one another, would actually bring you closer together. Would you like that, Mr. Caelum? If some of that pressure was relieved, and you could both relax and share yourselves with each other? Feel that lovely closeness again?"

Unexpectedly, I teared up. Nodded. Maureen touched my arm.

"So you would not feel upset, then, or threatened, Mr. Caelum, if Maureen used a marital aid to achieve self-satisfaction?"

"No, I guess not. Not when you put it that way. . . . This isn't something she'd pull out in the middle of . . . ?"

"No, no. This is something Maureen would do in private. Unless, of course, you and she decided mutually that you would like to incorporate this in your lovemaking."

"Oh. No, I don't think . . . but, like you said, in private, she could—"

"Perhaps you would like to speak directly to Maureen?"

"Oh. Sure." I turned to Mo. "Why not, right? To empower yourself or whatever. It's fine with me—not that you need *my* permission. Whatever floats your boat."

Dr. P threw her head back and laughed. "What floats your boat," she said. "That's marvelous! When I get home later today, I shall write that in my notebook of American colloquialisms. And I shall credit you, Mr. Caelum, as the source. 'What floats her boat.' Delightful! Now, please, my friends, when you return home, you should perhaps take a lovely walk, or cook a nice soup together, or enjoy a warm cup of tea. And with as much tenderness as possible, relax and enjoy each other's company. Remember, Mr. Caelum: *tenderness.*"

As it played out, it wasn't moonlight and roses but a couple of cans of diet Dr Pepper and the UConn-Villanova game. During a commercial, I asked her where she'd bought the vibrator. Ordered it on the Internet, she said.

"Oh," I said. "Well, I think it'll be good for you. And, you know, for us, too." She nodded. Smiled. "So you and she are figuring things out, it sounds like, huh? Untangling some of the shit from the past?"

She said they were definitely doing that. She had a ways to go, but she was definitely making progress.

"Good," I said. "Great. And about the other thing? Your 'marital aid' or whatever? As far as I'm concerned, consider yourself cleared for takeoff."

THE LAST ITEM ON MAUREEN'S personal goals chart was: *Go back to work.* Sometimes when I looked at her list, I'd think, Jesus Christ, let her nail this one. Let her start signing her name on the back of a paycheck. Lolly's washing machine had started seeping from the bottom, and I'd be damned if I could figure out how to fix it. That same month, Chet developed an abscess, so between him and Soph, our vet bill shot past four hundred. And our car and house insurance were due. "I can't, in good conscience, recommend it," the agent had said, when I asked her over the phone about downgrading our policy in the interest of lowering our bill. "But if it's this or nothing, Mr. Quirk." It was that or nothing, I told her. From the sale of our Colorado house, we had nineteen thousand left, and it seemed like every month we were subtracting more and more to meet our expenses.

Tricia, one of Mo's NarcAnon pals, told her the caterer she worked for needed extra servers for some big hospital fundraiser. It would be fun working together, she said. And so, Mo had bought the requisite black pants, white shirt, black vest, and red necktie. The bill for those duds came to a hundred sixty; her pay, with tip, was one fifty-five. But it's an investment, Tricia had reminded her; you only had to buy the clothes once, but you'd get paid for every gig. But serving crab puffs and mini samosas to snooty rich people had made Mo such a nervous wreck, she asked Tricia to tell her boss she wasn't available for upcoming jobs.

Home Healthcare Services, Inc. advertised for visiting nurses, offering flexible hours and a benefits package for full-timers. Maureen was reluctant to apply at first because of her drug problem, but I reminded her that (a) she had no record and (b) she was in counseling, went faithfully to meetings, and had been drug-free for almost a year. She prepared her résumé, mailed it, and got called for an interview. She must have impressed them, because they hired her on the spot. Over the next week, she read the manual, watched the instructional videos, and underwent the three days of mandatory on-site training. She was to start on a Monday morning, but had had the dry heaves most of the night before. At five a.m. on day one, she crept downstairs, called Home Healthcare's answering service, and left the message that she was not available to work for them after all.

She was down for a while after that, but she wasn't out. Then Jackie, her nursing friend from Rivercrest, called to tell her that Norma Dubicki had gotten in a huff about something and given notice. Jackie was Rivercrest's third-shift north wing nurse. If Maureen replaced Norma as third-shift south wing nurse, they could spell each other and hit Curves together when their shift ended at seven a.m. Third shift was "cinchy" compared to first and second, Jackie assured Mo: bed checks, temps and meds, and paperwork, most nights. No family members or pain-in-the-neck state inspectors, no docs or administrators walking around with God complexes. And third shift had the coolest aides, too: hard-working young Latinas, for the most part, who changed their kids' Pampers during the day and the residents'

Depends at night. Olga, Provi, Rosa, Esmerelda: they were great with the patients, and hilarious with one another when they got going. Rivercrest would hire Maureen back in a flash, Jackie told her. They'd *salivate* if they heard she was available.

Margaret Gillespie, the director of nursing, offered Maureen the job on a Friday and gave her the weekend to think it over. As third-shift R.N., Mo's salary would be about two-thirds of what she'd made before as nurse supervisor, but double what she'd made as a part-time school nurse in Colorado. And, hallelujah, the benefits package would include health insurance. Still, I didn't pressure her. Nor did I ask her about the one thing that was bothering me—until Sunday afternoon, when she wanted to know what I thought she should do.

"It's your decision," I said. "Which way you leaning?"

She kept going back and forth, she said.

"Oh, by the way, I meant to ask you. Paul Hay still work there?"

She shook her head. His wife had died, Jackie had told her. He and his son had moved to Minnesota, where Paul's family was from. Jackie had heard he was in divinity school.

I nodded at the news, trying to keep my face free of reaction. "Well," I said. "It'd be a relief to have health insurance. And you'd have Jackie for backup, right? Nothing says you have to stay if you don't like it."

She liked it well enough. There were trade-offs, of course. The shift passed more slowly than when she'd worked days. And she didn't get to know the residents as well now; they were mostly asleep while she was on duty. But, as Jackie had promised, the aides were competent and fun and the work was pretty low-impact. On really slow nights, she and Jackie chatted with each other on the phone from their respective nurse's stations.

It was nice, too, that our work schedules matched up. Afternoons, when I got back from Oceanside, she'd have cooked something for us. We'd eat, talk, watch a little TV. Then we'd unplug the phone, get into bed, spoon, and sleep. Sometimes, before I dozed off, I'd do some future planning. If she hung in there at the nursing home for, say, a year, then maybe I could drop one of my Oceanside courses. Lighten my load a little—cut that pile of student papers in half. Or, if the state lifted the hiring freeze and Oceanside offered me a full-time position, I could quit the bakery. I'd been cutting, proofing, frying, and frosting doughnuts since college, and it was getting pretty old.

The alarm would wake us up at nine p.m. She and I would get up, shower ourselves awake, get the dogs taken care of, eat a little ten p.m. breakfast. Then we'd dress for work and leave the house. Us and the raccoons, we'd say. Out all night.

DURING CHRISTMAS WEEK OF 2003, Maureen passed the six-month mark at Rivercrest. Her favorite patient, by far, was ninety-something-year-old Sally Weiss, a lifelong insomniac. If Mo wasn't at the nurse's station and one of the aides, or Lorraine, her LPN, needed to locate her, they usually looked first in room 5. More often than not, Maureen was seated bedside, listening to another episode of Sally's amazing life story. She'd been a New Yorker until her son had plunked her down, against her wishes, "here in the boondocks." She boasted often to Mo, and to me the first time I met her, that she had been kissed by three U.S. presidents: Grover Cleveland (as a baby, in her grandfather's restaurant on Forty-ninth Street), Jimmy Carter (a wet kisser), and Bill Clinton. ("It's those twinkly eyes that get him in trouble.")

Sally's mother had been a Ziegfeld Follies girl, and Sally herself had been a Broadway dancer and a USO comedienne during World War II. She had married and divorced four husbands, one of them a black playwright who was talented but "bitter as all get-out." She had babysat for Gloria Vanderbilt one afternoon in a suite at the Waldorf Hotel, had roomed with (and necked with once, "after too much gin") Ethel Merman, and, at a Broadway party, had given "mouth sex" to George Sanders, the actor who later married Zsa Zsa Gabor, and, later still, committed suicide, claiming he was bored by life. "Bored!" Sally had shouted, forgetting it was the middle of the night. "I've never been bored a minute of my life, not even at this joint!" At Rivercrest, Sally had established the Residents' Council, which she chaired until her ninety-first birthday. Her two greatest achievements, she told Mo, were shaming "that cheapskate Board of Directors" into coughing up course reimbursements for the nurse's aides enrolled in the LPN program and strong-arming the dietician into serving lox and cream cheese with the bagels they served on Sundays. "Not that those things are real bagels. You want a real bagel, you gotta go to H&H on Broadway or Pick-a-Bagel on the Upper East Side." Despite her son's skepticism about her participation in Rivercrest's annual Easter bonnet contest, Sally had emerged victorious three years running, wearing a creation made by her youngest grandchild, Ari, a fashion student at Pratt Institute. Ari had fashioned for his grandmother a purple picture hat, on top of which sat a styrofoam outhouse, in which sat a clay-sculpted Easter Bunny, on the toilet, with the door swinging open. In the Easter Bunny's hands was a tiny replica of *Time* magazine with Sally's picture on the cover, under the headline "Woman of the Century."

As far as I was concerned, Sally stole the show at Rivercrest's 2003 "December Holidays" party, which I attended. Wearing sweatpants, canvas Keds, and a sequined top, she upstaged the high school carolers and a somewhat inharmonious barbershop quartet by standing and singing, a cappella, "Jeepers Creepers" and "There's No Business Like Show Business." A trouper, Sally had ignored the fact that half of her audience was asleep in their wheelchairs and was unfazed when a sourpuss in a flowered housecoat asked loudly, in the middle of Sally's second song, "What makes her think *she's* such a big chunk of cheese? Damn kike. If you ask me, her singing stinks!"

But if Sally's attitude that evening was "the show must go on," later that night, Mo reported, she was uncharacteristically depressed. She had invited her family to come to the party, but none of them had shown, not even Ari, who, out of all of them, was the most special to her because he had inherited her zest for life. Mo had gotten no paperwork done that night, she told me. Instead, she'd sat with Sally. Mo told her she'd never really known either of her grandmothers. "So we decided to adopt each other," Mo said. "I now have a Jewish grandmother."

"And that would make you the shiksa granddaughter," I noted.

Mo laughed at that. "That's just what Sally said!"

Maureen worked Christmas Eve and Christmas night so that Claire, the other third-shift south wing R.N., could stay home and be with her kids. In gratitude, Claire had given Mo a two-decker box of Russell Stover chocolates and Rivercrest had given her a three-night midweek hiatus. She returned to work on December thirty-first and, having grown close to her staff, had prepared a New Year's Eve spread for them—shrimp, cheese and crackers, veggies and dip, and that big box of chocolates from Claire. She'd bought two bottles of sparkling cider, too. If it was quiet on the floor, she'd call the girls into the staff lounge maybe ten minutes before midnight. They could watch the ball drop on TV, drink a cider toast, have some snacks, and then get back to work. Esmerelda, her best aide, had told her New Year's Eve wasn't that big a deal to her, anyway, as long as she could get Three Kings Day off, and Maureen had seen to it.

Seeing Maureen struggling down the hall with her platters and plastic bags, Esmerelda had hurried down to help her. They'd inquired about each other's Christmases—yes, yes, very nice—and then Esmerelda had said, "Too bad about your little friend, huh?"

"My little friend?" Mo asked.

"Sally. She went quick, though. She was a nice lady, huh?"

Death was ever-possible at Rivercrest, but this one walloped Maureen. When she got to the nurse's station, she put down the party stuff and began to cry. Essie embraced her. "Aw, it's all right," she cooed. "She didn't suffer long, right? That's the good part. We all gotta go some time, right?"

Mo called me, she said later, to tell me the news and maybe get a little sympathy. But I was in a New Year's Eve slump myself, getting buzzed on red wine, watching Dick Clark's New Year's Rockin' Eve, and feeling sorry for myself. I figured it was Mo when the phone rang, but I didn't answer.

At midnight, Mo was in room 16 with Mrs. Civitello, who had spiked a fever and begun thrashing. Hallucinating, too, from what Mo could make of her paranoid mumblings about "those evil balloons." She could hear her staff down there in the break room, laughing and chattering, counting backwards. "Happy New Year!" "Happy two thousand four!" Qui'shonna, the newest aide, should remember where she was, and what time of night it was, and stop that loud whooping. Maureen liked Qui'shonna and was rooting for her success, but she wasn't convinced the woman was cut out for nurse's-aide work. She could get pouty when you pointed out something she'd done incorrectly. And she overwhelmed the patients—this oversized, overly effusive woman, with her cornrows and her on-the-lips kisses that Mo had spoken to her about twice. Most of the elderly white patients at Rivercrest had reservations about blacks. Okay, she'd say it: prejudices. Maureen was one of the few people who knew Qui'shonna had come to the nursing home by way of Bride Lake Prison. Sally had known this, too. An open-minded New Yorker, she'd befriended Qui'shonna, and assured her that Qui'shonna's Latina counterparts would become less aloof once they got to know her. Sally had been such a gift, and now she was gone. And no one had even thought to call her. . . .

According to her chart, Mrs. Civitello had been running a low-grade fever for the past forty-eight hours. Urinary tract infection, Mo suspected; she'd leave a note for the day shift, recommending she be tested, but she knew nothing would get done on New Year's Day. She'd better page Dr. Smiley—ask him if he wanted her to give Mrs. Civitello something to calm her down. She dreaded calling, though; Smiley was the worst of the walks-on-water docs—famously snotty if you disturbed him after hours with a question or a concern. One time, Mo's friend Jackie had had the audacity to *question* one of his med orders, and the next day he'd called Gillespie, the director, to complain. Mo just wanted to come home, she told me later, where she could sit with me, watch all the people in Times Square, and grieve for Sally Weiss. They *knew* how close she and Sally had become; that was the thing. Hectic holiday week or not, someone could have picked up the phone. Essie said none of Sally's family had been with her when she passed. If she'd known, Mo could have gotten over there, held her hand, made sure she was comfortable. She imagined herself kissing Sally's forehead, leaning close to her ear and thanking her for all her stories. On her way down the hall to page Smiley, she stopped at room 5 and stared at the sheetless bed, the empty, shiny floor. She opened Sally's closet door. Empty, except for the clothes hangers and, on the top shelf, flopped on its side way in back, that silly Easter bonnet.

Dr. Smiley sounded impatient. A little drunk, too, maybe. "Give her Xanax, one milligram now, and another in four hours." She didn't dare question the order, but she didn't agree with it, either. Two milligrams in a four-hour span? For a woman who didn't weigh eighty-five pounds? Mo wanted to calm her down a little, not knock her out for the next day and a half.

"Tablet or injection?" she had asked, and Smiley'd answered sarcastically. Hadn't she ever learned in nursing school that if you wanted quick results for a suffering patient, you used the stick? When she hung up the phone, she said it out loud. "Asshole!"

She went to the drug closet and prepared the IV. On her way back to Mrs. Civitello's room, she went to the break room door and told her girls to finish up and get back on the floor. She injected Mrs. Civitello slowly and carefully, giving her half the dose the doctor had ordered. The old woman calmed quickly; she didn't need more. Mo withdrew the syringe. She was about to walk down the hall to the north wing so that Jackie's sub, Louise, could witness the discard and sign off on it. Then she heard the crash.

They arrived at room 19 together: Mo, Essie, Olga, and Qui'shonna. Mr. Anderson had had diarrhea earlier, and had had to be washed, re-diapered, and rolled so that Olga and Qui'shonna could change his soiled bed linens. One of the two had forgotten to lock Mr. Ander-son's bedrails back into position. Qui'shonna, most likely, although now she stood there denying it, even though no one had accused her. Mr. Anderson must have gotten out of bed, gone to the bathroom, and passed out. And now, oh God, here he was, slumped on the bath-room floor, blocking the door so that they couldn't get in to help him. Through the three-inch opening, she called his name but got no re-sponse. She could see the gash in his forehead, the dent in the wall where he'd crashed, blood all over his face and undershirt. She had to get in there and stop the bleeding—get him off the floor. She'd better call the EMTs, and notify his doc. Oh, shit! Smiley was Mr. Ander-son's physician, too.

"What the hell's going on over there?" Smiley wanted to know. "What are you, all drinking on the job?"

"I don't drink, Dr. Smiley," she said, verging on tears. "Nobody's drinking." She saw one of the EMTs at the back door. Thank God they'd gotten here quickly. She told Smiley she had to get off the phone and let them in.

She ran to the door and turned the lock. Even as she swung the door open, she realized her mistake. There was only one man stand-ing there. No gurney, no ambulance. Whoever she had just let enter was unshaven, unbathed, and reeling drunk. And then, just like that, she was back there, at the doorway to the library break room, watch-ing them enter, armed. *Get up! Are you guys scared? Well, don't be, because you're all going to die anyway. . . .*

The drunk—balding, in his thirties, maybe—grabbed her right wrist. When he tried to kiss her, she jerked her head away. He pulled her, teetering, toward the row of chairs against the wall facing the nurse's desk. In daytime, some of the residents liked to sit there and watch the comings and goings. The drunk fell into one of the chairs and pulled Maureen down on his lap. He kissed her on the nape of her neck. She flinched, but she was too terrified to protest, to fight or beg. He told her she had nice breasts—small ones, the kind he liked—and with his free hand, began stroking them.

In her peripheral vision, she was suddenly aware of Qui'shonna, at the far end of the hall, staring. She saw Qui'shonna move slowly and deliberately toward the hallway phone. Please, she thought. Please be calling the police.

Five minutes later, the crisis was over. The EMTs arrived before the cops did. Ignoring his shouted orders to "stay away from that fucking door, you fucking spook!" Qui'shonna thundered past him and Mo and threw open the door for the ambulance guys. "We got us a situation!" she shouted.

The older, more experienced EMT sat two chairs away from where the guy was holding Mo. He smiled, wished the drunk a Happy New Year. He asked him if he'd been partying. Asked him what his first name was. "Bones? Yeah? Gee, that's a name you don't hear too often. . . . A nickname? Oh, okay. That makes sense. What kind of music you like, Bones? . . . Tom Petty? No kidding. Geez, that's a coincidence because I'm a *huge* Petty fan. Petty, Clapton, Steve Winwood. That's *real* music, right? Hey, Bones, what do you say you let go of her now? Because I bet she probably needs to go check on her patients. Okay, Bones? What do you say you let her go?"

The cops arrived shortly after he had released her and Mo had run into Qui'shonna's enveloping arms. "Oh, Jesus Christ, not this bozo again," one of the cops groaned. "Come on, Bonezy. Let's me and you and Officer Collins take a little ride, and let these nice folks get back to work."

He left peacefully. The EMTs hurried down to room 19 and wedged open Mr. Anderson's bathroom door. He'd come to by then, but he seemed dazed. Concussion, maybe. But the wound wasn't as deep as Maureen had feared. They strapped him onto a gurney and wheeled him out the back door to the waiting ambulance.

Maureen couldn't stop shaking, but she assured her staff, over and over, that she was okay. She was fine. Could they all just please stop looking at her like that? Because everything was fine. *Peek-a-boo! You want to get shot today? You think you look cool or something? You're a fucking geek. . . .*

She considered trying me again, she said later, although she knew I'd be sleeping. She thought about calling Dr. Patel's service and saying it was an emergency. Thought about asking Althea or Nehemiah, her NarcAnon friends, to help her. Instead, at around two a.m., she went into the med closet and closed the door behind her. She took from her pocket the syringe she'd used to medicate Mrs. Civitello, wiped the needle with alcohol, tapped at a vein, and injected herself with the remaining half-milligram of Xanax. She sighed, waited. In under a minute, she was calm, in control again. Crazy circumstances, she told herself. Just this once. She smiled. The Xanax had banished Klebold and Harris. Sent them back to 1999. In the log, she wrote, "Civitello, Marion, one mg Xanax @ 12:05 a.m. by injection, repeated @ 4:00 a.m., as directed by Michael Smiley, M.D." At four, she returned to Mrs. Civitello's room. She was awake now, but woozy. "I'm going to give you a shot now, Marion," she told her. "Doctor's orders. You ready?" Mrs. Civitello stared at her with glassy eyes, Mo said, as she injected her with another half-dose. She pocketed the syringe. By six a.m., she was jumpy again. She felt his hands pawing her, smelled his sour breath. "Going to the ladies' room," she told Lorraine. Sitting in the locked stall, she found a good vein in her other arm. Stuck the needle in and depressed the plunger.

OFF AND ON, DURING THE next months, Maureen would promise herself that this next injection would be her last. She was lucky not to have been found out, and she would stop after this one, and no one would be the wiser. It wasn't like she was depriving any of her elderly patients of meds they needed; she would never, ever do that. But most of the docs overtranquilized these frail, underweight elderly. She and Jackie had concurred about that.

In July, Jackie finally confronted her about her suspicions. Mo had cried, begged her not to go to Gillespie, made promises she had every intention of keeping. And she *had* kept them, too, until mid-September, that long stretch when she'd worked ten nights in a row because Claire's husband was so sick.

The accident happened on Saturday, October 9.

———

IN PART TWO OF "A Victim's Victims," investigative reporter Rosalie Rand shifts focus from the Seaberry family to the other two principals in her story: Maureen and Resident State Trooper Brian Gatchek. Gatchek, a thirty-two-year-old third-generation cop, was the first responder at the scene. He told Rand he had suspected from the start that there was more to it than a nurse's exhaustion after a long overnight shift.

Rand's depiction of Maureen is evenhanded. She first recounts Mo's troubles: the Columbine murders and the emotional and physical ravages that survival had cost her. On the advice of her lawyers, Maureen granted Rand an interview; in it, she talked frankly about her posttraumatic stress, her drug dependence, and—this surprised me—her father's sexual abuse. (Arthur had pledged to pay half of Mo's legal costs, but after the article ran, he withdrew the offer and, through his attorney, notified Mo that she'd been disinherited and disowned.) Rand does not, as I feared she might, reshape Mo's words to push a thesis or an agenda. Nor does she discredit the mitigating factors in the case. Instead, she presents them objectively and lets the reader decide: Should the quality of mercy be strained or unstrained, given the facets of the case?

For the section on Maureen, Rand also interviewed Jerry Martineau, Jackie Molinari, Connecticut Health Department attorney Peter Hatch, and Lindsay Peek. Jerry spoke candidly for a cop, second-guessing his decision not to arrest Maureen the day the system had red-flagged her as a substance abuser. ("The truth is, I felt sorry for her. What she'd been through out there in Colorado. She looked so pathetic and scared when my detective brought her in that day. I'll admit it. I let my sympathy cloud my better judgment.")

Jackie said she suspected Maureen might be using, and falsifying med log records to cover her tracks. "She kept asking me to sign off on witnessing discards when I *hadn't* witnessed them. We were friends; we worked the same shift; we trusted each other. It happens sometimes when you're in a hurry, or when you space out and squirt out the rest of an injection without thinking about it. But it started happening pretty consistently, usually with Ativan or Xanax. And I began to ask myself if she had a problem." Rather than report her suspicions to her supervisor, Jackie had confronted Maureen directly, and Mo had admitted everything: "doctor shopping," NarcAnon, and how she'd first injected herself on New Year's Eve when that creep had gotten in and it had triggered a flashback. Jackie believed Maureen's promise that, as of that moment, it was going to stop. "I'm convinced Maureen believed it, too," Jackie told Rand. "Look, she had an illness, but she was a great nurse. If I had reported her, the Health Department would have swept in, prosecuted her, and taken away her license. Do I feel horrible about what happened? Sure I do. Guilty? You bet. But what I want to know is, why the system lets doctors who have a drug problem keep their licenses and their anonymity, but if you're a nurse, you get publicly humiliated and they take away your career."

"Because drug addicts are in denial," the prosecutor told Rosalie Rand. "They won't stop until the profession stops them. Or until there's a dead kid lying in the middle of the road. Which do *you* prefer?"

"She was nice enough when she worked at Columbine," Lindsay Peek told Rand. "Kids liked her. I liked her. She's probably the main reason I decided to go into nursing. But nurses are supposed to heal people, not kill them. When you think about it, what she did dishonors all the kids who died that day at Columbine."

I tried to convince Maureen not to read "A Victim's Victims" when it came out, but she didn't listen. When she got to Lindsay's quote, she wailed like a wounded animal.

THERE WERE TWO EYEWITNESSES TO the accident that killed Morgan Seaberry that morning. Tawnee Shay, herself a recovering addict, was running down Route 32, late for work at McDonald's. Later that night, she'd watched the TV news footage: the car up on the lawn, the sign knocked crooked. They'd shown the victim's high school yearbook picture, and Gerry Brooks from Channel 30 had asked anyone who might have witnessed the event to contact the state police. Tawnee had not contacted them, though; she wanted nothing to do with cops. But Officer Gatchek had gone into full-bore investigative mode and, a few days later, had ferreted her out.

The other eyewitness was the victim's older brother, Jesse Seaberry. It had been a strange night, Jesse told Rosalie Rand—the strangest night of his life. His mom, his brother and sister, and he had arrived the night before at the Comfort Inn. They'd checked in and, on the recommendation of the desk clerk, had gone to the Chinese buffet in the mall, rather than to the Mickey D's across the road. The food had sucked, Jesse said; he and his mother had finally agreed on *something*.

When the four of them got back to the motel, Jesse told Rosalie Rand, his mother said she was going to arrange 6:45 a.m. wakeup calls for both rooms—hers and Alyssa's and his and Morgan's. She'd given a twenty-dollar bill to Morgan (not Jesse) so that they could buy some breakfast at McDonald's the next morning, if they got ready early enough. She said she wanted them outside, at the car, by seven thirty sharp. She wasn't quite sure where to go when they got to campus, and she didn't want to be still driving around when the thing was already starting. She was a typical Type A, she told them for the billionth time, and liked to arrive a little early to avoid stress.

Morgan and he had gone to their room, flopped on their beds, and agreed that the motel their mother had picked out was a shithole: burned-out lightbulbs, a broken lock on the bathroom door, cigarette burns in the drapes. And if those *weren't* cum stains on the carpet, it sure looked like it. Jesse told Morgan about a reality crime show he'd seen where the detectives had solved a rape-murder by bringing this special light to a hotel room, and turning off all the other lights, and the spots where there were body fluids had fucking *glowed*, and that was how they'd matched the dude's DNA or whatever. Morgan fell asleep listening to him, Jesse said, but he, Jesse, couldn't sleep, so he watched some pay-per-view and smoked a little of the weed he'd brought along to make the trip bearable. Then he'd gotten nice and mellow and fallen asleep, too.

The weirdness began later, at about four in the morning, Jesse said, when he woke up with some serious cotton mouth and needing to take a leak.

He didn't think to look over and see if Morgan was in his bed, which he wasn't. Morgan was in the bathroom with the broken lock, sitting on the toilet, butt-naked, and cutting slits in his pecs with a single-edge razor. "Get out!" Morgan had screamed, and Jesse was about to when he noticed these pictures on the floor around the toilet, which Morgan started snatching up, fast as he could—these computer printouts, skin pictures that, at first, Jesse assumed, were women, but then he realized were *dudes*. Muscle guys with stiffs. And Jesse had said to Morgan, who'd begun to cry, "Holy shit, you're *gay*? Mr. Perfect is *gay*?"

Morgan went at him, Jesse said, throwing punches, pretty fierce ones, too. Then Jesse got Morgan in a headlock and squeezed his neck so hard that Morgan said, "Okay! Stop! Please stop!" And after they'd both calmed down and caught their breath, they'd started talking.

They talked for a long time, an hour maybe, about everything: the divorce, their lives before their dad left, their mom's cancer. It was weird, Jesse said, but in a way, it was the best talk they'd ever had. The most *real* talk they'd ever had. Morgan told Jesse he cut himself to relieve the pressure. "What pressure?" Jesse had asked. "Everything in your whole fucking life's come super easy." Morgan said it was hard always trying to live up to their mother's expectations. To be the one person in the family who wasn't going to disappoint her. It was hard to explain, but sometimes, he said, his skin felt too tight from having to hold in his *real* self. Constricted, like, and it *hurt*. So he'd cut himself to relieve the pressure, and it would feel, not good, but better.

"Like when you pop a zit?" Jesse had asked, and Morgan had said no, not really, but kind of. Yeah.

Jesse wanted to know if Morgan had ever made it with a dude, and Morgan said he had, once, with one of the other actors in *Of Mice and Men*—this kid named Danny, who played one of the ranch hands. He'd almost had sex with this other guy, he said—this guy he'd met in a chat room. Morgan had driven to Asbury Park to meet him, but the guy had turned out to be in his forties, not twenty-two like he'd said, so Morgan had decided not to get in his car, and the guy had kept going, "What's *wrong* with you?"

Jesse said Morgan begged him not to tell their mother. She'd been through so much already: getting dumped by their dad, getting cancer. Instead of saying whether he would or wouldn't tell, Jesse had suggested they smoke together. Morgan said he couldn't, because the open house was in, like, three hours, and because weed was illegal. Jesse'd laughed at that. "You cut yourself, have sex with *guys*, and you won't smoke a blunt with your own *brother*?"

So they'd smoked. And the more Jesse thought about it—that his Mr. Perfect little brother was more fucked-up than *he* was—the freer he felt and the harder he laughed. But Morgan was one of those guys who smokes and, instead of kicking back and enjoying the ride, gets all paranoid. He started whimpering, thinking the cops were going to storm their room. He begged Jesse again not to say anything, and Jesse said he hadn't decided yet what he was or wasn't going to say, and then, all of a sudden, Morgan bolted.

Jesse ran after him, down the hallway, and out into the dim daylight. And Morgan, without looking, started across the road just as that woman's silver Tercel came out of nowhere and plowed into him without even tapping her brakes. And then the Tercel had jumped the curb and crashed into the sign, "Billions and Billions Sold" or whatever, and there was his brother, lying there in the road, not moving, and Jesse knew he was dead.

Carole Alderman told Rosalie Rand that Jesse was hateful—that he had been "pathologically jealous" of Morgan his whole life, and now, unforgivably, he had concocted this whole malicious story to discredit Morgan in death. Morgan had not ever cut himself intentionally, Carole said—he would never, *ever* do something self-destructive like that; Jesse was the self-destructive one. And Morgan was certainly not a homosexual; that was simply *ridiculous*. Morgan had been a normal, kindhearted boy whom everybody loved, and he had been the biggest blessing of her whole life. He had started across the road that morning to go to McDonald's and get himself some breakfast, just as they had planned the night before, and that woman, that Quirk person, had come along and *murdered* him. And, Carole said, she was sure, beyond the shadow of a slightest doubt, that Morgan had looked both ways before he ventured across.

———

WHEN MORGAN SEABERRY WAS STRUCK and killed, Officer Gatchek was just across the road, coasting slowly through the mall parking lot, front and back, checking on things to make sure everything looked "copacetic." He had recently learned that word, he told Rand, and he usually tried to use new words once he discovered them. He loved words. Kept a pocket dictionary in his cruiser and, when things were slow, would open to a random page, stick his finger somewhere on the page and, more often than not, increase his vocabulary. It helped him out when he played Scrabble with his wife and his in-laws. Sometimes, but not always. He couldn't, for instance, use "copacetic" because the word had three c's in it and there were only two "c" tiles in the Scrabble game. Well, unless he had a blank tile. "This probably sounds screwy," he told Rand, "but for me there's a correlation between police work and Scrabble. You stare at what you got in front of you. At first you don't see anything much. Then, boom, you do."

He was at the scene in two minutes, max. He called immediately for an ambulance, but it was just a formality; the kid was already gone. Later, in his report, he would estimate that Mo had hit him while traveling at an approximate speed of fifty-five miles per hour in a thirty-five-mile zone.

Officer Gatchek called for backup—someone to direct traffic, someone else to talk to the brother, who said he'd seen it happen, but who, Officer Gatchek had observed, looked and smelled like he'd been smoking cannabis. He'd smelled cannabis in the victim's hair, too, but would probably keep that information to himself, at least for now. The victim's mother had arrived on the scene by then and was hysterical. He decided he'd send her off in the ambulance; let the EMTs deal with her, maybe get one of the ER docs to give her something to calm her down. He told Maureen to just sit on the grass near her car. To not get back into the car. Could she just get her purse? He said no. She should just wait right where she was. "Oh, my God," she kept saying, over and over, like a chant. "Oh my God, oh my God, oh my God."

It was the dazed look in her eyes, he said later. The fact that her pupils were dilated. Maybe she was in shock, or maybe she was just exhausted after her shift, like she said. Dozing a little, maybe, though she hadn't copped to that. Or maybe, just maybe, she was DUI. People's pupils dilated when they were stoned, and also when they were lying about something, and hers were as round as saucers. The victim's brother said she hadn't put the brakes on *after* she hit him, let alone before. And he, Gatchek, hadn't heard any brakes, either, which he would have over in the mall parking lot. Hadn't seen any rubber in the road. Overtired or not, it was instinct, even if you *were* dozing: you felt your car hit something, you braked. But instinct, when you were DUI, could betray you. Liquor? A belt or two out in the parking lot before she took off? He didn't think so; he hadn't smelled it on her. Drugs? Downers, maybe? That was more likely. An RN would have the key to the candy store. She was wearing a wedding ring, he noticed, but she hadn't said anything about calling a husband. That was usually the first thing a wife in her situation would do. Maybe her marriage was in trouble and, to cope, she was swiping happy pills. There were things you had to do when there was a fatality—procedures you had to follow. Legalities you had to be cognizant of. But as he was following these procedures, he was fiddling with his observations like they were Scrabble tiles. And his instincts kept spelling out DUI.

He caught a break when he noticed that Maureen's hands had gotten burned by the detonated air bag—and that there was a small amount of blood oozing from the cut in her left eyebrow. "Ma'am, I think, to be on the safe side, we're going to call you an ambulance. Get you to the hospital and have them look you over." She told him she didn't need to go; her injuries were superficial. "Just to be on the safe side, ma'am," he repeated. He knew they'd take a blood sample when they examined her, and later on, if he could convince a judge to sign off on probable cause, he could get at that blood. Have her serum levels analyzed by the toxicologists at the State Police lab.

He caught a second break when the ambulance got there and Maureen complied. The EMTs strapped her onto the stretcher and hauled her up and in.

Officer Gatchek nodded in satisfaction as the ambulance pulled away. She hadn't said anything more about getting her purse. It was in the car, on its side on the floor of the passenger's seat. By rights, he couldn't look in it, not without probable cause. But he could certainly pick it up and put it back on the seat for her. And when he did, he felt something in the purse's side pocket. Damned if it didn't feel like a syringe.

He called for a tow. Her car was evidence, so they'd have to inventory everything in it when it got to the impound lot. That wasn't breaking any search and seizure rules: doing a standard inventory. And meanwhile, he'd have bought himself some time to write up the affidavit, go after probable cause. Once the judge had signed off—he'd ask Judge Douville, who never refused if it was a suspected DUI—then he could execute the search warrants. He wanted her blood tested. He wanted her medical records. He wanted a look at her employment history. And he wanted to talk to her coworkers, too—see if there were any issues there. Nurses covered for each other, he knew that. But even if it was inadmissable later on, he'd have another piece of the whole picture. Maureen Quirk: Who was she? He'd figure it out. He owed that to the hysterical mother, and to her lifeless son, splayed facedown in the middle of Route 32 and now heading off to the morgue.

———————

WE HIRED LENA LOVECCHIO, MY Aunt Lolly's pal and pallbearer—the lawyer who'd helped me out with the Paul Hay debacle. Lena had an associate now, her cousin Nicholas Benevento.

The four of us—Lena, Nick, Maureen, and I—sat at Lena's conference table. It was after hours, at Mo's request. She was too ashamed to go out in daylight. "Guys, I hate to be the one to tell you, but there's no sense bullcrapping you, either," Lena said. "In terms of an acquittal, we've got the proverbial snowball's chance in hell."

Mo nodded, resigned. She was on a pretty powerful antidepressant at that point, and it tended to stupor her out. The upside was that she was finally able to grab three or four hours of uninterrupted sleep, and she had stopped talking about suicide.

"A snowball's chance why?" I asked.

"Because they've got her on the blood serum, and they've got the second eyewitness who corroborates what the brother says. And, most of all, because she coughed it up to Gatchek about injecting herself before she left the parking lot. That's the real nail in the coffin."

"He told me it would be better if I cooperated with him," Mo said.

"Better for him, yeah. Not for you."

The bitter irony was that I'd been upstairs on the phone, arranging for Lena to represent her while, downstairs, Gatchek was knocking at the back door, wanting to know if she could answer a few questions.

"He didn't read her her rights," I reminded them.

"Didn't have to because she wasn't in custody," Nick said. "You're not required to Miranda-ize someone if you're just having a chat at their kitchen table. She handed it to him voluntarily."

"Therein lies our problem, kids," Lena added. "You never, *ever* talk to the cops without your lawyer there."

The fact that it was a high-profile case didn't help us either, Nick explained. The accident had caught the attention of the national media because of the Columbine angle. That had generated op-eds in both the *Daily Record* and the *Courant*, which had in turn generated over a dozen letters to the editor. "The public cares about this case," Lena said. "So the chief state's attorney is bound to take an active interest. As in, stick his finger into the wind to see which way it's blowing. And so far, it's blowing pretty hard against us. But I talked to that *New Yorker* writer today, and we may be able to use her to our advantage. Not sure yet; she and I are continuing our discussion. Maureen, I may want you to talk to her. We'll see. Of course, the *New Yorker*'s national. What we need more right now is a sympathetic in-state press."

"In terms of potential jurors?" I asked.

She shook her head. "We probably won't go the jury route. Too risky. Their case is just too damn strong. So we want to avoid a trial if we can. See if they're in the mood for some charge-bargaining."

Nick went over the chronology of what was coming. First, the arrest, probably sometime the following week. "I talked to a guy in the state's attorney's office and asked for a heads-up," he said. "Better for us, Mrs. Quirk, if you turn yourself in, rather than they take you in in handcuffs. Makes great theater for the cops and the TV guys, but it's bad for our side. People see a perp walk on TV, and 'innocent until proven guilty' goes flying out the window. We want to be able to control as much of the imagery as we can."

Maureen would be arraigned within twenty-four hours after they arrested her, Nick said. "They'll read the charge, we'll enter her plea. They'll give her a court date and set her bail. I'm guessing a hundred thou. I think we can get a reduction, though. She's got no priors. She's not really a flight risk."

"What we'll do is post a surety bond," Lena interjected. "Use the farm as security, if you're comfortable with that." I nodded. "Okay, now about her plea. I think our best bet is to have her plead guilty under the Alford doctrine. That'll open up a 'let's make a deal' situation."

"What's the Alford Doctrine?" I asked.

"It's when the defendant says, 'I'm not admitting actual guilt, but based on the state's evidence, I *am* conceding that, in all likelihood, I will be convicted. Therefore, I plead guilty.' Doesn't change the criminal penalties, but it gives you guys some leverage later on if the Seaberrys decide to file a civil suit. The insurance companies love it when their clients use the Alford. Makes it harder for the plaintiff to win a civil case."

"So is that what you're going to do? Use this Alford thing?"

"Yeah. Because, defense-wise, we just don't have much to work with. I'll argue that it was the *non*-Xanax circumstances that led to the accident. There'd been a death on her shift that night, and a shouting match between the two aides that Maureen had to put a stop to before it broke out into a fistfight. So Maureen was upset. Distracted. And since Columbine, she deteriorates when there's any threat of violence." She turned to Mo. "And I'm also going to emphasize that you've tried in earnest to wrestle with your demons, hon: psychotherapy, NarcAnon. I'm going to play Columbine for all it's worth. If we have an ace to play, that's it: the fact that *you're* a victim, too. That's what I think's going to bring them to the bargaining table."

"But why *would* they bargain, if their case is so strong?" I asked.

"Expediency, mainly. They get a conviction, which makes the public happy, but they don't have to put the manpower into it that a trial would require. And conviction's another notch on their belt that they can point to at reappointment time. These guys are politicians, first and foremost, okay? Now, they've also got to keep the Seaberrys happy. The last thing they want is for the victim's mother, say, to start spouting off in the papers and on the nightly news about how Maureen got off with just a slap on her wrist."

"It's a dance," Nick said. "First, they'll hit Mrs. Quirk with the toughest charge they can: manslaughter in the second degree with a motor vehicle. That's a class-C felony, which means that they could put her in prison for up to ten years. So we start charge-bargaining. Offer them the guilty plea in exchange for a lesser charge: misconduct with a motor vehicle. That's a class D. Carries a prison term of five years tops."

Maureen sighed in disgust. "Misconduct: it makes it sound like I should go to the principal's office. You all seem to be forgetting that I took a seventeen-year-old boy's life."

Lena smiled, softened her voice. "Hon, you may feel like waving the white flag right now. But there's a big difference between a ten-year sentence and a five-year one. You were a victim, too, Maureen. Don't lose sight of that. What happened to the Seaberry kid would *not* have happened if those little psychopaths out there in Colorado hadn't damaged you. Now you're definitely going to have to do some jail time; we don't see any way around it. But I'll be damned if we're going to let them lock you up for a whole decade. Okay?"

Looking down at the floor, Maureen nodded.

"So just to summarize," Nick said, "what we're looking for from the prosecution is a downgrade to class D, and what we're willing to give them in exchange is a guilty plea under the Alford. If we get what we want, Maureen's out in five years max, but we might have a decent shot at five, suspended after three. Or if we *really* get lucky, three years, suspended after two."

"One more thing," Lena said. "We've heard that the boy's mother is consulting with Jack Horshack, the victims' advocate for the state. Remember Arnold Horshack on that show, *Welcome Back, Kotter?* Not too far off. But the reason we've got to worry about Jack is, he sees things in black and white. There's good guys and bad guys, and you never show the bad guys any mercy. My guess is, if the kid's mother decides she wants them to throw the book at Maureen, Jack's the one who's fanning her fire. And like we said, the chief state's attorney's going to want Mom on board if they make a deal with us. What I imagine happening—*if* they deal—is that they'll tell Mama to go along with them on the criminal side of the equation. Then they can whack you guys in the civil case."

"What do you mean, whack us?" I asked.

Nick was opening his mouth to answer when Maureen began crying and banging her fists against the table. "It's all so calculating," she said. "Deals, politics. I'm guilty! I killed him!"

I got her calmed down, got her coat. On our way out, I asked Lena if there was anything else she needed me to do.

"Yeah. Pray we don't get Judge Douville or Judge LaCasse. Most of the others will be inclined to factor in the mitigating circumstances when they sentence her. But not those two."

We got LaCasse.

We got the deal: misconduct with a motor vehicle, class D. A five-year prison sentence, to be suspended after three years, if LaCasse gave his blessing.

Under Victims' Advocate Horshack's advisement, Carole Alderman invoked her allocution rights so that she might address the court before Maureen was sentenced. I heard later that Jesse Seaberry's request to address the court, too, was impromptu—that he had approached Horshack at the hearing and told him he wanted to speak, and that the blood had drained from Horshack's face.

Jesse was called first. Given what I'd read about their father-and-son acrimony in "A Victim's Victims," I thought it odd that the boy was sitting with his father. When he walked past his mother and nodded a hello, she turned away.

Judge LaCasse informed Jesse that in his courtroom, men didn't wear bandannas. "Yeah?" Jesse replied, as if he'd just been presented with an interesting but irrelevant factoid. Horshack stood and whispered something to him. "Oh, right. Sorry, Your Excellency," Jesse said, yanking off the bandanna. LaCasse told the kid he'd had an appointment to the bench, not a coronation. Jesse nodded in puzzled agreement. He turned and faced Maureen.

"I guess if life was fair, you should have killed me, not my brother," he said. "Because I'm the one who isn't worth much. My brother was, though. Morgan was my hero in a lot of ways, you know? Even though he was younger than me. But I never got the chance to tell him that. . . . He had a future, you know? He was good at things, whatever he tried." Jesse looked from Mo to his mother. "He wasn't perfect, though. And he didn't *want* to be perfect, either." Carole Alderman locked her arms around her chest and glared at him.

Jesse looked back at Mo. "But he was a great guy. And me, hey, I'm just a druggie, same as you. Except I didn't kill anyone. So, you know, you did the crime, you gotta do the time, right? . . . But I don't hate you or anything. I don't know. Maybe I should, but I don't. All's I want to say to you is that Morgan's death kind of woke me up, you know? Me and my dad made up at the funeral, and I'm living with him now. Him and my stepmother. I got a job at this furniture warehouse? Operating a forklift? And I been clean and sober for forty-one days now. Which is a somewhat large deal for me. . . . And all

I'm trying to say to you is that maybe you could do like I did. Let it wake *you* up, you know what I'm saying? While you're doing your time. Okay?"

Mo had been standing there, her hand over her mouth, her cheeks wet with tears. She had nodded at everything Jesse said. Her words, after he'd finished, were nearly inaudible. "Thank you."

"No problem. Peace out." He looked up at LaCasse. "You, too, Judge."

"And peace to you, sir," LaCasse said. "Keep up the good work."

Carole Alderman had brought two things with her to the sentencing hearing: a framed assemblage of snapshots that showed Morgan's progression from infancy to adolescence, and her leather-bound copy of *Who's Who in American High Schools, 2002–2003*. She asked that the assemblage be placed on the table in front of Maureen. The judge nodded and a sheriff took it from her and did as she asked. Carole Alderman, too, spoke directly to Maureen.

"Look at me, please," she said, and Mo, shaking violently, raised her eyes. Ms. Alderman was dry-eyed and composed. "Practiced," Lena said later.

"I understand you have no children, Mrs. Quirk, so I don't expect you to fully understand what this ordeal has been like for me. Mothers know things about life that women who aren't mothers don't know. Mothers love more deeply than any other people on earth. But I want you to try to understand as best you can what I have to say. All right?"

Maureen nodded. I took a breath because I was pretty sure things were about to get brutal.

"Morgan was the light of my life, Mrs. Quirk—the sweetest, kindest, most talented, most genuine young man you would ever hope to know. Someone who's here in this courtroom today told a reporter some malicious lies about my son—for which I will never, ever forgive that person—and that reporter, a woman whom I trusted and allowed into my home, saw fit to repeat those lies in a national magazine. But Mrs. Quirk, I assure you, the truth speaks louder than vengeful lies, and the beautiful truth is that people *loved* Morgan Seaberry. His teachers, his teammates, his wide circle of friends. They cheered him on the soccer field, applauded him on the stage, laughed at his jokes. We all bathed in the glow of Morgan's presence."

As Ms. Alderman spoke of her son's accomplishments, his listing in *Who's Who in American High Schools*, she raised the volume above her head, as if it was something sacred. Then she kissed the book and put it down.

"He had a wonderful life ahead of him, Mrs. Quirk," she said. "And please, once again, I ask that you look at me while I'm speaking to you. . . . Thank you. As I was saying, Morgan's future was a bright one. He would have given so, so much back to the world. But because you chose to steal drugs, inject them into your arm, and then get behind the wheel of a car, my son never got to live past October of his senior year. And so, the prom, the class trip to Six Flags, graduation day: he won't get to go to any of those, thanks to you. You snuffed out his life, Mrs. Quirk. Those two boys in Colorado used guns, and you used your car. But the result was the same."

Maureen stood there, wailing now, but Carole Alderman wouldn't stop.

"I'm told you were a good nurse, Mrs. Quirk—that your elderly patients, and the children at the school where you worked, liked you very much. That they trusted you. And I've heard, too, that you were devastated by the shootings at Columbine. But in spite of all that, you, who were, by profession, a healer, got into your car, drove under the influence, and killed my son. So I don't care how wondeful a nurse you were, or how much trauma you suffered because of those shootings out there. You murdered my son, Mrs. Quirk, and because of that, you rip the beating heart out of my chest every single day of my life. Several times a day, in fact. Because just as you will never

know the depth of a mother's love, you cannot ever know the depth
of a mother's suffering when she has to bury her child."

"I'm sorry," Mo wailed. "I'm so, so sorry." She was doubled over
in pain. Lena, standing beside her, rubbed her back. Nick, seated next
to me, grabbed onto my shoulder. "It's almost over," he whispered.

Carole Alderman turned to the judge. "Your honor," she said. "I
understand from Mr. Horshack that the prosecutor and Mrs. Quirk's
lawyers have come to an agreement that would allow her to leave
prison after the third year of a five-year sentence. And I ask you, I
beg you, sir, to reject that compromise, which I understand it is in
your power to do. Three years? Thirty-six months for the life of my
son? Please, your honor. Take into consideration that this woman
has given my family and me a life sentence of suffering. If her sentence is to be five years, then please, *please* make her serve the full
five years."

LaCasse twiddled with the pencil he was holding, swiveled back
and forth in his big leather chair. Under his breath, Nick whispered,
"Shit."

As we waited for the judge's response, a commotion erupted at
the back of the room. I glanced back quickly. A sheriff and a young
woman were arguing with each other in hushed tones.

"Ms. Alderman," LaCasse said. "I'm going to grant you your request." He was in the middle of explaining why when the woman in
back broke free and ran forward, calling to the judge.

"Don't! It's bogus what that lady said! She's nothing like that!"

By the time I looked away from the tussle between Velvet Hoon
and the two sheriffs who had wrestled her to the floor, a third sheriff
was hurrying Maureen toward the door.

"No, wait!" I called. "Please just let me—"

"Don't listen to any of that stuff she said about you, Mom! I'm
going to come visit you! I love you, Mom!"

I stood there, fingering the wedding band Maureen had taken off and handed to me before the hearing began. I hoped she might turn back to look at me, but she didn't. She was heading out the door and on her way to Quirk Correctional Institution, the prison that my radical great-grandmother had dared imagine into existence in the early years of the previous century, and which, ninety-odd years later, had strayed unrecognizably from her vision.

"Get your fucking hands off of me! I LOVE YOU, MOM!"

I held Mo's wedding ring tight in my fist and watched her go.

chapter seventeen

DRIVING THROUGH THREE RIVERS' DESERTED downtown, I passed the Savings and Loan sign at the exact second when the time changed from 11:59 to midnight.

Thursday, September 1, 2005.

Bodies were floating facedown in New Orleans. The death count in Iraq was ratcheting up. The shadow of 9/11 was over us all. "Yes, yes, Mr. Quirk. So much to grieve and worry about these days," Dr. Patel had acknowledged the day before, interrupting my CNN-fueled rant about the state of the world. "But tell me. What is the *good* news?"

"The good news?" She'd looked so anticipatory, I'd felt like a game show contestant. "I don't know, Doc. Can't be that we're stuck with Dubya and Darth Vader for another three-plus years. Or that I owe my wife's lawyers more money than I made in income last year. Or that, if the Seaberrys go ahead with the civil suit, they could end up owning the home I live in and the land it sits on. *Good* news, huh? Gee, you stumped me on that one."

But now I had an answer for her. If it was September 1, then the good news was that Maureen Quirk, State of Connecticut Inmate #383–642, had survived the first two months of her sentence.

Why was I behind the wheel at midnight? Because Alphonse had had to rush down to Florida. Mr. Buzzi had gotten tangled up in his garden hose, fallen, and broken his hip, and Mrs. Buzzi had gotten herself so worked up about it that her shingles had come back. And while Al was down there, running back and forth from the hospital to his parents' trailer park, his night baker had quit on him. "No notice," Al had said when he called in the favor. "Leaves me a fuckin' text-message that his keys are on the shelf above the prep table and him and his girlfriend are on their way to New Mexico. And you should see *her*, Quirky. Looks like she walked off the set of *Planet of the Apes*. If I had to drive cross-country with that, I'd shoot myself. Dipshit missing-front-tooth motherfucker. Good riddance. I'm *glad* he's gone."

I'd tried to get out of it. If I worked third shift, then I had to sleep days, and visiting hours at the prison were from two to three thirty. On top of that, the semester at Oceanside was starting in less than a week, and my department chair had saddled me, last minute, with another teacher's class. The good news, Dr. Patel, was that teaching three sections instead of two made me eligible for health care. The bad news was: How was I supposed to write a syllabus until I got the reading done, and how was I going to get the reading done if I was up all night cutting, proofing, frying, and filling doughnuts?

But mentioning semesters and syllabi was like speaking Sanskrit to Alphonse Buzzi. "Last couple months, I ain't even been making my expenses," he'd confided. "It's this fuckin' heat, man. Who wants coffee and doughnuts when it's ninety-eight degrees and you're walking around in your own pig sweat?" I'd almost mentioned global warming—Alphonse had voted for Bush in 2000 and, unforgivably, again in 2004—but instead I'd let him ramble. "I'm a month behind on my rent. I'm buying on credit from my coffee guy and U.S. Foods. And now Numb Nuts bails on me. If my morning regulars see the lights off and a sign on the door, they're gonna drive down the road to Dunkin' Donuts and never come back. Coolatas, smoothies, iced fuckin' Dunkaccinos. What are they gonna offer next—handjobs while you're waiting in the drive-thru line? Honest to God, Quirky, I wouldn't ask you if I wasn't desperate. Trust me. I'm *desperate*." And because he'd sounded close to tears, I'd agreed and gotten off the phone ASAP. Alphonse had cried in my presence once before, the night his brother died—had blubbered and choked and said it should have been him, not Rocco, who got leukemia. That it would have been easier on his folks if it *had* been him. Two months earlier, at the sentencing hearing, I'd heard the same thing from another surviving sibling: Jesse Seaberry. I wondered how he was doing now, sobriety-wise. Wouldn't want to bet the farm on *that* kid's staying on the straight and narrow. . . .

"Very stressful, Mr. Quirk," Dr. Patel had concurred. "A large debt, a worrisome lawsuit, a spouse in prison. I acknowledge that your burdens are heavy ones." She was nodding so sympathetically, I hadn't noticed the brass knuckles. "And we can continue this pity party if you'd like. But since we have just this one session together, might I suggest we take a different approach?"

Pity party? The hell with her. I hadn't gone there to be ridiculed. I'd gone so that she could call some colleague who'd call in a prescription—something to help me sleep. I'd been overdoing it on the Katrina coverage, then dropping across the bed, exhausted but too agitated to sleep. Eyes closed, I'd keep seeing people stranded on their rooftops, wading neck-deep through that bacterial stew. Blacks, mostly—just like over there at the prison. You sit in the visiting room, and it's maybe eight or nine to one, black to white. All that phony outrage about New Orleans from the politicians and pundits: it was a bullshit show. All Katrina did was shine a spotlight on what this country's been tolerating since the days of the slave ships. . . .

"What do you mean, a different approach?" I'd asked Patel.

"Tell me again, Mr. Quirk, the name of the new course you're to teach." So I'd told her: The Quest in Literature.

"The Quest in Literature. Ah, yes. Lovely. It's a shame my schedule won't allow it, because that is a course *I* would like to take myself. But I'm wondering if, as you teach this material, you might also launch *yourself* on a quest. A personal one, I mean." A quest for what? A yellow Mustang? "And, Mr. Quirk, I see from your countenance that you are immediately skeptical."

"I'm not skeptical. I'm . . . What kind of a quest?"

She smiled, sipped her tea. Didn't answer the question. . . .

———

MULTIPLY 365 DAYS BY FIVE, add one day for leap year, and you get a 1,826-day prison sentence. Subtract the 62 days she'd already served—July and August—and it equaled 1,764 more to go. I'd computed it the day before—had done the math on the inside of a paperback while I was cooling my jets in the waiting area where they corral the lawyers and loved ones. There's a lot of hurry-up-and-wait at Quirk CI. Two months has taught me that. Weekday visits are supposed to be ninety minutes long, but by the time their afternoon count clears and they search the women who have visitors, you're lucky if there's three-quarters of an hour left. Complaining is useless. I swear they must train corrections officers how to make that look-right-through-you face if you object to something. I've gotten that same look from three or four different COs. Now I just bring something to read and keep my mouth shut. *Ancient Myth and Modern Man*: that was the paperback I was reading. It was one of the books I'd be teaching.

The Quest in Literature. The guy who'd been teaching it was one of those hipster professors with the ponytail and the piercings. "But Caelum, you've been *asking* me to assign you something other than the composition course," my department chair reminded me.

"Yeah, but under different circumstances."

"Such as?" She was starting to climb up on that high horse of hers.

"Such as, how about more than five days' notice?"

"Well, Caelum, had Seth Wick let me know ahead of time that he had an amphetamine problem and was planning to have a meltdown and be rushed into rehab, then I certainly would have given you more notice." Dr. Barnes, she wanted everyone to call her now. For the first few years I taught at Oceanside, she was Patricia, but then she'd gotten the doctorate from Columbia, the Volvo, and a wardrobe of expensive suits and become *Doctor* Barnes. How had she put it in that e-mail she sent to everyone? Something about "Dr. Barnes" being her "preferred appellation."

But anyway, Seth the Speed Freak hadn't bothered to leave behind a syllabus, and the books he'd ordered were already sitting in the bookstore. I was told I had to use them. And it wasn't exactly a *light* list: *Ancient Myth and Modern Man*, Campbell's *Hero with a Thousand Faces*, Homer's *Odyssey*, *The Hero's Journey*. I could already hear the students whining about how hard the readings were, not to mention the feminists crabbing about the sexist titles. Those back-to-school feminists? The ones who'd postponed college until their kids were older? They're both the most conscientious students and the biggest pains in the ass. Which I appreciated, oddly enough. They're good consumers, those women—want their money's worth, which you can't fault them for. The majority of the nineteen- and twenty-year-olds are so goddamned passive. Don't want to come up with any of their *own* opinions about what they read; they just want to copy down *your* opinions and give them back to you on the test. Not those older students, though. They can be fierce.

Mo says they do pat-downs before the inmates enter the visiting room and full strip searches after the visit's over. The women officers do it, not the men, but it's still pretty degrading. What they're looking for is contraband: drugs, jewelry, stuff to barter or bribe someone with. They peer inside their ears and their mouths, have them lift their breasts and spread their toes, part their vaginal lips, spread their butt cheeks. Mo says there's this one CO who always says, when they have to spread for her, "And I better see pink!"

The two-month mark would be a milestone, the jailhouse shrink had assured Maureen during those rough first days. Woody, he has them call him—short for Dr. Woodruff. He urged Mo to set

September as a goal and, as she worked toward it, to stay focused on the recovery mantra: one day at a time. At two months, he said, she'd be better able to cope with those sudden loud noises that kept doing her in—the shouting and slamming cell doors, the out-of-nowhere shrieks of laughter and wounded animal wailing in the middle of the night. Woody told Mo there were probably more inmates at Quirk CI who suffered from posttraumatic stress than inmates who didn't—including some of the toughest cookies. She'd be surprised. At two months, he promised, she'd have a much better grasp of the rules and routines, the jailhouse culture. Meanwhile, she should listen to her gut and proceed with caution. Like any prison, Quirk was full of manipulators. He prescribed an antianxiety drug to help her cope with the noises, an antidepressant to quiet her crying jags.

When they let you into the visiting room, the inmates are already there, seated on one side of these big gray tables. Visitors sit on the opposite side. You're allowed a quick hug and kiss at the beginning and end of a visit. No long lip-locks or lingering embraces. They're awkward, those hugs. For one thing, you have to reach across a table that's four feet wide. For another, you're being watched. There's a camera room where they can look out at you but you can't look in at them. They've got four or five video cameras suspended from the ceiling, another one on a tripod next to the CO's raised desk. He's got a microphone and calls you by your seat number if you're doing something he doesn't like. It's weird: if you're a visitor, you're a seat number, and if you're an inmate, you're Miss So-and-So. "Table F, seat seven, please put your hands on the table where I can see them. . . . Miss Rodriguez, lower your voice or I'll send you back to your tier." *Miss* Rodriguez: sounds so mannerly, doesn't it? Like they're treating them with the utmost respect. Mo said a woman in her unit was walking to the chow hall and thought she saw a CO pointing to her. Goes over to him and asks, Does he want something? "No," he says. "I'm just pretending I'm at the shooting range."

Mo says the women officers are, in general, more decent than the guys, but that they can be chameleons. Depends on who they're part-nered up with. If it's someone who's fair, then they're fair. If they're working a shift with a hard-ass, then they turn hard-ass. My aunt, when she was a CO, sure as hell wasn't like that. With Lolly, what you saw was what you got. Which was probably why the good ole boys went after her with a vengeance.

Those first weeks? God, they were hideous. For one thing, Mau-reen had arrived with a target on her back because her last name was also the name of the prison. Inmates and staff alike drew all kinds of ridiculous conclusions about that surname. Mo was a rich bitch get-ting special treatment. She was a plant—a DOC spy. It's a culture of fear and distrust, that place. Everyone's looking over their shoulder at everyone else, doesn't matter if you're doing time or drawing a pay-check. Everyone's suspect. So the name "Quirk" gave Mo one more burden to bear at a time when her life seemed unbearable.

During those visits, she'd sit across from me, sobbing and hug-ging herself while I racked my brain for things to say. "You know that Korean family lives down the road? They painted their house purple. Looks weird. . . . I pulled two ticks off of Nancy Tucker yes-terday. This morning, she left me a present: a headless mouse. Pain-in-the-ass cat. By the way, she said to say hello." No smiles, no eye contact. She'd hardly say anything, and when she did, I couldn't hear her. There's a din in there—everyone jabbering in English and Span-ish, and the acoustics are horrible, all these different conversations bouncing off the cinder block. "What'd you say?" I'd ask, then wish I hadn't when she repeated it. "I don't think I can survive in here," she'd say. Or "I should've died that day." Which day, I wondered. The day they opened fire at Columbine? The day she killed the Sea-berry kid? I didn't have the heart to ask.

Half the time during those visits, she acted like she was someplace else—like I was boring her or something. But if I said I might not be able to come next time, her tears would spill onto the tabletop. And her fingers: she'd chewed her nails and the skin around them so raw, it looked like she'd fed them one by one into an electric pencil sharpener. I had to force myself to go over there, frankly. I'd look up at the CO at the desk sometimes, and he'd be looking back at me like I was guilty of something. Then I'd look back at Mo without a clue about how I could help her. I had to recover after those visits, to be honest—recovery being a couple of stiff scotches when I got back home.

I don't think I'm going to survive in here. . . . I should have died that day. Was she thinking about suicide? It's not unheard of over there—not even uncommon. I got scared enough to call the prison shrink. He took his time getting back to me, and when he did, he told me to call him Woody, too. He was pretty dismissive of what Mo had said. He hears that kind of stuff all the time, he assured me. Acclimation to prison—to any foreign culture—was a gradual process, depression a rational response to the reality of a long sentence. After a while, I was only half listening to him because I'd started making a list in my head of other Woodys: Woody Allen, Woody Woodpecker, Woody the bartender on *Cheers*. It wasn't exactly reassuring me. I tried to imagine Dr. Patel taking this guy's approach: *Lovely to meet you. I am Dr. Beena Patel, but please, call me Beena Baby.*

But as it turned out, Woody knew what he was talking about. At two months, Maureen *was* better. Less gaunt, less hangdog and weepy. During our last visit, she'd even smiled. So there's more good news for you, Dr. Patel. I might have missed it if I'd blinked, but I hadn't. Maureen Quirk, Inmate #383–642, had finally given me a smile.

Not that there'd been much for her to smile about. Her first cellmate was wacko—bipolar, Mo thought. Sherry? Cherry? She spent Mo's first few days sprawled out on her bed like roadkill. Then some switch got flipped in her brain and she started pacing, muttering, screaming for the guards. By the time they took her to mental health, Mo was a wreck. I mean, those cells are eight-by-ten. Got these toilet-and-sink combos parked right out in the open that, Mo says, when you have to take a crap, you sit there for all the world to see.

Cellmate number two was the really scary one. Denise, her name was, but everyone was supposed to call her D'Angelo after some singer. Apparently, she was the resident ladies' man—used to wad up socks and stick 'em down the front of her pants, Mo said—strut back and forth from the chow hall bowlegged, grabbing on to her bulge. First time I saw this D'Angelo in the visiting room, I thought maybe the prison had gone coed. I mean, this woman was a muscle-bound *beast*. First thing she told Maureen was that she hated white women. She sure loved Mo's stuff, though: swiped her shampoo, her deodorant, dumped her tea bags in the toilet. She ran out of toilet paper and used Mo's stationery instead. When D'Angelo realized that loud noises freaked out Mo, she began this thing where she'd hold a stack of books at arm's length and let them go. She started making these one-note yips and yelps. She'd sneak up behind Mo and yell, "Hey!" Laugh like hell when Maureen cried.

"*Tell* someone," I'd said.

"Who?"

"Woody."

There was a three-week waiting list for appointments, she said.

"The tier supervisor then."

"Why? So that he can speak to D'Angelo and she can retaliate?"

I told her okay then, *I'd* tell someone. She cried, begged me not to. She was shaking so badly that I promised I wouldn't. You want to know what powerlessness is? It's when you have to promise your imprisoned wife that you're not going to do anything about a psychopath who's terrorizing her.

I went home that day, got myself half-plastered, and got online. DOC has this database where you can get information on anyone in their custody: name, town of residence, conviction, length of sentence. It took a while, but I found her: Denise Washington, Bridgeport, Connecticut. Murder One. She'd slammed a woman's head against a sidewalk repeatedly and killed her. I didn't sleep at all that night, and by dawn I'd resolved to break my promise. I was going to howl like hell until I got her out of that cell and got her protected.

But I don't know, maybe there *is* a God, because the next morning, I got a call from Mo. (You can't call them; you can only accept the inflated service charges on their calls to you.) Mo said she had a new cellmate. D'Angelo had caught one of her girls in a clinch with another woman and had jumped the competition along the walkway, choked her within an inch of her life, and stabbed her eight or nine times with the jagged barrel of a Bic pen. The victim had been rushed to the hospital, and D'Angelo had gotten hauled off to the segregation unit. "Seg," Mo called it. She was starting to pick up the lingo.

Mo's cellmate since then has been Helen, a grandmother in her fifties and a former town comptroller. Embezzlement, the Web site says; she stole to stoke her gambling habit. Mo says Helen's nice enough but that she never shuts up. Hey, better a motormouth than a sadist, right? . . . I looked up Maureen's information on the DOC Web site once. They've got the facts right but none of the context. Nothing about Columbine, though, if she hadn't been in the library that day, she never even would have *been* in prison. Look, I know the state and the Seaberrys have to take their pound of flesh, as Lena LoVecchio put it; she stole sedatives, drove while she was out of it, and killed the kid. I'm just saying, there's nothing about the circumstances in that database of theirs. But I guess you could say that about any of them, maybe even D'Angelo. I mean, from the things I've read, nature trumps nurture. I *get* that. But does anyone really come out of the womb a psychopath?

Mo said the inmates refer to strip-searches as "drop, squat, spread your twat." She said this one woman, Gigi, is famous for cutting farts in the officers' faces when she has to bend over and show them her anus. She's like a jailhouse legend or something, from the sound of it. That was what Mo had smiled about, come to think of it: this woman, Gigi, passing gas in the guards' faces. I had tried to smile back when she told me about it, but I couldn't quite manage it. Makes me wonder, you know: If this is what makes her smile sixty days into it, what's she going to be like at the end of five years? Who's Maureen Quirk going to be by the time Quirk CI gets done with her?

"Grandma's prison," Lolly used to call it. The other day, I went into Lolly and Hennie's bedroom and stared at that wooden sign that used to hang on the wall above Great-Grandma's desk—the one Lolly took with her when they gave her the bum's rush out of there. Place had traveled light-years away from the place Lydia P. Quirk had run. They'd gone from "A woman who surrenders her freedom need not surrender her dignity" to "Drop, squat, spread your twat. And show me pink."

I PULLED INTO THE ALLEY between the Mama Mia and Mustard Insurance and parked by the back entrance. Grabbed my copy of *Ancient Myth and Modern Man* and got out of the car. I doubted I was going to get any reading done that night, though. I'd started dozing about an hour or so before it was time to leave, and now I was running a good forty minutes late. I was going to have to hustle. If you want full cases of product out front by six a.m., you'd better get your ass down there before midnight. Takes a good half hour for the oil to heat to three seventy-five, and in the meantime, you've got to get the mixes started for your cake doughnut and your yeast doughnuts. And believe me, yeast doesn't hurry for anybody. Back in college when I was working nights for Mr. Buzzi, he and I made everything from scratch, but these days Alphonse orders these kits where everything comes premeasured and premixed. It costs more, but it's cheaper than hiring a helper. The night guy can fly solo, but he'd better be organized and he better not be late.

I'd just barely gotten the lights on and the fryer fired up when the phone started ringing. That, and someone was rapping at the front door. I looked out and, Jesus Christ, it was her again. Velvet Hoon. Third night in a row. I held up a wait-a-minute finger and grabbed the phone. Alphonse was on the other end.

"I got Ma in her bedroom, whimpering rosaries all day to make the pain go away, and I got him over in the hospital, being a prick to everyone. You know what he pulled yesterday? Kicked the *priest* out of his room. Little Cuban guy—comes in, asks does Pop want to take Communion, and Pop goes, 'Get the hell out of here!' If Ma had been there, she woulda broken his other hip."

I asked him what his father had against the priest.

"Nothing. It's God he's pissed at. Hasn't been inside a church since my brother died. Ma's convinced he's going to hell, and after yesterday maybe—"

"Hey, hold on a sec," I said. I put down the receiver and went to unlock the door. I couldn't let her just stand out there. Two nights earlier? When she'd shown up the first time? I probably shouldn't have started it. But it was safer for her to be inside the bakery than out there by herself in the middle of the night. There's some seedy characters hanging around Three Rivers at night. She knows some of them, too, from the soup kitchen and the Silver Rail.

"What's up?" I said.

"Need any help?" She'd asked me the same thing the two previous nights and had gotten the same answer: "Nope." She nodded and strolled past me to the coffeemaker. I'd shown her how to use it the night before. Shouldn't have started that, either. By the time she left, she'd drunk a pot and a half, and it wasn't like she'd paid for it. *I'*d paid for it—threw a fin in the register and rang up five bucks.

I grabbed the phone again. "Yup."

"This trailer park they're in? It's like everything's miniature, Quirky. I've hit my head on the door frame so many times, I oughta wear a fucking helmet. A hundred fifty units here in Oldie-But-Goodyville, and I don't think anyone's taller than five-foot-three. I'm like whoozie-whatsis in that story—the one that lands where all the midgets live."

"Yeah, well, try clicking your ruby slippers together," I said.

"No, not the Munchkins. Smaller. The Lillipoppers or something."

"Lilli*putians*," I said, crooking the phone against my shoulder and prying the lids off the mixes. "*Gulliver's Travels.*"

"Yeah, that's it. I used to have the Gold Key comic."

"Probably the closest you've ever come to a literary experience," I said.

"Oh, yeah? Well, fuck you, professor, because it just so happens I been reading a book while I'm down here. What the hell else am I gonna do? No Internet, no NESN, and all's my parents have is basic cable. You can't get a Sox game to save yourself. *The Da Vinci Code.* You ever hear of it? I gotta hide it under the couch cushion because Ma thinks it's sacrilegious. Hey, by the way, did you know Jesus was doing Mary Magdalene?"

"Al," I said. "If you don't let me get off, I'm going to be serving raw batter to your early risers."

"Yeah, okay. Hey, before you go, you happen to know how we made out yesterday? Receipt-wise?" I reminded him that Tina, his day person, was taking care of the books—that he should call her later. "Yeah, okay. I'll let you go then. Hey, I heard the door before. You letting customers in?"

"Uh, no," I said. "Not really." Velvet was tearing sugar packets and pouring them into a paper coffee cup. She was up to four.

"'Not really?' What's that mean?"

"Look, Gulliver, I gotta go."

I got back to the business at hand, wondering, was *Gulliver's Travels* a quest story? Had Gulliver gone off in search of something?

Velvet had toned it down since high school, I'd give her that much—had lost the blue crew cut and the silver combat boots. Her hair was short, still, but brown now, her natural color. She still had that fire hydrant build, but her face had lost some of its baby fat. Army jacket, T-shirt and miniskirt, black tights bagging at the knees. She was what now? Twenty-two? Twenty-three?

The day of Maureen's sentencing? After Carole Alderman had begged the judge to throw the book at her and Velvet had caused that commotion? She'd followed me out of the courthouse. I'd just watched them haul my wife off to prison, and all I wanted to do was get the fuck out of that parking garage before my head exploded. And Velvet had run after me, calling, "Mr. Quirk! Wait up!"

I'd pivoted and faced her. "What are you *doing* here? How'd you even find out about this?"

She said she'd been cleaning offices someplace down South and had lifted a bunch of magazines from waiting rooms. Taken them home, and opened up to "A Victim's Victims" in the *New Yorker*. It was "a sign," she'd said. She'd started hitchhiking up to Connecticut the next morning.

"Well, hitchhike back," I said. "There's nothing for you up here."

Yes, there was, she said. Her "mom" was here, and she was going to stand by her. Visit her and give her moral support. She asked me if I wanted to go someplace and talk—get a pizza or something.

"A pizza?" I said. "Velvet, after what just happened in that court-room, do you think I've got an *appetite*?" I got into my car and slammed the door. Backed out of my space and took her out of reverse. But just as I was about to give it the gas, she stepped in front of the car.

"It was Columbine," she said. "That's what messed up her head."

"Gee, really? You think? Get out of my way."

"Could I crash at your place? Until I get a job and a room some-place?"

"No!" I was fighting back tears.

"Can I borrow some money then?"

I fished two twenties out of my wallet and threw them at her. And when she bent to pick them up, I swerved around her and got out of there.

That was the last I'd seen of her until two nights earlier, when she'd shown up at the locked door of the Mama Mia. Which is not to say she didn't call me five or six times in between—so much so that I thought about getting caller ID. She kept bugging me about asking Maureen to add her name to her visitors list. Mo had enough to contend with, I figured, so I kept saying no, it's not a good idea, maybe down the road sometime. What were they going to do: reminisce about Littleton? I could spare Mo that much. And anyway, when an inmate puts someone on her visitor list, they do a security check to make sure the person doesn't have any felony convictions. I figured Velvet might very well have racked up one or two of those, and that it might raise a red flag with DOC.

Velvet circumvented me, though. Wrote to Mo, Mo put her on her list, and, what do you know, they approved her. I didn't know all this had gone down until after the fact—after Velvet's first visit. It was hard seeing her at the place, Maureen said, but she appreciated the kid's effort. "She's still so needy, Caelum. And it's not like I can help her while I'm here."

"You two talk about Columbine?" I asked her.

Tears welled up in Maureen's eyes. She looked down at the tabletop and shook her head.

"Let Velvet take care of herself," I said. "You take care of *your*self."

THOSE FIRST TWO NIGHTS AT the Mama Mia, over all those free cups of coffee, Velvet filled me in about her life since I'd gunned it out of the parking garage. It was the edited version, I was pretty sure. She was renting a room downtown. She'd gotten a job on a cleaning crew, but then the company had done urines on all their employees and fired her.

"What did you test positive for?" I asked. Marijuana, she said, but I had my doubts. Who wears an army jacket during a summer heat wave? And why were there blood stains on the cuffs of that jacket? Jesus, if she was doing heroin, I didn't want her going anywhere near Maureen and I'd told her as much that first night. "Heroin?" she'd said. "God, I'm not *that* stupid."

Yeah, and I'm not that naïve, I thought.

She was on town welfare now, she said—had established residence and qualified. She did some dishwashing and maintenance work at the Silver Rail, and they paid her under the table. I suspected she might be turning tricks, too—she'd mentioned hanging out at the highway rest stop on I–95 and at the all-night diner where a lot of the truckers eat. She and I had a don't-ask-don't-tell policy about that, though. I didn't want to know, because I was damned if I was going to become her surrogate dad again. I'd tried that once before back in Littleton, and she'd burned me pretty bad.

"Mom seemed good yesterday," Velvet told me now, matter-of-factly. She'd picked up *Ancient Myth and Modern Man* and was leafing through it while I mixed a bucket of butter cream. "She said there's a Survivors of Violence group down there and she went to one of their meetings."

"I know she did," I said. "I visit her three times a week. She's my wife."

"And she's my mom."

"No, she's not," I said. "You need to back off from that 'mom' crap."

Her eyes narrowed angrily. "Why? Because you hate my guts?"

"No, because she's got enough to deal with without having to feel responsible for you."

"Who says she's responsible for me?" she shot back.

"You imply it when you call her Mom. Mothers take care of their daughters."

"Not all of them," she said. We stood there, facing each other. She emptied the rest of the coffee into the sink and started a new pot. "It's just a nickname," she said. "God."

I did end up putting her to work that night, though—mainly because somewhere around three a.m., when I figured I'd pretty much gotten things under control, it dawned on me that I'd forgotten to check the "special orders" book. And when I did, it said that someone from the junior high was coming at seven to pick up three dozen assorteds and three dozen muffins for a teachers' meeting and that half an hour later, Yankee Remodelers was picking up a half-sheet cake, marble with butter cream frosting, "Happy Retirement, Harry!"

"Fuck!" I shouted, louder than I meant to. When I looked up, Velvet was staring at me. "God," she said. "Why can't you just let me *help* you."

"Take off your jacket then," I said. "And wash your hands."

I got her an apron. Showed her how to cut doughnuts. Taught her how to use the pump for the filled ones. The hand pump, not the electric. You can fill two at a time with the electric pump, but it takes a while to get the hang of it. I glanced at her arms a few times, but I didn't see any tracks. That didn't necessarily mean there weren't any. When she was done with those jobs, I had her make muffins and bake a few dozen of those frozen hockey-puck bagels Alphonse sells, much to the disdain of his father.

Truth is, Velvet saved my butt that night. By six a.m., the cases were full, the special orders were done, and I was reading chapter four of *Ancient Myth and Modern Man*. Daedalus, Theseus, the Minotaur, the maze. "Throw me a pen, will you?" I said to Velvet. I'd just read something I wanted to underline: "The labyrinth is simultaneously inextricable and impenetrable. Those inside cannot get out and those outside cannot get in." Like Maureen and me, I thought. For the next four years and ten months.

By eight a.m., Velvet had taken a hike and Tina, Alphonse's day shift gal, had taken over. I was seated in a booth, reading still, and having a coffee and a cruller. Tina reached up and turned on the TV in the far corner. The *Today* show was all about New Orleans still: the fiasco inside the Superdome, the mayor's frustration with FEMA's and Bush's bullshit. Gunfire had been exchanged between looters and police.

"'Scuse me," the guy at the next table said. "Y'all mind if I turn that thing off?" He was black or part-black, unshaven and baggy-eyed. The sad-eyed white woman sitting across from him looked like she'd been through the wringer, too. We were the only three out front. I told him no, I didn't mind.

"Good," he said. "Because she and I been on the road for three days driving away from that particular nightmare."

"You're from New Orleans?"

"Used to be. Now, who knows?"

He got up and deadened the TV. Back at the table, he extended his hand. "Moses Mick," he said. "This is my wife, Janis."

"Caelum Quirk," I said. I shook hands with both of them. The bones in hers felt as fragile as a bird's.

"Pleased to meet you," Moses said. "You don't know, by any chance, where she and I could rent a place short-term?"

I told him Three Rivers had two motels, and that there were three hotels down at the casino, two high-end and one not.

He shook his head. "I'm talking about a couple of months maybe. Our game plan was, we'd head north to Cape Cod, because Janis has been there and says it's pretty. But I'm damn sick of driving. Y'heard me?"

→→ chapter eighteen ←←

MOSES AND JANIS MICK WERE a handsome couple, mis-matched in intriguing ways. Moses was a big guy—biracial, blue-eyed, blue-collar. He had an easy smile and a slow, deliberate way of moving that was in sync with his Louisiana drawl. Janis, a petite, wide-eyed academic, was Type A all the way— and cute as hell. She had a cute little body on her, too—not that a guy whose sex life was on hold for five years would notice. That morning at the bakery, I put down *Modern Man and Ancient Myth* and listened to the details of the Micks' Hurricane Katrina ordeal.

Their shotgun house was on Caffin Avenue in the city's Ninth Ward, they said—flanked by a beauty parlor and a Family Dollar. Fats Domino's blond brick place—a palace in comparison to the rest of the neighborhood—was half a block away.

"What's a shotgun house?" I asked.

"Narrow but deep," Moses said. "Bedrooms up front, kitchen in the back. No hallway. You want something to eat, you gotta walk from room to room to get to where the food's at." He gave a nod to Janis. "House drove her crazy at first. California girl."

"I love that house," Janis said. Stroking his arm, she turned to me. "Moses was born there."

At first, they had planned to stay put and ride out the storm, they said, but sometime after midnight on Sunday, with the predictions so dire and the TV showing live shots of the necklace of headlights inching along I–10, they'd relented. "My mother kept calling from Sacramento and begging us to leave," Janis added.

"Begging *her*," Moses corrected. "Her mama don't have much use for the black guy who kidnapped her daughter and dragged her down to the big, bad Lower Nines." It jolted me a little to hear him put it that way. When they'd entered the bakery, I'd just been reading about Persephone's abduction to the underworld and the creation of the seasons.

"My mom's pretty conversative," Janis said. To which Moses added, "Big Limbaugh fan. 'Mega-dittoes, Rush. It's an honor and a privilege to speak to a bigot and a drug abuser such as yourself.'"

"Moze, stop," Janis said. "We don't know what this guy's politics are."

I assured her they fell well to the left of her mother's.

"We'd already boarded up the windows, so that was done," Moses said. "I figured the rain gutters and some of the roof shingles'd go. Maybe even the roof itself if the chinaberry tree fell the wrong way. Figured a category four or five might uproot that ole boy." He stopped, swallowed hard. "I thought we might get *some* flooding, but I was picturing a foot or two. I didn't calculate the levees'd fail and the whole damn Lower Nine would go under. We left everything there, pretty much. Packed up her computer and my molds and tools and drove off."

"What kind of molds?" I said.

Moses said he was a sculptor, angels and gargoyles his specialty.

Their cat, Fat Harry, had probably drowned, Janis said. They'd delayed leaving for over an hour, calling him and shaking his box of treats. But Harry hadn't come home. "That ole rascal's gone fat and lazy, but he's still got an interest in the ladies," Moses said. His smile was rueful. "And if he died tomcattin', well, I guess there's worse ways to go." Janis rested her head against the tabletop, and he reached over and massaged the small of her back. He said it softly. "Sugar, we gotta get you some sleep."

I invited them to crash at the farmhouse. I had the room, and they seemed like decent people. And I mean, Jesus Christ, their whole goddamned life had gone underwater.

An hour later, Janis was sacked out across Lolly and Hennie's bed and Moses and I were downstairs, drinking ten a.m. beers and staring at the havoc on CNN. I thought about confessing that, six years earlier, I had stared at that same TV, that same channel, watching Columbine unfold—watching the beginning of the end of *our* shared life as we knew it. Instead, I kept my mouth shut. What was I going to say? That if he thought things were bad now, he should brace himself for the repercussions? That if his sleeping wife had come away from Katrina with posttraumatic stress, they were fucked far worse than he could imagine?

"You married?" he asked.

"Yeah. Yup." He waited. "My wife's away for a while."

He nodded. "Where's she at?"

Rather than answer him, I asked if he knew Fats Domino.

"The Fat Man? No, not really. See him sometimes, driving past in his big pink Cadillac. I was at his house once, helping a friend of mine move a piano. Mr. Antoine wasn't there, though. That's his given name: Antoine. I know his wife a bit. Miss Rosemary. She was church friends with my mamaw."

"Your mother?" I asked.

"*Grand*mother. Some of us families go back to when the Nines was neighborly. My Granddaddy Robichaux built our place back in nineteen-fifty, way before crack and crime took hold. I inherited it after Mamaw passed—what you'd call a mixed blessing, I guess. But even *with* all the problems, a neighborhood's a hard thing to let go of, y'heard me?" He looked back at the TV, shaking his head. He said he recognized some of the rooftops from the aerial footage, and a few of the people stranded on those roofs.

"My granddaddy built his house square and true," he said. He was picking at his beer bottle label and talking more to the images on the TV screen than to me. "That place survived three of his and Mamaw's kids, six of Mamaw's and my step-granddaddy Mr. Clarence's, nine of us grandkids, and Hurricane Betsy." He turned and faced me. "Betsy's how I come by the name of Moses. I came into the world just as she was blowin' through. That ole she-devil put the Nines underwater, too. My mama'd been in labor the better part of the night before, but when the water come, she got up out of bed, put me in a dresser drawer, and waded in neck-deep. Sixteen and single, and Mamaw said she pushed me along inside that drawer past bodies and debris until me and her reached higher ground. Two days later, she died from infection. 'Name him Moses,' she told Mamaw. It was Mamaw who raised me—her and Mr. Clarence and Miss Delia next door. Auntie, I always called her, but she wasn't really blood. Might as well have been, though. Used to run Delia's High Classe Beauty Shoppe before her legs swelled up bad. Ain't no way she survived this, or that ole shop of hers neither."

"Maybe she did," I said. "Maybe it's not as bad as you think."

He shook his head. "Miss Delia's two hundred pounds and wheelchair-bound. We asked her to come with us, but she said no. Figured if she'd survived Betsy, she'd weather Katrina, too. . . . No, she's gone. Who was gonna hoist *her* up onto her roof? Her son in prison? Her crackhead granddaughter who steals her blind? I shouldn't have taken no. Should have insisted."

The six-pack was sitting on the couch between us: five empties and one last beer in the carton. I picked it up, twisted the cap off, and handed it to him. "Miss Dee?" he said. "When I was growing up? At Christmastime, after midnight church, we'd head back to her house for *reveillon* dinner. Eggs and grits, red beans and rice, cherry bread pudding, turtle soup. Crawfish boil on top of all that other. She'd of been cooking for days." He drank his beer in two or three long gulps, then rose abruptly. Staggering a little, he left the room, then left the house.

A banging sound brought me to the parlor window. I stood there, watching him kick the driver's side door of his pickup, over and over, until he'd dented it pretty badly. In the process, he'd spent himself. Slumped to the ground and rested his forehead against his knees.

———————

"WHAT DOES SHE LOOK LIKE?" Maureen wanted to know.

"Janis?" I shrugged. "I don't know. She kind of reminds me of that little actress. What's her name? *Legally Blonde?*"

"Reese Witherspoon," Mo said.

"Yeah, her." I caught a flash of disapproval and amended the comparison. "Well, half Legally Blonde, half Energizer Bunny. She vacuumed the house yesterday, cleaned out the refrigerator, went grocery shopping. She's cooking supper tonight. Says she feels better when she keeps busy."

Maureen's frown was pensive.

"But it's kind of buggy, you know? All that manic energy."

"Do they know about me?" Maureen asked.

"Some," I lied. "Not all of it." Janis had inquired about Mo's whereabouts, too, and I'd made up a story about her needing to go back to Colorado to help with a family emergency. Because she's a nurse, I'd said.

"They figure their cat drowned. It hadn't come home yet when they had to evacuate. Nancy Tucker's kind of adopted them, though. Janis, especially. Follows her around, sleeps on their bed."

"It's not their bed," Maureen pointed out. "It's Lolly's bed."

The visitors' room racket was worse than usual that afternoon. Two seats down, a Latina with Cheeto-colored hair and the inmate across from her were arguing in breakneck Spanish. Two tables over, a black guy with gold front teeth was singing "Happy Birthday" to a pretty inmate in orange flight risk scrubs. Mo said something I didn't catch, and I cupped my hand behind my ear. "Come again?"

"I asked you what *he* was like."

"Moze? Well, older than she is. Forty or so. She's twenty-eight. They're one of those opposites-attract couples, I guess: he goes maybe six-four, six-five, and she doesn't quite clear five feet. She's halfway to a Ph.D. at Tulane, she says. In women's studies. But all that's in limbo for the time being, I guess."

Mo reminded me that she had asked about Moses, not Janis.

"Oh," I said. "Right. Well, let's see. Says he dropped out of high school to work on a shrimp boat. Smart guy, though. He knows carpentry, electrical, plumbing. Says he started sculpting about four or five years ago. On the side at first, but then he caught a break when *Frommer's New Orleans* listed his studio in its 'Shopping A to Z' chapter. Says he made 'beaucoup bucks' in 2004 and the first half of 2005. But of course, that's over now. When they evacuated, he took his molds and equipment, but none of his stock. Says he lost a couple hundred sculptures."

Mo looked impatient. "I meant, what does he *look* like? If these people are living in my home, I'd at least like to be able to picture them."

Our home, I thought. My family's home. The one we might lose in a lawsuit because of you. "Tall," I said. "Burly. Black hair, goatee." I described Moze's African facial features and his pale blue eyes. "Croatian on his father's side, he says. Haitian Creole on his mother's. Rhymes, now that I think of it."

"What?"

"Haitian, Croatian."

Mo didn't return my smile. "So she's pretty?"

Because I knew better than to say so, I shrugged. "More like . . . perky. I feel bad for them, you know? All they took with them when they left were . . . What is it, Maureen? Something bothering you?"

She gave me one of those never-mind shakes of the head.

"Is it about them staying at the house? Because as soon as they get their bearings—"

She shook her head. "There's a new second-shift CO in our unit," she said. "A transfer. Officer Sibley."

"Yeah? He harassing you or something?" I could feel my body clench.

She said no, that Sibley was one of the more reasonable ones. "It's not rational. It's just that . . . he reminds me of . . ."

"Which one?"

"Harris." I nodded. Waited. "I had a flashback yesterday. It's okay, though. It only lasted a minute. Hey, I'm in prison. I'm *supposed* to suffer."

I reached across the table and took her hands in mine. "You taking your meds?" She said they'd told her in Med Line that they couldn't dispense any more of her antianxiety medication until Woody okayed it. "Well, that's not a problem, is it? He knows your history. If you're having flashbacks, then—"

"The earliest appointment I could get is October," she said.

"That's unacceptable. Did you explain it was an emergency?"

It *wasn't* an emergency, she said. "Sibley doesn't even really look that much like him. It's just that he's short and wiry and . . . "

"And what?"

"The way he smiles. He was smiling that day, Caelum. They both were. Like it was all a big joke." She closed her eyes and shuddered.

"Maureen, look at me," I said. I squeezed her hands and spoke slowly, deliberately. "Rational or not, the fear is real. Right?"

She looked at me in a way I couldn't read.

"So we need to *do* something about it. Don't we?"

She just sat there, staring through me.

"So I'm going to call Woody and let him know what's going on. Insist that he see you, or at least write you a prescription. And in the meantime—"

She shook her head emphatically. "Don't call. I'll handle it. I'll speak to my unit manager."

"Will you? Because I don't like hearing this 'I'm in prison, I'm supposed to suffer' stuff. I don't want you to hit the skids in here."

"Can we please just change the subject?" she said.

"Mo, I just want to make sure—"

The CO's microphone clicked on. *Tap, tap, tap* through the amp sitting on that elevated desk of hers. "Table D, seat three. Hand-holding during visits is not permitted." I looked up at the reprimanding officer: a black woman with auburn dreadlocks, red lipstick, red talons like Edward-fuckin'-Scissorhands. I held her gaze for maybe two or three seconds longer than I should have, then released Maureen's hands and raised my own, palms up. I was suddenly aware of how quiet the room had gotten, all the jibber-jabberers having stopped talking to stare at the wicked handholders, the visiting-room criminals.

Mo's face was flushed. Her hands were trembling. "What?" I said.

"Nothing. It's just that they're going to hassle me now. After the visit, when they strip-search me. . . . Or maybe they won't. Never mind. Tell me more about these Micks."

"What do you want to know?" I said.

She shrugged. "Anything. What's she getting her Ph.D. in?"

"I told you," I said.

"Tell me again."

"Women's studies."

✦ chapter nineteen ✦

Friday morning
September 17, 1886

My Dear Lillian,

Please excuse my hideous penmanship today. I am writing these words aboard the early train bound for Hartford from the Union depot. We were to have traveled from New Haven yesterday and spent last night at the home of Grandmother's friend from the War, Reverend Twichell. Then, the deluge! This morning there are dark clouds and muddy roads but no more Heavenly torrents. The newspaper reports that this day's ceremony will proceed, rain or shine, but that the parade may be sacrificed. However, on this matter, I have sanguine spirits and feel the sun will shine and the marchers will march.

Sister, we travel with the hordes this *matin*! All seats are taken (two by Grandmother and me) and fifty or more passengers stand shoulder to shoulder in the aisle. Most are men, and so there is jostling, coarse talk, hearty laughter, and huffing and puffing. Tobacco smoke hangs so thick in the air that, a moment ago, the conductor, calling for tickets, emerged from the fog like the ghost of Hamlet's father!

Like Grandmother and me, most of our fellow sojourners appear bound for today's dedication of the Memorial Arch. Many former soldiers and Naval veterans are aboard, dressed in the uniforms they wore more than twenty years ago. A few of these aged warriors cut a dashing figure, but most have frost in their beards and bellies that strain the buttons of their jackets. There is a one-legged veteran across the aisle and down from us and two others whose sleeves hang empty. At the New Haven station, I saw a darkie with a shadowy hole where an eye should have been. "I wish that man had thought of others and worn a patch," I remarked, innocently enough, but Her Majesty pounced and pontificated. "If he was good enough to sacrifice an eye to help preserve the Union, then I should think you might be generous enough to sacrifice a bit of comfort to see him, or else look away." Honestly, Lil, I find the Old Girl's righteousness so very dreary.

When we boarded, Grandmother said she was amused to think that some of the veterans might be wearing the very uniforms sewn by the Ladies Soldiers' Relief Society. I asked her what that organization might be and was surprised by the answer. After the defeat at Fort Sumter, it seems, our grandmère directed two hundred women from New London and Three Rivers Junction in the making of uniforms, bandages, and compresses for the First Connecticut company. I was well aware of her battlefield nursing, her letter-writing to the mothers of wounded soldiers, and her coaxing of the injured back to health with nourishing beef teas and wine jellies. I had not, however, heard about this earlier shepherding of seamstresses and bandage-makers for the good of the Union. She is full of surprises, our grandam!

As ever, dear Sis, I struggle with two minds about Grandmother. Here, seated beside me, is the esteemed Elizabeth Hutchinson Popper, brave abolitionist, valiant battlefield nurse, and tireless champion of orphans and fallen women. But here also is the cold woman who has yet to remember her granddaughter's fifteenth birthday, now eleven days past. Madame Buzon and the girls at the school remembered, gifting me with a lovely cut glass cologne bottle, a Chinese box, a pair of five-button scallop-top kid gloves, and a volume of poems by Christina Rossetti. My flesh and blood relation, however, has forgotten me. Had Lizzie Popper been in charge during the time of the Biblical flood, she might well have led all of God's creatures onto the ark, two by two, then closed the door against the torrent and floated away, having forgotten her poor granddaughter at the pier!

Overheard just now amongst the veterans: If the rain holds off and the parade proceeds as planned, two guns will be fired at the east end of Bushnell Park. That will be the signal for the bands and regiments to assemble. On the matter of marching, what will be will be. I suppose I can most certainly live without a parade. Our dinner engagement for this evening is a different matter. If *that* were snatched away, I should probably die from disappointment! I am most curious to see the Clemens manse, which I am having trouble imagining. Reverend Twichell has described the house to Grandmother as being "one third riverboat, one third cathedral, and one third cuckoo clock." This I shall have to see for myself.

Mr. Twichell says that Mr. and Mrs. Clemens's eldest daughter, Susy, will dine with us, as will his own daughter, Harmony. This was Mrs. Clemens's idea, says Mr. Twichell, as she imagined I should feel more at home with dinner companions closer to my own age. It was a most thoughtful consideration. To think, Sister, in twelve hours I shall be at table in a house next door to greatness. Perhaps I will even get a glimpse of Greatness Herself as she strolls past a window! Grandmère says I mustn't go on and on about Mrs. Stowe tonight in the presence of Mr. Clemens, who is also a writer of some note. To be sure, Mark Twain's books are amusing, but Mrs. Stowe's works are sublime.

Do you love reading, Lillian? Which authors play the strings of your heart? Here are my favorite authors and poets at present: Shakespeare, Mrs. Stowe, Robert Browning, and Christina Rossetti. Grandmother disapproves of the last name on my list. Elizabeth Popper's sympathies for darkies and fallen women most certainly do not extend to mystical poets or tellers of fairie stories. Last night, she picked up my book of Miss Rossetti's poems and examined it like a damning piece of evidence. "That Buzon woman will turn you into a Papist before she's through with you," she mumbled. I quickly informed Grandmère that Christina Rossetti is an Anglican, not a Catholic, but, of course, no apology was offered. Of course, she never misses a chance to disparage Madame Buzon and the finishing school. It is so tedious to have to hear this steady stream of remarks, and all because my tuition is paid for by the mysterious Miss Urso. This reminds me—I owe my benefactress my yearly letter of appreciative thanks. Some day I shall meet in person this famous traveling violinist, and when I do I shall plague her with questions about our mère et père. She knew them both.

Sister, I do find Christina Rossetti's verse quite extraordinary. Her "Goblin Market" is my particular favorite. In this mysterious poem, two sisters are tempted and must resist the ripe and luscious melons, gooseberries, peaches, and figs of a band of goblin fruitmongers. "Come buy! Come buy!" they call, and the food looks and smells as delectable as the apple offered to Eve in the Garden. One sister forbears; the other succumbs, selling a lock of her golden hair for a taste of the goblins' wicked harvest. She eats and falls into depravity. It is the stronger sister who must save her by confronting the

demon peddlers, resisting temptation, and securing the antidote. I have committed portions of the poem to memory and
here are the final lines:

> *For there is no friend like a sister*
> *In calm or stormy weather;*
> *To cheer one on the tedious way,*
> *To fetch one if one goes astray,*
> *To lift one if one totters down,*
> *To strengthen whilst one stands.*

Would that I were that strength for you, Lil—that sister to
fetch you from your miserable fate!

Oh, and now I must tell you about a rude young man aboard
this train—a tall, strapping fellow of perhaps twenty-eight or
-nine who stands facing me in the crowded aisle. He has a
swarthy complexion and a prominent nose and is wearing a
shabby coat with frayed sleeves and a missing button. He looks
foreign-born to me, but from where he originates I could not
say. Wherever it is, they must not teach common courtesy.
Each time I look up from this page, I catch his eyes leaving
me. It is most vexing. Grandmother has her packet of letters
from Reverend Twichell in her lap and has begun dozing in
the midst of rereading them. If I could do so without waking
her, I would give this lout some sharp words and do not think
I would not. Look elsewhere, please, Mister Tatty Suit!

Overheard just now: a quarrel between husband and wife.
Their seats are directly behind ours. It is quite dreadful to
listen to, but also quite impossible not to listen. He accuses
her of sloth, slovenliness, and discombobulation; she mur-
murs limp objections and teary excuses. "Go to grass, then,
why don't you!" he has just shouted, in a sharp voice for all
to hear. She makes no answer except a whimper. I have a

mind to stand, turn and face this brute, and inform him that if his better half were indeed dead and buried, at least her ears would fill with dirt and she would no longer have to listen to the likes of him!

And now Grandmother has begun to snore, spilling Mr. Twichell's letters from her lap. I suppose I should wake her for propriety's sake, but who but I on this noisy train can hear her?

Of course, I remain furious that Grandmother is not to be seated today on the dignitaries' platform and lauded for her good works during the War as Reverend Twichell had earlier promised would be the case. Colonel Bissell's complaint that it would "dilute" the dedication ceremony to have a woman on the platform alongside senators, judges, and distinguished military heroes is most infuriating. I should like to know who brought this Bissell into the world if not a woman!

Reverend Twichell agrees that this is a most grievous slight. The poor man has made numerous efforts to reverse the dedication committee's decision, but ultimately he is bound by the wishes of the majority. Grandmother dismisses the fuss, of course. She may have broken with the Society of Friends years ago, but she has retained her Quaker modesty along with her Quaker speech and dress. She has written Mr. Twichell that she is content to stand in the shadows rather than bask in the sun. Better, says she, to procure her precious letters of support from these influential men than to sit amongst them and be glorified with no useful outcome. Mr. Twichell wrote back that if anyone might persuade these movers and shakers to consider the plight of our state's fallen women, it is she. Grandmother chuckled when she read his words to me: "Whosoever wishes to spur Connecticut's lawmakers to action for their cause would do well to save themselves the trip to Hartford and send the little Quaker lady in their stead."

To be sure, Sister, I do not dispute that the "little Quaker lady" is a woman of numerous achievements. Still, she can at times be a most irksome grandmother and traveling companion. Here is a fine and dandy example. At the Union depot before we boarded, I picked up a discarded newspaper from the bench beside me and happened to turn first to the advertisements. I saw that the Bee Hive department store was offering, free of charge to every purchaser, a beautiful colored engraving of the new Memorial Arch. The notice promised that those Bee Hive shoppers who secured one would possess "not a worthless picture, but one worthy of a place upon the walls of any household." I passed the paper to Madame and remarked that I should like one of those pictures as a souvenir of the day. She eyed the page suspiciously and then asked in an accusing voice if I was drawn to the engraving of the arch or to the black Ottoman silks and indigo dress velvets on sale at the Bee Hive. (If Grandmother had her wish, I would mimic her and wear the Quaker cap and shawl and speak in "thees" and "thous," I suppose.) Rather than defend myself, or suggest that a few yards of velvet might make a suitable birthday gift for a granddaughter who had been forgotten, I changed the subject.

"I see from the newspaper that thirty thousand visitors are expected in Hartford today," I stated. "And that these will be joined by another thirty thousand city residents along the parade route if weather permits. I have never seen such a throng as sixty thousand."

"A drop in the bucket," she snapped. "In the war, six hundred thousand fell—ten times that many."

"Mon dieu, Grandmère!" I replied, more to plague her than to practice my French. (She says my French-speaking makes me sound like a Catholic.) Grandmother has suffered dyspepsia and insomnia these past few days, and so I have been made to suffer her dismissals and criticisms. Did you know, Lillian, that, according to Grandmère, I am too affected, too hasty to pass judgment on others, too covetous, and "too modern for my petticoats"? This latter charge was launched in response to my simple voicing of a desire to try bicyle-riding. "Thou had best travel the road of the true woman and not the modern one," she advised. "Bicycle-riding can damage thy reproductive capacity." I promptly informed her that I wanted neither husband nor babes, a statement to which her only answer was a frown and a shaking of her head. This proves, dear Sis, that despite her many virtues, the old girl is a hypocrite. Was it not she who went on and on about Mrs. Sedgewick's "splendid" novel, *Married or Single*? The story advances the idea— drearily, in my view—that a woman might be as happy in one state as the other. I disagree. Happy to be single, miserable to be married, if you should ask me!

And here he goes again, the bad-mannered lout with the jumping eyes. I have caught him, too, peeking at my words to you, which he is trying to read upside down. Have I mentioned, Lil, that Sir Wandering Eye has a mass of unruly black hair which he has tried (unsuccessfully) to tame with a pound or more of pomade? That large head of his smells so wretchedly sweet that if I closed my eyes, I should think I was lying in an apple orchard amidst the rotting drops. Perhaps he would have better luck with axle grease! And now, the impudent fellow stares down at this page. Well, I shall fix him then.

SIR, YOU ARE RUDE BEYOND ALL REASON. KINDLY PLACE YOUR EYES ELSEWHERE OR I SHALL BE FORCED TO COMPLAIN TO THE CONDUCTOR!

There! He has given me his back. Rubbish to him and good riddance!

Sister, a shocking thing has just happened in the moments since I wrote my words above. When the train pulled into the station at Middletown, another throng stood waiting on the platform, bound for the dedication. Two dozen or more passengers squeezed into this car, and in the shuffle, Sir Tatty Suit was turned back toward me again—all but pushed by the crowd into my lap. Propriety forced me to look past Grandmother and out the window. Where else was I to look? I fixed my eyes so, until the constant rush of the countryside made me dizzy and I thought I should be sick if I did not look away.

One of the passengers I'd seen board at Middletown was a thin, nervous man of middle age. Despite the crowded conditions, he was pushing and shouldering his way about the car. He was not a vagabond from what I could see, neither unshaven nor ill-dressed. Still, I watched him take pains to elude the conductor. I assumed the fellow was down on his luck and had no money for a ticket. Well, let it stand, I thought. With all of the extra paying customers today, the Consolidated line can well afford the loss of one fare.

Whether this curious fellow had money or not, he was enterprising. I watched him accost several of the veterans aboard, attempting to interest them in the purchase of what looked like half-penny postal cards. A few bought them, most did not, but all studied them with serious interest.

The trouble began when the strange salesman approached Sir Tatty Suit with his wares. I reached into my bag for a penny and spoke. "Sir, if those are engravings of the Memorial Arch you are selling, I should like one." Well, Sis, it was as if I were the ether and not a living, speaking person.

"Sir, I should like to purchase one of your engravings," I said again, this time in a voice he could not ignore.

"Hey!" someone shouted from behind. "I thought I told you to stay off my train!" And at that, the seller threw his cards at me and pushed past so violently that Sir Tatty lost his balance and landed on my lap! He rose immediately, only to be knocked down again by the portly conductor in pursuit of his scoundrel. We all watched the chase, of course, and the last view I had of the salesman was from the window to my left. He had leapt from the train and was tumbling down a grassy embankment! In what state his hasty exit left him I should not venture to guess, but he was gone and good riddance.

Gathering himself, Tatty Coat offered me a hundred embarrassed apologies, as well he should have, the clumsy oaf. I acknowledged him with the curtest of nods and no words whatsoever. It was then that I noticed the fugitive's disgusting wares, sitting still in my skirts.

They were photographs mounted on cardboard such as I had never seen and hope never to see again. Each image was more filthy than the next. In one, a woman stood admiring herself before the glass. She was naked except for the lavaliere around her neck and the high-button shoes on her feet. In another, this same wicked woman leaned forward to be spanked by a man with a paddle. In the third, a different woman, fully displayed, and a naked man with a hideous horselike deformity were . . . well, it was as if human beings were beasts.

Lil, I sat there, frozen. I could neither touch the loathsome cards to rid myself of them nor look away from them. It was as if their wickedness had cast a spell. I felt light-headed and began to tremble. I did not know what I should do.

It was Mr. Shabby Jacket, of all people, who helped me. Without speaking a word, he gathered the cards and ripped them into pieces. Then he reached past me and Grandmother and tossed the ruined things out the open window. To save me further humiliation, I suppose, he then pushed past the others and found a place elsewhere in the car.

I must end now, Sis, because we are fast approaching the station. The crowds are milling about and it looks as if every building in Hartford has been gotten up in patriotic bunting. Grandmother snorts and awakens, having missed most of this wretched ride. I am glad that the sun has come out and that tonight we will dine with the Clemens family. Still, my spirits are a good deal less sanguine than they were. What I had imagined would be a red-letter day has turned into something else. Still, I have this evening's dinner to anticipate and can barely wait for it to come.

I shall write you more anon.

Yours ever so truly,
Lydia

⤚ *chapter twenty* ⤛

FATS DOMINO AND HIS WIFE had been rescued and were okay. The body of the Micks' next-door neighbor, Delia Palmer, was found floating in the wreckage of what had once been her home and beauty parlor. Moze learned from a cousin who'd traveled by rowboat up Caffin Avenue that the chinaberry tree he'd worried about had fallen, dislodging his house from its foundation and breaking it in half. The back rooms were smashed. The front rooms were floating diagonally in floodwater. On the night he received the news, Moze got drunk and got into a knockdown drag-out fight with Janis, their shouting back and forth and then her sobs carrying down the front stairs so that I had to turn up the television to give them and their grief some privacy.

The good news was that the Micks' cat had survived. Moze's cousin had found Fat Harry sitting "like an exiled king" in the fallen tree's inverted root system. "Soon as they give the okay, I got to go down and retrieve that ole fleabag and see if there's anything else left to salvage," Moses told me. "But I can't see as we're ever goin' back there to live if the Nines is unlivable."

He asked me if we could make a deal.

The rental agreement I forged with the Micks obliged me to consolidate Maureen's and my stuff to the first floor of the farmhouse, convert the pantry into a bathroom, and provide an outside exit from the upstairs—now Moses and Janis's apartment. *Egress*, the building inspector called the necessity of a second-floor escape route. No egress, no certificate of rental.

Moze, who had moonlighted on and off for a company called Big Easy Remodelers, said he could tackle most of the required renovations. He cut a door in the upstairs south wall, and together he and I built and installed the staircase that led from what had been Great-Grandma Lydia's bedroom to the backyard. Moze roughed in the plumbing for the downstairs bathroom, guided me through the finish work, and installed showerheads upstairs and down. (At long last, it was possible to take a shower at 418 Bride Lake Road.) The building inspector returned, strolling upstairs and down with his clipboard and his poker face, reexamining things he'd already examined. I figured I was in for a hassle, but he surprised me by pronouncing the place rentable.

In return for Moze's help, I waived their security deposit and their first two months' rent. That's not to say I couldn't have used that seven hundred and fifty bucks times three. Maureen's legal bills had totaled about fifty thou, and that was just for the criminal case. The civil suit was yet to come, and I was probably going to have to hire a high-end law firm if I had any hope of keeping the Seaberrys from getting at the farm property. Still, I figured, letting the Micks ride for a few months was an investment. They seemed solid enough, and I sure as hell couldn't have done those renovations on my own. I also agreed to let Moze set up his studio in the barn—free of charge for the first six months, three hundred a month after that. By February, I'd have a rental income of a thousand a month.

I told the Micks about the specialty shops over in Olde Mistick Village, but Moze said he'd had it with the tourist trap thing. Mail order was the way to go. He registered a domain name, www.cherubs&fiends.com, and figured he'd go online once he'd built his stock up to about three hundred pieces and figured out how to put up a Web site. He told me his New Orleans customers had preferred the grotesque to the angelic by about four to one, and he guessed that ratio would hold once he went national.

"Or international," I said. "With the Internet, you never know."

Moze nodded in sober agreement. "I'm sayin'."

With Tulane University's operations suspended, Janis's academic work was on hold. That was a blessing, Moze said. Now she could help him in the studio, first with the castings and later with accounting and shipping. He calculated an ambitious pouring schedule—three fiends for each cherub—but said he'd need to generate more capital before he could make his plan happen. What *I* needed was a reprieve from the night shift at the Mama Mia. I spoke to Alphonse about it. Al's parents had stabilized, and he was back from Florida but still down a night guy. He agreed to my proposal: I would train Moze, then phase out. I was chafing at the bit to be done with baking and babysitting for Velvet Hoon. To be fair, Velvet pitched in sometimes, but only when the spirit moved her. When it didn't, she'd sit on her ass all night, reading paperbacks and drinking Quirk-subsidized coffee. That, plus I'd have to keep reminding her that if she wanted to smoke, she was obliged to go outside and do it.

Sharing the farmhouse was a comfort in some ways—Janis kept the place in better order than I did and, as it turned out, Moze was a damn good cook. Fish stews, filé gumbo: more often than not, they asked me to join them, and it was nice not to have to eat alone. Still, having tenants took some getting used to. Because I'd given the Micks kitchen privileges, I had to train myself to put on pants before stumbling out to make my morning coffee. And there was the acoustics issue. The radiator pipes passed between us, so I'd often hear snatches of their conversations—their arguments, especially, which flared often enough. Stress, I figured. Why *wouldn't* they be stressed after all they'd been through and all they'd lost?

He didn't hit her, far as I knew, although when they went at it, I kept an ear cocked for that possibility. I knew firsthand how a guy who'd been cornered by things out of his control could turn into his worst self. I thought about how I'd gone off on Maureen the night I found out about her and Paul Hay. How I'd seen Hay out there at the house he was building and swung that pipe wrench out of some kind of temporary adrenaline-fueled craziness. What had that ball-busting anger management instructor called it? The cardiology and endocrinology of rage. Coincidentally, I'd run into her a few weeks back in the middle of the renovation project. Moze and I were buying plywood at Home Depot, and there she was. I recognized her immediately, and I think she might have recognized me, too. Gave me a tight little nod, as if to say, *I'm still watching you, buddy.* She'd given Moze the evil eye as well. "God*damn*," he'd quipped. "What'd we do to *her?*"

I tell you one thing, though. Those fights of Moze and Janis's didn't seem to put a damper on their sex life. When I'd moved downstairs, I'd set up our bed and bureaus in what had been the dining room. Once upon a time, Great-Grandma Lydia had used that room to feed and politick with state and federal officials, even a U. S. attorney general—Hoover's, I think Lolly'd said. The problem was that the Micks' bedroom was directly above mine. Between us hung Lydia's Victorian-era ceiling light with its suspended glass lampshades and lead-crystal doodads. Whenever they went at it, that damn fixture would sway and tinkle to the rhythm of their lovemaking. At first, I tried to respect their privacy—get out of bed and walk around the downstairs rooms until things quieted down again. After a while, though, I just stayed put and listened. I'd get to thinking about Mo and me back at the beginning. Or Francesca—the way she looked coming out of the water at that nude beach we went to a few times. My hand would drop between my legs while I watched that swaying light so that I could get some relief. Get some sleep. . . . And I'll admit it: sometimes I'd lie there and banish him. Imagine myself upstairs with her. Hey, don't get me wrong. It's not like I was obsessing about her or anything. But having a good-looking younger woman in the house, well . . .

Mornings? When she'd come into the kitchen after her run? Her hair would be pulled back in a messy ponytail and she'd be wearing that cropped pink T-shirt and those little gray gym shorts with "Tulane" written across the ass. Her skin would have that patina of sweat.

"I used to run pretty regularly," I told her one morning. "Kind of fell out of the habit the last few years."

"Oh, you should start up again," she said. "We could run together. Motivate each other." I said I'd think about it.

Her back was to me during this conversation—she was at the stove cooking eggs—and I kept looking up from my newspaper for another glimpse of that grabbable ass. Then she'd turned around and caught me looking. My eyes jumped back to the headlines, and I felt myself blush. It was a matter of forbearance, I figured. And anyway, it was kind of pathetic. I was old enough to be her father. It wasn't like I ever caught *her* looking at *me*. She was getting all she needed, according to that swinging ceiling light.

———

MAUREEN WATCHED MY APPROACH. WHEN I reached her, she stood and we gave each other the DOC-approved hug across the table, the prison-sanctioned smooch. "I didn't recognize you when you first came in," she said.

"No? Who'd you think I was?"

Her fingers grazed my temple. "I hadn't noticed how gray you've gotten." I felt like asking her whose fucking fault that was.

I was already in a pissy mood. I'd just come from teaching my Quest in Literature class. Half of them hadn't done the reading, and the half that had had spent the first fifteen minutes of class bitching about it: it didn't make sense, they couldn't relate to it, blah blah blah. Hey, I felt like telling them, I got *dealt* this class; you guys *signed up* for it. Halfway through class, the skateboarder had started dozing. The soldier in camouflage kept checking his watch. The blonde's cell phone kept ringing. She *couldn't* turn it off, she'd snapped back at me. Her kid was running a fever. *Okay?*

"I met an old friend of yours yesterday," Maureen said. She was in an upbeat mood that afternoon. She'd been moved to a less restrictive unit. She liked her new cellmate, Camille.

"Jesus, what is this now, your third move?" I asked.

Her fourth, she said.

"What's Camille in here for?"

Embezzlement, Mo said. "She convinced me to go to church with her yesterday—the Catholic mass. First I said no, but then I changed my mind." Mo said she felt less heavy-hearted than she had since coming to Quirk.

"Yeah? That's cool. So who's this friend of mine?"

"Father Ralph," she said. "I don't know his last name. He said you guys doubled to the high school prom and ended up marrying each other's dates."

"Oh, okay," I said. "Ralph Brazicki."

"At first I was like: he's *married*? But Camille said he was a widower."

I nodded. "Betsy Counihan. Breast cancer, I think it was. So what did your new roomie steal?"

She'd been an accountant for a chain of carpeting companies, Maureen said—had been cooking the books and hitting the casino three or four nights a week. Once she struck it big, she was going to give her son and daughter-in-law the money for a down payment on a house and put back everything she'd "borrowed."

I noted that Camille was Mo's second cellmate doing time for "creative accounting." And the fourth out of four whose bid was connected somehow to an addiction. Five out of five, counting Mo herself.

"Speaking of which," I said. "You still going to your NA meetings?"

"I do when I can get to the sign-up sheet fast enough," she said. "They cap the number at fifteen. It's ridiculous. If you need a meeting, you need a meeting." The warden was always giving lip service to recovery, she said, but that was all it was. "The only time you see him on the compound is when he's giving some politician or media person the tour. And he'll stop a group of girls and say things like, 'Remember now, one day at a time,' and 'It'll work if you work it.' But *he's* the one who limits the attendance at meetings. And it was *his* big idea to cut the number from six to three meetings a week."

I was getting antsy. Eager to change the subject. "*Father* Ralph, huh? I'm still trying to imagine that one. Back in high school, Ralphie Brazicki would've been a shoo-in for Least Likely to Become a Priest. So what's prison church like?"

Strange, Mo said. But nice. They set up plastic chairs in the hallway of the industrial building. Bring in an altar-on-wheels. "It's right outside where they do food prep, so there's bags of surplus onions and flats of canned tomatoes lining the walls. And all kinds of noises coming from the kitchen. Camille's one of the singers. The No Rehearsal Choir, they call themselves. But, I don't know. The singing sounded so beautiful to me. The windows look onto the loading dock where the Dumpsters are. Where all the seagulls congregate."

"Maybe one of them's the Holy Ghost," I said.

"Maybe," she said, minus a smile. She said Father Ralph had given her a set of rosary beads.

"When I was a kid?" I said. "My mother used to pray her rosary every single damn night. Drag me to St. Anthony's on Sunday. You know what I liked best about going to church? After it was over, if I'd sat still and behaved, she'd take me to this luncheonette for a Coke and a Devil Dog. . . . That, and looking at the stained-glass windows. All those suffering, pious faces. And the Holy Ghost flying above it all."

Maureen started looking fidgety. "So what's new with you?" she said. "What's new with the Minks?"

"The *Micks*," I said. "Let's see. Remember all those boxes of stuff of my great-grandmother's out on the sun porch? Janis has started digging through it. Says for someone like her in Women's Studies it's like hitting paydirt. You know what she found a couple days ago? My great-grandma Lydia's diary entry about the night she and her grandmother ate dinner at Mark Twain's house up there in Hartford. So that's pretty interesting, huh?"

Mo nodded halfheartedly.

"And Moze is working solo at the bakery now. Says Velvet's driving him nuts, same as she did me."

"Velvet came to visit me Sunday," Maureen said. "I didn't get to see her, though. There were clusterfucks all day long, and by the time they were ready to release us to the visiting room, Velvet had already left."

"Too bad," I said. "What are clusterfucks?"

Human traffic jams, she said. The COs tell them to hurry and line up, then they make them wait. It was one of their many ways to make them feel worthless—just what people wrestling with addiction *didn't* need. If she had started our visit in a good mood, it sure as hell hadn't ended that way. My fault pretty much, I figured. I'd wanted to leave since I'd gotten there. She was saying something about rosary beads—how she'd begun praying the rosary.

"Just like my mother," I said. "Hail Mary, full of grace, blessed is the fruit at Stop & Shop."

"Is that supposed to be funny, Caelum? Or is it supposed to negate the fact that going to mass made me feel uplifted a little bit?"

"You know what?" I said. "I'm tired. I don't need this."

———

THAT NIGHT, LYING IN BED, I tried to recall the words of the Hail Mary. *Hail Mary, full of grace. The Lord is with thee. Blessed art thou amongst women, and blessed is the fruit of thy womb, Jesus. . . .* How did the rest of it go? Damned if I could remember.

But in a sudden rush, I remembered something else—something Mo had told me about her ordeal that day at Columbine. As she'd sat inside that cabinet while Klebold and Harris lobbed their bombs and killed their classmates, she'd prayed the Hail Mary, over and over and over.

Holy Mary, mother of God. Pray for us sinners, now and at the hour of our death. Amen. . . . In a way it *had* been a kind of death for Maureen that day. And now she was stuck in that hell hole down the road. *There were clusterfucks all day long.* . . . With only one tenth of her sentence served, she was already speaking jailhouse slang like a pro. "Now and at the hour of our death." I spoke the words aloud, and a shiver passed through me.

ONE MORNING, WHEN IT WAS just the two of us at the kitchen table, Janis asked me if I'd mind driving her over to Ocean-side some morning when I taught my class. "Sure," I said. "Anytime. Why?"

The official reason, she said, was because Moze was stymied about how to build that Web site and had given her the assignment of locat-ing some techie-type student who might agree to design them some-thing on the cheap.

"And what's the *un*official reason?" I asked.

Her eyes filled with tears. She had lost her work as well as her home, she said. She missed her colleagues and her professors, who were scattered, now, around the country. She e-mailed back and forth with some of them, but it wasn't the same. She missed sitting in a library with a stack of books and articles—losing herself in her discoveries so that, when she checked her watch, she'd be shocked at how much time had gone by. "So I thought it might make me feel a little better to hang out for a few hours at a college campus."

"I'm happy to give you a lift over there, but I think you better lower your expectations," I said. "I suspect the library at Oceanside Community College is going to look pretty pitiful next to Tulane's."

"Doesn't matter," she said. "The thing is, helping Moze get his business started? It's what *he* wants, not what I want. And if this mail-order thing takes off, I'm afraid I'll get trapped. That I'll never get back to the work I love."

"None of my business," I said. "But did you tell him how you feel?"

She said she'd tried to the day before, but that it had caused a fight. I knew something had. "Selfish bitch!" I'd heard him shout.

"But anyway, that's enough about me," she said. "What do you hear from your wife? I can't wait to meet her. Is she coming back soon?"

I took a deep breath. It was time. Past time, really. "Not for another four and a half years," I said. "Unless by some miracle she gets a reduction in her sentence."

Janis looked at me, wide-eyed and confused. "She's . . . ?"

"Right down the road," I said. "In the slammer."

Then everything spilled out of me: Columbine, Mo's addiction, Morgan Seaberry. It was like some emotional levee had finally failed to hold, and all the pain of the last several years had come flooding forward. I mean, I didn't just cry. I *wailed*. And when I had quieted down—was back to just sniffling and shuddering—she reached across the kitchen table. "Take my hands," she said.

I took them. She squeezed. And her doing that, making that simple gesture, offered me more intimacy than I'd felt in . . . I don't even know how long. Never, maybe. It's hard to explain, my hands in hers. It wasn't really sexual—had nothing to do with the semen I'd spilt watching that hanging light rock and sway above my head. But . . . it wasn't completely nonsexual, either. Like I said, I don't know how to describe it, except to say it was, what? . . . Powerful, I guess. Hopeful.

And then the kitchen door swung open and there was Moze, wearing his checkered baker's pants, smelling like fried dough. There was flour in his eyebrows and his goatee. "Look what I found sitting on y'all's back stoop," he said. He held out his cupped hand for me to see, then opened it.

On his palm was a praying mantis.

chapter twenty-one

September 18, 1886

My Dear Lillian,

I am writing this from the Hartford station, where we will be delayed for how long we do not know. It seems the train we were to have boarded has collided with a runaway bull between Springfield and here and a derailment has resulted. This is according to the ticket agent, who grows more cross with each would-be sojourner's inquiry and who has, by the way, a most unsightly goiter. The delay vexes Grandmother. She has been out of sorts all morning because of the rich food we were served last night and because she leaves Hartford without the firm promise of a letter of support for the ladies' prison from "the Great Twain," as she has taken to calling Mr. Clemens. Grandmother pronounces him "vainglorious" and "clever by one-third of what he supposes himself to be." When I reminded her a few minutes ago of what she has many a time reminded me—judge not lest ye be judged—her response was a rude harrumph.

As for me, I say let New Haven wait. I am content to sit here on this wooden bench and relive with these words the most glorious evening of my life! I must write it all down lest

I forget even a moment. Was it all a dream, Lil? It would seem so, save for the proof I have that it was not. I have never before pilfered a thing and vow never to do so again. Yet it is a small enough token, which I hope our hosts will never notice. I should not like the Clemenses to think ill of me. Am I wicked, Lil? For I am happier to have the proof of my enchanted evening than I am conscience-stricken for having taken it. This morning, I have a thousand times fingered the soft thing with its deep blue eye, which I have hidden between these pages. It thrills me to do so. You stole, too, Lil, and so perhaps would understand my sin, whereas a certain ancient paragon who sits and sulks two seats away would pronounce me reprehensible and wicked. If Lizzy Popper's ladies' reformatory were ever to become a reality, she would probably make me its first penitent!

Yesterday certainly did not begin as wonderfully as it concluded. First there was the trying train ride to Hartford—that hideous man hawking his filthy wares and Mr. Tatty Suit gaping at me as if I were a mannequin in a storefront window. Then there was the jostling crowd. Upon our arrival at the Hartford station, Grandmother took my arm and told me to stay close, saying she would not like to lose me in the throng making its way to the dedication ceremonies. Lillian, I have never seen such numbers in one place as those assembling at Bushnell Park. The decrepit aged had come, and newborn babes gotten up in patriotic garb, and every age between. Most prominent were the honorees—those thousands of veterans who had saved the Nation in the days before you and I were born. Many were mangled or maimed. Most wore their old uniforms and badges. Bushnell Park was a swirling sea of faded Union blue!

Grandmother and I arrived at the easterly end of the park in the company of Mrs. Twichell and several of her brood, the

bottoms of our skirts soaked from the wet ground after yesterday's deluge. Tents had been erected and an early lunch was
being readied for the veterans, who would march with their
former companies. At one long table, young ladies from the
High School put out sandwiches, grapes, and doughnuts—a
ration of each on each plate. At another station, a big steam
boiler heated barrels of water in which floated bags of ground
coffee—enough for the thousands who had come to be honored. Alas, even in the midst of the morning's bustle, I was not
to be spared Grandmother's plaguing. I had not eaten breakfast before we left New Haven, and my empty stomach had
begun to snarl. To quiet it, I took one of the doughnuts from
one of the plates and was promptly scolded. "Those are not
for thee!" the Old Girl chided. It was humiliating to be up-
braided like a child in front of Mrs. Twichell and her daughter
Harmony, and I would have treated her to a sharp retort had
a clumsy horse not caused a clamor at that very moment. The
poor beast had become tangled in a tent rope and crashed to
the ground not five feet in front of us. With the attention thus
drawn away from me, I took a large bite from the doughnut
and disposed of the remainder beneath a table.

   The Memorial Arch is an imposing structure, Lil—a work
of art deserving of all the attention it has received. When
Grandmother first laid her eyes upon it, even <u>she</u> was moved
to tears. Fashioned of Connecticut brownstone, it consists of
two medieval towers connected by a Roman arch into which
have been carved friezes in the Greek style on both the north
face and the south. The former tells the story of the War—
farmers turned into soldiers, General Grant surveying his
men, and so forth. The latter tells the story of the Peace that
followed when the North prevailed. In it, the City of Hartford, embodied as a goddess, welcomes home her returning
warriors. The structure spans the bridge under which flows

the Park River. This same river passes behind the Clemens manse, as I later learned. Mr. Clemens's nickname for it is "the Meandering Swine." I know not why.

Speech-making preceded the review of regiments by Mayor Bulkeley. Grandmother's friend Mr. Twichell arrived at the speaker's platform in grand style, riding atop the old warhorse which he had ridden all those years ago and which was taken out of its pastoral retirement for yesterday's event. The day's chief orator was General Hawley, who spoke poignantly in remembrance of those who had fallen on Land and Sea. I stayed with him for the first several minutes of his address, but when his remarks wandered from the battlefield to the discovery of Connecticut by Thomas Hooker in sixteen-hundred-and-I-know-not-when, my attention began to wane. Instead of listening, I found myself watching a small band of boys who were skylarking unperturbed on the riverbank and pestering the ducks. Colonel Bissell then addressed the crowd. It was he who had insisted Lizzie Popper be denied a seat on the dignitaries' platform for the sin of being a member of the fairer sex, and it was all I could do not to hiss and boo the man. When Bissell made the formal presentation of the memorial to the City of Hartford, the applause was thunderous!

After the speech-making, shots were fired and the parade commenced. Such a display of pageantry, music, and flag-waving I have never before witnessed. For as many times as Grandmother has spoken of the Terrible War, I had always regarded it as much a part of ancient history as the rise and fall of the Roman Empire or the campaigns of Napoleon. Yet now that I have witnessed yesterday's review of the regiments, the war comes closer. It was a right and noble thing for these men to have freed the darkies and preserved the Union. When I am home again, I shall go to the parlor and gaze anew upon the memorial busts of Uncle Edmond and Uncle Levi, who gave their lives to the righteous cause. Perhaps it was Grandmother's slain sons whom she was remembering when the sight of the Arch made her cry. But what of our papa, Lillian? I know he did not serve in the war, but I know not why, or why Grandmother has remained so steadfastly tight-lipped on the subject. Perhaps someday when I meet my benefactress, the mysterious Miss Urso, she will avail me of the details. Until then, I remain in the dark about our late *paterfamilias*. But now I must continue to tell you of my most amazing day.

Following the festivities, Grandmother and I returned to the Twichells' home on Woodland Street in the lovely Nook Farm neighborhood where the Clemens family and Mrs. Stowe also live. Whilst Grandmother met with Reverend Twichell about the ladies' reformatory, Harmony took my hand and spirited me away to Farmington Avenue so that I might meet her friend Susy Clemens. Susy is the eldest of Mr. Twain's three daughters. Passing Mrs. Stowe's home next door, it was as if my heart would stop. I had been hoping against hope that the great authoress might be one of those who would dine with us at the Clemens home that evening. Alas, I learned from Harmony that Mrs. Stowe's husband had succumbed last month and she remained in seclusion. Indeed, all the windowshades were drawn, and the house was as still as a painting.

Not so the Twain home, where there is hustle and bustle outside and in. The house is splendid, not at all the queer-looking thing I had expected from its description as "part cathedral and part cuckoo clock." It is built of brick and wood and trimmed handsomely in black and red. There are turrets, porches upstairs and down, and a glass-roofed conservatory so that plants can be brought indoors and enjoyed in wintertime. When Harmony and I arrived, Mr. Twain himself was outside with Susy and her sisters, Clara and little Jean. They had a bottle of soap bubble water and it was with this that they were amusing themselves, Susy and Clara blowing bubbles and Jean chasing them. The bubbles were a beautiful opaline color in the late afternoon sun, and to see them made me feel light-hearted and gay. Mr. Twain blew bubbles, too, filling his with smoke from his cigar. When these burst, they released small puffs of blue.

Harmony introduced me to Mr. Twain. Because he has traveled the world, I extended my hand and said, "Enchantée, Monsieur," to which he answered, "And parlez-vous to you, too, Mademoiselle. Your French is magnifique, but how's your arithmetic?"

"My arithmetic?" I asked, somewhat confused.

"Oui," said he. "If Pierre buys a horse for two hundred francs and Jacques buys a mule for a hundred and forty, and the two enter into a partnership and decide to trade their creatures for a piece of land that costs four hundred and eighty francs, then how long will it take a lame Frenchman to borrow a silk umbrella?"

"An umbrella, sir?" I said. Now I was greatly confused, but Susy laughed and said, "Pappa, you mustn't tease poor Miss Popper so."

"Oh? Mustn't I?" said he. "Then please, *Mademoiselle*, forgive me." And with that, he bowed to his waist and returned to his bubble-blowing.

Little Jean approached me next to report that at her aunt's house, where the family summers, there are ten cats. She named each, and curious names they were: Pestilence, Famine, Soapy Sal, and so on. "Sour Mash is Pappa's favorite," Jean announced. "He calls her his tortoise-shell harlot."

"Yes, well," Mr. Twain mumbled, somewhat chagrined, I think. He said he must be getting inside to see if the butler had any chores for him to do. Susy said I mustn't mind her father. "Mother has tried her best to civilize him, but the cause is hopeless," said she—in jest, I suppose. Susy is fair-haired, rosy-cheeked, and pretty. Her eyes, behind spectacles, have an eager look. She says she has tried the mind cure for her nearsightedness but it did not take.

Once inside the Clemens home, my own eyes were dazzled! The walls and ceiling of the entrance hall are painted red and patterned in dark blue. The paneling is stenciled in silver. There is also a closet with a telephone inside. I have read of these contraptions but had never seen one. Jean whispered to me that the telephone, when it is not working properly, makes her father speak bad words, and that each time he does, he must pay a penny to her mother.

Susy led me through the drawing room—one of the most splendid I have ever seen with its settees and drapes of celestial blue. My eyes would have liked to linger on the array of fine things displayed, but it was on to the kitchen to meet Susy's mother, who was reviewing the details of the coming dinner with the family's colored cook. Here is a queer thing: the Clemens kitchen is located at the front of the house, not the rear. Susy said her father had insisted the architect design it thus, so that the servants could look out on the daily "circus" passing by on Farmington Avenue.

As for Mrs. Clemens, she is the picture of loveliness and grace—the kind of mother any girl would adore. She said she was pleased to make my acquaintance, and that she was very much looking forward to meeting Grandmother, as she admires her work on behalf of the downtrodden. Susy was excited about the evening, too. This was to be the first time she would be seated at table at one of her parents' dinner parties. Usually, she is confined to the top of the stairs with her sisters and obliged to eavesdrop from on high.

Susy, Harmony, and I proceeded from the kitchen to the upstairs schoolroom. Susy and Clara have a tutor, a Miss

Foote, and Mrs. Clemens instructs them in the German language. Harmony also studies German, and both girls said they were quite envious of me because of my French studies at Madame Buzon's school. We three had a delightful conversation about literature. Harmony's favorite writers are Shelley, Charlotte Brontë, Mrs. Stowe, and Mr. Twain. Susy's are Shakespeare, Swinburne, her father, and Christina Rossetti. She was most impressed with my recitation from memory of stanzas from Miss Rossetti's "Goblin Market." In ten minutes' time, we had become fast friends, and Susy said she wished I lived closer—that if I did, she would cast me in the theatricals they perform downstairs in the Clemens library for the enjoyment of their Nook Farm neighbors. "Does Mrs. Stowe attend?" I inquired. Susy and Harmony said she had done so once. "What is she like?" I asked, and these were the words they used to described her: "quiet," "dignified," and "gentle-natured." Harmony said she has read *Uncle Tom's Cabin* many times, and that Little Eva's sad passing never fails to bring her to tears. I said the same.

Susy, Harmony, and I played a jolly game of charades and also a game of whist, for which I have discovered a talent. Thank goodness Grandmother was not there to disapprove, as she thinks card games are "a bridge to wickedness." Harmony and Susy said both their mothers play whist, and also bridge and bezique. Oh, how I long for a modern mother!

Back at the Twichells', Grandmother and I rested and readied ourselves for the evening ahead. When it was time to leave, I saw with some dismay that Harmony and her mother had changed into lovely evening frocks. I, however, was doomed to wear the same mud-spattered brown dress that I had been wearing the live-long day, wrinkles and all. Grandmother wore her usual drab Quaker garb. We returned on foot to the Clemens manse, for it is but a short distance. Grandmother and Mr. and Mrs. Twichell led the way, and Harmony and I strolled arm in arm behind them. It amused me to see the eminent but tiny Lizzy Popper betwixt the Twichells, both of whom are tall of stature. A study in opposites these three truly made!

We were the first guests to arrive. Susy descended the stairs in a satin dress of sky-blue—cerulean, she called it—which she had complemented with a hair band of matching color and a clutch of artificial violets at her waist. Mrs. Clemens was the picture of elegant refinement in a high-collared gown of sea-green silk. Mr. Clemens looked more respectable than he had earlier, blowing bubbles in his open collar and rolled-up shirtsleeves.

No sooner had introductions been made when Grandmother pounced on her quarry, asking Mr. Clemens if she might have a word with him about a matter of import. She was foiled, however, by the boisterous arrival of two other guests, Mr. William Gillette and his wife, Helen—a fetching couple, indeed. Mr. Gillette is a stage actor and a former Nook Farm neighbor of the Clemenses. "Young Will owes his acting career to the many games of charades he played here as a youth," Mr. Clemens declared. "I have often suggested to him that we should share in his box office receipts now that he has made a success of himself, but he has thus far resisted the notion resolutely." There was laughter all around, except from Grandmère, whose opportunity to exact a promise from Mr. Clemens had slipped away, and who, after all, has opined many a time that actors are humbugs lacking in moral character.

Here, Lillian, is a list of last evening's dinner guests: Reverend and Mrs. Twichell and Harmony, the Gillettes, Mr. Walter Camp (a Yale man employed by the New Haven Clock Company), Grandmother, and myself. A ninth guest—Mr. Tesla—was also invited but had failed to materialize nearly an hour after we others had arrived. "Oh, he will be here, poor fellow," Mr. Clemens kept saying. "He may be lost, or thinking up some grand new invention. Scientific geniuses are not ruled by their pocket watches." They could only wait so long nonetheless, Mrs. Clemens said, and so, the party proceeded to the dining room.

A magnificent room it is! Flocked wallpaper of red and gold in a pattern of repeating lilies, Oriental vases filled with bouquets of ostrich plumes and peacock feathers, and a splendid view of the adjacent library and conservatory. The table was draped with a covering of fine Irish lace and set beautifully with silver candlesticks and blue and white willow pattern china. At each place was a small card, also in the willow pattern, which told where we were to sit. Mr. Clemens sat at head of table. To his left was Mr. Camp and to his right was the empty chair for the missing Mr. Tesla. Mrs. Clemens sat opposite her husband and was flanked by Grandmother to her left and Susy to her right. My place, I was happy to see, was between Susy and Harmony. Next to Harmony sat the Gillettes, and to Grandmother's left sat the Twichells.

Here were the courses served: a delicious cream soup of celery and leeks, poached Fishers Island oysters, roasted ducks with potato cakes and root vegetables, a lettuce leaf salad with chestnuts and figs, and for dessert, charlotte russe and ice cream in the shapes of cherubs. Spirits flowed freely throughout: aperitifs, sherry, champagne, and after-dinner liqueurs of vivid colors, one of which I recognized as the crème de menthe which Madame Buzon sips in her office to aid digestion. Susy, Harmony, and I abstained from these, of course, as did Grandmother—ever the virtuous Quaker! All of the modern ladies partook, even Mrs. Twichell, though she is the wife of a clergyman.

Oh, Lil, the dinner conversation was lively and gay! Mr.

Clemens was asked by Mrs. Gillette what novel he was writing at present, and he said he has been laboring for some time on a story about a modern man who finds himself misplaced in the medieval past. From there, he spoke comically about how his books are edited. Mrs. Clemens reads each new chapter aloud, says he, taking out all of the "delightfully terrible parts" and editing these "into the stove." If Mrs. C. had not performed surgery on *Huckleberry Finn*, he said, that book would have run to a thousand pages! The jest produced laughter from all, even from Mrs. C. herself. "Oh, Youth, our guests will think me a tyrant," she said, to which Mr. C. responded, "Only when there is an editor's pencil in your hand, my dear." It is plain to see that Susy's parents share a great fondness for one another. I think it amusing that Mrs. Clemens calls her gray-haired husband "Youth." Mr. Twain's youth is long past! He is forty if he is a day.

From Mr. Twain's books, the conversation turned to Mr. Camp, who is an athlete as well as a clock maker. He spoke of the need of humans to imitate the beasts of the jungle and exercise their muscles lest their health fail. He has designed a calisthenics regime which he calls his "daily dozen" and says that those who adhere to it will lengthen their lives. Much fun was had at Mr. Camp's expense when he gave the names of these contortions he has designed: "the grind," "the grasp," "the roll," "the crawl." Mr. Camp also spoke at length about football, a gentlemen's game about which I know not a jot or care to.

I was far more interested in Mr. Gillette's tales of his life on the theatrical stage. He says he is an advocate of "natural acting" rather than melodramatic declaiming. He has played Benvolio and Shylock, as well as Rosencrantz to Edwin Booth's Hamlet. There was ample discussion around the table about this Mr. Booth's troubles—a wife gone mad, horrid

in-laws, dizziness mistaken for drunkenness during a performance and reported in the newspapers as such. Mr. Gillette
also spoke of "the terrible burden of brotherhood" which Mr.
Booth bears. It was only then that I realized they were speaking of the brother of the black-hearted villain who murdered
President Lincoln! What must that be like, I wonder? To share
common blood with one so infamous? Does one go on loving
his wicked relation, or does he join the multitudes in reviling
him? The burden of brotherhood, indeed!

From Mr. Booth and his many trials, the talk shifted to mer-
rier matters. Mrs. Clemens and Susy spoke of a New York theatrical they had attended this past spring, a musical farce called
The Mikado. Mrs. Clemens called it "merriment to relieve the
strains of the day," and Susy said the elaborate sets and costumes made her feel as if she had been transported by magic to
the Orient. Mr. Clemens saw *The Mikado* as well and called it
"phantasmagoric." He then turned to Susy, Harmony, and me
and asked which of us could spell "phantasmagoric."

"Oh, Pappa, you know I am a dreadful speller," Susy la-
mented. Harmony, too, declined to essay. I, however, spelled
the word correctly and was declared by Mr. Twain to be "a
brilliant intellect of the highest order." It made me blush to be
described so and to have all eyes upon me, but I must admit I
do have a talent for spelling. Have I not won the upper-level
bee at Madame Buzon's school not once but twice? Still, I
was relieved when the conversation shifted from my spelling
prowess to those bomb-throwing labor agitators in Chicago
and the capture of Geronimo and his renegade band.

But alas and alack, Lil, my relief was short-lived. When the
discussion lit upon the government's ill treatment of the Red
Man, Grandmother climbed upon her soapbox and spoke her
familiar refrain about the grave injustices done to the poor by
the greedy upper classes and their apologists, the evil Social

Darwinists. And at the end of her speechifying, she turned to our host and challenged him directly. "Mr. Clemens, does thee not agree that it is more a matter of society's failure than one of personal failure when the downtrodden fall prey to vice?"

I knew what she was up to, for had Grandmother not accepted this dinner invitation in pursuit of an endorsement from Mr. Twain concerning the building of her precious penitentiary? But if her question was cheese in the mousetrap, Mr. Clemens proved himself a sly and crafty rodent. With a twinkling in his eye, he asked Grandmother to which vices she referred. "Because my good woman, if you mean cursing and smoking, I confess I am guilty of both." All chuckled at this remark except Grandmother. Oh, Lil, was there ever a woman so earnest and yet so humorless as she?

"I refer, sir, to the city vices to which the female of the species in particular is vulnerable," Grandmother responded.

"Such as?" someone asked.

"Such as prostitution and rape. And along with these, the wages these sins exact from both the sinner and her society: children born outside of holy wedlock and the spread of syphilis!"

Oh, Lil, to hear such matters spoken of at that elegant table to those elegant people—by my own relation, no less! I have never been so ashamed. But Grandmother would not be silenced. Nor would she look away from our host. "And what, sir, becomes of the unfortunate females who fall prey to these vices and afflictions? Are they granted asylum? Delivered to a place where they can be guided back to feminine virtue by God-fearing Christian women? No, sir, they are not. They are thrown into prison alongside the masculine criminal element—tossed like meat to hungry dogs!"

There was sympathetic murmuring from the ladies at the table and stony silence from the men. Susy and Harmony looked at each other, wide-eyed, and I was relieved that neither looked at me.

It was Grandmother's friend Reverend Twichell who came to her rescue. "Mrs. Popper has a solution to the problems she so forcefully articulates," said he. Turning to Grandmother, he asked if she might be so kind as to tell those gathered about her vision. She did so, describing the curing of female criminals with fresh air and farmwork, penitence and prayer. "I am firm in my belief that those women who have fallen can rise again," she said.

"And so, Mrs. Popper has been traveling the state in pursuit of letters of support," Mr. Twichell said. "For she feels that a chorus of voices from esteemed individuals will help persuade the legislature of the need for a ladies' reformatory quite separate from the harmful male element."

I saw Grandmother's hands tremble as she spoke the next. "And toward that end, Mr. Clemens, I should be grateful to thee, sir, if—"

Here the poor old soul was foiled once more, for Mr. Camp interrupted her in the middle of her request. "But with all due respect, Mrs. Popper," said he, "I cannot see why women who have fallen to wickedness deserve deliverance to this Elysium you would create. Nor, for that matter, can I entirely discount the theories of the Social Darwinists. Like it or not, in both nature and capitalism, there will always be the powerful and the weak."

The interruption flummoxed poor Grandmother. "With all due respect, sir," said she, cheeks flushed and nostrils a-flare, "that sounds like the reasoning of one more attuned to calisthenics than to Christian charity." A period of awkward silence followed. I half-expected the Old Girl and her humiliated granddaughter to be shown the door!

"Yes, well, I met Charles Darwin once," Mr. Clemens finally said. "Our mutual friend Mr. Howells introduced us. I told Darwin that I had read and enjoyed his *Descent of Man*, and he told me that he kept a volume of mine by his bedside because it helped him to fall asleep. I chose to take it as a compliment."

Having regained the reins of the discourse, Mr. Clemens steered it in an entirely different direction—namely, his love for darky spirituals. He jumped from his chair like a jack-in-the-box, ran to the piano in the adjacent drawing room, and began to sing and play, comically off key and out of tune, "Swing Low, Sweet Chariot" and "Go Chain the Lion Down." I dared to glance at Grandmother but once during this musical interlude and saw that she was flushed with pique. I likewise saw her friend Mr. Twichell reach over and pat her hand in a kindly gesture of reassurance. Mrs. Clemens, too, leaned to her and seemed to offer a soothing word or two. Whatever was said, Grandmother sulked a bit more, then began to look more weary than peeved.

As the oyster plates were being cleared away, Mr. Twain told a silly story about how his dog Hash had trained <u>him</u> to fetch sticks. The servants, a darky butler and an Irish maid, midway through serving the next course, stopped to listen and laugh. Mr. Twain took note of this, announcing to his guests that both preferred listening to working and that we should not be alarmed should they pull chairs to the table and force the rest of us to serve ourselves. The butler laughed heartily at this jest, but the maid seemed mortified. She finished passing the potato cakes, then hurried, red-faced, back to the kitchen.

During our devouring of the ducks, Grandmother made one last attempt to broach the subject of the penitentiary but once more was thwarted—this time by a clamorous knocking at the front door. "Tesla!" Mr. Twain ejaculated. He jumped to his feet and all but galloped to the entrance hall.

I heard this Mr. Tesla before I saw him. In English so atrocious that it was barely comprehensible, he spoke a hundred apologies and his host in return gave a hundred reassurances that these were unnecessary. When the two entered the dining room, I was aghast! Horror-struck! For there before us stood none other than Mr. Tatty Suit from the morning train! And in seeing him, my mind's eye saw once again the images on those filthy postal cards which had landed in my lap—the woman naked as a jaybird save for her shoes and lavaliere, the man with his beastly protrusion. I am quite sure Mr. Tesla recognized me, too, for when his eyes fell upon me, he appeared quite startled. To my great relief, he did not look at me again for the remainder of the evening.

If I was unnerved by Mr. Tesla's presence, Mr. Twain was made ecstatic by it. He explained to us that the two—inventor and lover of inventions—had been introduced earlier in the year at a New York gentlemen's club by their mutual acquaintance, a Mr. Edison. Mr. Tesla had come to America from Austria-Hungary two years earlier in hopes of interesting this Mr. Edison in some sort of electrical motor he had designed. "Now, my good fellow, tell our guests the story of how your brilliant invention came to you," Mr. Twain entreated. In his atrocious English, Mr. Tesla then related a tale that to me seemed less fact than fancy. In Budapest, said he, as he was walking through a city park and reciting poetry, the idea for his motor had come to him fully realized, as if delivered by a bolt of lightning. He grabbed a stick and sketched in the sand a diagram of his idea.

Mr. Twain clapped his hands in delight. "The revelation of

an instantaneous truth!" he declared. "And I daresay, friends, Mr. Nikola Tesla's invention will change the world. Here among us is an electronical wizard!"

An electronical wizard perhaps, I cannot say, but the man certainly is no diplomat. When Mrs. Twichell inquired of him how he finds America, he opined—while eating with his mouth open, the brute—that ours is a country a century behind Europe in civilization. That whereas his homeland reveres aesthetic beauty and high culture, America loves only money and machines. 'Tis a pity you feel thus, I felt like interjecting. Perhaps you should return from whence you came, and until you do, kindly eat like a gentleman, not a hooligan.

At the conclusion of the dinner, girlish giggling called us all to the Clemenses' library. In the company of her sister Clara, little Jean, dressed for bed in her nightclothes, demanded a story from her father. He indulged her, fashioning a tale from items displayed on and about the fireplace mantel—an Oriental ginger jar, a cat statue, and the like. It was quite a clever narrative, enjoyed by all. Its chief antagonist was a runaway tiger because, as Mrs. Clemens explained, "Jean must always have a tiger in her stories."

After Mr. Twain spoke the words, "The End," Jean was sent off to bed. Mrs. Clemens led the ladies of our party to the drawing room for quiet conversation and a game of bezique. Grandmother declined to play, of course, but at least she neither scowled nor voiced disapproval. Seated by herself at the far end of the settee, she promptly fell asleep.

How Grandmother could slumber through the adjacent racket I do not know, for the gentlemen, who had remained in the library to drink brandy and smoke their Havanas, were quite boisterous, Mr. Twain and Mr. Gillette most especially, and Reverend Twichell to a lesser degree. At one point, Mr.

Twain persuaded Mr. Camp to lead them all in a round of his "daily dozen." It was quite peculiar to see those men of mark rolling and writhing on the floor like apes. All partook of the exercises, even Mr. Tesla, though he looked quite frightened to be thus engaged.

Toward the end of the evening, the men joined us in the drawing room. Coffee was served, and Mrs. Clemens and Susy passed pralines and tiny sugared delectables on a silver tray. It was during this interlude that Mr. Tesla rose to his feet and delivered a strange and quite unexpected tribute to his host, Mr. Twain. At the age of seventeen, Mr. Tesla told us, he had had the misfortune of contracting cholera. He was bedridden for several weeks, during which time his condition grew steadily worse. The doctors declared that his was a hopeless case and advised Mr. Tesla's parents to prepare for the worst. Prior to his illness, Mr. Tesla said, his father had insisted that his son was to follow in his footsteps and become an Orthodox priest. Mr. Tesla, however, was inclined more toward science than religion and had dreamed of studying engineering. In that respect, he was less like his father and more like his mother, who had herself invented a mechanical egg-beater and a superior clothesline reel. Mr. Tesla grew weaker and weaker from the cholera, and it was while he was in this withered state that his father made him a tearful promise: if he survived, he could study engineering. Mr. Tesla's mother, unable to comfort her son in any other way, went each week to the lending library and lugged home books for her son to read in bed. It was amongst those stacks of borrowed books, Mr. Tesla said, that he discovered the works of the great Mark Twain. With each of Mr. Twain's books he read, he seemed to grow more sanguine. And after a while, he was able to leave his bed, rejoin the world, and attend the Austrian Polytechnic Academy. "And so, Mr. Mark Twain," Mr. Tesla said, "I salute you for having written the books that saved my life!" It was all quite strange, Lil. Having heard Mr. Tesla's story, Mr. Twain, that man of laughter, was reduced to tears.

By eleven o'clock, the evening was winding down. Grandmother was gently wakened. Susy, Harmony, and I made promises to write faithfully to one another. Because the night had turned damp and foggy, the Clemenses insisted that their driver bring 'round the carriage so that we should ride rather than walk the short distance back to the Twichells'. I was loath to leave that grand house and to bid farewell to a most magical evening, though all good things must end. Grandmother was helped into the carriage. The long day had exhausted her and her failure to exact a promise from Mr. Twain had disappointed her, but she thanked her hosts and said she hoped we should all meet again. Then, just as I was about to climb into the carriage, Grandmother said, "My shawl. I have forgotten my shawl."

Mr. Twain said he would go back inside and retrieve it, but I said no, I would do it. I knew exactly where it was. I did, too, for I had seen the shawl slip from Grandmother's shoulders to the floor during dinner. My real reason for wanting to retrieve it, however, was so that my eyes, one last time, could look upon that magnificent house with all of its magnificent things.

Lil, it was when I reentered the Clemenses' dining room, picked up Grandmother's shawl from the floor, and was about to leave that I committed my theft. It was an impulsive act. I heard the soft clatter from the kitchen, the voices outside through the open window. I was completely alone in that beautiful room and felt I must take away some small part of it. I walked over to the vase that held the peacock feathers. When I bent the top third of the tallest and most beautiful, its thin shaft snapped easily. I hid the purloined feather in the folds of Grandmother's shawl and returned outside. I know it was wicked of me, Lil, but I am glad I did it and am today strangely without remorse.

Last night, as I lay in bed next to Grandmother in the Twichells' guest room, my head filled with the sights of my amazing day: those thousands of gray-haired soldiers, the majestic brownstone Arch, Mrs. Clemens in her elegant green gown, the delicate ice cream cherubs. "He's a cock of the walk if you ask me," Grandmother muttered. "Such comforts and luxuries will prove detrimental to his character and his soul. . . . He calls that singing? I call it caterwauling." I drifted off to sleep to the sounds of our disappointed grandmama's myriad disapprovals and her gaseous digestion.

And now, Lil, just a moment ago, an unexpected surprise! The ticket agent emerged from his cage to announce that the train to New Haven will be arriving momentarily. A cheer rose up from the crowd to hear the news, and as I looked from traveler to traveler, my eyes fell upon the face of a man I recognized but could not immediately place. I watched this man's approach to Grandmother and realized, suddenly, that it was Mr. Twain's carriage driver—he who had delivered us back to the Twichells' last evening. "He was going to post this to you, Missus," the driver told Grandmother. "But then we heard about the delay here at the station and he said to bring it to you direct. He wrote it this morning before he come downstairs." And with that he handed an envelope to her. Inside was a typewritten, hand-signed endorsement letter from Mr. Twain, his signature at the bottom so big and bold that I could read it from two seats away. Strange, Lil. Until yesterday, I have never known our stoic old gran to shed tears. Yet here in Hartford, I have seen her cry twice.

Yours ever so truly,

Lydia

P.S.

Here is a queer thing, Sis—something I had forgotten to record until this second. As if I had not yesterday already seen far too much of the curious Mr. Tesla, during the night I dreamt of him as well. A strange dream it was. Mr. Tesla was himself but also somehow a stallion in a field, and I was astride him, riding swiftly and recklessly without benefit of a saddle.

→ chapter twenty-two ←

I HAD TOURED HARTFORD'S MARK Twain House many times with my high school students but drove there on that beautiful Indian-summer Sunday so that Janis could see for herself the place where my adolescent great-grandmother had dined with the country's most renowned author, the inventor of alternating electrical current, the architect of American football, and the stage actor who would later don inverness coat and deerstalker cap to become the quintessential Sherlock Holmes. "Caelum, you've got to read this! Oh, my God, what a find!" Janis had said, wide-eyed, when she unearthed from the chaos of sun-porch clutter young Lydia's account of her Hartford trip and rushed downstairs to show me. After I'd finished reading the diary entry, she'd handed me a stack of printouts— the result of her Google searches on Nikola Tesla, Walter Camp, and William Gillette.

We, the assembled ticket buyers, were a motley group: five clucking Red Hat Society ladies, two gaunt design students who'd driven up from NYU to check out the house's Tiffany flourishes, a Minnesota couple and their bored-out-of-his-mind teenage son, plus Janis and me. At the start of the tour, our guide—"Hope Lunt," her name tag said—had asked us to tell a little about ourselves. "A teacher," I'd said, and Janis had identified herself noncommittally as someone interested in history.

"Now the mantel we're standing in front of was salvaged from a Scottish castle destroyed by fire in the early nineteenth century," Hope said. She was one of those well-heeled West Hartford women of a certain age: tanned, tastefully dressed, and of an economic level that allowed for volunteer work and gold jewelry. "Sam purchased it during one of his European lecture tours and had it shipped here with the instruction that this date be carved into it." She touched her fingertips to the numerals *1874*.

We were in Twain's library. To our right was the conservatory, with its lush greenery and softly trickling fountain. To our left was the room where Lydia had eaten poached oysters and ice cream cherubs and later swiped herself a peacock feather. Miraculously, that feather had remained hidden between the pages of her diary for a hundred and twenty years. Despite the "Dear Lillian" salutations, that was apparently what all those entries had been: never letters meant to be sent, but daily reflections bound between hard covers. When Janis had shown me the feather, I'd picked it up and it had fallen apart in my hand.

"Eighteen seventy-four? Any guesses as to the significance of that date?" Hope asked.

One of the Red Hats wondered if that was the year the family had moved in.

"Exactly! And here they lived happily for the next seventeen years."

Hope told us about the family's storytelling ritual: how the Clemens girls would demand their father tell them impromptu tales by incorporating the paintings and knickknacks on and around the mantel. "And little Jean always had to have a tiger," Janis whispered. We shared the look of coconspirators.

"But by 1891, the troubles had begun and the family found it necessary to close up the house where they'd shared such happy times," Hope said.

"What sorts of troubles?" the Minnesota mom asked.

"Well, Sam's disastrous financial investments for one. And for another, the untimely death of the eldest daughter, Susy." From Janis, standing beside me, I heard a sharp intake of breath. "Now this mantel was eventually removed and installed at Stormfield, Sam's retirement home in Redding. That building, too, was destroyed by fire and curators assumed that the mantel had been lost in the blaze. But fortunately, it was discovered stored away in a barn and in 1958 was returned here to its rightful place on Farmington Avenue."

"How did Susy die?" Janis asked.

"Oh, it was sad. Sam had fallen so deeply into debt that he was forced to mount a grueling year-long lecture tour that took him as far away as California and Australia. Mrs. Clemens and the couple's middle daughter, Clara, traveled with him, but Susy and Jean, the youngest child, stayed behind. They were to join the others in England that summer, but Susy contracted spinal meningitis shortly before they were to sail. She deteriorated quite quickly, poor thing, and as her condition worsened, the congestion in her brain caused her to hallucinate and go blind. Friends and family thought it might comfort her to be in familiar surroundings, so they reopened the house and brought her back here. Sam stayed in England, but Mrs. Clemens and Clara rushed back to be with Susy. Unfortunately, they were still two days from port when the end came. Mrs. Clemens could never bring herself to set foot in this house again. Sam came back here once, shortly before it was sold. We know from his letters that he felt terribly guilty about his daughter's death—that if he hadn't been so reckless with his finances, Susy would not have had to be without the comfort of her mother at the hour of her death."

Sad sighs from the Red Hat ladies. Janis looked close to tears. I caught myself mumbling the phrase my mother had repeated over and over each night while fingering her rosary beads: *Pray for us sinners now and at the hour of our death.*

The teenager from Minnesota groaned out his boredom, and his dad reached over and swatted the back of his head. *"What?"* the kid said, scooping his baseball cap from the floor. I couldn't help but smile. Sometimes I missed all those high school lunkheads I'd taught.

"Well, on to more cheerful subjects!" Hope announced. "We'll move on now to the second floor, so if you'll follow me back to the entrance hallway. Please use the banister on your way up."

It happened as I was climbing the stairs. Thinking about "fair-haired, rosy-cheeked" Susy Clemens dying alone, I heard, out of nowhere, the explosion of rifle fire and shattering glass. I saw kids scrambling to escape. Saw Rachel and Danny, struck and lying there, dying alone outside the school. Nauseous, I took another step and saw Morgan Seaberry starting across the road, Maureen's car bearing down on him without braking. When I heard the ugly thud of the impact, it dropped me to my knees. . . .

I LOOKED UP AT RED hats and concerned faces. Had I just passed out? "I'm all right," I kept insisting. "Got a little dizzy and missed a step, that's all. I think I'll go out, get some air." When Janis started to leave the tour with me, I insisted she stay. "I'm fine. Really. I'll meet you in the gift shop. Enjoy."

I sat out in the sun for a few minutes, gathering myself, waiting for my hands to stop shaking. I was grasping for the first time, maybe, the terrible power of Maureen's flashbacks. Or maybe not. I mean, how can you flash back to things you never experienced in the first place? Whatever the hell had just happened in there, I knew one thing: I was going to shut up about it. I'd tripped on the stairs. That was my story, and I was sticking to it.

Killing time in the gift shop, I browsed through a book of Sam Clemens's correspondence. I knew the Mark Twain everyone knew—the witty curmudgeon in the white suit who, according to Lydia's account, stayed in character even at his own dinner table. Maybe his letters revealed the man behind the mask. I turned to the year 1896—to what he'd written from England in the wake of his daughter's death. To his grieving wife, tending to Susy's burial without him, he wrote,

> It rains all day—no, drizzles, and is sombre and dark. I would not have it otherwise. . . . She died in our house—not in another's; died where every little thing was familiar and beloved; died where she had spent all her life till my crimes made her a pauper and an exile. . . . The beautiful fabric of her mind did not crumble to slow ruin, its light was not smothered in slow darkness, but passed swiftly out in a disordered splendor. Think of it—if she had lived and _remained_ demented. For Dr. Stearns once told me that for a person whose reason is once really dethroned there is no recovery, no restoration.

When I closed my eyes to his words, I saw Maureen, seated across from me in the Bride Lake visiting room—a pale, rail-thin prisoner who almost never smiled. A damaged woman crumbling to slow ruin. . . . I recalled our brutal separation that day: me, stranded across the country, unable to reach her, unable to fly back fast enough, and Mo hiding inside that cabinet, mouthing her silent Hail Marys. . . .

———

"WHAT'S IN THE BAG?" JANIS asked.

"Hmm? Oh. Book of Twain's letters. I'm not sure why I bought it."

She suggested we skip Bushnell Park and just drive home. "I'm fine," I said. "Hungry, too. We didn't pack that picnic lunch for nothing."

"But you said you got dizzy before. At least let me drive."

"Hey, who knows Hartford? You or me?"

She shook her head and smiled. "You men."

Fifteen minutes later, we were standing before the Soldiers and Sailors Memorial Arch. Janis said it looked pretty much the way she'd pictured it from Lydia's description. "Except for the addition of these aesthetically pleasing cement barricades," I said. I explained that the

Arch had been on the news a while back. Someone's SUV had bashed into it and done damage. It had been repaired since, from the looks of it, but the barricades had remained to prevent further collisions between gas guzzlers and historical landmarks.

"But where's the river?" Janis said.

"Hmm?"

"Lydia wrote that the Arch spanned a river—the same one that ran behind the Twain house. But I didn't notice any river there either."

I said maybe it had dried up, or maybe the city had filled it in for some reason—forced it underground.

"You can do that? Make a river go underground?"

"Civil engineers can. Sure."

We grabbed a picnic table and unpacked the lunch we'd brought. There were mallards in a pond, and twenty-first-century kids "skylarking" along the water's edge. "Santiago!" a young mom screamed. "Don't bother those ducks!"

Janis took a bite of her sandwich. She looked lost in thought.

"Yoo-hoo," I said.

"Oh. Sorry. I was just thinking that that's what your ancestry's like. Anyone's ancestry, really—not just yours, but yours is what's on my mind because of Lydia's diaries." I told her I wasn't following her. "Think about it," she said. "What do we do when our elders die?"

"Call the undertaker and start fighting over the will," I quipped.

"No, really. We put them in the ground, right? But we also carry them forward because our blood is *their* blood, our DNA is *their* DNA. So we're intimately connected to these people whose lives—whose *histories*—have gone underground and become invisible to us."

"Like that river," I said.

"Right. Except in your case, a spring has bubbled up. Your great-grandmother is speaking to you, Caelum."

I started humming the *Twilight Zone* theme, but the reference went flying past her. Hey, why wouldn't it have? The week before, Janis had turned twenty-nine. "I think Lydia's speaking more to you than me," I said.

"To both of us, maybe. And, oh! I can't believe I forgot to tell you this. This morning? Before we left? I was looking in that old gray filing cabinet—the one with the wide drawers? The bottom one was jammed, and I had to keep yanking, but then, wham, it came flying open. And guess what was in there. Lizzy Popper's letters! Your great-great-*great* grandmother!"

"Wow," I said, amused by her enthusiasm. "Whoopee."

"No, seriously, Caelum. Letters written *to* her and what looks like carbons of letters *she* wrote to other people. Bundles of them, tied up with velvet ribbons. I haven't gone through any of it yet, but if she wrote about her nursing during the Civil War? Or her lobbying efforts? Oh, my God, that filing cabinet's a treasure chest! It's okay if I look through it all, isn't it?"

"Have at it," I said. "I'm just glad someone's interested. After my aunt died and we moved back here, I tried donating all that old stuff. One historical society said they didn't have the space to house it, and the other never even called me back. I was going to heave it all, but I never got around to it."

Janis winced at the thought.

"I remember her, you know."

"Remember . . . ?"

"My great-grandmother."

"Lydia? You *do*?"

"Uh-huh. I must have been about eight or nine when she died. Hard to believe that feisty girl in the diary and the tappy old white-haired lady I remember were the same person."

"Tappy as in senility?"

"Or Alzheimer's maybe. Is Alzheimer's hereditary? That's what her son died from. My Grandpa Quirk."

Janis wanted to hear more about Lydia.

"Well, let's see. She smelled mediciny—like liniment or something. And when she crapped her pants, well, that was a different aroma."

"She was incontinent?"

I nodded. "And she was always taking her teeth out. Unless she was being fed, her upper plate would be sitting on her tray, smiling at you. She was bedridden, pretty much, but sometimes they'd bring her out on the sun porch. I didn't like going near her. Used to sneak past in the hallway because . . ."

In the act of conjuring Great-Grandma for Janis, I was becoming a kid again, demoted back to a childhood I preferred to keep a lid on, snapped tight as Tupperware.

"You snuck past her because—?" Janis coaxed.

"Because if she saw me, she'd call out. 'Boy! Come here, boy!' And then I'd have to go in there and let her pat me like a dog. Have to kiss her doll. She was always holding this rag doll and she'd . . . used to . . ." I looked up at Janis. "Jesus Christ."

"What?"

"I just remembered her doll's name. 'Kiss my Lillian,' she'd say."

"She named the doll after her sister?"

"I guess. God, why was she so fixated on this Lillian?"

Janis shrugged. "Who took care of her? Your mother?"

"No, no. Mother worked at a bank, so she pretty much dodged that bullet. Used to do her laundry, but that was it. Lolly worked, too—on the farm during the day and then over at the prison at night. This housekeeper we had? Hennie? She took care of her during the day. And at night, after Grandpa was done with the milking and had had his supper, he'd take over."

"Her son, right?"

"Uh-huh. He was good to her, I remember. On Sundays, he'd carry her down the stairs and out to his truck. Take her for a drive."

As I spoke, I saw them drive off together. Saw my high-strung mother upstairs, stripping Great-Grandma's soiled sheets with a vengeance. She did Lydia's bed linens on Sunday, her day off, the same day she did the priests' laundry. Mother was clearly pissed at this extra assignment, I remember: having to tend to the needs of a troublesome old relative of her ex-husband—someone whose DNA had nothing to do with her own. God, Mother'd been intense—brittle to the breaking point half the time. And when she did break, *whack!*

"So Grandpa Quirk was your father's father?"

"Hmm? Yeah. . . . He used to get Lydia ready for bed every night, I remember. And after he tucked her in, he'd sit on her bed and sing to her. 'Rock of Ages,' 'Amazing Grace.' She loved it when he sang those old hymns to her. She'd smile, mouth the words."

"He sounds like a nice man."

"Grandpa? Yeah, most of the time. He was good to me. My father had pretty much abdicated, so he pinch-hit for him. Grandpa and my Aunt Lolly. Lolly liked guy stuff: fishing, roughhousing on the parlor floor. She and Hennie? Our housekeeper? They were a couple. Of course, nobody back then dared to say the word 'lesbian.' But, hey, they went on vacations together, slept in the same bed. . . . But yeah, Grandpa was a good guy. He could be a son of bitch when you didn't measure up, though. He and I had a few go-arounds when I was in high school. You know how teenagers are. I started thinking I knew everything there was to know, and he took it upon himself to convince me otherwise. This one time? Right after I got my license? I came home cocked, and he caught me. Slammed me up against the wall, jabbed his finger in my face, and told me in no uncertain terms that he'd be goddamned if he was going to let me go down the same path as my father."

"Meaning?"

"Daddy'd been a drunk. A bum, pretty much. He was dead by then, though. Died when I was fourteen."

"How?"

"Got hit by a train. Cops thought he probably passed out. Either that, or it was suicide."

"Oh, God, Caelum. That's awful."

"Yeah, well . . . the conventional wisdom was that it was the Korean War that screwed him up. But Lolly had told me one time that Grandpa Quirk blamed my father for his wife's death, so I don't imagine that did wonders for his psyche either. They were twins, my father and Lolly, and no matter how badly he messed up, she always came to his defense."

Janis asked why Grandpa blamed Daddy for his wife's death.

"Because she died having him. Lolly was born first, no problem. But Daddy's was a breech birth. Tore up their mother pretty bad, and she started hemorrhaging. Died a day later, I think Lolly said it was. Grandpa was left with these twin babies to raise by himself. Well, he and his mother, I guess."

"Lydia," Janis said.

I nodded. "Must have been quite a balancing act for her—running a prison and raising a couple of grandkids. And she was no spring chicken by then. Would have been what? In her sixties, maybe? . . . But anyway, Lolly said that after my father got back from Korea, he never would talk about it. Built a wall of silence around whatever happened to him over there—with beer cans and liquor bottles, pretty much."

Janis said her grandfather had fought in the Pacific Theater during World War II, and that he'd never talked about his experiences either. "That 'greatest generation' stoicism," she said. "Maybe that's what made them 'the greatest': the fact that they spared everyone at home the details."

"Well, if that's the case, then my father would have had a leg up. We Quirks were good secret-keepers. Our family motto should have been, 'Shh, don't tell. What goes on in this house *stays* in this house.'"

As I spoke, I saw Daddy, dirty and seedy-looking, parting the cornstalks and entering the clearing at the center of the maze—him and that girlfriend of his, the one who'd shown up at Daddy's wake and been given the bum's rush out of there. Bums, they'd been: both of them. His-and-her derelicts, dependent on a little boy's thievery and secret-keeping. *Don't tell your grandpa we're out here. Okay, buddy? Because that's a secret between you and me, right? Now what do you got there? What'd you bring us?* I liked it better when Daddy *didn't* show up—when I could just hide the stuff I'd stolen in the baby buggy and go. Get away from those stuffed, pumpkin-headed replicas of who the Quirk family was supposed to be. No lesbians or drunks or divorcees. It was funny the way townspeople would come in droves every autumn weekend to wander through our maze and find, at the center, the Quirks we weren't.

"Caelum?"

For a second or two, I couldn't quite place her. "Sorry," I said. "I was someplace else. What were you asking?"

"If your grandfather ever remarried."

"Uh, no. Nope. He had lady friends from time to time, but . . . God, do you really want to hear about all this?"

She said she did.

"Before? When I said Grandpa was good to me? According to Lolly, he was just the opposite with my father. Beat him, threw it in his face all the time about how my grandmother would have lived if it wasn't for him. . . . I guess Daddy's big mistake was going right back to the farm after he got out of the service. Signing on for another tour of duty as Grandpa's whipping boy. Lolly said he'd work for his old man all day, then go downtown and get shit-faced at night. Then he started drinking day *and* night, and that was when Grandpa gave him the boot. . . . At school? I used to lie about him."

"Your father?"

I nodded. "Tell the other kids my dad was dead—that he'd died a war hero. And they bought it, too, until this one big-mouthed girl in my class, Bunny Clauson, brought in a newspaper clipping for current events, and it was about my father. How he'd staggered, drunk, off the downtown pier and had had to be rescued by police frogmen.

Having to sit at my desk and listen to that and not cry, not show *any* emotion: man, that had to be one of the hardest moments of my life. . . . But like I said, Grandpa was good to me. That time I came home drunk was the only time he laid a hand on me. And, you know, you can see where *that* was coming from."

Janis sighed. "Families are so hard," she said.

Neither of us spoke for a minute or more. Then she stood and said she wanted to walk back over to the Soldiers and Sailors Arch, study it some more. Did I want to come? "No, I'll stay here," I said. "Take your time."

Sitting on that picnic bench, I put my head in my hands and thought about that weird flashback-like experience I'd had a few hours earlier. Families are hard, she'd said: well, I couldn't argue with that. But better to have had Alden Quirk the Third for a father than Eric Harris or Dylan Klebold for a son. A brother. I'd known them both: Eric's and Dylan's older brothers. Nice kids, good students. How were *they* surviving? How had *they* managed to go on after life dealt them the hand it did, courtesy of their little brothers? . . . It made me think about something I'd read in Lydia's diary—the part where, at the Clemenses' dinner party, the conversation had come around to the burdens of John Wilkes Booth's brother, the actor Edwin Booth. How had *he* carried on after his brother's infamous deed? Head down and one foot in front of the other, probably. The way *I'd* gone on after Maureen killed the Seaberry kid. . . .

Morgan Seaberry: he'd been a secret-keeper, too. And when his brother'd threatened to blow the whistle—out him to their mother— he'd run out of that motel room and gotten himself killed. But what if that *hadn't* happened? What if Mo had left Rivercrest five minutes earlier, or been held up and left five minutes later? Hell, *one* minute later. That poor kid would have crossed the road safely, and the dominoes would have fallen a whole different way. Maureen would have come home from her shift that morning, and gone to bed, and never have gone to prison. . . . And Morgan might have gone to UConn like he wanted to, come out to his dad and stepmom first maybe, and then to his mom. Become himself, finally, and stopped pretending to be the paragon she wanted him to be. He might have met some nice guy and fallen in love. Told his lover about how hard it had been for him in high school, before he'd found himself, claimed his life as his own. . . .

I cleaned up the picnic stuff, brought the cooler back to the car. The book I'd bought was on the front seat, and I opened it and read.

I did know that Susy was part of us; I did not know that she could go away, and take our lives with her, yet leave our dull bodies behind. And I did not know what she was. To me she was but treasure in the bank; the amount known, the need to look at it daily, handle it, weigh it, count it, realize it, not necessary; and now that I would do it, it is too late; they tell me it is not there, has vanished away in a night. . . .

When Janis got back, she said she'd been thinking that maybe none of this was an accident.

"This?"

Maybe she and Moze had been *meant* to meet me at the bakery that morning. Maybe she'd been *meant* to move into the farmhouse and find those old diaries and letters.

I smiled. "So it's not all just a crapshoot, then? Some Master Puppeteer's up there in the sky, yanking everyone's strings according to his Master Plan?"

If by that, I meant did she believe in God, she said, then yes. She did.

"Yeah? And why's that?" I asked.

She couldn't exactly say why, she said; it was just a trust she had that some benign presence was making sure that good overpowered evil.

"Really? Then how do you explain Hitler and Columbine and 9/11? Or Katrina, for that matter. Why'd your 'benign presence' okay that one?"

She neither answered me nor looked away.

"This guy I met once?" I said. "This chaos theorist I got stuck sitting next to on an airplane? He was a total nut job, but he said something to me that I've never forgotten. He said maybe God wasn't Allah or Jesus Christ or any of the other deities that people are always using as an excuse to go to war over. That maybe all 'God' was was mutation. Mutability. The thing that happens when the DNA we're 'carrying forward' from our ancestors suddenly jumps the track. Gets altered in some unpredictable way and, for better or worse, sets the first domino falling in a different direction."

For a little longer than was comfortable, we held each other's gaze. Then she came over and sat down beside me. Hitched her hair behind her ear. Touched her earlobe. "So I take it you and Maureen never had children?"

Children? "No," I said. "Or me and my other two wives either."

"Was that your choice or . . . ?"

Where were *these* questions coming from? "Patti and I were only in our mid-twenties when we got divorced. We probably would've had kids if we'd stayed together. She and her second husband have them—daughters, I think. And Francesca was . . . "

God, she was cute: those smoky blue eyes, that little mole to the left of her lip. . . .

"Francesca was what?"

"What? Oh. On the fast track, career-wise. Didn't want anything or anyone to stand in the way of her ride up the corporate elevator. Including me, as it played out. And with Maureen, it was a nonissue. She'd had her tubes tied during her first marriage. So that was that."

She shifted positions a little, and when she did, her knee bumped up against my thigh and stayed there. "Do you ever regret it? Not having kids?"

I shrugged. And when I opened my mouth, what came out of it surprised me. "A little, I guess. Doesn't occupy major portions of my day but . . . Maybe it's all this ancestor stuff you've been digging up. It's got me thinking about how I'm the end of the Quirk line. How the river's not going underground, it's drying up." A little bit after the fact, I realized she was touching my arm, rubbing her hand up and down it. "I read once that that's why guys cheat—that we're hard-wired to want to spread our seed." Now why had I just said that? Why was I shallow-breathing? "What about you and Moze? You guys see kids in your future?"

"Moses doesn't want any more," she said.

"Any more?"

She said he had an eleven-year-old daughter by a former lover. He and the mother had an agreement: no child support, but no contact, either. They lived in Oregon. "And before that, there was a little boy by a different woman. He died, though, when he was very young. Two, I think. I don't know the circumstances. Moses doesn't ever want to go there."

"That's got to be the worst," I said. "Losing a child." To spinal meningitis, I thought. Or to a couple of psychopathic kids with rifles. A nurse driving home stoned on painkiller. "So is that okay with you, then? No kids because he doesn't want them?" I shifted a little, got an inch or so closer to her.

"Sometimes it is," she said.

I nodded. Watched the rapid blinking of her eyes, shiny with un-spilled tears. Watched the moisture that had pooled in the little valley above her top lip. What was that indentation called? I always forgot. But God, didn't it feel nice the way her fingertips were grazing the veins on the back of my hand? And wouldn't it feel nice to lean forward and poke my tongue into that little valley and taste her salt, taste her . . .

I'm not even sure which one of us started it, but we were kissing each other—openmouthed, tongue to tongue. When I felt her begin to pull away, I placed my hand against the back of her neck and kissed her some more. Right there in public, in Bushnell Park, in front of Santiago and his mom and the ducks and whoever else might have seen us—the pretty blonde who wasn't even thirty yet and the gray-haired guy who was old enough to be, but was not, thank God, her father. I kissed her again. And again. Those kisses felt more necessary than right.

We were quiet on the drive back—both of us a little embarrassed, I think, by what had happened. Maybe she hadn't kissed me, I thought. Maybe she'd just been kissing her access to Lydia's diaries and Lizzy's letters.

It wasn't until I reached over to turn on the radio that she spoke. "Caelum, what happened back there shouldn't have happened," she said.

"What happened?" I said. "*Nothing* happened. I don't even know what you're talking about."

"Oh," she said. "Okay. Yeah."

I turned up the music. Van Morrison's "Brown-Eyed Girl." We both stared ahead, our eyes on the highway ahead of us.

Back in Three Rivers, on Bride Lake Road, I passed the prison without looking at it. Put my blinker on, turned in, and drove up the long driveway to the farmhouse. Someone was outside, sitting on the front step. Was it a woman? A child?

"Oh, my God," Janis said.

I cut the engine. Got out and walked warily toward her. Her face was bruised and puffy. There was a nasty-looking gash above her left eyebrow. She had dried blood on the front of her shirt, bloodstained teeth.

We sat down on either side of her. "What happened, Velvet?" I said.

"What do you *think* happened? I got beat up, that's what."

Janis took her hand. "Sweetie, who did this to you?" she asked.

"Some asshole at the rest stop. Gives me twenty bucks to go down on him, and when I start doing what he's just paid me to do, he yanks me back up by my hair and starts slamming my face against his dashboard. Opens the door of his truck when he's done, throws me out onto the ground, and drives off. Cocksucker."

I stood up. Held my hands out and pulled her up. "Come on in," I said. "Let's get you cleaned up. See if that cut you got is going to need stitches."

Velvet began to cry. "I want my mom," she said.

"Your mom's in jail," I said. "You're stuck with me."

Janis looked back and forth between us.

THAT NIGHT, LYING AWAKE IN bed, I listened to their voices murmuring above me, their footsteps: Moze's, Janis's, Velvet's. I couldn't sleep. Couldn't stop thinking about everything that had happened that day: the flashback or whatever it had been, the feel of her kisses.

I put the light on. Opened the book I'd bought. I found a letter he'd written to his friend Twichell shortly after his daughter's death.

> *You know our life—the outside of it—as the others do—and the inside of it—which they do not. You have seen our whole voyage. You have seen us go to sea, a cloud of sail, and the flag at the peak; and you see us now, chartless, adrift—derelicts; battered, waterlogged, our sails a ruck of rags, our pride gone. For it is gone. And there is nothing in its place. The vanity of life was all we had, and there is no more vanity left in us. We are even ashamed of that we had; ashamed that we trusted the promises of life. . . .*

I closed the book, turned off the light, and cried in the dark. For

the Clemenses, the Columbine families. For Morgan Seaberry's parents, the Harrises and the Klebolds. I cried, too, for Moze and Maureen. I wished I hadn't kissed Janis, but I had and wanted to kiss her
again. Wanted to undress her, hold her nakedness against my own,
and spill my seed inside of her. . . . She'd lit a match to a loneliness
that, for years, I'd tried hard to bear. *What* happened? I'd said. *Nothing* happened. But something had. Something had jumped the track
back there in Bushnell Park. Some first domino had fallen.

↠ chapter twenty-three ↞

From: studlysicilian@snet.net
To: caelumq@aol.com
Sent: Friday, October 27, 2006
Subject: offer u cant refuse???

Yo Quirky—U busy tommorow? Theres a car show/
auction up in Springfield MA. Pretty big one—
mean machines from all over NY and N. Eng.
Thinking about checkin it out. Wanna go? Maybe
we could hit Outback on the way back, get some
steaks.

From: caelumq@aol.com
To: studlysicilian@snet.net
Sent: Friday, October 27, 2006
Subject: offer u can't refuse???

Can't, Al. I've got plans. FYI: "tomorrow" has
one m, two r's.

From: studlysicilian@snet.net
To: caelumq@aol.com
Sent: Friday, October 27, 2006
Subject: offer u cant refuse???

Yeah thanks spelling nerd. Who you got plans
with—your dick and Fanny Five Fingers?

From: caelumq@aol.com
To: studlysicilian@snet.net
Sent: Friday, October 27, 2006
Subject: offer u cant refuse???

Doctor's appointment.

———

"WHAT DID YOU CALL IT again?"

"Vicarious traumatization. It can happen to those who bear secondary witness to the traumas of others. Therapists, for instance—an occupational hazard to which those in my profession must be alert."

"So it's like . . . transference or something?"

Dr. Patel nodded. "But I'm not sure about flashbacks, Mr. Quirk. More typically, vicarious traumatization manifests itself as hypervigilance or an inabilty to focus. Nightmares, sometimes. All classic symptoms of—"

"Posttraumatic stress," I said.

"Yes, yes. Now I'm thinking the episode you experienced—vicarious flashback or not—may have triggered a rapid drop in your blood pressure. And that, in turn, may have been the reason you seem to have lost consciousness for a second or two. Were you alone when this happened?"

"No, I . . . well, yeah. Yes, I was." I looked away from her curious face. Looked back. There was no way in hell I was getting into the subject of Janis and me. "Vicarious traumatization, huh? Weird."

"My concern is that if it happens again, you might fall and hurt yourself, and there would be no one to help you."

I shook my head. "I'm sure it was just some weird, onetime thing."

"Perhaps you should see your physician, Mr. Quirk. Have some tests done to rule out physiological causes. And, should symptoms persist and the problem *does* seem to be psychological in nature, I would be happy to work with you. But at any rate, it's lovely to see you again."

"You, too. And I see you've got a new office mate since the last time I was here." I pointed past her puzzled face to the marble sculpture on the table behind her: elephant head, human body, four arms flailing.

"Ah, you mean Lord Ganesha! Are you familiar with him?" I shook my head. "Ganesha is the destroyer of sorrows and the remover of obstacles. A fitting 'office mate,' don't you think, given what we try to accomplish here?"

I nodded. "And four hands instead of two. Must be a multitasker."

She laughed. "Yes, yes. A Hindu deity well suited to busy Americans. You should remember to rub his big belly before you leave. It's said to bring good luck. More tea?" I held out my cup. She poured. "I must say, Mr. Quirk, you are looking quite well despite your recent episode."

"Am I? Well, I've started running again. Helps with the stress."

Janis and I were doing three or four miles together, first thing in the morning. We'd get back at about the time Moze drove in from night baking, and the three of us would have breakfast together. The *four* of us, actually, on the days when Princess Velvet managed to drag herself out of bed and saunter downstairs. I'd agreed to let Velvet move in with the Micks—temporarily, I'd stipulated. I wasn't crazy about the idea, but I figured it would keep her out of harm's way for a while. I'd also said yes as a favor to Janis. Velvet was helping Moze set up his sculpture business, and that freed Janis to work on all the stuff she'd discovered in those old filing cabinets. *Caelum! You're not going to believe this! I found Lizzy's Civil War letters! And old photographs, too—a whole big envelope of them!* Jesus, she'd acted like a kid on Christmas morning.

"You're smiling, Mr. Quirk," Dr. Patel noted.

"Hmm?"

"Your face just broke into a lovely smile. A penny for your thoughts."

I shook my head. "I'd be overcharging you."

Her eyes moved from my face to my tapping left foot, then back. "And so you are running again. And teaching your new course: The Quest in Literature, as I recall. Are you enjoying that?"

I nodded. "Students are a little resistant, though. They keep wanting to know what all these classical Greek myths we're reading have to do with them. Community college students tend to be pragmatists, you know? Can't blame them. A lot of them are balancing school, work, kids."

"Multitaskers," Dr. Patel observed. "And when they ask you what the ancient stories have to do with them, how do you respond?"

"Last week, I threw the question back at them. Told them each to pick a myth and write a personal essay about its relevance to their lives."

"Ah, that's an interesting assignment, and a useful one, too, I should think. The archetypal stories address human needs and longings so marvelously. Which is why they have lasted since antiquity, yes?" I nodded. "And did your assignment yield good results?"

"Don't know yet," I said. "Papers are due next Tuesday."

"Well, Mr. Quirk, your resistant students are fortunate to have you as their teacher. Now tell me, please. How is Maureen?"

"Mo?" I looked away from her for a second. Looked back. "Doing okay for the most part. She's got a cellmate she's compatible with now, so that helps. Gambling addict. In there for embezzlement." I pulled at an unraveling thread on my sweatshirt sleeve. "She seesaws from visit to visit. Mo, I mean. Some days she's up, some days she's down."

"And how often are you able to see her?"

"How often?" I shifted in my chair, folded my arms in front of me. "It goes by the last digit of their inmate numbers. Odds can have visits one day, evens the next. So, theoretically, I can go every other day."

Dr. P's head tilted slightly. "Theoretically?"

I took a sip of tea. Over the rim of my cup, I watched her watch me.

"No, it's just . . . I *was* getting there every other day at first. Because that's what she needed, you know? She was so intimidated by everything. And everybody."

"Well, that's understandable."

"Yeah. It is. All the loud noises really freaked her out at first, you know? Doors banging, people screaming and swearing at each other. This one little darling on her tier realized that noise bothered her, so she'd rile her up on purpose. Sneak up behind her and clap in her ears, go 'Boo!'"

Dr. Patel shook her head. "Assimilation to such a harsh environment would be difficult for anyone, but particularly so for someone with PTSD."

"But she's better now. Like you said, assimilating. Other day I was down there and she said she heard 'on the down-low' that there was going to be a shakedown that weekend. A shakedown's where the goons herd them over to the gym and strip-search them while another bunch pulls their cells apart, looking for contraband. Drugs, weapons. That kind of thing." I shook my head. "On the down-low: like she grew up on the streets or something. Part of her assimilation, I guess. Learning the lingo. Next thing I know, she'll be getting a jailhouse tattoo."

I sat there, waiting for her to say something. Watching her wait.

"They got this thing down there called 'five on the floor,' okay? Which means that once an hour, the CO at the control desk pops their cell doors. Everything's controlled electronically, okay? So the CO pops their doors and they get a whopping five minutes to go out to this common area where there's phones, and a TV, and a pot of hot water so they can make themselves instant coffee or tea or whatever. That's when she can call me, okay? During 'five on the floor.' Except after we get through the rigmarole of me accepting the phone company charges and the State of Connecticut surcharge and all that yadda yadda, we've got maybe two, three minutes to talk. And, you know, all the time we're trying to have a conversation, the TV's blaring and everyone's yapping away in the background with *their* volume jacked up. And so, half of our conversation is me repeating two or three times what I already said because she can't hear me over the racket. Gotta stick her finger in her ear the whole time, she says, and even then. . . . Plus, there's this intermittent beep-beeping coming through the receiver to remind you that Big Brother may be eavesdropping."

Dr. P shook her head. "Face-to-face visits are preferable, then. Yes?"

"Yeah. Somewhat. . . . But it gets hard, you know? I mean, I'm teaching, conferencing with students, going to these bullshit committee meetings that drag on forever. You know academics: love to hear themselves talk. All that plus I've got a forty-minute commute twice a day. . . . And now? With the civil suit coming up? The lawyer I hired says he needs all the documentation from the criminal trial, plus all the information about our assets. Takes *time* to gather all that stuff, you know? She doesn't realize that I can't just put the brakes on everything from three to four thirty every other day and get over to see her."

"So this is an issue between the two of you?"

"An issue? No, not really. Not a *big* issue."

In the dead air that followed my bogus denial, her eyes moved from my eyes down to my crazily tapping foot, then back again.

"Hey, I can understand it from her perspective, you know? I mean, what's *she* doing all day while I'm running from one thing to another? Sitting in her cell, waiting for three o'clock. So when they *don't* call her down. . . . I mean, I *get* that, but . . . She's applied for a job, though. That should help. She'd like to get assigned to the infirmary—use her skills, you know? But her unit manager told her he doesn't think it'll happen because of her drug history. Says she'll probably get food prep or janitorial or something. Which would be okay, too, I guess. Anything to eat up some of her day. Make the time go by quicker."

"Indeed," Dr. Patel said. "Well, I hope—"

"Trouble is, whenever they apply for something at that place, the paperwork takes forever. I swear, the entire system's being run by *in*efficiency experts. It's ridiculous."

"And so it goes with large institutions, I'm afraid."

"And then? When I *do* bust my butt—drive back from school like a bat outa hell and rush over there? It's hurry-up-and-wait. They've got this rule: inmates have to be seated in the visiting room before they let us enter. And Mo says a lot of the guards take their sweet time calling them from their units. Or they hold them up at the walk gate—hassle them for the simple reason that they can get away with it. Make themselves feel like big shots."

"An abuse of their authority," Dr. P noted.

"Right. Exactly. And meanwhile, I'm parked in the bullpen with all the other visitors, thinking about all the things that aren't getting done while I'm just sitting there. . . . Sometimes? You wait there for half, three-quarters of an hour, and then they come strolling out and tell you visits have been canceled for the day. No explanations, no apologies for anyone's wasted time. It's like, see ya, don't let the door hit you in the ass on your way out."

"That must be very frustrating, Mr. Quirk."

"Hey, it's not even that big a deal for me. I live right up the road. You know who *I* feel sorry for? The grandmothers. These poor, exhausted-looking women who are stuck raising the daughter's kids while she's doing time. They drive an hour, hour and a half from Bridgeport or Stamford, some of them, in these rusted-out old gas guzzlers that look like they might not make the trip back. Got the toddlers strapped into their car seats in back. Haven't even had time to change out of their work clothes, a lot of them—they're still wearing their nursing-home smocks or whatever. Then they get there and the goon at the gate goes, 'Sorry. No visits today.' . . . Sucks for those little kids, you know? And for the grandmothers."

Dr. Patel nodded sadly. "As it sucks for the prisoner who has anticipated seeing her loved ones." She stopped, cocked her head to the side. "Something is humorous, Mr. Quirk?"

"No, I just . . . You usually speak the Queen's English. Struck me funny to hear you say something 'sucked.' Another occupational hazard, eh, Doc? Assimilating the slang you have to listen to all day long from us boneheads?"

By way of an answer, she gave me a noncommittal smile.

Her smile faded. She glanced at her clock. "I'm afraid we'll have to end in a few minutes, Mr. Quirk. But tell me something, please, before we do. Maureen's failure to understand how busy you are: Would you say your frustration about that stems more from anger or from fear?"

"Neither, really. It's just . . ." I shrugged. "It is what it is."

"That's a circumlocution, Mr. Quirk—the kind of time-wasting response which, I imagine, you would not accept from your students. Suppose I were to insist you choose one or the other. Which would it be? Anger? Or fear?"

As if she *wasn't* insisting. "I don't know. Anger, I guess."

"And what would be the source of that anger?"

We held each other's gaze for several seconds.

"This lawsuit we're facing? *I'm* facing. Hey, *I'm* the one who had to go out, get a lawyer, get all this stuff ready while she's sitting down there at the human warehouse. . . . I keep going back to this Sunday night several years back when my aunt called me. My aunt Lolly—the one I inherited the farm from. This was back in ninety-seven, ninety-eight—after she and I reconciled and we moved out to Colorado. So my aunt calls me, okay? Says she's having her will done. Asks me, do I want her to put the farm in just my name, or in both our names. Maureen's and mine. 'Both,' I said. Hey, we'd moved out there to save our marriage, right? Clean slate, new beginnings. And it was working pretty well. Things *were* better. So I said, without really thinking about it, 'Put it in both our names.' As an act of faith, or whatever. So that's what she did. But now . . . because of that . . ."

"Yes? Go on."

"If they win the civil case . . . Look, it's not like I'm unsympathetic toward that woman. She lost her *son*, you know? And from what I heard, that kid was a great kid. Had his problems, but . . . But *I* wasn't the one at the wheel that morning. *I* didn't kill him. How's taking what's mine going to make things any better? It's not like it's going to bring him back from the dead, is it? Pulling *my* life out from under me? . . . I mean, I've already lost her, you know? For five years, anyway. And after that? It's not like she's going to bounce out of that place unchanged. 'There's going to be a shake-down. I heard it on the down-low.' . . . And now, on top of that, I might have to lose my house? My farm? That farm's been in my family for years. Generations. But because of what she did, and be-cause, on the night my aunt called, I said, 'Put it in both our names.' . . . You know how old I was when I lost my father? Fourteen. I mean, I'd lost him to alcohol long before that, but that's when he got killed—when I was fourteen. Freshman in high school, and my aunt shows up outside my algebra class. . . . Lost my mother when I was thirty. Kept a vigil by her bedside, and you know who she wanted in her dying hours? Not her son, her only kid. She wanted Jesus, with his big brown eyes and his honey-colored hair. . . . I have no kids, no siblings. No cousins, even. Well, technically, I've got cousins on my mother's side, but I don't really know any of them. Haven't seen any of them since I was a kid. Aunt Lolly was the only relative left who I cared about, and then she died. And so the farm. . . . That farm's all I've got left."

She handed me the box of tissues. Waited.

"And the thing is, I really *tried*, you know? After the shootings? When I saw how scared to death she was of everything? How trau-matized? Jesus, I tried everything I could think of to help her get past it. Get back to the person she'd been. It's fucked up, you know? Three wives, three marriages, and it wasn't until after Columbine that I finally figured out how to be a halfway decent husband. . . . Only it wasn't enough. No matter what I tried, no matter what I did. It was almost as if . . . as if . . ."

"Say it, Mr. Quirk."

"It's like she died inside that cabinet. Said her prayers, wrote me a good-bye note, and then the SWAT team got there and this other, damaged stranger crawled out instead. And Maureen was dead."

She was the one who broke the silence. "I am thinking, Mr. Quirk, that perhaps the flashbacklike episode you experienced may have been some subconscious attempt to be a good husband to Maureen. To bear a little of her terrible burden for her."

I shrugged. Sat there looking at her. "I went to the convenience store the other day? For a coffee? I go, 'Medium black, no sugar,' and the kid at the counter—must have been all of eighteen or nineteen— she gets me my coffee, goes over to the register, and she says, 'Do you get the senior citizen discount?' And I go, 'Oh, no, God, no. Not yet, ha ha ha.' . . . But you know something? By the time she gets out of there? I *won't* be too far from their friggin' senior discount. Still teaching, still chipping away at our mountain of legal debt on my shitty thirty-five, thirty-six thousand a year—and that's *if* they give me tenure. Living in some crappy little apartment because we lost the house. *My* house. *My* family's farm. So yeah, I guess I feel angry."

"And what is it that you feel *beneath* your anger?"

Several seconds passed. I held her gaze.

"I'm afraid."

"Of what, Mr. Quirk? Can you tell me?"

"Of ending up with nothing. With no one."

I WROTE HER A CHECK. Rubbed the belly of her elephant-head statue for good luck. Promised to call her if I had another flashback, or if I just wanted to talk some more. I knew I wouldn't, though. All I wanted to do was get home, put a couple of drinks into me, and see Janis. Hold her and lie naked with her. But that was never going to happen. After we'd come back from our runs and Moze got home from the bakery? They'd touch each other, tease each other, pass food while I sat there and watched.

At the door, Dr. Patel wished me good luck with my students. "It's a curious thing about quests, isn't it, Mr. Quirk?" she said. "The seeker embarks on a journey to find what he wants and discovers, along the way, what he needs."

"Yeah," I said. "Yup." If I thought she'd have gotten it, I would have started singing her that old Stones song: *You can't always get what you want.* But I was pretty sure Mick and the boys weren't on Doc Patel's iPod.

We'd gone over our allotted time, so her next patient was sitting in the waiting room—Dominick Birdsey, a guy I'd known since grade school. It was a little weird for both of us. "Hey, how's it going?"

"Good. Great. You?"

"Going okay. Good to see you, man."

"Yeah, you, too."

Passing what had to have been his black BMW on the way to my car—ours were the only two in the lot—I smiled, shook my head. If we were both doing so goddamned great, why were we both seeing a shrink? Guess life wasn't happily-ever-after even when you were a casino millionaire. Well, I'll be a son of a bitch. . . .

Back home, Moze's truck was gone and all the upstairs lights were off. Velvet must have gone out, too.

I fed the cat, poured myself a drink. I would have preferred scotch but I was drinking vodka now—the low-end stuff. Junior was billing me seventy-five bucks an hour so that I could keep what was already mine.

I re-microwaved the rest of the pizza I'd microwaved the night before.

Washed my supper plate.

Poured myself another couple of inches of rot-gut and sat down at the computer. I Googled "vicarious traumatization." It said pretty much what Doc Patel had said. Should have saved myself the money I'd handed over to her. Googled "Ganesha." *The son of Parvati the Destroyer and Shiva the Restorer. . . . His big belly is "a pitcher of pros-*

perity." . . . *He is propitiated at the commencement of important work.* I
backed out of Google and checked my e-mail.

From: janis.mick@tulane.edu
To: caelumq@aol.com
Sent: Saturday, October 28, 2006
Subject: Great News!

Caelum,
   I got the most exciting news today! A few
days ago, I emailed Amanda, my adviser from
Tulane, to tell her about your family's archives. She called me this afternoon and we
talked for over an hour. She's invited me to
submit a proposal for a paper at a huge Wom-
en's Studies conference in San Francisco next
February. (Luckily for me, she's on the selection committee!) Amanda thinks I should focus
on Lizzy Popper. She thinks Lizzy would be a
great subject for a thesis project, and that
it could maybe even be enough for a book! It
will be a TON of work for me to pull it all
together by February, but I am SO EXCITED.
Moze is taking me out to dinner to celebrate
and we've invited Velvet, too. We wanted you
to come, but we didn't know where you were.
If you get back in time, come join us (Asian
Bistro, 6:30 reservation). Caelum, none of this
would have happened if it wasn't for your generosity. I can't say enough how grateful I am
to you. Tell you more tomorrow. Are we running
in the morning? If so, see you then.

From: studlysicilian@snet.net
To: caelumq@aol.com
Sent: Saturday, October 28, 2006
Subject: my search may be over!!!!!!!!!!!!!!!!!!!!

   Quirks—your not gonna fucken believe this.
I go to the auto show this afternoon, okay?

And me & this guy who kinda looks like one of
those long beard dudes from ZZ Top—we're both
checkin out the Mustangs. So we start shootin
the shit and guess what. This guy's a contractor, okay, and this sheetrocker he use to
use had a heart attack and died a few months
ago & GUESS WHAT! He (the dead guy) owned a
4 BARREL, 289-CUBE, 1965 PHOENICIAN YELLOW
'STANG!!!!!!!!!!!!!!!. Dude, how freaky is that?
I been checkin eBay and the Yellow Mustang
Registry for eight, nine years thinkin if I'm
lucky one might show up in Idaho or Arizona
or someplace. And now here's my DREAM MACHINE
only 25 miles away in Easterly Fucken Rhode
Island!! Little Rhody, Man!! I was trying to
act casual, like I might be interested might
not, and meanwhile I'm so excited I'm practicly
shootin off in my shorts. I know I know, probably shouldnt get my hopes up until I see the
car. Lonnys gonna check with the guys wife and
get back to me but he heard she probably wants
to sell it. SHE BETTER!! Dude, I been blastin'
my old Beach Boys and Jan & Dean tapes ever
since i got home. U and me are goin' cruisin',
mutha fucka!! Later, Al. ☻ ☻ ☻

Half in the bag, I clicked on reply and e-mailed him back.

From: caelumq@aol.com
To: studlysicilian@snet.net
Sent: Saturday, October 28, 2006
Subject: my search may be over!!!!!!!!!!!!!!!!!!!!!

Asshole,
  Beware! He who goes questing for what he
wants may discover, along the way, what he
needs.

chapter twenty-four

DEVIN, A DOMINO'S PIZZA DELIVERER, identified with Hermes, the Greek god who dispatched messages from Olympus on his winged feet. "Also, he's the dude who invented the lyre and I play electric guitar."

Ibrahim zeroed in on Icarus, likening his fall from the sky to the September 11 victims' suicidal leaps from the top floors of the World Trade Center towers. Those remembered images haunted him, Ibrahim wrote, as did the terrorists' actions. His essay spoke of what it was like to be an Arab and a practicing Muslim in post–9/11 America: the presumption of guilt by others, the assumption of an unearned guilt of which he could not rid himself.

"The first time I stuck that needle in my vein, it was like opening my own personal Pandora's box," Kahlúa wrote. By special arrangement with the halfway house where she was completing the last months of her sentence, she was delivered to and retrieved from Oceanside Community College in an unmarked van.

Glum, withdrawn Private First Class Kareem Kendricks, home from Walter Reed Hospital, likened Iraq to Hades, himself to Sisyphus. "I'll be alright for a few day's and think I'm gaining on it than have a nightmare or a daymare that sets me back. For example, the other day I was reading my little daughter this book *Green Eggs and Ham*. I must of stopped right in the middle and didn't even realize it because the next thing I knew I heard her saying 'Mommy, I keep telling Daddy to turn the page and he won't do it.' Right in the middle of that silly story, I was back there, in that gunner, on the day I lost my right hand and my best buddy lost his life. Iraq is my rock that I have to keep pushing up this big hill called Moving On and every day it rolls back down to the bottom again and I have to start all over."

Littered with syntactical and grammatical errors, they were the best papers they'd written all term, and they triggered the class's most worthwhile discussion. It was almost time to wrap things up when Kyle, a quiet boy in a backwards baseball cap—a near-nonpresence in the class until that moment—asked me, point blank, "What's yours, Professor Quirk?"

"My . . . ?"

"Myth?"

They waited. Watched me.

The fact was, I *had* done their assignment—in my head, during my ride from Oceanside CC to Quirk CI—had, in fact, come up with not one but two resonant myths. But I spared them our Columbine connection: Maureen's having become lost in the labyrinth and my own failure to slay the monster and rescue her, or to rescue Morgan Seaberry *from* her. They all looked so wide-eyed and expectant that they might have been my children to keep safe.

I came out from behind my desk, pulled up a chair and sat closer to them. I looked first at Private Kendricks. "Mine's about Hades, too," I said. I scanned their faces. "Orpheus and Eurydice. You guys remember that one?"

Devin spoke. "That's the one where the dude goes down to Hell to get his wife back. Then he forgets he's not supposed to look back at her while she's following him out, so she has to stay."

On a less unusual day, I might have corrected him: reminded him that Hell was a Christian concept, different from the Ancient Greeks' netherworld. But on that day, I nodded, let it go. "My wife's in prison," I said.

The slouchers sat up. Several students leaned forward.

"And . . . when I visit her? I've got this thing—this superstition, I guess it is. . . . They've got a rule down there: inmates stay seated when visiting time's over. They don't get dismissed until after everyone's company has cleared out. And so at the end of a visit, when I get up to go? I've got this thing where I tell myself not to look back at her. That if I let myself look over my shoulder, take another glimpse, she's going to stay stuck in there. She'll never get out."

There was commotion out in the hallway, the changing of classes. But in our classroom, no one moved.

When Marisol raised her hand, I figured I knew what was coming: What had Mo done? Why was she in prison? "Yes?" I said.

"What's your wife's name?"

"Her name? Maureen. Why?"

"Because I'm going to pray for her," she said.

Tunisia nodded. "My mom's a minister," she said. "I'm gonna ax her to ax our congregation to pray for her, too."

I nodded, smiled. "Well, we'd better wrap up," I said. "Good class today. Remember that Joseph Campbell essay for next time. Check your syllabus."

"Is there going to be a quiz?"

I smiled, lifted my eyebrows. "You never can tell."

After class, four or five of them stayed behind to talk with me. Nothing out of the ordinary there, but this time it wasn't to challenge a grade or offer an excuse about why an assignment hadn't been done. This time, the ones who stayed wanted to tell me they had people in prison, too. Hipolito's dad, Cheyenne's brother. Plus Kahlúa, who had done time at Quirk CI herself, as had her alcoholic mother. "How you think I got the name Kahlúa?" she said.

"Could've been worse," someone noted. "She could have named you Jello Shot."

"Fuzzy Navel."

"Saki Bomb."

It felt nice, you know? Hanging with them for a few minutes, sharing a laugh, a little of the pain. Even Private Kendricks had smiled. And those papers they'd written—not just the poignant ones, but all of them, even the one by fleet-footed Hermes with his pepperoni pizzas. It reminded me that they were more than just their scholarly shortcomings and gripes about the workload. Each had a history, a set of problems. Each, for better or worse, was anchored to a family. That assignment, that class, buoyed me a little. And I don't know, maybe it buoyed a few of them, too.

But if I arrived at the prison that afternoon feeling pretty good about things, Mo put the brakes on that. Approaching her, I was struck with how distracted and pale she looked. I kissed her and sat down, trying to read the jumpiness in her eyes, the ragged skin and dried blood around her cuticles.

"I didn't think you were coming," she said.

"No? Why not?"

She shrugged. "You were here on Sunday."

"And today's Thursday," I said. "I would have come Tuesday, but Velvet told me she was visiting you, so I figured you were all set." No response. "You two have a good visit?"

She shook her head. "All she could talk about was Mr. and Mrs. Wonderful. How she loves working on his stupid gargoyle statues, how easy she is to talk to. Oh, and I heard how you cooked pancakes for everyone last Sunday. Sounds like you four are quite the happy little family over there."

"They're my tenants, Maureen. They pay rent, they have kitchen privileges. Sometimes we share a meal." It pissed me off the way she rolled her eyes. "What's the bug up *your* ass?" I said, although I wasn't sure I wanted to hear the answer. Had she found out somehow about what had happened up at Bushnell Park? Was my desire for Janis readable?

Camille had been reassigned to a different tier, Mo said. No prior notice, no explanation. Just a guard at the door throwing Camille a couple of garbage bags and telling her to pack. Mo was just leaving to go to her NarcAnon group. When she returned an hour later, a new woman was sitting on Camille's bunk—Irina, a Russian immigrant, who had a chip on her shoulder a mile wide. She coughed constantly; Mo said; she had kept her up all night with that cough. In the morning, as the two stood side by side at the bathroom sinks, Mo had advised Irina to put in a request to go to Medical and have herself checked out. Irina had misinterpreted her concern as criticism and launched into a profanity-laced invective. A third inmate—a "drama addict" named Iesha—had jumped in, calling Mo "Miss High and Mighty" and accusing her of thinking she was better than everyone else.

Mo had tried to explain that she was worried about Irina's health. That she was a nurse.

"*Used to be* a nurse, maybe!" Iesha had screamed. "Now you're just a jailhouse 'ho like the rest of us!" A guard who'd heard the shouting barged in, threatening disciplinary tickets for the three of them. For the rest of the morning, Irina had paced their cell, mumbling in Russian, coughing and spitting phlegm on the floor and the walls.

At lunchtime, there'd been a second incident, Mo said. She and Camille had located each other in the chow hall and sat together. On their way out, they'd been stopped by CO Moorhead. The pepper shaker was missing from the table where they'd been eating, and Moorhead accused Mo and Camille of having stolen it. When they denied it, she'd ordered them into the restroom to be strip-searched. Camille had given her some lip about it, and Moorhead had retaliated by humiliating her during the search, shoving her plastic-gloved fingers deep into Camille's vagina and leaving them there for several seconds "while she stood there, smirking."

Since her arrival at the prison, Maureen had tried her best to fly beneath the radar with the custody staff. But now Camille was preparing to file an incident report, and Mo, the only witness to the abuse, would be questioned. She'd have to tell the truth, she said—Moorhead had gone way over the line—but there would be retaliation. Moorhead's crony, CO Tonelli, was "borderline psychotic," according to Mo. Tonelli usually treated her like she was invisible, but that would change once she gave her statement. She was afraid, she said. She felt nauseous. "And it's not going to do any good anyway. They'd never take an inmate's word over a CO's. God, I hate this place." She began to cry.

"You want me to say something?" I asked. "Call someone?"

Her expression changed from dismay to contempt. "Like who, Caelum? Who would you call?"

"I don't know. Your unit manager? The warden? Hey, fuck it, I'll call our state senator if I have to."

"Just stay out of it, Caelum. Just go home to your little family."

I took a breath. "You know what I do with the Micks' rent check, Maureen? I deposit it in an account so that I can pay the lawyer who's trying to make sure we don't lose our goddamned house to your victim's family. Okay?"

She looked away, shaking her head in disgust.

"Okay?" I repeated.

She turned back, facing me with a vengeance. "The last thing I need right now is you guilt-tripping me!" Heads turned. Conversations around us came to a halt.

To counteract her raised voice, I lowered my own. "I'm not guilt-tripping you," I said. "I'm giving you a reality check."

"Shut up," she said. "Just leave."

Without another word, I rose, walked across the room, and stopped at the metal door. The CO at the desk notified Big Brother that someone was leaving early. A few seconds later, the door slid open and I stepped through to the outside. I did not look back.

HOME AGAIN, I FOUND MOSES in the kitchen, standing at the open refrigerator. "Getting myself one of those damn-Yankee beers you introduced me to," he said. "You want one?"

"*Need* one's more like it," I said.

"Yeah? Why's that?"

I answered him with a shrug. Moze uncapped two Sam Adams and handed me one. "So how are things going with you?" I asked.

"They're going," he said. "Web site's done. Looks pretty decent. And I been talking to a couple of shipping companies. DHL's offered me the best deal, so I'll probably go with them. Me and Velvet started casting yesterday. She tell you?"

I shook my head. "How's that working out, anyway? She more of a help or a hindrance?"

Moses smiled, swigged his beer. "Nah, she's good, man. Got some rough edges, but she works hard. Comes by it naturally, maybe. She says her granddaddy was a sculptor."

I nodded. "Lived up in Barre, Vermont, and there's a big granite quarry up there. He did cemetery statuary, mainly."

"Yeah, we got on the Internet and she showed me some of his work. Pretty impressive. Velvet says she wants to try designing some gargoyles, so I told her maybe later on, after we got rolling, she could work up some sketches and we'd see. First things first, though. I want to get a hundred pieces poured and finished by the end of next week. I'm hoping to put the business online as soon's I get back."

"Back from where?" I asked.

"N'Orleans. Gotta go down, get our cat, check in with my cousins. They're staying with friends, waiting on one of them FEMA trailers. Hey, you don't have one of them cat caddies, do you? Last thing I need is Fat Harry getting between me and the brake pedal on the ride back."

I said there might be one up in the attic—that I'd look.

"Appreciate that. When I was talking to my old cuz, he says, 'You know what FEMA stands for, don't you? Fix Everything My Ass.'"

I nodded, smiled. Asked him how long he was going to be away.

"About a week, give or take. Alphonse gave me the time off. Says he'll have Tina do the daytime baking and take my night shift his damn self. Man, that ole boy's been in such a good mood since he found that Mustang, I probably could have hit him up for the gas money as well's the time off."

"So the widow's going to sell it to him?"

"Still hasn't made up her mind, he says, but he *thinks* she's leaning toward selling. Says she told him to stop calling and pestering her about it—that she'll contact him once she decides. Kind of a goofball, that Alphonse, idn't he?"

I nodded. "A good-hearted goofball, though."

"Yeah, but shit, man. How many guys his age get jazzed up because PlayStation's coming out with a new version of *Grand Theft Auto*?"

"You'd understand if you met his parents," I said. "His mother still sends him an Easter basket."

Moze shook his head. "Man, that's fucked up with a capital F. Hey, before I forget, that folder yonder? Janis left it for you." I glanced over at the legal-sized manila file folder on the counter. "Stuff she found in one of those boxes upstairs. She's got some questions. Wants you to take a look at it."

"Yeah, well, like you said before, first things first. Mind if I grab another one of your beers?"

He shook his head, finished the rest of his. "As long as you're up."

Standing at the fridge with my back to him, I tried to make the next sound as casual as possible. "So is Janis going down there with you?"

It wasn't until I turned and faced him that he responded. "No, she's not. Why you asking?"

"No reason," I said. I handed him his beer. Watched him watch me as he uncapped it and took a sip. I could feel the pace of my heartbeat pick up.

"She says she's working against that conference deadline and can't spare the time." He placed his beer bottle on the table. "She's living and breathing those ancestors of yours."

"Better her than me," I said. "All that moldy old stuff. Well, don't worry. We'll take good care of her while you're away."

He cocked his head. "That right? You figure she needs taking care of?"

It felt like something had just shifted gears—that we'd gone from two buddies having a couple of beers to something else, something vaguely hostile. Why was he smirking?

"No, check that," I said. "She's a grown woman, right?"

"Right."

I wanted out of there. Wanted to get away from that fucking smirk of his. "Well, I guess I'll get out of these teacher clothes. I'll look for that cat carrier. Thanks for the beers."

"Not a problem," he said.

In my bedroom, I changed into a sweatshirt and jeans. A few kisses, that was all it had been. By mutual agreement. Had she said something to him? Laughed about kissing the old fool landlord whose archives she was "living and breathing"? Kissing a guy who was old enough to be her father? . . . I thought about what Maureen had said: how that guard had smirked while she was "searching" her friend, Camille. That was when people smirked, wasn't it? When they had the upper hand?

When I reentered the kitchen a few minutes later, he was gone, thank God. I rinsed out the beer bottles, put them in the recycling tub by the door.

That folder Janis had left for me caught my eye. The note she'd paper-clipped to the front read, "Caelum—Found these today. Lydia is mentioned in a few of the articles but who are Ethel and Mary Agnes Dank? And what's with this sexist old beer ad? The Rheingold 'girls'?? Thank God feminism came along! Love, Janis."

Inside the folder were several old news clippings: "Sentence Woman for Immorality". . . "Local Woman Among Boston Fire Victims". . . "Girl, 17, Attempts Suicide Over Thwarted Love of Boy, 14". . .

When I looked from the clippings to the kitchen door, I nearly jumped out of my skin. Someone was standing there, looking in at me. I rose and started toward the door, recognizing who it was: Lolly's not-so-handy handyman. "Hey, Ulysses," I said. "What's up? Come on in."

He was nervous, shaky as hell. He was three weeks sober, he said. He'd gone back to AA and was working the steps. He needed to apologize.

For what? I asked.

For having betrayed my trust, he said—crashing here at the farmhouse when all I'd wanted him to do was check in every few days and feed Lolly's cat. He was sorry, too, that he'd tried to take on those teenage punks who'd been trespassing down at the apple house. He should have picked up the phone and called the cops. Let them handle it. "I was cocked and I wasn't thinking straight," he said.

Water under the bridge, I assured him. I was just glad those twerps hadn't hurt him. Why didn't he have a seat?

He nodded. "So how's Nancy doing?" As if on cue, Lolly's cat sauntered into the kitchen and sidled up to him. "Hey, here's my girl!" he said. She jumped onto his lap and nuzzled his chest, apparently as happy to see him as he was to see her.

"You want a cup of coffee?" I asked.

He glanced over at the empty beer bottles. "Nah, I'm all set. Thanks. You know something? You look like your dad. Anyone ever tell you that?"

I shook my head. It wasn't true. Lolly'd said plenty of times that I resembled my father, but I'd never seen it. Had never appreciated the comparison, either.

"Me and him were buddies growing up, you know. Grammar school, high school. Went down and enlisted right after graduation, the both of us."

I nodded. "And Jerry Martineau's dad, too," I said.

"That's right. Then the three of us got shipped over to Korea."

And came home screwed up, I thought. Mr. Martineau held it

together for years, then put a shotgun to his head. You and Daddy became lushes. What I *said* was, "Well, Ulysses, as far as your AA steps, consider yourself forgiven."

"Aw right," he said. "That's good of you. Your aunt was always good to me, too, you know. Always helped me out, no matter how bad I screwed up."

"She helped *me* out from time to time, too," I said.

He nodded, teared up a little. "That day I found her wandering out in the yard? When she had her stroke? Jesus, what a heartbreaker that was."

"I'm just grateful you came by and got her to the hospital," I said. And I *was* grateful to him, too, but he'd already gotten his forgiveness and he wasn't going to be offered a beer no matter how many times he glanced over at those empties. I stood, took a few steps toward the door. "So. Congrats on your sobriety. Keep up the good work, okay?"

"Yeah, okay," he said. He took the hint. Scooted Nancy Tucker off his lap and got up from his chair. I was just closing the door behind him when he stopped and turned back to face me. "Oh, Jesus Christ, I almost forgot. I wanted to ask you something. I was wondering if maybe you had any work for me to do around here. You wouldn't have to pay me much. Just a little something under the table to keep me in smokes, more or less."

Smokes and booze, I figured. "You know, Ulysses, money's pretty tight right now, to tell you the truth."

"Yeah, okay. No problem then. . . . But what I was thinking was maybe I could take down the apple house for you. Kinda dangerous leaving it half-collapsed like that. If those fuckin' kids come sneaking back and the rest of the roof falls down on them, they could sue your ass, right?"

I nodded. "But like I said, I just don't have a whole lot of capital right now. I'd help you out if I could, but . . ."

"Yeah, okay then. Don't worry about it. I was just thinking I could pull the boards down, stack 'em up, get the nails out. Builders pay good money for salvage, you know. And then, after the building was down, you probably wouldn't want a concrete slab just sitting there, so maybe I could take a sledgehammer to it, bust it up and wheelbar-row it the hell out of there for you. You wouldn't even know that fuckin' apple house had been there."

I shook my head. "But I tell you what. You stay on the straight and narrow and come see me next spring. April, let's say. First of April. Come back and see me then. And if you've stayed sober, and if my finances have improved a little, maybe we can work something out then. Okay?"

"Okay," he said. He thrust his hand out and we shook on the deal.

Watching him trudge up Bride Lake Road, I was reminded of that Sunday afternoon long ago, when I'd stood there watching my father retreat from the farmhouse, Grandpa Quirk's whiskey bottle in hand, after Daddy'd fought with Mother and broken Lydia's soup tureen in the scuffle. After he'd gone, Mother had sat there at this same kitchen table, flush-faced and defeated. Then she'd hugged me and accused me of not hugging her back.

I'd denied it, I remember, though it was true. "I *do* hug you back."

"No, you don't. You never do."

"I do, too."

I opened the folder of clippings Janis had left and read.

Three Rivers *Evening Record*,
October 13, 1935

SENTENCE WOMAN FOR IMMORALITY

Mrs. Adolph (Ethel) Dank, 28, formerly of 113 Green Street, this city, was sentenced to the State Farm for Women for a term of 90 days by Judge Micah J. Benson in town court today following her guilty plea to charges of lascivious carriage, intoxication, and breach of the peace. Mrs. Dank admitted to having no lodging place since leaving her home recently. She told the court that she and her husband are estranged.

Ethel Dank was taken into custody by Police Lieutenant David F. O'Connor early yesterday morning after she was found in the company of two navy sailors at the White Birch Motor Court on Rural Route 3. Lieut. O'Connor stated he responded to a complaint by motel officials that Mrs. Dank, clad only in her undergarments, was causing a disturbance by banging on the door of the sailors' rented room and pleading to be let back inside, apparently after an altercation. Lieut. O'Connor reported that, by the time he arrived to investigate, the defendant had been readmitted to the room and was subdued. She was bruised about the face, legs, and neck but refused treatment at William T. Curtis Memorial Hospital.

The servicemen involved in the incident told Lieut. O'Connor they had been on a spree following their return from a period of overseas duty and had met Mrs. Dank at the Silver Slipper, a local tavern. The defendant had been imbibing and dancing with both white and Negro clientele, according to the sailors.

Lieut. O'Connor said he did not bring charges against the two servicemen involved because Mrs. Dank had been soliciting male company and because he was satisfied the sailors were sufficiently ashamed of their actions. "I'm certain these young men have learned their lesson," the officer told Judge Benson.

Upon being sentenced to a six month term, Mrs. Dank pleaded for a lesser confinement, stating that her imprisonment would represent a hardship for her daughter, who is seven. Judge Benson told Mrs. Dank her actions demonstrated she was an unfit mother and the child was probably better served by her absence than by her presence. He then agreed to reduce her sentence by half, to 90 days, provided she leaves the area upon her release. In sentencing Ethel Dank, the judge charged her to use her time at the state farm to express remorse to her husband and others and to restore herself to womanly virtue. "The word 'penitentiary' derives from the word 'penitent,'" Judge Benson told Mrs. Dank. "I would advise you to contemplate that."

Three Rivers *Evening Record*,
December 23, 1935

STATE FARM FUGITIVE HELD FOR HIGH COURT

A young woman who escaped from the State Farm for Women at Three Rivers a few days ago, stealing articles from the institution and a nearby farmhouse, has been bound over from the Stonington Borough justice court to the superior court. Ethel Dank, 29, was apprehended by local police in a wooded area of Bride Lake Farm, which borders the state facility. She had been at large for about six hours before her capture.

Mrs. Dank was brought before the Stonington court on the complaint of Mrs. Lydia P. Quirk, superintendent of the State Farm for Women, who described the fugitive as being "a bad apple" who was the source of continuous trouble there. The value of the articles the police said Mrs. Dank admitted stealing was placed in excess of $50 by Superintendent Quirk. These items included articles of clothing, food, and toys from the institution's nursery. From the neighboring farm, the escapee stole a child's music box, a necklace, and a number of silver dollars. Bride Lake Farm is owned and operated by Superintendent Quirk and her son, Alden Quirk, Jr.

Mrs. Dank told police she escaped because she could not bear to be separated from her child during the Christmas season. She is the mother of a seven-year-old girl.

Pending arraignment at the next criminal session of the

superior court, Mrs. Dank was committed to the county jail
in default of bonds of $500 each.

And these had been the "good old days," right? I shook my head.
Whoever this Ethel Dank was, my guess was that her chief offense
had been "dancing with both white and Negro clientele." And that
she'd obviously taken the hit for those two unnamed sailors after
they'd brought her to that motel, liquored her up, and, most likely,
raped her. Blame the victim: probably business as usual back then.
Well, now, too, except not *this* blatant. In sentencing Ethel to six
months in the pokey—releasing her "to the custody of State Farm
Superintendent Lydia P. Quirk"—the judge had advised her to use
her time to "restore herself to womanly virtue." I had to smile at
that one. You'd swear that some of the women walking around over
at the jail these days were men. Shaved heads, bulked-up bodies.
Strutting like roosters in the hen house. . . .

Was the "nearby farmhouse" Ethel had broken into after her big
escape *this* place? Had she been "bad apple" enough to commit a b &
e at the home of the prison matron? Ballsy enough to sneak upstairs
and do some last-minute Christmas shopping for the daughter that the
judge had said would be better off without her? Big mistake, Ethel,
if you ripped off Superintendent Quirk, no matter how progressive
her practices were. Maureen had said more than once that prison was
hardest of all on the women who were separated from their kids. It
was a whole different era now, but I guess *that* hadn't changed.

Time Magazine, December 1, 1942

CATASTROPHE: BOSTON'S WORST

Holy Cross had just beaten Boston College. Downtown Boston was full of men and women eager to celebrate or console. Many of them wound up at Cocoanut Grove night club.

They stood crowded around the dimly lighted downstairs bar and filled the tables around the dance floor upstairs. With them mingled the usual Saturday night crowd: soldiers and sailors, a wedding party, a few boys being sent off to Army camps. Motion picture cowboy star Buck Jones was there with an entourage, too. Jones was in Boston on a combination war bond selling tour and promotional junket for Monogram Films, producers of *The Rough Riders*, a Western series.

At 10 o'clock Bridegroom John O'Neil, who had planned to take his bride to their new apartment at the stroke of the hour, lingered on a little longer. The floor show was about to start. Through the big revolving doors, couples moved in and out.

At the downstairs bar, a 16-year-old busboy stood on a bench to replace a light bulb that a prankish customer had removed. He lit a match. It touched one of the artificial palm trees that gave the Cocoanut Grove its atmosphere. A few flames shot up. A girl named Joyce Spector sauntered toward the checkroom because she was worried about her new fur coat.

Before Joyce Spector reached the cloakroom, the Cocoanut Grove was a screeching shambles. The fire quickly ate away the palm tree, raced along silk draperies, was sucked upstairs through the stairway, and leaped along ceiling and wall. The silk hangings, turned to balloons of flame, fell on tables and floor.

Men and women fought their way toward the revolving door; the push of bodies jammed it. Nearby was another door; it was locked tight. There were other exits, but few Cocoanut Grove patrons knew about them. The lights went out. There was nothing to see now except flames, smoke, and the weird moving torches that were men and women with clothing and hair afire.

The 800 Cocoanut Grove patrons pushed and shoved, fell and were trampled. Joyce Spector was knocked under a table, crawled on hands and knees, and somehow was pushed through an open doorway into the street. A chorus boy herded a dozen people downstairs into a refrigerator. A few men and women crawled out windows; a few escaped by knocking out a glass brick wall. But most of them, including Bridegroom John O'Neil and Motion Picture Star Buck Jones, were trapped.

Firemen who broke down the revolving door found it blocked by bodies of the dead, six deep. They tried to pull a man through a side window; his legs were held tight by the mass of struggling people behind him. In an hour, the fire was out and firemen began untangling the piles of bodies. One hard-bitten fireman went into hysterics when he picked up a body and a foot came off in his hand. They found a bartender still standing behind his bar, a girl dead in a telephone booth, a nickel clutched between her thumb and finger.

At hospitals and improvised morgues which turned into charnel houses for the night, 484 dead were counted. One Boston newspaper ran a two-word banner headline: BUS-BOY BLAMED, but the busboy had not put up the Cocoanut Grove's tinderbox decorations, nor was he responsible for the fact that Boston's laws do not require nightcubs to have fireproof fixtures, sprinkler systems, or exit markers.

Three Rivers *Evening Record,*
Tuesday, December 1, 1942

LOCAL WOMAN AMONG NIGHTCLUB FIRE VICTIMS

—

**Former Three Rivers Resident
Was Hollywood Actress in Buck Jones Entourage**

—

Husband, Daughter Identify Remains

—

**Jones Succumbs to Injuries,
Becomes 481st To Die**

Mrs. Ethel S. Dank, 35, formerly of Three Rivers and more recently of Van Nuys, California, has been identified as one of more than 480 victims who perished in Boston's Cocoanut Grove fire Saturday evening. Positive identification of Mrs. Dank's body was made late Sunday by her husband and daughter, Mr. Adolph P. Dank, 58, of 113 Green St., this city, and Miss Mary Agnes Dank, 14, of the Three Rivers County Home for Girls. Father and daughter were among hundreds of loved ones who stood for hours in long lines outside the Park Square garage on Sunday, awaiting their turn to view the dead. The garage, located across the street from the scene of the disastrous blaze at 17 Piedmont Street in the city's Back Bay section, had been emptied of automobiles and converted to a temporary morgue.

A 'House of Ghouls'

"There were rows and rows of bodies, hundreds of bodies," Adolph Dank said, describing the grim task of identification that awaited family members as they entered the garage. "You'd pass by each, shake your head, and move on. It was a house of ghouls." Many of the deceased were burned beyond recognition, except by a ring or necklace or other non-perishable item, according to Deputy Coroner John W. Troyer. Other victims, Troyer said, were untouched by the blaze, indicating that the cause of death was suffocation from smoke inhalation or ingestion of poisonous gas.

Victim Described as 'Sleeping Beauty'

Of the identification process, Mr. Dank reported, "People went about it quietly, but every few minutes, someone would cry out a name or shout 'Oh, my god!' or 'That's him! That's her!' Then they'd wail like the dickens." Mr. Dank said his wife's body was untouched by flame. He was told by a rescuer that she had been discovered slumped in a telephone booth near the Cocoanut Grove's coat check area in the front foyer, a nickel clutched between her fingers. "It looked like she was sleeping," Mr. Dank said of his late wife. "She was all dolled up. Fur stole, pretty dress. Sleeping Beauty—that's what came to my mind when I saw my Ethel." Mr. and Mrs. Dank had remained legally married but were estranged.

Victim Attended Buck Jones Party

Mary Agnes Dank, the victim's daughter, said she had spoken to her mother by telephone Saturday afternoon, hours before her death, and that Mrs. Dank had told her of her plans to attend a dinner party that evening at the popular Boston night club. Employed by Monogram Motion Pictures as a personal assistant to Francis "Buddy" Gifford, producer of Monogram's Rough Rider series of Western films, Mrs. Dank was part of an entourage of about two dozen guests attending a testimonial dinner honoring cowboy actor Charles (Buck) Jones, 52, a long-time favorite of American boy movie fans.

Jones Succumbs

Rescued by a Coast Guardsman and a taxi driver, both unidentified, Buck Jones survived the Saturday night blaze and was hospitalized at Massachusetts General Hospital. He died yesterday from smoke inhalation, burned lungs, and third and second degree burns on the face and neck. Jones' name was the 481st added to the death roll.

Appeared in Motion Pictures

Mary Agnes Dank said her mother was a Monogram Pictures secretary and actress, having appeared in two Rough Rider films under the stage name Dorinda DuMont. "She was friends with Joan Blondell and Constance Bennett," Miss Dank said. "She was going to be a big movie star."

Ethel (O'Nan) Dank was born in Cranston, Rhode Island in 1907, the daughter of the late Mr. and Mrs. Michael (Sioban) O'Nan. She wed Adolph Dank in Cranston in 1924. Funeral arrangements for Mrs. Dank are incomplete.

Sleeping Beauty, huh? Well, bad apple or not, Ethel had followed the judge's orders. Had left Three Rivers and hightailed it out to Hollywood. Become a secretary and a starlet and probably provided other "services" to the men of Monogram Pictures. Wasn't that how it worked out there? Well, whatever she had or hadn't done, the restoration of her "womanly virtues" had landed poor Ethel feet up at a makeshift morgue.

I recalled reading once or twice about that Coconut Grove fire— or *Cocoanut* Grove, as they apparently spelled it. Wasn't it after that horror show that they made illuminated exit signs mandatory?

For whatever reason these old newspaper articles had been stuck in there with Great-Grandma Lydia's old records, it was interesting stuff. Still, I told myself, if I were smart, I'd put them down and get started on my work.

Instead, I kept reading.

Three Rivers *Evening Record,*
Thursday, December 3, 1942

FIRE VICTIM LAID TO REST

—

Daughter, 14, Bids Emotional Farewell

Mrs. Ethel S. Dank, formerly of Three Rivers and later of Van Nuys, California, was laid to rest this morning at St. Eustace Cemetery, this city, following a Mass of Christian Burial at the Roman Catholic Church of Five Wounds. Mrs. Dank perished Friday in the tragic inferno at Boston's Cocoanut Grove night club, which has now claimed 486 lives. Monsignor Giacomo A. Guglielmo of the Diocese of Three Rivers officiated at the funeral Mass.

State, Town Dignitaries Pay Tribute
Mrs. Dank's graveside service was attended by more than

two hundred mourners, including The Honorable Arthur M. Tillinghast, Lieutenant Governor of Connecticut, Zachary M. Potter, Mayor of Three Rivers, and Mrs. Lydia P. Quirk, Superintendent of the State Prison Farm for Women. Ethel Dank was confined at the prison farm from 1935 to 1937, where she was "fully rehabilitated," according to Mrs. Quirk.

Lieutenant Governor Tillinghast brought words of condolence from Governor Robert A. Hurley. In eulogizing Mrs. Dank as "our beloved native daughter," Mayor Potter ordered that the flags at Three Rivers' schools and office buildings be flown at half-mast in her memory for the coming week. Mrs. Quirk spoke of the deceased as "a woman who had wandered down a wrong path in life" but who had then had "the strength and the wherewithal to turn back and travel a better road."

Victim's Daughter Overwrought

Superintendent Quirk's remarks were interrupted by Miss Mary Agnes Dank, 14, the victim's daughter. Addressing those gathered, Miss Dank said she wanted to honor her mother's memory with a special farewell gesture. She began singing "Life Is Just a Bowl of Cherries," which she identified as Ethel Dank's favorite song. Halfway through her musical tribute, however, Miss Dank became overwrought and could not finish. She then attempted an impromptu eulogy, describing Ethel Dank as "the greatest mother in this whole wide world." Miss Dank became angry as she spoke, telling mourners that when her mother had lived in Three Rivers, "people had no use for her, and after she left, she had no use for any of you." Adolph Dank, the victim's estranged husband, attempted without success to subdue his daughter. Miss Dank was removed from the premises by officials of the Three Rivers County Home for Girls, where she currently resides. Ethel Dank's service ended with a blessing by Monsignor Guglielmo and the singing of the hymn, "Lead Me, Lest I Stray."

Three Rivers *Evening Record,*
May 25, 1945

GIRL, 17, ATTEMPTS SUICIDE OVER THWARTED LOVE OF BOY, 14; SURVIVES, PAYS PEACE BREACH, CONTEMPT FINES

Miss Mary Agnes Dank, 17 year old daughter of Mr. Adolph Dank of 113 Green Street and the late Mrs. Dank, was fined $10 today in town court on a breach of peace charge stemming from an attempt to take her own life last Friday. An additional $10 was levied against Miss Dank for being in contempt of the court, the result of her verbal exchanges with Judge Joseph P. Wool.

In response to the thwarting of what police characterized as her youthful love affair with a boy of fourteen, Miss Dank attempted suicide by self-poisoning last Friday. She pleaded a demurrer to the peace breach charge, stating that she had become desperate when the boy's grandmother forbade the couple from seeing each other. Miss Dank argued to Judge Wool that she and the boy remained deeply in love and it was his grandmother, therefore, rather than she, who had disturbed the peace. Judge Wool overruled the demurrer.

Investigation by Patrolman Leo T. Jakes revealed that Miss Dank had on three occasions trespassed on the property of the boy's family, demanding to see him. On the last of these intrusions, she stated that unless the affair was resumed, she could not survive. When there was no resolution, she consumed a concoction of India ink and oil of wintergreen, which contains methyl salicylate, a poisonous agent.

Adolph Dank told police that when he returned home from work last Friday evening, he found his daughter in an agitated state, complaining of dizziness and ringing in the ears. Later, she became nauseous and appeared to be having trouble breathing. Questioned by her father, Miss Dank revealed that, upon her return from school that afternoon, she had drunk three ounces of the wintergreen mixed with an equivalent quantity of ink. She told her father that her action was the result of a suicide pact she had made with the boy she had been forbidden to see, and that he had pledged to end his life, too. When questioned later by Patrolman Jakes, the boy stated that Miss Dank had suggested the double suicide, but that he had not agreed to it.

Adolph Dank, an employee of the Three Rivers Bleaching Dyeing & Printing Company, sought to get a physician for his daughter but was unsuccessful. He then ran to the Curtis Memorial Hospital's School of Nursing, where an unidentified nurse advised him to administer milk as an antidote and to treat the girl's fever with sponge water baths. If that failed, he should send her to the hospital. After drinking the milk, Miss Dank rallied, her father said, but at about 8 o'clock that evening, she began to convulse and hallucinate. The police were notified and Patrolman Jakes was dispatched to the house. Officer Jakes reported that he gave Miss Dank more milk, but when she failed to rally a second time, he called for an ambulance. Miss Dank was admitted to Curtis Memorial shortly after midnight on Saturday and responded successfully to treatment.

In overruling Miss Dank's demurrer, Judge Wool advised her that a pretty young woman such as she had much to live for. He urged her to consider her father before committing further rash acts, to concentrate on her studies, and to socialize with youngsters her own age. Appearing before the court without counsel, Miss Dank was defiant in the face of Judge Wool's advice. She informed the judge that her deceased mother had served as housekeeper for his wife's family and reminded him that he, Judge Wool, was married to a woman fifteen years his junior. Miss Dank also questioned what "a white-haired man in a black robe" knew about true love. Judge Wool chastised the girl for her flippancy and fined her an additional $10, citing her contempt of the court.

In a related matter, Judge Wool issued a restraining order

which forbids Miss Dank from trespassing at the home of her former beau or from having written or verbal contact with him at the Three Rivers High School, which both attend. She must maintain a distance of twenty-five feet from the boy at all times. So that there would be no question about what was expected of Miss Dank, Judge Wool instructed Bailiff Harold Timmons and Adolph Dank, who had accompanied his daughter to court, to demonstrate the distance of 25 feet with the aid of a tape measure. Miss Dank appeared not to look at the measured distance between the two men. She exited the courtroom before being dismissed.

Mr. Dank addressed the court, apologizing for his daughter's behavior. He stated that she had always been a headstrong girl and that she had had a particularly difficult time since her mother's death three years earlier. Judge Wool responded that many young people faced hardships in life without resorting to extreme behavior. The judge wished the girl's father good luck and said he hoped never to see Miss Dank in his courtroom again.

Tough little cookie, she must have been, I thought. Survives her suicide cocktail, and when she gets hauled into court, she gives the judge some shit. . . . Who had saved these clippings? And why? Damned if I knew. And damned if I hadn't better shove them aside and get to that Joseph Campbell essay I'd assigned them for our next class. I went to my desk, grabbed a highlighter and my copy of *The Hero with a Thousand Faces*, and headed back to the kitchen table.

This first stage of the mythological journey—which we have designated the "call to adventure"—signifies that destiny has summoned the hero and transferred his spiritual center of gravity from within the pale of his society to a zone unknown. . . . The hero can go forth of his own volition to accomplish the adventure, as did Theseus when he arrived in his father's city, Athens, and heard the horrible history of the Minotaur; or he may be carried or sent abroad by some benign or malignant agent, as was Odysseus, driven about the Mediterranean by the winds of the angered god, Poseidon. . . .

Hoo boy, I thought. I could hear their bellyaching already. And why not? Campbell was tough going. Sometimes I felt like throttling that speed-freak professor whose syllabus I'd inherited. I knew one thing: if I taught this class next semester—and I had *better* teach it after the sweat equity I'd been putting in—I was going to revamp the book list. But until then . . .

A blunder—apparently the merest chance—reveals an unsuspected world, and the individual is drawn into a relationship with forces that are not rightly understood. As Freud has shown, blunders are not the merest chance. They are the result of suppressed desires and conflicts. They are ripples on the surface of life, produced by unsuspected springs. And these may be very deep—as deep as the soul itself.

It reminded me of what Janis had said that day up in Hartford: how Great-Grandma Lydia's diaries and Lizzy Popper's letters were "unsuspected springs" that had bubbled up to the surface. That those words from my ancestors were speaking to me.

My eyes wandered from the Campbell text to the folder of newspaper clippings at the other end of the table. Stay focused, I advised myself. Get the essay read and underlined. I picked up the folder and tried tossing it onto the counter, but I didn't quite make it. The contents spilled onto the floor. And when I stooped to pick them up, I saw the magazine ad that was in there, too.

"It's time to elect Miss Rheingold 1950! Your vote may decide!" Beneath the banner headline were photos of six pretty, girl-next-door types from that bygone era: short bangs, identical outfits, red lipstick smiles. And beneath their pictures, more verbiage. "So pick your favorite Rheingold Girl and vote for her in the U.S.A.'s second largest election! And while you're at your neighborhood store or tavern, why not try some thirst-quenching Rheingold Extra Dry? You'll join the millions who say, 'My beer is Rheingold, the dry beer!'"

I looked again at those six young women. Must be what? In their seventies by now? The most striking, a blue-eyed brunette, smiled back at me. "Jinx Dixon," the name beneath the picture said. She looked familiar somehow—unsettlingly so. Where had I seen that smile? . . .

> *This first stage of the mythological journey—which we have designated the "call to adventure"—signifies that destiny has summoned the hero and transferred his spiritual center of gravity from within the pale of his society to a zone unknown. . . .*

I stopped, stared again at Jinx Dixon. That was when it clobbered me: she was clearly, unmistakably, my vagrant father's vagrant girlfriend. The kerchiefed woman who had smiled at me so unnervingly whenever I met them at the corn maze with their stolen food. The woman who had freaked out Mother when she showed up at Daddy's wake.

I sat there, sifting again through those yellowed articles, looking back at that old ad. I couldn't put the pieces together. . . . But maybe someone else could. I closed *The Hero with a Thousand Faces* and grabbed my car keys.

He'd gotten maybe a mile and a half up the road. "You know, you're right," I said. "It *is* dangerous leaving the apple house like that. Someone *could* get hurt. I'll figure out a way to pay you. Why don't you come by Monday afternoon and get started?"

He nodded. We shook on it. I did a U-turn and headed back to the house. Truth was, that dilapidated old building was the least of my worries. But if Ulysses had known my father all those years ago, then maybe he'd known this Jinx Dixon, too. Whoever she was, and for whatever reason her picture was in that folder, I was going to get to the bottom of it.

Later that evening, Janis came downstairs to heat up some soup for herself and Moze. "So I solved the mystery," she said.

"Did you?" I said. "What mystery's that?"

"Who those women in the clippings were. God, how weird is that, huh? Your maternal grandmother does time at a prison run by your paternal great-grandmother."

I gave her a look. "What are you talking about?"

"Ethel Dank. The woman who died in the nightclub fire. She was Mary Agnes's mother."

"Yeah?" I said. "So?"

"So she was your mother's mother."

I shook my head. "My mother's mother was Moira Sullivan."

Janis looked confused. "Wait a minute," she said.

When she came back downstairs, she handed me a bent-up eight-by-ten envelope. "I found this later today, after I found those clippings. It had fallen behind the bottom drawer of the file cabinet, and when I went to close it, I heard something crinkling. So I wedged my hand down there and fished it out. You probably need this, right?"

I opened it and pulled out a birth certificate. *My* birth certificate, it looked like, except something was screwy. It had my name, my birthday. It listed my father as Alden J. Quirk Jr., my town of birth as Three Rivers, Connecticut. But they'd gotten my mother's name wrong. Instead of Rosemary Sullivan Quirk, they'd listed her as Mary Agnes Dank.

I didn't say much. I couldn't. Couldn't fathom what was in front of me. But after Janis went back upstairs, I opened our strongbox and took out my birth certificate. Back in the kitchen, I put it on the table next to the birth certificate Janis had found. I killed the rest of Moze's six-pack looking back and forth between the two: the one that bore the impression made by the official Town of Three Rivers seal and the one that didn't. I kept touching those raised letters. Kept touching her name: Mary Agnes Dank.

chapter twenty-five

ON MONDAY, OUT AT THE apple house, Ulysses verified what by then I had pretty much figured out: "Jinx Dixon" was Mary Agnes Dank. "He was nuts about her, your dad, and she was just plain nuts. In and out of the bughouse. Beautiful girl, though. Your family tried their damnedest to keep the two of them away from each other, but it never did no good. She and the old lady locked horns more than once, I remember."

"The old lady?"

"Alden's grandmother—the one who ran the prison. Guess in her line of work, she knew a troublemaker when she seen one. Your father'd swear off her for a while. Then the next thing you know, they'd be back at it. It was like she had him under a spell or something. But yeah, the family couldn't stop it. Maybe if they hadn't pushed so hard, it would've run its course. But Mary Agnes was as bullheaded as she was beautiful. Had a chip on her shoulder, too. I remember that about her. Probably told herself she'd be goddamned if she was gonna let Alden's family push her around."

I asked him if he knew what had happened to her.

"Died young, same as he did. I want to say a month or two later, but I could be wrong. My memory's kinda fuzzy these days. All the booze, I guess."

IN CLASS ON TUESDAY, I passed out a quiz on the Campbell essay that was so difficult, all but three of them flunked it. Well, tough, I told myself. If they can't do college-level work, then they shouldn't be in college. Screw 'em.

Driving to and from Oceanside that week, I honked my horn at any asshole whose driving got in my way. At the bank to deposit the Micks' rent check, I went off on a teller who'd infuriated me by waiting first on a customer who'd come in after me. Back home again, when Velvet hit me up for a ride over to Target, I didn't just say no. I said I thought it was kind of pathetic that someone in her twenties still had to bum rides off of other people. That someone her age should have her own car. Run her own errands.

"What's *your* problem?" she'd shot back.

"Oh, I got a bunch of them," I said. "You, for one."

Slouching away, she said it under her breath. "Jerk."

Hey, I *was* being a jerk. And I felt completely justified in being one. I'd finally figured out *why* I'd never been able to hug my mother: because she'd been a fucking fraud. If my brain hadn't known that when I was a kid, I guess maybe my body had. My disengaged muscles.

Every night that week, I'd lie in bed, stewing and sputtering instead of sleeping: about my father's fatal attraction, about the battle between Mary Agnes and the Quirks. My mother had fought back with the only two weapons available to her: her looks and her defiance. I was furious on her behalf, and on my own. And when sleep refused to come, I'd climb out of bed, slip my clothes on, and walk down the road—by moonlight one night, by the first weak light of morning another couple. I'd walk the field where the maze had been, where my mother had emerged, smiling hungrily at me but never speaking. And now, forty-something years after the fact, I kept squinting into the tree line as if—like that ghost bride the inmates used to claim they saw walking along the lake shore—Mary Agnes might appear. Walk into the clearing toward me and reach out. Hold me. Hug me and let me hug her. They had had no right to keep us from each other. No fucking right at all.

I stayed away from the prison that week.

I walked and walked that field.

I drank.

By Friday, the apple house was nothing more than stacks of lumber, a pile of roof shingles, and a concrete slab exposed to the sun. "I'll come by next week and start busting up that cement for you," Ulysses said.

I nodded, opened my wallet, and gave him two twenties and a ten. "You remember anything else about Mary Agnes?"

I had asked him that same question all week. This time his answer was different. "Come to me this morning," he said. "Something that happened when you were just a little fella. She took you."

"Took me? What do you mean?"

"Grabbed you. Kidnapped you. It was over quick, I think. That same day or the next, maybe. I don't remember the particulars."

I stood there, shaking my head. My mind reeled. "How old was I?"

"Just a little fella, like I said. Two or three maybe. But my memory—"

"Did they arrest her?"

Ulysses shook his head. "Never pinned it on her. See, she had moved away by then—went down to New York and become a model, I think it was, and your dad had married the other one on the rebound. But then later—maybe five, six years after it happened—Alden and me were down at the VFW, getting soused together on twenty-five-cent beers. That's when he told me."

"Told you what?" I said.

"That it was Mary Agnes who come out here and took you that time. Her and some guy she'd hooked up with who had a car."

"What do you mean 'came out here'? To the farm?"

"Yeah. Drove out here and snatched you right in the yard. In broad daylight, I'm pretty sure. Her and that guy. She never had trouble attracting the fellas, you know? But it was always your dad she come back to, even after he'd moved on, married the other one. She kept showing up like a bad penny."

"Why did she take me?" I said. "For money?"

He shrugged. "Maybe she just wanted to see you for a little while. Have a visit with you. She dropped you off someplace, I think. At a store or something. But don't trust my memory. I probably killed off more brain cells than I got left."

――――――――――

"WE'RE CLOSING IN FORTY MINUTES," Tillie, the keeper of the *Daily Record*'s "graveyard," told me. "It'll probably take you a while to find what you're looking for, especially if you don't have the specific dates. Nothing's indexed. Why don't you come back earlier in the day on Monday?"

"Please," I said. "I just need to . . . If I could just . . ."

She must have realized I was fighting back tears, because she put aside her resistance. Took a key from her drawer and stood up. "This way," she said.

The old newspapers were bound in dusty, oversized books with hard covers: Jan-Mar 1950, Nov-Dec 1951. By luck, I found what I was looking for almost immediately in the book labeled July-Aug 1954.

CHILD'S ABDUCTION ENDS HAPPILY; PARENTS RELIEVED, GRATEFUL

What Mrs. Rosemary Quirk of 418 Bride Lake Road, this city, called "the most frightening day of my life" ended happily last evening for her and her husband, Alden Quirk, Jr., when the couple's son Caelum, age 3, was found alone and unharmed at the Frosty Ranch, the popular ice cream emporium at the juncture of Routes 2 and 165. The boy had been abducted that morning from the family's home.

The kidnapper or kidnappers remain at large. Town and state police are on the lookout for a 1947 or 1948 green Hudson Commodore with whitewall tires, the vehicle they believe may have been used in the snatching.

"It all happened so quickly," Mrs. Quirk said of the abduction of her little boy. "I was outside hanging laundry on the clothesline and he was running back and forth between the sheets playing peekaboo. The phone rang and I went in to answer it. When I got back outside a few minutes later, he was gone." Mrs. Quirk's husband was away in Rhode Island at the time, attending a livestock auction with his father, Alden Quirk, Sr. The Quirk family owns and operates Bride Lake Dairy Farm.

Mrs. Quirk said she initially thought young Caelum had wandered down to the nearby cow barn where his aunt, Miss Louella ("Lolly") Quirk, of the same address, was working. Miss Quirk informed her sister-in-law that she had seen a green Hudson head up the driveway toward the family farmhouse and then, a moment later, drive away at a high rate of speed. "I had a feeling something fishy was going on, but I sure didn't think anyone was kidnapping Li'l Bit," Miss Quirk said. She tried to get a look at the license plate but was unable. "Whoever was at the wheel was driving like a bat out of h–," she noted. Miss Quirk said there may have been a person in the passenger's seat but she could not be certain.

The kidnapping occurred at approximately ten a.m. yesterday. The Three Rivers Police Department was promptly notified and a search was begun under the direction of Detective Francis X. Archambault. By mid-afternoon, the search for the boy had widened to three surrounding counties. The Bride Lake State Farm for Women, which lies adjacent to the Quirk farm, was also searched. Prison authorities ascertained that each woman under their supervision was present and accounted for and that none had witnessed the abduction.

Little Caelum was discovered seated alone atop a picnic table outside the Frosty Ranch Creamery shortly after eight p.m. by Miss Josephine Lenkiewicz, a Frosty Ranch patron. Miss Lenkiewicz said she had heard about the boy's abduction on the radio earlier in the day and had remembered the description of the tyke's clothing, a Hopalong Cassidy polo shirt, blue dungarees, and Buster Brown shoes. "I had to look twice because whoever took him must have bought him a chocolate cone, and Hopalong was sort of hiding beneath the stains," Miss Lenkiewicz said. "Luckily, I remembered his name. When I said it, he looked right up so I knew it was him."

The boy appeared calm when approached by police minutes later. "He had a mayonnaise jar in his lap with a praying mantis inside, and he was more interested in that bug than he was in us," Officer Felix Delmore noted. "Someone had poked air holes in the top for him, probably the kidnapper." Detective Archambault said later that the boy did not appear to have been harmed or mistreated.

The abduction was unusual in that it had occurred at the victim's home, Detective Archambault noted. "A kidnapper will usually make a grab at a grocery store or a country fair, some public place like that where he can disappear into a crowd with the victim and make a getaway. This was different. This was pretty brazen."

Mr. and Mrs. Quirk said they were not contacted by note or telephone about a ransom. Yet money may have been the motive, Detective Archambault said. "Whoever took him may not have had time to communicate his demands, or he may have lost his nerve and decided it wasn't worth it," he said. The investigation is continuing.

Little Caelum's parents arrived at the Frosty Ranch a short time after he was identified and were reunited with their son. "My prayers were answered," his mother said. The Quirk family wishes to extend their gratitude to the

Three Rivers Police Department and the Connecticut State Police. To reward Miss Lenkiewicz for her keen eye and quick thinking, the family will provide her with a dozen eggs and two quarts of milk each week for a year.

Anyone who may have information about the abduction is asked to contact Detective Francis X. Archambault of the Three Rivers Police Department at Turner 7–1002.

"Sir?" Tillie said. "Five more minutes. Okay?"

"Okay," I said. "I just need to find one more thing."

Ulysses had said he thought she died shortly after my father. Daddy'd been killed in May of 1965. I pulled two books from the shelf: May-Jun '65 July-Aug '65, Sept-Oct '65. I found what I was looking for in the latter book.

STATE FARM PRISONER DROWNS; SUICIDE SUSPECTED

The body of State Farm for Women inmate Mary Agnes Dank, 36, was recovered on Monday from Bride Lake, a body of water located within the confines of the prison compound. The victim, missing since Saturday, was reported to have been distraught in recent days.

Coroner Asa T. Pelto, who has examined the body, has concluded that Miss Dank died from drowning, most likely at her own hand. There were no signs of foul play, he said.

Miss Dank, a Three Rivers native, had been serving a six-month sentence for vagrancy, disturbance of the peace, and the assault of a law officer. She had once worked as a fashion model, registered with the prestigious John Robert Powers Agency of New York City, but more recently had fallen on hard times.

BACK HOME, I CLIMBED THE stairs to the attic. There, on the floor next to a box labeled "Xmas Decorations," was the cat caddy Moses had asked about. And there, leaning diagonally against the south wall, was the wooden sign that had hung first in my great-grandmother's office over at the prison and later on on the wall above Lolly and Hennie's bed. I'd taken it down and exiled it when the Micks moved in. Atop Grandpa Quirk's bureau with its missing drawer, in a cardboard box, was *The Absent Boy*, the book I'd written in my early thirties and had almost gotten published. I lifted the manuscript out of the box and flipped through the yellowing typewritten pages. How could I have written an entire novel about the kidnapping of a little boy when I had no recollection whatsoever of my own abduction by the mother who had been denied me?

I dropped my book back into the box. Walked over to Great Grandma's sign and cocked my head to read the words her husband-to-be had burned into the wood the year Bride Lake Prison had opened. I spoke Lydia's manifesto aloud: "A woman who surrenders her freedom need not surrender her dignity." Well, my mother had had to surrender hers; the Quirks had made sure of that. First, they'd made my father inaccessible to her. Then they'd separated her from me. Then they'd imprisoned her. A woman who surrenders her freedom need not surrender her dignity. No? Then what was so dignified about having your water-bloated body pulled out the lake and hauled off to the coroner's?

She'd never had a chance against them, and neither had her mother. The Quirks versus the Danks had been an unfair fight from the beginning. And so, I lifted my foot and brought it down hard against Lydia's sign. Broke it in two. Grabbed the cat caddy and went back downstairs.

The following week, while Moses was away, I bought two bottles of red wine, invited Janis down for dinner, and got us both drunk. Got to talking about how hard it was to be married to Maureen. Got

Janis talking about all the ways Moze didn't understand or appreciate her. All those times we'd gone running, that day up in Hartford:
I'd wanted so badly to take her to bed and make love to her. But that
wasn't what I did that night. I just got her drunk and fucked her.
Pulled out just before I got there and spilled my stuff—my Quirk-
Dank DNA—into the rucked-up sheets. There'd been nothing
loving about it, and my despair overtook me before I'd even gone
limp again.

I rolled over and gave her my back.

"Caelum?" she said. "Are you all right?"

I didn't answer her.

Didn't speak a word when, to my relief, she slipped her clothes on
and went back upstairs. Alone again, I lay there, thinking to myself
that maybe I should track down Paul Hay and call him up. Tell him
I'd joined the brotherhood: guys who fucked other guys' wives.
What had they called it in anger management class? The cardiology,
neurology, and endocrinology of rage? Well, I was enraged all right.
I was fucking *furious*. They had goddamned lied to me, all of them:
my grandfather, my no-good father, the mother who hadn't been my
mother. Even Lolly, the person I trusted the most out of all of them.
They'd gone so far as to make up a bogus birth certificate. Who had
done that? Which one of those fucking liars? . . .

She had had to kidnap me to spend a day with me. . . .

Somewhere around three in the morning, I got up and got dressed.
Walked down the driveway and headed up the road toward that
empty field again, to the place where she once had been. Where she
wasn't.

→→ chapter twenty-six ←←

Transcript of an interview with Sheldon "Peppy" Schissel
Recorded at the Inn Between, Astoria, New York
February 18, 2007

Would you like something to eat before we start, Mr. Schissel?

Sure. How about a shrimp cocktail, a porterhouse steak, and some cherries jubilee for dessert?

Uh. . .

Nah, I'm just kidding you, Jake. You eat a steak at this joint, you'd probably get mad-cow disease. Maybe we should have a little something to wet the whistle, though. And by the way, you keep calling me "Mr. Schissel," I'll have to go home, put on a necktie. My friends call me Peppy.

Peppy it is then. What are you drinking?

Chivas and milk.

Excuse me?

Chivas and milk. I got a bum gut, but I can get away with a nip here and there, long as I keep it coated. Just don't tell my daughter, will you? The Enforcer, I call her. Worse than her mother was. So what do I do now? Pick up this little microphone, and talk into it?

No, it's recording already. Just speak in your regular tone of voice, and it should pick you up fine from the table here. Let me just get you your drink.

Sit down, sit down. What are you having, Jake?

Just coffee, I guess. My name's Caelum, by the way.

Gonna make me drink alone, eh? Well, let's see if we can wake the barkeep up from his siesta over there. Hey, Jake! Yoo hoo! We'll take a Chivas and milk, rocks, and a cup of coffee. You got any half 'n' half back there? . . . Atta boy. Chivas and half 'n' half then. And a coffee. . . . Did I already tell him the coffee?

Uh, yeah. Yup.

Memory's a funny thing. Ask me what I had for breakfast today and I couldn't tell you. But I can still name all the families lived on our street in the Bronx when I was a kid. Can still recite the ditties we learned in school. You ever hear this one?

Starkle starkle, little twink
Who the hell you are you think?
I'm not under the alfluence of inkahol
Although some thinkle peep I am.

You learned that in school?

Yeah, school o' hard knocks. So, Shirley Nussbaum said you wanted to talk about my career at Rheingold?

Right—particularly your connection with the Miss Rheingold beauty contest. Mrs. Nussbaum said you used to chauffeur the contestants?

That's right. I drove the Rheingold girls, not to mention quite a few of the Mets when they were a new team—Gil Hodges, Bobby Klaus, those guys. Drove Nat King Cole and Lionel Hampton around one summer, too, when the brewery was cozying up to the Harlem market. Nice guys, they were—first-class gentlemen. Hey, you know how Shirley tracked me down, don't you? Through the hoozy-whatsis.

The Internet.

Right. That and a matchbook cover. See, Shirley and I were in Public Relations together, and we were pretty good friends. No hanky-panky or anything, just, you know, office pals. So when my daughter Rochelle got married in 1966, we invited Shirley to the wedding and she kept the matchbook. Collects matchbooks, I guess. So that's how she found me. Put my daughter's married name—which is Skolnick—into her computer and got her number. And guess who answers the phone when she calls? Me! Because I'm living with Rochelle now, since my wife passed on. "Who?" I said. "Shirley *Nussbaum*? You gotta be kidding me." Hadn't talked to her in . . . well, let's see. Pepsi Cola bought out Rheingold in '73, and they shut us down for good in '76. We all saw the writing on the wall, of course, but you know what the bastards did? Halted production right in the middle of a work-day. Didn't even bottle what we had in storage; they just dumped 100,000 gallons of good beer into the East River. Some of us old-timers stood there watching, holding our notices and crying like babies. . . . Well, life goes on, right? So what's the story now, Jake? You writing a book?

Uh . . . just researching for now.

That right? What are you researching?

Well . . . the old breweries. Their, uh . . . their marketing.

Business book, then. Well, if you want to know about my career at Rheingold, I guess I better begin at the beginning. I was twenty years old when I started there. Now this was war-time, see? Nineteen forty-two. I had tried to enlist, but they wouldn't take me on account of my flat feet and something else I didn't even know I had: an inguinal hernia. That thing gave me trouble later on, but that's a different story.

Actually, the time period I'm interested in is—

The Brooklyn plant, this was. The *main* plant. I'd been moping around for a while, kind of lost because most of my buddies had enlisted. But I had this cousin worked for Rheingold, see? My cousin Hyman. And he was always saying how Weismann Breweries treated their workers right. Sponsored a bowling league, a summer picnic, gave out turkeys at Thanksgiving, that kind of thing. It was a family-owned operation back then, see? The Weismann family. German Jews, they were. But anyway, I guess I better back up a little and tell you about the Weismanns, because anyone reading a business book's gonna want to know how a family starts from scratch over in Germany and ends up with the top-selling beer in New York. So tell me something. You writers are smart guys. What was happening back in 1864?

Well, like I said, the time period I'm looking at is—

See, you struck pay dirt with me, Jake, because I'm not only a thirty-four year employee of Weismann Breweries. I'm also a student of history. I read it, think about it, connect the dots between this thing and that thing. You ask my daughter what's the two things I watch on television, and it's either *Law & Order* or the History Channel. When I can get her away from the shopping channel, that is. All day long, those yentas with their junk jewelry, Joan Rivers and her face cream. Funny gal, but those plastic surgeons have stretched her face tighter than a sheet of Glad Wrap over a bowl of leftovers. Don't look natural, in my opinion. Okay, so answer my question. What was happening in 1864?

Uh, well . . . the Civil War.

That's right. Can't argue with that. But listen, Jake. It's a big world out there. The North and the South may be going at it on *this* side of the ocean, but over in London, Karl Marx is writing *Das Kapital*, and to the east, in Bavaria—where the Weismann family's from—they've just crowned a new king. King Ludwig

II, his name was—eighteen years old. His old man kicks the bucket and *boom*! They stick the crown on his head and hand him the scepter. See, Germany's not united at that point in time; it's all these different states: Prussia, Bavaria, etcetera, etcetera. So, Ludwig's the new king of Bavaria. Now you tell me what kooky teenager, past or present, is gonna be fit to run a country?

I'm afraid I'm not making the jump here.

Then *listen*, already. Okay, so Ludwig's a young, good-looking kid—very popular with the people, like what's his name, over there in England, Princess Diane's son. The Swan King, they nickname Ludwig. The Fairy Tale King. There's only one problem: poor kid doesn't want the job. And he stinks at it. The politics are way over his head, he's scared to death of the public. The only thing he's really interested in is opera, see? You much of an opera buff, Jake?

Me? No, I'm not.

Well, Ludwig's a goner for it, and you know who his favorite composer is? That no-good, Jew-hating son of a bitch Wagner, that's who. Ludwig idolizes the guy. Knows his operas, memorizes the librettos. So one day he says to himself, "Hey, I'm the king, right? If I want to meet the maestro, I can summon him here." So that's what he does: has his ministers track down Wagner and bring him to the palace.

But Mr. Schissel? Peppy?

And the two of them hit it off: the teenage king and his musical hero. And the kid starts making promises: he's gonna build Wagner a big festival theater in Munich, finance productions of his four *Ring of the Nibelung* operas. They figure they'll start with the first one in the series, *Das Rheingold*. You know the *Das Rheingold* story, Jake? The golden treasure hidden at the bottom of the Rhine River, guarded by the beautyful Rhinemaidens? Then the dwarf steals it and the brave hero, Siegfried, has to steal it back?

Not ringing a bell, Peppy.

No? One of the most famous legends in Germany! Well, anyway, Ludwig and Wagner talk into the night, and they get so hepped up about their big plans for *Das Rheingold* that they decide to take a moonlight ride out in the country. They wake up the carriage driver, and two or three of the royal ass-kissers, and the party takes off. Only it starts snowing, see? It's the middle of the night by now. So they pull up to this little roadside guesthouse. Zum Stern, it's called—nice little family inn where they make their own beer. And who do you think owns the place?

Couldn't tell you.

The Weismanns!

Ah, the family that—

That's right! Now, at this point in time, you're maybe saying to yourself, "Gee, you ask Peppy for the time of day and he tells you the history of the cuckoo clock." But let me ask you something, Jake. When a contractor builds an apartment house, what's he start with? The fifth floor or the foundation?

Okay. So—

So start writing some of this stuff down already.

Well . . . the tape recorder's on.

Oy! You see that—what I mean about memory? The gizmo's sitting here, staring me right in the face! Okay, so there's a bang, bang on the door at Zum Stern, and the Weismanns' son, Otto, gets up and answers it. Tells them they're closed for the night. Then the others step aside and who's standing there, wearing his fancy frock cloak and fur hat?

King Ludwig.

Right. It's a moment in history, see? The king and the commoner, probably about the same age, standing face to face. So Otto swings the door open and lets them in—the king, the composer, the royal *tukhes lechers*. Couple minutes later, the whole family hustles down and goes to work: start cooking up a feast and pouring the *Weismannbrau*. . . . Now, by the time the sun comes up, the bellies are full and the snow's stopped and the whole world is beautyful white. The maestro, who's half in the bag, tells everyone to grab a farewell glass of beer and follow him outside for a toast, and so they do: the king and his lackeys, the Weismanns, and I don't know who else. And word's leaked out by now, see? So there's a little crowd out there— everyone waiting to get a peek at the Fairy Tale King and the big shot composer. Wagner raises his glass. "To Ludwig, Bavaria's very own Siegfried!" he shouts. Now, you remember who Siegfried is?

He's, uh . . . the character in *Das Rheingold*.

Not just the character, Jake—the *hero*. So, it's quite a compliment, see? "May King Ludwig forever rule in the light!" Wagner says. And everyone drinks up. Then Ludwig—who's probably as soused and happy as he's ever been—*he* steps forward and makes his own toast. "To Bavaria!" he says. "To Bavaria!" everyone answers. And just then, Ludwig happens to notice the way the sun's caught his glass of beer. He looks at its golden color, twists the glass back and forth, then says, "To the best beer in all of Bavaria—the Weismanns' *Rhein gold*." You get it, Jake? The Rhine river, the golden treasure hidden on the bottom? "To the Weismanns' Rhein gold!" the crowd shouts. And with that, the king and his party chug-a-lug their beers and take off. Now, Mr. Business Book Writer, what do you think happens next?

Well, the Weismanns have just gotten a pretty big celebrity endorsement. So I'd say they probably cash in.

Correct! Word spreads about the king's visit, and now everyone wants to stop at the inn where the Fairy Tale King stopped to taste "Rheingold," the best beer in all of Bavaria. From then on, the Weismanns are in business. And speaking of business, I have to take care of a little myself. Excuse me a minute, Jake. Hey, barkeep! Where's the men's room? And where's our cocktail and our coffee?

Yeah, give me another minute, Pops. I'm just finishing up my inventory.

What? Your inventory's more important than your paying customers? *Oy!*

———————

So, Peppy, that was quite a story. Where'd you hear it?

Hear it? Who heard it? I *read* it, before you came to pick me up. *Re*read it, I should say. When you said you wanted to learn about Rheingold, I dug around in my old stuff, found the book the company came out with on their seventy-fifth anniversary. *The History of Rheingold Beer*, it's called. A lot of employees, when they got that memorial book, probably tossed it out, but not me. Because, like I said, I'm a student of history. I got it back at my daughter's if you want to take a look at it.

No, that's okay. Now, if we can switch gears to when you were involved with the Miss Rheingold contest—

Not so fast, Jake. There's more. See, when Ludwig walked through the door at Zum Stern that night, politics walked in with him, and the Weismanns' business got hitched to the king's fortune. Which didn't turn out so good after all. As king, the kid was a disaster! He pulled temper tantrums with his ministers, hit the servants, hid behind the potted plants at state functions. He was engaged to an Austrian princess for a while, but her family broke it off. Don't ask, don't tell, right?

You read all this in *The History of Rheingold Beer*?

No, no, this I got from another book, *Roots of the Third Reich*. I connect the dots, see? That's what us history buffs do. Then this crazy Ludwig starts raiding the royal treasury for his two cockamamie obsessions. One of them's opera, like I already told you about. The other is castle-building. See, he commissions these expensive, full-scale Wagnerian operas—costumes, sets, the best singers and musicians in Bavaria—but nobody can see them except him. Says when there's an audience, everyone stares at him with their opera glasses and it ruins it for him. Worse than that are the castles—these medieval replicas he has built all over Bavaria, and when they're done, they just sit there, empty. And Ludwig's goofy make-believe is breaking the bank. He was like what's-his-name—that *shmekel* with all the plastic surgery.

Joan Rivers?

No, no. The goofy one with the one glove. The singer.

Michael Jackson?

Right. So no one's too happy about the way things are going. Now, the Prussians are watching all this, see? Circling Bavaria like vultures. Bismarck's already got the other German states to sign on to his North German Alliance, but Bavaria's the biggest prize and the only holdout. So Bismarck comes up with a plan. He goes to Ludwig's old buddy, that son of a bitch Wagner. Wagner's all for a big German Empire, see? So he pays a little visit to the kooky king, and by the time he leaves, he's got a letter for Bismarck that says Ludwig's joining the Empire and is gonna transfer power to the Prussian Kaiser. Now when the loyalists find out their king's signed away their Bavarian sovereignty, the wind shifts for the Weismanns. The famous inn where Kingy Boy stopped on that snowy night becomes a target, see? They take the torch to Zum Stern, burn the place down to the ground!

No kidding.

I kid you not! Now, it ended bad for Ludwig. They declare the royal *schlemiel* insane and jail him inside one of his fancy castles. Put him in the care of the doctors of the Munich Asylum. Then one night, Ludwig and his head shrinker go for a walk by the lake and guess what? They find them both the next morning, floating facedown in the water. Was it murder? Suicide? No one knows. But, of course, everyone knows what happened once Bismarck unified Germany. What *that* led to. . . . Give me a minute, will you?

Here. Take a napkin. . . .

But, Mr. Business Book, a king can fall and a commoner can rise! Because after Zum Stern burned down? Otto Weismann didn't sit around, crying in his beer. He booked passage and came to the U.S. of A. Started all over again, with just his brewing recipes and his business smarts. And in 1886—the same year they fished King Ludwig out of the lake—Otto opened the Weismann Brewing Company of Brooklyn, New York. Corner of Forest and Bremen Streets. Rheingold beer—named by a German king after a German myth—becomes as American as apple pie! So there.

So there.

And look who finally finished his inventory.

Sorry for the wait, guys. You wanna pay for these now or run a tab?

Run us a tab, Jake. And why don't you make me another one, so it'll be ready by the time I finish this one.

You got it, Pop.

Pop? Nah, it wasn't me. Must have been the milkman. If I was your father, you wouldn't have turned out so goddamned good-looking. . . . See, there's a good tip for you, Jake. Compliment the barkeep and he might get a little heavy-handed when he's pouring your next one.

Right. Hey, Peppy, I'm sorry to rush us along, but I promised your daughter I'd have you back by six o'clock, and what I'm really interested in—

So we call her, tell her we're running late. So I don't get home in time to watch Judge Judy read the riot act to some poor *schmuck*. So what? You want to hear about Miss Rheingold or don't you?

I do. Particularly the—

Okay then. So Otto opens the Brooklyn brewery. It's slow for a while, but little by little, sales pick up. Brewery gets its lucky break in 1898, when New York consolidated the boroughs. Before that, Brooklyn was a separate city, see? But now—

Hey, but you know what? Since my focus is on the contest years, why don't we cover that stuff today? Then maybe we can schedule another time to discuss the earlier era. Because it's fascinating, but—

Go *backwards*? Doesn't make sense to do it that way, Jake. History's all cause and effect. If I'm gonna show you how Rheingold became a success story, I gotta show you how they met the challenges along the way: anti-German backlash during WW1. Then Prohibition, the Depression, WW2.

And I *want* to hear all that. But let's table it for next time, and then I'll cut and paste it all together later on. That's what writers do, you know?

Well, I don't see the sense of it, but you're the expert. How about if I tell you about the year I come aboard? Nineteen forty-two?

Fine. Start there.

Because, come to think of it, that was when the Miss Rheingold promotion was just getting started. Company'd put the gals at a table in the lunchroom, have them sell War Bonds to the workers. "Keep on buying, keep our boys flying!" If you signed up, they'd take it right out of your paycheck, see? Which I did, of course. I'm a young guy with all my parts working, including the part that responds to the opposite sex, and I'm going to say no to some of the most beautiful girls in Manhattan? By the way, I'm just curious. How old would you say I am?

Couldn't tell you. So you started in forty-two and—

Go on. Take a stab. Not gonna cost you anything. Just keep in mind that I walk two miles in the mall every morning with the Senior Strollers and that every single tooth in my head is *au naturel.*

Seventy-three? Seventy-four?

Eighty-four, this coming April!

No kidding? Wow. Okay, let's get back to business.

You're the boss. Now Otto Weismann was long gone by the time I started at Rheingold, and it was the *second* generation of Weismanns running the show: Otto's sons, Isadore and Herman, and their kid sister, Sadie. All three were in their fifties by then, each going about their business the way their father had laid it all out. Isadore oversaw the plant's day-to-day operation and Herman was their chief buyer. He was on the road a lot, making deals with the grain merchants, the tin and glass companies. Now as far as the hops, the old man had been a shrewd one, see? He'd arranged a marriage between his son Herman and Greta Schein, daughter of Gustav Schein, who was the biggest hops merchant back in Munich. Can't brew beer without hops, right? So Rheingold married into the family discount. Of course, Otto hadn't figured on Hitler. Nineteen thirty-seven, thirty-eight, the Nazis arrest Schein and seize his business. This was before the U.S. of A. entered the war, of course. Lot of American companies, Jewish included, were still looking the other way at what was going on over there. But not the Weismanns. The company took a stand: refused to trade with the Nazis on principle. So Rheingold took a hit—had to reduce production, lay off some of their people.

Meanwhile, Herman Weismann found out his in-laws— Greta's family—had been sent to the camps. He got the State Department involved, went over there himself two or three times to try to get them out. But after the Japs bombed Pearl Harbor, everything fell through. Poor Greta lost everyone—parents, grandparents, brothers, and sisters. Later on, Rheingold put up a memorial park in their honor. Right across from the Brooklyn plant, this was. Had a fountain, a wishing pond, a beautyful flower garden. Sometimes you'd see Greta Weismann over

there, fussing with the flowers or brushing off the stone benches
with a whisk broom. They had people coulda done that stuff for
her—the Weismanns were millionaires by then—but she had to
do it herself. It was a sight to make you cry: this fine and fancy
lady, watering plants, pulling weeds. Trying to make something
nice out of her terrible loss.

Now Sadie Weismann—you remember her? Otto's daughter? Usually it's the eldest son who calls the shots, but it was
Sadie who had inherited her father's business smarts and the old
man knew it. So before he died, he set things up so that Sadie
held the purse strings and had final word on the big decisions.
And what was even *more* unusual about the Weismanns was that
both brothers went along with it. No power struggles, no hatchet
jobs. Nothing like that. . . . Odd duck, Sadie was, though—six
foot tall and three foot wide. She was married for a little while,
but it didn't take. Never had kids of her own. But you know what
I always liked about Sadie? She was never too good to speak to
her rank-and-file. She'd look you right in the eye, ask you how
things were going, ask your opinion on things. Then she'd *listen*
to your answer. That's smart business, see? Creates loyalty. I tell
you, Jake, I loved working for Rheingold. I'd come up from the
subway every morning, get a whiff of the aroma coming from
the plant, and walk a little faster just to get there.

Worker loyalty. Got it.

Now, they started me down in the government cellar, which
was where they *stored* the beer, see? Called it the government
cellar because that's where they calculated the tax by what the
pump read. Then from the g.c., I went to blending and brewing.
Then to pasteurizing. You did three-month rotations, so you'd
understand the entire crafting process. Again, smart business.
Creates pride in your worker so he gives you a better effort. You
see?

Yes.

I worked in sales for a while. I wasn't too keen on that, but it was better money. By then, Cookie and I had gotten hitched and our daughter was on the way. Rochelle—the one you talked to. You know what the brewery did when she was born? First, they sent Cookie a big, beautyful bouquet at the hospital. Second, when I opened up my paycheck that week, there was a fifty-dollar gift certificate from Macy's. I took the subway downtown, bought a bassinette and a hobby horse. Cookie had wanted the bassinette but we couldn't afford it. So I bought that and the rocking horse, carried 'em out of Macy's, and hired a cab. Cabbie and I roped the stuff to the roof and we rode all the way from Thirty-Fourth Street to Roosevelt Avenue in Queens. When Cookie come home from the hospital and there's the bassinette, she broke out in tears. Beautyful person, my Cookie was—active in synagogue, hospital auxiliary. Couldn't do enough for people. Three years now since I lost her and I still . . . How about you, Jake? You married?

Separated.

Well, if you want my advice, bury the hatchet and get her back. Life's too short for "separated."

It's a circumstantial separation, not a legal one.

Yeah? So what does that mean?

I'd rather not go into it.

Okay, okay. Let's lighten up the party, shall we? You ever hear this one? Jewish girl tells her college roommate, who's a Catholic, that she's going home for Roshashanna. "Oh," the Catholic girl says. "That's the holiday where you light the eight candles, right?" Jewish girl says, "No, no, you're thinking of Hannukah." Catholic girl says, "Oh, right. Roshashanna's when you eat the unleavened bread." "Wrong again," the Jewish girl says. "That's Passover. Roshashanna's when we blow the shofar." Catholic girl says, "See, that's what I admire about your people. You're always so good to the servants." You get it? Blow the shofar. Blow the chauffeur? . . . Oy, such a chest-heaving sigh from you, Jake. Did I offend you? You a Catholic? Because I'll tell you who told me that joke. Father Frank McElwain, that's who! Retired priest. He's one of the Senior Strollers.

I'm not offended, Peppy. I'm frustrated.

You're not a Jew, are you?

No.

No, I didn't think so. By me, a Jew knows another Jew. So what are you then?

Look, *you're* being interviewed. I ask *you* the questions.

You believe in God?

Peppy, I—

Do you or don't you? It's a simple question.

Let's just say I have my doubts.

Yeah? That right? Well, let me give you a little piece of advice, Mr. I Have My Doubts. Next time you're in a bad way and you're asking this god you have your doubts about to help you, just remember that the question you gotta ask isn't Why? or If? The question is How? You got that? Not *why*. Not *if. How.* You wanna write that down? Oh, that's right. You got me on tape.

So you were in sales. Then what?

Then they transferred me to public relations, which was where I found my niche. Now *that's* when I got involved with the Miss Rheingold contest, see? When I was in PR.

The archivist said you used to—

The who?

The Rheingold archivist. Your friend, Mrs. Nussbaum.

Yeah, well, I don't know from archivist, but Shirley Nussbaum was Gus White's secretary. Don't let that name throw you, now. Gus was third generation Weismann—Herman and Hennie's son. He went out to Hollywood for a while—tried to be a movie actor but it didn't take. Leaves Brooklyn as Gustav

Weismann, comes back and he's Gus White. Good-looking guy, Gus was. Beautiful set of teeth, quite the ladies' man. And once he got California out of his system, he turned into a damn good businessman. Course, it didn't hurt that he was his Aunt Sadie's favorite nephew, either. Sadie groomed Gus for big things.

Shirley Nussbaum said it was Gus White who thought up the idea of the Miss Rheingold election.

No, no, that's wrong—although I'm not surprised Shirley would give her boss the credit. Little case of idol worship there, my friend. Like Bush and that colored gal he's got working for him—what's her name?

Condoleezza Rice.

That's the one. Condoleezza Rice-a-Roni. But no, it was the photographer for the ad campaign, guy name of Pete Hazelton, who come up with the idea for Miss Rheingold. He was a prima donna, that guy, which is Eye-talian for "pain in the *tukhes*." Mr. Perfectionist at those photo shoots! Every shadow had to fall just right, every sleeve straight, every eyelash curled and hair in place. Yeah, it was Hazelton who sold Gus White on the idea of using a pretty face—same girl from month to month, so that she got identified with the product. First year, Hazelton just picked the Rheingold Girl. Second year, he gets a bunch of lookers from the modeling agencies, dresses them alike and photographs each one. Then Rheingold takes the pictures around to all the distributors and tavern owners and lets *them* pick their favorite. Democracy, you see? End of the year, Rheingold's sales numbers are up maybe twenty percent. The voting gimmick went over so big that, in the third year, they got the bright idea to open it up to the public. Put cardboard ballot boxes with the girls' pictures on them in bars and liquor stores and delis, and I tell you Jake, you never seen anything like it! Rheingold's sales took off like a rocket. We go from number six or seven in New York to number one. Plant starts operating seven days a week instead of five and we *still* couldn't keep the shelves stocked. "Elect Miss Rheingold. Your vote may decide." Sex and democracy, see? It was brilliant!

Mrs. Nussbaum said Miss Rheingold used to get more votes than the mayor.

Oh, *millions* more! Course, people used to stuff the ballot boxes. Guys sitting at the bar, kids at the corner market. Everyone was crazy to pick Miss Rheingold, see? In the early days, they hired an accounting firm to count all the votes. But the contest got too big—took too long and cost too much to count nineteen, twenty million paper ballots. So they changed the system. Put out six barrels, one for each candidate. And as the ballots come in, day by day, they'd have their workers—see, what they'd do is hire housewives part-time—and they'd sort 'em and dump the ballots for each girl into her barrel. Then they'd *weigh* the barrels instead of counting votes one by one, see? So instead of Suzie Q got 62,000 votes that day, she'd get 400 *pounds'* worth. But what a formula: democracy plus sex equals beer sales! Now, of course, it was *safe* sex, like they say now. No Jayne Mansfields or what's-her-name? The blonde from *Baywatch*, married that screwball rock star with the tattoos?

Pamela Anderson?

Bingo! That's the one! You ever see that home movie those two made? Her and her screwy husband? I went to a bachelor party a while back—my friend Hekkie Fishkin's grandson—and they shown that tape before the stripper come on. I tell you, my Cookie bought me an eight-millimeter camera for Father's Day one year, but I never took any home movies like that! But no, Jake: no sexpots running for Miss Rheingold. It was always the girl-next-door types, in their white gloves and summer dresses. Always shiksas, of course, or Jewish girls with shiksa names. No coloreds, no Spanish girls. I'm not saying it was right—hey, my people don't know from prejudice? Ha! Like hell we don't. But business is business. I'm just saying what working-class whites would have put up with back then and what they *wouldn't* have. . . . But here's why Sadie Weismann was a shrewd businesswoman, see? She had a survey done, and what they found out was that the lady of the house buys more of the beer for the Frigidaire than her hubby does. So what Rheingold was selling along with the beer was *class*. Rheingold puts Miss Rheingold in the latest fashions, starts running ads in ladies' magazines like *Gourmet*, *Harper's Bazaar*. Company spent *millions* on promotion—print ads, billboards, car cards in the subway, radio, and then TV—and every year it paid off bigger and better. Saturation coverage, see? You couldn't walk down the block in New York without Miss Rheingold smiling at you from half a dozen storefronts. That contest was a cash cow like advertising had never seen before! Thanks to Miss Rheingold, we were moving three, four million barrels a year!

Wow.

Wow is right, my friend! Only, with the stakes this high, the contest had to be orchestrated like one of Wagner's big operas. First they'd have the all-call. Couple thousand girls, or their modeling agencies, would send in pictures. They'd whittle it down to about two hundred of the best lookers and invite 'em to an all-day cattle call at the Waldorf Hotel. Separate 'em into three groups—blondes, brunettes, and redheads—and the gals would parade in front of the judges, schmooze a little, show 'em their portfolios. End of the day, they'd announce the six finalists and two alternates and give the rest of the gals their walking papers. Then the finalists had to be investigated. The ad agency would hire private detectives and they'd do background checks to make sure each Rheingold girl was squeaky clean. I remember one year, they gave a finalist the boot when they found out she was rooming with some bull-dyke poet down in the Village. Beautyful girl, too—probably would've won it. Another gal, they found out she'd been out to the Stork Club with some nephew of the Cosa Nostra. Next things you know, she's kaput and one of the alternates is in. Hell of a lot riding on Miss Rheingold, see? A scandal would've sunk the ship.

And where exactly did you come in? Because what I'd like to get to is—

For the personal appearances. Company bought two brand-new Cadillacs every summer when the girls were on the road. White convertibles, top of the line. We'd get the weekly schedule and drive them wherever they had to go: county fairs, supermarket openings, a ride around the diamond before the game at the Polo Grounds. Rheingold was one of the Giants' sponsors when they were a New York team. Later on, it was the Mets. But yeah, we used to put some mileage on those two Caddies. Girls always traveled with their chaperone, of course—gal name of Pam Fahey. Good egg, but she could get her Irish up when she needed to.

How often did she need to?

Not too often. They were good girls, most of them. Course, we drivers acted as chaperones, too, if the situation called for a fella to step in. Guy in the crowd starts running his mouth, or getting a little grabby with one of the gals, we'd have to step in and defuse the situation.

We?

Me and the other driver, Georgie Gustavson. You didn't think I drove two Cadillacs at once, did you?

So, you probably got to know these women pretty well, right?

Oh, sure. Between the promotions department and the ad agency, they ran the Rheingold Girls ragged. We'd do four, five appearances a day, seven days a week, while the contest was running. August and September, this was. On weekends, we were hauling them up to New England or down to the Jersey shore,

Pennsylvania. But like I said, they were sweet girls. Couple of pips here and there. College kids, a lot of them, who did modeling on the side.

Do you remember many of them?

Some. The winners mostly, because I'd work with them year-round. I used to get a birthday card every year from Nancy Woodruff, the winner in '55, but we lost touch after they closed the plant.

Do you remember a woman named Jinx Dixon? . . . Peppy?

Hmm?

Jinx Dixon?

Who?

Jinx Dixon.

Can't say that I do. She couldn't have been one of the winners, because I remember them. Was she one of the final six?

Yes.

What year?

Nineteen fifty.

No, not ringing a bell. Maybe if I saw her picture. Blonde? Brunette?

Brunette. Some of my research says she won that year, but most of the old ads from 1950 feature another woman named Estelle Olson.

Yeah, I remember Estelle. Classy blonde from California.

Hey, Peppy? I'm going to be blunt here. I think you're holding back on me.

What's that supposed to mean?

You say you don't remember Jinx, but when I said her name just now, you looked a little panicky. And now you're not looking at me.

What do you mean, not looking at you? I'm looking at you. . . . Look, that stuff's ancient history. Nothing you need to know for a business book. What are you asking about Jinx for?

Like I said, there's a discrepancy. I did a LexisNexis search, and—

A Lexis whatsis?

It's a computer search. Very comprehensive. And almost every item says Estelle won that year, but there's this one item in an old Ed Sullivan column that says Jinx has won and is about to be named—

What'd you say your name was, again?

Caelum Quirk.

Well, Caelum Quirk, I'll be blunt, too. I'm not quite sure who's been holding back on who this past hour. Because to tell you the truth, I don't think you're even writing a business book. You tell me you're researching the old breweries, but when I say you can look at my copy of *The History of Rheingold Beer*, you don't so much as take a nibble. . . . She wasn't a bad kid, Jinx. She just got in over her head.

What do you mean? What happened?

Nothing happened. Pass me my coat, will ya? I gotta get home before my daughter sends out the search party.

Hold on, Peppy. I don't mean for things to go south here, because I really appreciate your agreeing to talk to me and giving me so much of your time. You're like a walking history lesson. How about another drink?

No thanks. Two's my limit.

Because I thought maybe I'd join you after all. Have a drink with you.

Yeah? Well . . .

Tell you what. Let me dial Rochelle's number on my cell phone here so you can check in, and while you're doing that, I'll get us both a drink. You sticking with Chivas? Okay, Chivas it is. I tell you one thing: I hope I'm as sharp as you are when I'm eighty-four.

I'm eighty-three. Eighty-four next April.

Well, you could have fooled me. I would've guessed seventy-five, tops.

Now?

Yeah, tape's going again. Go ahead.

She was a living doll, that one. Big blue eyes, that shy little smile of hers. Hazelton, the photographer, was rooting for Jinx to win the thing, and you couldn't blame him. The kid ate up the camera. But it was neck and neck that year, between her and Estelle. Estelle was your more glamorous Miss Rheingold type, but there was just something special about Jinx. Something sweet, but at the same time, a little mischievous. Naughty, you know? . . . Anyway, it went down to the wire between those two, but in November, by the time they got all the ballots sorted and weighed, Jinx had beaten Estelle by a nose. So they bring her in, have her sign her contract, take her measurements for the wardrobe they're going to design for her. Now, within the company, it circulates that Jinx has won it, but the public won't find out until later because Hazelton has to shoot the announcement ad, which they always ran in January. New year, new Miss Rheingold, see? "Here's the lucky girl you, the voting public, have elected!" So Hazelton takes her picture. And they're expensive, these photo shoots: photographer's assistants, hairstylist, makeup gal, fashion people. But the pictures come out great, because, like I said, Jinx loves the camera and the camera loves her right back. Only, there's a problem, see? And man oh man, it's a doozy. See, Jinx and Gus White had been seeing each other on the sneak since the summertime. And Gus was a married man, so that complicated it. Hardly anybody knew about this, but *I* did because Gus was having *me* drive Jinx to their rendezvous spot—this little roadside motel in North Jersey. Only that wasn't all. You remember how I told you Rheingold was courting the Negro market? Well, one of the things they'd do was have the girls pose with Nat Cole or Satchmo or Monte Irvin, first baseman for the Giants. General public never saw these pictures, but they'd run them in the Negro papers, you see? Circulate autographed glossies to the liquor stores in the colored neighborhoods. So somewheres along the line, Jinx meets one of Irvin's teammates, an outfielder name of Calvin Sparks. His batting average was nothing to write home about, but he's a handsome son of a gun, light-skinned, and he's got an eye for the white girls. So one thing leads to another and *those* two start cozying up. Sparks and Jinx. So Gus White's two-timing his wife with Jinx, and Jinx is two-timing Gus with Sparks. I'm telling you, Jake. That summer, I was chewing Tums nonstop. Because the only two people that know the whole story are me and Jinx. Put me in a tough position, you see?

How did you know about Jinx and Sparks?

How did I know? I'll tell you how. Because just before the big announcement, Rheingold throws a little cocktail party for the bigwigs so they can meet the new Miss Rheingold—their "super-salesgirl," they used to call her. Jinx ends up having one or two Manhattans too many at this wing-ding, gets a little tipsy, and when I drive her back to her apartment on Sutton Place, she starts up with the true confessions. Says things started off great with Gus, but now she's just going through the motions because what she and Sparks have is the real deal, and that neither of them can help themselves. Well, you know what I did? I pulled over to the curb, put 'er in park, and I turned around so I could look her right in the eye. And I said, "Look, little girl, I'm going to speak to you like a father would speak to a daughter. You're playing with fire here, and if you're not careful, you're gonna get burnt to a crisp. Now when you get out of this car, you go up-stairs to that nice all-expenses-paid apartment of yours, pick up the phone, and end it with Sparks." And you know what she says to me? She says, "Well, Peppy, if you think *that's* possible, you must not know what true love is." Which, I'm thinking, she's probably defining "true love" as a good *schtupping*. Because, believe me, Jake, married to my Cookie, I think I knew a little more about true love than *that* pretty little pipsqueak.

So what happened?

What happened was, I had a real dilemma on my hands, see? I mean, I liked Jinx—I really did. Lot of the models back then come from money, see? Kinda snooty, some of them. But not Jinx. She'd gotten where she was on moxie and the good looks God give her. But Winchell, Earl Wilson, Hedda Hopper: they had snoops all over the city digging around for *shmutz*. One of those gossip columnists gets wind that Miss Rheingold's seeing a colored ballplayer and it shows up in the *Daily Mirror* or the *Daily News*? Rheingold's million-dollar promotion'd go down the toilet and maybe take the brewery with it. And like I told you, the Weismanns had always been good to me. They and I had a history, see?

What did you do?

I go to Gus. And he's mad as hell. Says he'll be goddamned if he'll stick his dick into *anyone's* sloppy seconds, let alone some *schvartze*. Says there's no way in hell Jinx is gonna be Miss Rheingold, popular vote or not. It's partly a business decision and partly a get-even thing—at least that's how I see it. What he does is, he goes to his aunt Sadie. Drags me into her office with him, as a matter of fact. Gus doesn't say word one about his *own* little fling with the girl, but he tells Sadie they got a crisis: their new Miss Rheingold's sleeping with a Negro. Next morning, there's this top-secret meeting in Sadie's office. The lawyers are there, Hazelton, the top marketing guys. I'm pulled into it, too, because, for one, they know I can keep my mouth shut and for two, I've been driving Jinx around all summer, so I'm the guy who can best predict how she's going to react when they give her the heave-ho. At least everyone *thinks* I'm the guy who knows her the best, except I don't know her the way Gus White does. But I'm not saying anything about that, and neither is Gus!

So they decide they've got to get rid of Jinx—get Estelle Olsen in on the next plane from Los Angeles and make her Miss Rhein-gold. Hazelton balks at first because he's got some beautyful pictures of Jinx—says he doesn't care if the guy she's screwing is black, white, or purple with yellow polka dots. But he finally comes on board, because that contest is *his* bread and butter, too. Now the *good* thing is, the announcement ad hasn't run yet, so the public won't need any explanations. The *bad* thing is, the accounting firm that oversees the contest has already registered the election results. In pounds of paper, right? Remember the barrels? It's on the books that Jinx has won by about x number of pounds, I can't remember how many.

So here's what they do. Everyone at that meeting, myself included, goes down to the warehouse and into the government cellar. It's all hush-hush, top secret. They bring in all the unused ballot pads—boxes and boxes of 'em, maybe two, three hundred pads of ballots in each box. They have a couple of the warehouse guys roll in four or five empty barrels. Then all of us—Gus, me, the lawyers—we spend the better part of the day checking off ballots for Estelle. Next morning, they make up this cocka-mamie story about how someone's discovered these barrels of ballots in the warehouse that accidentally never got counted. So now they have to do a recount, see? A re-*weigh*. They get the accounting guys back in, and the loading dock guys roll both Jinx's and Estelle's barrels out to the weigh station. And whataya know? Estelle's got Jinx beat by eighty, ninety pounds. So they reregister the election results and Estelle Olson becomes Miss Rheingold for 1950.

What happened to Jinx?

She took it bad. Trashed that fancy apartment the day they evicted her. Broke all the mirrors, slashed the upholstery. At first, she swore up and down she was gonna fight them—go to the papers, go to Gus's wife, sue the company. But she backed down. The company's lawyers put a pretty good scare in her, I guess. In the meantime, they put a *team* of private investigators on her, and these guys dug up something really screwy: turns out, the kid wasn't really Jinx Dixon. I forget what her real name was, but the real Jinx had been a roommate of hers who'd gotten fed up with modeling and left the city. So this one "borrowed" her name—to get past the background check, see? But once they found out who she really was, they had the goods on her. She'd had a couple scrapes with the law, see, and she'd signed a contract that said she was clean as a whistle. So there was no way she could've sued. By contest rules, she was ineligible. We coulda saved ourselves all that writer's cramp, checking off all those ballots. . . . The sad thing was, after Rheingold fired her, Sparks dropped her like a hot potato and so did her modeling agency. Word got out, so no other agency would touch her either. She hung around for a while—kind of stalked Gus, I guess. It got pretty ugly. One afternoon, she showed up at the Brooklyn plant where Gus's office was and they called the cops—had her removed from the premises by armed guards. They hushed it up, though. I heard she made some trouble for Sparks out at the Polo Grounds, too. I guess she went a little off the deep end. I felt kinda lousy about my part in it, but the girl dug her own grave. *Schtupping* two men at the same time, one of 'em a black guy? Bad mistake. Miss Rheingold had to be pure as the driven snow. . . . Funny thing was, the white-black thing was what finally killed off Miss Rheingold anyway. About fourteen, fifteen years later—the summer when all the race riots were breaking out—Rheingold pulled the plug on the contest. They claimed the public had lost interest, so it was no longer cost-effective. But the real reason was, the company was between a rock and a hard place. On the one hand, they were getting pressure from the blacks to run a colored contestant. You remember Adam Clayton Powell? Congressman from Harlem? He kept calling, giving Gus White the needles about it. Sadie had passed on by then and Gus was president of Rheingold, and I was his driver. So one afternoon, I got the boss and Powell in the backseat and Powell says, "Now Gus, the good people in my district buy a lot of your beer. Lot of folks wondering when you're going to give us a beautiful Negress to vote for in that little contest of yours." But back then, if they'da run a black girl, there woulda been a backlash from the whites. Maybe old Otto Weismann would have done the right thing, but Gus wouldn't risk it. The Rheingold girls were about fun, see, not politics. So rather than run a colored girl, they killed the contest.

Okay, but back up a minute. You ever hear anything more about Jinx?

Heard *from* her. Got a call one Sunday morning, out of the blue. At first, I thought she was calling to give me guff for blowing the whistle on her. It had to have dawned on her that I was the one. But no, that wasn't it. She says, "Peppy, can you do me a favor?" What she wanted was for me to drive her back home to Connecticut. She wanted to get the hell out of New York, she said, because there was nothing left for her here, and because that's what the head shrinkers at Bellevue said would be best for her. To pull up stakes and go home. She'd landed in the nut-house, see? Admitted as much. So I said, "Sure, okay, Jinx." I was still calling her Jinx, see? Playing as dumb as possible, for her sake as well as mine. I didn't want to drive her up there, but what was I going to do? Say no? I made sure Cookie rode up with us, though. We got a babysitter for Rochelle, and me, Cookie, and Jinx drove up to Connecticut. I mean, I liked the kid, I really did, but she was bad news. I didn't want any trouble. You get what I'm saying?

Yes.

We picked her up outside this little coffee shop way downtown on Delancey. You should've seen her. She was wearing bobby sox, rolled-up dungarees, kerchief on her head. No makeup. No trace of Miss Rheingold. She looked like some sweet, innocent high school kid. On the drive up there, we stopped at a diner for pie and coffee, and when I went off to the men's room, she told Cookie she was pregnant. Didn't say who the father was, so I don't know if it was Gus or Sparks or maybe even someone else. She said there was a boy back home—a guy who loved her, would take her back. We dropped her off at some little town called . . . geez, I can't remember the name. When she said Connecticut, I was thinking Danbury or Bridgeport, maybe. But it was way the hell over on the other side of the state. Little town in the boondocks.

Three Rivers.

Yeah, that might've been it. We had a hell of a time getting back to the city, I remember. It had started snowing, see? One of those crazy March blizzards and I didn't have any chains on my tires. So all the way back to . . . Hey, you all right? You look a little . . . emotional. Did you know Jinx?

No.

Here. Now *you* need a napkin.

I'm okay. It's. . . . I'm fine.

This isn't really a business book you're writing. Is it, Jake?

No.

Well, whatever it is, I better go home now. You okay to drive? Because if you need to take another minute, maybe have a cup of coffee—

I'm okay.

And I have your word, right? I'm not gonna see any of this Jinx stuff in some book down the line?

No. It's all off the record.

Okay, then. Good. Well, I guess I talked your head off, eh? About King Ludwig, and the Weismanns and all that. Now you just give me a call when you're ready to have me fill you in about the other stuff. Because remember what I said: history is all cause and effect. Connecting the dots.

Yeah, speaking of that, did you ever wonder about what became of her after you dropped her off?

Jinx? I did, as a matter of fact. From time to time, I'd—

She killed herself. They found her floating facedown at the edge of a lake, same as your buddy, King Ludwig. Suicide, the paper said.

No kidding. Gee, that's a shame. How do you—

Bride Lake, it's called. It's on the grounds of the prison where she ended up. So there's your cause and effect. You fed my mother to the fat cats, and she ended up dead.

Your mother? Jinx was your . . . Look, she had problems. You can't say—

Here's your coat. Let's get out of here. Because to tell you the truth, I'm sick of listening to you.

I stood, flung Peppy's coat at him, and threw a bunch of bills on the table. Grabbing my tape recorder in one hand and his forearm with the other, I hustled him out the door of the Inn Between a little faster than his feet wanted to move. Damned if, at that moment, I could remember a single one of those anger management strategies I'd learned. Damned if I wanted to.

In the parking lot, Peppy lost his balance and stumbled forward, and I broke his fall at the expense of my tape recorder. It hit the asphalt and cracked, sending double-A batteries rolling. I got him off his knees and into the car, then walked back to the broken recorder. Picked it up and hurled it, hard as I could. It rattled a chain-link fence and ricocheted into a patch of dead weeds.

I got in the car and started the engine. "Look, you don't understand," he said. "If it got out what she was doing, it would've cost the company—"

I shouted it without looking at him. "Don't talk!"

On the drive back to his daughter's, he sat ramrod straight, staring ahead. His hands, illuminated at the traffic lights, danced with tremors. One of his pant legs gaped open, exposing a bloody knee. It wasn't until he was safely out of the crackpot's car that he issued his two-sentence defense. "The Weismanns were like *family* to me! There was something *wrong* with her!"

I stomped on the accelerator.

Trying to escape Queens, I got good and goddamned lost, and none of the bodega cashiers or glassed-in gas station attendants I stopped to ask seemed to have heard of the fucking Whitestone Bridge. . . . She was already pregnant when she went back? With me? Had they lied about who my father was, too? Did I have a half-sibling somewhere? . . . Lost in a maze of unfamiliar streets, I somehow passed the Inn Between again. Braked, backed up. I found my tape recorder. Popped the cassette and slipped it into my coat pocket.

I never did find the Whitestone. Instead, I followed signs to the Throgs Neck, which got me to the Bruckner Expressway, which became the New England Expressway. Somewhere along dreary I–95, my shame kicked in. Yes, he'd taken the scenic route through Bavaria on his way to coughing up what I needed to know. But on the subject of my birth mother, Peppy Schissel had been far more forthright than my own family.

Then why did you get so angry with him?

Because he ratted her out. And because I saw the outcome: her out there at the corn maze, at Daddy's wake. Dirty, seedy looking. . . . Eight years old and I had to steal them food, for Christ's sake—my mother and father. If he even *was* my father. . . .

So which do you prefer? The lies or the truth?

The truth! I just want the truth!

You sure about that, Quirk? The Minotaur took victims before he was slain.

Yeah? What's that supposed to mean?

The truth might eat you alive.

In Branford, I pulled off the highway and into a McDonald's rest stop. I parked at the outer edge of the lot and cut the motor. Picked up the cassette I'd salvaged from that busted recorder and shoved it into the tape player of my car.

"It was a sight to make you cry: this fine and fancy lady, watering plants, pulling weeds. Trying to make something beautyful out of—"

I hit fast-forward. Stop. Play.

"— that the question you gotta ask isn't Why? or If? The question is How?"

I slammed the dashboard so hard and so many times that I sprained my fucking wrist.

I GOT BACK TO THREE Rivers a little after midnight. Drove past the glow from the casino, onto Ice House and then onto Bride Lake Road. Drove past the jail. A "circumstantial separation," I'd told him—a bullshit euphemism for "my wife's in prison."

I drove up the driveway and around to the back. The lights were on in the barn; Moze's Web site business had taken off, and he and Velvet were hustling to keep up. The upstairs was dark. Janis had left for San Francisco that morning to deliver her paper at that conference.

I entered through the kitchen door and fumbled for the light switch. I saw it first thing: the slim, spring-bound book with its burgundy leather covers.

I approached it tentatively. When I opened it, a card dropped out—a note.

Dear Caelum,

    I hope you enjoy the finished product. Thanks so much for your encouragement. You come from an amazing family.

Love,
Janis

>>*chapter twenty-seven*<<

ELIZABETH HUTCHINSON POPPER (1804–1892):
An Epistolary Self-Portrait of a Remarkable
Nineteenth-Century Woman

By Janis S. Mick,
Ph.D. Candidate in Women's Studies,
Tulane University

Social activist Elizabeth Hutchinson Popper's extraordinary life spanned the presidencies of Thomas Jefferson and Grover Cleveland. Her acquaintances included such nineteenth-century notables as writers Louisa May Alcott and Mark Twain, reformers Dorothea Dix and Lucretia Mott, and the many politicians and captains of industry whom she lobbied for support of a variety of social justice causes. A staunch abolitionist, "Lizzy" Popper was an agent of the Underground Railroad and, later, a Civil War nurse. A lifelong crusader for the betterment of the downtrodden, she worked tirelessly on behalf of orphans and poor women, slaves and free blacks, and female prisoners. Popper left behind a treasure trove of documents, diary entries, and saved letters. Because it was her long-standing practice to slip a sheet of "carbonated paper" beneath the letters she wrote to others, what survives is a rarity: a record of both sides of written exchanges between Popper and her correspondents. From these it has been possible to reconstruct the details of a life fully lived and to gain intimate access to the psyche of the remarkable nineteenth-century woman who lived it.

Elizabeth Hutchinson Popper was born in 1804, the eldest child of William and Freelove (Ashbey) Hutchinson, devout Hicksite Quakers of Philadelphia, Pennsylvania. The eldest of four children, Elizabeth assumed the role of surrogate mother to her siblings after her own mother died, probably of cerebral hemorrhage, while birthing her youngest child, Roswell (1817). In addition to her domestic responsibilities, "Lizzy" Hutchinson, during her teens and twenties, ran a small private Quaker school for girls. At the urging of family friend Lucretia Coffin Mott, she also wrote abolitionist pamphlets and articles for the Society of Friends. Following the death of her father in 1834, Lizzy Hutchinson closed her school and traveled to Connecticut to visit her sister Martha, the wife of New Haven harbormaster Nathanael Weeks. For the remainder of her life, Elizabeth Hutchinson Popper called Connecticut home.

Lizzy Hutchinson was a founding member of the Ladies' Division of the New Haven Abolitionist Society and a delegate to the New York Antislavery Convention of 1838. It was at this gathering that she met her future husband, fellow abolitionist Charles Phineas Popper. Seven years Lizzy's junior, Popper was a traveling subscription bookseller and a member of the American Bible Society, a Congregationalist organization whose goal was to place Bibles "without note or comment" in homes where there were none. As a young man, Popper had toured the country with his brothers and sisters in a popular abolitionist singing act. The Popper Family Singers were headliners at antislavery fundraisers, spreading the abolitionist message to the settlers of westward territories preparing to vote on the issues of statehood and slavery. Two of Charles Popper's songs, the rousing "Swing Open, Freedom's Door!" and the sen-

timental "Mother's Tear-Stained Bible," were widely published in songsters and as sheet music—the nineteenth
century equivalent of hit records. Although Popper had
made no money from these compositions, they lent him
celebrity at the contentious 1838 New York Anti-Slavery
Convention, at which factions argued bitterly about whether
or not female and male delegates should conduct business
separately or "intermingle promiscuously," and whether or
not "our sable brothers and sisters"—free blacks from New
York and New England—should be allowed to fraternize
with white delegates. Lizzy Hutchinson and Charles Popper both spoke out in favor of the intermingling of all, and
it was this shared stance that first united them. In a letter to
her fiancé dated May 6, 1839, Lizzy would later write:

> I confess that I first assumed thee a popinjay, more in love
> with the looking glass than with the idea of freedom for all,
> but later I saw that thy heart and thy intentions are true.
> I am often too quick to judge, dear Charlie, and this thee
> should know about the woman to whom thy troth will be
> pledged.

In October of the same year, Charles wrote to his sister
Winifred:

> Miss Hutchinson is a native Philadelphian and a woman
> of admirable intellect and high moral character, nothing at
> all like the fetching but frivolous lasses of New Haven and
> New London. Since our engagement, she has separated
> herself from the Society of Friends and embraced Congre-
> gationalism. Yet she retains the Quaker garb and the plain
> Quaker ways, which I find appealing and quaint. She is
> plain rather than pretty, Sis, but lovely in her own way. I
> have a great fondness for her.

Assumed a spinster, Lizzy Hutchinson surprised her family when she married Charles in 1841 at the age of thirty-

seven. The couple was wed at the North Church of New Haven, the Congregational house of worship where Charles served as a deacon. She birthed three sons in quick succession: Edmond (1842), Levi (1843), and, at the age of forty, her beloved Willie (1844). Subsequently, she suffered at least two miscarriages and, on New Year's Day of 1846, gave birth to a "severely imbecilic" daughter she named Phoebe. The child's death ten days later triggered a depression in Lizzy Popper that lasted through the winter and spring of 1846. Records reveal that her sister Martha Weeks financed a six-week stay at the Hartford Retreat, a sanitarium, and cared for the Popper children during this time. Among the family's private papers was a March 26, 1846, letter to Charles Popper from the Hartford Retreat's Dr. Elihu Foot, advising Popper to offer his wife, upon her return:

> . . . *gentleness, sympathy, and encouragement toward a gradual return to the charity work which seems to sustain her. I would furthermore advise that, from hereon in, you desist from carnal relations with your wife, as another pregnancy might seriously threaten her physical well-being and exacerbate her nervous condition. If you desire information about alternatives to sexual intercourse, I shall be happy to advise you on the subject when I see you next.*

It is unknown if Charles Popper heeded Dr. Foot's warning, but by the autumn of 1846, Lizzy had reengaged wholeheartedly in her "charity work" and Charlie had begun the first of his extramarital affairs.

———————

Two events in 1841 galvanized and further deepened Elizabeth Hutchinson Popper's commitment to the abolitionist movement. The first was an incident involving her youngest brother, Roswell, by then an instructor at a boys' preparatory academy in Richmond, Virginia. The second was the *Amistad* trial.

After Roswell Hutchinson had made remarks to his students that revealed his abolitionist sympathies, his lodgings were broken into and ransacked, and antislavery tracts were discovered among his possessions. He was attacked by "cowardly hooligans" the next night, and beaten so savagely that he lost an eye and suffered subsequent "lapses in sound judgment." Accused of "attempting to poison the minds of Southern youth," Roswell Hutchinson was jailed for his own protection. At the time, Lizzy Popper was five months pregnant with her first child. Although this was an era in which women rarely traveled without a male escort and pregnant women confined themselves to home, upon hearing of her brother's plight, Lizzy sojourned alone to Richmond. She convinced the constabulary there to release her brother to her custody and to assist her in smuggling him out of Virginia and back to her home in Connecticut. Later in her life, she would identify this incident as the first of her many successful attempts at lobbying men in power for the sake of just causes.

The second event that heightened Lizzy Popper's resolve to fight against slavery was the arrest in New Haven harbor and subsequent trial of the *Amistad* defendants, fifty-six kidnapped Africans who had killed captain and crew members of the Spanish-owned schooner *Amistad* and commandeered the ship in a failed attempt to sail home from Cuba. Following former president John Quincy Adams's successful defense of the would-be *Amistad* slaves, they were supported by Farmington, Connecticut's Congregational First Church of Christ while awaiting the collection of private funds to finance their return voyage to their homeland, now Sierra Leone. Members of New Haven's North Church were active in this fund-raising initiative as well, and Lizzy Popper solicited and obtained significant contributions from prominent businessmen in New Haven, New London, and Windham. This cooperative effort between the Farmington and New Haven churches most likely initiated Lizzy and Charles Popper's association with the Underground Railroad, as

Farmington was Connecticut's "Grand Central Station" of the secret system by which escaped slaves made their way north to Canada. Following the passage of the Fugitive Slave Act of 1850, agents of the "railroad" were subject to arrest for aiding and abetting runaways; therefore, arrangements were covert and documentation is scant. It is believed, however, that both the Poppers' attic and the barn of Lizzy's sister, Martha Weeks, were used to harbor fugitives.

Atypical of married women of her era, Lizzy Popper was the nineteenth-century equivalent of the "working mother," frequently leaving her children in the care of the childless Martha Weeks when she traveled on behalf of one of her social justice causes. At the invitation of Lucretia Mott, Popper attended the 1848 Conference on Women's Rights at Seneca Falls, the historic New York gathering that launched the struggle for women's suffrage. More a moderate than a radical thinker, Lizzy Popper was ambivalent about women's suffrage. Aboard the train returning her home, she wrote to Martha Weeks:

While I support many of the agreed-upon points of the Declaration of Sentiments, I fear that the demand that women be granted their "sacred right" to elective franchise will cost us dearly. We can accomplish far more by appealing to the better instincts of men of mark than by battling for access to the ballot box. Extremism will negate our efforts, and here is a perfect example. Three or four of the delegates advocating suffrage saw fit to promenade up to the podium wearing pantaloons! Thee would have laughed the livelong day, dear sister, to see what I saw: women in trousers asking to be taken seriously! Liberate women from toil and drudgery, yes, but why from skirts and petticoats? I trust that my three babes have minded their manners in my absence. Thee can rest assured I shall spank the bottom of any boy who has not.

An 1851 letter from Charles Popper to his wife, when their sons were nine, eight, and seven, reveals that Lizzy's frequent travels became a source of conflict between the couple. A somewhat remote parent who was himself frequently on the road selling books, Popper accused Lizzy of saving the world at the expense of his children, and of ignoring "the sound, common-sensical guidance of Miss Beecher, whose book you stubbornly refuse to open." Of the volumes he sold to his subscription customers, Charles Popper's perennial best-seller was Catharine Beecher's *Treatise on Domestic Economy for the Use of Young Ladies at Home and at School.* (Beecher was the sister of author Harriet Beecher Stowe and feminist Isabella Beecher Hooker.) Written in an autocratic tone, the book instructs women and girls on cooking, laundering, and household sanitation, and advocates the sublimation of the female's personal ambition for the sake of her family. "I lay any future flaws in our sons' character firmly at your feet," Charles Popper warned his wife. But Charles's criticisms failed to slow Lizzy's momentum; her ledger of travel expenses reveals that she took seven trips in 1851, eleven in 1852, and sixteen in 1853. As for *A Treatise on Domestic Economy,* Lizzy Popper apparently read Catharine Beecher's book after all—or tried to. In a letter to her sister, Anna Livermore of King of Prussia, Pennsylvania, she observed wryly that Beecher had taken seven pages to instruct readers on the proper way to prepare a garment for ironing "before the iron is allowed to touch the cloth." Dismissing the work as "well-intented poppycock," Popper concluded, "Let Miss Beecher attack her wrinkles. I shall attack injustice. There is no short supply of either!"

In addition to her antislavery efforts, Lizzy Popper was active in the—

I STOPPED THERE. PUT IT away. I had to.

Because if Peppy Schissel was right—if Mary Agnes had been pregnant when she left New York—then it was possible, maybe even probable, that I was *not* the great-great-great-grandson of the amazing Lizzy Popper. That I was not a Quirk at all but the bastard son of Calvin Sparks or Gus Weismann. . . .

But if that was the case, then why didn't the math add up? Peppy had told me "Jinx" was already pregnant when he drove her back to Three Rivers in March of 1950. I was born in October of 1951. . . . Or was I? If they'd gone out of their way to lie about who my mother was, maybe they'd fudged my date of birth, too. Paid off some town clerk or something. Was I a year older than I'd been led to believe? Half Jewish? Half black? Was I someone's half-brother?

Not knowing what to think, I kept my mouth shut. But *not* knowing, *not* telling anyone, was making me crazy. I caught myself slamming things, dropping things, muttering to all the dead liars in my life. One afternoon, at the wheel of my car, I couldn't recognize where I was or remember what I was supposed to be driving toward. One night, battling insomnia, I became lost in the corridors of our old corn maze. A woman's voice was calling my name. Was it Maureen? Mary Agnes? I ran along the twisting packed dirt paths, getting closer and closer to the voice. Velvet's voice—I recognized it now. But when I reached the center of the maze, instead of Velvet, I found Harris and Klebold, armed and smirking. It was Eric who spoke. *You know what I hate? Cuuunnntry music! And people who think that wrestling is real! And idiots who are so fucking clueless, they don't even know who their parents were!* As they raised their shotguns and took aim, I bolted upright in bed, gasping, flailing for the light.

———————

JANIS HAD WOWED THEM AT the Women's Studies conference—had returned from San Francisco with business cards and e-mail addresses from department chairs and university press editors. Her adviser had assured her that, with a few strategic expansions and some fine-tuning, "Elizabeth Hutchinson Popper: An Epistolary Self-Portrait" would serve beautifully as both a detailed proposal for her doctoral thesis and her gateway to the job market. If she could complete her revisions by April, they would call her committee together so that she could present her proposal and get the green light to proceed.

"Did you read it?" she asked me the evening she got back. She'd come down to the kitchen and found me leaning against the counter, eating canned ravioli out of the saucepan. In the week she'd been away, I'd both missed Janis and been relieved she was gone.

"Started it," I said. "Great job. Lizzy was quite a gal, huh?"

She asked how far I'd gotten.

"Uh, well . . . Seneca Falls. The suffragists wearing pantaloons." Watching her smile turn from anticipation to disappointment, I changed the subject. "So did you hear about the big feline smack-down?"

In the month or so since the Micks' cat had arrived from New Orleans, there had been no love lost between him and Nancy Tucker. Fat Harry and little Nancy had had several howling, arched-back face-offs. But while Janis was away, the fur had finally flown. Nancy had come out of it with a torn ear and a bald spot on her back. Harry, sporting a rakish gash over his eye, had been banished to the barn.

"Moses says he loves it out there," Janis said. "He left him a dead bat as a thank-you present yesterday."

"Is he sure that wasn't Velvet?" I quipped. "She's kind of got that Vampira thing going on."

Janis smiled, said I was awful. "So when do you think you'll be able to read the rest of my paper? Because I'd really love to hear what you think."

"Hey, don't worry about what *I* think. It's your doctoral committee you've got to impress. Not me."

"This isn't about impressing you, Caelum," she said. "This is about your having given me the gift of access to your ancestor's archives and my giving you a gift in return."

"Yeah? What am I getting—an iPod?"

But I couldn't back her off with sarcasm. "You're the blood of Lizzy's blood, Caelum," she said. "You exist because she married Charlie after everyone had written her off as a spinster, and because they had babies together: Eddie, Levi, and then your great-great grandfather, Willie—Lydia's father." Damned if I could hold her gaze when she started that blood-of-her-blood stuff, which I probably *wasn't*. I dumped the rest of the ravioli in the garbage. Started washing the pan and whatever else was in the sink. Problem was, Janis grabbed a dishtowel and came up beside me. "Willie was an entertainer—a star on the minstrel circuit. Did you know that?"

"Nope."

"You know what everyone at the conference was talking about after I presented my paper? The incredible ironies in your family history."

"The ironies?" I glanced at her for a second, then looked away again.

She nodded. "In 1863—the middle of the war? Willie was performing on the New York stage, entertaining audiences with these hideous parodies of black women. And meanwhile his sixty-year-old mother was down in Washington, nursing the wounded and defying the terms of the Emancipation Proclamation—sending slaves from the border states off to safe havens before their masters could catch them. And then there's the irony that—"

"Hey, not to interrupt," I said. "But what does Moze think?"

That stopped her short. "About what?"

"Your paper. He's read it, right?"

Now it was she who was struggling to keep eye contact. "I haven't asked him to, Caelum. Moses doesn't really value my scholarly work."

"Oh," I said. "Well . . ." I promised her I'd read the rest of it as soon as I could—probably that weekend.

But two weeks later, Lizzy Popper was still stuck on that train coming back from Seneca Falls. When Janis asked again if I'd finished, I told her I'd been crazy busy. School stuff, plus a situation over at the prison—something I hadn't anticipated.

"Is everything okay with your wife?" she asked.

"It is now," I said. "But it took some doing to get it fixed."

"Get what fixed?"

I told her I didn't have the energy to go into it. "I *do* want to read your thing, though. It's not that I don't."

What had happened was: Mo's former cellmate, Camille, had filed that complaint about Officer Carol Moorhead, the CO who'd sexually assaulted her during that cavity search for the missing pepper shaker. There'd been an investigation, and Maureen, the only witness, had been questioned by two of Moorhead's supervisors. The surprise was that they'd taken Mo's word over their officer's. Moorhead got a letter of reprimand and a transfer to the juvenile detention center in Hartford. That had been good for Camille but bad for Maureen, because Moorhead's fellow officer and paramour, Officer Tom Tonelli, had targeted her for some payback.

Tonelli began harassing Mo in quiet ways: shadowing her when she walked to and from the chow hall, making inaudible remarks under his breath, chuckling at nothing. One afternoon, he gestured to Mo when she was on her way to her NA meeting. She approached tentatively and asked if he wanted something. "Nah," he told her. "My trigger finger's just a little itchy today."

Tonelli upped the ante when he did a third-shift rotation. They do hourly head counts over there—daytime, nighttime, twenty-four/ seven. At night, when the women are sleeping, most of the COs just enter their cells quietly and shine a light on them. Try not to wake them up. But if a CO wants to be a prick, he'll throw on the overhead light, make noise. Maureen's roommate, Irina, was sleeping through all these intrusions, but Tonelli would wake up Mo three, four times a shift. Then one night, she opens her eyes and there's Tonelli, his face about six inches away from her face. "Boo!" He whispers it, okay? Laughs under his breath and leaves. I mean, come on. After what she lived through at Columbine, and everything after that. And she's got to put up with some vindictive low-rung state employee who's trying to screw with her sanity?

The trouble was, I didn't *know* this was going on. She and I had had that argument, see? That day in the visiting room, when she told me to just get up and leave. And so I'd left. Walked out of that room, and stayed away for maybe the next six or seven visits. And when I finally *did* go back there, I was like, Oh shit, because I could see it immediately on her face: the PTSD, the hypervigilance. It was like she'd spiraled back to Littleton. And when she told me why—told me about what that asshole was doing to her— well, I went a little ballistic. But this time, instead of picking up a pipe wrench, I picked up the phone. Called and complained to everyone I could think of: the warden, the deputy warden, the Corrections commissioner, my legislators. I *kept* calling the ones who wouldn't speak to me directly until they finally got on the line. I wrote letters, e-mails. Contacted Dodd's and Lieberman's offices, the governor's. I was goddamned if I was going to let her get "Columbined" again.

And guess what? It worked. Tonelli got transferred. Maureen got to see the jailhouse shrink without waiting the usual three or four weeks for an appointment. She got new meds—an antidepressant and an antianxiety drug. And once those kicked in, she was better. Much better. She began to come out of herself a little, and then a little more. So it was better for me, too. Because I tell you, it's a hell of a lot easier to walk across that visiting room floor toward a smile than toward a face that's suffering. "Thank you," she said, two or three visits in a row, and I told her she didn't have to thank me—that I'd done it because I loved her. "I love you, too," she said, and God, I don't think we'd told each other that for three or four months.

I was grading papers at the kitchen table when Janis came downstairs to make herself some tea. I asked her how the revisions were going. She had finished them, she said; she had e-mailed them off to her adviser and was waiting for a response. She asked me again if I'd read Lizzy's story.

I shook my head. Grabbed a bunch of student papers and held them up to her as evidence. "I really want to, though," I said. "Because from what I've read so far? Wow."

"Do me a favor," she said. "Don't patronize me."

"I'm *not*. I'm *going* to read it. But I can't just drop everything and—"

I stopped mid-sentence because that's exactly what I was doing: patronizing her, bullshitting her. I'd been doing it for weeks.

The kettle whistled. She poured her tea and started to leave. But at the doorway, cup in hand, she stopped. Turned and faced me. "Caelum, the thing that happened between us while Moses was away? It just happened, that's all. We were both feeling a little vulnerable that night, a little sorry for ourselves. We'd both had too much wine."

Nodding in agreement, I began to gather my stuff together so I could work someplace else.

"We made a mistake. It doesn't have to be a wedge between us."

"A wedge?"

"Oh, come on, Caelum. You know what I mean. We don't run together anymore. You don't share meals with us like you used to. Half the time when I talk to you, you won't even look at me. And this refusal of yours to read my work: it's passive-aggressive. And it *hurts*."

"Being busy makes me passive-aggressive?"

"You couldn't read sixty pages in six weeks? About your own ancestor? No one's *that* busy, Caelum. Look, we didn't plan for it to happen. It just—"

"*I* planned for it to happen, okay? I kept pouring you that wine *hoping* it would happen."

That stopped her, momentarily. "And I kept drinking it," she finally said. "So maybe I was hoping it would happen, too."

"Does he know?"

"Moses? Oh, God, no. I would never—"

"Good," I said. "Great. Because you know something? I've *been* the husband who got cheated on. And you know what? It sucks when you find out. It hurts like hell."

She blinked back tears. "Caelum, why are you so *mad* at me?"

"I'm not. I'm mad at . . ." At who? I wondered. The uptight mother who wasn't really my mother? The mother who was screwing two guys that summer? My straight-talking aunt who had kept it from me, too? "Never mind," I said. "I can't go into it."

"Can't?" she said. "Or won't?"

I had to pull the plug on this going-nowhere conversation, so without answering her, I stuffed my students' papers inside my grade book and stood. *Let* her think that my not reading that damn thing was about what we did that night. *Let* her flatter herself that that's all that was on my plate. . . . And besides, it *had* hurt like hell—getting that phone call out of the blue that night from Hay's wife's meddlesome friend. *We just wanted you to know, in case you don't know, that your wife is having an affair.* That phone call had lit a fire in my head, and it had spread as fast and wild as the one that killed all those people at the Cocoanut Grove that night, Ethel Dank included. . . . If things hadn't gone the way they did—if that pipe wrench had crushed Paul Hay's skull like I'd meant for it to do—then it might have been *me* sitting in prison for having killed someone. . . .

Janis? Yeah, I still wanted her. But she was someone else's wife, and telling her the truth about *why* I couldn't bring myself to read her paper would have been another kind of intimacy between us. No. Uh-uh. If I was going to get into my paternity problem with anyone, it wasn't going to be Janis.

———

"BUT IT DOESN'T MAKE SENSE, Cae," Maureen said. "Why would some town clerk affix her seal to a phony birth date?" I had just confessed my confusion about who I was and wasn't in, of all places, the ugly gray-walled visitors' room, under the gaze of surveillance cameras and a scowling CO with a buzz cut and a bulked-up torso.

"I don't know. Money, maybe?"

"From who?"

"From whoever wanted my birth hushed up. The married beer executive, maybe. Or the ballplayer. I Googled him. He was married, too."

"But Cae, hold on a minute. If you're not a Quirk, then why do you look like your father?"

"I *don't* look like him. There's no resemblance between him and me. It's just that Lolly used to say it so often, everyone took it as the truth."

Mo shook her head. "You know those family photos Lolly used to have up in her bedroom?" she said. "One time, she put your high school yearbook picture next to your father's. I *saw* the resemblance, Cae. It wasn't just Lolly telling me."

"That's what pisses me off the most," I said. "The fact that she was just as big a liar as the rest of them. Lies and secrets: that's what the Quirks were all about. And Lolly was as much a part of the big cover-up as any of them."

Mo said she hadn't known any of the others, so she couldn't vouch for them. "But I knew Lolly, Cae. She loved you. And in spite of how confusing this must be for you right now, you should try to remember that. Lolly never would have done anything to hurt you intentionally."

"Well, she *did* hurt me. Never used to shut up about Quirk this, Lydia that. But she couldn't let me know who my *mother* was? That hurts like hell."

"I understand that. And it *was* wrong for her to withhold it from you. You had a right to know. But Lolly must have been torn about it: whether to tell you the truth or protect you from it. She was very protective of you, Cae."

"Protective? Really? Jesus, my neck still hurts from some of those headlocks she used to put me in."

Maureen smiled. "I'm serious, though, Cae. You know what Lolly told me once? That before Hennie, she'd been involved with another woman. Someone named Maggie, who she was crazy about. There'd been a plan in the works. Lolly was going to 'get out of Dodge,' as she put it. Get out from under her father's yoke and move down to Florida with Maggie. They had it all figured out; there was this trailer park they were going to move into—a lesbian community that sort of flew under the radar, I guess. But in the end, she broke it off and stayed put. And do you know why? Because she couldn't leave *you*, she said. Her brother wasn't reliable, and she felt that your mother had her limitations: her temper, her resentment about the way your father—"

"Rosemary *wasn't* my mother," I said. "I was just tricked into believing she was. . . . When was this, anyway? Because Hennie was around for as far back as I can remember."

"You were pretty young, I guess. I remember that that was how she put it: that she'd wanted badly to go to Florida with her girlfriend, but that she couldn't leave 'Little Bit' unprotected. I think I assumed at the time that she was talking about protection from your father. And now that we know Mary Agnes snatched you, it makes more sense. Doesn't it?"

"Nothing makes sense right now," I said.

She nodded. "I know. I'm so sorry you have to go through this, Cae. But the point is: Lolly sacrificed her own happiness to stand by you. Protect you. That's love, Cae, whatever mistakes she made. Just remember that."

I sighed. Rubbed the back of my neck. Looked around at the rest of the motley crew in that visiting room—Mo's counterparts and mine. "Well, maybe I am a Quirk and maybe I'm not," I said. "Let's change the subject. What's new with you?"

Mo said she'd applied for the prison's hospice program, and the program director had said she'd probably have a good shot at getting accepted. Comforting dying inmates—the majority of them addicts suffering from HIV and hepatitis—would give her purpose, she said. It would be the closest she'd ever get to nursing again. Oh, and she'd heard that morning that she was getting a new roommate, thank God.

I asked her what had become of Irina the Terrible.

She'd gotten into an argument with another inmate during "five on the floor," Mo said—something about who should have refilled the hot pot during the previous hour. There'd been a dispute about whether Irina or the other woman had thrown the first punch, but because Irina was as unpopular with the COs as she was with the other inmates, it was she who'd been presumed guilty and hauled off to "seg."

"So how does the new roommate look?" I asked. Mo said she hadn't met her yet, but that CO Santerre had told her it was a young Spanish girl who hadn't yet been sentenced—the defendant in a high profile case.

"What did she do?" I asked.

Maureen said she didn't know. "But I was just thinking, Cae, if you want closure on this paternity thing? Maybe you should think about a DNA test."

"Yeah? How am I supposed to do that? Dig up my father's grave?"

She shook her head. Lolly had shown her something once, she said: locks of her own and her twin brother's hair from when they were children—curls scissored and saved from their first haircuts. "They were in her bedroom, in a bureau drawer. What did you do with Lolly's stuff when those Mick people moved in?"

Those Mick people: Mo was still resisting the idea of Moze and Janis living in our house. "Dumped a lot of it," I said. "Threw the rest in boxes and carted them up to the attic. . . . But you know something? I think I remember seeing those locks of hair. Right after

Lolly died, when I was getting some things for the funeral. I don't remember seeing them later, though, when I was clearing things out for the Micks. I probably chucked them."

"Maybe not," Mo said. "You should look."

I found them at three a.m. the next morning: the two envelopes inside a jewelry box, each labeled in what I now recognized from those old diary entries as Great-Grandma Lydia's distinctive handwriting:

Louella's first haircut, June 1, 1933.
Alden's first haircut, June 1, 1933.

The closest testing center was in New London. The woman on the phone explained that a one-week turnaround on test results would cost me three hundred seventy-five bucks. Results in three days would set me back six hundred. If I had to know by the next business day, it would be a thousand. And though I needed to know the truth, I also wasn't sure I wanted to know. I was grateful that I could just barely afford the one-week option.

"Wow, this is *vintage*," the freckle-faced woman in the lab coat noted when I handed over the envelope containing the remnant of Alden Quirk Jr.'s first haircut. "Okay, have a seat and open your mouth so I can swab the inside of your cheek. This will take like two seconds."

"That's all you need to do?"

"Yup."

"And that hair's not too old?"

"Nope."

A week later, a receptionist slid open her glass window and handed me a manila envelope. You'd have thought I would have torn it open, wouldn't you? But I didn't. I couldn't. Instead, I opened the trunk of my car, dropped the envelope in, and slammed it shut.

I drove home, went inside empty-handed. Velvet was seated at the kitchen table. Facing her were three snaggle-toothed, pointy-eared gargoyles. There was a bunch of art supplies on the table, too: brushes, little jars of paint, glitter, glue. I picked up a bag of garishly dyed feathers and asked her what she was doing. "Experimenting," she said.

She'd had this idea that she wanted to try decorating the drab plaster statues—that maybe their customers, some of them, anyway, would want their gargoyles made up. "Like drag queens," she said. "That's what I'm aiming for, anyway. Drag queens are cool. I got to know some of them when I was living in Slidell." Moses had made her no promises, she said, but he'd given her some defective pieces and fifty dollars for art supplies. If he liked what she came up with, he said, he might put her creations up on the Web site and see what happened.

"Well, good luck," I said. "If you're going to paint, spread some newspapers first."

"Don't sweat it, Dad," she said.

Dad? I rolled my eyes and left the room. I was lying facedown on my bed when I heard her calling me. "Caelum? . . . Hey, Caelum!"

I recalled that dream I'd had about the maze—the way Velvet had been calling me and how, when I thought I had finally reached her, I'd found Klebold and Harris standing there instead. "What?" I called back.

"I'm gonna make some scrambled eggs. You want some?"

"No, thanks."

I thought about how she'd been there that day—in the line of fire. How she'd lived, run away, wound up in Louisiana, and then had traveled north and found us again. She never had talked to me about having witnessed the slaughter that day. Having dropped beneath a table and survived. Did she talk about it when she went over there and visited Mo? Was that day what they talked about? . . .

That night, the Micks' argument woke me up—Janis's end of it, anyway. "I *don't* think I'm better than you, Moses! . . . Well, what do you expect me to do? Forfeit my career?" I couldn't make out Moze's murmured responses, but her retorts came through loud and clear. "All these years, I couldn't even bring up the subject, and now you *want* us to have a baby?"

After awhile, everything was quiet up there. I squinted at the clock radio. One forty-eight a.m. Half an hour later, I gave up on sleep and went out into the kitchen. When I put on the light, there they were in all their garish glory: Velvet's leering, colorful grotesques. Customers would either love them or hate them, I figured. They'd either bomb or sell a million.

I thought about what Maureen had said in the visiting room: that despite the mistakes Lolly may have made, she had loved me enough to stay and protect me, to give up her plans, her lover. From the window, I looked out at my car, illuminated by a three-quarter moon. Maybe that was why those test results were still out there, locked in the trunk. Maybe I was afraid they'd show that Lolly had never really been mine, either.

See that? What did I tell you? The truth can eat you alive!

Yeah? Well, let it. Because not knowing the truth is doing a pretty good job of that, too.

I grabbed my keys. Grabbed the door handle. The bottoms of my bare feet were wet and cold against the dew-covered grass. I popped the trunk and took out the test results.

Back inside, by the light of the kitchen stove, I opened the envelope with shaking hands and read the report.

It was a match. I *was* Alden's son, Lolly's nephew. . . .

And so maybe Janis had been right that day up at Bushnell Park. Maybe my ancestor *was* trying to talk to me. Because here was the scientific proof in black and white, wasn't it? I was a Quirk. Lizzy Popper's blood was my blood.

→→chapter twenty-eight←←

In addition to her antislavery efforts, Lizzy Popper was active in the Children's Aid Society of Connecticut and the Society for the Alleviation of the Miseries of the Public Prisons of Connecticut. In 1849, she initiated a correspondence with French statesman and writer Alexis de Tocqueville. A decade earlier, Tocqueville had toured the Connecticut State Prison at Wethersfield and, in his famous study *Democracy in America*, had written favorably about the degree of order, obedience, and penitent silence maintained inside America's penal institutions. In her own tours of the Wethersfield prison and other state jails, Lizzy Popper was appalled by what she saw: the squalor of inmates' living conditions ("tethered veal calves being readied for slaughter receive more charitable treatment"), the imprisonment of "lunatics better suited to modern insane asylums than to the Medieval dungeons the State maintains," and the easy access of male guards to the handful of "godforsaken female wretches banished to the prison's attic." One such "wretch," an Irish immigrant named Maude Morrison, surreptitiously slipped a letter to Lizzy during a prison tour. Morrison complained that guards and favored male trusties "gratified their lusts" at will with the female inmates; that rum and trinkets fell into the hands of women willing to oblige these urges; and that false charges of incorrigibility were made against women who resisted them. "We who try to fight them off are stripped naked and lashed in front of whatever man wishes to gape at our shame, jailer and jailed alike," Morrison wrote. In response, Popper wrote letters of complaint to prison superintendent Silas Norrish and Connecticut governor Joseph Trumbull; this intervention resulted not in improved conditions but in Morrison's abrupt release. When Popper also wrote of this matter to Alexis de Tocqueville, Tocqueville wrote back. Their occasional correspondence, exchanged over the next several years, constituted a lively philosophical debate as to the balancing of society's obligation to "suppress vice" against its obligation to "restore female sinners to sacred womanhood." In the 1870s and 1880s, Lizzy Popper would again take up the cause of female prisoners, lobbying for a separate reformatory where women could be held "apart from the abuses of malevolent men." However, the issues of slavery and secession would dominate her political activism during the decade that began with Abraham Lincoln's bid for the presidency in 1860 and ended with the securing of voting rights for blacks through the passage of the Fifteenth Amendment in 1870.

On March 6, 1860, at the urging of her eldest son Edmond, Lizzy Popper attended a speech by Illinois senator Abraham Lincoln, who was then campaigning for the Republican presidential nomination. Edmond Popper had recently joined the Wide Awakes, a Republican society comprised mostly of unmarried young men who organized and marched in torchlit spectacles in support of such causes as antislavery. Speaking to a large, enthusiastic audience at New Haven's Union Hall, Lincoln advocated forbearance for both North and South, a settling of differences by peaceful means, and the prevention of slavery's expansion to the western territories. Lizzy liked what she heard that day and supported Lincoln's candidacy, although she would later become disenchanted with Lincoln when, as president, he concluded that war against the Confederacy was inevitable.

The Civil War further frayed the deteriorating marriage of Charles and Elizabeth Popper. Reverting to the Quaker values on which she'd been raised, Lizzy Popper took an unequivocally pacifist stance, arguing that it was a "monstrous fallacy" to assume the Union could be saved and slaves freed "by an armed hand." Conversely, Charles Popper saw the fight as a "Holy Cause"—and a necessity in preserving the Union and ridding the nation, once and for all, of slavery's evils. "Of war and slavery, slavery is the greater sin," he wrote to his wife from the road. Edmond Popper and Levi Popper, the couple's elder sons, sided with their father in this regard. Against their mother's wishes, they mustered in as privates in regiments organized at Norwich, Levi with the Connecticut Volunteers, 18th Regiment Infantry in August of 1862 and Edmond with the Connecticut Volunteers, 21st Regiment, one month later.

In response to her sons' signing on as Union soldiers, Lizzy Popper, too, joined the war effort. She organized a "sanitary fair" in New Haven to raise money and medical supplies for the newly formed U.S. Sanitary Commission, a forerunner to the American Red Cross. She also directed two hundred women from New Haven, New London, and Three Rivers Junction in the making of uniforms, bandages, and compresses for several Connecticut regiments. Yet she continued to speak out against the war whose Union soldiers she abetted. Upon signing on, Lizzy Popper's sons had each received thirteen dollars (the equivalent of one month's army pay), plus a thirty-dollar bounty from the State of Connecticut. "Blood money," their mother called this bounty in a letter published in the *Hartford Daily Times* in September of 1862. "As Rome handed Judas Iscariot thirty pieces of silver to betray Christ, Connecticut hands her sons thirty dollars apiece to betray their Christian values and slay their Southern brothers," Popper argued.

Charles Popper was furious that his wife had gone public with sentiments at odds with his own and those of their soldiering sons. In a response published in the *Hartford*

Daily Times one week after Lizzy's letter appeared, he, too, invoked scripture—not to condemn the Union effort, but to justify it. The Book of Jeremiah, chapter 4, verses 16–18, Popper contended, warned those southerners who would maintain "the bondage of God's mahogany-skinned children" against His will:

> *The besiegers are coming from the distant land, shouting their war cry against the cities of Judah! Like watchmen of the fields they surround her, for she has rebelled against Me, sayeth the Lord. Thy conduct, thy misdeeds, have done this to thee; how bitter is this disaster of thine, how it reaches to thy very heart!*

Charlie Popper ended his argument with a couplet from "The Building of a Ship," an 1849 poem by Henry Wadsworth Longfellow:

> *Sail on, O Ship of State!*
> *Sail on, O Union, strong and great!*

A heartfelt letter from Lizzy Popper to her spouse, written in the wake of their public disagreement, revealed the private toll taken:

> *Husband, I cannot and will not apologize for my beliefs, but I regret the publication of same because I know this has caused thee suffering. The stony silence that has grown between us saddens me, and when thee walk past me as if I am some invisible wraith instead of thy lawfully wedded wife, it pains my heart.*

Sadly, Lizzy Popper's reference to "blood money" proved prophetic. Neither Edmond Popper nor Levi Popper survived the war. Upon leaving Connecticut, Edmond Popper's regiment was attached to the 2nd Brigade, 3rd Division, Army of the Potomac. The soldiers' mission was to

keep Washington secure from Confederate attack. Toward
that end, Edmond died of injuries sustained at the Battle of
Fredericksburg, Virginia, in December of 1862.

Levi Popper's regiment was first attached to the Defenses of Baltimore, Maryland, 8th Corps, Middle Department, and later moved on to Winchester, Virginia, joining
General Robert Milroy's Command. Wounded at the Battle
of Winchester, Levi Popper was captured as a prisoner of
war on June 15, 1863. He died eight days later at a makeshift Confederate hospital and was buried with other Union
casualties in an unmarked communal grave, the exact
whereabouts of which were never discovered by the Popper
family, much to the consternation of his grieving mother.

The location of Edmond Popper's remains likely would
have stayed a mystery like his brother's, if not for the kindness of a young Union Army chaplain. In January of 1863, a
letter addressed to "The Mother of Private Edmond Popper
of New Haven, Connecticut" arrived at the Popper home,
forwarded from Washington. The sender was twenty-four-
year-old Joseph Twichell,* a native of Southington Corners,
Connecticut, and an assistant chaplain in New York's Excelsior Brigade. Edmond Popper had died in Twichell's arms,
and Twichell wrote Lizzy Popper to tell her of her son's final
words: "They as raised this war have done a terrible wickedness, I know it now. Tell Ma I will see her in the bye and bye."
Lizzy had been inconsolable, but hearing her son's words
comforted her, as did the information about the location of
his remains. Concerning the latter, Twichell wrote:

*Many a mother's heart, for years to come, will yearn over
some spot of earth, she knows not where, which holds the
ashes of her brave son. You, however, shall know where*

---

*After his war service, Reverend Joseph Twichell would become pastor of Hartford,
Connecticut's Asylum Hill Congregational Church and a close friend of his world-
famous Nook Farm neighbor, Mark Twain. Twichell also became a lifelong friend and
correspondent of Lizzy Popper and lent his support to a number of her social justice
causes.

your boy is buried. We gave Private Popper a brief but honorable service, then laid him to rest in the back field of Robert Hatheway's farm, which lies south and to the west of Fredericksburg, four miles from Spotsylvania. He rests fifteen or so rods behind the barn, ten or twelve steps to the east of the stone wall at its corner.

The deaths of their sons, six months apart, rocked both Charles and Elizabeth Popper. Sadly, neither seemed able to console the other, perhaps because of their fundamental disagreement about the necessity of what Lizzy Popper called "Mr. Lincoln's fratricidal war." In an October 3, 1863, letter written on stationery from Manhattan's Hotel DuMont, Charles Popper referred to the couple's New Haven home as "an empty shell to which, at present, I am loath to return." Popper instructed his wife that all necessary communication should be forwarded to him in care of the New York office of his employer, the Century Publishing Company. This period of estrangement lasted for fourteen months, during which time Charles Popper began an extramarital affair with Mrs. Vera Daneghy, a subscription customer to whom he sold penny novelettes and by whom he later fathered a daughter, Pansy, born in 1870. Letters Vera Daneghy sent to Lizzy Popper after Charles Popper's death suggest that Popper saw little of his illegitimate daughter but deposited small sums for her in a secret bank account.

Elizabeth Popper's fifty-ninth year was one of profound and confusing loss. Compounding her grief for her slain sons and the defection of her husband was the abrupt and mysterious disappearance, during Christmas week of 1863, of her youngest child, nineteen-year-old Willie. Lizzy became consumed with fear that her surviving son had followed his brothers into the Union Army and would perish as they had. Alone and afraid, she spiraled into a second immobilizing depression.

Worried about their sister's "addled state" and "unkempt person," Martha Weeks and Anna Livermore came to Lizzy Popper's aid. As she had done before, Weeks financed a "rest cure" for Lizzy at the Hartford Retreat. She also commissioned Boston sculptor Aldo Gualtieri to create, from existing daguerreotypes, memorial busts of Edmond Popper and Levi Popper. Anna Livermore traveled from Pennsylvania to stay with Lizzy following her release from the sanitarium, and it was she who promoted her sister's brief but influential foray into Spiritualism. Like many nineteenth-century feminists, Livermore was both a suffragist and a Spiritualist. "Spiritualism and women's rights drew from the same well," notes author Barbara Goldsmith. "For women—sheltered, repressed, powerless—the line between divine inspiration, the courage of one's convictions, and spirit guidance became blurred."

For the grief-stricken Lizzy Popper, the possibility that she might communicate with sons who had "passed over" was irresistible. Could she learn the location of Levi's remains? The whereabouts of her missing Willie? A séance was arranged, to be conducted by Spiritualist minister Theodore W. Cates of Boston, a friend of Livermore's. An account of what transpired that evening—no doubt a subjective one—was later published in a Spiritualist newspaper, *A Beacon from the Beyond*. The article's author was Anna Livermore.

On a snowy evening in late February of 1863, Livermore wrote, Reverend Cates and seven others gathered around the Poppers' dining room table and grasped hands, forming a Spirit Circle.

Then prayers were spoken, incantations uttered, questions posed to the dead. A response came first in the form of notes played on a vacant piano in the adjacent drawing room. (All three of Mrs. Popper's sons~Edmond, Levi, and William~had played the piano.) As instructed by Reverend Cates, Mrs. Popper then placed articles of her sons' clothing across her lap and touched her fingers to the planchette of Mr. Cates' Ouija board. Placing his own fingers on the planchette's opposite side, Reverend Cates closed his eyes and asked in a commanding voice if spirits were present. Mrs. Popper immediately reported feeling tingling sensations in her arms and hands. Magnetic forces had entered her body, Mr. Cates explained. These caused the planchette to move across the board, gliding first to the letter E, then to the letter P. "Is Edmond Popper in this room?" Reverend Cates inquired. The planchette pointed to the word "YES." Mr. Cates then inquired of Edmond if he was in the company of other spirits. The planchette roamed the board, stopping on the numeral one. When Mr. Cates called on the second spirit to identify itself, three people in the room—Reverend Cates, Mrs. Popper, and the author of this account—heard a baby cry. Mrs. Popper called out, "It's the girl! It's my Phoebe!" referring to a daughter she had lost in infancy. Mr. Cates asked the spirit of Mrs. Popper's infant if she had a message for her mother, but the planchette remained still. Mr. Cates then reported seeing the ectoplasm of a small babe float through a window to the outside. The child had left, he announced, but Edmond Popper was still present.

Through Cates, Lizzy asked Edmond if he was in contact with either of his brothers. The planchette failed to budge. A number of follow-up questions went unanswered as well. Then, wrote Livermore, Cates pushed a pencil through a hole at the head of the planchette and placed a sheet of paper between the planchette and the board. Cates asked if Edmond had a message he wished to impart to his mother. The planchette glided again, and as it did, the pencil spelled out, much in the manner of a modern Etch-a-Sketch toy, the message: "healthemma." (The *Beacon from the Beyond* article is illustrated with a drawing of Lizzy Popper's hand and the supposed message.) According to Livermore's account, it was Lizzy herself who decoded the communiqué, staring at the cryptic swirls, then shouting, "Heal them, Ma!"

Recalling the séance years later, Lizzy Popper would express skepticism that she had, in fact, made contact with her dead son and daughter that night. She nevertheless took to heart the "message" she had received. Putting aside her personal grief, Popper wrote to the Union Army's Superintendent of Women Nurses, Dorothea Dix, whom she had met fifteen years earlier at Seneca Falls. "I am nearly sixty years of age and have had no formal medical training, but my constitution is strong and I can learn as swiftly as any. Having lost sons to this war, I should like to come to the aid of other mothers' sons."

JANIS WALKED INTO THE KITCHEN, looking the worse for wear.

"Hey," I said. "Coffee's just made. Help yourself."

She nodded. Her eyes lit for a second on Lizzy's manuscript, opened before me on the kitchen table. Then she turned away and busied herself pouring coffee, adding milk from the fridge. "So I suppose you heard the fireworks last night," she said. Her back was to me.

Play dumb, I told myself. "Fireworks?"

"Moze and me. We had a fight about . . . oh, never mind." She sipped her coffee and sighed. "I don't think I got two hours' sleep last night. God, I didn't need this. I've been so stressed out anyway."

"About what?"

"They're convening my Ph.D. committee. I fly down to defend my thesis proposal on Monday. 'Defend': sounds hostile, doesn't it? And it probably *will* be. I keep thinking I rushed it—that it needs more work."

"Could have fooled me," I said. "It's reading beautifully, Janis."

She walked over to the counter and stared at Velvet's row of grotesques. "This is probably what my committee's going to look like when I walk into that room," she said. Ignoring my smile, she stuck her hand into the pocket of her robe and fished out a pack of cigarettes. "Smart of me, isn't it? I stop running and take up smoking instead." She turned and faced me, her eyes glistening. "You know what he hit me with last night? He's changed his mind. Now he *wants* us to have a child together. Kind of coincidental, don't you think? Just when my career may be . . . and it's bullshit, too. Moses doesn't want a baby. He just wants to throw a net over me so that I can't get away."

Get away? She was thinking about leaving him?

The temporary insanity of my sexual attraction to Janis had long since subsided. She was a cute, intelligent, somewhat neurotic rent-paying tenant, and I'd been a lonely, angry idiot that night that I'd poured her all that wine and taken her to bed. But like she'd said before: she'd drunk the wine; she'd gotten into bed with me, too. This disclosure about a baby was a red flag, though. Becoming Janis's kitchen confidante now would be another kind of intimacy, and if there was one thing I didn't need, it was further entanglement. But when I opened my mouth to say something like "You'll work it out" or "Well, this is between you and him," she held out her hand like a traffic cop and headed out the back door.

Still, I felt for her. She'd worked hard to bring Lizzy back into the light of day, and if her career was poised for takeoff, it was because she'd earned it. I watched her out there for a minute or two, sitting on the stoop, puffing away. Then I folded a napkin in half, bookmarking the place where I'd stopped reading. I grabbed the spring-bound manuscript and went out there. "Scoot over," I said.

"Caelum, I'd just better be by myself, okay?"

"Nope. Push over." I sat down beside her on the chilly stone stoop. "Thank you," I said.

"For what?"

I tapped my knuckles against her manuscript. "For this," I said. "My aunt used to try to interest me in all this family history, but I *wasn't* interested in it back then. And then, after she died and Maureen and I came back here, life had just gotten too complicated. If it wasn't for you, it'd all still be sitting up there on the sun porch. Or lost to the landfill, maybe. But you rescued it for me and, well, *synthesized* it. Brought Lizzy to life for me and, you know, for other people, too. So I'm grateful for all the hard work you did. Thanks."

She nodded. Mumbled it almost inaudibly, "You're welcome."

Somewhere in the woods beyond the farm, rifle fire exploded—three blasts in quick succession. It was mid-November now, hunting season, the trees bare and the ground carpeted with papery leaves.

"A guy came by to see you yesterday," she said. "I forgot to tell you."

Junior had called a couple of times that week about the upcoming civil suit. The Seaberrys' attorney had called him about some clarifications about deeds or something. I'd purposely not returned those calls. "Did he give you a name or a business card?"

"He wasn't exactly the business-card type. He said something about you hiring him to do some work around here. Something about the apple house."

"Oh, okay. Old, skinny guy, right? Was he drunk?"

"Not that I noticed. He was jittery, though. Who is he?"

"Nobody. Just some old rummy who used to do odd jobs for my aunt. He's harmless." I held *Elizabeth Hutchinson Popper: An Epistolary Self-Portrait* in front of her. "Listen, Janis. You've got publishers interested in this thing, inquiries from colleges. Your committee's not going to give you any trouble."

"Ha! Too bad *you're* not on it. How far have you gotten?"

"The sons' deaths, the séance. Shit, it's no wonder she fell into that depression. Her kids get killed in a war she opposed, her husband bails on her. It's sad, isn't it? That she and Charlie couldn't have grieved together."

"Charlie was a pig," Janis said.

"Maybe. But he had to have been struggling with the loss, too."

"So that justifies his moving out? Getting his mistress pregnant?"

"I didn't say that. I'm just pointing out that they were his sons, too. And, hey, it couldn't have been easy living with someone like Lizzy."

She turned toward me, frowning. "Meaning?"

"Meaning she was relentless—the tireless little crusader for social justice. Maybe Charlie needed her to be less of a crusader and more of a wife. It's kind of like what's-her-name, that antiwar mom who lost her son and camped out near Bush's ranch, demanding to speak to him."

"Cindy Sheehan," Janis said.

"Yeah, her. She and her husband split up; it was in the paper. Because of her activism, I think it said. All I'm saying is, the cause may be righteous, but when they go into overdrive—"

"And 'they' means women, right? Why are you men all so insecure?"

I smiled. "All of us, huh? Now there's a broad indictment."

"I'm serious, Caelum. Why is it so threatening to men when a woman feels compelled to engage with the world? Look at the grief Hillary Clinton always gets." She took an angry drag off her cigarette. "For five years he tells me he doesn't want us to get pregnant, and now he does?"

Rather than debate her on gender politics, I brought the subject back to her book. "Tell me something," I said. "The missing son? Willie? He was my great-grandma Lydia's father, right?"

Janis nodded.

"Which means he was what? My great-great-grandfather?"

She nodded again.

"So why'd he go missing? Don't tell me he got killed in the war, too?"

She looked disbelieving of my stupidity. "You're *here*, aren't you?"

"So where was he then? Where'd he disappear to?"

She stubbed her cigarette against the stone step. "I wrote the goddamned thing, Caelum. You want the Spark Notes, too?"

"No, ma'am. I get the message. I'll just keep reading."

She said she didn't mean to snap at me—that it was nerves, sleep deprivation, their fight the night before. She lit another cigarette.

Out in the woods, there was more gunfire. I thought about Maureen—how, after we moved back here to the farmhouse from Colorado, those random gunshot blasts during hunting season would make her flinch, set her on edge. Return her, over and over, to that place, that day. . . .

"Wow," Janis said. "Where were you just now?"

"What?" I looked away from her gaze. "Nowhere. Just thinking."

"About what?"

I shook my head. "Nothing."

"You know what I find depressing?" she said. "That between Lizzy's era and ours, nothing's really changed."

"Oh, I don't know. Ouija boards and horse-drawn carriages have kind of fallen out of fashion, haven't they?"

"Really, Caelum. Think about it. We still enslave black people. We still put kids in uniform and send them far away from home to kill and be killed. Do you know what our military is paying in 'blood money' these days so that they can make their recruitment quotas? I heard it on NPR yesterday. Twenty thousand dollars! And who's vulnerable to bribery like that? Well-heeled kids from the suburbs? No, poor kids. Inner city kids. Twenty thousand dollars so they can go over there and get themselves killed in Bush and Cheney's bullshit war. It's disgusting."

"Okay, the deck's still stacked. I'll grant you that. But 'enslaved'? That's a stretch, isn't it?"

"You know something, Caelum? You don't live in New Orleans for five years without having your eyes opened. You don't marry a black man without seeing the million little ways this country chips away at his dignity. And not just in the South either. Do you know how many times Moze has been pulled over and profiled since we came to Blue State Connecticut? Three times. Do you know how many banks he had to go to before one of them would give him a small business loan? Four. And do you know why the fourth one said yes? Because *I* was with him that time. Because that stupid loan officer addressed everything he had to say to me and treated Moze like he wasn't even there."

"All right, I'll give you institutional racism. But that's not—"

"Tell me something, Caelum. When you go to visit your wife, what's prevalent at that prison—and every other prison in this country, for that matter? Light skin or dark?"

"Dark," I conceded. "Eight or nine to one."

"And who gets a longer sentence for the same conviction? That one white woman or the nine black women who can't afford good lawyers?"

She shook her head in disgust. "Poor Lizzy. She must be rolling over in her grave. And Lydia, too."

"Maybe so. But here's a little friendly advice. When you walk in there to present your thesis proposal? I think you'd better check your guns at the door."

"What's that supposed to mean?"

"It means, don't start talking about 'blood money,' and how blacks are still enslaved. Because if there's a couple of conservative professors in that room and you start sounding like Al Sharpton, they might just take you on. And then things *could* get hostile."

She said she hadn't been in grad school for five years without knowing what people's politics were, and how to talk the talk.

"Then you'll do fine," I said.

She stood, said she'd better go back upstairs. But instead of opening the door, she just stood there.

"What?" I said, knowing it was a risky question.

"I got pregnant once. Not too long after Moze and I moved in together. I wasn't sure whether I wanted it or not, and he was pretty definite that he *didn't* want it. So I had an abortion. I was afraid if I didn't, he'd leave me."

I nodded. Said nothing.

"That child would be in kindergarten by now. I was lying awake thinking about that last night. I'd be the mother of a five-year-old."

"First things first," I said. "Go down there and get your degree. Then you can come back here and figure things out, you and him."

After she went inside, I stayed out there for a while. She'd forgotten her cigarettes, and I took one out of the pack and lit it. I don't think I'd had a cigarette in a decade.

Boom! Boom! A deer had either escaped or been struck down. . . .

I closed my eyes and saw the two of them out there on the side of the school building, armed to the teeth, taking aim at their own. *Go! Go! This is awesome! This is what we always wanted to do!* . . . Saw Rachel's body in the grass near the top of the stairs. Saw her white casket, scrawled with messages of grief and love. . . . Rachel, Danny, all of them: they'd been their parents' precious children, just as Edmond and Levi had been Lizzy's. As Morgan Seaberry had been *his* mother's pride and joy. . . .

Nothing ever changes, Janis had said. It did, though. We lived, lulled, on the fault line of chaos. Change could come explosively, and out of nowhere. What had that chaos theorist on the plane called it? I couldn't recall the word. Began with a *b*.

I checked my watch. My papers were graded, my lessons prepared, I was showered and dressed. I had another twenty minutes or so. I could either get to Oceanside a little early for a change—run off those handouts, answer some emails. Or else I could . . .

Putting aside her personal grief, Popper wrote to the Union Army's superintendent of women nurses, Dorothea

Dix, whom she had met fifteen years earlier at Seneca Falls. "I am nearly sixty years of age and have had no formal medical training, but my constitution is strong and I can learn as swiftly as any. Having lost sons to this war, I should like to come to the aid of other mothers' sons."

While Lizzy Popper awaited a response from Dix, she received, to her great relief, a letter from the missing Willie. Lizzy's fear that her surviving son would become a casualty of war proved unwarranted. As his letter explained, Willie Popper had taken a far different path.

Earlier correspondence between Lizzy Popper and her brother, the troubled, one-eyed Roswell Hutchinson, sheds light on the Popper family dynamic, and on the ways in which Charles and Elizabeth Popper's youngest child differed from his siblings. In an 1859 letter to the sister who had raised and later rescued him from his troubles in Richmond, Hutchinson criticized what he perceived as his sister and brother-in-law's "immoderate mollycoddling" of Willie. The letter was a parting shot of sorts; after an extended stay with the Poppers, Hutchinson had been asked to leave because of drunkenness, "dicing," and unemployment. Said the wounded and wounding Hutchinson:

Even a one-eyed shipwreck of a man such as I can see that Crown Prince William is worshipped by his fawning father and doting mother, and that he is ill served by these extreme attentions. Would that you had offered me one-tenth of the affection you bestow on this spoiled whelp, Lizzy, back in the day when you were young and I was younger, and the mother who would have loved me was mouldering in the ground. Perhaps if you had been more loving, I would not have taken as my consort the demon drink.

In a letter written but apparently never sent, Lizzy answered her brother's charges with Quaker frankness: "If thee was ill raised by me, I say only that I did my best. I will not be held responsible for thy intemperance. Willie's gift sets him apart, but he is neither better nor more prized than his brothers."

By "Willie's gift," Lizzy Popper most likely referred to her son's musical talent. Charles Popper had detected in his youngest son an aptitude for music and had taught him to play piano, banjo, and fiddle, and to sing much of the catalogue from the old Popper Family songbook. Willie shared his father's love of performance, executing the abolitionist songs with passion and zeal, but later confessed to his mother that he gave little notice to the political messages the lyrics conveyed. During the second half of 1863, Willie Popper had been working unhappily as a longshoreman under the direction of his uncle, New Haven harbormaster Nathanael Weeks. Slight of build, Willie hated the work and was intimidated by the other dock workers—"coarse Irish," he later wrote to his mother, "whose great sport is to mock me for my small frame and small hands, and the absence of whiskers on my chin." It was at the harbor, however, that Willie became seduced by what he called "the siren's song": placards and broadsides advertising the Broadway melodramas and minstrel shows a short ferry ride away. On a winter afternoon, Willie Popper snuck aboard one of those ferries, crossed Long Island Sound, and arrived in Manhattan. He never saw his mother again.

During the bleak years when the Union battled the Confederacy and mothers on both sides of the Mason and Dixon line wept for their slain sons, there were no fewer than twenty blackface minstrel shows playing in and around lower Broadway. Willie Popper auditioned and was hired as an "Ethiopian delineator" by one of the most successful of these entertainments, Calhoun's Mississippi Minstrels at Waverly Calhoun's Musee and Theatre, located at the corner of Broadway and Prince Street. Promotional posters for this large-cast show promised that ticket-buyers would witness "The Darky As He Truly Is—At Work! At Rest! In Song and Dance!" But if authenticity was advertised, what

Calhoun's show delivered was the usual costumed extravaganza and comic stereotype.*

Willie Popper began with Calhoun's Mississippi Minstrels as a blackface chorus member in the opening and closing production numbers, but his voice and stage presence quickly brought him to the attention of owner-producer Waverly Calhoun, who renamed him Fennimore Forrest, dressed him in drag, and made him a featured player.

By the mid-nineteenth century, women had broken the gender barrier in New York theater, among them actress-producer Laura Keane and soprano Jenny Lind, the popular "Swedish Nightingale." Minstrel shows, however, continued to cast males in female roles, most likely for comic effect. As a longshoreman on the docks at New Haven, Willie Popper's slender frame and beardless chin had been liabilities, but on the minstrel stage, they became assets.

Wearing gaudy dresses and ocher-colored makeup, Willie titillated and repulsed audiences during the walk around as Lucy Long, a seductive, sashaying "yaller gal" who made fools of her would-be "darky" lotharios, and whose "lips are so big, they can't be kissed all at once." In the show's afterpiece, Willie segued from comedy to melodrama, playing a suffering young slave named Minnie May. Minnie May was a blatant imitation of Eliza, the heroic escaped slave mother

---

* Most minstrel shows adhered to a standard three-part structure: the act-one "walk around," the act two "olio," and the act-three "afterpiece." In the "walk around," the entire cast sang and danced, then left the stage to a dozen or so featured players, seated in a semicircle. At center stage sat Mr. Interlocutor, a white master of ceremonies who served as straightman to the "end men" in the corner chairs—white comedians, their faces smeared with burnt cork, their lips exaggerated with contrasting white makeup. Called Tambo and Bones, or Gumbo and Sambo, or Jim Crow and Zip Coon, the end men were comic buffoons who swapped boasts, insults, and malapropisms, reinforcing the belief that "Ethiopes" were dim-witted, lazy, and happy with their lot in life. For the "olio," the curtain was lowered. At the front of the stage, singers, fiddlers, jugglers, sleight-of-hand artists, and Shakespearean parodists performed a fast-paced variety show while, behind the curtain, stagehands readied the sets for the "afterpiece," an elaborate production number set on a Southern plantation.

in Harriet Beecher Stowe's ever-popular *Uncle Tom's Cabin*. Dressed in ragged skirts and cradling a black baby doll wrapped in bunting, "Fennimore Forrest," as Minnie May, apparently galvanized New York theatergoers. According to an April 3, 1863, *New York World* account, "The talented Mr. Forrest, in the midst of the third-act plantation frolics, stops the show with a poignant anthem that brings tearful audiences to their feet and reminds us of the Union's Holy Mission." For his showstopper, Willie had converted his father's abolitionist hymn "Swing Open, Freedom's Door!" into a melodramatic tour de force.

In the letter Willie Popper sent to his mother, he enclosed a clipping of the *World* article and wrote that, despite lingering sorrow about the deaths of his brothers,

I am far happier now than I have ever been. You who worked so hard to liberate the slaves will hopefully appreciate that my life in New Haven was one of enslavement. When I stepped aboard the ferry that took me to New York, it was my escape from bondage! Cast aside your mourning and your Quaker resistance to theatricals, Mother. Come and see my show!

No evidence exists that Lizzy complied, but her estranged husband, then ensconced at Manhattan's DuMont Hotel, did attend a performance of Calhoun's Mississippi Minstrels. Charlie Popper promptly disowned his surviving son. A subsequent letter from Willie to his mother is ambiguous as to the exact reason, or reasons, for the break with his father. Perhaps it was because Willie's reworking of "Swing Open Freedom's Door!" insulted Charles Popper, or because Willie's taking of female parts embarrassed him, or because he disapproved of minstrel shows in general. The possibility also exists that Willie Popper may have been engaged in a sexual relationship with Waverly Calhoun, the show's owner and producer, and that Charles Popper broke with his son for this reason. If Willie Popper was, in fact, having an affair with Calhoun, he hardly would have stated so in a letter to his politically liberal but socially conservative mother. The social mores of the time dictated that "the sin that dare not speak its name" was never referred to directly. But in Willie's letter to his mother, he stated, "Waverly has become a friend to me—the dearest I have ever known." The letter's return address indicates that Willie was living at Calhoun's Park Avenue apartment.

Whether or not Willie Popper and his producer were involved sexually, their relationship ended abruptly in January of 1864, when Waverly Calhoun's Musee and Theatre was destroyed by fire. Calhoun had fallen asleep in his office while counting the evening's box office receipts and had died, apparently of asphyxiation. A *New York Sun* account of the blaze and its aftermath describes the removal of Calhoun's body from the destroyed building, "while his young star, Fennimore Forrest, looked on, distraught and in *dishabille*." Willie Popper disappeared from New York shortly after and did not communicate with his mother again until ten years later, in 1874. By then, Charles Popper had died. He and Willie had not resolved their differences.

In March of 1863, Lizzy Popper received by telegram a succinct response from the Union's nursing superintendent Dorothea Dix: "You will suffice. Come as soon as possible."

I went back inside. Fed the cat, packed my briefcase for the teaching day ahead. On my way out, that word came to me: bifurcation. I checked my watch, looked over at the computer. The screen saver was on; I'd forgotten to close it down the night before. I sat. Googled *chaos theory bifurcation*.

And son of a bitch, what was the first listing that rose up from cyberspace? An article by my airplane buddy, Mickey Schmidt. I'd called him, slurring drunk, at midnight on Y2K as the tectonic plates of time were shifting from the twentieth century to the twenty-first. *Sure you remember me*, I'd insisted. *You said you were writing a book about gambling. You asked me to hold your hand during takeoff because you were afraid to fly.*

And did you? No, you didn't. You couldn't do that one small thing. . . .

Why don't you ever hug me back? she'd wanted to know—the mother who hadn't really been my mother. The mother they'd passed off as mine. . . .

"Emotional castrato," Francesca had etched onto the face of my computer monitor the day she left me. Wife number two: she'd had the same complaint as wives number one and three. I saw Maureen, standing there in our Colorado living room, our signal, the lit candle, flickering between us. *Come upstairs. Love me. Be close to me.* But I'd withheld myself, as usual, and now withholding myself was one of the house rules: a quick embrace across the visiting room table, a peck on the cheek, no handholding. Guards and surveillance cameras were watching. . . .

I clicked the mouse. Scrolled down. And there it was, in Mickey Schmidt's own words: "Bifurcation occurs when the environment of a potentially chaotic system destabilizes due to stress over time, or to some inciting disturbance, explosive or catastrophic. When perturbation occurs, an attractor draws the trajectories of the disturbance and, at the point of transition, the system bifurcates and is propelled to a new order of self-organization, or else it disintegrates."

I thought about all this on my drive over to Oceanside, where the lawn signs and bumper stickers I passed—"Let's Support Our Troops," "Sleep Well Tonight—Our Marine Has Your Back," "There Were No WMDs—They LIED," "Impeach Bush"—spoke of our deep division, our *bifurcation* since 9/11. . . . Whether it was "Bush and Cheney's bullshit war" or "Mr. Lincoln's fratricidal war" or the vengeful war against their own that Eric and Dylan had waged: war begat chaos and altered everything. I thought about Private First Class Kendricks in my Quest class: who had Kareem Kendricks been, I wondered, before he went over there to fight the insurgency and got his hand blown off? . . . Thought about how chaos had descended on the Columbine families. They'd sent their kids off to school that morning, lulled by the assumption that school was safe. . . . Thought about Charlie and Lizzy—how the war had pretty much ended their marriage, how their children's lives had bifurcated. Levi and Edmond had marched off to war to end slavery and had lost their lives to the cause. Their brother, my great-great-grandfather, had marched out onto a Broadway stage to reinforce all the ugly stereotypes and had been lauded and rewarded for it—at least until the night his benefactor went up in flames. But there was more to Willy's story than that. There had to be. Because as Janis had put it, I was here, wasn't I?

Perturbation, chaos, bifurcation: it was just as Mickey Schmidt had written: some explosion—as local as rifle fire, as worldwide as war—can set things reeling in a whole different direction, can cause a fork in the road. And one path may lead to disintegration, the other to a reordered world.

So maybe Janis had been right that day when we'd gone up to see the crumbling Memorial Arch that Lizzy and her granddaughter Lydia had seen unveiled and dedicated. Maybe my ancestors *could* teach me something. . . .

And maybe I'd better put all of that aside for now, because my mission that day was to try and somehow convince seventeen skeptical community college students that the ancient myth of Theseus and the Minotaur could inform their lives. Well, good luck with that one, Quirk. Wishing you all the best with Mission: Impossible. . . .

→→ *chapter twenty-nine* ←←

Order → *Inciting disturbance* → *CHAOS* → *Order Restored*

Recapping the felt pen I'd used to scrawl the myth's equation, I turned from the whiteboard back to them. "So by the end of the story, Theseus has slain the Minotaur, sacrificed his kill to the gods, and escaped from the imprisoning maze. Athens has been restored to order, until the gods' next intervention for good or ill. But let's backtrack, okay? What would you identify as the 'inciting disturbance' of this story—the thing that called the Minotaur into existence in the first place?"

Hipólito's leg pumped up and down with restless boredom. Devin dozed beneath the brim of his ball cap. Kahlúa miscalculated that her text-messaging would be undetectable from my vantage point. My eyes moved from her dancing fingers to Private First Class Kendricks. As always, he was dressed in sand-colored camouflage. As always, he was seated in back, apart from the others. His eyes shifted nervously. His hands rested against his desktop, the fingers of his good hand steepled with the metal fingers of his prosthesis.

"The inciting disturbance?" I asked again. "The thing that threw everything else out of kilter?"

I waited for them. They waited for me.

"Kahlúa? What do you think?" Busted, she dropped her cell phone into her oversized orange bag and shrugged guiltily.

"Someone else?"

No one else. Well, okay, they owned this uncomfortable silence. Let them live with it.

Marisol raised a tentative hand. Poor, sweet Mari: the student most willing to volunteer and least likely to have a correct response. "Was it when the monster ate all the human sacrifices?"

I scanned the others' blank faces. "Mari proposes that the Minotaur's periodic devouring of the seven youths and seven maidens is the inciting disturbance. Agree? Disagree?"

Ibrahim's eyes bounced to the board and back. He shook his head. "That's a result, not the cause."

"Yeah, man," Manny agreed. "That's like saying that the soldiers coming back in body bags caused the war in Iraq."

Iraq: the word triggered my involuntary glance at Private First Class Kendricks back there. A few of the others looked back, too. Until then, Private Kendricks had been having one of his less kinetic mornings, but our glances set him in motion. It had begun three or four classes ago: Kareem Kendricks's pacing and desk-switching back there. There'd been a complaint—a hushed after-class conversation with Daisy and Marisol. "He kinda freaks us out," Marisol had said. "Makes it hard to concentrate." Reluctantly, I'd promised to speak to him about it without mentioning them specifically.

And I had, too, in the hallway before the next class. PFC Kendricks had responded defensively. How did I think he'd survived numerous gun battles during three tours of duty? he asked. By making himself a hard target—*that* was how. I'd wanted to point out the obvious: that no one in class was shooting at him. Instead, I'd suggested that maybe we could take a few minutes at the beginning of class so that he could speak briefly about his experiences over there—that the others might better understand his restlessness if they had a context for it.

He'd shaken his head emphatically. Did I want him to drop the class? Was that what I was trying to say? No, no, I'd assured him; of course not. Instead, I'd dropped the issue, letting him wander at will, despite our collective discomfort. I mean, what did it matter if he moved around back there? Who did it hurt?

"Okay. Good point, guys," I told Manny and Ibrahim. "But if we rule out the sacrificing of Athens' youth to the voracious Minotaur, then what *was* the inciting disturbance?"

"When the queen did it with the white bull?" Hipólito asked.

"Eww," Ashleigh said. "She had sex with a *bull*?"

"Yeah, like *you* read the assignment," Ozzie noted.

"Shut up, Oswaldo. I had to work a double shift yesterday. Okay?"

"All right, let's stay on course here," I said. "Let's go back to the beginning. King Minos asks the gods to give him a gift that will signify he's a favored son. Poseidon obliges, and the spectacular white bull emerges from the sea. But as the saying goes, be careful what you wish for. Minos's queen becomes so enamored of the creature that she craves him sexually. Why??"

"Same reason the ladies can't resist me," Ozzie said. "Just too damn fine a specimen."

"Pfft," Ashleigh fired back. "Your mirror must be cracked."

"Because Poseidon put a spell on her," Daisy said. "So that whenever she looked at the white bull, she got . . ."

"Damp in her drawers," Ozzie stage-whispered. The guys around him grinned. Devin came out from under his ball cap.

"Daisy's right," I said. "But *why* did Poseidon put a spell on her?"

"To embarrass her husband, King Midas or whatever," Hip said.

"It's Minos, not Midas—that's a whole other myth. But yes. Poseidon wanted to humiliate Minos by having his wife cuckold him with the white bull. Why?"

"Whass 'cuckold'?" Hipólito asked. At the back of the room, Private Kendricks chuckled at some private joke.

"When a wife cheats on her husband," someone said.

I saw Paul Hay, up there on his roof. Saw the pipe wrench. . . .

"Because after Poseidon sent him that bull, he was supposed to kill it," Marisol said. "Sacrifice it or whatever."

"Show Poseidon some props," Hip concurred. "Only he didn't do it."

I nodded. "Why not?"

"The 'inciting disturbance' was Minos's pridefulness. He failed to humble himself to his higher power." At first I didn't realize that it was Private Kendricks who had spoken. Then I saw him back there, bouncing up and down on his heels, hyper-engaged. We were three weeks past mid-semester. This was the first time he had volunteered in class.

"Mr. Kendricks is right!" I said, more enthusiastically than I'd meant to. "Minos was so proud of his prize bull that he couldn't bring himself to slaughter it in gratitude. So Poseidon answers his arrogance by afflicting his queen with a sort of sexual madness. She commits bestiality and gives birth to a freak of nature—a dangerous half human half beast who must be imprisoned inside the labyrinth and who can only be appeased by the slaughter of innocents . . . by the slaughter of . . . and uh . . . and . . ."

They were there, at the rear of the classroom, instead of Kendricks. Eric and Dylan, geared up and smirking at me. A wave of nausea overtook me. I faltered, grabbed the edge of my desk. "Excuse me," I said.

In the safety of the empty corridor, I squatted, bent my head, took some deep breaths. I broke out in a clammy sweat.

"You okay, Mr. Quirk?" I turned and faced Ibrahim's dark worried eyes.

"Yeah. Yeah, I'm good. Got a little dizzy for a second there, that's all." He followed me back in. "Okay," I said. "Sorry about that. Where were we?" I sat behind my desk. Kept my hands in my lap so they wouldn't see that they were shaking.

It was Manny who brought us back. "Mr. Quirk, ain't pride one of the whataya-call-its? Seven deadly sins? We were just talking about them in my ethics class."

They were watching me, waiting, each face a study in innocence.

"Well, the uh . . . the seven deadly sins is a Christian concept. But certainly the ancient Greeks would have exerted an influence on the Christian value system. Their philosophers and storytellers . . ."

Were they gone now? Were we all safe again?

"Excuse me," I said. "Lost my train of thought. Where was I?"

"The philosophers."

"Oh, right. Well, I think . . . I think it's fair to argue that the ancient Greek philosophers and storytellers laid down the cornerstone for the ethics of Western culture. Because what are all these age-old stories we've been studying, if not lessons about how to manage the human condition? How those of us in civilized society should and shouldn't live our lives?"

Someone wanted to know what the other six deadly sins were.

"Being a glutton's one, I remember," Manny said. "And being lazy."

Tunisia, the daughter of a minister, chimed in. "Greed. Anger. Lust."

"Passing gas in public," Ozzie quipped. "Talking on your cell phone while you're driving."

Everyone laughed except Private Kendricks, who volunteered for the *second* time that semester. "The seven deadly sins are pride, envy, wrath, sloth, greed, gluttony, and lust." He'd begun pacing again, looking at nothing, at no one. "And the seven contrary virtues are humility, kindness, patience, diligence, generosity, abstinence, and chastity."

"Chastity?" Ozzie said. "What fun is that, man?"

Private Kendricks stopped in his tracks and addressed him directly. "This is a class, not a comedy club. Show a little respect."

His reprimand triggered an uneasy silence. They lowered their eyes, shifted in their seats. Chagrined, Ozzie retaliated. "Hey, G.I. Joe. Take a chill pill, man."

"Man?" Kendricks shot back. "What do you know about being a man?"

Before I could summon the words to put out this little brush fire, Devin opened his mouth and fanned the flames. "Yo, Oz. He just got you bad, man."

"Yeah, man," Ozzie said. "Let's all give G.I. Joe a hand. Cuz, you know, he could use one."

All eyes—my own included, unfortunately—tracked Private Kendricks's prosthesis. "Okay, knock it off!" I said, my voice raised. "This is a college class, remember? Save your trash-talking for the playground."

Ozzie covered his smile with his hand. Kendricks crash-landed in a seat. He was breathing hard, nostrils flared.

Mercifully, it was almost time to wrap things up anyway. I reminded them to check the syllabus for Thursday's assignment and told them they could go. "Come by my office if you have any questions about the paper that's coming up." Private Kendricks bolted out the door.

"That was a cheap shot," I told Ozzie as he passed me on his way out.

"Whatever," he said, neither facing me nor stopping.

"You make another remark like that, and I'll toss you out of here."

"Yeah, whatever," he said again. His gait was a little cockier than usual, a little more face-savingly macho. In the corridor, his buddies welcomed him with hoots and high fives. Asshole, I mumbled. Assholes. . . .

I stared past the empty desks to the back of the room—the spot where their ghosts had been. Why, out of nowhere, in the middle of a class . . . But hadn't they threatened as much, in those basement videos they'd left behind? Hadn't they warned us they were coming back to haunt us?

IN THE FACULTY LOUNGE AT lunchtime, I tried my best to filter out the usual verbal spam: how Maggie Bass's search for a mother-of-the-bride dress was going, how the planned relocation of the faculty parking lot from the east side of campus to the west was going to ruin everyone's lives. In the four years I'd been teaching at Oceanside, I'd made no real friends. Once an adjunct, always an adjunct. Plus there was the notoriety factor, I figured: he's the husband of that woman who . . . But truth be told, I hadn't exactly extended myself to any of them either. So there was no one, really, to run things by after that unsettling class—no one to ask what I might do about Kendricks's distracting behavior and the class's intolerance of it. Unless I called Counseling Services. Maybe I could get someone there to call him in and talk to him. If it *was* PTSD, then Kendricks denied it at his peril. He needed treatment. Medication, maybe— something to calm his agitation. . . . But hey, was that *my* business? There were limits, lines not to overstep. I was only his lit teacher. And anyway, the semester would be over in another three weeks. I was the only one who had to face him when he was back there, doing his thing. If the others didn't like it, they should just ignore it and face the front.

I finished my lunch in silence, give or take a few perfunctory pleasantries, then headed down to the copying room to run some stuff off. Wendy Woodka, two teachers ahead of me in line, had a whole *folder* of material she was running off, thirty copies at a clip. There was a paper jam, a toner cartridge replacement. What should have taken me five minutes took fifteen, which made me late for my office hours. Well, no big deal, I told myself. No one usually showed up anyway.

But someone had. Approaching my office from the other end of the corridor, I watched him in silhouette against the staircase window. He was pacing, checking his watch, his cell phone. "Kareem?"

He pivoted so abruptly that I reared back. Catching someone off guard like that in Iraq could probably get you killed, I thought.

"Sorry to keep you waiting." I fumbled with my key ring. "Kind of a madhouse at the copying machine. You been here long?"

Instead of answering the question, he informed me that he had to be in New London for a four p.m. appointment. So what was the problem? I wondered. It was ten past one. New London was only twenty minutes away.

I swung the door open and gestured toward the swivel chair opposite my desk. "Have a seat," I said. "You here to talk about the paper?"

He shook his head. He sat. I sat. He didn't look at me. Didn't speak.

"So I was glad to see you volunteer in class today," I said. "I hope you'll keep contributing like that. You have a lot to offer."

He nodded. Still no eye contact.

"And about that crack Ozzie made? I checked him on it after class. I suspect it was more face-saving than malicious. Try and let it go, okay?"

He smiled. Swiveled. "They're all so young, aren't they? Maturity-wise, I mean. Not age-wise. Ozzie and I went to the same high school. He's actually a year older than me, believe it or not."

"Well, I suspect Ozzie hasn't seen as much of the world as you have. The army must grow you up pretty fast, I imagine. In wartime, especially."

He spoke not to me but to the philodendron on my filing cabinet. "I drove down to Pittsburgh to visit my dad last weekend. Him and his 'shack-up'—the woman he met online and left my mother for. He hadn't bothered to come and see me when I was in Walter Reed, but he'd bought us tickets to the Steelers game on Sunday, and he thought that was gonna make everything all right again. I was supposed to stay the weekend and head back on Monday. But I took off early

Sunday morning, while they were still sleeping. I had to. I couldn't take it."

"Couldn't take what?" I asked him.

"Well, for one thing, I don't condone adultery. And okay, those weeks that I was at Walter Reed, he says he could get off of work—and I accept that, I understand it. But *he* could have called *me* every once in a while, instead of *me* always calling *him*? But you know what was *really* messing me up when I got down there to Pittsburgh? Was how young he seemed. He kept asking me things like, what did I think of Kanye West's music, and did I think he should hold on to Kevin Garnett in this fantasy basketball league he was in or trade him. And how he wasn't just *in* this league; he was *commissioner* of it. Like that was some big mark of distinction: commissioner of make-believe. And I wanted to slam him, one-handed, against the wall, the way he used to do to me, and scream in his face, 'Stop it! Act your age!' . . . I didn't do it, though. I wanted to, but I couldn't. 'Honor thy father,' you know what I'm saying? So instead, I grabbed my car keys, got out of there, and took off. It was messing with my head, you know? You get out of there alive, more or less, wait for your father to come see you at the hospital you're stuck at, and when you finally go to see him, he's younger than you are."

My mind searched for something useful to say, but all I could come up with was something to ask. "How long were you over there?"

"Thirty-six months total. Got home for Christmas in oh-five. An eight-week furlough, it was supposed to be, but they pulled us back twelve days early. Rumsfeld's orders. 'Rummie's dummies,' we used to call ourselves."

"So every time you turn on the TV, someone who's never been over there the way you have is giving an opinion on Operation Iraqi Freedom. Pull out. Stay the course. I'm curious, Kareem. What are your politics?"

"My *politics*?" He shot me a quick glance, then looked away again. "I voted for W, if that's what you mean. Both times. No way I was voting for Kerry."

"You think it's worth it? That we're over there for the right reasons?"

He shrugged. "Politics is a luxury you can't necessarily afford when you're over there. You just get up, do your job, and embrace the suck."

He raised his prosthetic hand and made the wrist rotate. A soft mechanical whirring accompanied the back and forth motion. "I was a 'single-digit midget' when *this* happened. That's what they call you when you got less than ten days left before you get out. Only had seventy-two hours to go when we got waxed. Me and my buddy Kelsey, this guy from North Carolina."

I asked him what happened.

"We were on patrol together in a Humvee, Kelsey and me. And Kelse goes, 'What's that up yonder?' and I go, 'What do you mean? Those trunk monkeys on the bridge?' And Kelsey goes, 'No, no, not them, that black thing.' And I go, 'What black thing?' because I didn't see any black thing, okay? And that's all I remember.

"They said that, after the explosion, I was wandering around in a daze, gushing like Old Faithful, and trying to pick up pieces of my buddy with a hand that wasn't there anymore. I took some sniper fire, they said—couple of Ali Babas shooting at me from a rooftop. Trying to finish the job, I guess. The trunk monkeys who were covering us got one of 'em, they said, but the other one got away. I don't happen to remember any of it.

"They medevaced me to a hospital north of Baghdad. Stabilized me and sent me on to Germany. I was there for ten days. Then they flew me back stateside. I was stuck in Walter Reed for six weeks. My wife and my mother came to see me a couple of times. And Kelsey's family—his mom and dad and his sister. Which was pretty decent of them, I thought, because, you know. Lose your son like that, your brother, and then you drive all those miles to give comfort to the guy who was sitting right there next to him and survived it?'"

I asked him when he'd finally gotten back home to his family.

"In May. End of May. They had a party for me—my mother's people. It was at my aunt and uncle's. You know those yard signs— 'Let's Support Our Troops'? They'd stuck them up, all over their lawn, signs and balloons. And there were maybe sixty, seventy people at that party. Friends, relatives, some cousins from Florida that I hadn't seen in years. My aunt had gotten this sheet cake made and, I don't know how they did it, but there was this big picture of me on it. This picture of me in my dress uniform. But it was edible, you know? And my daughter? Keesha? When they cut the cake? She was sitting on my lap, eating her piece, and she says, 'Look, Daddy, I'm eating your face.' And everybody thought that was so funny, you know what I'm saying? Everybody in that crowded room was laughing but me. Because Kelsey? When his family came to see me at Walter Reed? His father told me, when it was just me and him in the room, that that bomb had blown Kelsey's face off. So I didn't think it was funny what Keesha said. And I got so mad that I shoved her onto the floor. Hard, they said. She fell facedown, dropped her cake, started crying. And it was bad, you know? Me, losing it like that with my daughter? With my family watching? . . . The thing is, you get into these situations over there. Exchange gunfire with four or five hajis, maybe, and when you pursue them, they duck into private homes, apartment buildings. And there's *kids* living in these places. But it's self-defense, you know? You see someone rearing back to lob a grenade at you, you got to shoot whether there's kids caught in the crossfire or not."

I thought about what Lolly had said about my father—how, after he returned from *his* war, he'd drink himself useless rather than talk about it. This was healthier, right? Talking about it? Getting it out? I just wasn't sure why Kendricks had picked me to be his sounding board.

"I was . . . I was thinking about that paper you wrote a while back—the one where you said that, post-Iraq, you felt like Sisyphus, pushing a heavy rock up a hill every day." He nodded in recognition. "How's that going? Things going any better on the home front now?" I asked.

He stiffened. Looked at me directly for the first time since he'd sat down. "Why are you asking?" he wanted to know.

"Oh. Well . . . that paper. How you were reading your daughter a story and, in the middle of it, you had . . . what was it? A flashback?"

He stared at me and swiveled, not answering.

I grabbed at anything. "So how does that thing work, anyway?" I asked, indicating his artificial hand.

He extended his arm, so that the hand was halfway between us, six inches or so above my desk. "Battery-powered," he said. It opened and closed, opened and closed. "There's wire sensors in the fingers that read the electrical impulses in my muscles and nerves."

"No kidding," I said. "And were you—*are* you—right-handed or left?"

"Left."

"Well, that's a break at least, huh? Less to have to readapt to."

Open, close, open, close, open, close.

Did *I* own this awkward silence, or did he? "This uh . . . this guy I knew? Grew up with? He developed schizophrenia when he was in college. His freshman year, I think it was. In and out of the state hospital most of his adult life. And then, when Saddam invaded Kuwait back in—when was that? Nineteen ninety? Guy goes into the library over there in Three Rivers, sits down, and cuts off his hand. Some kind of crazy antiwar sacrifice, I think it was supposed to be. And after? I'd see him sometimes. Him and his brother. Twins, they were. I'd see them at the grocery store, or in Friendly's. The brother and I had run track together in high school, but I knew them both. They were twins. Did I say that? . . . Anyway, that guy—he just had a stump. Nothing high-tech like you've got. I mean, sensors in the fingers: wow. . . . Sad story, though, that guy. He drowned. Suicide, I guess it was. The paper never put it in so many words, but that's what people were saying at the funeral."

"And are you telling me all this because you think I'm crazy, too?"

"Oh, God, not at all, Kareem. I didn't at all mean to imply that—no, no. Nothing like that."

Apropos of nothing, he asked me if I knew what the seven acts of Christian charity were.

"The seven . . . ?"

"Acts of Christian charity. There's the seven deadly sins, the seven contrary virtues, and the seven acts of Christian charity."

What the hell was going on, I wondered. Why *was* he here? I shook my head. "I don't know them. No."

"I'm not surprised. I take it you're like most professors."

"How do you mean?"

"You're a nonbeliever, right? Too highly educated to humble yourself to a higher power?"

It's none of your business what I believe or don't believe, was what I *felt* like saying. Instead, I spouted off some bullshit thing about how my policy was not to discuss my personal beliefs with my students. For emphasis, and a little facetiously, I guess, I stuck out my index finger and, in the air between us, drew a question mark.

We stared at each other for five or six seconds. Then Private Kendricks closed his eyes and spoke slowly and deliberately, with exaggerated enunciation. "Feed the hungry. . . . Give drink to the thirsty. . . . Clothe the naked. . . . Shelter the stranger. . . . Visit the sick. . . . Bury the dead. . . . Minister to the prisoner." His eyes sprang open. "Speaking of which, how's your wife?"

I leaned back a little. Grabbed onto the edge of my desk. "My wife?"

"That day you told us she was in prison? I looked her up on the Internet. She got five years for killing that boy, right? Negligent homicide?"

"Vehicular homicide. She's okay, thanks. How's *your* wife?"

His blinking became rapid. His smile was bizarre. "I couldn't tell you because she's taken out a restraining order against me. That's how off-base the justice system is in this country. *She's* the one who broke the ninth commandment, but *I'm* the one who gets court-ordered to stay away from my own home."

"I'm sorry," I said. And I was, too, but I was also just about done with this conversation. I stacked some already-stacked papers. Looked up at the clock. "So you have that appointment at four, right? I guess we better—"

"This is the value system I risked my life to protect? So that some clueless female judge can sit there and accept another woman's lies as gospel? Tell a father who's served his country to the best of his ability that he can only see his child for one hour, twice a week? Under the supervision of a *social* worker?"

He stood up, but rather than heading for the door, he walked over to my bookcase. His back was to me. I felt a trickle of sweat from my underarm. Proceed with caution, I told myself.

"You know, don't take this the wrong way," I said. "I'm not at *all* saying that you're . . . but are you getting any counseling? Because, after all you've been through, it might be good to talk with someone who can help you over the rough spots. Get you back on track with . . . your domestic situation. Maybe someone who works specifically with vets on these kinds of—"

He did an about-face. He was wild-eyed. "I'm *not* a vet. I'm active duty."

"Oh. Okay, sure. My only point is, talking to someone could—"

"I *am* talking to someone," he said. "I'm talking to you."

———

I GOT TO THE PRISON late, and once I did, they took their sweet time calling her up from her unit. By the time I was okayed to enter the visitors' room, we had twenty minutes.

She studied me as I approached her, the way she always did. We embraced across the table and sat. "Crazy day," I said.

"I can see that. Something wrong?"

"Nope." I smiled. "You look nice today. You get a haircut?"

Mo smiled back. Cut *and* styled, she said. She'd finally gotten an appointment with someone in the cosmetology class. First time since she'd become an inmate that she hadn't had to cut her bangs with her nail scissors.

"They teach cosmetology here?"

"Oh, yes. Hairdressing, industrial cleaning, nurse's aid training, data entry. They're traditionalists here at DOC. They like to prepare us for the kinds of crappy minimum-wage jobs that are waiting for us when we get out." She reached up and touched her hair. "Thanks for noticing, Cae."

"Hey, no problem."

"So why was your day so crazy?"

I gave her an edited version: told her about the in-class skirmish between Ozzie Rivera and PFC Kendricks, but nothing about Kendricks's office visit later on. (I was still trying to process that one.) Told her about the shimmy in my steering wheel, but nothing about Eric and Dylan's having shown up in my class. Had to have been a mini-version of that "vicarious flashback" I'd had up at the Mark Twain House, I figured. I'd never told her about that episode either. Figured the less said about flashbacks—vicarious or otherwise—the better. Far as I knew, she hadn't had any in quite a while. But maybe I was getting the edited version of her life, too.

"So what else is new?" she asked.

"Well, let's see. Moses told me cherubs&fiends.com has started turning a profit. They're getting two, three hundred hits a day some days. Says he has to hire a third person to keep up with the orders."

"What's selling better?" she asked. "The cherubs or the fiends?"

"Oh, the fiends, definitely. Four to one, he says."

"And what about the civil suit? Anything new there?"

I shook my head but must have given myself away because she looked skeptical. "Well, maybe there is. Junior left me a message. Says he's talked with the Seaberrys' attorney and wants to run a few things by me."

"Are they talking about a settlement?"

"I don't know, Maureen." I said it a little more defensively than I'd meant to. "I haven't had a chance to call him back yet."

"You haven't had a chance, or you're avoiding calling him back?"

I cracked a half-smile. "You know me too damn well. You know that?"

"Well, I just know how hard it must be for you to think about losing the farm. It's so tied up with your family history. I must say to myself fifty times a day, 'If only I hadn't—'"

I stuck my hand up like a traffic cop. "Don't, okay? Wasted energy. Whatever's going to happen is going to happen."

"But this Brandon guy you hired: he's good, right?"

"Lena LoVecchio thinks he's good, so that's what I'm going on. Hey, speaking of my family history? I've been reading the thing Janis wrote about that ancestor of mine. It's pretty interesting, actually. Old Lizzy was quite a gal."

She reached across the table and took my hands in hers. "I love you, Caelum," she said. She was blinking back tears.

"I love you, too. And you know something? After you get out of here, we're going to have a decent life again, you and me. No matter what we end up owning or not owning."

The mic clicked on. *Tap, tap, tap.* "No handholding, Miss Quirk. You know the rules." Maureen withdrew her hands from mine and gave the CO an apologetic nod. Held up her palms so that he could see them. I looked over at him, sitting up there on his elevated platform like Zeus on Mount Olympus. I flashed him a snarky smile and held up my hands, too. Clenched and extended them the way Kareem Kendricks had done a few hours earlier.

"So how's Velvet?" Maureen asked. "I haven't seen her for a while."

"She's good, I guess. Moze has been giving her some creative license with those gargoyles of theirs, and she's come up with some pretty freaky variations. Not that *that's* any big surprise. She's heading up to Boston this weekend for some big rave thing—bunch of bands that play the kind of noise she misidentifies as music. The Micks are away this weekend, too. Nancy Tucker and I are gonna have the whole place to ourselves."

"Nancy's doing okay?"

"Getting a little forgetful about where the litter box is," I said. "Follows me around squawking, wanting to eat, after I've already fed her. You think there's such a thing as feline Alzheimer's?"

Maureen smiled. "How's she getting along with the Micks' cat?"

"Just fine, now that they've got separate accommodations and never see each other," I said.

"So where are they going?"

"Hmm?"

"You said the Micks are going away this weekend."

"Oh. Different directions, actually. He's heading down to New York for some big trade show at the Javits Center. Trying to woo some bigger accounts, I guess. He's a pretty good businessman, that guy; his wheels are always turning. And Janis: she's flying down to New Orleans. Proposes her dissertation game plan on Monday, and if that goes okay, she's well on her way to getting her Ph.D."

Maureen said she wished she could read Lizzy's story.

"Yeah, well, I can't exactly carry it in here and hand it to you. How about if, after I finish it, I mail it to you?"

Mo reminded me that inmates could only receive books shipped directly from Amazon or Barnes&Noble.com

"Makes a lot of sense, doesn't it?" I said. "That the history of how this esteemed institution came into existence would be disallowed as contraband?"

Mo said that I could donate a copy of the manuscript—mail it to the prison library. Then she could check it out and read it.

"Good. Great. You know how Lizzy's campaign for a separate female penitentiary got started? She was on this committee for the betterment of prisoners or something, and while she was taking a tour, this one inmate slipped her a letter. Back then, they used to throw 'fallen women' in with the men. I guess the conventional wisdom was that they were just throwaways, anyway. Beyond saving. So in her letter, this woman describes how the women who let the guards and trustees have sex get special treatment, and how the ones who don't got abused. So Lizzy reads the letter, starts lobbying for a separate women's prison run by women. She kind of got sidetracked by the Civil War, I guess—that's the part I'm up to now, but . . . What is it, Mo?"

A sadness had come over her face. Things hadn't changed much, she said; sex was one of the few things that women on the inside could barter with, and some of them weren't above making deals with the officers who were interested. It was all about power and powerlessness, she said. "I think the ratio of fiends to angels may be about four to one at this place, too. Some of those fiends get to go home at the end of an eight-hour shift and some don't."

I opened my mouth to respond, but a *tap-tap* of the CO's microphone interrupted me. "Miss Quirk, I need to see you for a moment." Oh, Christ, this wasn't about our handholding, was it? Mo and I exchanged worried looks. Then she got up and started across the room.

As I watched their exchange, I thought about the coincidence: how Maureen had just said the same thing Janis had said out on the back stoop that morning—that from era to era, nothing really changed. And they were right, to some extent: about all the ways that blacks were kept down, still. All the ways that women were exploited. But they were wrong, too. After Columbine, every damn school in the country developed a lockdown policy, same as the prisons. Schools weren't safe havens anymore. Every damn parent in America sent their kids out the door in the morning and, for the rest of the day, kept an ear cocked for trouble. . . . And 9/11: chaos had come rushing in that day, too. Mohammed Atta and his henchmen fly those planes into those buildings, Bush says "Bring 'em on," and now we've got Guantánamo, Abu Ghraib. Torture's okay now, Cheney says, because these enemies live in the shadows, the dark places, and so we've got to go to those dark places, too. Kareem Kendricks goes off to fight a war against the wrong enemy and gets his hand blown off and his mind fucked up. Comes home again, and he's older than his father. . . .

Mo came back over and took her seat. "Everything okay?" I asked. She nodded. There'd been a message. They wanted her to go over to the Med Unit after our visit. One of her hospice patients was asking for her.

"How's that hospice thing working out for you, anyway?" I asked. "Not too depressing for you, I hope."

Just the opposite, she said. It made her feel good to be useful again. And some of the deaths she'd witnessed were beautiful.

"Beautiful?"

"I don't know, Cae. I guess it's one of those you-have-to-be-there things. I witnessed death all the time at the nursing home, and a lot of them were moving, too. But it's a different experience here. Near the end? Their last couple of days? They finally get to put down all their pretenses and defenses, all their guilt and regret. And this . . . peacefulness comes over them. And, hey, death isn't pretty, especially for someone dying of AIDS-related complications. But I don't know. I guess it's their smiles that are beautiful. Their courage. Strange as it sounds, I'm finding that hospice is the most hopeful and life-affirming place on this entire compound."

"Reminds me of something I read in a Flannery O'Connor story once," I said. "This selfish old lady's about to get shot, okay? By this escaped criminal? And right at the moment when he lifts his rifle to blow her away, she reaches out to comfort him. And O'Connor says something like, it's too bad we can't all be dying all the time, because that's when we're our best, most decent selves." The smile dropped off Mo's face and she looked down at the table. Too late, I realized what a stupid fucking idiot I was—that Mr. English Major's stupid literary reference had just sent her back to Columbine.

"Mo, I'm sorry," I said. "I wasn't thinking."

She looked up, smiled bravely. "It's okay, Caelum."

"So tell me," I said, desperate to change the subject. "How are things going with the new roommate?"

"Crystal? Oh, it's just so sad. Prison is the last place that poor kid should be. She's just a scared little girl."

"How old?"

"Sixteen. But she looks and acts like she's about twelve. And she's slow. I'm not sure, but I think she may be mildly retarded."

"You find out what she's in for yet?"

She nodded. "Homicide. Her baby wouldn't stop crying, so she shook him until he stopped. Dislodged his brain. Sunshine, she'd named him; he was only three weeks old. The father was her mother's boyfriend."

"Jesus, that's . . ." I couldn't even find the words.

"There's this group of women on our tier who are so cruel to her. It's like a blood sport, you know? They'll do that here: travel in a pack, pick off the weakest member of the herd. At night, after lights out? They do this thing where they call to her. 'Mmmomm-my, ssss-stop shhhh-shhaking me.' And they *laugh*. They think it's hilarious."

Ozzie's remark came flying back at me: *Give G.I. Joe a hand*. The way his buddies had high-fived him in the hallway after class. "Amazing how cruel people can be, isn't it? What's that about, anyway?"

"I don't know. Self-loathing? Survival of the fittest? . . . Some nights I just climb up onto her bunk and hold her, rock her until she cries herself to sleep. I could get in trouble if they caught me. We're not supposed to be on each other's beds. But she's just a baby, Caelum. She *needs* to be held."

She looked so sad, so beaten down by it. Even her new hairdo seemed to have wilted. A few minutes later, the guard at the desk announced that visiting time was over. I stood, embraced her across the table and gave her a peck on the cheek. "See you day after tomorrow," I said.

Maybe yes, maybe no, she said. According to the jailhouse grapevine, a lockdown was coming, sooner rather than later.

"God, I can't wait until you get out of here," I said.

She sat down again, and I walked away from her and toward the door. Silly superstition or not, I held to my policy. I did not look back.

→→ *chapter thirty* ←←

PASSING THE GUARD STATION ON my way out of the prison, I swung right and started the quarter mile up Bride Lake Road to the farmhouse. Then, spur of the moment, I braked, U-turned, and headed into town instead. I pulled into the strip mall on Franklin Street. Got a six-pack at Melady's and a foot-long at Subway. Decided to swing by the Mama Mia to see if Alphonse was still there. Al was always good for a few laughs, something I sorely needed.

But the bakery was dark. A sign taped to the door, scrawled in Al's handwriting, read "Re-open soon. Sorry for the incovience. We appreciate your buisness." Two misspellings in one sign: the guy was hopeless. Was it his folks? Had he had to go down to Florida again? If so, why hadn't he called to let me know? . . . Well, I guess I knew the answer to that one. He'd left several e-mails and phone messages in the past weeks. *What's shakin' Quirky? How's Maureen?* Did I want to get together and grab some dinner? Did I want to go for a spin in the "dream machine" that widow from Rhode Island had finally sold him? I'd deleted all his overtures.

Home again, I tossed my sandwich onto the table and put the six in the fridge, minus the bottle I opened and emptied in two long gulps. Went into the bedroom to change out of my teaching clothes. That's when I heard it, echoing from somewhere out back. *Bang . . . Bang! . . . Bang!*

Was someone stupid enough to be hunting deer at dusk? Didn't sound like gunfire, though. It was loud and percussive—something slamming against something else. What the hell was it?

Bang! . . . Bang!

Standing at the back door, I tried to pinpoint where it was coming from. Grabbed my jacket off the hook and headed out toward the orchard. There was a motorcycle parked in front of the barn and, beside it, Moses and some guy shaking hands. "Okay, then," I heard Moze say. "I won't be back from New York until midday Monday. Why don't we start you on Tuesday morning?"

"Hey!" I called. "You know what that sound is out there?"

Moze shrugged. "I was wondering that same thing my damn self. Hey, breaking news, man. This here's our new guy."

I nodded at the lanky kid standing next to him: shaved head, hooded sweatshirt, baggy hip-hop jeans. He looked familiar—a former student, maybe? Whoever he was, my mind was elsewhere. "Nice to meet you," I called, although we hadn't really met.

Bang! . . . Bang! . . . Bang!

I took a few more steps toward the orchard, then stopped, called back. "Hey, Moze! You talk to Alphonse lately?" He shook his head. "I just went over to the bakery. It's closed." He shrugged.

I walked through the abandoned orchard. Most of the trees were just standing dead wood, and those that were still hanging on had yielded the pathetic, nugget-sized apples that littered the ground. Would've sickened Grandpa Quirk to see what had become of things.

I stopped when I got to the clearing. Stood there a moment and took it in: Ulysses swinging a sledgehammer over his shoulder and bringing it smashing down against the concrete slab that had been the apple house floor.

"Hey!" I called. "What the hell you doing?"

He stopped, turned and looked at me for a second or two. Then he tossed aside the sledgehammer and started picking up chunks of the busted cement and throwing them onto the pile in the wheel barrow.

"I can't pay you now."

"You don't have to pay me," he said. "This is just something I gotta do."

"Yeah? Why's that?"

"Unfinished business."

He picked up the sledgehammer again and swung it.

Bang! . . . Bang! . . . Bang!

I could feel the violence of each blow in the pit of my stomach. Technically, he was trespassing.

"Getting too dark out here," I called. "Another twenty minutes and you won't even be able see what you're swinging at. You could get hurt."

"Full moon," he said, pointing to the sky as proof. "They give me some tests at the clinic. Said my liver's shot. I'm living on borrowed time."

I told him I was sorry. Told him he could come back tomorrow if that was what he needed to do. "And I'll give you a hand. We can finish it up together. Come on. I'll drive you home."

He stood there, panting, his hands trembling badly. "Tomorrow? Yeah, okay. How about if I stay here tonight then? Sleep on your couch, maybe?"

"No, I don't think—"

"I ain't seen Nancy Tucker in a while. Kind of like to have a little visit with her, if that's okay. And that way, I can save myself the trip back here. Get an early start. I do better in the morning."

Against my better judgment, I agreed.

"You're good people," he said. "Take after your aunt."

Maybe things weren't as bad as they'd said they were, I told him. Maybe he should get a second opinion.

"Nah. When your time's come, it's come."

In the house, under the harsh kitchen lights, he looked like he was dying: his skin tone was ghastly, the whites of his eyes were yellow. He had an odor about him, too—b.o. and alky stink, sickening and sweet, the way Daddy had smelled near the end.

"You hungry?"

"Nah. I ain't got much of an appetite these days. I could use a little nip, though, if you got one. Little something to calm the jitters, help me get to sleep. That way, I can get up bright and early tomorrow and finish the job."

"You don't *have* to finish it on my account," I reminded him. "And maybe you shouldn't be taxing yourself. Busting concrete's hard work."

"So what do you think? Can you spot me a little something to drink?"

As long as he ate a little something, I told him. I put half of my sandwich on a plate and placed it in front of him. Put a shot glass and an unopened quart of vodka on the table. What did it matter at this point?

"None better than Lolly," Ulysses said. "That gal was salt of the earth. Whenever I think about that day I come over here and found her wandering out there by the clothesline. Socks on her hands, talking gobbledy-gook. . . ."

He was right about the jitters. As he poured his first shot, he got more vodka on the table than in his glass. Spilled some more on the way to his mouth. He downed it in one gulp. I poured him his second.

"Tell you the truth, I was always a little bit sweet on Lolly," he said. "All the way back to high school, when I used to come over here and pal around with your dad. Didn't dawn on me until later that I had the wrong equipment. You know what I mean?"

I nodded.

"I was a little dense about that kind of stuff back then. I knew from the service about queers. But I didn't realize that some women . . . You know when it dawned on me? About Lolly? Happened right here in this kitchen, before your dad and me shipped out to Korea. We were sitting around the table, having some beers. Just wasting time, you know? And we started horsing around, roughhousing and such. Tipped over a coupla chairs, I remember. And Lolly come in from the barn and said she'd take us both on in arm-wrestling and come out the winner. And we said yeah, yeah, *sure* you could, and then that's just what she goddamn did. Took me on first and beat me without much of a problem, and she'd just beaten her brother when the old lady walked in. The grandmother. She was getting up there by then, but she still ruled the roost. She looked around at the empty beer cans and the tipped-over chairs, and I thought, uh-oh, Alden and me are in for it. But she didn't say nothing to us. What she done was, she lit into Lolly like nobody's business. Read her the riot act about what a sad state of affairs it was that she could teach all those prisoners next door how to act like ladies but her own granddaughter was a lost cause. Alden just sat there, kinda smirking, I remember. Enjoying not being the one who was in trouble for a change, I guess. But that's when it dawned on me. Hit me like a ton of bricks: Lolly had more man in her than woman. Probably all that farm work she did, I figure. Turned her mannish."

"It's not about what kind of work you do," I said. "It's about who you are. Gay or straight's something you're born with."

"Oh. That right?" He reached again for the vodka bottle. "But she was always good to me, Lolly. Helped me out plenty of times."

"You know, Ulysses, maybe after you finish your sandwich, you'd like to clean up a little. Get out of those clothes and grab a shower."

"Nah, that's all right," he said.

"Because to tell you the truth, you smell a little funky."

"Oh. I do? Okay then."

"I can lend you some clothes. Put yours in the washer."

He lifted his arm and sniffed. "Yeah, all right. I didn't realize."

When I heard the water going, I made him a little pile: sweat-shirt, sweat pants, underwear, socks. Thinking he was already in the shower, I opened the bathroom door to place them on the hamper. He hadn't stepped into the tub yet. He stood there, naked and cadaverous, sobbing at his steam-clouded image in the mirror. He turned and faced me. "I fucked up my whole goddamned life, didn't I?"

He had; there was no denying it. Still, I tried to think of something. "You were never a mean drunk," I said. "That counts for something." I handed him the clothes and left the room.

I put sheets down on the couch. Got him a blanket, a pillow. By eight o'clock, the vodka bottle was half empty and Ulysses was face-down and fast asleep. Nancy Tucker had climbed aboard and made herself at home on the small of his back. She was sleeping, too.

Standing there, watching the two of them, I couldn't help but smile. He'd had a crush on Lolly? Good thing he'd never acted on it; she probably would've clocked him. . . . Another couple of months, I thought, and the last of the trio would be gone: those three naïve buddies who'd strolled down to the recruiting office on their last day of high school and signed on to help fight the Commies in North Korea. Poor, old, cirrhotic Ulysses was finishing his unfinished business. . . .

I thought about Kendricks then—his shoving his daughter off his lap after she'd made that innocent comment; his need to make himself a "hard target" in a classroom where no one was shooting at him. . . . Thought about those poor Columbine kids—how they'd hidden in plain sight under tables, behind counters and copy machines, and then the two of them had marched in and shot them like fish in a barrel. . . . Thought about how, strange as it was, that one of their potential victims had followed us back East and ended up living right here at the farmhouse. Velvet had found herself a safe haven, first down at the bakery when I was working the night shift, then here, upstairs with the Micks. She'd found work she liked, too, or maybe even loved: mixing, pouring, and finishing those foot-high sculptures, then packaging and shipping them off to strangers. Decorating her grotesques. . . .

In the bathroom, I pissed away the beers I'd drunk and picked Ulysses's clothes off the floor. I set the washer—small load, hot water—

and started the cycle. "Long freakin' day," I announced, out loud, to no one. I grabbed Janis's manuscript off the counter where I'd left it that morning and headed into the bedroom. Propped my own and Mo's pillows against the headboard, climbed between the sheets, and opened Lizzy's story to the place that, that morning, I had bookmarked with a napkin. I read.

In March of 1863, Lizzy Popper received by telegram a succinct response from the Union's nursing superintendent Dorothea Dix: "You will suffice. Come as soon as possible." Suffice, indeed: Popper was just the sort of nurse Dix sought. Strident and unpopular with the medical personnel she often confronted, Dix had little use for nurses who were young and pretty because, intentionally or not, they might "awake the lusts" of the battle-weary men they served. Dix was equally wary of the Catholic Daughters of Charity who served the sick and wounded without army pay; the nuns, she suspected, preyed on the sickest patients with an eye on accomplishing deathbed conversions. Dix specifically sought Protestant nurses of proven character who were "plain-looking, over thirty, and competent." Lizzy Popper qualified on all three counts.

Freed now from the fear that her beloved Willie had perished, and armed once again with a righteous cause, Lizzy Popper returned to form. With the help of Martha Weeks, she reactivated the Ladies' Soldiers Relief Society, putting two hundred women to the tasks of sewing, baking, canning, and gathering needed supplies. She traveled the state to collect donations from the executives of textile mills, department stores, distilleries, and apothecary supply houses. The woman who had been immobilized with grief in January had, by mid-May, closed her house, informed her husband of her plans, taken a week's worth of nurse's training in New York, and traveled by ship, train, and carriage to her assigned post at Washington's Alonzo P. Shipley Hospital, a converted lyceum hall and ballroom on Connecticut Avenue. She did not arrive empty-handed.

Popper reported for duty accompanied by no fewer than four carriages weighted with bags, barrels, and boxes of supplies. These provisions included clean bandages, linens, shirts, and stockings for the bedridden; cakes, tonics, pickles, and beef and wine jellies for the malnourished; whiskey for amputees in need of anesthetic; and medicinal plants and herbs such as sassafras, mayapple, pomegranate, ginger, and horseradish for the treatment of maladies ranging from diarrhea and constipation to bronchitis and nervous agitation. For months, there had been a bloody stalemate between Union and Confederacy on the war's eastern front, and as the numbers of sick and wounded had increased, government supplies had dwindled. Lizzy Popper's replenishments, perfectly timed and greatly appreciated, afforded her an instant cachet with the hospital's ward masters and executive officers. At first, Popper's favorable reputation pleased Directress Dix, as it affirmed her stance that plain-looking elder nurses served the cause most effectively. Later, however, Popper's popularity would become a source of conflict between the two.

In a June 7, 1863 letter to Martha Weeks, Popper recounted her duties at Shipley Hospital, revealing the physical and emotional challenges of her service.

Sister,

No doubt thee has waited for words from me these past weeks, and I have meant to send thee some, but the days here are long and full, and by nighttime my bones remind me of their years. After my sick have had their supper and the gas lights have been set aglow, I surrender to the night matron and climb the stairs to my attic quarters. I mean only to rest my eyes and lift my swollen feet from the floor for a moment before taking pen in hand or putting hands together to pray. Next thing I know, there is clatter downstairs and, in the muddy street below, the clip-clopping of horses' hooves and the caterwauling of Irishwomen. "Milk for sale! Warm still from the cow! Come buy your morning

milk!" More reliable than the rooster's cry are these "Don-
negal Dames," as another nurse calls them. Time to rise,
wash, give thanks for the new day, and serve again.

When I arrived here a fortnight ago, much was made of
the provisions thee and I had collected from the good folk
of Connecticut. Indeed, my entourage of boxes, bins, cakes,
and casks gave me immediate prominence with both the
medical staff and the sick. "Mother Bountiful" some of the
men took to calling me, and "Mother Christmas." Thee who
knows me, sister, knows that, while I do not love attention
drawn to myself, I am happy to use the prestige for the good
of others, particularly the contrabands.

Many darkies have attached themselves to this hospital.
They serve as attendants in the kitchen and laundry, and
on the wards. Some are freemen. Others are contrabands
on the run. All live in fear of slave hunters, and for good
reason. Several of the doctors at this hospital are Southern sympathizers. Dr. Winkle, a Kentuckian, has made it
clear to me and others that if an owner from Lexington or
Louisville came looking for his lawful property, he should
be obliged to surrender it. "It, yes, but never he or she," I
said. Dr. W answered that even abolitionists were obliged
to observe the laws of the land. I told him I was obliged to
observe the laws of human decency before any man-made
laws, then walked away, so that I should have the last word
on the subject and not he. Father Abraham was hailed when
he issued his Emancipation Proclamation earlier this year,
and rightfully so, but he made a grave mistake when he ex-
cluded from liberation those slaves from the border states.
Last Sunday afternoon, I walked past Mr. Lincoln's grand
white wedding cake of a house on Pennsylvania Avenue and
had a mind to knock on his front door and scold him for this
error. Thee who knows me best knows I would have had
the gumption to do it, and may do it yet. Freedom for some
slaves, but not for others. Pshaw!

Sister, I shall do my best to describe to thee what my surroundings are like. Shipley Hospital is a three-story brick

*building in the Georgian style, one of many here on Con-
necticut Avenue. Before the war, it was a lyceum hall with a
grand ballroom upstairs, and I pray it will soon be so again.
Better Virginia reels and elevating lectures than young men
torn and dying. The first floor houses doctors' quarters,
kitchen and dining area, chapel, morgue, and a twenty-bed
ward for injured officers. On the high ceiling of the second
floor, a great painted Federalist eagle flies to remind the sick
that they have sacrificed for the salvation of the Union. The
ballroom has been divided into two wards. Each has forty-
five beds with barely a space between them. The Daughters
of Charity serve one of these wards, Miss Dix's nurses the
other. Surgeries are performed at the back of the room behind a curtain, but the cries of pain can be heard throughout. The third floor is a low-ceilinged attic and has been set
up as a dormitory for the female staff. My quarters there are
simple but satisfactory.*

*Each day, great mounds of soiled and bloody bed linens
must be made clean again. The Sanitary Commission in-
sists on this, and rightfully so. Laundering is done outside
the back door. The fires beneath the washerwomen's kettles
burn all day and into the night. Behind the laundry, what had
been a courtyard is now the darkies' tent village. Behind that
is a pest house for those afflicted with smallpox. The nuns
minister to the sick there, and I am thankful for that.*

*The stench is the first thing to which a new nurse must
accustom herself here at Shipley. Death, decay, and human
waste hang in the air, but the windows are nailed shut per
the orders of Dr. Luce, the chief of surgery, who fears fresh
air will bring smallpox inside. Louisa Alcott, a pleasant and
clever nurse from Massachusetts, gave me a vial of laven-
der water and told me to sprinkle it liberally and often. I
did, and it saved me from swooning during my first hours.
Each day brings new challenges, but there is the comfort
of routine here, too. We eat breakfast first, seated at long
tables just off the kitchen. There is one table for the doctors, another for the nuns, a third for us "Dixies." (The nick-*

name is meant to mock us. D.D. is resented by the medical men, and so there is disdain for those of us who serve at her will or, as Louisa puts it, "at her mercy.") Breakfast is corn-meal porridge, bread, jam, and tea, warm rather than hot, drunk from tin mugs. On Sundays, we each have an egg. The darkies pass among us carrying trays and we pluck our morning victuals from these. Sister, forgive my longing for worldly things, but how I yearn for good, hot tea with sugar sipped from one of thy delicate bone china cups!

My mornings are taken up with the wetting of wounds, the changing of dressings, the bathing of bodies, and the cooling of fevers with soothing cloths and soothing words. I spoon medicine, soup, and tonic into open mouths as once upon a time I did with my own babes. In the afternoons, if there is time, I write to wives, mothers, and sweethearts. I read to those who wish to listen—Scripture, for the most part, but also poetry and tales of frontiersmen and savages. I do what I can to make a hospital a home for these poor, damaged boys and men because I have quickly come to think of them as my children. No doubt the surgeons would shudder to hear me say it. They see only the bullet that needs removing or the leg that needs severing, and so they pick up their pliers or their saw and do the job. I see the boy to whom the wounded thigh or the dying limb is attached. Still, I do whatever the doctors tell me. Charlie would be shocked to find me so obedient!

Martha, most of the damaged and dying are so young. Most suffer bravely in silence, or ask only for small favors. "Would you write a few words to my gal, Ma'am?" "Mis-sus, could I trouble you for a cup of water?" A drummer not more than fourteen years of age, shot in the stomach, died yesterday with nary a sigh. Oh, but there are groaners and moaners, too, and from some angry mouths come words no decent woman should hear, and no wicked woman either. Fever sometimes scrambles their senses. One young soldier from Delaware had had his foot so badly burned and man-gled by cannonfire that it turned black as a plum and had to be removed. That night he became agitated and insisted he could wiggle the toes on his missing foot. "I'm going to get up and go home to my Ma and my Josie!" he announced, and promptly fell from his bed with a resounding crash. When I rushed to him and knelt, he struck me twice across the face. The blows caused my nose to bleed and my eye to swell and later blacken. The sight of my blood brought him back to his senses. "I'm sorry, Missus! I was thinkin' you was Johnny Reb! I'm scared! I want my Ma!" I pulled him against my breast, cradling him and whispering not to be afraid. He was clenched at first, and it was as if I held one of my own small boys when, on a winter's night, they suffered so from colic or croup. Then, like a small boy, this soldier—Erasmus, his name was—relaxed his limbs, and I could feel that merciful sleep had come to him. One of the nuns, Sister Claire, came to help me, but I waved her away. What a sight we must have been, one-footed Erasmus and me, sprawled on the hospital floor together, one asleep, the other looking as if she had been brawling! Still, for those moments, I was his Ma and he was my Eddie, or my Levi, safe in my arms. He (Erasmus) died from infection two days later. I wrote to his Ma and his Josie and have received a grateful letter from the mother. She says I am welcome in their home whenever I should wish to visit Delaware.

Sister, I hope this missive finds thee well, and thy beloved Nathanael, too. I do hope his gout is improved. I have had a letter from Charlie, and he writes that he is proud of the sacrifice I am making to the Holy Cause of Liberty. He says he may travel by train to visit me here. We shall see about that. Charlie makes promises more easily than he keeps them. Write soon and know that thy letters are always treasured and that thee are as ever dear to

Thy sister,
Elizabeth

There was a soft *tap-tap-tap*. "Come in," I said. Ulysses's head poked around the bedroom door. "Hey. What's up?"

"Nancy's crying at the door to go out," he said. "I wasn't sure if you let her out at night."

"That's fine," I said. "Put her out and get back to sleep." But instead of closing the door, he just stood there. "You all right?"

He nodded. "Fisher cats have made a comeback around here, you know. They been gone for a while, but now they're back. . . . They're weasels."

"I know what fishers are."

"They eat cats, you know. Maybe she ought to stay inside."

"She's a farm cat, Ulysses. She knows how to take care of herself."

"Oh. Okay. Let her out then?"

"Let her out."

"A farm cat, and there ain't even a farm here anymore," he said, shaking his head in disbelief. Jesus H. Christ, what did he expect me to do? Start milking Holsteins again?

"See you in the morning," I said.

"Yup. See you in the morning."

The door closed. I heard the kitchen door open and close. Heard the toilet flush. Then things were quiet again.

Charles Popper did, in fact, visit his wife in Washington that summer. A letter from Lizzy to Charles dated June 27, 1863 refers to a Congregationalist service they attended together and to a Sunday supper they shared at Charles's hotel dining room. Lizzy thanked her husband for having managed the latest unspecified "unpleasantness" concerning her brother, Roswell, and for the donation of Bibles and Century Publishing Company "seconds" to the convalescents of Shipley Hospital.

The tomes have been well used, by those who can read and those who take comfort in being read to. Yesterday, Thomas Simmons, a sergeant from Vermont, lost his battle against typhus and the Holy Book thee provided was a comfort to him during his final hours. We buried him and

two others today in the post cemetery, preceded by sober
words from the chaplain and a dirge played by the hospi-
tal band. As he had asked, Sergeant Simmons' Bible went
with him into the ground.

Discussion of the Poppers' errant son would have surely
come up during their visit together in Washington, but, curiously, Lizzy's letter makes no mention of Willie. Willie
also goes unmentioned in letters his mother wrote to Martha Weeks during this period. It remains unclear whether
or not Elizabeth Popper, like her husband, had estranged
herself from her son, now a rising star of the minstrel stage.
As for the Poppers' marital estrangement, Charles's trip to
Washington began a thawing that would result in his even-
tual return to the family home in New Haven in February
of 1864, even as his affair with Vera Daneghy continued.
Lizzy, too, would return to New Haven during the winter of
1864, following her abrupt dismissal from service at Shipley Hospital. Popper's conversion from "Mother Bountiful"
to persona non grata at Shipley would come in the wake of
the war's bloodiest battle and the strain it put on the caretakers of its thousands of wounded and sick.

The scope of the three-day Battle of Gettysburg was profound, the loss of life staggering. By the time the last shots
had been fired and Lee's army had retreated, the Confederacy had suffered twenty thousand casualties, the Union
seventeen thousand five hundred. The most severely injured
were treated at emergency tents erected at the battlefields'
perimeters. Many thousands more traveled on foot and by
train, carriage, wagon, and ship, and over others' shoulders
to existing hospitals and makeshift facilities from Boston
to the Carolinas. These overwhelming numbers of sick and
wounded resulted in neglect, haphazard care, and death for
the many who had survived the battlefield only to lose their
lives to infection and disease. Shipley Hospital was no exception to this phenomenon. The facility had beds for one
hundred and twenty patients, but in the days following the

Gettysburg conflict, over four hundred sick and wounded arrived. The attendants' village behind the hospital was disbanded, trees were felled, and shrubbery was uprooted to make room for seven emergency medical tents. These were badly understaffed. In a letter to Charles, written six days after the battle's end, Lizzy Popper wrote

Oh, shit. Another knock. I knew this was a bad idea. At least he didn't open the door this time. "Yup?"

"I just wanted you to know I let her back in."

"Yeah, okay. Thanks."

"Did her business and then she wanted to come right back in."

"Uh-huh. Good night."

"Night."

No footsteps. "Anything else?"

"Nah, I guess not. Thanks again for letting me stay here."

"No problem."

In a letter to Charles, written six days after the battle's end, Lizzy Popper wrote:

Husband,

There is no time to write thee at length. I am sad tonight because I have just said goodbye to my friend and fellow nurse, Louisa. I shall miss her terribly, as she was a beacon of light in this terrible darkness, but her ill health necessitates that she be sent home. The needs here at Shipley are *overwelming* [sic], *the sorrows manyfold. Each day more*

---

*Popper most likely refers to Louisa May Alcott, who contracted typhoid fever during her nursing service. A hospital physician treated Alcott with calomel, which cured her of the disease but left her with the mercury poisoning that eventually took her life in 1888 at the age of fifty-six. Upon leaving her hospital post, Alcott returned home to Concord, Massachusetts where she wrote a poignant but humorous account of her nursing experiences, published as *Hospital Sketches*. Her novel, *Little Women*, followed six years later and made her famous.

of the Gettysburg warriors arrive. Most are in pitiful condi-
tion. One group had been left inside a deserted schoolhouse
for days without food or water. After their canteens were
emptied, they were forced to drink and wet their wounds
with their urine. We lost twenty-two men yesterday, seven-
teen the day before. Ten more were carried to the morgue by
noon today. Some of these might have been saved, but we
are far too few serving far too many. From dawn to dark, I
move through a maze of suffering soldiers. At night, I close
my eyes but cannot sleep, for I see their hands reaching for
me, their frightened faces. I have seen the Devil's den now, I
think, where the wretched doomed cry out in vain. Pray for
my sick, Charlie, and for the end of this hellish war, and for
the forebearance of

> *Thy aggrieved wife,*
> *Elizabeth*

Lizzy Popper's forbearance held, but her tolerance of in-
competence and deceit did not. Her dismissal from service at Shipley Hospital came as the result of several
skirmishes with male authority and a showdown with
Directress Dix.

   In the midst of the post-Gettysburg chaos, Shipley Hospital's chief surgeon, Dr. Reuben Luce, suffered a heart attack
and was retired from active duty. Lizzy Popper had enjoyed
a cordial relationship with Dr. Luce, and the departing
physician recommended her to his successor, Dr. Palmer
Pettigrew. Pettigrew, a thirty-three-year-old Missourian,
assigned Lizzy to assist him with his surgeries. The two disliked each other from the start, but the acrimony escalated
when Pettigrew altered existing hospital policy, directing
that sand, instead of linens, be spread on operating tables
between surgeries for the purpose of better absorbing patients' blood. Lizzy objected, arguing that pebbles were a
further discomfort to supine patients already in misery. To
placate her, Pettigrew ordered that surgical sand be sifted,
but Lizzy's protest continued. Sand clung to the men's

wounds and stumps, she argued, causing in them the urge to scratch and poke at that which needed to be left alone to heal. Joseph Lister's breakthrough discovery of carbolic acid as an antiseptic agent and Louis Pasteur's founding of modern microbiology were still years into the future; during the Civil War era, the causes of infection were not yet understood. Yet Elizabeth Popper seemed to understand on some intuitive level that sand-covered surgery tables further compromised vulnerable patients. She wrote to Superintendent Dix about her concern. Dix wrote back, advising Popper that sand was not a problem as long as wounds were "properly, thoroughly, and frequently wetted." Dissatisfied with her superior's response, Lizzy wrote two more letters, one to Eugenia Trickett, a Sanitation Commission executive, the other to surgeon General William Hammond. In her letter to Hammond, Popper added the further complaint that, of the dozens of amputations Pettigrew performed daily, a fair number were, in her opinion, unnecessary—that Pettigrew was "more butcher than surgeon." The charge was investigated by Hammond's office and found to be unwarranted. During the inquiry, Pettigrew was shown Lizzy's letter. In response, he wrote Hammond a letter of his own, charging that his surgeon's assistant was "an overweening hag who assumes, quite preposterously, that her knowledge of medicine is superior to my own—indeed, that all of Eve's descendants enjoy a natural superiority to any of Adam's." Lizzy's letter to Hammond also incurred the wrath of Dorothea Dix; one of her Dixies had flouted the chain of command, going not through her but over her head with the serious charge that surgeries were being performed capriciously. Dix reprimanded Popper and demoted her to the position of stewardess of medical supplies. But in this capacity, also, Lizzy drew fire. The issue this time was whiskey.

Lizzy Popper was a firm believer in temperance, but she was also a realist who understood whiskey's value as an anesthetic in the lessening of patients' suffering. Each month,

Shipley Hospital received from the federal government a barrel of "spirituous liquor" to be used for medicinal purposes. The whiskey was kept locked in the supply room and drawn in pints and quarts as ordered by staff physicians. Hospital policy required that withdrawals be made only by the house apothecary or the provisions steward, and that each withdrawal be recorded in the log that sat atop the whiskey barrel. Not long into her new position, Popper became aware of a discrepancy between the amount of alcohol recorded withdrawn and the greater amount missing. In a letter to her sister Martha, she wrote of her dilemma, and also of a disturbing rumor she'd heard: that a certain Dr. Peacock had been intoxicated while performing surgery on a young soldier shot in the cheek, and that he had botched the stitching of the boy's face and given him a permanent smile. Popper wrote, "My suspicion is that some of my doctors are drinking spirits meant for my sick. I shall have to set a trap." When she did, hiding in the dark recesses of the supply room after hours beneath a canvas covering, she caught her thief, the apothecary, who confessed he had been providing four of Shipley's doctors with whiskey at a modest profit. Lizzy complained once again to Dorothea Dix. An investigation was launched. Three of the guilty physicians, including Dr. Peacock, were reprimanded, and the apothecary was dismissed. Popper had secured the patients' monthly allotment of anesthetic, but, in the process, had made more enemies. One was Abner Winkle, the Kentucky physician and Southern sympathizer whose political opinions were antithetical to Popper's.

Lizzy Popper enjoyed many friendships with the free blacks and contrabands who worked at Shipley Hospital. She had become particularly fond of two runaway slaves from Kentucky, George Ruggles and his common-law wife, Mazie Spinks. Spinks was one of the hospital's washerwomen, and Ruggles served as an attendant in the upstairs wards. Affable and efficient, George Ruggles was popular with both the staff and the sick of Shipley Hospital. Because he exhibited an aptitude for medical procedures, the doctors under whom he served had begun giving him responsibilities beyond the scope of most attendants. Lizzy Popper recognized Ruggles's potential, too, and began teaching him to read and write. In a letter to her husband Charles, she pronounced Ruggles "an apt and eager pupil who will thrive as a free man if the forces of good prevail and the war is won."

Ruggles and Spinks had escaped from the estate of Quentin J. Cheeks, a wealthy shipping merchant from Covington, Kentucky, who, by the terms of the Emancipation Proclamation, retained legal claim to the couple. Acting on a tip he had received, Cheeks took out an advertisement in the *Washington Observer*, a Southern-leaning weekly. The ad carried drawings of both Ruggles and "his wench Mazie" and offered a twenty-five-dollar reward for information leading to the couple's recapture. At Shipley, news traveled quickly that Dr. Winkle had seen the plea and contacted his fellow Kentuckian. Cheeks subsequently telegraphed the hospital's administrators that he would arrive in a fortnight to claim his property. Shipley's executive officer was reluctant to surrender Ruggles and Spinks to the police, but the law was the law. Lizzy Popper, however, would have none of blind obedience to a federal dictate she deemed unjust. In collusion with Sister Agnes O'Hara, one of Shipley's Daughters of Charity, she hatched a plan.

Earlier that same week, a prostitute who had been haunting the hospital environs had been apprehended and arrested. Sister Agnes had taken pity on the woman and accompanied her to court. Through the nun's advocacy, the judge had allowed the streetwalker an alternative to prison: she could surrender herself to the Daughters of Charity's convent in Philadelphia. The woman accepted, and Father Joseph Cassidy, a Philadelphia priest, was dispatched to accompany and deliver her to her destination. Father Cassidy had traveled to Wasington alone, but when he and the to-be-reformed prostitute boarded the return train to Philadelphia, they did so in the company of two dark-skinned Daughters of Charity. On the evening of the escape, a gleeful Lizzy wrote to Martha Weeks:

Thee should have seen Mazie and George in their borrowed habits. Just as the newly-made Papists were about to board the train, a wind came up and their white bonnets flapped like pigeons' wings. It's a wonder they did not lift into the sky and fly to Heaven or Rome!

Lizzy's glee ended soon enough. When an outraged Cheeks learned of her part in the escape of his slaves, he moved to have her arrested. A letter signed by seven of Shipley Hospital's twelve physicians, stating that she was indispensable to the sick there, saved her from the jailhouse. Abner Winkle wrote a letter of complaint to the Union's Secretary of War, charging Popper—a paid employee of the United States government—with the flouting of federal law. The letter also accused Nursing Superintendent Dorothea Dix of an inability to control her subordinates. The already embattled Dix was furious at having been unfairly implicated, and she excoriated Popper. In a letter to Anna Livermore, Lizzy gave a colorful account of the exchange between the two:

For a quarter of an hour, DD railed against me. I was told I was guilty of arrogance, pridefulness, and treachery. She said she knew full well what I was up to—that from the start I had been plotting to unseat her as Directress so that I might have the position for myself. As she spoke this piffle, it was with such spleen that her face turned red, her eyes bulged like a frog's, and I wondered if, at any moment, she might express steam from her ears! My nursing was passable, I was informed, but I was more trouble than I was worth. In turn, I informed DD that if helping the Lord's children break the chains of slavery made me a troublemaker, then I accepted the title gladly, and if she could

not support me in what I had done, I should call her not
Dragon Dix as the others did, but Traitor to the Cause!

Dix dismissed Popper on the spot. Lizzy surrendered her
keys, signed her dismissal papers, and left on the evening
train "with neither protest nor teary farewells." Her service
as a Civil War nurse had come to an end.

Although Lizzy Popper continued to support the Union
cause through her work with the Ladies' Soldiers Relief Society, her efforts were greatly reduced during the final year
of the war. Charles had returned to their New Haven home,
and the couple seemed to have entered a period of domestic calm. For Lizzy, it was a time of reflection rather than
active engagement with the world. On April 11, 1865, two
days after Lee's surrender at Appomattox, she wrote in the
diary she had begun to keep:

At last, the gunfire has ceased, the last soldier has fallen.
No more new widows will be made today, no other moth-
er's heart will break. Today is a day for taking stock. The
Union has been saved, but at astounding and hideous
cost. The Lord has returned Charlie to me as I have asked
Him to do, but my Willie wanders I know not where. The
marble busts of his slain brothers sit atop their pedestals
in the drawing room, cool to the touch and far too smooth,
no substitute for flesh and blood and human imperfection.
Many times each day, my mind returns me against my will
to Shipley Hospital, and I hear once more the stifled sobs
and delirious shouting, the phlegmy death rattle of men
breathing their last. I see the piles of severed limbs being
carried away for burning. I feel a dead man's eyelids as
I thumb-shut them, feel my fingertips press against the
pulsing artery of a frightened boy who will die when I let
go. What fools men are, and what an evil thing is war.

Yet today I threw open the kitchen window and heard
birdsong in the trees, the rush of melted snow in the brook
at the wood's edge. In the yard I saw squirrels at frolic and

that burst of yellow the forsythia bush delivers faithfully to us each spring. Gifts from God, these sights and sounds, this placid here and now, and I wonder—was my hospital life the dream, or is this?

Lizzy Popper's diary entries and letters, so forthright and soul-baring, tempt the twenty-first-century reader to assign modern diagnoses to her psychological state. What to make of her descriptions of the horrific things she saw, heard, and touched when her mind involuntarily transported her back to Shipley Hospital? Was she merely processing difficult memories or, perhaps, suffering the flashbacks associated with posttraumatic stress disorder? Did her earlier swings between heightened productivity and immobilizing depression indicate that she was responding to the needs of a nation and to difficult personal losses, or that she suffered from bipolar disease? There is no way to know. What can be concluded from Popper's postwar life, however, is that in her later years she arrived at a state of emotional stability. Lizzy was sixty-one years old when she returned home from the war, and would live another twenty-seven years. Further personal hardships and professional obstacles awaited her, but she would confront these with a newfound equanimity.

I shifted the pillows, glanced over at the clock radio. Only nine twenty-three? God, it felt more like midnight.

In the years following the Civil War, many female abolitionists transferred their energies to the causes of . . . In the years following the Civil War, many female abolitionists . . . their energies to the causes of . . .
    many female abolitionists . . .

I fought it for as long as I could, attempting over and over to get to the end of that same sentence. Then I surrendered to sleep. . . .

———

THE PHONE WOULDN'T STOP SCREAMING. I lunged for it, more to shut it up than to see who was calling. Lizzy's story fell off the bed with a thunk.

"Yeah? What?"

"Oh. Hi. Can I please speak to Mr. Quirk, please? . . . The teacher?"

A young woman's voice. What the hell time was it, anyway? Two a.m.? Three? Who'd be calling me at . . . But when I squinted at the red numerals on my clock radio, they said 10:16 p.m.

"Speaking."

"Oh, hi, Mr. Quirk. It didn't sound like you. I'm sorry to be bothering you, but I been crying all night and my mother keeps going, 'Call your teacher, call your teacher.' I got your number off the Internet White Pages cuz I remembered one time you said you lived in Three Rivers. I hope it's all right I'm calling you. I didn't wake you up, did I?"

"Who *is* this?"

"Mari. From your class. Marisol Sosa. I just keep crying and thinking about how, maybe if I had just talked to him—asked him how he was doing or whatever. And about how me and Daisy complained to you about him. And how Ozzie said that thing to him. . . . And then last week, Mr. Quirk? Me and my friend Melanie? We were in the Student Union having lattés and talking about our soaps? And he came in, and I go, 'That's that weird army guy from my class who's always switchin' his seat.' And then right after I said that, he walked over to our table and said hi, and I said hi, and he asked me, he said, did I mind if he sat down with us? And Melanie was all trying not to look at his hand, and I said, 'No, sorry, cuz we're kinda busy studying.' But we didn't, you know, we didn't even have no books out or anything. We were just talking about our soaps. But now, all's I keep thinking about is that maybe if I had said, 'Yeah, sure. Have a seat. This is Melanie,' then—"

"Marisol, I don't . . . What happened?"

"That guy from our class," she said. "The army guy. Oh, my God, you didn't hear about it?"

ON THE ELEVEN P.M. NEWS, they showed pictures: Kareem Kendricks's high school yearbook photo, a portrait of him in his dress uniform. In the third photo—one of those group portraits that families have taken at Sears or someplace—Kendricks, both hands intact, stands with one arm around his daughter, all pigtails and plaits, and the other arm around the pretty, petite young wife he wounded that afternoon in the Department of Children and Families parking lot. At that hour, the news anchor said, Taneeka Hawkins-Kendricks, a dental hygienist and part-time waitress, remained in serious but stable condition. The social worker who had been supervising Private Kendricks's parental visit had been shot, too, but hers was a superficial wound. She was being kept overnight for observation and would most likely be released in the morning. Private Kendricks was dead—a bullet to the neck, self-inflicted. His daughter had witnessed the injuring of the social worker but not of her mother, the news anchor said, and not her father's suicide. She had been placed in protective custody pending the arrival of her maternal grandparents from out of state.

"It was the war that messed him up," I had kept reassuring a near-hysterical Marisol over the phone. "Not anything you said, or did, or didn't do. It was the war." She hated George Bush, she said. She tried hard not to hate anybody, but she hated President Bush and Vice President Cheney and that Condi lady—all of them. She couldn't help it. In the morning, she'd pray for forgiveness, but that night she was just going to let herself hate them. Her cousins, Frankie and Modesto, had both been injured in that stupid war, and a guy whose family lived in the apartment down the hall in their building had been killed. "And he was nice, too," Mari said. "He was always laughing."

I turned off the news, reached over to turn out the light. I saw Lizzy's story on the floor, facedown, where it had dropped when I'd reached for the phone. I picked it up, smoothed out the bent pages, and read a random snatch:

"'I'm sorry, Missus! I was thinkin' you was Johnny Reb! I'm scared! I want my Ma!' I pulled him against my breast, cradling him and whispering not to be afraid. . . ."

Some nights, Mo had said, she climbed up onto that girl Crystal's bunk and held her. She had to, whether she got in trouble or not, because that girl was just a baby herself. She *needed* to be held.

Lying there in the dark, I kept telling myself the same thing I had told Marisol over the phone: that none of us could have anticipated he'd do something so desperate. That nothing we could have said or done would have prevented it. . . .

But what if, that afternoon in my office, I had stood up, come out from behind the safety of my desk, and held out my arms to him? Let him fall against me and release some of that pain and fear and unbearable isolation? . . . *Do you ever regret not having children?* Janis had asked me that day up in Hartford, and I'd surprised myself by saying I did. . . . *Dad*, Velvet sometimes called me, and I'd roll my eyes, not let on that I kind of liked it. . . .

Kareem's father had walked out of his life, had not even made it to Walter Reed. Well, I knew what paternal abandonment felt like, didn't I? What if, that afternoon in my office, I had stood and risked fatherhood? Offered him a pair of sheltering arms? Would it have been enough to keep him from going down there and doing what he did? What if? What if? What if? . . .

———

Bang! . . . Bang! . . . Bang!

I cracked my eyes open and squinted at the clock. Fucking 5:43 a.m., and he was already up and at it. Well, I had promised I'd help him. The sooner I got out there, the sooner we'd finish and I could put him in my car and take him home. I felt sorry for the guy, but I wasn't about to turn this place into a hospice. I was no Maureen.

I got out of bed, stumbled into the kitchen and started some coffee. Went to the front door. The newspaper was there—Kareem Kendricks in his army uniform, the same picture, I figured, that they'd superimposed on his welcome-home cake. Had his wounded wife survived the long night? Was his daughter okay? How was his dad doing—the guy who'd thought fatherhood could be bought back for the price of a couple of football tickets?

Bang! . . . Bang!

I pulled his wet clothes out of the washer. Threw them in the dryer and hit start. I poured two mugs of coffee, checked the outside thermometer. Cold out there: twenty-six degrees. I pulled on my hooded sweatshirt, my stocking cap and gloves. I figured I'd better get something warmer for Ulysses to wear, too. As I grabbed for my frayed old wool-lined canvas jacket, a memory fired off in my brain: me tossing this same jacket to Velvet on that chilly morning way back in Littleton, when she'd sat on top of our picnic table—a tough little cookie scared to death of the two wimpiest dogs in the world. God, that had been a lifetime ago: Maureen's and my Colorado life. Our lives before they'd said, "Go! Go!" and started shooting.

Bang!

"Okay, okay. I'm coming."

Both of the Micks' cars were gone. Janis was probably in the air by now, en route to Tulane; she'd said she had an "insanely early" flight. Moze was probably halfway to New York with his display cases and order forms—his angels and fiends.

Bang! . . . Bang!

Passing by the barn, I recalled Moze's near-introduction. *Breaking news, man. This here's gonna be our new guy.*

I'd seen that kid from somewhere. A student at Oceanside? One of my high school kids from further back? Whoever he was, he'd better be trustworthy. There was no toilet out there in the barn. When Moze or Velvet had to go, they came back to the farmhouse and used my bathroom rather than climb the back stairs to the Micks' apartment. I supposed this new guy would expect access, too. Well, Moze had better have done a background check then, or checked his references at the very least, because I wasn't crazy about letting someone I didn't know have the run of—

I stopped, took a sharp intake of breath. I knew who he was. Moze's new hire was Jesse Seaberry, Morgan's bad-news older brother.

Bang!

→*chapter thirty-one*←

"DIG RIGHT ABOUT THERE," HE said. "No, not that far. Two or three feet to the left of that. . . . No? Nothing? Son of a bitch. I was thinking we buried it on the north side, but now I'm not so sure." *We* was Ulysses and my father. Surrounding us was a chaos of disturbed earth and busted-up cement.

We'd been at it for an hour, and I was getting tired of humoring him. Tired, too, of his cat-and-mouse evasiveness. I'd asked him two or three times what it was, exactly, we were trying to locate, but he'd kept deflecting the question. I figured it had to be stolen money or stolen goods of some kind—that I'd soon be adding burglary, or maybe even robbery, to my father's illustrious résumé. But now I was beginning to wonder if this treasure hunt had been triggered by the imaginings of a brain pickled in alcohol.

"Good thing the ground's not frozen over yet, huh?" he said.

Yeah, I thought. Lucky us. Three more shovelfuls, I told myself, and I'm done. It was getting a little old: him acting like my job foreman.

He faced east, took eight or nine steps away from me, and tapped the toe of his boot against the ground. "Try here." When I did, I both felt and heard metal hit metal. Ulysses heard it, too. "That's it," he said.

A few minutes later, I had loosened and pulled from the ground the dented gunmetal-gray footlocker that Ulysses identified as the one they'd buried that day. "Jesus, it's heavy," I said. "What'd he steal? Bricks?" He shook his head, eyes fixed on what I'd just unearthed.

Squatting before the trunk, I brushed away the caked dirt still clinging to it. But as I moved to open it, his hand stopped mine. "Not out here," he said. "Bring it inside." I'd have ignored him had he not looked so sick and stricken.

We each grabbed a handle and started back toward the house. He got winded a few times, and we had to put it down. I offered to lug it myself or go get the car, see if I could fit it into my trunk. He shook his head.

As the barn came into view, my eyes bounced from Jesse Seaberry's motorcycle to the kid himself, shaking the door handle at the side entrance of the barn. I motioned to Ulysses to put down the trunk. "Hey!" I yelled, approaching Seaberry. "What are you doing?"

When he'd come by the day before, he said, he'd taken out his cell phone to silence it and put it on Moses's desk instead of back in his pocket. Then he'd forgotten to grab it when he left. Had Moze left for New York yet? I said he had. Did I have a key to the studio? I did, I said, but I was busy. He'd have to wait until Moze got back.

"Dude, I rode all the way here from Glastonbury. I really need that phone, man. It'll just take a minute." I waited until he looked away from my gaze. Then I pulled my key ring out of my pocket. The quicker he got his phone, the faster I'd get him off my property.

But as I slipped the key into the lock, I couldn't resist. "Why is it you want to work here?" I asked. "So that you can check out the lay of the land? Start planning what you're going to do with it if you guys win?"

That wasn't it, he said. He'd been loading trucks for FedEx for a while, but that job was getting old. He'd seen Moze's ad on Craigs-list.

"Yeah? Gee, there's a funny coincidence."

He nodded, seeming not to register my note of sarcasm. "I've always kinda liked gargoyles and shit. And Mr. Mick seems like he'd be a pretty cool boss to work for."

"Don't be too sure you're *going* to be working for him," I said. "Because when he gets back, I'm going to let him know who you are and what your family's trying to do."

"He knows, man. I told him. He said it made no difference to him. Dude's a businessman, you know? I guess he figures he'll be able to stay put no matter which way the lawsuit goes."

That stopped me. He was probably right about Moze.

"Dude, it's not me or my dad so much. It's more my mom. She's still pretty bitter. And, you know . . ."

"What do I know?"

"She killed him. While she was driving stoned." This time I was the one who looked away first.

I unlocked the side door and flipped on the lights. "Yes!" he said. "There it is, right where I left it. Thanks, man."

I turned the lights back off, locked the door. I followed him as he walked back toward his bike. "Just so that you all know, my aunt signed a preservation agreement with the state back in 1980-something. And it's binding, too, no matter who holds the deed. This property has to remain farm land. So it's not like you guys are going to be able to turn around and sell it to some condo developer or something."

"Yeah, we know that," he said. "But farming would be cool. I was thinking about that the other day."

"Really? What would you cultivate? Pot? Poppies?"

I had said it to piss him off, but he smiled at me instead. "Been clean and sober for 597 days now. But who's counting, right?"

I kept my face expressionless. Said nothing. If he was looking for a high five or a congratulatory pat on the back, he was going to have a long wait on his hands. He was going to have to fucking wait forever.

"The thing is," he said. "That morning? Just before she hit him? I was busting his stones. Scaring him, okay? I'd just found out some shit about him, and I was threatening to tell my mom and everyone else who thought he was perfect. Which was basically everybody. But then he bolted, and *bam*. . . . So, in a way, I'm responsible, too. And I've had to live with that, okay? That, and a whole bunch of other crap I did. Because if someone had to get killed that day, it should have been me, not Morgan. That's what my mother thinks, I guess. She still won't speak to me, have anything to do with me, and she probably never will. And if I could've changed places with him, I would have done that for her. But I couldn't. The only thing I could do was deal with my shit and clean up my act. Get straight and stay that way. Work the steps. . . . Which is why farming would be kind of cool, you know? Something positive. Grow stuff, produce stuff. Have you ever, by any chance, been to Epcot?"

"Epcot?" I was still trying to negotiate his remorse. Why were we suddenly going to Disney World?

"They got this building there called The Land. And you go downstairs and there's this ride, okay? You get in these little boats and they take you past these farms of the future. You know what hydroponics are? Because I was thinking that might be cool: hydroponic farming."

Two hundred acres of farmland, and he wanted to grow things in water?

"Or herbs, maybe," he said. "Not, you know, *herb*. Herbs like parsley and paprika and shit. You ever watch the Food Channel?"

I reminded him that I was busy.

"Yeah, okay. Thanks again, man." He walked over to his bike. "Or llamas, maybe. A llama farm would be cool. But hey, you never know. Maybe we won't win and you'll be able to stay put. I'd be cool with that, too." He straddled his bike. It roared to life. "Thanks again, man! See you soon!" he yelled. He lurched forward, helmetless, down the rutted dirt driveway and onto Bride Lake Road.

———————

ULYSSES AND I LIFTED THE trunk and carried it from the back stoop to the kitchen. I got an old sheet and spread it so that the floor wouldn't get crapped up with dirt and whatever else was in there. "Mind if I have a drink to steady my nerves?" Ulysses asked. His hand was already on the vodka bottle that I'd forgotten to put away the night before.

"Not now, U," I said. "Let's get this done."

I knelt before the footlocker. The left-side clasp opened no problem, but the right one was bent beyond cooperating. "There's a screwdriver in that drawer beneath the microwave," I said. "You want to grab it for me?"

"Funny you just called me U," he said. "That's what your dad always called me." He held out the screwdriver, sharp end out, and the damn thing was dancing so crazily in his trembling hand that I had to steady his wrist so I wouldn't get jabbed. "Take it easy," I told him. "We found it. We dug it up. It's all good, right?"

He shook his head. "Just so you know, I had no idea what was in there the day we buried it," he said. "I asked him, but he said I was better off not knowing. He didn't tell me till later. *Years* later, it was. He was cocked and I wasn't, and he says, 'Hey, U, remember that day you and me buried that trunk out past the orchard?' And that's when he come out with it."

"Uh-huh."

I got the clasp pried apart and raised the lid. The smell of dead air and dry rot hit my nostrils. It was no wonder the thing had had some heft to it.

I unpacked the contents one by one, lining things up like Russian nesting dolls. Jammed inside the trunk was one of our old wooden apple crates, its label "Bride Lake Farms" still vivid with color. Inside the crate was something that had clearly been my mother's: some kind of zippered suitcase from her modeling days—oval shaped, light blue, vinyl covered. The name she'd gone by ran diagonally across the front of it, professionally lettered in darker blue with gold trim and punctuated with an exclamation point: "Jinx Dixon!"

This was different than the other stuff I'd recovered—the magazine ad and newspaper clippings, the cassette of my interview with Peppy Schissel. Here was something my mother had used and carried. I lifted it out of the crate and placed it in front of me. Sat back on the floor with my legs bracketing it. I took hold of the zipper's metal tab and pulled, slowly, hesitantly. It stuck a little in one spot where the teeth had rusted, but when I pulled a little harder, it gave. I lifted the lid.

Inside the suitcase was a small cast-iron chest—an antique, could have been, from the looks of it, though I was no expert on that kind of thing. Its lid was shut tight with spring-held clamps. I loosened the tension and removed the cover. For a second or two, I didn't know *what* I was looking at. Then, Jesus Christ Almighty, I *did* know. Lying side by side on a bed of fine-grained white sand were the remains of two human infants.

Palms against the floor, I crab-walked away from them, only half-aware of my own mantra: *What the fuck? . . . What the fuck? . . .*

Ulysses was saying something, but his words weren't quite registering. He was crying. He had hold of the vodka. I stood up, reeling a little, and snatched the bottle away from him. Grabbed a glass, poured him an inch or so, and poured the rest down the sink. "Here!" I said, shoving his drink at him. "Drink up! And as soon as I come back here, I want some answers!"

"Why? Where you going?"

I wasn't so much going someplace as getting away. I hurried, stumbling, from the back of the house to the front, knocking into things as I went. Banged open the front door and broke into a run, down the porch stairs, down the driveway. Crossing Bride Lake Road, I barely noticed the screech of brakes, the rebuke of some faceless driver. "Asshole!" I ran alongside the road, weaving in and out, muttering to myself. They hadn't fucked me up enough already with all their lies and secrets? Now *this*? . . .

I ran past the prison and into our fallow cornfields. Ran to where the maze had been—the place where they'd come out of hiding to take their stolen food, the table scraps of decent people's lives. I screamed it over and over as if, with enough repetition, it might travel back in time so that they'd get the message: *I hate you. I love you. I hate you. I love you.* . . .

I don't know how long I was out there, but by the time I was limping back up the driveway, the sun was halfway across the sky and my throat was raw, my foot throbbing from having kicked something out there, I didn't recall what. The front door gaped open. I went back in the house.

In the foyer, I stopped before the framed photo hanging at the bottom of the staircase, the one that pilot who'd had to emergency-land on our property had flown back later and taken as a gift to my grandfather: "Bride Lake Farm, Aerial View, August 1948". . . . My eyes moved left to right—from the neat and orderly rows of corn to the prison compound with its ant-sized inmates, its brick buildings and sparkling lake—the lake where the legendary largemouth bass, Big Wilma, had swum, uncaptured and uncapturable, and where my mother had drowned herself. . . . Near the photo's right border was the apple orchard and the open field beyond it. No apple house. It hadn't been built yet, and so those babies out in the kitchen hadn't yet been buried under it. I stood there in front of that old picture, rocking back and forth on the balls of my feet, dreading what I had to do. I started back toward the kitchen.

Ulysses was gone. I walked slowly up to the iron chest and stood there, peering down at them, willing myself not to look away. . . . They weren't twins—they couldn't have been. They didn't look like they'd come from the same planet, let alone the same mother.

The bigger one, dressed and bonneted, looked like some kind of weird freak-show attraction. Its smiling face was partly missing and partly mummified, upholstered in leathery brown skin. Its jaw and cheekbone were partially exposed on the left side where the skin had deteriorated. The bonnet it wore had a wide, old-fashioned brim decorated with colorless ribbon. Along the hem of its dingy, half-rotted dress someone had stitched a prayer or a plea in thread of a color now faded and nondescript: "God Bless This Child."

The other, smaller one was an unclothed skeleton. Its legs were drawn up toward its chest. Its fists, no larger than walnuts, were clenched in front of its face as though it had died in pain. Had my mother given birth to it? And what was its connection to its bizarre companion? Why had they been put together in that chest? . . . I kept looking away from them, then looking back. My gaze returning, over and over, to the smaller of the two—the one frozen in suffering.

When I glanced back at the empty blue suitcase, I saw, on the bottom, something I hadn't noticed when I'd lifted out the chest: a letter or note, torn into small pieces. I gathered them up and carried them open-palm to the counter, then pieced it together like a jigsaw puzzle. It was printed, not written: capital letters, fountain pen ink from the looks of it—a man's forward-leaning, no-nonsense script on stationery from some Chicago hotel. I figured some of the pieces might be missing, but it was all there. The letter was undated.

DEAR JINX,

I GAVE YOU 50 IN OCTOBER TO GET IT DONE AND ITS YOUR PROBLEM NOT MINE IF YOU DIDN'T. HERE'S ANOTHER HUNDRED FOR YOUR TROUBLES, BUT THIS IS ALL YOUR GETTING FROM ME SO CHASE THOSE DOLLAR SIGNS OUT OF YOUR EYES. I DON'T WANT TO MAKE TROUBLE FOR YOU, BUT YOU NEED TO KNOW OUR ORGANIZATION HAS PEOPLE WHO PROTECT US WHEN SITUATIONS LIKE THIS COME UP AND SOME OF THESE GUYS ARE ROUGH CUSTOM-

ERS. DON'T CALL OR WRITE ME AGAIN (IF YOUR
SMART) AND I HOPE <u>FOR YOUR SAKE</u> THAT WHAT
YOU SAID ABOUT CONTACTING MY WIFE WAS AN
EMPTY THREAT BECAUSE I DON'T WANT TO THINK
OF THE TROUBLE YOU'LL BRING DOWN ON YOUR-
SELF IF YOU DO SOMETHING THAT STUPID. LIKE
THEY SAY, IT TAKES 2 TO TANGO, JINX. WE HAD FUN
BUT ITS OVER.

TAKE CARE OF YOURSELF,
CAL

Cal. Calvin Sparks. The ballplayer.

So now I knew that much at least: when Peppy Schissel had driven her back from New York that day, it was Sparks's baby she was carrying, not the company nephew's. Why else would he have paid her money to "get it done"? Not out of altruism, from the tone of his letter. But shit, if one of the babies in that chest was hers and Sparks's—and I was pretty sure it had to be the smaller one, not the Ripley's Believe It or Not oddity lying beside it—then where did my father fit into all this? Why had *he* been the one to bury those babies? The only person who might be able to answer that one had taken a powder.

Yet rather than going out and looking for him, I pulled up a kitchen chair and sat there with the babies. Kept a kind of vigil, I guess. They'd been lying out there under the cold ground, alone with only each other for company, for longer than I'd been alive. Now that, for better or worse, they'd been brought back into the light of day, I was reluctant to leave them.

I must have sat there for an hour or more, the way you'd sit at a wake—contemplating their too-brief lives, wondering about the people who'd brought them into existence. As usual, I had so many questions, so few answers. . . . Somewhere during that hour, I felt the need to reach in and touch them. Comfort them in some small, belated way. But my hand inside the chest was as big and clumsy as a catcher's mitt, and when my knuckles grazed the dress of the mummified one, I flinched. Drew my hand back.

I tried again. Touched the smaller one—the one whose mother, I felt pretty sure, had been my mother, too. I cupped my hand around its skull, the curve of its tiny shoulder. Touched its femur, its foot. Had it been a little girl? A boy? There was no way to tell. . . .

The skin on the other one's face had looked sturdy as leather, but it wasn't. When I touched it lightly at the temple, the skin and bone beneath it crumbled and caved in. Its fragility both frightened and repulsed me, and when I pulled my hand back, I saw that my fingertips were covered with a powdery residue of long-dead skin cells. I brushed my hand against my pant leg, but some of the residue had settled into the whorls of my fingertips. I looked across the room to the sink, the faucet I could have used to wash away its traces. But for some reason, I didn't, or couldn't, do it.

I stood, opened the back door, and called out to him. "Ulysses!"

If he had wandered back to the field where we'd dug up the trunk, and then had wandered into the woods behind, he might have been oblivious to the sharp drop-off. I thought about Zinnia, the Bride Lake prisoner who had worked for us when I was a boy—who had hugged me so tightly and later had fallen from that sheer drop-off to her death. . . . So I left the babies and went outside—walked the path to the orchard, the field. Walked past the hole I'd dug a few innocent hours earlier and into the back woods. "Ulysses! You out here, U? . . . Hey, Ulysses!" A couple of times, I thought I heard his footsteps, then saw it was only the squirrels running over dead leaves. Standing at the edge of the drop-off, I looked down, looked from side to side. I called his name again and again, but the only answer I got was my own echo.

Approaching the house again, I looked at the empty places where the Micks' cars were usually parked. I was grateful that they were both away for the weekend. Velvet, too. The way she was drawn to freaky stuff, she'd have probably thought my grisly discovery was "fuckin' rad!" or something, and her enthusiasm for the macabre was about the last thing I needed. . . . What I *did* need was to talk to Maureen—lean on her a little and get her opinion about what I should do as I tried to wrestle with this . . . this what? Could you call the discovery of two dead babies on your propery a crisis? I wasn't sure, but crisis or not, it wasn't like I could pick up the phone and call her. It didn't work that way. Under DOC rules, she could only call me. *This is the operator. I have a State of Connecticut prisoner on the line. Do you wish to accept the charges for a call from Maureen Quirk?* There was no telling what Mo's reaction was going to be—to the babies, to the news about Kareem Kendricks's rampage. She'd been in a pretty good place lately, pretty stable, and I didn't want anything to set her back. Still, I'd have to tell her when I visited the next day. *If* the scuttlebutt about a coming lockdown was wrong, which it probably wasn't. The jailhouse grapevine was pretty reliable, Mo said, given the liaisons between COs and inmates. A heads-up about what was being planned was power, and power could be bargained for. If they did go into lockdown, she'd be unreachable for the better part of a week. . . .

And Alphonse was away; I couldn't call him either. Not that the Mustang King would've been much help. Al had always been a little creeped out by death. Dead babies, one of them mummified? Forget it. . . .

I had Jerry Martineau's home number, but I hesitated for a while, weighing the pros and cons. But Jesus Christ, I needed to talk to *somebody*. When his wife answered, I told her it was "semi-urgent." And when Jerry called back a few minutes later, I was vague. I told him I needed some advice about something I'd found on my property.

"What kind of 'something' we talking about?" he asked.

"Something kind of strange. Can you come out here as a friend, rather than as a cop?" He said he could come over in that capacity,

but depending on what it was I was going to show him, he wasn't necessarily going to able to *leave* as such. He said he needed to hit CVS
on the way over, but that he'd probably be by inside of an hour.

"YOU KNOW, I REMEMBER MISS Rheingold," he said.
"Cardboard box with their pictures on it, a pad of ballots, little pencil
on a string. Every summer, my sister and I would walk down to my
Aunt Dot's package store, pick who we wanted, and stuff the ballot
box." He kept rubbing his cheek and looking back and forth between
the old *New Yorker* ad he was holding—"It's time to elect Miss Rheingold 1950! Your vote may decide!"—and the two small corpses at his
feet. "My old man drank Rheingold," he said. "Had a can every night
with his supper."

"*One* can?" I said. "Well, there's the difference between your old
man and mine."

"Hey, they may have taken different routes, but neither one of them
saw their fortieth birthday," Jerry noted.

"And scrawny little Ulysses outlived them both by over forty years.
Man, he better be okay, because I've got some questions for *his* ass."

Jerry nodded. "So do I."

"Officially, you mean? Why? What's the point?"

"The point is, what we've got here, I'm guessing, is two deaths that
were covered up and never accounted for. Which means I'm going to
have to call in the coroner, see if she can determine whether or not
these two died of natural causes. Because if they didn't, that hole you
dug out there is a crime scene." He peered in again at the remains,
and I watched a shiver pass through him. "I tell you, Caelum, I've
seen a lot of bodies over the years, investigated a lot of screwy domestic situations. But this one may just take the cake."

"Look," I said. "If a crime *was* committed, it happened over fifty
years ago. By people who've been dead for decades."

"Except for one of them maybe. If he helped your dad cover up a homicide—or *two* of them; I'm not ruling anything out at this stage of the game—then that makes him an accessory."

I shook my head. "He's dying, Jer. Why put him through that kind of an ordeal at this point?"

"Because he picked up a sledgehammer and started busting up that concrete. And because you two opened Pandora's box here. *You* called *me*. Remember? What do you expect me to do? Look the other way again?"

Again: fair enough. Jerry had looked the other way after Maureen had been caught "doctor-shopping," and down the line, a seventeen-year-old kid had ended up dead in the road. I flashed on Jesse Seaberry, the way he'd looked as he'd spoken of his own culpability in his brother's death.

"Ulysses say where he was going when he left here?" Jerry asked.

"Nope. But wherever he is, he's not drinking any more of the vodka I let him have last night when he slept over here. I poured the rest down the sink."

"You gave him liquor? In his condition?"

"Yeah, well . . . give drink to the thirsty, right? It's one of the seven acts of Christian virtue." Jerry gave me the kind of quizzical look I must have given Kareem Kendricks the day before in my office. "You see that thing on the news last night? About the soldier who opened fire at that office over in New London?"

"Yes, I saw it. What about it?"

"Student of mine. A few hours before he did what he did, he was in my office, reciting the seven acts of Christian virtue: feed the hungry, give drink to the thirsty . . ."

"Jesus," Jerry said. "You've had a hell of a couple of days, haven't you?"

I nodded. "I was up most of the night, letting the what-ifs do a number on me. What if I'd realized what he was planning and been able to prevent it? Said just the right thing that might have brought him back to his senses and . . . Then, of course, there's the bigger, scarier what-if."

Jerry cocked his head. "Meaning?"

"He'd been acting pretty unstable in class that morning, and one of the other students said something to antagonize him. He could have just as easily pulled out his gun and started taking victims then and there instead of . . . could have found ourselves in the middle of another . . ."

He finished it for me. "Columbine."

I turned my back to him and walked over to the window. "I've been trying for eight years to wrap my head around *that* one," I said. Outside, a hawk lifted off a sycamore limb and flew through the grim gray sky. I turned back and faced him. "You're a cop, Jerry. Maybe you can tell me. Why is it that these damaged people who can't take the pain anymore have to pick up firearms and go out in a blaze of glory? Destroy other people's lives along with their own?"

"I don't know, Caelum," he said. "How's she doing over there, anyway?"

"Okay. Better, actually. Although I'm not exactly looking forward to our next conversation when she asks me what's new." I looked down again at the babies. "Come on, Jerry. Think about it. What good's some long, drawn-out police investigation going to do these two at this point?"

He rose and walked over to me. Put his hand on my shoulder. "I don't know, my friend. Acknowledge their existence maybe? Give 'em a little belated justice?"

"When that train smashed into him, it dragged him along for several hundred feet. Severed both his legs. She was doing time for vagrancy when they fished her out of Bride Lake. What's the matter, Jerry? Cosmic justice not enough for you?"

"Not when I've got regulations to adhere to. Protocols to follow."

"Yeah, well, you've got your protocols, and I've got a lawsuit hanging over my head with my land and my home hanging in the balance.

I don't exactly need a lot of negative attention drawn to this place right now."

He sympathized, he said, but he wasn't going to put his job on the line for me *or* Ulysses. "But let's not get ahead of ourselves, okay?" He pulled a pen and a small notepad out of his pocket. "Read me again what that letter says."

I walked over to the counter. As I read him Sparks's letter, he jotted some notes. "This is conjecture on my part," he said. "But from that comment about 'dollar signs' in her eyes, I'm guessing she may have been trying to extort money out of him," he said. "Threatening to go public about her pregnancy, maybe. So he would have had to either pay her off or scare her off, and it sounds like he opted for the latter. When was it Jackie Robinson broke through to the majors? Forty-six?"

"Forty-seven," I said. "Why?"

"Well, put it in context. Robinson's a great player on the field and a stand-up guy off of it, and when he broke through, *he* was getting death threats, for Christ's sake. Couple of seasons later, this Sparks comes along, and not only is he cheating on his wife with some pretty little white model, but then he gets her pregnant on top of that? You know what would have happened if the papers got ahold of a story like that? He played for the Giants, you said? Probably would have brought his career to a screeching halt. Hell, there'd have probably been a lynching party right there at the Polo Grounds. So let's say his letter works. Scares her into shutting her mouth. *Now* what the hell's she going to do? . . . Interesting that she ripped up his letter and threw it in there, isn't it? That's hostile. Shows how pissed off she must have been when she realized she wasn't going to get what she wanted from him. But, you know, this is all guesswork. I could be way off base."

I shook my head. "She had a temper when people thwarted her. I know that much." I told Jerry about the old newspaper article—the one about how, as a seventeen-year-old, Mary Agnes had swallowed India ink after Great-Grandma Lydia forbade her from seeing my fourteen-year-old father. And about how, after she got hauled into court and the judge ordered her to stay twenty-five feet away from him when they were at school together, she ripped into His Honor and got slapped with a contempt fine. "And after Rheingold fired her? Before she vacated the fancy apartment they'd set her up in? He told me she trashed the place. Broke mirrors, slashed the furniture."

"Who's he?" Jerry asked.

"The old guy I talked to down in Queens. The former driver."

"Okay, so what we've got then is a behavior pattern: she's volatile when she doesn't get what she wants—which, in this case, let's just say, for example's sake, might have been blackmail money."

It was hard to hear him describe her as being that devious, that unstable—hard because it sounded plausible. In the face of all that was coming to light, it was getting harder, too, to romanticize about my mother. I'd been outraged about the way the Quirks and everyone else had bullied her. Used their power against her. But I was beginning to see that, for whatever reason, Mary Agnes Dank had engineered most of her own troubles.

"The old guy you talked to down in Queens—the Rheingold driver. He said she was pregnant when he drove her back here from New York, right? Any idea when that was?"

"Yeah, nineteen fifty. Wintertime, because he said it started snowing on his way back to the city. March, I think he said. Pregnant with *me*, I thought—either by Sparks or the other guy she was seeing. The heir apparent at Rheingold, also married. But the math didn't add up. If she was pregnant with me in March of 1950, then how the hell could she have given birth to me in October of '51? So then I figured, okay, maybe if my family had gone to the trouble to have that bogus birth certificate made up—to hide the fact that Mary Agnes was my mother—then maybe they'd lied about my date of birth, too. Maybe I was a year older than I'd been led to believe. I started thinking about things like how, by the end of sixth grade, I was already shaving. Already having wet dreams. I came up with all kinds of—"

"Sixth grade? Jeeze, I didn't have my first one until high school. On an Explorers campout. Woke up dreaming about Joey Heatherton, and I started firing off like Mount Vesuvius. Thank God for sleeping bags, you know?" He was making wavy lines on his notepad. "Joey Heatherton: where is she now?"

"Probably in a nursing home," I said. "But it was driving me nuts, you know? Not knowing how old I was, who my father was. Then this DNA test I had done said I definitely *was* a Quirk. That my father *was* my father."

I told Jerry what I'd found out from Ulysses and later verified in that old newspaper article about my kidnapping. Told him about how I'd been taken away from Mary Agnes and "legitimized"—given a different mother who was passed off as the one who'd given me birth.

Jerry glanced down at the babies. "So who the hell are these two then? That's what *I've* got to figure out." He took out his cell phone and started punching buttons. I asked him who he was calling. "The station house. I'm going to have a couple of my patrolmen drive around, see if they can find our buddy Ulysses so that I can talk with him."

"So you're going to question him yourself?"

"Yeah, I figure he'd be more forthcoming if—Yeah, Gina? This is Captain Martineau. Who's on this afternoon? Tanaka? . . . Okay, tell him I want him to see if he can find someone for me. And put Bill Meehan on it, too, while you're at it. You know that old rummy who—"

"Hold up," I said. I pointed toward the back door. Ulysses was sitting on the stoop, his head in his hands.

chapter thirty-two

HE WAS PRETTY SHAKEN UP. Pretty scared. "You drunk?"
Jerry asked him.

He shook his head. "I wish I was."

I started a pot of coffee, and Jerry told Ulysses, as gently as he
could, that he had some questions he needed him to answer.

Ulysses looked back and forth between us. "Questions about
what?" he asked. Jerry extended his hand toward the babies. "Oh.
Yeah, okay." He said he didn't mind answering Jerry's questions,
but he'd just as soon not have to do it in the same room as "those
things."

"Fair enough," Jerry said. They adjourned to the living room.

When the coffee was ready, I poured three mugs and went in there.
"Mind if I sit in on this?" I asked. Jerry said it was okay with him if it
was okay with Ulysses. Ulysses said he'd feel better if I did.

"And Jer, before you get started, do you think he needs to
lawyer up?"

Jerry rolled his eyes. "What *I* think is that you've maybe been hitting the *Law & Order* reruns a little too hard."

We exchanged smiles. "Point taken," I said.

Ulysses said my father and he had buried the trunk and laid the
cement floor over it in September of 1953.

"You sure about that?" Jerry said. "Because we've been trying to piece this thing together, and we're thinking it might have been 1950."

Ulysses shook his head. It was about a week or so after he'd gotten his discharge from the navy, he said, and that was Labor Day of '53. Grandpa Quirk and Lolly had gone out of state to a cattle auction, he remembered, and left my father in charge of the milking. "That and looking after the old lady."

"My great-grandmother," I said.

Ulysses nodded. "She wasn't too tappy at that point, but it was heading in that direction. They kinda had to keep an eye on her. Anyways, Alden called me up, asked me if I'd help him milk."

My father had been released from the service sometime before, Ulysses said. "Something happened to him over there, and it made him snap, I guess. The navy couldn't use him any more. Medical discharge, I guess it was. Alden never did say what it was. Lolly told me he was in bad shape when he first come home. Stayed up in his room most of the time. Didn't eat, couldn't sleep. By the time I got out, he was okay, pretty much. Drinking heavy, but other than that, the same Alden as before, far as I could tell. Except that he was a married man. He'd married on the quick, see? After Caelum here come along."

"Yeah, speaking of that, where were Caelum and his mother that day you guys buried the trunk?"

Ulysses shrugged. Said all he remembered was that we weren't around.

"We might have been up at the Cape," I said. "Buzzards Bay. When she and I would visit her family, we'd usually stay over for two or three nights."

"Okay, then," Jerry said. "Go on, Ulysses."

Grandpa Quirk had been after my father to help him build the apple house, he said. He was anticipating a bumper crop that year, and with it, he hoped, a bump in customers, too. "See, he'd just shelled out for that big cider press they used to have here. Thought it'd be a draw to get people out to the farm. Families with kids, that kind of thing:

show 'em how cider's made, and then they'd buy a jug or two and a basket of apples." Ulysses looked from Jerry to me. "He was pretty shrewd, your grandfather. Knew how to tease out a dollar. But he wasn't too happy with your father, because Alden had been dragging his feet on the building project, see? On purpose, see? Because he was waiting for an opportunity."

"What kind of opportunity?" Jerry asked.

"A time when the old man wasn't around. See, Alden had something he needed to do when nobody was around to see him do it."

It was a scorcher that morning, Ulysses remembered. After he and my father finished morning milking, they'd begun drinking. "Working our way through a couple six-packs, and then, out of the blue, he says to me, 'Come on, U! There's something else you need to help me with.' So I follow him up to the attic. And it was hotter'n hell up there, too. Like walking into a furnace."

First, they had lifted a large highboy away from the wall. Then my father, with the claw end of a hammer, had pried off a wooden panel that that highboy had been parked in front of. "And there was this crawl space behind it, see? Alden said he'd discovered it back when he was a kid—that his grandma's rule was that him and his sister were never supposed to go up in that attic unless she went up with them. And of course, the way Alden was, that was like handing him an open invitation to go up there and snoop around whenever he thought he could get away with it. And that's what he done back when he was a boy: snooped around and found that secret passageway."

My father got down on his hands and knees and disappeared into the crawl space, Ulysses said. And when he backed out again, he was dragging the footlocker. "And I remember, I says to him, 'What do you got in there? Pirate treasure?' And he laughed, said he wished it was. Only he wouldn't say what *was* in it. He told me it was better for me if I didn't know.

"We put everything back the way we found it—tapped the wooden panel back in place, put the highboy back in front of it. Then we hauled the trunk downstairs and out to the spot where the old man was planning to put up his apple shack."

Ulysses said they dug the hole, lowered the trunk, and shoveled over it. Then they rolled the ground to level it, built the staging for the floor, and started mixing cement. "I said to him in the middle of it, I said, 'Jesus, it's hot out here. How about we quit for a little while now? Wait till it cools off a little?' But Alden said No, no, we had to keep going so's we could get everything done by the time his old man got back. So all afternoon, we mixed and poured cement, two wheelbarrows at a time. Then we . . . then . . ."

He had been staring into the distance as he recalled that long-ago day, but suddenly he was back in the present, back in the farmhouse living room. He looked at me, surprised. "I just remembered something," he said.

"What's that?" Jerry asked.

"The old lady. Alden's grandmother."

Now that he had retrieved the memory, he said, he could picture it plain as day. "In the middle of all that cement mixing we were doing, she come wandering out from the house. She'd always been the prim and proper type, you know? But when she come out there, she was barefoot and her hair was kinda helter-skelter. Wearing a housedress that was buttoned up all wrong. . . . See, Alden'd been so busy rushing around, trying to get everything finished, that he'd forgotten about her. But then, there she was. When Alden seen her, he kinda froze up. Because this thing we were doing was supposed to be top secret, see?

"She walks up to him, barefoot like I said—walks right through the slop from the spillover around the wheelbarrow. Grabs Alden by his wrist. Now, I'd seen her do that same thing often enough when I was a kid—grab him by the wrist with one hand and start hitting him with the switch with the other, because of something bad she'd caught him doing. But that day, she walks up to him, grabs his wrist, and she says to him, close up to his face, she says, 'What did you do with it?' Meaning the trunk, see? We hadn't realized it, but she must have seen us that morning, carrying it down from the attic. And I said to myself, Uh-oh, the jig's up now. Alden's in trouble again. But then—and this surprised me—Alden looked right back at her, kinda bold-like, and he says he done what should have been a long time ago: put it in the ground where it belonged. And the old lady stood there, not saying anything at first. It was like a face-off, you know? Like a contest between the two of them. Then she nodded, decisive-like, and said, 'Good.' And then Alden took her by the arm and brung her over to the water bucket. Washed that wet cement off her feet and walked her back to the house. . . . Funny how memory works, ain't it? All those years ago, and now that I remember it, I can see her standing there plain as day. Hear her saying that one word when he told her that he'd buried the trunk: 'Good.'"

Ulysses clunked down his empty coffee mug. "More?" I asked.

"Nah. I could use a little nip of something, though."

"No way, José," Jerry said. "We're not through yet. And you're not supposed to be drinking anyway."

Ulysses nodded and turned to me. "How about one of them beers you were drinking last night, then? You got any of them left?" But before I could respond, Jerry asked him if there was anything else about that day that he remembered.

He shook his head. "Just that, when the old man come home that night, he was pleased as punch. Kinda shocked, I guess. Not only hadn't the farm gone to hell in a handbasket with Alden in charge, but the building project had moved forward, too." He said the next to me. "Didn't happen too often that your grandpa was pleased about something your dad had done. But he was that night. He was falling all over himself about how we'd laid down that floor. Course, he had no idea *why* Alden had gotten so hardworking all of a sudden—that he'd been waiting for the chance to get that chest out of the attic, bury it, and make sure it stayed buried."

Ulysses told us he had to stop talking and take a leak. But when he got up, he started heading toward the front door instead of the bathroom. "Wrong way," I said. "It's off the kitchen. Remember?" He said he'd just as soon relieve himself out in the yard if it was all right with me—that he'd rather not walk past "those two" again if he didn't have to.

While he was outside, I told Jerry that it didn't sound to me like Ulysses had been an accessory to anything except helping out his buddy. "So far, I'd say you're right," Jerry said. "But we're not through yet." He took out his phone again. Called the station house and directed his dispatcher to contact the coroner and give her a heads-up. He wanted the babies' remains and the other contents of the footlocker picked up and brought to the forensics lab later that afternoon. He said he also wanted Officers Meehan and Tanaka to meet him here at three o'clock so that they could have a look up in the attic and cordon off the hole out back.

When he got off the phone, I asked him if he thought he could keep the media away. He couldn't make any promises, he said. He'd urge his people to be as discreet as possible, but if the paper or the TV news people got wind of the investigation, he wouldn't be able to withhold information from them. "I think you better brace yourself, Caelum," he said. "Some of my guys are pretty chummy with the reporters. And I won't be able to control what does or doesn't come out of the coroner's mouth. Let's face it: hidden remains, a mummified baby—it's pretty sexy stuff for *Live at Five* and '*Eyewitness News*, details at eleven.' I wouldn't be surprised if you got some national media sniffing around out here. Maybe not. Maybe I'm wrong. I hope I am."

I looked at him and sighed.

When I went outside to retrieve Ulysses, I found him leaning against the side of the house, looking exhausted and sick. "You all right?" I asked. He shook his head. All he wanted to do, he said, was go back to his place, get a few drinks in him, maybe, and go to sleep.

"Well," I said. "Come on in, then. Let's get this thing finished, and then I'll drive you home."

"Yeah, okay," he said. "You're not mad, then?" The answer to that one was pretty complicated, but I told him no, I was weary but not mad—not at him, anyway. He was one of the few people in my life who had told me the truth. I put my hand on the small of his back and led him back inside.

"Okay," Jerry said. "So if Alden wouldn't tell you what was in the footlocker the day you buried it, when did he tell you?"

Ulysses turned to me. "What year was it that train hit him?"

"Nineteen sixty-five," I said. "May the twenty-second."

He nodded. "That'd be about right. It was springtime, I remember. He told me maybe a week or two before he got killed. Right at that same spot, too."

"The same spot?" I said. "What do you mean?"

"Me and him were fishing for buckies off the trestle bridge. I was on the wagon at the time; I'd been sober for the better part of that year. Minister and his wife at the Lutheran church had kinda tooken me on as a project. But Alden, he was drinking pretty heavy that day. And outa the blue, he starts spilling his guts about Mary Agnes. It was kinda unusual, see? Alden could be a happy drunk, and he could be a mean one, but that was the only time I ever seen him get weepy when he was cocked."

Ulysses said my father started pouring out his heart about how he should have listened to his grandmother when she'd warned him all those years earlier that Mary Agnes was bad news, same as her mother, and that she would ruin him. "The way he put it was, that she was a disease he picked up when he was a kid and hadn't ever been able to shake. Alden had a way with words, you know—a way of saying something so's you'd remember it. Back in grammar school—we were in the same class together, him and me—the teacher'd be cracking the ruler against his knuckles one minute because of something bad he done, and the next minute she'd be handing him a gold star and having him stand next to his desk and read his paper out loud because it was the best one in the class."

I had never heard anything about my father's having had a gift for words and would have liked Ulysses to tell me more, but Jerry said he needed to get back to that day at the trestle bridge.

Ulysses nodded. "Alden said he thought he'd finally got himself free of her after she moved away—went after bigger fish down there in New York. But then she come back and 'reinfected' him all over again. She'd gotten herself pregnant, see? By some guy who hadn't done right by her. Alden was in the navy by then, but this was before they sent him to Korea. He was home on leave from Portsmouth, waiting for his orders. And Mary, she come back with her tail between her legs and a bump in her belly. She was renting a room up in Jewett City—one of those places where they let you pay by the day and nobody bothers you with questions. What she done was, she tracked Alden down at the Cheery-O and begged him to help her. She had no money, she told him, and no future, either, if she was gonna get stuck raising that kid." Ulysses leaned in and whispered the next. "See, it was a colored fella who'd knocked her up, so that complicated things even worse."

Ulysses said my father promised he'd help her out, but he refused to marry her. "That's what she wanted, see? For them to get hitched on the quick. Have him make her an honest woman, and if they sent him over and he got killed, she'd be a widow entitled to some benefits. She'd always had a kind of power over him, everyone knew that, but this time he stuck to his guns. See, if he did what she wanted, he'd end up with a half-colored baby. And, you know, back then . . ."

What my father had offered Mary Agnes instead of marriage, Ulysses said, was money: for an operation, if that was what she wanted to do and could find someone who'd do it, or money to help her and the kid get by, once she had it. "But she was holding out for a wedding ring, see? And she got mad as hell when he wouldn't budge. Started hitting him, throwing things at him. Scratched his face up pretty bad, too, he said. So Alden said the hell with her. Borrowed his sister's car and took off for a few days. And when he come back, he said, he walked in the door and seen a telegram sitting on the front table. His orders had come. But then the phone started ringing, so he picks it up and who is it but her."

"Mary Agnes?"

"That's right." She'd taken some kind of concoction, Ulysses said—tincture of something or another that she'd mixed with Coca-Cola and drunk to terminate her unwanted pregnancy. "That girl brung her troubles on herself, always did, but she was pinning everything on Alden. Told him that, thanks to him, her baby'd be dead in a few hours and she was probably going to die along with it. And that, later on, he could go to the cemetery and find her grave and spit on it." Ulysses turned to me. "She could play your father like a fiddle, see? She was a pro at that."

Ulysses said my father told him he jumped back into Lolly's car and broke every speed limit between here and Jewett City. And sure enough, by the time he got to her, Mary Agnes was vomiting and convulsing. And the baby was coming.

"'Course, Alden had helped birth plenty of calves, so he knew the basics about what to do. How to get a baby out of its mother. Or he *thought* he did, anyway. But things got complicated, he said. It was coming out wrong, or trying to, I guess, and it tore her up pretty bad. Alden said she lost so much blood that he got scared. He was worried that she was going to die, see? Same as his mother when she had him.

"Baby was dead by the time he got it out of her, he told me. It was a boy, or woulda been. Alden said he didn't know what to do with it, where to put it, so he wiped it off a little and put it in a dresser drawer. He cleaned up the mess as best as he could—the blood and such. Cleaned her up a little. Then he just sat there with her, holding her hand. It was one hell of a long night, he said. Mary Agnes was sick as a dog—burning up with fever and rambling wild, thrashing back and forth. He said he kept making her drink water, lots of it, because he figured whatever that stuff was that she'd taken, she'd be better off if she could flush it out of her system. He was scared to bring her to the hospital, see? Because they'd start asking questions. But he was scared to *not* bring her, too. After a while, he tried convincing her that that was what they better do, but she carried on so bad that he give it up."

By mid-morning the following day, my father had told Ulysses, Mary Agnes had come around a little. She was weak, still, but lucid—improved enough so that he could leave her for a few hours—get Lolly's car back to her, grab a little sleep, and then head back there. Before he left, she asked him what he'd done with the baby, and he told her. He offered to take it with him, but she told him no. He should leave it for the time being, in case she wanted to look at it.

"And then, wouldn't you know it?" Ulysses said. "He gets back here to the farmhouse and there's that telegram. With everything else happening, he'd forgotten about it. And sure enough, it was his orders. The United States Navy wanted him to get to San Diego inside of a week. And you know what San Diego meant, don't you?"

"Korea," Jerry said.

"That's right. But when he got back to Mary Agnes's and told her he had to shove off, she got hysterical. Begged him to ignore his orders—go AWOL and stay with her. She didn't care that he'd get in trouble, get himself thrown in the brig, long as she got what *she* wanted. That's the way she was. But Alden said no, he had to get down to New York, get on a train, and go. That made her furious, Alden said. Didn't matter that he'd sat up all night with her—got the baby out of her and probably saved her life. When he went to kiss her good-bye, Alden said, she wouldn't let him. Told him to just get the hell out and take the baby with him. Alden said he opened that dresser drawer, but it wasn't in there. 'It's in there,' she said, and she was pointing to her suitcase—the one you found inside the trunk, I guess. Alden told me he couldn't risk walking out of there carrying a lady's suitcase. Didn't want to draw people's attention to it, you see? Not with what was inside of it. So he took his coat off and put that over it. And just before he left, he told me, he asked Mary Agnes to wish him good luck, tell him she hoped he'd come back in one piece. She wouldn't do it, though, he said. Wouldn't even look at him. He hadn't done what she wanted, see. So as far as she was concerned, he could go pound sand."

Ulysses said my father told him there'd been no time to bury the baby—not with Grandpa and Lolly around. So he'd snuck it up to the attic and hidden it away in the crawl space. The next morning, he packed his sea bag and said his good-byes to his father and grandmother, and Lolly drove him down to Grand Central Station. "And I still remember this, because Alden was crying to beat the band when he said it: he said that, when him and his sister got to the station and it was time to board his train, Lolly give him the kind of send-off that he'd wanted from Mary Agnes—held on to him so tight, and for so long, that he thought he was going to miss his train. And he says to me, he says, 'You know something, U? That sister of mine's the only person in my life who ever really loved me.' And it was kinda sad, you know? Because it was true, I guess."

Mary Agnes recovered, Ulysses said. Got a little money together and hightailed it out to California. "Got there a week or so before Alden shipped off for Korea. You're the proof of that, Caelum. Your father told me that's where you got made."

It suddenly made sense to me—why he'd sometimes called me his "California kid."

"She made her way back here after he shipped out. And after she had you, she went to Alden's father and hit him up for money. But the old man wouldn't budge. Then Mary Agnes did something stupid. You were only a month old or so, and she left you with a neighbor lady. Just for the evening, it was supposed to be, but what she done was, she went off on a toot with some fella and didn't come back for a week. By the time she did, Alden's father and his grandmother had filed the complaint, gone down to see the judge, and gotten custody of you. And after Alden come back and got himself right again, they convinced him to find someone else—someone who'd make you a good mother. The grandmother couldn't have raised you, like she raised your father and Lolly, see? She was starting to fail. And Lolly, well, your grandpa needed her on the farm. She might have been working over at the prison by then, too. I can't remember. But that's when Rosemary come into the picture. Alden met her at a dance hall, I think it was, and they got hitched pretty quick. But it never really took, Alden said; he just married her to give you a mother, and to try and get on his father's good side. But Mary Agnes still had a hold on him. He'd go off and meet her on the sneak. If his family'd gotten wind of what he was doing, they'd have raised holy hell. See, they meant well, the Quirks. But one way or another, they'd never let Alden get out from under their thumb."

For a minute or so, no one spoke. Then Jerry broke the silence. "How you doing?" I'd assumed he was asking Ulysses, but when I looked over at him, I realized he was talking to me. Realized, too, that I'd been holding on to myself and rocking back and forth in my chair.

"Me? I'm okay," I said. "I'm fine."

"Yeah?"

"Yeah. Yes. Or I will be."

Jerry turned back to Ulysses. "So do I have the sequence right? She aborts the baby in 1950. He stashes it up in the attic here, then takes off for California. She follows him out there, gets pregnant with Caelum, and he ships out to Korea. Gets his medical discharge, then he marries the woman they pass off as Caelum's mother. And then in September of 1953, you get out of the navy. The two of you take the trunk out of hiding, bring it out to that field on the other side of the orchard, and bury it."

Ulysses nodded. "Sounds about right."

"And you're telling me that you had no idea whatsoever until 1965 that what you two buried inside that footlocker was the baby she'd aborted?"

He nodded. "That's right, too. I didn't know until that day him and me were fishing off of the bridge."

"Okay, one more thing. Whether you realized it at the time or not, you guys put *two* babies in the ground that day. So eleven years later, when your buddy was letting it all hang out at the bridge, did he happen to say anything about who the second one was?"

"Well, that's the screwiest part of it, if you ask me," Ulysses said. "See, that's what give him the idea to hide Mary Agnes's baby up in the crawl space. He said it had always bothered him that the other one up there was lonely. Said he wanted to give it some company."

Ulysses said my father had confided something else to him that day: that he had discovered the remains of the mummy-baby when he was a boy of nine or ten—that he'd come upon the little iron chest hidden at the back of the crawl space one afternoon when he was poking around where his grandmother had forbidden him to go. That he'd pulled out the chest, opened it up, and there it was. He told Ulysses that, until that day on the bridge, he had never confided to another living soul the secret about what he'd found up there in that attic. "Kinda peculiar, ain't it? Alden said he used to sneak up there from time to time and pull it out of its hiding place. Take the lid off and visit with it, like, *talk* to it, even, so's it wouldn't be so lonely up there. He said he had no idea whose baby it was or how it got there. The only thing he was sure of was that it had been hiding up there for a long, long time."

Jerry closed his notepad and hooked his pen onto his shirt pocket. He told Ulysses he'd done a good job.

"We're done, then?" Ulysses asked.

"We're done. No more questions."

"I have one more for you, U," I said. "You could have gone to your grave without saying a word about what was under there. Why didn't you? Why were you so bent on bringing those two babies into the light?"

"Because of you," he said. "They kept you in the dark about so much, and when you started asking me all those questions about Mary Agnes . . . But the thing is, I kept going back and forth about it, see? Because it's not a very pretty story. It's an *ugly* story, is what it is. Doesn't put either one of them in a very good light. Her *or* him. But Alden . . . your father . . . hey, he fucked up plenty. I'm not saying he didn't. But he was my friend, see? And Lolly was my friend. And you're my friend, too. So I said to myself, I said, Ulysses, why don't you have some guts for once in your life? Ugly story or not, why don't you let the poor guy know the truth?"

"Thank you," I said. He nodded.

Jerry left the room. Left Ulysses and me to our tears.

———

I DROVE ULYSSES HOME, THANKED him again, and declined his request for "a little bit of booze money." I told him he needed rest more than alcohol.

"Yeah, okay," he said. "Well, don't be a stranger."

Driving home again, I realized it was a visiting day. But when I checked my watch, I realized, too, that there was only thirty minutes left. Sometimes it took that long just to get them past the walk gate and up to the visiting room. But I figured I'd try to see her anyway.

For once, there weren't the usual delays. By the time she was seated and I was allowed in, we had twelve minutes together. "Oh, my God, Caelum," she kept saying. "Oh, my God." She said she'd need time for it all to sink in, but that she was going to help me through it. Help me sort it all out.

When the CO called time, I stood. Gave her one of those awkward across-the-table embraces. Kissed her once. Again. I didn't want to let her go.

When I was halfway between the exit door and the table where she was seated, she called my name. I stopped, turned, and looked back at her. "Love you," she said.

"Love you, too."

———————

BY THE TIME I GOT back to the farmhouse, there were several vehicles in the driveway: cruisers, unmarked sedans, a crime lab van. When I walked in, Jerry was all business. "Mr. Quirk, this is Officer Tanaka. He has a few things he needs to ask you."

"Anyone else living here?" Tanaka asked.

I nodded. "Upstairs tenants. A married couple and a young woman who lives with them. She works for the husband. They're all away for the weekend."

"Beautiful," he said. "Let's head on up to the attic, okay? I'd like you to show me that crawl space."

When I came back down again, Jerry pulled me aside. "You know something? You should get the hell away from here for a few days. At least for an overnight. We'll be here for most of the evening, and probably a good part of tomorrow."

"Where would I go?" I asked him

"Anywhere. Just throw some things in a bag, get in the car, and drive until you're tired. You got a lot of thinking to do, Caelum, and if you're like me, you do your best thinking at the wheel."

And so that was what I did. Packed a bag, gave Jerry a key, and started toward the door. Then I stopped. I went back into the bedroom and grabbed Lizzy Popper's story. Wherever the hell I was going to sleep that night, I would take it along. Finish it before I crashed.

➤➤ *chapter thirty-three* ⬿⬿

In the years following the Civil War, many female abolitionists transferred their energies to the causes of temperance and women's suffrage. Lizzy Popper gave tacit support to both of these movements, but she was active in neither. A chance reunion with Maude Morrison, the former Connecticut State Prison inmate for whom Popper had once advocated, reignited her interest in prison reform for women, and it was this feminist cause that would become the focus of her later years.

Maude Morrison's imprisonment at the age of seventeen had been a classic case of blaming the victim. Morrison had emigrated from Ireland the year before and had found work as a barmaid at a New Haven tavern popular with Yale College students. Morrison was raped and impregnated by two inebriated but well-connected collegians who charged that she had seduced them. She was found guilty of "being in manifest danger of falling into vice" and sentenced to the state prison at Wethersfield.

Sequestered with a handful of other female inmates in the windowless attic of the Wethersfield facility, Morrison resisted the sexual demands of guards and trusties and was flogged for insubordination. Midwifed by her fellow inmates, she birthed a stillborn in the sixth month of her pregnancy and nearly died from subsequent infection.

An ability to read and write and a resourcefulness born

of desperation won Morrison her freedom during the second year of her incarceration. With stolen paper and pen, she recorded the details of her prison life and slipped these pages to Lizzy Popper in March of 1849 during the latter's tour of the facility on behalf of the Society for the Alleviation of the Miseries of the Public Prisons. Popper's subsequent letters of complaint to government officials resulted in Morrison's release.

Like many women with prison in their past, Maude Morrison might well have become a pariah, destitute and unemployable, if not for the intervention of a wealthy socialite with whom Lizzy Popper put her in contact. Mrs. Hannah Braddock, whose husband's family owned J. J. Braddock & Company, a popular New Haven department store, arranged for Morrison to work in the store's millinery department, where she fetched and fitted hats to the heads of Braddock's well-heeled customers. Within a year, Maude Morrison was designing hats. Her elegant creations, veiled with fine Irish lace, sold briskly and afforded her status at J. J. Braddock, and later at Gimbel's in New York. Under Hannah Braddock's tutelage, Morrison was schooled in the manners and mores of polite society. At the age of twenty-seven, in Newport, Rhode Island, she was married to Lucius Woodruff, a New York financier twenty years her senior. A year later, Woodruff was deceased and Maude was a wealthy widow.

Maude Morrison Woodruff was the picture of refinement when, in May of 1868, her carriage passed Lizzy Popper as she walked along a busy New Haven street. Woodruff recognized the little Quaker woman who had once acted on her behalf and instructed her driver to stop. The two women took tea together and, at the end of an hour, decided to join forces for the betterment of "fallen" women.

Possessed of a first-hand understanding of the plight of female prisoners, Woodruff pledged a portion of her wealth to advance their lot. Her generosity fueled Popper's resourcefulness. Lizzy designed and Maude funded a boarding house, farm, and school for women exiting the state prison. Located away from the temptations of the city in the coastal village of Noank, Connecticut, the twelve-bed Lucius Woodruff Charitable Home and Farm for Women sought to provide a safe haven for "women who have run afoul of the law, so that they may rise again and be restored to their natural feminine dignity." Opened in November of 1869, it was, in effect, Connecticut's first halfway house.

The Woodruff Home ran quietly and successfully at first. Its residents assimilated discreetly, marrying local farmers and fishermen and becoming mothers. One woman opened her own tailoring shop in nearby Mystic. Another, illiterate when she entered the home, became the secretary of a New London shipping company scion. Yet the Woodruff Home faltered in its fourth year. A group of villagers who had objected to the admittance of the home's first Negro resident stole onto the property and burned down a hayfield and a chicken coop. Blight killed off most of that summer's crops. A deranged resident laced a supper stew with rat poison, killing one woman and making several others violently ill. The press gave the story lurid coverage, and the matron resigned as a result. Lizzy Popper was forced to step into the role of acting matron, even as she attempted to quiet the negative publicity and the calls for closure of the facility. The final blow came when Maude Woodruff learned that her late husband's business partner had swindled her out of several hundred thousand dollars. Her financial advisers told her she could no longer provide the funds needed to run the home and farm. The residents were dispersed and the doors were nailed shut in January of 1873. The property sold at auction the following month.

To her husband Charles, supposedly traveling through Massachusetts on business, Lizzy wrote philosophically about the closing of the Woodruff Home. Interestingly, the letter also presents a blueprint for Popper's later life as a Hartford lobbyist on behalf of "fallen women":

And so, our noble experiment dies an early death. Poor Maude is beside herself, but I am not, for I am convinced that our model is sound and can be made to work if we are not reliant solely on the generosity of a private benefactor or benefactress. Society must bear its burden, for in most cases, it is society's ills—poverty, prostitution, and whiskey chief amongst them—which subvert the female and make her a criminal. Government, therefore, must become involved, and so I must convince the politicians. I have been in this world and see how it works, Charlie. My shortcomings at Shipley Hospital can be attributed to a failure of diplomacy. Mrs. Dix was a worse "politician" than I—sincere in her advocacy for the sick, but all vinegar. In my advocacy for the betterment of female prisoners, I shall make honey drip from my tongue. Better to spend a productive thirty minutes in the wood-paneled office of a state official or bank president than to spend a hundred hours with ladies' societies whose members are well-intentioned but powerless to exact change. Mrs. Mott and Miss Anthony may yet win us the vote—it is a worthwhile goal—but as for me, I shall politick with men of mark and, when I deem it useful, bend the ears of their spouses, too, for more often than not, a wife serves as her husband's moral compass and can steer him in the direction of benevolence and Christian charity.

Lizzy's letter, dated February 13, 1873, never reached its intended recipient. Charles Popper, supposedly in Boston, died in Manhattan that same evening. Having drunk a flask of brandy during a sleigh ride with his mistress, Vera Daneghy, he stood, lost his balance, and fell from the sleigh, breaking his neck. Popper succumbed three days shy of his sixtieth birthday. His widow had turned sixty-seven the week before. Vera Daneghy was thirty-eight.

Compounding the shock of her husband's death was Lizzy Popper's sudden awareness that he had kept a mistress for the previous eight years and fathered a child by her—a girl,

Pansy Rebecca, now nearly five years old. Among Lizzy's trove of papers and letters, a thin file labeled "Daneghy woman" survives. Inside are six letters bound together with string: the three Vera Daneghy wrote to the wife of her deceased lover and carbon copies of Popper's three responses to Daneghy.

Vera Daneghy's first letter to Lizzy, dated ten days after Charles Popper's death, informs his widow of her own and Pansy's existence, and of her expectations in the wake of her lover's demise.

We was going to be married, him and me, after we both got free of our situations. Now that day will never come. Charlie told me once about your baby girl that weren't right in the head and died. When Pansy come, and Charlie held her and seen she was all right, he cried. He said over and over how, come Hell or high water, he would always do right by his daughter so she could enjoy the good things in life and not have to do without. Now that promise falls to you.

Daneghy's letter ends with instructions as to how Lizzy is to make monthly deposits to the bank account which Charlie had established for Pansy's well-being. Daneghy suggests a sum of nine dollars per month but warns, "I can't make do on any less than eight. Charlie would be mad if you was stingy."

Lizzy's response is curt and to the point: "This is to inform you that I have not the means, the intention, or the moral obligation to help with the support of a child conceived of thy own and my husband's sin."

Vera Daneghy's second letter, dated one month later, is exasperated and self-pitying. It informs Lizzy that, in a fit of remorse, she has confessed to her husband that he is not Pansy's father. In response, Seamus Daneghy has disowned his wife and the girl and put them out of his house. Her own and her husband's families have spurned her and she has been forced to take a menial position "peeling potatoes and worse" at Delmonico's, a fine restaurant where Charlie had twice taken her to dine. She wishes to remind Lizzy that it was she, not Lizzy, who, on the night of the accident, had to deal with the police, the corpse in the road, and "that skinflint of a sleigh driver who insisted he be paid, no matter the circumstances, may he rot in hell." Had it not been for Lizzy's husband, "him with his fancy airs, big promises, and books I never even read, most of them," her life would not now be in tatters. The woman who rents her a room and cares for "Charlie's child" while she is at work robs her of most of her wages and she cannot make due on what's left. She is *owed* some help, and if Lizzy Popper will not provide any "then you are as cold a fish as Charlie always said you was."

Popper's measured response to Daneghy's demands restates her disinclination to offer assistance and advises Daneghy that it is not the intrusion of her late husband into her life, but rather the wages of her own sinning, which find her in her current predicament.

Vera Daneghy's third and final letter, written fourteen months after the last in May of 1874, is markedly different in tone; Daneghy is resigned and frightened. In desperation, she has turned to prostitution to provide for herself and her daughter. She writes from a charity ward of New York's Bellevue Hospital, where she has just learned she is suffering from a "womanly cancer" that is expected to kill her before summer's end. Daneghy apologizes to Lizzy for the grief she has caused her and acknowledges that she has no right to beg for what she must: that Lizzy retrieve Charlie's daughter, give her his name, and raise her "like she was yours."

Daneghy's dilemma presented Popper with one of her own. Her husband's mistress had become one of the fallen women to whom she had dedicated the last several years of her life. If she did not claim the innocent child, Pansy would be abandoned to a city orphanage or handed a worse

fate. Her final response to Daneghy was, once again, curt
and to the point:

> I shall make arrangements to collect the child at a time
> and place to be determined. My one stipulation is that thee
> not be present when I do so. I think it best that thee and I
> not meet face to face. I am sorry for thy suffering.

Of the many challenges life presented Lizzy Popper, perhaps none was more incongruous and ironic than what
transpired next. On May 30, 1874, she returned home from
New York with her red-haired, freckle-faced four-year-old
charge in tow. A letter awaited her. Its author was her long-
lost son, Willie.

Dear Mother,

*I hope this letter finds you and father in fine spirits and
robust health. I regret that I have not been a more faithful
correspondent, but an actor's wayfaring life leaves little time
for letter-writing. This missive comes to you from Virginia
City, Nevada Territory, where I have been appearing these
past weeks at Maguire's Theatre in the role of the frontier
hero Davy Crockett. Maguire's is as majestical a palace
as any at which I have walked the boards. The Comstock
lode has made this a land of lucre, and the silver kings who
own the town demand the best entertainments and have the
means to pay for them. Yet today I depart. A coach leaves
in an hour, and I must post this letter before I climb aboard
and begin my long sojourn east. The pages you hold in your
hand will travel east as I do, and hopefully will reach you
first, for reasons I shall explain. There is much to tell and
little time to tell it.*

*Eight years ago, at the funeral of my mentor and friend,
Mr. Waverly Calhoun, it was my great good fortune to have
been approached by one Mr. Harry Truitt. Mr. Truitt and his
wife, Nina, are two of the best theatrical booking agents in
the business, and they have since put me on stages from*

*Boston to San Francisco. Under the stage name of Fenni-
more Forrest, I have played the parts of Rip Van Winkle,
Shakespeare's Romeo, and Dumas's Count of Monte Cristo.
In Utica, New York, after the renowned actor Edwin Bixby
took sick, I hastily replaced him as the noble aboriginal
savage Metamora, Last of the Wampanoags. (Many have
noted that my own interpretation eclipsed Bixby's.) As the
frontiersman Crockett, I wear buckskin breeches and a
leather frock coat trimmed with fringe. Just before the curtain falls, ending the fifth and final act, I rescue a family
of homesteaders from a fierce prairie storm while reciting
Sir Walter Scott's "Lochinvar." The applause is enthusiastic
and prolonged. Some nights I imagine that you, Father, Ed,
and Levi are in the audience, witnessing my triumph. On
the stage, I am loved!*

*This next will surprise you, Mother, but I shall say it direct:
I had a wife, and I have a child. Five years ago, I was wed to
Miss Clara Chapman of Peoria, Illinois. At the time, I was
touring in Jay Rial's theatrical of Uncle Tom's Cabin. In the
role of Little Eva's father, I sang a mournful psalm during
the climactic scene of the girl's death and apotheosis, and I
daresay it was my singing, as much as the waif's ascension
from sickbed to celestial heavens, which, night after night,
rendered audiences lachrymose. Clara was a fellow traveling performer engaged by the Truitts~a violinist who was
one fourth of the Diederich String Quartette, performing in
Nancy Potter's Seven Pleiades. The Pleiades show was, that
season, appearing in tandem with our own. Clara fell in love
with me, and I with her. We were wed in Danville, Pennsylvania, during a two-week run at that city's Opera House.
When I learned that a child was coming, I sent Clara back
to Peoria so that she might observe her period of confinement in familiar surroundings. Alas, the rheumatic fever my
frail Clara had suffered as a child left her with a weakened
heart and she died giving birth. The child, however, thrives.
Mother, you have a granddaughter, Lydia Elizabeth. Though
I have seen her but twice, I am told she has become a sweet*

and obedient child whose looks favor myself rather than her departed mother. You shall meet her soon.

The first leg of my journey eastward will take me to Peoria. My father-in-law has written me that his wife is ill and they are unable to continue caring for Lydia. I therefore will reclaim her and transport her to New Haven. The girl needs the steadfastness of grandparents far more than the thousand kisses of an adoring father whose life's work makes of him a costumed vagabond, and so I will do the unselfish thing and surrender her to your own and Father's care.

Mother, you may be shocked by what I must next impart. Father will not approve, I know, but I am in hopes that you, who worked so faithfully on behalf of the darkies' freedom, will rejoice that your son, too, has been emancipated from another form of bondage. Along with several others of our company, I have come to embrace the tenets of the American Free Love League as espoused by our guiding spirit, the forward-thinking Stephen Pearl Andrews. Mother, I reject the notion that a marriage sanctioned by church and state is an exclusive and indissoluble bond. I subscribe instead to the philosophy that physical knowledge of others be based only on spiritual affinities, and that these, by virtue of human nature, are in constant flux. I have broken free of the notion that Man should know only one wife or that Woman should know but a single husband. After I deliver Lydia to your care, I shall travel on to New York, where I will board a ship bound for Europe. By mid-summer, I shall be ensconced at the palazzo of the Famiglia Urso on the sun-baked Amalfi coast of Italy. I shall be in the company of those I most adore in this whole world: the harpist Edwina Mathers (another of Miss Potter's Seven Pleiades), the novelist Gaston Groff, and the love of my life, violinist extraordinaire Camilla Urso. Rejoice, Mother! Your son is unfettered and in love!

By my calculations, we should arrive during the week of May 15. It is my hope that Father and I might repair the trouble between us before my departure, but for that to be so, he must be willing to utter the words "I apologize." The cruel things he said to me some years ago still ring in my ears. My ship departs for Europe on May 28. Until I see you, adieu.

Your loving son,
William

Willie Popper had come and gone by the time his mother sat in her parlor, reading the shocking news that she was now, at the age of seventy, the custodian of not one, but two, four-year-old girls—the first fathered by an unfaithful husband, the second by an irresponsible son. In her diary, she wrote poignantly of what happened next:

I sat there, trembling, wanting to rise and run from the room but was unable to move. In my lap was Willie's letter, with its dozens of I's, me's, and my's. He had learned humility in our home, and it troubled me to read how prideful he had become. Free love? Pish! What a fine and fancy term for lechery! . . . Last of the Wampanoags, indeed! If he has a child, he should be playing none other than the role of father-provider. . . . And what do I know of raising little girls? I had raised sons, and that with a husband's and a sister's help. Now the one was dead, and the other old like me and spending half her days in Florida. What would become of my work for the prisoners, and the traveling needed to accomplish it? . . . As I was mulling all this, I chanced to look over at the Daneghy woman's daughter. That gaudy hair and freckled face were, I supposed, her mother's, but her eyes gave her away as Charlie's child. It pained me to see it. She was sitting on the settee, staring at me as if I, not she, were the curiosity. I realized then that I had been speaking my thoughts aloud. "And what, pray tell, is the matter with thee?" I demanded.

"Nothing, Missus," said she. "I only wonder that, with all your jabbering, do you hear that banging?" I was suddenly aware of the rapping of the brass knocker against the front door.

"Well, miss, if this is to be thy home and we have a visitor, then I entreat thee to go to the door and say I am not receiving callers." It was not proper for a child so young to be put to such a task, but I feared that, were I to rise and try to answer the door myself, my legs might collapse beneath me or I might burst into sobs. Such was my addled state.

I stared after the waif as she hied to her task. How was I to explain this Irish imp? Was I to bring her to the town green and proclaim, "Here is Pansy, the fruit of my husband's adultery"?

And then, the four of them were standing at the parlor threshhold. The two children were in front, holding hands as if the steps from front door to parlor had made them friends. Behind them stood Martha, my sister and my rock, and our ne'er-do-well brother, Roswell, he with his eye patch and his leering smile. "Hallo, Sis. I'm back," Ros proclaimed, as if this were welcome news, and not one more grievous burden heaped upon me.

Because I could not yet bear to look at the smaller, darker girl standing beside Pansy, I looked instead at the doll she clutched—its gingham dress, its porcelain head and black painted hair. My eyes, again, fell upon the two girls' clasped hands, and that was when I knew what I would do: I would announce them as sisters. . . . Pansy: a gaudy flower, a gaudy name, a gaudy mother. I would rename her Lillian. They would be Lydia and Lillian, the twin daughters of my widower-son, Willie, and his poor, doomed wife. . . . And Willie: he would not be a foolish stage-actor, but rather a respectable government agent, posted to Italy. No, not to Italy but to England, where people embraced not "free love" and Pope-worship but proper Protestant values. It was pretense, yes, motivated by pride, and pretense and pride are sinful, but by this treachery the two little girls and I could save face and survive this cruel assignment which fate had given us. They would be sisters, and I the grandmother of not one but both. . . . With my

plan hatched, I was able to look now into the eyes of Wil-
lie's girl. And when I did, I was lost with looking at her. Her
black hair, her pale eyes and pale skin: she was plain, not
pretty like the one whose hand she held. She was Hutchin-
son, top to toe, and my eyes filled with tears, and my head
with thoughts of my beloved father, and my sons. I loved
Lydia immediately, and when she gave me a shy smile, I
gave her one in return. I turned then to the Daneghy girl. I
knew that, though I would claim her and call her Popper,
I would never love her. She somehow must have read my
thoughts, for until that moment, she had acted as good as
gold, but now her eyes went dead and her nostrils flared.
She snatched the other's dolly away from her and dashed
it against the parlor wall. Its head exploded into a million
shards.

This outburst was apparently the first of many for Pansy
Daneghy, now known to the world as Lillian Popper. In diary
entries and letters, Lizzy variously described her charge as
"tetchy," "petulant," "sulky," "a fibber," "a thief in the making," and "a red-haired blackguard in banana curls." In
contrast, Lydia was "docile" and "sweet-natured"—a "shy
but helpful girl with her head always in books." Numerous references are made to Lillian's tormenting of Lydia:
the snatching away of trinkets and sweets, the ruining of
clothing and keepsakes. Lydia's knees were "scraped and
bloodied" when Lillian "shoved her to the ground without
provocation as the two walked home from Miss Bridges's
Sewing School." Lydia's wrists were sprained in a desperate jump from a tree swing after Lillian pushed her higher
and higher, refusing to stop. An 1880 letter from Lizzy to
Martha Weeks in Florida reveals details of the household
dynamic when both girls were ten.

Although Lillian never tires of plaguing her, Lydia remains
a devoted sis, absorbing each insult, forgiving every
trespass. In this regard, my granddaughter is a model

of Christian forgiveness, and her grandmother suffers in comparison. I am at my wits' end about this troubled and troublesome creature who causes such havoc in our household. I suppose I am partly responsible for her troubles, for the girl believes as gospel what I have told her for her own protection: that her father and Lydia's father are one and the same. Would it not be worse to say the truth: that she is the daughter of fornicators? Still, the child suffers when fine gifts arrive for Lydia but not for her. In the days before and after her birthday, Lil stood on the front porch in the cold, awaiting the postman's arrival. Each day when he came into view, she would run up the lane to meet him. "Anything for me? Anything for me?" When at last she was reconciled to the fact that no packages were coming to her from Italy, she set about destroying the ones her sister had received. She took scissors to the red velvet cloak which that Urso woman had sent Lydia. She defaced Lydia's favorite book, The Adventures of Alice in Wonderland, a gift from Willie. Across each page, she scrawled, "Lydia is ugley." Page after page of that mean-spirited insult, and misspelled to boot. (Lillian is a poor speller, Lydia an excellent one.) Poor Lyd cried and cried for her losses. Yet when her Uncle Roswell grabbed the hickory switch to whip Lillian for her wickedness, who was it intervened on behalf of the sinner but she who had been sinned against! She hadn't liked that red cloak anyway, Lydia told her uncle. She had read Alice in Wonderland so many times that she had grown tired of it. Roswell whipped Lillian about the legs and buttocks, but he said he gave her an easier thrashing than he had planned because it upset Lydia so.

Truth be told, Sister, it was with dread that I granted Roswell permission to take up residence in our home again. Yet I have been grateful for his help, for I doubt I could have dealt with Lillian on my own. When she has one of her conniption fits, it is "Uncle Ros" who can bring her back under control, sometimes with nothing more *than a fierce look in her direction, or by placing his fingers against his eye patch. For all her bluster and boisterousness, the girl is terrified that she might be made to look at what lies beneath Roswell's patch, and it is a threat he holds over her head, the better to control her.*

In thy last letter, thee asked if Roswell had embraced temperance. No, sad to say, he is still under the curse of the bottle. Yet, for the most part, he has done as I have asked and confined his consumption of spirits to the privacy of his room after he retires for the evening. With two young girls to raise, my life has become one of compromise, and Roswell is one of these. As the man of the house, he may be somewhat lacking in industry and moral rectitude, but without him, I would have to forsake my work. In the months when thee and Nathanael are away in Florida, how could I sojourn otherwise on behalf of my prisoners?

Sojourn on behalf of her prisoners Elizabeth Popper did. Her travel log reveals that she crisscrossed Connecticut numerous times in the years when Lydia and Lillian were in her care, calling on mayors, influential clergy, and prominent citizens to enlist their support for the separate state-funded women's reformatory she envisioned. In a second log, Popper recorded the ups and downs of her lobbying efforts. Beside the name of each member of the Connecticut General Assembly she approached, she wrote "yes," "no," or "?". In 1882, Popper presented Governor Hobart Bigelow letters of support from such illustrious Connecticut citizens as Aetna Life Insurance Company president (and future Hartford mayor) Morgan Bulkeley, the Hartford Retreat's Dr. Eli Todd, social crusader Josephine Dodge, Norwich industrialist William Slater, Trinity College president John Brocklesby, and her friend the Reverend Joseph Twichell of Hartford's Asylum Hill Congregational Church. But Popper had also picked up an articulate enemy of her cause, Yale professor William Sumner. The brilliant Sumner, an ardent Social Darwinist, championed laissez-faire, warning that man must not tamper with the natural laws of social development. He spoke out against trade unions, government regulation, and such "meddling" social legislation as that for which Lizzy Popper advocated. In June of 1879, the Social Darwinist and the social reformer skirmished in the editorial pages of the *Hartford Daily Times*. Sumner fired the first shot, writing that criminals, the great majority of whom belonged to the lower classes, could not be reformed. "The little Quaker lady who now bustles about the State Capitol on behalf of incorrigibles would squander the government's money on a futile endeavor," Sumner maintained.

Popper's response, published the following week, dismissed Sumner's argument as "elitist claptrap" that flew in the face of democratic ideals and biblical teachings.

Perhaps Professor Sumner would be more at home amongst England's queen-lovers or Rome's papists, for here in America we reject the notion that the rich and powerful are designated by divine right. Ergo, we must also reject the arrogant assumption that the criminal, driven more often than not by grinding poverty, is doomed by the hand of Almighty God. Nay, he is made poor and desperate not by natural laws as directed by the Great Overseer, but by the greed of the upper classes. Does not the New Testament exhort us to extend a hand to one who has fallen? Professor Sumner would have us place a foot on the fallen one as he lies prone and pitiable, the better to remain his superior.

The dozens of letters from *Hartford Daily Times* readers that followed this exchange ran two to one in favor of Popper's argument and won her new support among Hartford's lawmakers. Yet, curiously, just as Popper's campaign for prison reform was gathering momentum in the General Assembly, she abruptly halted her lobbying efforts. Little is known about why the travel log of the "little Quaker lady" lists no trips from April of 1883 to October of 1885, or why this otherwise meticulous chronicler, letter-writer, and letter-saver saved none of her own or others' correspondence from this period, or recorded no diary entries. From this time period there exists only the faded five-sentence beginning of a letter from Popper to her sister Martha dated April 6, 1883—a communiqué that apparently was never finished and never posted, and which indicates that Popper's retreat from politics was triggered by a domestic crisis involving her ward, Lillian, and her brother, Roswell.

Sister,

Thee must burn this immediately after reading. It is with anger and shame that I write of a vile thing that has happened, and has been happening, inside my home while I have been away. Since yesterday, I have been borne back over and over to a time long ago when my boys were young and Charlie warned me that I would save the world at the expense of his neglected children. Alas, that is what now has come to pass, although I thank the Good Lord that in this instance it is "child," not "children." To the best of my knowledge, Lydia has been spared. The injured party is not one of mine, but one with whom I have shared a surname and a home. The injurer, it pains me to say, is our brother. Yesterday, quite by accident, I discovered the

Popper stopped herself mid-sentence, then put a large X through what she had written. Interestingly, she did not follow her own dictate and burn the unfinished letter. Had Roswell Hutchinson's whippings of Lillian led to greater violence against her? Had she become the victim of sexual abuse? The details of what happened are left to the conjecture of the modern biographer. All that is known is this: Roswell Hutchinson left the Popper home abruptly in April of 1883, the troubled Lillian ran away the following year, and Lizzy Popper entered a long and atypical period of disengagement from politics.

Both Roswell Hutchinson and Lillian Popper suffered untimely deaths. Among Lizzy's papers are certificates of death for both. Hutchinson's, issued at Baltimore, Maryland, is dated June 5, 1884. Cause of death: cranial bleeding from mortal blows to the head, suffered during a barroom altercation. Lillian Popper died in March of 1885 while incarcerated in the notorious New York City Tombs. Her death certificate indicates that, following her flight from Lizzy Popper's home, she retained her father's surname but reclaimed her given name of Pansy. As Pansy Popper, she was exiled to the Tombs for "the use of fisticuffs in the settling of a dispute" and "frequenting a chop suey house of bad repute." The latter charge suggests the possibility that Charlie Popper and Vera Daneghy's child had become a prostitute, a drug addict, or both, as "chop suey houses" of this era sometimes served as fronts for parlors at which opium and sex were bought and consumed. Pansy was fifteen when she died, her cause of death listed as "consumption," the nineteenth-century term for pulmonary tuberculosis.

The bitter irony of these tragic outcomes surely must have caused Lizzy Popper to suffer. Like her birth mother, the obstreperous girl Lizzy had reluctantly agreed to safeguard had become another of the "fallen women" for whom she had advocated so faithfully. The brother whom she had raised, supported, and enabled had become one of the "malevolent men" from whom Lizzy had worked so hard to protect imprisoned females. Yet it was during her extended absences on behalf of these women that her home had become, for young Lillian, a prison run by a "jailer" who had clearly abused his power.

Whatever the stirrings of Lizzy Popper's conscience, she left behind no written reflections of her own or others regarding this matter. Perhaps she burned these, or perhaps she suffered in silence. Perhaps her withdrawal from the world indicates that her old nemesis, depression, had descended once again. A lack of documentary evidence leads only to speculation.

What is known, however, is that in 1886 Lizzy Popper reengaged with the world and resumed her political efforts with a vigor that defied her eighty-two years. Her granddaughter Lydia was now enrolled at a private boarding school in Massachusetts, her tuition paid for by Willie Popper's wealthy *inamorata*, Camilla Urso. Back on the road, Lizzy procured new letters of support for a women's reformatory from biblical scholar Calvin Stowe and his famous wife, Harriet Beecher Stowe; retired United States senator Lafayette Foster; *Hartford Courant* newspaper scion Joseph Hawley; and, through the intervention of their mutual friend, Reverend Twichell, the illustrious Mark Twain. Remarkably, Popper also managed to obtain a letter from investment banker and Hartford native J. P. Morgan. The supremely wealthy and powerful Morgan was a member in good standing of the avaricious upper classes of which Popper was so critical, and he was not otherwise a supporter of social welfare. It remains a mystery how Popper accomplished this epistolary coup, as she left behind no documentation as to the circumstances by which she managed to get Morgan to endorse her vision.

In her later years, Elizabeth Popper wrote and spoke out about other political issues of the day. Following the May 1886 Haymarket Massacre in Chicago, at which both police and labor protesters were killed, Popper published a *Hartford Daily Times* editorial in support of the controversial Knights of Labor, lauding the Knights' efforts to lessen the disparity between America's "filthy rich and her desperate poor."

Following the well-publicized September 1886 surrender of the Apache chief Geronimo to federal troops, while walking across the New Haven green with her granddaughter, Lydia, Lizzy Popper came upon an amateur orator who was lauding the victory of the U.S. military over the "renegade savage." In response to the man's comments, Lizzy gave an impromptu speech of her own in support of the captured warrior. In her diary, she wrote the following about what ensued:

I was hissed at and booed, mine being the unpopular sen-
timent, but I persevered. Halfway through my remarks, I
had to stop and remind a loutish young man in a tweed
cap that he and I lived in a land where free speech was
guaranteed, and if he was assaying to take away my right
to say what was on my mind, I should be glad to step over
to where he stood and box his ears for him, or else to find
his own grandmother and have her do the job for me. He
left then in a huff and I was able to resume my speech-
making.

In October of 1886, Popper ferried to New York City in
the company of her granddaughter, Lydia, now sixteen, for
the purpose of witnessing the dedication of the Statue of
Liberty. Of that historic event, Lizzy wrote the following
reflection to her now-bedridden sister, Martha Weeks:

There was a grand parade, and a hundred or more boats
afloat in the harbor. Lydia and I were amongst the lucky
ones to have secured a place on Bedloe's Island itself, close
to the dais. Bartoldi, the statue's maker, was there, and
Senator Evarts, and the President himself and several
members of his Cabinet. Mr. Cleveland is the third Presi-
dent these now old and rheumy eyes have espied. The
others were Jackson and Lincoln. Oh, yes, General Grant,
too, when he visited the sick at Shipley Hospital. So the
number is four, not three, and of these Grant cut the most
dashing figure and Lincoln, all arms and legs, the most
awkward.

I chuckle now to recall for thee, Martha, the mishap
we who had gathered witnessed in the midst of the glori-
ous pomp and hoopla over Lady Liberty's debut. Before
the grand unveiling, Senator Evarts was speaking on and
on. (Pity he had not learned the value of Quaker concise-
ness!) Then, midway through the Senator's lengthy disqui-
sition, the nervous Bartoldi pulled the cord, accidentally
and prematurely. The drapery dropped and Miss Liberty

was revealed in all her splendor. This set off the cheers of the crowd, the boom of cannonfire, the screeching of boat whistles, and joyful music from any number of bands on the mainland and in the harbor. The Senator continued moving his mouth through this hubbub but at last gave it up for lost and resumed his seat. Would that all politicians could be so soundly silenced!

As for Lady Liberty, she is a fitting goddess to symbolize the American ideal, though as I stared up at her, I could not help but think of the many thousands who, two decades earlier, had to die to expiate America's sin of slavery. It made my eyes wet to think of my Edmond and my Levi amongst those who perished. Eddie, in particular, would have relished this dedication which his Ma and his niece Lyd were lucky enough to have witnessed.

After the ceremony ended, the President and his entourage passed by, not ten or twelve steps away from Lydia and me. Mr. Cleveland's demeanor is reminiscent of Charlie Popper's, and it pained me to think of that other thing they had in common: the fathering of children outside of wedlock. I hated so that ditty that commonfolk chanted in jest during the campaign two years ago: "Ma, ma, where's my pa? Gone to the White House, ha ha ha!" It made me glad then and now that women do not vote, for whom would I have chosen: Blaine the Swindler or Cleveland the Fornicator?

In addition to the dedication ceremony, Lizzy and Lydia's New York itinerary that week included a ride on the Third Avenue el, a visit to the newly opened Bloomingdale's department store, and a matinee performance of the Gilbert and Sullivan opera *Princess Ida*, in which the title character concludes that men are "little more than monkeys in suits," then promptly retreats to Castle Adamant to run a college for women. In her diary, Lizzy dismissed the musical as "piffle" and complained of an inability to stay awake beyond the first act, "but Lyd has talked ever since about how 'marvelous' were the performances and the music, and how she would be elated to attend a college exclusive to females, for she wishes to have as little as possible to do with men."

Another diary entry, written shortly after the former, reveals that, even as an old woman, Lizzy Popper was still processing her traumatic experiences as a Civil War nurse. Responding to a newspaper article about Robert Wood Johnson's manufacturing of Johnson & Johnson sterile dressings, individually packaged, the invention of which had been inspired by a lecture Johnson had heard James Lister deliver, Popper reflected in her diary:

> This medical discovery is significant but twenty-odd years too late in coming. It might have saved hundreds who died in their beds at Shipley. Those boys would be middle-aged men now, gray-haired or bald with children of marrying age. Their mothers would not have outlived them, subverting the natural order of life. I have outlived Edmond and Levi for two-score years and three now. Where is God's plan in that?

The years between 1886 and 1892 were, for Lizzy Popper, ones of declining physical health and painful personal losses. Her beloved sister Martha died of heart failure in 1889. Her surviving sister Anna Livermore died of the same the following year. Although Popper's mind remained clear and productive until her final days, she became unsteady on her feet and was often confined to a wheelchair in her last two years. In May of 1892, while attempting to move from her chair to her bed, she fell and broke her hip. The fracture hastened Popper's decline and she died of complications nine days later, on May 30, 1892.

Lydia Popper was with her grandmother during her final days and reported that Lizzy drifted in and out of consciousness near the end. During one of her lucid hours, Lydia reported, Lizzy said to her, "My failures were far too many, Lyd, and my successes far too few. I can say only that I did my best." At her grandmother's bedside when she died, Lydia later wrote that Elizabeth Popper's final words were, "Listen. The girl is crying for me. Come, shadow, take me now."

Elizabeth Hutchinson Popper may have failed during her remarkable lifetime to achieve her goal of establishing a separate state-funded women's reformatory administered and run by women, but her dream was realized posthumously when the granddaughter she had raised, sociologist Lydia Popper Quirk, became the inaugural superintendent of the Connecticut State Farm for Women at Three Rivers in 1913. Quirk held the position until 1948 and, during her long tenure, instituted many progressive changes that bettered the lives of the incarcerated women under her supervision. "The prison that cures with kindness," people often said of the institution that was the realization of Lydia P. Quirk's grandmother's vision. Throughout her years as Superintendent, a wooden plaque stating her philosophy hung on the wall behind Lydia Quirk's desk. It said, simply and eloquently, "A woman who surrenders her freedom need not surrender her dignity."

➤➤chapter thirty-four➤➤

REMAINS OF TWO INFANTS
FOUND ON LOCAL FARM

State's Medical Examiner to Conduct
Autopsies on Long-Buried Babies

CONDITION OF SOLDIER'S
WOUNDED WIFE IMPROVES

Iraq Veteran's Widow Says Husband Was "Still at War"

MUMMIFIED REMAINS TO BE ANALYZED
BY STATE ARCHAEOLOGIST

Second Exhumed Infant Died 50 Years Ago,
Test Indicates; State's Attorney: Criminal Prosecution Is
"Moot Point"

FAMILY OF TRAUMATIZED VETERAN
DECRIES IRAQ WAR

Widow Declines Military Funeral, Refuses Purple Heart

State Archaeologist Concludes:

"MUMMY BABY" LIVED, DIED IN 19TH CENTURY

PFC KAREEM A. KENDRICK, 1983–2007:

A Body Maimed, A Mind Impaired,
An American Warrior Forsaken

BEHIND THE GLAMOUR:
A BEAUTY QUEEN'S LIFE OF PAIN AND DELUSION

Mental Illness Was Family Curse, Scarring Legacy for Unearthed Baby's Mother

Over the next few weeks, as the enticing front-page headlines lured readers to the concurrently unspooling stories, I kept my head down and limped through the final classes of the semester. "No comment," I repeated to each inquiring journalist; nevertheless, my name was linked to every new episode. Photos of the farmhouse, taken from the neutral ground of Bride Lake Road, illustrated the coverage. There was a recurring photo, too, of my mother as one of the six red-lipsticked, white-gloved women campaigning to be Miss Rheingold of 1950. And as I had feared, two or three of the journalists covering the story exhumed, along with my mother's provocative past, the unrelated story of Maureen's having survived Columbine, killed Morgan Seaberry while under the influence, and gone to prison for her crime.

My Oceanside colleagues said nothing to me about my connection to the babies' remains or the Kareem Kendricks tragedy. Yet whenever I entered the faculty lounge, my presence scattered some of my peers and silenced others, even those who loved nothing more than the sound of their own clever pronouncements. I had never felt so exposed and alone as in their midst during those difficult days of disclosure.

My students were kinder. Daisy Flores handed me a card at the end of our first class meeting after Kareem Kendricks's suicide. I delayed opening the envelope until the room was empty and was glad I had because it made me cry. "With Deepest Sympathy for the Loss of Your Brother," the outside said. Inside were the signatures of each surviving class member. It felt both odd and touching to receive condolences for a fetal half-sibling whose death had occurred before my birth, and about whom I'd been in the dark until the morning I had unwittingly pulled him, with his mummified companion, from the ground. My discovery of "Baby Boy Dank," as the newspapers had taken to calling him, had confused and challenged me, and had complicated my response to a birth mother for whom I had hungered unknowingly most of my life. But the class's sympathetic acknowledgement of my loss invited me, finally, to acknowledge that it *was* a loss, and so to grieve. Baby Boy Dank had been my older half-brother. Claiming kinship with Mary Agnes's *other* son meant that I had never been, as I had always assumed, an only child.

At the beginning of that first class after Kareem's rampage, I invited my students to share their thoughts and feelings. Only two did, and only to make businesslike announcements. Marisol Sosa gave the time and place of the college's memorial service for Kendricks. Ibrahim Ahmed invited the others to join him at the weekly anti-war demonstration outside the student union. The rest were mute. I took note, especially, of Oswaldo Rivera's sullen silence. It spoke, I was pretty sure, of his regret for having ridiculed Kendricks on what had turned out to be the last day of his life. Having seen through a glass darkly in Iraq, Private Kendricks had marveled at how "young" his contemporaries now seemed to him, Ozzie in particular. Now Ozzie's vision, too, had darkened. Whatever the course curriculm had taught him, Ozzie seemed, because of his interaction with Kendricks, to have put away the persona of the cocky manchild and become a sadder but wiser adult.

We'd been through a lot together, these Quest in Literature students and I, and so for their final exam, I gave them an essay question that they could not answer incorrectly.

That best known of modern artists, Pablo Picasso, often drew on ancient myth for inspiration. He seemed particularly fascinated with the Minotaur, a creature to which he returned repeatedly. In a 1935 etching titled *Minotauromachia*, Picasso features the monster as the dominant figure in a dreamlike scene. A young girl, seemingly unafraid of the imposing man-beast, faces him while clutching a bouquet in one hand, a lit candle in the other. The monster reaches toward the candle flame, but it is unclear whether his gesture is one of acceptance or rejection. Between the girl and the Minotaur, a wounded female matador lies draped across a wounded horse. At the left of the composition, a man in a loincloth looks over his shoulder while on a ladder. Is he climbing down into the chaotic scene or escaping from it? To the man's right, two women with doves are detached observers of what is happening below. In the far distance, a boat sails away, and in the sky above the Minotaur, a storm cloud releases dark rain.

How does Picasso's *Minotauromachia* investigate what we have discovered this semester: that ancient myth informs and illuminates modern life? In other words, what do <u>you</u> see in this picture? What does it say to you about the human condition and the world we inhabit and share?

I went to Kareem's memorial service, a sparsely attended event at which those few who spoke struggled to eulogize a sacrificial lamb who had been heroic, destructive, and deranged. When Marisol spoke, she reminded us to be kind to one another "because you never know." She was followed by an army chaplain who assured us that God's plan, unfathomable at times, was just and merciful nonetheless. Around me, the faithful nodded in glum agreement, and I envied them their belief in a Divine Father who loved us and knew best.

For Kareem's sake—and for Ibrahim's—I went to the antiwar demonstration, too. "This song's called 'Peace Call,' and it was written by a dude named Woody Guthrie," a skinny, stocking-capped student announced as he strapped on his guitar. "And if any of you want to join in on the chorus, that'd be cool." In a voice both plaintive and assured, this scraggly troubadour sang of dispiriting "dark war clouds" and the arrival of "heavenly angels." And as he had invited us to do, we joined him on the refrain:

Peace, peace, peace, I can hear the voices ringing
Louder while my bugle calls for peace

Back home again, I sat at the kitchen table and tackled my students' blue books. Their *Minotauromachia* essays, to the last student, were poignant and thoughtful. A few seemed almost profound. In the menacing Minotaur, they saw Kareem Kendricks, the threat of terrorism, man's inhumanity to man, and the dual capacity of humans for evil and good. The bare-breasted female matador was a rape victim, a suicide bomber, and Private Kendricks's wounded wife. For one student, Kendricks was the wounded horse who carried her. Many identified Jesus as the man on the ladder, but they were divided as to whether the figure was arriving to save the day or evacuating. The little girl was the wisdom of youth over age, the personification of courage, and the triumph of light over darkness. Over the duration of the long semester, Devin O'Leary had been the class's least engaged member and its most likely to snooze. But in the end, it was he, perhaps, who best summed up what they'd learned. "This picture shows us what all the myths we studied told us," he concluded. "Life is messy, violent, confusing, and hopeful." In the end, I realized that The Quest in Literature had been that *best* kind of class—the kind where teacher and students had taught one another. I gave all of their exams A's and said good-bye to them with the click of my mouse—the electronic filing of their final grades. Then I walked into the winter sun and down to the prison to see Maureen.

THE VISITING ROOM WAS LESS crowded that day, which was nice. With fewer people chattering away, Maureen and I were able to speak without raising our voices. The week before, I had donated *Elizabeth Hutchinson Popper: An Epistolary Self-Portrait of a Remarkable Nineteenth-Century Woman* to the prison library. Mo had asked the librarian, Mr. Lee, if she could be the first to check out the volume, and he'd said sure. By the time I visited, she had read Lizzy's story from cover to cover twice.

"I guess there's no way to tell for sure," Mo said. "But don't you think the mummy baby might have been Pansy's by that creepy Roswell?"

I told her that was my hunch, too. "Maybe that's what shut down Lizzy for a while: having to face the fact that she hadn't protected the girl from him."

"And then having to deal with the shame and secrecy of her pregnancy," Mo said. "However that baby died, they hid the body rather than bury it. I did the math, Cae. Pansy would have only been fourteen years old."

I nodded. "And if we're right about whose baby it was, what's also creepy is that someone had to have taken it out of hiding and moved it from Lizzy's house in New Haven to the farmhouse here in Three Rivers."

"Who would have done that?" Mo asked. "Lydia?"

"Had to have been. Which, in a way, would explain why, after Pansy died in the Tombs, Lydia started addressing all of her diary entries to 'Dear Lillian.' In one of those entries, she goes on and on about this poem she loved—this thing called 'Goblin Market.' I read it online a while back. It's about this brave girl who rescues her sister from temptation and sin. Which, in real life, Lydia hadn't done. For me, it begs the question: Where was Lydia while Uncle Ros was victimizing her 'sister'? Did she know what was going on?"

"If she did, Cae, why wouldn't she have gone to her grandmother? Or for that matter, why didn't Pansy?"

I shrugged. "Maybe Uncle Roswell scared them both into keeping their mouths shut. Isn't that how predators operate? By telling their victims about all the horrible stuff that will happen if they blow the whistle?". . .

I felt his breath on my face, heard him whisper it. *I killed a dog once. Tied a rope around its neck, threw the other end over a tree branch, and yanked. You got a dog. Don't you, Dirty Boy? Maybe he'll have to get the Stan Zadzilko rope treatment.* . . .

"Well, whatever the reason they didn't tell, Lizzy would have had to realize what had been going on after Pansy started showing," Mo said.

"At which point, she would have had to wrestle with some pretty intense guilt. The Tombs: doesn't sound like a day at the beach, does it?"

"And Lydia must have felt terribly guilty, too," Maureen said.

Survivor's guilt, I thought: Mo knew all about how hard that was.

"You know, I can still picture her, up there on the sun porch in her wheelchair. Holding out that doll and telling everyone, 'Kiss my Lillian. Love my Lillian.' Now it seems so much like . . . a plea. And who knows? If Lydia carried all that guilt and shame into adulthood, maybe that's why she took up her grandmother's mission. Dedicated her life to saving 'fallen women.' With one glaring exception, that is."

"Your mother, you mean?"

I nodded. "But it's understandable, I guess. Lydia must have seen Mary Agnes as a kind of predator, too—which she was, in a way. Ulysses told me that, from the beginning, she could manipulate the hell out of my father. Get him to do whatever she wanted whenever she wanted him to. So I can see how Lydia would have done everything in her power to protect her grandson—her flesh and blood—from someone so . . . what? Reckless? Ruthless?"

"Oh, sweetie, this must all be so painful," Mo said. "How *are* you?"

Okay, I told her. I was handling it, processing it. "It's gotten a little easier now that the Quirk family skeletons aren't showing up on the front page day after day. Not that I don't still have my bad moments— my bouts of anger about the way they kept things from me that I had a right to know. . . . For a while there, I was *really* wrestling with the fact that Lolly never told me. But what you said helped: that she may have still been trying to protect me from the truth. I've checked in with Dr. Patel a couple of times, too, and she's been helping me sort it all out."

"That's good, Caelum. That's great."

"Yeah. The thing is, I can't ignore the fact that Mary Agnes was so unstable that she was dangerous—that I probably *needed* to be protected from her. You ever hear of 'borderline personality disorder'?"

Mo said she'd heard of it but didn't know much about it.

"Patel says that's what my mother might have been suffering from. She took out this reference book, the DSM-something or other, and read me the symptoms: reckless, self-sabotaging, paranoid about abandonment. It's plausible, isn't it? The way she sabotaged her career as a model? The way, whenever my father got himself free of her, she'd sink her hook into him and reel him back in? There's this other borderline symptom called 'identity disturbance.' That fits, too. She leaves the small town for the big city, becomes Jinx Dixon."

"The same as Lydia's father," Mo said.

"Hmm?"

"Willie Popper. He went to New York and became Fennimore Forrest."

I nodded. "Hadn't thought about that. 'Identity disturbance' on both sides of my family. Lucky me, huh? Maybe I'll go out of town for a while and come back as, oh, I don't know . . . Derek Jeter."

"Isn't he a Yankee?" Mo said.

"Oh god, you're right. What was I thinking? Lolly's probably rolling over in her grave. She hated the Evil Empire almost as much as the Lady Vols."

It felt good to exchange smiles. "Hey, speaking of Lolly," Mo said.

She told me she'd run into Lena LoVecchio the day before—that Lena had come to the compound to see a client, and she and Mo had chatted for a few minutes. "I mentioned that I was reading Lizzy's life story, and I said how we wouldn't have known any of these things if you hadn't rented out the upstairs to someone whose field was Women's Studies. And Lena said that Janis wouldn't have found any of that stuff if Lolly hadn't hijacked it."

"Hijacked?" I said. "What did she mean by that?"

"That's what *I* asked her. Do you remember when they started harassing Lolly? Bullying her so that she'd resign?"

"How could I forget?" I said. "She gave me the blow-by-blows every single Sunday night."

"Well, according to Lena, Lolly saw the writing on the wall. She knew they were gunning for her. For some reason, all of her grandmother's old records and diaries and letters were still here at the prison. Stuffed in a storage closet someplace. But when Lolly said she wanted it all back, they said no. That it was state property, even Lizzy's correspondence. And, come on. Lizzy had written and received those letters before this place even existed. And it wasn't because DOC was actually interested in Lydia's archives. They just were saying no to spite her."

"Sounds about par for the course," I said.

"So, according to Lena, Lolly said screw it, and she took it all home anyway. Carried everything out of here piecemeal, a box at a time."

"No shit," I said. "I knew she'd defied them about taking Lydia's wooden sign, but I didn't know she'd boosted all the other stuff, too. God, there's a *ton* of it up there—filing cabinets full. Must have taken her weeks. How the hell did she get away with it?"

"I asked Lena that. She said Lolly told her that was one of the benefits of working second shift. When you left the place at eleven o'clock at night, you could walk out of there with the warden's desk strapped to your back and nobody'd bat an eye."

I laughed, shook my head. "She was a gutsy one, wasn't she?"

"She was more than that, Cae. Janis may have put all the pieces together, but Lolly's the one who carried those pieces out of here. She rescued your family history for you. . . . Oh, I'm sorry, Cae. I didn't mean to make you cry."

"No, it's just that . . ." I wiped away my tears with the back of my hand. "I loved her so much, you know? I just can't remember ever telling her I did."

"Well, whether you did or not, she knew, Cae. I know she knew."

I nodded. Sniffled a little more. "God, lately? I'm like a human fountain or something. I cry so much, they ought to put me on *Dr. Phil*."

"I think some of those tears have been waiting a long time to come out," Mo said. "And it's good that they are, Cae. It's healthy."

"Yeah, okay. So anyway, that's enough about me and my screwed-up family. How *you* doing? Everything okay here at Camp Quirk?"

More or less, she said. She'd written to the deputy warden about the women's harassment of Crystal. And miracle of miracles, he'd taken it seriously, she said. Had the ringleader transferred to a different tier, warned the others that he wanted it stopped, and told his COs to be on the lookout and let him know if it didn't. "So far, so good," Mo said. "Oh, and Crystal's going to start hospice training. Her approval just came through today. I think it'll be good for her, Cae. Whatever did or didn't happen that day her baby died, the guilt she feels has paralyzed her. Comforting the dying will allow her to do something merciful. And maybe that will help her to . . ."

"Forgive herself?"

Maureen shook her head. "You never really forgive yourself. At least *I* haven't been able to. But if you can find ways to be useful to others, you can begin to figure out how to live inside your own skin, no matter what you did. The girls who commit suicide here? They're the ones who *can't* figure out how to do that. Their guilt just becomes too hard for them to bear. A girl over in Travers Hall killed herself day before yesterday. Hung herself with a plastic garbage bag. She just couldn't take it anymore." Maureen asked me if I remembered a cellmate she'd had a while back. "Irina? The Russian woman?"

I nodded. "Irina the Terrible. The one who was always coughing. Was *she* the suicide?"

Mo shook her head. "She's in hospice now. I've been taking care of her. It probably won't be more than a couple of days."

"What's she dying from?"

Multiple problems, Mo said. Because of confidentiality, she couldn't really go into the specifics.

AIDS? Hepatitis? Hadn't I read something a while back about an outbreak of TB in Russia? "Tell me she's not infectious," I said.

Instead, Mo assured me that she was careful—that, as a nurse, she knew how to take precautions and make sure the other volunteers took them, too. "But you know something, Cae? Now that Irina's close to the end, that hostility has left her. And god, she's so appreciative of small efforts: if I feed her ice chips when her mouth gets dry, or comb her hair. Sometimes at night when she gets scared, she asks for me. And the third-shift COs are pretty good about waking me up and letting me go to her. . . . She likes me to listen to her stories about when she was a little girl, or sometimes she just wants me to hold her hand. I never would have predicted it when we were stuck in that cell together, but Irina and I have become friends."

"She's lucky she's got you," I said.

"But I'm lucky, too, Cae. That's what's so cool about working with hospice patients. It's reciprocal."

Kareem Kendricks came suddenly to mind—his recitation of the seven acts of mercy: *minister to the prisoner, bury the dead*. . . .

"You know something?" I said. "You're a damn good nurse."

She broke into a beautiful smile. "I am, aren't I? Thank you, Caelum."

The CO at the desk announced that we should begin our good-byes. Visits were over in five more minutes.

"Hey, before I forget," I said. "Dr. Patel said to say hi. Velvet, too."

"Oh, speaking of Velvet, that reminds me," Mo said. "Father Ralph's gotten the warden's okay for a special family mass. We can each invite two people on our visitors' list. It's two Sundays from now, January twentieth. I thought maybe you and Velvet?"

"Could be dangerous for you," I said. "If she and I show up in a house of worship, that God you believe in will probably start hurling thunderbolts."

"But seriously, Cae. Will you come? And ask Velvet?"

I told her she could count me in, but that Princess Voodoo might be a tougher sell to get to a Catholic mass.

"Father Ralph's even gotten the warden to spring for a light lunch after the service. So we'll be able to share a meal and hang out to-gether for a while, without these stupid tables between us. Which is *huge*, huh? Father Ralph is awesome."

I said I expected nothing less from one of my fellow Four Horsemen.

"Four Horsemen?" she said. "Oh, okay. Your relay team. Right?"

"State record holders for umpteen years."

"And wasn't Captain Martineau on that team?" she said.

I nodded. "Who'd have thunk, back when we were those four skinny high school seniors passing off the baton to one another, that we would have turned into a cop, a priest, a casino big shot, and yours truly. . . . A lunch, huh? Guess I'll finally get to taste some of that five-star jailhouse cuisine you're always raving about."

"Cuisine?" Mo said. She got a kick out of that one.

It had been a good visit—one of the best we'd had since she'd gone in. Thinking about it as I walked back up Bride Lake Road, I caught myself smiling. And as that smile faded, I subtracted in my head the number of months she'd now served from her sixty-month sentence. Twenty-nine down, thirty-one more to go. The day of that family mass, she'd be right about at the halfway mark.

> **From:** studlysicilian@gmail.com
> **To:** caelumq@aol.com
> **Sent:** Monday, December 17, 2007
> **Subject:** I'm Baaaaack!
>
> Yo, quirk. Back home with the parental units
> in toe. Long story. My father fell again. Took
> some doing but I got them both into St Joe's,
> that nursing home over on Rte 14. Bakery's
> open again. For now anyway. Stop in when u get
> a chance. Got a lot to catch you up on.

"A girlfriend, Al?" I said. "And we're talking about a *real* woman here, not the vinyl blow-up kind that arrives in a UPS truck?"

"Geeze, Quirky, that was so funny, I forgot to laugh." We were having coffee in the booth by the front window. Seeing him again, I realized how much I'd missed him.

"So who *is* this lucky lady?"

The woman who'd sold him his car, he said.

"The Mustang widow? Really?"

She had telephoned him a few weeks after he bought it, he said. "Her stepson was cleaning out her garage for her and he found the 'Stang's mud flaps. Her husband had had them custom-made at some specialty shop. I think the guy might have been more of a Mustang lunatic than I am."

"Yeah, but I'm sure you'd take him in the general lunatic category."

"Shut up, asshole. Anyways, I drove over to Easterly to pick 'em up, and she goes, 'Do you want to stay for dinner?' I got there maybe four, four thirty in the afternoon and I didn't leave until after eleven. She's easy to talk to, you know? When you're with her, you don't even notice the time. Plus, she's funny. Sarcastic, kind of. I don't know, we just hit it off."

"So Big Al's romantically involved," I said. "Thanks to mud flaps."

"Hey, flap *this*," he said. "And it didn't start out as a boyfriend-girlfriend thing either. It was more like, we were just two people talking, telling each other about our lives. Except now it's kinda turned into something else."

He said that after his father's most recent mishap—it was the third time in six months that Al had had to rush down to Florida—he'd had some tough decisions to make. Had had to lay it on the line to his folks. He couldn't keep trying to be in two places at once; he had the business to run. "And at night? After Ma and me would get back from the hospital and she'd go to bed? I'd call Dee on my cell. Just to talk to a friend, you know? And after I hung up, I'd feel better about things. Calmer, like. And this one night I called her, she was like, 'Okay, I've done some research for you.'"

"Research about what?"

"Old people stuff: home health care, nursing homes, Medicare. She's the one who found St. Joe's for us, and believe me, Quirky, that place has saved my ass. Whether or not I'm gonna be able to save *this* place is another story. I can't keep operating in the red every month. Hey, if I thought it would beef up business, I'd put my counter girls in thongs, you know? Hell, *I'd* wear one."

"Them, maybe," I said. "You? Nope. *Bad* move. . . . So your parents are okay with going into a nursing home?"

"They balked at first—my mother, especially. Didn't want to go someplace where she'd have to live with a bunch of 'old people.' And the food thing: nobody can cook the way she can. But she's getting used to it. And Pop, well, he just kinda goes with the flow. Doesn't hurt that they got a chapel there, so Ma can walk down the hall to Mass every morning. And the priest they got there's Italian. I *really* lucked out there."

"And what's Mama's take on the girlfriend?"

"Likes her okay, I think. First time I brought Dee over there, Ma was giving her the evil eye. You know that Sicilian thing: anyone who's not *famiglia*'s a little suspect. But Dee's Catholic, so that helps. Picked up some points when she told Ma she went to parochial school. Her husband who died? That was her second marriage. I haven't exactly mentioned to Ma that she and her first husband got divorced. Or that she's a *lapsed* Catholic."

"Well, what the old *signora* doesn't know won't hurt her," I said. "But cut to the chase, will you? Have you and the widow, uh . . . ?"

"Have we what?"

"Done the deed yet?"

"You writing a book, Quirky? Make that chapter a mystery."

"Gee, lover boy's blushing a little," I observed. "I'd say that solves *that* particular mystery. So when do I get to meet your little honey?"

"Stick around," he said. "She's driving over later on. We're gonna do Chinese, maybe see a movie. You wanna come with us?"

I declined the offer. Told him I'd swing by St. Joe's in the next few days to see his folks. Al said if I wanted to see his mother, I could save my gas money. She was in the back. "Got her apron on and her pizelle iron fired up. It's like she never left the place."

And as if on cue, Mrs. Buzzi, all four-foot-ten of her, emerged, lugging the once-famous statue of the Blessed Virgin whose eyes, back in the seventies, had bled a map of Vietnam. "Alfonso!" she said. "What the hell you got this stuck in the back for? Put her in the front window where she belongs."

"But, Ma—"

"Don't 'but Ma' me. This is a Catholic bakery and don't you forget it." Ever the dutiful Italian son, Alphonse rose to do her bidding. "And when you're done with that, get a hammer and some nails and put Padre Pio's picture back up, too." I wasn't sure whether to smile or wince. After the Holy Trinity, the Virgin Mary, her deceased son Rocco, and Popes John XXIII and John Paul II, Padre Pio was *the man* for Mrs. B. For decades, she had prayed daily to the memory of the mystical, miracle-working priest and had twice made pilgrimages to his birthplace. If Mrs. Buzzi ever sat down and made a list, I was pretty sure her surviving son and her ailing husband would hold spots well below her beloved Padre Pio.

"Hey, Ma," Al said. "You see who's here?"

She pushed her glasses onto her forehead, squinted over at me, then broke into a smile. "Oh, jeepers Christmas! I didn't recognize you, sweetheart. Come over here. You got any kisses for an old lady?" We approached each other, arms extended, embraced and smooched. "Oh, my gosh, look how gray you got," she said, tousling my hair. "Hey, how's your wife?"

"Pretty good," I said. "You still saying those novenas for her?"

" 'Course I am, the poor thing. And I'm praying for those poor little babies you found, too. Terrible thing that was, huh? Just goes to show you how much respect there is for human life these days. I don't know what this world is coming to." Rather than point out that the babies in my backyard had died a century and a half century earlier, I asked her how Mr. Buzzi was doing.

She shrugged. "Eh. He's an old man. What do you expect?"

"And how about you? Looks to me like St. Joe's is agreeing with you. You like it over there?"

"Eh," she said again. "The food's lousy. They don't put enough salt in anything. Their marinara sauce comes out of a can, for Christ's sake." When she realized she'd just taken the Lord's name in vain, she made a hasty sign of the cross. "But it's easier for this one," she said, pointing her chin at Al. "So I put up with it. What the hell else am I gonna do?"

Hammer in hand, Alphonse pounded a nail into the wall. "Yeah, but he's a good boy, though. Isn't he, Mrs. B?"

"Yeah, he is. Don't tell him, though. I don't want him to get a big head."

A few minutes later, Alphonse had restored the Mama Mia to his mother's specifications. The Blessed Virgin had been reinstated in her place of honor and plugged in so that her halo, once again, was aglow. Padre Pio's scowling portrait had been restored to the side wall gallery alongside the framed pictures of President Kennedy, Rocco Buzzi, Mother Teresa, Sergio Franchi (who had once enjoyed biscotti at the Mama Mia), and the curse-breaking 2004 Red Sox, Alphonse's only decorative flourish.

"Well, it's nice to see you again, sweetie pie," Mrs. B told me. "I gotta get back to my pizelles." And with that, she hustled, stoop-shouldered, back to the kitchen, wiping her hands on her apron.

Al and I shot the shit for a little while longer, and I got up to go. I was putting on my coat when the little bell over the front door tinkled and a smiling, middle-aged woman entered the bakery. "Hey, *here* she is!" Alphonse said, beaming at the plump, pretty redhead who approached him. "Come over here, hon. I want you to meet some-one." He took her by the hand and brought her to me.

"Caelum, this is Dolores Kitchen," Al said. "And Dee, this is my best buddy, Caelum Quirk. But you can call him what I do: Quirk the Jerk."

She rolled her eyes and gave him a swat. "Oh, Alfie, grow up," she said.

"Yeah, Alfie," I said. "Pleased to meet you, Dolores." And I was, too. I liked this woman already.

———

FOR THE PRISON MASS, WE invitees gathered in the front foyer, presented our IDs, and, once the COs had located our names on their "approved" list, passed through the metal detector and entered the compound. But instead of stopping, as usual, at the sliding metal door of the visiting room, we were escorted by two COs into the inner sanctum. We walked en masse through a series of doorways, a maze of passageways, and finally reached the wide gray corridor where the special Sunday service would be held. Each of a hundred plastic putty-colored chairs, their backs stenciled with the words "Quirk CI," had been set up in neat rows, divided by a center aisle. A folded, photocopied program had been placed on each seat. A sober-faced CO wheeled a portable altar through a set of open Plexiglas doors and brought it to rest at the front. For this event, the usual visiting rules had been reversed. Now it was the visitors who took seats and waited for the arrival of the inmates.

Velvet, seated beside me, was dressed in a black turtleneck, black jeans, black socks and blood-red sneakers. She'd grown her hair long over the past several months and recently had dyed it jet black. She'd painted her fingernails black, too. It was like being accompanied by a niece of the Addams Family.

"Psst," she whispered. "Why do I smell onions?"

She followed my gaze to the dozens of fifty-pound bags of onions stacked against the corridor walls. "Oh, okay. What are they here for?"

I shrugged. "I don't know. To make people cry, maybe."

"Oh," she said, not realizing I was kidding. Then I told her what Maureen had said: that church was held in the food service wing.

A minute or so later, Velvet tapped me on the shoulder. "I only been to church one other time, you know," she whispered. "So I don't know about all that standing and sitting and kneeling shit."

"Well, don't look at me," I whispered back. "I haven't been to Mass in several decades. Just follow what everybody else does. And don't worry about kneeling. There's no kneelers. They're not going to make us kneel on the floor."

She nodded, relieved. "My mother was into Satan-worship for a while," she said. I was pondering that new piece of information when she tapped me again. "Look. Here comes Mom."

Maureen was at the head of a line of forty or fifty women, identically dressed in their maroon T-shirts and pocketless blue jeans. She approached us, beaming. "Hey, you guys. Thanks for coming. Wow, I like your hair, Velvet." I scooted over a seat so that she could sit between us. She put an arm around each of us. Squeezed my shoulder and, I was pretty sure, Velvet's, too. "I feel so happy," she said.

Led by an inmate who was carrying a yard-high wooden cross, Ralph Brazicki marched in wearing his priestly robes. He looked more full-faced and baggy-eyed than the last time I'd seen him. Thinner on top, too. Well, we were all getting up there, myself included.

Ralph welcomed everyone to what he said he hoped would be the first of many family masses. It was up to all of us, inmates and visitors, he said; the smoother things went, the more inclined the warden would be to okay the next one. And with that, he introduced the No Rehearsal Choir.

Eleven women rose from their chairs, assembled up front, and began a song called "On Angel's Wings." As they sang, I thought about my stepmother: how fervent Rosemary Sullivan Quirk's love of God had been in spite of the many crosses she'd borne: a drunken husband who had never really loved her, an unforgiving father who left whatever room she entered because she'd married and then divorced a non-Catholic, a stepson who had stood as rigid as that wooden cross up front, waiting for her hugs to be over. The Mass in this prison corridor was about as far away as you could get from the solemn services Mother and I had attended at stately St. Anthony's Cathedral. And yet, as I studied the faces of the No Rehearsal Choir—many of them ravaged, I could see, by addiction, by violence endured and committed—I was struck by their resemblance to the tortured faces of the saints and martyrs rendered in stained glass at that church of my childhood.

Mo's friend and former cellmate, Camille, approached the podium and gave the first reading, an Old Testament account of God the Father's justifiable smiting of some deserving transgressor. I meant to pay attention, but my mind wandered, and before it could refocus on the business at hand, Camille was genuflecting and starting back to her seat.

Next, two African-American women walked to the front. One was a tall and muscular androgyne; the other was short, fat, and womanly—a living Venus of Willendorf. Rosalie and Tabitha, their names were, according to the program. They harmonized beautifully on a gospel song called, "Must Jesus Bear This Cross Alone?" *There's a cross for everyone, and there's a cross for me*, the tall one sang, and in response, her partner wailed a snatch from of a hymn more familiar to me. *Amaze-amaze-amazing grace, how sweet the sound that saved a wretch like me*. It had been Great-Grandma Lydia's favorite hymn— the hymn Grandpa would sing to her those nights after he'd gotten her ready for bed. The hymn that Lolly, in honor of the grandmother who had raised her, had requested for her own funeral, a service that had gone on without me as I flew back to Colorado on that nightmarish day, not knowing if Maureen was alive or dead. As the song crescendoed, they raised their voices, in tandem, to a fever pitch.

I found in Him a resting place . . .
And now my heart is glad . . .
I'm not alone! . . .
Not alone! . . .
Not alone! . . .
No, not alone! . . .

To me, the loinclothed Christ figure in Picasso's *Minotauromachia* was clearly climbing *up* that ladder, bailing out on the sufferers, but Rosalie and Tabitha's song walloped me nonetheless. I looked to my right and saw that Maureen was crying. And that Velvet, to Mo's right, sat there dry-eyed but looking stunned.

After Tabitha and Rosalie took their seats, Maureen rose unexpectedly and started toward the podium. "Our second reading comes from the New Testament Acts of the Apostles," she announced. She scanned the gathering, smiling at one and all, and, in a voice both calm and assured, began.

"Now when Herod was about to bring him forth, that same night Peter was sleeping between two soldiers, bound with two chains, and outside the door sentries guarded the prison. And behold, an angel of the Lord stood beside him, and a light shone in the room; and he struck Peter on the side and woke him, saying, 'Get up quickly.' The chains dropped from his hands. And the angel said to him, 'Gird thyself and put on thy sandals.' And he did so; and the angel said, 'Wrap thy cloak about thee and follow me.'

"And Peter followed him out, without knowing that what was being done by the angel was real, for he thought he was having a vision. They passed through the first and second guard and came to the iron gate that leads into the city; and this opened to them of its own accord. And they went out, and passed on through one street, and straightway the angel left him."

Father Ralph's homily homed in on the passage Maureen had read. His message was a radical one, given that six sober-faced correctional officers stood at attention and watched us, their shoulder blades against the cinderblock wall, their eyes searching for trouble. Like Peter in Acts, Ralph said, the women of Quirk CI might likewise slip their chains of confinement and escape, even as they served their sentences. "We *all* have the power to free ourselves from prisons of our own or others' making, but doing so depends on our willingness to take that crucial leap of faith and realize that angels are real, not merely the products of wishful thinking, and that they are all around us. We are, my friends, or *can* be, angels for one another. But this is real life, not La-La Land. And as we heard in the passage that Maureen read to us, the angels can lead us to freedom. But then they will leave us to chart our own path toward righteousness. And that, my friends, is a solitary journey. Each of us passed individually through the birth canal when we came into this world, and each of us will be alone once again at the hour of our death. 'From dust we came, to dust we shall return.' What matters is how, in the interim, we treat each other."

A burly inmate across the room popped up like a jack-in-the-box. "I hear you, Father! That's some righteous truth you're speaking!"

"Sit down, Miss Fellows!" one of the younger, more intimidating COs shouted. He took a step or two in her direction. "Show some respect or I'm going to take you out of here."

"I'm just feeling the feeling is all," Miss Fellows protested.

Another scowling CO entered the fray. "Then 'feel the feeling' with your mouth shut!"

"Everything's cool," Father Ralph assured the guards and the assembled. "Everything's fine." But when Miss Fellows opened her mouth again, she was escorted by two officers down the corridor and around the corner. "You say one more word and I'm giving you a ticket," I heard one of them threaten.

After Holy Communion was dispensed—Mo partook, Velvet and I refrained—Ralph gave the final blessing and invited Rosalie and Tabitha to return to the front for the closing song. They delivered a jubilant, no-holds-barred foot-stomper called "I'm So Glad Trouble Don't Last Always." Throughout the room, singly at first, and then in pairs, and finally in entire rows of people, inmates and guests rose from their chairs to clap, shout, dance, and sing along. When Mo got on her feet, Velvet followed suit. I held back at first, then suspended my skepticism and joined the rapture, partly in solidarity with the banished Miss Fellows, but also in celebration of the notion that trouble might not last always. In the midst of our impromptu group response, I glanced over at the bewildered COs. They looked nervously at one another, hard pressed to know what, if anything, to do. I was pretty sure their paramilitary training had not covered the appropriate response to spontaneous joy, and I pitied them the stolid joylessness that was, no doubt, a part of their job description. For all I knew, the majority of them might be good and decent people when they got home and changed out of their uniforms.

The luncheon buffet had been set up in the visiting room, and as we all made our way back there, Maureen introduced Velvet and me to Crystal and her mom, Camille and her husband and daughter, and LaToya, one of her fellow hospice volunteers. The wide tables that, on normal visiting days, served to separate us from our loved ones, were now covered with long white tablecloths and silver serving dishes. Inmate servers wearing hairnets and white jackets, stood poised and ready to feed us. The smiling, wiry guy in toque and chef's whites called out, "Okay, everybody. We got pasta with meat sauce, salad, cake, and fruit punch. Come and get it! Enjoy!"

"Let's hear it for Mr. Price-Wolinski!" someone shouted and the inmates all cheered.

"He runs the culinary program," Mo explained. "He's awesome. Everyone loves him."

En route to the buffet line, I felt someone grab my shoulder and turned to see who it was. "Good to see you, Caelum," Ralph said. "I've got a fair amount of table-hopping to do first, but I hope we get a chance to talk a little later on. We've got some serious catching up to do."

"Sounds good," I said. "Nice job today, by the way."

He deflected the compliment by turning to Maureen. "This gal's one of my mainstays. Didn't she do a great job with that reading?"

As he walked away, Maureen noted that his comment was typical. "He does all the work and gives everyone else the credit."

We got in line, Velvet first, then Mo, then me. Maureen picked up her Styrofoam plate, then dropped it on the floor. She turned abruptly, her hand reaching out for me. "Oh," she said. "Oh."

"What's the matter?" I asked.

"I don't know. I'm seeing double."

I opened my mouth to ask her if she wanted to sit down for a minute, but she screamed out in pain. "Oh, my god! My head! It hurts! It *hurts*!"

Her eyes rolled back. Her legs buckled, and she fell backward against Velvet. "Mom?" Velvet screamed. "Mom!"

A female officer kept insisting that I was not allowed to ride with her to the hospital. "Sir, I understand your situation, but this is a security issue. You're going to have to follow behind in your own vehicle."

When I attempted to climb up into the ambulance anyway, two of her male counterparts grabbed me and pulled me back. "Get the fuck away from me!" I yelled, trying without success to yank myself free. "That's my wife! I need to be with her!" Still fighting against their hold, I watched the ambulance, alarm blaring, speed away.

Cerebral aneurysm, the autopsy report would later conclude. She died en route to the hospital.

→→ *chapter thirty-five* ←←

Where would I go? I had asked Jerry Martineau the day I dug up the babies and he advised me to get away. Didn't matter where I ended up, he said. At the wheel, I could think about where I'd been. I would know where I was when I got there. And so I had grabbed Lizzy's story and gone.

From Route 32, I'd picked up 6–West to I–84. In Hartford, I got onto I–91 heading north. Passed Springfield and Northampton and drove into the Berkshires. "Mountains," some people call those hills, but they've never lived in the shadow of the Rockies. At White River Junction, I'd had to make a choice. Québec? Burlington? To avoid the rigmarole of border patrol, I chose the latter and eased into the flow of traffic on I–89 North. It was getting dark and I was getting tired as I approached the sign for Montpelier. I put on my blinker and exited. Got a room, a bottle of screw-top red wine, and a pizza. Took off my pants, ate, drank, and read about the final decades of Lizzy's life. About how both her husband's dying mistress and her narcissistic son had dumped their daughters on the old girl's doorstep. About how, as busy and as tired as she was, she'd taken on the task of sheltering them both. And between the lines of Lizzy's letters and diary entries, in her troubled silence, I read about how she had loved and inspired one of those girls and had failed the other. Elizabeth Hutchinson Popper was a complicated and thorny ancestor, more admirable than loveable, and somewhere in the middle of my reading that night, I began to connect the dots between my formidable forebear and my less than formidable stepmother. At the cliff's edge of a bleak and lonely future, Rosemary Sullivan had defied her austere father, taken a leap of faith, and cast her lot with a troubled man she'd met at a dance hall—a man whose infant son had needed a mother. My father, for all his flaws and failures, had done that at least: had gone looking for and found me a decent and dutiful mother. . . . Like Lizzy, Rosemary had been driven more by duty than love. And because of this, she had stayed after my father abdicated—had lived with and tolerated the in-laws who tolerated her so that I might have, if not my father, a reliable grandfather and a loving aunt. . . .

I thought about the newspaper account of my kidnapping—that long-ago day when Mary Agnes and whichever man she'd manipulated into driving the getaway car had trespassed once more on Quirk property and snatched the three-year-old boy she'd birthed and then abandoned. Mary Agnes had only wanted to borrow me for the day, as it had turned out. At dusk, she had delivered me to a public place and left my life once more. In the hours between my disappearance and reappearance—those hours when I had been "the absent boy," the missing child who might well have been harmed or even killed— Rosemary must have been in the same kind of terrifying free fall as the Columbine families when they gathered at Leawood Elementary School on that worst of days, waiting to hear if their missing children had been murdered. Rosemary must have prayed to—begged—her god for a happy ending. And then, at sunset, she'd gotten one. There I was, unharmed on a picnic table at the Frosty Ranch, wearing the dungarees and Hopalong Cassidy shirt she'd dressed me in that morning. There I was, transfixed by a praying mantis that someone—who else but Mary Agnes?—had imprisoned inside a mayonnaise jar on my behalf. . . .

Rosemary had told the newspaper reporter that, until its happy conclusion, that day had been "the most frightening of my life."

Hadn't it been her love for me, not her duty to me, that made it that? As anxious and limited as that love might have been, it had been love nonetheless. In that drab, nondescript Montpelier motel room, I had finally admitted to myself that, all along, I had *had* a mother's love. And so I had closed Lizzy's story and held it tight against my beating heart. Hugged that book as if it were Rosemary herself. At long last, I could fully return the embrace of the lonely woman who had stepped forward to mother a motherless boy.

In the morning, I showered and dressed, itchy to get the hell out of there. But should I go home? Keep driving in the opposite direction? In the motel office, while the desk clerk was printing out my receipt, my eyes fell upon a tourist brochure—an invitation to travelers to visit Barre, Vermont's Rock of Ages Granite Quarry and the nearby Hope Cemetery, a graveyard filled with the funerary sculpture of the area's artisans. Velvet's grandfather had been one of them, I recalled. Back in my car, brochure against the steering wheel, I followed the map. Hope Cemetery: kind of oxymoronic, I remember thinking. What was so hopeful about being dead?

Fifteen minutes later, I drove through the gates, parked, and roamed.

They moved me, those strange and poignant stonecutters' efforts to immortalize the dearly departed. In bas-relief, a woman materializes from the cigarette smoke of her brooding widower. . . . A man and woman hold hands while lying in beds that double as their coffins. Above them floats an inscription from the Song of Solomon: *Set me as a seal upon thine heart, for love is strong as death.* . . . Some stonecutter with a sense of humor had freed a death angel from a slab of rock. There she sat, one leg across the other, chin resting in hand, looking impatient with the cluelessness of mortals. . . .

I had no idea which works were Velvet's grandfather's, but as I headed back toward my car, I came upon a sculpture signed in stone by a name that sounded familiar: Colonni. When I looked up from that signature, I found myself standing before a life-sized gray granite Pandora, her arm raised in front of her face as if to shelter herself from the wide-mouthed jar she has just opened—her gift from the vengeful gods. Too late, now, to undo what's been done. Behind her, in bas-relief, Colonni had sculpted a quartet of human skulls, labeled "pain," "war," "pestilence," "suffering"—the horrors she has just unleashed on humanity. Inside the jar, easily missable by the casual stroller through this garden of graves, was a sweet-faced infant wearing a necklace of flowers. The child, as my Quest in Literature students might have remembered, embodied the one thing that has not escaped from Pandora's jar: hope. Above its head were carved these words: *By this, we dreamers cross to the other shore.*

I drove out of Hope Cemetery and back onto the interconnecting roads that would bring me back home. En route, I thought about Maureen—how, hidden inside her dark womb in that cramped library cabinet, as she heard the pleas and screams, the taunts and explosions, she had mouthed her prayers to Mary. How she had scribbled onto the wood, in anticipation that I might somehow, some day, find them: her messages of hope and love.

———

I CHOSE CREMATION OVER BURIAL. No calling hours, no funeral, no newspaper obituary. There were certain mandatory procedures to follow, certain services I was required to purchase. I handed my credit card to Victor Gamboa and told him to charge whatever it was I was supposed to pay for. I signed whatever paperwork he put in front of me.

In those first bitter days, I faltered. Drank too much. Ate too little. Didn't bother to bathe or get dressed. Whenever Moses or Janis walked into the kitchen, I got up and left. One afternoon, from behind a window curtain, I watched the yellow Mustang come up the driveway, Alphonse at the wheel, his mother riding shotgun. Rather than answer the doorbell, I lay face down across my bed and waited them out. Later, at the front door, I found the things they'd left me: a mass card for Maureen, a potted plant, and one of Mrs. Buzzi's ricotta pies. I left the plant out in the cold, tossed the mass card onto a pile of unopened condolences, and dumped the pie in the garbage.

Velvet was hurting, too, I knew, but it was hard enough negotiating my own grief. I didn't have the energy to take on hers. So I avoided her as much as possible, and she took the hint and avoided me. Until, that is, the afternoon she knocked at my bedroom door and asked if she could borrow some pictures of Maureen. What for, I wanted to know. So that she could make a collage, she said. I shook my head. Told her I didn't want her cutting up Mo's photos.

"I *won't* cut them up," she said. "I'll get them copied at Staples and give them right back."

"No," I said again.

She stood there, as obstinate as ever. "Why not?"

Because in gathering together photos of Maureen, I would have to look at them. Confront, in those captured moments from her life, the kick to the groin her sudden death had been. Not that I explained that to Velvet.

"Because I said so."

"Okay, fine. Whatever. You don't have to be such a dick about it." I saw that she was on the verge of tears and closed my door against them.

The next morning, when Moze came down to make coffee, he caught me dozing face-down against the kitchen table. I'd been up most of the night.

I raised my head and looked at him groggily. "Morning," he said.

"Morning."

When I rose and started for my bedroom, he put his big body between me and my escape. I watched his eyes bounce from my unwashed hair to my week's worth of beard growth before they settled on *my* eyes. "Look, man, I know it's hard," he said. "But you've gotta snap out of it."

"You know it's hard, Moze? How's that? You ever lose a wife?"

"No, I haven't. But I've lost a son. Lost a home. A city."

I tried to outlast his gaze but couldn't. "Back off," I said.

He threw up his hands. "Yeah, okay, man. I'm just saying. But I guess you gotta go through whatever it is you gotta go through." He walked over to the coffeemaker, filled his mug, and started for the back door.

"Hey," I said. "I've been meaning to ask you. How's your new guy working out? You know, the one whose family is suing me. The kid whose mother demanded that the judge max out her sentence."

"He's working out fine," he said, over his shoulder. It pissed me off when he merely closed the door instead of slamming it.

Later that day, I stared at the ringing telephone instead of answering it. Stood there listening to Ralph Brazicki record his voicemail message. They were putting together a memorial service for Maureen over at the prison, he said. Would I come? I shook my head at the machine.

Two days later, Ralph left a second invitation. "She had a lot of friends here, Caelum, and they'd like to pay you their respects. Appreciate it if you'd get back to me." When I didn't, he showed up at the door.

"Mind if I come in?"

"Actually, yeah," I said. "I do."

He nodded. Stood there. "They keep asking me if you're coming, Caelum. They *need* you to come."

To get rid of him, I said I would.

"Okay then. Good. Great. Now before I go, can we pray together?"

By way of answering him, I laughed and closed the door.

In the few minutes of our exchange, he had kept looking at me funny. Curious to see what he'd seen, I went into the bathroom. Stood before the medicine cabinet mirror and cringed at the train wreck cringing back at me. At long last, I could see what everyone else had always seen: my resemblance to Alden Quirk the Third. It scared me shitless.

It didn't happen all at once. I re-engaged with life in small increments, baby steps. I showered and shaved. Changed the sheets on my bed. Cleaned out Nancy's litter box. In the midst of filing away some papers from the previous semester, I found myself holding the final exam I'd given my Quest in Literature class. The *Minotauromachia*, I saw clearly, was a struggle for dominance: the lurching Minotaur versus the little girl, her candle raised. . . . In those signals Mo and I had devised when we'd gone to Dr. Patel to save our marriage, a lit candle had meant, *I need you. Be with me. Love me.* But Mo had become the slain woman draped across the horse. The Christ figure was climbing out of the picture, and the two women in the window were as disengaged as the dead. My options were limited. I could either love the monster or the brave little girl. . . .

"Here," I said. "You wanted these?"

I watched Velvet's delight as she looked through the photos I'd gathered for her: Maureen in elementary school, as a high school cheerleader, a nursing school graduate. . . . Mo and me on our wedding day. Mo with her arms around Lolly and Hennie at some Christmas past. With Sophie and Chet, running along the water's edge at Long Nook Beach. "Thanks, dude," Velvet said.

"No problem, dude. Sorry I was a jerk before."

"That's okay. I'm used to it." She smiled. I smiled. "Sometimes I forget that she's . . . something will happen, and I'll go, 'Oh, I have to tell Mom that.' Then it hits me. Weird, huh?"

"No, it's normal. . . . Probably the first time anyone's ever used *that* word in connection with you, right?"

She flipped me a good-natured middle finger. "You want a hug?"

As we clung to each other, both of us crying for Mo, I thought about how far Velvet and I had traveled from *You want a blow job?*

I told her about the memorial thing they were having over at the prison. "You want to go to it with me?"

She shrugged. Made a face.

"Yeah, okay. I understand. . . . I'd appreciate it if you did, though. I don't particularly want to walk into that place by myself."

"All right then," she said. "I'll go."

"OH, HONEY, SHE WAS ALWAYS talking about *you*," Camille informed Velvet. "I think she thought of you as the daughter she never had." Several of the others gathered around her nodded in agreement.

Velvet smiled. Said it almost inaudibly. "She was my mom."

The warden gave a generic tribute to a woman he obviously had not known then made a hasty exit. But the deputy warden stayed, as did Mo's unit manager and Woody the jailhouse shrink. It meant something to me that a few off-duty COs had shown up, too. "She never gave us no trouble," one of them assured me. "Always acted like a lady." It made me think of Lydia: how, in her bygone era, the restoration of ladylike behavior had been one of the prison's primary goals for incarcerated women.

The music was celebratory, not sombre. Rosalie and Tabitha reprised "I'm So Glad Trouble Don't Last Always." When Ralph introduced the No Rehearsal Choir, he said they had belied their name and rehearsed all week. Their song, "O Happy Day," rocked the house.

Ralph gave the eulogy; Mo would have liked that. "This was not a place she would have chosen to live out the last years of her life," he said. "But she had come to understand, I think, that suffering can become a pathway to redemption. Maureen Quirk made the best of a challenging situation. Made a life here, made friends, contributions. In her hospice work, especially, she made this prison a more humane and merciful place. And we will honor our sister of mercy—keep her spirit alive—whenever we respond mercifully to one another."

Brawny, tattooed Wanda Fellows, who at the family Mass had "felt the feeling" and gotten the boot for it, stepped forward to end the service. "This song was written by Mr. Sam Cooke," she said. "He was da bomb, and so was Miss Maureen." She raised her eyes heavenward and called out, "This is for you, Mo!" And with that, she let loose a wrenching *a capella* rendition of "A Change Is Gonna Come" that raised goose flesh and made tears fall like rain. When it was over, I approached her and, though it was against the rules, held out my arms. And man, that woman could hug back. I hadn't been squeezed so tightly since the days when Zinnia had helped run the cider press.

"I'm so glad I came today," I told Wanda.

"Thass good," she said. "You comin' back?"

Father Ralph overheard us and laughed. "You could, you know," he said. "There's an opening at the school."

Before I could respond, a CO bellowed, "Line up, ladies! Time to get back to your units for count!" He and another guard herded them out as if they were dumb animals, not thinking, feeling women.

Ralph escorted Velvet and me out of the compound. "How about I take you two to lunch?" he said.

"Can't," Velvet said. "I've gotta get back to work." For some reason, she and Ralph shared a conspiratorial smile.

"What do you say then, Caelum?" Ralph said. "My treat."

We dropped Velvet off at the farmhouse, then headed over to the Three Rivers Inn. "Oh, hi, Father," the hostess said. "You can go right in. The others are already here."

The others? Wondering what was going on, I followed Ralph to a table all the way in back. There sat Jerry Martineau and Dominick Birdsey. "Here ye, here ye," Jerry said. "This reunion of the Four Horsemen of the Apocalypse is now in session."

I OPENED THE SYMPATHY CARDS. There were several from my students, sent to me in care of Oceanside and forwarded on by the department secretary. Patti, my first wife, had sent condolences. So had Maureen's father and stepmother. Scrawled at the bottom of their ostentatious card was a single chilly sentence in Evelyn's handwriting: *Her father and I hope she has finally found peace.* Inside a padded envelope at the bottom of the pile I found a thoughtful handwritten letter from Dr. Patel and a gift, enveloped in a protective bubble wrap sleeve: a small soapstone replica of Ganesha, remover of obstacles and destroyer of sorrows. Holding him in the palm of my hand, I couldn't help but smile. And as I did, I saw that his elephant's face was smiling back at me, his four human hands reaching out.

———

SOMEONE IN THE CHIEF STATE'S Attorney's office sent me a registered letter informing me that their official investigation into the deaths of the unearthed infants had now been closed. They were ready, therefore, to release the corpses to my custody; I was to contact them as soon as possible with instructions as to how I wished them to proceed.

At first, I didn't know what to do with them. Then I did. I sought and was granted permission to have the babies interred on the grounds of the prison that Lizzy Popper had envisioned and Lydia Quirk had actualized. They would join the other long-forgotten babies that Quirk CI volunteers had reclaimed and named. There was a modest healing ceremony, a blessing of their graves by a Methodist minister and two women from the Quakers' House of Friends. And so Baby Boy Dank and Baby Popper of undetermined gender now rest in the little cemetery along with the children born to Bride Lake prisoners of the past. Their small stones face the modest meditation park where current inmates with good behavior records can go to sit, think, and pray. Camille, who has taken Crystal under her wing, wrote to tell me that the two of them stop by once or twice a week to pray for the children, and for Maureen.

———

ULYSSES DIED AT DAYBREAK ON a gray day in March. I was with him at the end—me and Nancy Tucker, who had tucked herself like a death angel under his armpit and kept a vigil through the night. For some reason, cats were a comfort for the dying, the hospice director had told me. "You're like my own kid," Ulysses had whispered to me the day before he passed. In the final seconds, he seized, turned purple, and then was still. Nancy untucked herself, stood, and yawned. She licked his neck a few times, then jumped off his bed. I watched her stroll out of the room and around the corner. I left her there with the dying. I'm told she likes her new home and is treated like a queen.

Mr. Buzzi died one day after Ulysses did, so I guess you could say that Alphonse and I both buried fathers that week. Mrs. Buzzi, no surprise, was a Sicilian stoic about her husband's passing, but Al took it hard. After the funeral luncheon, seated at the bar in the front of the restaurant, he made his third or fourth toast to his father and said, red-eyed, "Well, at least he didn't live to see the day when the business he started went under." When he went teetering off to the men's room, Dolores confided to me that, at Al's request, she'd begun researching the pros and cons of filing for bankruptcy. "He went down to the casino last week and filled out an application for the food service department," she whispered. "Don't tell him I told you. Let *him* tell you. And for god's sake, don't say anything to his mother."

But Vincenzia Marianina DeLia Buzzi is a crafty old girl. She knew.

At least I suspect she did, because the week after Mr. Buzzi was laid to rest, the Mama Mia became the scene of a second "miracle." The statue of the Blessed Virgin, once again, began to weep. It shed its bloody tears for two days and, on the third day, went dry-eyed. At Mrs. B's suggestion, the statue was removed from the front window "for security purposes" and placed atop the front counter, below which was showcased Al's array of doughnuts, muffins, sweet rolls, and Italian cookies. The white cloth that had been placed beneath the statue in the window—and which had therefore absorbed its bloody lachrymal discharge—was framed and hung on the wall, where it could be analyzed by the Mama Mia's burgeoning clientele. Opinions varied, but the majority could see in the rusty blood stain a map not of Vietnam this time but of the United States of America. "Bush and Cheney and Rove and Rumsfeld's America," one of the *Daily Record*'s letters to the editor speculated—the one written by yours truly. The *Record* was the first newspaper to cover the story. Over the next few days, the *New London Day*, the *Hartford Courant*, the *New Haven Register*, and the *Boston Herald* followed suit. By the second week, TV journalists with their camera crews arrived to investigate the strange phenomenon: the *Today* show, Fox News, *Inside Edition*, CNN. Two high school students from Long Island drove up and, with a cell phone camera, recorded a narrated tour of the Mama Mia that Alphonse (the kids' tour guide) says has had more than thirteen thousand hits on YouTube. That same week, none other than Conan O'Brien came to see the statue for himself and stuck around long enough to sign autographs, crack jokes, and chow down on a chocolate doughnut and Al's newest creation. "The nun bun" was a variation on the traditional hot cross bun whose sales were not restricted to the Easter season. Mrs. Buzzi had no idea who Conan was, but she got a kick out of him. "Carrot Top," she called him. Before he left, she made him an honorary Italian.

Mrs. B greeted the media with open arms and free samples, but she gave the heave-ho to two graduate students from the University of Connecticut's Chemistry Department who wanted to borrow the blood-stained cloth so that its chemical composition might be analyzed for scientific purposes. I happened to be at the bakery when they made their request and thus was eyewitness to the skirmish between faith and skepticism. "You two have got a hell of a nerve marching in here and questioning the will of God!" she yelled, as loudly as she had that time when Alphonse spilled a full glass of orange soda on her just-washed kitchen floor. "Get the hell out of here! Scram! And don't come back!"

After she'd fended off the infidels, I sidled up to Mrs. B and whispered, "Methinks the lady doth protest too much."

"Hey, Mr. Smarty Pants, speak English," she said. Then she winked and walked away.

———

AFTER THREE POSTPONEMENTS AND NUMEROUS continuances, I didn't so much lose the civil suit as surrender to the inevitable. For one thing, I couldn't afford to keep shelling out for Junior's billable hours. For another, I had come, little by little, to the realization that I was finally ready to unyoke myself from long-held Quirk family property. My Scottish ancestor had purchased Bride Lake Farm with bribe money he'd received from a wealthy father-in-law who had wanted to rid his daughter of an unfaithful husband. A failure at farming and life, my namesake had hanged himself, Lolly once told me, leaving his widow and son cash-poor but land-rich. And although Adelheid and Caelum MacQuirk's son and grandson, Alden Quirk and Alden Quirk, Jr., had loved the land and been good stewards, my father, Alden Quirk the Third, had dedicated his life not to dairy farming but to drink. He had once quipped, in reference to his decision not to name me Alden Quirk the Fourth, "Well, *somebody* had to come along and break the family curse."

In fairness, the Seaberrys had said they would not evict me—that I could remain at the farmhouse for as long as I wanted. I chose, instead, to pack up my things and move. In the process of doing that, I rediscovered, up in the attic, three long-forgotten treasures: my unpublished novel about a young boy's kidnapping; the wooden sign that once had hung on the wall behind Bride Lake Prison Superintendent Lydia Quirk's desk; and, miraculously, packed away in a wooden crate filled with excelsior, the marble busts of Lizzy Popper's slain sons, Levi and Edmond, who gave their lives to free the slaves and save the Union.

I like my new place: it's one of those downtown condos they built a few years back—the ones that look out on the merge of the rushing Sachem and the meandering Wequonnoc, two of the three rivers for which our town was named. The thing I like best about my new digs, to tell you the truth, is the constant sound of that moving water. No matter what the weather, I keep a window cracked open to it because it reminds me of something Janis said to me that day up at Bushnell Park: that our ancestors move along with us, in underground rivers and springs too deep for chaos to reach.

The busts of Edmond and Levi have come to rest on a table in the living room of the condo. On the wall behind them I've hung Velvet's collage, "The Amazing Maureen," and the hinged high school graduation portraits of my father and my aunt, and the framed print I bought of Picasso's *Minotauromachia*. I've been reworking *The Absent Boy*, partly in salute to my father who, according to Ulysses, had had a gift for words. I have no idea if it'll ever be published or even publishable, but whatever happens, I'm thinking of changing the title; the revamped story seems somehow to have outgrown it. Oh, and I've Super-glued and wood-puttied the two halves of Lydia's wooden sign. Did a good job of it, too. You'd have to go looking to see that I'd busted it in anger during that dark period when my family's withheld secrets began to come to light. *A woman who surrenders her freedom need not surrender her dignity*: it still sends an important message, I think. I hung it up in my classroom over at the prison. I went back and forth about teaching there, but switching from Oceanside to the Quirk CI School has turned out to be a good move for me, too. My students are like sponges, I swear to god. I teach GED English and creative writing. Mostly, the women want to write about themselves, and it helps them, you know? Gives them wings, so that they can rise above the confounding maze of their lives and, from that perspective, begin to see the patterns and dead ends of their pasts, and a way out. That's the funny thing about mazes: what's baffling on the ground begins to make sense when you can begin to rise above it, the better to understand your history and fix yourself.

JANIS IS OUT IN CALIFORNIA now—she took a job teaching Women's Studies at Redwoods University. Moze decided to stay put, and cherubs & fiends.com is thriving. The Micks' divorce became final a couple of months ago.

Alphonse and Dolores got married. I was Al's best man and Mrs. B was Dee's matron of honor—wore a corsage that was half as big as she is. She and I waved the newlyweds goodbye when they drove off to their honeymoon in the Phoenician Yellow Mustang. It's like Dr. Patel told me once: sometimes when you go looking for what you want, you run right into what you need. After the Mustang disappeared around the corner, I turned to Mrs. B and said, "Well, you're a widow and I'm a widower. Maybe *we* should hook up."

"Nah," she said. "You're not my type."

"No?" I said. "Then who is?"

She thought about it for a few seconds. "Tony Bennett," she said. "You know what his real name is, don't you? *Benedetto*."

LIKE AL AND DEE, VELVET and Jesse Seaberry started out as friends and then it turned into something else. I'd gotten to know Jesse by then and had come to like the kid. He isn't the sharpest tool in the shed, but he's got a good heart and he's remained faithful to his sobriety. It was Jesse, in fact, who brought me to my first meeting and later became my sponsor. It's helped, too. I'm working on the second step.

I'm sleeping better these days. Most nights when I hit the sack, I lie there in the dark and listen to the moving water below. Then I talk to Maureen. Catch her up on what's been happening. "Velvet's pregnant," I'll say. "Been sick as a dog. She's due in August." Or, "Velvet had an ultrasound yesterday. They're having a boy." Or, "Well, Mo, you're never going to believe this one. Today I went and got myself a tattoo."

"*You?*" Velvet said when I told her about it.

"Yup. It's true. I've become a marked man."

"Holy shit. Let me see it." When I pulled up my pant leg and showed her my calf, she said, "Cool. What is it? A grasshopper."

"Praying mantis," I said.

"SHE'S SHOWING NOW, MO," I told Maureen the other night. "I can't believe she's already halfway through her second trimester. I'm taking her on a field trip this weekend. So on Sunday I'll probably be talking to you from up there in the Green Mountain State."

Velvet yacked nonstop for the first couple of hours. Pregnancy this, pregnancy that. But somewhere between White River Junction and Barre, she became quiet. I was quiet, too, lost in my memory of the last time I'd made that trek. After twenty minutes or so of neither of us saying anything, I reached over and turned on the radio. Listened to Van Morrison's "Moon Dance," then Paul Simon's "Graceland," and then that ubiquitous Cher song from several years back: *Do you believe in life after love, after love, after love, after love.* . . . After it ended, the news came on. The war, the nomination battle between Barack and Hillary, and then something about Columbine. The Jefferson County Sheriff's Office had just released a bunch of previously-withheld evidence: things they'd written, videotapes they'd made. When I looked over at Velvet, she was looking back at me.

"In all these years, you've never spoken to me about that day," I said.

She nodded in agreement. Said nothing.

"I'm curious. Did you and Mo ever talk about it with each other?"

She shook her head.

A mile or so later, her eyes on the road ahead, she broke her silence. "I was under a table by myself, over near the wall, when they started killing kids. And I kept saying, not out loud or anything, 'Don't see me. Please, please don't see me.' And then one of them walked over to where I was. The tall one. All I could see were his boots with his pants tucked inside them. 'Don't see me, don't see me.' And then he bent down and smiled at me. 'Peekaboo,' he said. 'What do *you* say, you fucking freak? Would *you* like to die today?' . . . And I shook my head. I was too scared to speak, but I didn't want to make him mad, so I just kept shaking my head. And I remember thinking, okay, this is it. This is the end of my shitty fuckin' life. Just please, not my head. Don't shoot me in the head. . . . And then he asked me something. He said, 'Tell me, mutant girl. Do *you* believe in god?' . . . And I couldn't . . . I didn't know what answer would make him not shoot me. So I just . . . I didn't say anything. I just wanted him to pull the trigger and get it over with, if that was what he was going to do. And to not shoot me in the head. So I closed my eyes and waited. But then nothing happened. And when I opened my eyes again, I saw that his boots had walked away. Had walked to the next table. And then there was this flash. Gunfire or riflefire. He had killed another girl instead of me. And I don't . . . I never told anybody about this before, but I've thought about it a million times. Not as much as I used to, but . . . And what I always wonder is why, instead of shooting me, he walked away. But now, lately, it's kinda been making sense. Because maybe . . ."

I waited. "Maybe what?" I finally asked.

"Maybe I had to stay alive so I could have this baby."

With my left hand on the steering wheel, I reached over and took hold of her hand with my right. Squeezed it. Unsqueezed. Squeezed it again. I didn't let go until we'd passed through the gates of Hope Cemetery.

I took her first to see Pandora. Velvet touched the statue's cheek, its hair. Then she knelt down before the open jar, reached in, and caressed the tiny granite baby. It sort of shocks me to say it, but I think Velvet may turn out to be a damn good mother.

"Do you mind if I wander around by myself?" she asked.

"Course not," I said. "Go to it." So we set off in different directions.

Later, I found her standing in front of an angel in flight—another of her grandfather's works, she told me later. "Hey!" I called. "You about ready to go?" As she turned to face me, she was blocking off the angel's torso but not its wingspan. For a second, it looked like Velvet herself could fly.

WE GOT BACK TO THREE Rivers a little after midnight, and when I dropped her off at the farmhouse, she hesitated before getting out of the car.

"I Googled your name the other day," she said.

"Quirk?"

"No, Caelum. It's from astronomy—the name of a constellation or something."

I nodded. "It's in the Southern Hemisphere."

"I've always liked your name. Jesse does, too. How do you think this sounds: Caelum Morgan Seaberry?"

"I like it," I said. "I like it a lot."

"Yeah, I like it, too. Grandpa."

"Grandpa?" I said. "So I'm your father?"

"Yup. Sucks for you, huh? Whoa." She laughed and touched her stomach. "Baby's kicking. Want to feel him?"

She pulled up her shirt and I placed my hand against the curve of her big, veiny belly. "Man, Bruce Lee's got nothing on *this* kid," I said.

She thanked me for the trip and got out of the car. I cried all the way back to the condo.

IN AA, THE FIRST THING you have to do is cop to your own impotence and surrender to a higher power. How you define that higher power is up to you. . . .

God: big G, little g? Buddha? Allah? The Holy Trinity? Is god the DNA we bring forth? The genes that mutate on the cliff's edge of chaos? Beats me. For all I know, god may be nothing more—or nothing less—than the sound of the moving water outside your window.

What I do know is that we *are* powerless to whoever or whatever god is. That was your tragic mistake, Eric and Dylan: your assumption that the power of the gods was yours to wield. That vengeance solved anything.

Anyway, I'm Grandpa now—eligible for the senior citizen discount at Dunkin' Donuts whether I want it or not, so I guess my best course of action is to stop resisting and grow old gracefully. Wisely. In the fifty-plus years of my life so far, I've known many sorrows, but I also have been the recipient of many valuable gifts, the student of many wise teachers. Among them are these.

An old woman who had witnessed the horrors of war returned home and still could see a forsythia bush's explosion of yellow in springtime, still could hear the music of melted snow rushing past in a nearby brook. "Gifts from God, these sights and sounds," she wrote. "This placid here and now."

"The question you gotta ask isn't Why? or If?" a wise old man once advised me as we sat in a bar in Queens, New York. "The question is How?"

"I can't do it," I had insisted on a dark and lonely road between Boston and home, but my loving aunt had insisted I could. And when I tried again, that stubborn lug nut, miraculously, had loosened and turned.

When I was a boy, I saw a laughing man perform a dance of hunger that turned, without pause, into a dance of love. And in my third and final attempt at marriage, I learned, alongside Maureen, how to master the steps of Mr. Mpipi's dance. . . . Hi, Mo. It's me again. I just wanted to let you know that I *do* believe that there's life after love, and also that there is love, still, after a life is over.

———————

AFTER I DELIVERED VELVET BACK to the farmhouse that night, I entered the condo and walked over to my *Minotauromachia*. And as I stood before it, it was crystal clear to me that the terrible monster was doomed in the face of the powerful little girl.

I looked away, then, from the impotent man-beast and down at the bust of Levi Popper, one of my fallen ancestor-uncles. I reached out and placed the curved palm of my hand against his cool marble skull. And in my hand resided, too, the tactile memory of what I had felt half an hour earlier, when I'd placed it against Velvet's swollen belly. Feeling both at once—the cool, silent pull of the dead-but-living past and the rigorous kick of the future: that was when I finally understood what had until then eluded me.

Yes, that was when and how it happened.

That was the hour I first believed.

⇥ afterword ↤

I HAD A TERRIBLE TIME starting this story. A year's worth of promising beginnings fizzled into false starts. I had a waiting readership, a book contract, and a deadline . . . but no story. In the midst of this creative drought, I agreed to teach a writing seminar at the Tennessee Williams Festival in New Orleans. It was my first visit to that city, and I mostly avoided the conference socializing in favor of walking the streets alone. My wandering led me to St. Louis Cathedral on busy Jackson Square in the city's French Quarter. Outside there was revelry—street musicians, mimes, dancing, drinking—but the cavernous church was empty. In my forlorn state, I lit a candle, knelt, and prayed to . . . well, I don't know who, exactly. The muse? The gods? The ghost of Tennessee Williams? "Whoever or whatever you are," I said, "please let me discover a story." Shortly after that trip, I began this novel in earnest. This was the first sentence that my then-nameless, identityless protagonist spoke to me: *My mother was a convicted felon, a manic-depressive, and Miss Rheingold of 1950.*

In the nine years it's taken me to construct the novel, the ground has shifted beneath us all. School shootings, 9/11, Hurricane Katrina, the protracted war in Iraq: these have altered us, collectively and as individuals. As I struggled to understand what was happening to our nation and our world, I looked to and was guided by ancient myth. I placed my fictional protagonist inside a confounding nonfictional maze and challenged him to locate, at its center, the monsters he would need to confront and the means by which he might save himself and others. Along the way to discovering Caelum Quirk's story, I, too, wandered down corridors baffling and unfamiliar, investigating such topics as the invisible pull of ancestry, chaos-complexity theory, and spirituality—my own and Caelum's. The former strand is given voice in the letters and diary entries of Caelum's forebears, Lizzy and Lydia. The latter two strands are symbolized by a pair of totem creatures from the natural world, the butterfly and the praying mantis.

My volunteer teaching at York Correctional Institution, a maximum-security women's prison, has been concurrent with, and integral to, the discovery and execution of this story. I began facilitating a writing workshop there the same month I started work on the novel—a dozen or so weeks after the massacre at Columbine High School. On the afternoon of April 20, 1999, my wife Christine and I were in Boston, where I was to receive a lovely writing award. I was tying my necktie in front of the bathroom mirror of our hotel room when I heard, from the other side of the door, Chris's distress: "Oh! Oh, no! Oh, god!" A few seconds later, I was staring at CNN's live coverage of the chaotic events unfolding at Columbine.

Two and a half years after Columbine, I sat before the television again, along with the rest of America, staring in disbelief at the smoke rising from the Twin Towers and the Pentagon, the file footage of Osama bin Laden kneeling and firing his rifle at a terrorist training camp. On impulse, I turned off the TV and drove to my sons' schools, where I circled the parking lots, trying to decide whether to let my kids carry on with their classes or to go inside and sign them out so that I might keep them safe. But safe from what? From whom? My fear was at the wheel that day, and I see now that I was confusing the actions of the terrorist hijackers with the actions, two years prior, of Eric Harris and Dylan Klebold.

In the months after September eleventh, the White House assured us that Iraq's leader was complicit in the attacks and had weapons of mass destruction which he would not hesitate to use against us. "Bring it on!" our president said, and we became immersed in the "shock and awe" of war. At first a trickle and later a steady flow of American military personnel began returning from Afghanistan and Iraq with maimed bodies and damaged psyches, or in flag-draped coffins which government officials decreed must not be photographed. In the name of combating terrorism, Congress passed the Patriot Act and the Administration bypassed the rules of the Geneva Conventions governing the humane treatment of prisoners of war. And as the tactics and conditions at Abu Ghraib and Guantánamo came slowly to light, my inmate students, through their writing, began to enlighten me about some equally disturbing realities: the correlation between incest and female crime; the racist and classist nature of the American justice system; and the extent to which our prisons fail to rehabilitate the men, women, and children in their custody. And yes, I did say children. One of my students entered prison in 1996 at the age of 15 and is scheduled to be released in 2046, the year she turns 64. She has, since her incarceration, attempted suicide three times.

Although *The Hour I First Believed* is a work of fiction, it explores and examines such nonfictional tragedies as war, catastrophic fire, violent weather, and school shootings by interfacing imagined characters with people who exist or existed. Why did I choose to access the actual instead of taking the safer and more conventional novelist's approach of creating fictional approximations of easily recognizable nonfictional people and events? Why, specifically, did I take on the tragic events that occurred in Littleton, Colorado, on April 20, 1999? My reasons are twofold. First, I felt it was my responsibility to name the Columbine victims—the dead and the living—rather than blur their identities. To name the injured who survived is to acknowledge both their suffering and their brave steps past that terrible day into meaningful lives. To name the dead is to confront the meaning of their lives and their deaths, and to acknowledge, as well, the strength and suffering of the loved ones they had to leave behind. Second, having spent half of my life in high school—four years as a student and 25 as a teacher—I could and did transport myself, psychically if not physically, to Littleton, Colorado. Could I have acted as courageously as teacher Dave Sanders, who sacrificed his life in the act of shepherding students to safety? Would I have had the strength to attend those memorials and funerals to which I sent my protagonist? Could I have comforted Columbine's "collaterally damaged" victims, as Caelum struggles to comfort his traumatized wife? The depth and scope of Harris and Klebold's rage, and the twisted logic by which they convinced themselves that their slaughter of the innocent was justified, both frightened and confounded me. I felt it necessary to confront the "two-headed monster" itself, rather than concoct Harris- and Klebold-like characters. Were these middle-class high school kids merely sick, or were they evil? What might their words and actions, their Internet spewings and videotaped taunts, tell us about how to prevent some future tragedy? Were they anomalies, or harbingers of school violence to come? Sadly, that latter question has been answered in the years since Columbine, at middle schools, high schools, colleges, and universities in California, Minnesota, Colorado, Arkansas, Mississippi, Ohio, Pennsylvania, and Virginia. And it is a bitter irony that, on the day I finished this manuscript and mailed it off to my publisher, a graduate student emerged from behind a curtain inside a lecture hall at Northern Illinois University, raised his gun, and shot twenty-one victims, five of them fatally, before taking his own life.

Why all this rage? Why all these deaths and broken-hearted survivors?

I hope and pray that, in using the names of those involved in my fictional/nonfictional exploration of the whys and wherefores of school shootings, I have not, in any way, added to the suffering of those directly involved, including the Harris and Klebold families, who also grieve and who did nothing wrong. And I hope and pray, as well, that this story, in some small way, might broaden understanding, the better to prevent future tragedy.

The year I began this novel, my elder two sons were a college freshman and a high school freshman. Today they are both teachers, working with the storm-tossed children of New Orleans. Whenever I visit them there, I make it a point to stop in at St. Louis Cathedral, where I give thanks to the greater power than I that allowed me to locate and tell my story. Having affixed its last period to its final sentence, I now release it to my readers and invite them to find in it whatever they want or need to find. Still, I hope the book advances the notion that power must be used responsibly and mercifully, and that we are all responsible for one another. These things I believe:

—That, as James Baldwin once put it, "People who treat other people as less than human must not be surprised when the bread they have cast on the waters comes back to them, poisoned."

—That wars, because of the terrible cost they exact, are never won.

—That love is stronger than hatred.

—W. L. APRIL 14, 2008

→notes from the author←

ABOUT COLUMBINE: For the reasons explained in the After-word, I have cited the actual names of the Columbine victims, both those who died and those who survived. All other characters in the Columbine-related chapters are fictional creations, with the exception of the following: Brian Anderson, Robyn Anderson, Brooks Brown, Frank De Angelis, Phil Duran, Patrick Ireland, Mark Manes, Patricia Nielson, Tim Walsh, and Greg Zanis.

ABOUT QUIRK CORRECTIONAL INSTITUTION: Although the work of my students at Connecticut's York Correctional Institute has informed the writing of this book, readers are reminded that Quirk CI is a fictional construction set in a fictional town and run by a fictional administration and custody staff. Those interested in reading about York CI, and its previous incarnations, the Niantic Correctional Institution and Connecticut's State Farm for Women, are encouraged to examine Andi Rierden's *The Farm: Life Inside a Women's Prison* (University of Massachusetts Press, 1997), a nonfictional examination of the facility, past and present. Also available to readers are two collections of our York writers' autobiographical essays, *Couldn't Keep It to Myself: Testimonies from Our Imprisoned Sisters* (ReganBooks, 2003) and *I'll Fly Away: Further Testimonies from the Women of York Prison* (Harper, 2007).

ABOUT MISS RHEINGOLD AND RHEINGOLD BEER: The first Miss Rheingold was selected by brewery executives in 1940. The second was chosen by distributors of the beer. From 1942 to 1964, the winner was chosen by the popular vote of customers at taverns, package stores, delis, and supermarkets that sold Rheingold. As it is described in the novel, the annual "election" was a promotional juggernaut that made Brooklyn-brewed Rheingold one of the biggest-selling beers in New York and New Jersey, New England, Pennsylvania, and later, California. But in reality, there was never a Miss Rheingold scandal, the likes of which are depicted in my novel. Nor does the fictional Weismann family represent in any way the Liebmann family, the original owners of Rheingold Beer. Readers who wish to read about the actual Rheingold story, as opposed to my fictional version, can access Rolf Hofmann's "From Ludwigsburg to Brooklyn—A Dynasty of German-Jewish Brewers," originally published in *Aufbau*, June 21, 2001, and available online or through the Harburg Project, a Jewish genealogical initiative. In 2003, Rheingold beer was reintroduced to the New York market and the Miss Rheingold contest was briefly revived. However, the tattooed, pierced, and midriff-baring twenty-first-century candidates—bartenders in and around New York—bore little resemblance to the demure, white-gloved contestants of past "Rheingold girl" glory. In 2006, the brand was sold to Drinks America, a Wilton, Connecticut–based beverage company, which now distributes Rheingold beer.

⤞ *acknowledgments* ⤝

I COULD NOT HAVE WRITTEN this novel without the support and help of my family. Christine, my bride of the past thirty years, as ever, lent me to my characters, responded to my umpteen drafts (armed with Post-it notes), and gave me the invaluable gifts of her patient understanding and her love. Our son Jared's teaching experiences in New Orleans's Lower Ninth Ward led me to the creation of Katrina refugees Moses and Janis Mick. Jared's brother Justin, a writer and performance poet, offered critical feedback to my work in progress and exposed me to some of the great music—classic r&b, gospel, and hip-hop—that helped me tell the story. Teddy, our youngest, on his final day as a third grader, carried home from school a praying mantis egg case—a science experiment that had failed because the insects had never hatched. Later that summer, Teddy's dormant egg case exploded with the hundreds of eyelash-sized mantises which became, in the novel, a symbol of good's triumph over evil and an invitation to hope. Our sons' honorary aunt, Ethel Mantzaris, one of my best and closest friends, was *The Hour I First Believed*'s head cheerleader. She told me so often and with such assurance that I could and would finish the novel that, after a while, I began to believe her.

What a lucky writer I am to have Terry Karten as my editor and Kassie Evashevski as my literary agent. Terry, who edits some of the finest authors in the world, agreed to take on my imperfect monster of a manuscript, and in doing so, helped me make the book more wisely, deeply, and sharply observed. Kassie is, in equal measures, savvy, sweet, and supportive; I'm grateful for her guidance and fortunate to have her first-rate representation. I'm thankful, too, for the HarperCollins team—for Jane Friedman's and Michael Morrison's wise stewardship and Jonathan Burnham's brilliant editorial direction, for the enthusiasm and expertise of Kathy Schneider, Tina Andreadis, Beth Silfin, Leslie Cohen, Miranda Ottewell, Leah Carlson-Stanisic, Sandy Hodgman, Christina Bailly, and Christine Boyd. Special thanks to Art Director Archie Ferguson for his patience, imagination, and keen artistic eye. And a tip of the hat for the Harper sales team, the best in the biz. My German publisher, Dr. Doris Janhsen, was kind and generous enough to read my manuscript at the halfway mark and offer me her valuable insights. ("Velvet may be the key to the meaning of the entire novel," she said, and lo and behold, she was right.) My former editor and publisher, Judith Regan, championed my writing from the very beginning, and for her faith in me and my work I remain deeply appreciative. I am thankful, as well, to Oprah Winfrey and her staff; the Oprah's Book Club endorsements of my two previous novels have led me to a readership far wider than I could have ever imagined.

On the homefront, I'm indebted to my two office assistants, Lynn Castelli and, later, Aaron Bremyer. Lynn's research during the early stages of this book was thorough and impeccable. Aaron's research was invaluable as well, and his willingness to listen to various drafts of chapters in progress and offer his response is deeply appreciated. And I am both indebted to and in awe of the members, past and present, of my two writing groups, talented scribes all, without whose help I could not have written this novel. They are: Doug Anderson, Susan Campbell, Bruce Cohen, Susanne Davis, Leslie Johnson, Terese Karmel, Pam Lewis, Sari Rosenblatt, and Ellen Zahl. Thanks as well to Margaret Hope Bacon, whose book *Abby Hopper Gibbons: Prison Reformer and Social Activist* inspired the character Lizzy Popper.

Thanks to my students and friends at York Correctional Institution. Each of the incarcerated writers I have worked with has added to my understanding of crime and punishment in America and has taught me the importance of helping the silenced find and use their voices. The following DOC staff members, past and present, have also been supportive of me in the writing of this book: Dale Griffith, Jeri Keltonic, Evva Larson, Joe Lea, Monica Lord, Karen Oien, and Leslie Ridgway. And my deepest gratitude extends, of course, to Susan Cole and Careen Jennings, my fearless workshop co-facilitators.

A number of professionals shared with me the two-pronged gift of their time and their expertise. Attorneys Steven Ecker and Thomas Murphy advised me as to Maureen Quirk's legal difficulties. Pharmacist Bob Parzych, one of my oldest and best buddies, advised me as to Maureen's chemical dependency issues. Toward that end, Bob also consulted with Dr. Evan Fox of Hartford Hospital. Dr. Steven Dauer read the manuscript from a psychologist's viewpoint and gave me valuable feedback and advice. Nick Buonocore, owner of the late and still-lamented Sugar Shack Bakery, taught me everything I needed to know about doughnut-making. Photo archivist Rick Goeren shared his knowledge of all things Miss Rheingold. Joline Gnatek, whose father served as farm manager of Connecticut's State Farm for Women, provided period details about what life on "The Farm" was like "back in the day." Literary agents Leigh Feldman, Linda Chester, Laurie Fox, and Jennifer Walsh offered friendship and guidance. Vic Butsch gave me a valuable assist with the Civil War material. Jonny Marks helped me with Peppy Schissel's Yiddish idiom. I am grateful to the staff and volunteers of the Mark Twain House and Museum in Hartford, Connecticut, and to its directors past and present: John Boyer, Debra Petke, and Jeffrey Nichols. Bernice Bennett, owner of the home in which my office is located, provided comic relief and sustenance (gingerbread, pudding, Swedish coffee cake, etc., etc.) throughout my writing of this book. Much appreciated, Bunny! Thanks to Jerry, Deb, and Matt Grabarek for information about dairy farming, corn mazes, and ghost sightings. Thanks as well to the late Matthieu Keijser, who gifted me with a copy of *Kaos*, Paolo and Vittorio Taviani's 1984 film based on the works of Luigi Pirandello, and further piqued my curiosity about chaos theory. Matthieu, rest in peace.

Finally, as a graduate of the Norwich Free Academy and the Vermont College of Fine Arts MFA in Writing program, and a past recipient of a National Endowment of the Arts fellowship, I remain ever grateful to these institutions for having launched me on my way.

➤ *a list of sources consulted* ◂◂
(I hope I've remembered them all)

Anton, Mike, and Ryckman, Lisa. "Mundane Gave Way to Madness" in *Denver Rocky Mountain News*, April 25, 1999.

Associated Press. "Forgiveness Not Needed Say Klebold's Parents," May 16, 2004.

"April 20, 1999," Jefferson County, Colorado Sheriff's Report, 1999.

Bacon, Margaret Hope. *Abby Hopper Gibbons: Prison Reformer and Social Activist*. Albany: State University of New York Press, 2000.

Bai, Matt; Glick, Daniel; Keene-Osborn, Sherry; Gegax, T. Trent; Clemetson, Lynette; Gordon, Devin; and Klaidman, Daniel. "Anatomy of a Massacre" in *Newsweek* Magazine, May 3, 1999.

Bartels, Lynn, and Bunn, Dina. "Dad Cuts Down Killers' Crosses" in *Denver Rocky Mountain News*, May 1, 1999.

Bartels, Lynn, and Crowder, Carla. "Fatal Friendship" in *Denver Rocky Mountain News*, August 22, 1999.

"Boston's Worst," *Time* Magazine, December 7, 1942 (slightly altered).

Bowser, Betty Ann. "Remembering Columbine," *NewsHour with Jim Lehrer* Transcript, April 20, 2000.

Brooke, James. "70,000 Mourn in Quiet Tears, Song and Rain" in *New York Times*, April 26, 1999.

Brooks, David, "The Columbine Killers" in *New York Times*, April 24, 2004.

Brown, Brooks, and Merritt, Rob. *No Easy Answers: The Truth Behind Death at Columbine*. New York: Lantern Books, 2002.

Brown, Fred, and Lowe, Peggy. "Tears from Heaven: Crowd, Tears Overflow at Service," in *The Denver Post*, April 26, 1999.

Campbell, Joseph. *The Hero with a Thousand Faces*. Princeton: Princeton University Press/Bollingen, 1972.

Carlston, Liz. *Surviving Columbine: How Faith Helps Us Find Peace When Tragedy Strikes*. Salt Lake City: Desert Book, 2004.

Cloud, John; Gwynne, S. C.; Harrington, Maureen; Shapiro, Jeffrey; Rivera, Elaine; and Woodbury, Richard. "Portrait of a Deadly Bond" in *Time* Magazine, May 19, 1999.

Cullen, Dave. "The Depressive and the Psychopath," posted in *Slate* (slate. msn.com), April 20, 2004.

Crowder, Carla. "'Your Courage and Commitment to Christ Have Gained You a Special Place in Heaven'" in *Denver Rocky Mountain News*, April 27, 1999.

Fitzpatrick. Michael F. "The Mercy Brigade" in *Civil War Times Illustrated*, October 1997, pp. 34–40.

Foster, Dick. "Mourners Recall Respectful Teen" in *Denver Rocky Mountain News*, April 24, 1999.

Gibbs, Nancy, and Roche, Timothy. "The Tapes: In Five Secret Videos They Recorded Before the Massacre, the Killers Reveal Their Hatreds and Their Lust for Fame" in *Time* Magazine, December 20, 1999.

Goldsmith, Barbara. *Other Powers: The Age of Suffrage, Spiritualism, and the Scandalous Victoria Woodhull*. New York: Knopf, 1998.

Gonzales, Manny, and Weber, Brian. "Students, Teachers Go Back to Class" in *Denver Rocky Mountain News*, May 3, 1999.

Gutierrez, Hector. "Smiling, Gentle Giant Buried with Military Honors at Fort Logan" in *Denver Rocky Mountain News*, April 28, 1999.

Harris, Jean. *They Always Call Us Ladies: Stories from Prison*. New York: Scribner's, 1988.

Harris, Mary B. *I Knew Them in Prison*. New York: Viking, 1936.

Hudson, Alice, and Cohen-Stratyner, Barbara. *Heading West and Touring West: Mapmakers, Performing Artists, and the American Frontier*. New York: New York Public Library, 2001.

Jones, Rebecca. "Young Athlete's Love for Soccer Always Brought a Smile to His Face" in *Denver Rocky Mountain News*, April 29, 1999.

Kelly, Guy. "He'd Rather Be Outside Than Anywhere Else, and His Favorite Place Was the Fishing Hole" in *Denver Rocky Mountain News*, April 28, 1999.

———— "In Memory of Lauren Townsend" in *Denver Rocky Mountain News*, April 27, 1999.

Lauck, Joanne Elizabeth. *The Voice of the Infinite in the Small: Revisioning the Insect-Human Connection*. Mill Spring, NC: Swan. Raven & Co, 1998.

Luzadder, Dan, and Vaughan, Kevin. "Amassing the Facts: Bonded by Tragedy, Officers Probe Far, Wide for Answers" in *Denver Rocky Mountain News*, December 13, 1999.

———— "Biggest Question of All" in *Denver Rocky Mountain News*, December 14, 1999.

————"Inside the Columbine Investigation" in *Denver Rocky Mountain News*, December 12, 1999.

Magers, Boyd. "Cocoanut Grove Controversy" in *Western Clippings*, #8, November/December 1995.

Mawhiney, Shawn. "Mummified Remains of Baby Found in Vacant City House" in *Norwich Bulletin*, Febuary 26, 2002.

McCombs, Brady; Oulton, Stacy; and Seibert, Trent. "Extensive Report Full of Surprises" in *The Denver Post*, November 22, 2000.

McCrimmon, Katie Kerwin. "'Pomp and Circumstance' and Tears" in *Denver Rocky Mountain News*, May 23, 1999.

Meadow, James B. "Teens 'Radiant, Forever Young'" in *Denver Rocky Mountain News*, April 26, 1999.

Melone, Katie. "Exhumation, DNA Could Identify Mummified Baby" in *Norwich Bulletin*, March 1, 2002.

Meskauskas, Mary C. "Nurse Pember and the Whiskey War" in *Civil War Times Illustrated*, August 1999, pp. 56–59.

Messent, Peter, and Courtney, Steve (eds.). *The Civil War Letters of Joseph Hopkins Twichell: A Chaplain's Story*. Athens, GA: University of Georgia Press, 2006.

Ochberg, Frank M. "Bound by a Trauma Called Columbine" www.giftfromwithin.org/html/columbin.html.

Petree, Judy. "Chaos Theory" www.fu/edu/~petrejh4/chaos.htm.

Powell, Barry B. *Classical Myth*. Upper Saddle River, NJ: Prentice Hall, 1998.

Raab, Scott. "Men Explode: A Special Report on Men and Rage" in *Esquire*, September 2000, pp.244–258.

Reuters. "Tape Shows Columbine Gunmen Mulling Murder" October 23, 2003.

Rierden, Andi. *The Farm: Life Inside a Women's Prison*. Amherst: University of Massachusetts Press, 1997.

Ryckman, Lisa. "17 Year Old Girl 'Shined for God at All Times'" in *Denver Rocky Mountain News*, April 25, 1999.

Salsbury, Edith Colgate (ed). *Susy and Mark Twain: Family Dialogues*. Mattituck, NY: Amereon House, 1965.

Scanlon, Bill. "'Dave Bled the Ultimate Blue and Silver; He Will Never Ever Be Taken from Us'" in *Denver Rocky Mountain News*, April 27, 1999.

Seibert, Trent. "Klebold Essay Foretold Columbine, Chillingly" in *Denver Post*, November 22, 2000.

Sheppard, Erika. "What Was Mine" in *Double Talk* Magazine, Spring 2003.

Sullivan, Bartholomew. "Family, Teammates Bid Final Farewell to Columbine High School's No. 70" in *Denver Rocky Mountain News*, April 28, 1999.

———— "In Memory of Daniel Rohrbough" in *Denver Rocky Mountain News*, April 27, 1999.

———— "70,000 Join Together in Sorrow" in *Denver Rocky Mountain News*, April 26, 1999.

Van Der Post, Laurens. *A Mantis Carol*. Washington, DC: Island Press, 1975.

Waldman, Hillary. "A Punishing Dispute: Anonymous Treatment vs. Public Prosecution" in *Hartford Courant*, May 4, 2003.

Washington, April M. "Talented Athlete Known for Generosity 'Would Give You the Shirt Off His Back'" in *Denver Rocky Mountain News*, April 30, 1999.

Wendel, Vicki. "Washer Women" in *Civil War Times Illustrated*, August 1999, pp. 30–36.

Zeller, Bob. "Smoketown Hospital" in *Civil War Times Illustrated*, May 1996, pp. 36–43.

⤙ *charitable donations* ⤚

READERS MAY WISH TO CONSIDER making charitable donations to the following not-for-profit organizations:

NAMI (NATIONAL ALLIANCE ON MENTAL ILLNESS)/VETERANS
www.nami.org/veterans
Toll free: (800) 950.NAMI
info@nami.org

"The National Alliance on Mental Illness (NAMI) has established an online Veterans Resource Center to help support active duty military personnel, veterans and their families facing serious mental illnesses such as depression, posttraumatic stress disorder (PTSD) and schizophrenia."

    • *Almost a third of veterans returning from Afghanistan and Iraq confront mental health problems. Families of soldiers deployed in Afghanistan or Iraq face increasing pressures from repeated and longer tours of duty. Unlike civilian suicide rates, greater numbers of young soldiers are taking their own lives, with broken relationships and marriages considered to be a factor.*

    • *Approximately 40% of homeless veterans have mental illnesses. Approximately 57% of this group are African-American or Hispanic veterans.*

———————

MAKE IT RIGHT
P.O. Box 58009
New Orleans, LA 70158-80009
Toll free: (888) MIR-NOLA (647.6652)
Local: (504) 208.9265
www.makeitrightnola.org

"Inspired by the courage and hope of the [Lower 9th Ward] residents he met, Brad Pitt resolved to do whatever he could to help them rebuild. Just as importantly, he wanted to help recreate and nurture the unique culture and spirit of the 9th Ward, which symbolized the soul of New Orleans ... The Make It Right mission is clear: to be a catalyst for redevelopment in the Lower 9th Ward by building a neighborhood of safe, healthy homes inspired by Cradle to Cradle thinking and high quality design that celebrates the spirit of the community."

STUDENTS AGAINST VIOLENCE EVERYWHERE
National Association of SAVE
322 Chapanoke Road, Suite 110
Raleigh, NC 27603
Toll free: (866) 343.SAVE
Local: (919) 661.7800
Fax: (919) 661-7777
www.nationalsave.org

"SAVE is a student-driven organization. Students learn about alternatives to violence and practice what they learn through school and community service projects. As they participate in SAVE activities, students learn crime prevention and conflict management skills and the virtues of good citizenship, civility, and non-violence."